WHEN THE DEAD COME A KNOCKIN'

B. L. BRUNNEMER

To Robert, thank you for sharing me with all the fictional people in my head.

Also to Darryl and James, you two would have gotten a kick out of this.

PROLOGUE

My name is Alexis Delaney, most everyone calls me Lexie. I'm your typical seventeen-year-old girl. Except I'm a Necromancer. I can see the dead, control the dead, and interact with the Veil. Or I'm supposed to be able to. I'm still trying to figure out how it all works. So far, all I've managed to do is see the dead, almost die, and wipe a girl's soul from existence. I have visited the Veil once; that place between life and death where all souls go to move on. And someone has fucked with it. They shut off the Veil, so souls can't reach it to move on. So everyone who dies now, can't move on; they're stuck here. Which is pretty much fucking with the amount of energy a soul should have.

The more energy a ghost has, the more dangerous they are. Oh, and the energy also fucks with the soul's personality, and makes them not them anymore. So, bonus danger. The longer the Veil is shut, the more the energy builds in this world. Someone is planning something big. And I'm supposed to figure it out and stop it. Right... me. The seventeen year old. Yeah. I'd think it was impossible but my friends keep reminding me that nothing is. My friends are pretty great. You know that weird girl in every high school with only guy friends? Yeah, that's me. Other girls don't seem to like me. That might have something to do with this bitch at school spreading rumors, but I can't be a hundred percent on that. Oh, and the bitch is my friend Asher's sister. So fun! Feel the sarcasm. Anyway, that's my life so far. Are you sure you want to keep reading? Cause shit's getting real around town. You're sure? Okay, don't say I didn't warn you.

CHAPTER 1

WEDNESDAY NOON

"*O*kay guys, it's the Wednesday before Christmas vacation, and I still need to know what you all want for Christmas," I said, pointing it out to the guys.

I looked at Asher, who was sitting on the bench to my left. He was your boy next door, only with model good looks, high cheekbones, and a sharp chin. His sandy blond hair was still short and near his head, but it was starting to grow out. He needed a trim. But one of the things I liked best about him were his eyes. He had both light and dark blue streaks with flecks of white throughout. He literally had eyes that looked like an ocean wave crashing. His athletic build was wrapped up in his black wool coat and gray pants.

He swallowed his food before answering me. "If we tell you, then it's not a present, Ally," Asher explained in his rich baritone.

The other thing I liked about Asher, well, besides the fact that he's him, was his voice. It was like rich hot chocolate to my ears.

"I tell you, you go buy it and give it to me. It's an errand then, not a gift," he said.

I rolled my eyes and looked past him to Isaac, who was sitting further down the bench.

Isaac's square jaw was covered in some black scruff today. His

3

slightly pouty, wide lips were the envy of every girl around. And surprisingly, he had a straight nose still. Mixed Martial Arts matches hadn't broken it yet. I knew it was coming, but so far, he'd been lucky. Isaac wasn't handsome so much as striking. Though most of your attention went to his hair. His hair was buzzed on the sides and left long on top. That wasn't the strange part. It was blue, a vibrant, bright blue. He had finally added darker blue streaks to his hair like he'd been talking about for the last two months. He was going for a Cookie Monster thing. While you were looking at his hair, you might miss the fact that his athletic build was wrapped in a neon blue snow jacket and blue jeans.

His chocolate eyes met mine as he shook his head.

"Cookie Monster..." I all but whined.

He smiled at me, which instantly made me want to smile back. Isaac just had that effect on me.

"Red, you're on your own," he said. His voice was oddly like honey; sweet, creamy and smooth.

I playfully growled at him before looking further down the table to Zeke. Big, strong, intimidating-as-hell Zeke. You know the poster child for the death penalty, as in the one for it? That was Zeke, at least in looks. His broad cheekbones and wide, strong jaw gave his face a rough, frightening look. It wasn't just his face or angry glares that were intimidating. It was his frame. He was huge. My head just met the middle of his chest. It wasn't only height either, oh no. Zeke had wide shoulders and was like a mountain of muscle. That mountain was currently wearing a black snow jacket, black jeans, boots, and his ever-present wallet chain. Zeke's clothes never changed much, and I was starting to think it was so he never had to match anything. A couple of weeks ago, during lunch, he said he liked the blue flower I had been drawing. The flower had been violet; I didn't tell him. Zeke's rough and scary looks didn't intimidate me anymore; the guy was like a teddy bear who argued all the time. Well, unless you hurt a girl around him, then he was your worst nightmare.

I met his sky-blue eyes and threatened to pout. He glared at me.

"No, Lexie," Zeke warned me.

My lip started to stick out.

"No, nope, not dealing with that fucking lip," Zeke snapped as he turned his back on the table until all I saw was the back of his short black hair. "Tell me when she fucking stops," he growled.

The guys burst out laughing. Zeke just kept his back turned.

I looked over to Ethan, Isaac's twin. The only difference was, well, everything but their faces and builds. His black hair was straight and reached his jawline. On his right ear, he had five silver loop rings running up his earlobe. His athletic build was also in a black snow jacket and black jeans.

"Ethan, please, give me a hint? Something you need?" I asked sweetly.

Ethan sighed. "Beautiful, we don't need anything. Gifts are supposed to be fun, not something you need," he said. Ethan's voice was smooth and smoky; it rolled over my ears like fog. It wasn't his toe-curling voice, but it didn't matter. I could listen to him talk all day.

I looked over to Miles and raised an eyebrow. Miles was cute until he smiled, then you saw how handsome he was. It felt like the world's biggest secret, and I was the only one who knew about it. He had high cheekbones and an angled jaw. His chestnut hair was short but had a wave to it. Though it was getting long enough now, that it was starting to curl around his ears. He had lovely dark green eyes behind his black-rimmed glasses. He was leaner than the other boys, but his shoulders were still broad with some muscle to them. Right now, his lean frame was wrapped in a dark green snow jacket and brown cargo pants.

"Miles?" I asked, knowing I wasn't getting anywhere.

He gave me an understanding smile. "I'm sorry Lexie, you're going to be on your own for this one," Miles said gently.

I cursed and buttoned up my long black wool coat. The guys had finally made me give up my leather jacket for a thicker coat this winter. The shit heads took me to the mall and wouldn't bring me home until I bought one. It had taken me awhile to find one I liked; well, that and making the guys go to three different stores was fun revenge. The coat was fitted through the bust, tucked in at the waist, then flared down to just above my knees. I also loved the hood; it was very cloak like. It looked great with my mass of curly copper hair.

"Fine, I'll figure it out," I groused, then pointed a gloved finger around the table at each of them. "But if you get shit you don't like, you have only yourself to blame."

They just smiled at me. Zeke turned back around now that he knew I wasn't pouting. Use a pout once, and the guy avoided it like the plague.

I felt my phone vibrate in my jacket pocket. Already knowing who it was, I pulled my phone out and checked my text.

Dylan: It's the last day of school before vacation! Wanna ditch?

I smiled. It was tempting. I had only seen Dylan a few times since we met at Vegabond in October. Though we texted or talked every day, we still weren't dating. I would ask him, but it seemed he didn't think of me that way. Though he had flirted hard in October, he'd eased back since. His dad had a couple of people quit at the hardware store in Dulcet and Dylan had been stuck picking up the slack. Which meant no time to see me, even though I was willing to drive up there. It seemed I had been friend zoned. I sighed.

Feeling resigned, I texted him back.

Alexis: Can't, I have to turn in that final art project today.

I set my phone on the table. The guys were talking about plans this week while I looked around at all the snow. There had been snow on the ground since November, and I was still trying to get used to it. Coming from the southern desert states, this was a complete turn-around. And it was fucking freezing.

"What are we doing out here, guys?" I asked, tucking my hands back into my pockets.

I heard my phone vibrate. I didn't want to answer it right now. Ethan's hand shot out and snagged my phone.

"You snoopy shit!" I snapped. I reached for it as he read my messages.

Ethan frowned down at my phone as I came off the bench to snatch it back.

"You don't have an art project due today," Ethan pointed out before letting me take my phone back.

I sat back down and ignored him. I checked my text.

Dylan: Shit, I was hoping to get a chance to see you.

I snorted before texting back. Yeah, sure you were.

Alexis: Sorry.

A shadow fell over my phone; I brought it to my chest to hide the screen. Asher was leaning across the table.

"Yes?" I asked, smiling through clenched teeth.

His eyebrows went up; his eyes widened before he gave me his sweet smile. "What's Dylan up to?" Asher asked, going back to his side of the table.

"He wanted to ditch to see her, and she said she couldn't," Ethan ratted me out.

I kicked my foot out and hit him in the shin. He hissed and shot me a look back.

"Wait. You have a chance to see Dylan, and you're not taking it?" Asher asked, his eyes running over me.

I glared at Ethan and mentally began planning my revenge. The thought of putting bleach in his shampoo so his hair turned orange entered my mind.

"I've been friend-zoned," I said, hating to admit it. "You guys think it sucks to be friend-zoned as a guy? Try it being a girl." They looked confused, so I continued, being blunt. "I have boobs, these things are supposed to be a free pass into a relationship. But nope, I've been friend-zoned."

The guys started laughing, even Asher, though he was trying to stop so he could say something.

"What do you mean friend-zoned? You guys talk all the time," Asher pointed out when he finally stopped laughing.

My phone vibrated again.

"Yes, we talk on the phone, we text." I sounded irritated, which I was. "And we don't see each other." I shrugged and picked up my phone.

Dylan: Which painting did you end up finishing?

Alexis: I went with the seascape. How's your day going?

The guys were still looking at me like they didn't believe me. I snorted at them.

"You want proof?" I slid my phone across the table and gestured towards it. "Have at it."

Ethan snatched up my phone and scooted down the bench to share with the others.

"Why don't you just ask him out?" Miles asked, closing his book.

"I was going to, but he stopped flirting. I'm not asking out a guy who isn't even flirting with me anymore." I felt like sulking. This sucked.

Miles reached out and patted my shoulder awkwardly. Miles still wasn't comfortable touching me on his own.

"Sorry, Lexie," Miles said gently.

I shrugged. "It is what it is," I muttered.

"What the hell man?" Asher grumbled as they went through my messages. Asher looked over at me, confused.

"Told ya," I said then gestured towards my breasts. "They're defective; I need trade-ins."

The guys chuckled. And to be honest, I laughed a little too.

"That sucks, Lexie," Zeke said, sliding my phone back towards me.

It vibrated before I picked it up. I decided not to check the message this time.

"Want me to kick his ass?" Isaac offered cheerfully.

I smiled at him. "It's fine. I just wish he'd told me he wasn't interested. Would have saved my ass a lot of time."

The guys were sending each other strange looks. I made a guess as to why we were outside at a picnic table.

"Okay, someone's got a girlfriend, and now you guys think it's a bad time to tell me?" I gave it a shot.

Isaac squirmed. Oh, this was fun.

I leaned forward and eyed each of them. "Come on, spill, I have to live vicariously through someone."

They chuckled.

Zeke met my eyes. "It's actually all of us, well, except Miles," Zeke announced.

My mouth dropped open. Holy shit! "Where the hell have I been?" I asked, looking at each of them in surprise. "Who are they? Where are they? And when did this happen?" The guys smiled. "This had to have happened recently because you guys are not that sneaky."

They chuckled.

"I've been talking to Riley at parties and at Vegabond since October," Zeke admitted.

I raised an eyebrow and pointed at him. "Purple hair girl?" I asked.

Zeke smirked. "Yeah."

I looked at Asher expectantly.

"I've been talking to Trisha for a couple weeks now. Mostly on the phone since we're still practicing for the playoffs," Asher admitted.

I looked over at Isaac who had a shit eating grin on his face.

"Cece is that girl I've been hitting on for the last two years, I finally got her," Isaac announced. He looked happy. I loved it when Isaac looked happy. Hell, I loved it when all of them looked happy.

I looked at Ethan.

"I met Faith the last time we played at Vegabond. She stayed after to ask why I played the E minor chord the way I do." He shrugged with a small smile on his face.

"You were hooked instantly," I guessed.

He gave me a big smile. "Totally hooked," Ethan admitted.

I chuckled and looked around the table at them. They were all smiling and happy. It made me happy. Just like that, the day was better. "That's awesome. But you guys didn't have to hide this from me, I want to meet your girls. If you like 'em, I'll like 'em," I assured them.

They sent those looks at each other again.

I felt a knot forming in my gut. "Just spill it."

"Some of the girls are a little weirded out that we have a friend that's a girl," Asher admitted reluctantly. "And with Jessica's rumors..."

My heart dropped. They were ditching me for their girlfriends. The day just turned shittier. Asher's sister, Jessica, had a bug up her ass about me and had spent every moment of her time since October trash-talking me around the school. I didn't care. But now...

"They don't want you hanging out with me. Right?" I picked up my phone and grabbed my bag. I didn't want to hear this today. This just fucking figured. "Tell me when they lose the sticks up their asses." I snapped as I got to my feet and headed for the parking lot. Fuck today. I was going home.

"Lexie, get your ass back here!" Zeke barked at me.

I turned around. "Why? So, you can tell me your girlfriends believe Jessica's bullshit?"

"How about so I can meet you and make up my own fucking mind?" a sarcastic voice shot from one of the hallways.

A tall, willowy girl walked out into the open. She wore black skinny jeans, black boots, and a purple shirt. She also wore a black snow jacket. I took all that in while I was looking at her oval face. She was damn pretty, with nice cheekbones and almond shaped eyes. A simple nose ring was the only jewelry she was wearing. She had thick, shoulder-length, lilac hair.

I met her brown eyes. "Really?" I asked, holding back a smile.

She smirked, revealing a cute dimple. She was fucking adorable when she smiled.

"Yeah, I wouldn't take that bitch's word even if she was just telling me the time," the girl, who had to be Riley, said.

I liked her instantly. I eyed her and smiled. I looked at the boys still sitting at the picnic table and pointed at Riley. "I like her," I announced. The guys burst out laughing. Riley did too.

I turned back to her. "I'm Lexie."

"I'm Riley." She pointed to the boys, who were still laughing. "They thought it would be better for the girlfriends to meet you one at a time."

I thought about it and nodded. "Yeah, I'm usually better one-on-one," I admitted. "My day was already sucking, and they said their girlfriends didn't like that they had a friend that was a girl, then they mentioned Jessica's shit."

"Wow, they really suck at giving news," she said, her eyes wide.

I snorted. We headed back to the table.

She walked up to Zeke and narrowed her eyes at him. "Did you guys really start off with 'we have girlfriends who listen to rumors?'" Riley asked.

Zeke's face grimaced as he ran his hand through his hair. Riley waited.

"I guess we did," Zeke admitted awkwardly.

Riley shook her head and gave him a hug. Zeke wrapped an arm around her waist, gave her a couple pats then let go. I looked away, it was so fucking weird seeing Zeke hug a girl. When Riley pulled away, Zeke made room on the bench for her. I walked back to the table and sat down where I was sitting earlier.

"Not the way to go, cutie," Riley told him gently. She looked over at me. "Why's your day sucking already?"

"Got friend-zoned by a hottie I've been talking to since October," I grumbled.

Riley winced. "Ouch,"

I pointed at her and looked at the boys. "See what I mean? A guy friend-zoning a girl who's into him shouldn't really happen." I knew that it wasn't true, but I felt like complaining, so I went with it.

Everyone burst out laughing.

"She's right," Riley said. "Unless he's gay?"

I looked at Asher with fake suspicion. "Is he gay?" I asked, my voice serious.

Asher just shook his head, looking a little stunned by the direction the conversation was going. "Nope, not gay."

I looked back to Riley and sighed. "I should just cash in my girl card, and go live in a cabin."

Riley grinned. "Actually, I know a couple guys who would absolutely love you," she said cheerfully.

My mood perked up. I looked at Zeke, with his tense shoulders. I met his eyes. "Best girlfriend ever," I told him earnestly.

The boys chuckled. Zeke relaxed, and everyone started talking about their plans for the day. Feeling stupid, I reached into my pocket and checked my text.

Dylan: Not bad, might get some time off soon.

Yay, good for you. Not like you'd use it to see me anyway. Am I bitter? No, no. Of course, I'm a bit bitter.

Alexis: Good, you need some time off.

Alexis: I just met Zeke's new girlfriend. She's fucking awesome.

"And you keep texting him back," Asher pointed out, his voice full of disbelief.

I put my phone back in my pocket and pointed at him. "I train with you guys now; you've all made me a sadist," I told him honestly. The boys chuckled.

"I mean it, with those fucking seven in the morning sessions on the weekend..." I was glaring at Isaac now. "Who does that?"

"MMA fighters, Red," Isaac countered, grinning his shit eating grin. "And people with packed schedules," he reminded me.

I made a face at him. He was right; my schedule was packed lately. With rock climbing lessons, MMA training, and meditation exercises, I barely had a night free anymore.

I looked over at Riley and leaned on the table. "Talk to me about girly shit that will make them uncomfortable," I begged.

The guys groaned.

Riley's eyes lit up with mischief. She leaned on the table, mirroring me. "Did you see what Jessica was wearing this morning? How the hell do you wear that little clothing in this weather?" she said in an exaggerated girly voice.

The guys started cursing. Oh, this was fun.

"Did you see her shoes? They were awful," I offered, exaggerating just as much. "Did you see Mary McNull's hair this morning?"

Riley made a fake, shocked face. "I know! She had total bed head! I call walk of shame,"

"Oh my fucking God! Zeke, what the fuck did you do?" Isaac shouted across the table.

Zeke just looked pained. Riley and I started laughing; we didn't stop for a while. The guys finally realized we were messing with them and looked so relieved that it set us off again. I was wiping tears from my face when they stopped glaring at us.

"Oh, that was priceless," I said between breaths.

Riley was still snickering; Zeke was shaking his head. He was probably wondering if introducing me had been a good idea. It kept a smile on my face as I looked at the others.

"So, when am I meeting the others?" I asked sweetly, then narrowed my eyes at them playfully. "Or are you all dreading that now?"

Isaac groaned and held his face in his hands. Ethan was shaking his head, and Asher rolled his eyes. I loved bugging my friends.

"Well," Asher began, rubbing the back of his neck. "Since we're all going over to my house tonight, we thought we'd stagger the girls showing up to meet you."

I nodded; it made sense. "And Jessica is going to be where?" I asked as I raised an eyebrow, waiting.

Asher snorted. "She'll be on her way to a spa in Missoula for the next couple of weeks," Asher assured me.

I did a little dance on my bench. "Best Christmas present ever," I declared.

My phone vibrated in my pocket. I sighed and pulled my phone out while the others started talking about what movies to take over.

Dylan: Zeke has a girlfriend? Wow.

Alexis: That's not all. So, do Isaac, Ethan, and Asher.

I put my phone back down and returned to the conversation.

"No sappy romantic movies, I don't care if the girls like 'em." Isaac was adamant.

I snickered and raised my hand. "I second that,"

Asher sighed. "If the girls want to watch a love story, we need to compromise," Asher pointed out.

I snorted. "Okay, I got one," I announced. Everyone looked at me. "Deadpool." They burst out laughing. I shrugged. "What? It's funny, there's some romance, and it's not that thick sweet shit either. Plus, a body count."

When they kept laughing, I started wondering if there really was something wrong with me. I didn't like the sweet, sappy stuff; it made me uncomfortable. Okay, occasionally during that time of the month,

I would watch a romantic comedy. But it always had a happy ending. I realized that the other girls were probably going to want to watch at least one of those movies tonight. Shit.

I waited till they all calmed down.

"If your girls want to watch some sappy movie, it has to have a happy ending. Please? None of this tragic love story crap. I get enough of that in English," I begged, looking at them with pleading eyes.

They all agreed.

My phone vibrated. I picked it up and checked it.

Dylan: When did this happen?

Alexis: Apparently in the last two weeks. I'm meeting the rest of them at Asher's tonight.

Dylan: Oh yeah, movie night. What's the theme? Horrible monster movies?

I snorted.

Alexis: No, that would be awesome. I have a feeling we're going to be watching some girly shit.

Dylan: LMAO

Yeah, laugh it up, buddy. You're not the one who has to sit through it.

Everyone started suggesting movies. Riley suggested binge watching Game of Thrones. I smiled. I was going to get along great with Riley. Soon enough, the bell rang, and we all headed off to class.

BEFORE HEADING HOME, I decided to drop by my locker and leave my books here over break. I was already pissed off at myself due to my latest attempt at painting an ocean scene. I had liked it yesterday, but today I saw all the mistakes I had made. The waves were wonky, the colors didn't work, and, oh yeah, I sucked. I wasn't even going to finish the damn thing. First garbage can I saw it was going in. Otherwise, I'd end up lighting the damn thing on fire. I was berating myself over the stupid mistakes I had made while trying to juggle the large rolled up canvas as I was trying to put my non-dead people sketch book away when I turned a corner.

Smack! I hit something tall and firm. There was an "oomph." My bag was knocked off my shoulder as I stumbled back a couple of steps. I managed to stay on my feet. I looked up to realize I had run into some guy. His face was grimacing as he rubbed the middle of his stomach. It was probably where my shoulder hit since he was two heads taller than me. He had a tall, lean, broad-shouldered build, with shaggy dark hair and dark eyes. That was all I had noticed before I was apologizing.

"Sorry," I sighed, this just followed the pattern of the day.

I knelt and focused on putting my books back in my bag, pushing the painting out of my mind for a minute. "I wasn't looking where I was going."

The guy squatted down to help me. "No, it's my fault. I wasn't really looking either," he mumbled as he passed me my World Civ. book.

"Thanks." I took it from him and stuffed it into my bag. I reached for my Algebra book. "So, we're both at fault," I said before looking over at him with a half a smile. "I'll have my people call your people to settle the damages."

He gave me a tense half grin as he kept his gaze on the ground. He handed me my Chemistry book. When I finally finished putting everything away, he gave me my canvas.

"Thanks."

"You paint?" he asked, his voice so quiet I could barely hear him.

We both stood back up.

"I try. This is a massive failure. I'm not even finishing it," I said absently as I put the canvas under my arm, not caring if I was crushing it. "I'm seriously thinking of having a Viking funeral for it." I looked up at him just in time to see his gaze jump back to the ground. He was shy, worse than Miles shy. I was probably making him uncomfortable. I gave him a small smile. "Thanks for the help." I went to step around him. "And sorry again, for the crash."

I headed down the hallway towards my locker. When I passed a trashcan, I didn't even stop as I threw the canvas away, never wanting to see it again. Stupid fucking waves and their bitchiness.

Turning around another corner, I went down the hall to my locker, still cursing myself as I opened it. There was a folded-up piece of paper inside. Weird, I usually always cleaned out my stuff. Thinking it was class notes, I picked it up and opened it. It wasn't class notes; it wasn't even my handwriting.

YOU LOOKED BEAUTIFUL TODAY. *I just had to tell you.* - *Your Secret Admirer*

I BLINKED hard and read it again. Okay, someone was fucking with me. I didn't look great today, let alone beautiful. My hair was just pulled off my face, and I was in blue jeans and a gray thermal shirt. And the secret admirer thing? Nah, I wasn't buying it. It was one of the guys fucking with me. I stuffed the note into my jacket pocket and began unloading my books. I put it out of my head as I shut my locker and headed back out to the parking lot.

I drove home and picked up several movies I liked. All with a body count. I also grabbed Rory's Lord of The Rings trilogy; maybe that would be enough romance to keep the girlfriends happy.

I was in a somewhat better mood as I drove over to Asher's, which was right next door to the twins' house. I didn't have training tonight or climbing lessons, and I didn't have to try any of my meditation exercises. I had the night off. It usually only happened once a week, and I was going to enjoy it.

I pulled up to the curb. Asher's house was an old farmhouse with a wraparound porch. It was a nice house. I parked and grabbed my bag of stuff for movie night. I hurried up to the door and tried the knob. It was locked, so I rang the bell, not wanting to deal with my keys. It was freaking freezing out here.

I was bouncing on my toes when the door opened. It wasn't Asher. It was a girl with long, curly brown hair and hazel eyes. She had a beautiful face. A small sharp chin and angled jaw gave her cute, smooth cheeks. Her eyebrows had been plucked, and her makeup was flawless. Her slender body was clad in designer jeans and what looked like a cashmere sweater. Surprised, I looked at the address, thinking I just went to the wrong house. No this was it. I looked back at her and smiled.

"Either Asher moved and forgot to mention it, or you are Trisha." I held my hand out to her. "I'm Lexie."

Her eyes ran down my body then back to my face. She gave me a tense smile that didn't reach her eyes. She shook my hand with her fingers like she was trying to avoid touching my hand as much as possible. A knot formed in my gut. I took my hand back and waited for her to let me in.

"Nice to meet you, but movie night isn't until, like, six tonight," she said. Trisha's voice was soft but held a sharpness underneath.

Okay. This is Asher's girlfriend, Lexie, play nice.

"Yeah," I pointed into the house. "Asher threatened me with no snack privileges if I didn't help make them this time."

She ran her eyes over me again like she was deciding something.

I tried again. "Seriously, have you had those chips? They're so addicting."

When she didn't open the door further, I was about done trying to be polite and getting no response. I kept my smile friendly as I looked past her. "Is Asher here?"

She seemed to decide something. She smiled again, it didn't reach her eyes. "Yeah, of course. Come on in."

She stepped back and opened the door further. I walked into Asher's house and dropped my bag by the stairway in the foyer as usual. "Ash! Where you at?" I shouted out like I always did when I walked into his house. I started taking off my jacket.

"You really don't need to shout," Trisha said, frowning at me.

By the horrified look on her face, I must have done something she considered terribly rude.

I was about to explain, when Asher shouted back, "Kitchen, where else woman?"

I chuckled at that. Trisha's eyes widened a bit before going back to pleasant. I started to explain as I pulled my cell from my jacket. "The first time I showed up here I went looking for him. Almost walked in on him changing." I grimaced and shook my head. "No, thank you. Since then I just shout for him." I tucked my phone into my pocket.

"Oh," she said quietly. Her face was pleasant, and her voice was friendly. But her eyes were still cold. I decided to ignore it for now and play nice.

"Come on, let's go make some chips." I turned and headed straight down the hall to the kitchen, rubbing my hands together. "Chips, chips, chips," I said in my happy kid voice, trying to make her laugh. It didn't work.

Trisha was acting like I had interrupted some special alone time they were having. But if that were true, Asher wouldn't have told me to come over and make my share of the snacks. I pushed it out of my mind as I stepped through the doorway to find Asher surrounded by food. He was adorable as hell in his blue and white striped apron.

"She's so cute," I whispered.

Asher chuckled as he cut the ends off the potato and reached for another one.

"I think so." He grinned, as he chopped the ends off another potato. Trisha walked into the kitchen as I was washing my hands.

"So, how did you two meet?" I asked, hoping to get her talking. Maybe if we talked more then she might like me a little.

"We met at school a couple weeks ago," Trisha began, her voice warming. Yay! "I had a fashion club meeting and came out to find I had a flat tire."

I turned, leaned against the counter and looked at her. Her eyes had become soft as she looked at Asher.

"Asher was leaving from practice and saw the flat. He fixed it, asked for my number, and we clicked." Her cheeks had gone rosy.

She really was beautiful. Way to go, Ash.

"That is so romantic, I might barf," I said dryly.

Her eyes flashed sharply at me.

Asher chuckled. "Trish, just so you know," Asher began, not looking up from the cutting board. "That's Lexie speak for 'aww.'"

I snickered and looked at Trisha again. She didn't look like she believed him. I tried to explain. "Romance makes me uncomfortable.

It's something I need to work on," I admitted honestly before looking back at Asher. "So, what am I supposed to be doing?"

He gestured toward the cut potatoes with the knife. "Get the mandolin out, start slicing, and lay them out on the paper towels. We want as much water out of them as possible," Asher said as he continued cutting.

I went to the cabinet with the mandolin and set it up the way Asher had shown me last time we used it.

"And don't cut yourself or I'll never hear the end of it," he added.

I snorted. Zeke's lectures could go on, and on, and on. I lined a couple layers of paper towels on a baking sheet. Then I started slicing.

"So, is that what happened with Dylan? He got romantic, and you became a smart ass?" he asked.

Trisha made a small noise.

Asher winced and said, "Mouth, smart mouth."

I raised an eyebrow at him. "Um, what was that?"

"Trisha doesn't like swearing," he said, pulling another potato from the pile.

"So, we can't swear?" I asked, horrified. Did he not know me at all? I swore in just about every fucking conversation I had.

He finished cutting the potato before answering. "She can stand some swearing, but she has a limit," Asher explained, looking over at me. "And with you, Zeke, and Riley in the same room tonight...."

"Oh, yeah. That's a lot of swearing," I admitted, wincing. I went back to slicing. "We're going to need a swear jar or something."

Asher nodded as he put another potato on the to slice pile. "Then we'll need more jobs to pay the swear jar." Asher chuckled.

"I just don't appreciate swearing; it makes me uncomfortable," Trisha said defensively from across the kitchen.

I waved my hand dismissively. "To each their own, honey; we want you to feel comfortable around the rest of us," I assured her. Then I had a thought and snickered. "Wait till Zeke hears he can't swear." Asher and I both started laughing. "Oh, it'll be so funny!" When I finally stopped laughing, I started slicing again.

"You still didn't answer the question," Asher pointed out.

I shook my head. "No, you guys don't get to keep your girlfriends a secret and then get to go snooping in my love life," I told him firmly. "Or lack thereof. Not happening."

"Fine, I'll stop asking," he muttered.

I started setting the slices onto the paper towels, then added more paper towels, then more slices. We were making a ton of chips tonight.

"So, Trisha, tell me about yourself. Have any siblings? What movies do you like?" I asked, hoping to get the ball rolling.

"I have one sister. And I like all kinds of movies," Trisha said. "The Fault in Our Stars is one of my favorites."

I winced. Sad girly movie, damn it. "I've never seen it, what's it about?" I asked as I started slicing again.

She began telling me about the book and then the movie. When I stopped slicing to grab another potato, Asher nudged my arm with his elbow. I looked up at him. He mouthed "thank you." I winked at him. When Trisha started talking about the scenes they left out of the movie, the front door open.

"Hey!" Isaac shouted.

A girl's voice started speaking softly in the hall.

"Kitchen!" Asher and I shouted at the same time.

The footsteps on the hardwood floor came towards the kitchen. That knot tightened in my stomach. I don't think Trisha liked me; was Cece going to be the same way? I turned around and leaned against the counter as they came in.

Isaac came in first, his arm behind him. He stepped further into the room, pulling Cece with him.

Cece had a sweet, heart-shaped face. A cute chin and arched brows. Her nose was just slightly too big for her face, but it made her look unique to me. Her skin was pale, not redhead pale but the kind of pale light blondes get. She had long, straight, white-blonde hair, and she was wearing a loose blue beanie that hung off the back of her head. She was dressed simply. Jeans, a shirt, a scarf, and her jacket. Her big, dark green eyes ran around the kitchen nervously. She had a death grip on Isaac's hand.

"Red, this is Cece," Isaac introduced us. Isaac looked down at her, his face softening. "Lexie to everyone else."

She gave him a nervous smile before looking over to me. I gave her a big smile.

"Hi, want to come help slice potatoes?" I asked in my friendly voice. "It's so fun."

Asher shot out with an elbow and hit me just under the shoulder. "You're not getting out of this, Ally, so stop trying," Asher chided me. "You eat more of those chips than anyone else, so now you gotta make them."

I looked up at him and saw that he was grinning at me. He knew what I was doing. I stuck my tongue out at him. Both Isaac and Cece laughed. Yay! I turned back around and started stacking again.

"So, how did you two get together?" I asked, hoping to get her to relax.

Footsteps moved across the kitchen to the counter to the right of the corner sink. Isaac hopped up, then pulled Cece until she was standing in front of him between his knees, his hands rubbing her shoulders. It was sweet.

"We've known each other for a few years," Cece said, her voice was sweet and a bit uncertain. "Isaac always went out of the way to talk to me, even when he was busy."

"Yeah, I was kind of stalking her for a while," Isaac admitted.

Cece smacked his knee lightly. "Oh, you were not," Cece scolded him. I smiled. "I had broken up with my ex a couple months ago, and Isaac was there. It was just the right time."

"That's a sweet story." I looked up at Isaac and smiled. "You went for the long game, huh?"

He chuckled. "Yeah, I went for the long game," he admitted, giving Cece's shoulders a squeeze. "And it actually worked."

Cece rolled her eyes.

I kept working. Over the next half hour, I finished slicing and had the chips in both ovens. The timer was set, and we were just standing around the kitchen getting to know each other when the front door opened again.

"How can you say that?" a girl's voice shot out.

"It's very easy to say that. You're wrong." Ethan's voice came down the hall towards the kitchen. "See easy."

I winced as we all went quiet and listened.

"The Gibson L-5 was the first orchestra guitar, that alone makes it better," the girl, who must be Faith, pointed out.

Ethan scoffed.

I smiled, they were fighting over guitars? That was incredible.

"The Gibson Les Paul sounds better, and it plays better. So, it wins hands down," Ethan shot back.

"Bullshit." Faith scoffed.

Trisha winced.

I leaned over to Asher. "We're going to need that swear jar," I whispered.

Asher chuckled but went looking for one anyway.

"You know, you're cute when you get all pissed off." Ethan's voice changed to that smoky, low toe curling one. He used that voice, the shithead.

"So are you," Faith said, the fight leaving her voice.

"Oh, he cheats," I mumbled.

Isaac snickered.

There were footsteps down the hall, then Ethan stepped into the kitchen, followed quickly by Faith. Faith was hot, there's no other way to say it. She had the curves that most girls would kill for. Her black hair had red streaks running through the pixie cut. Her face was pretty, high cheekbones, small chin, angled jaw, and a cute freaking nose. Her olive skin made it seem like she had a tan. I noticed the eyebrow stud and the small hoop nose ring. She looked around the kitchen and stopped when her amber eyes found me. My stomach knotted. I just wanted to get along with them. That was all.

"You must be Faith," I said from my spot on the counter.

She ran her eyes over me and nodded. "And you must be Lexie," she replied; she sounded like a soprano to me, but I wasn't sure.

"Yep, that's me, all day, all the time," I said cheerfully. "You totally won that argument by the way. He cheated."

Faith raised an eyebrow at that.

Ethan's mouth dropped with fake shock. "I would nev-"

"Oh, stow it; you know you did." I called him on in.

Ethan glared at me for a second then nodded. Faith smacked him on the shoulder.

"Ha, ha. That's for snooping today," I shot at him.

Ethan's eyes promised retaliation.

Asher came back in and set an empty jar on the island. "Okay, guys, swear jar," Asher announced. "Trisha isn't comfortable with swearing, and we have Zeke, Riley, and Lexie tonight." The guys winced like I had. "You swear, put a dollar in. We'll use the money for next movie night snacks."

We all mumbled an agreement. Then everyone started talking, trying to get to know each other. Well, the girls were trying to get to know me, and I was trying to get to know them. The other guys seemed to have already met the girls. The knots in my stomach eased as I talked to Faith. She seemed awesome; she was a music devotee like Ethan. She was even in a band herself. She didn't mind me being a smart ass either. Then Ethan slipped up.

"Hey, Beautiful, did you bring Monty Python tonight?" he asked absently, stealing a chip that was still hot from the rack.

My gut knotted even worse than before. My eyes flicked to Faith to see how she was taking my nickname. Her face was completely blank. I looked back to Ethan who was juggling the chip from hand to hand.

"Yeah, I brought it. Along with the Lord of The Rings trilogy and Hellboy I and II," I said to the room like I hadn't noticed anything different. When Faith didn't say anything, I started to relax.

"So, Lexie, are you seeing anyone?" Trisha asked from her spot next to Asher on the far side of the island.

I stopped myself from groaning. I kept my face pleasant as I answered, "I have been talking to a guy since October." The girls looked interested. "But I think I've been friend-zoned."

"Just talking?" Faith asked bluntly.

The room went silent; the tension ramped up as all the guys

frowned at Faith. My stomach knotted hard. This was Ethan's girl-friend, I couldn't just tell her off. I could see Ethan becoming angry, getting ready to say something. I answered before Ethan could say anything.

"Yep, never even kissed the guy," I admitted in front of everyone, which totally sucked.

"I still don't think you got friend-zoned," Asher said, changing the way the conversation was heading.

I chuckled as the other guys chimed in.

"You saw his texts, he's not flirting with her," Isaac pointed out.

"Ouch. Thanks man," I said, my voice pained.

Isaac sent me an apologetic look.

"He is really busy," Ethan offered.

The front door opened and closed.

"Oh God, please stop," I pleaded, my face going into my hands.

"I still think he's into you," Asher said confidently.

"I think she should stop wasting her time," Ethan countered. "And ask him out."

"Can we please, not do this?" I asked no one in particular.

"And if it's a no, he'd stop talking to her," Isaac reminded Ethan.

"Would that be so bad at this point?" Miles asked, coming into the kitchen. His face went white as he realized there were other girls in the room. His body tensed immediately. I jumped to help.

"Miles, as the only other almost single person here, come save me?" I asked pitifully, patting the counter next to me.

Miles gave me a small tight smile then walked over and lifted himself to sit next to me. His fingers started a staccato rhythm against the counter tile. I hadn't seen it in a while. I bumped my shoulder into his and gave him a smile. He gave me a half grin and bumped back.

"The question still stands," Miles told me.

Traitor. I took a deep breath and let it out slow. Everyone was still listening. Fuck. "No, it wouldn't be so bad," I admitted.

"Just ask him out." Miles' voice was gentle and quiet; he knew I liked Dylan a lot more than I admitted to anyone else. Miles always managed to get the truth out of me. He was right. I was tired of this almost dating but not dating place I'd been stuck in.

"Fine, I'll get it over with and ask him out tonight."

The front door opened and closed. Big feet walked down the hall towards the kitchen. Zeke walked in and found a place to lean, Riley following right behind.

"So, what did we miss?" Zeke asked the room.

"Oh, just tearing my lack of love life apart," I answered grumpily.

Zeke looked at the guys, his face becoming hard.

I looked at Asher, pleading with my eyes. "Can I tell him? It'll cheer me up," I begged.

Asher grinned as he nodded.

I looked at Zeke with a big smile and pointed at the jar. "We have a swear jar! No swearing tonight!"

Zeke looked like he'd been hit in the head with a board. The guys and I started laughing. Even Riley joined in.

Not a minute had gone by and the first thing Zeke said was "Fuck."

CHAPTER 2

WEDNESDAY NIGHT

A couple hours later, we were watching Romeo and Juliet, with Leonardo DiCaprio and Claire Danes. Trisha had insisted on it, and we had to be completely quiet during the movie.

Asher's family room wasn't huge. The green couch was under the front windows on the left wall, and two wide blue armchairs against the wall across from the pass through. With the entertainment center, end tables, and coffee table it was a comfy room. Though with the lack of seating, a couple of us had to sit on the floor. The guys and I made a point to make sure Ethan had a spot on the couch. His back had been hurting him more lately. He never said anything, but we'd all caught him wincing over the last week.

I sat near the doorway to the foyer, watching the screen. I was miserable, and it was only halfway through the movie. I pulled my cell phone out and texted Asher.

Alexis: I hate you for this.

I watched as Asher pulled his cell phone out and read my message. He smirked and typed back.

Asher: We'll watch something with action and shooting next.

Alexis: We better or I will mutiny.

Asher snorted as he read my messages. He put his cell away and continued cuddling with Trisha. My phone vibrated. I checked it.

Isaac: Next, an action movie, please?

I snorted, he hated this too.

Alexis: If not, I'm planning a hostile takeover, you in?

Isaac snorted. My phone vibrated.

Isaac: Just give the signal.

I smiled to myself. I got another text.

Ethan: What are you guys doing?

I snickered quietly.

Alexis: We're planning a rebellion if the next movie doesn't have high body counts. You in?

Ethan snickered. My phone vibrated.

Ethan: YES!

I laughed silently. I was about to put my phone away when it vibrated. I checked it.

Miles: What are you three up to?

I grinned; Miles always watched me and the twins carefully when we were snickering. Chaos usually ensued soon after.

Alexis: Just planning a coup if the next movie is boring. Want in?

I looked across the room to watch Miles look at my message. His lips made a half grin.

Miles: Are there explosives involved?

I snickered as I answered.

Alexis: Could be...

I watched as Miles read it. He looked up from his phone, a full grin on his face. I winked at him. He shook his head before looking back down at his phone. My phone vibrated.

Miles: I'm in.

I looked up from my phone and raised an eyebrow. Miles was never usually willing to create havoc; then again, this movie was boring. He gave me a small nod; he was serious. I gave him a big smile. He smirked at me. I put my phone away and watched the movie.

We were at the part where Juliet was going to take the potion that would put her to sleep. I couldn't take it anymore. I got up to walk into the foyer to pull my jacket on.

"Red?" Isaac whispered.

I looked at him and made a walking motion with my fingers. Isaac nodded then went back to watching the movie. I looked over at Miles, made the same gesture and pointed over my shoulder.

Miles looked around the room and noticed the couples getting touchy with each other, well except for Riley and Zeke. Those two seemed to be playing a game on their phones together. His ears started to turn pink; Miles quickly got to his feet and crossed the room, apologizing for blocking the television. No one seemed to notice. I waited in the foyer as he pulled his green snow jacket on over his shoulders. His green sweater pulled up as he pulled on his coat, flashing me a glimpse of hard abs. Miles was the State Swim Champion for the last three years, and his body showed it.

I turned away and headed outside. Rule one of being friends with guys: don't get caught drooling. The cold bit into my skin as I buttoned up as fast as possible. Miles stepped onto the porch, closing the door behind him.

"I thought you might like to get out of sitting through the make-out session about to start," I said, smirking up at him as we headed down the porch steps.

He nodded, his ears almost back to his usual pale. "Thank you." He grinned down at me gratefully. "I have been mentally calculating the odds of an asteroid entering the atmosphere and only hitting the DVD player."

I snorted as we headed down the shoveled walkway. "And what did you come up with?" I asked as I pulled out my black skulls scarf and wrapped it around my neck.

"I started with the house: 1 in 4,5755,561,741,716," he told me confidently.

I smiled as he pulled out his own gloves to put on.

"I was still working on the calculations for it hitting the DVD player."

I laughed as I began pulling out my own gloves. "Not a fan of tragedies?" I asked, watching him pull out his own gray wool beanie and pull it on.

"If they are done right," he admitted. "I think plays should be done in a theater and not turned into a movie. It loses something."

I thought about that then shrugged. "I've never seen a play, so I will take your word for it."

He looked down at me, his brow furrowed. "You've never been to a play?" he asked slowly in his 'careful what you say, don't insult her' voice.

I had to bite back a smile as I shook my head. "Never had a lot of extra time,"

I watched his grin fade out of the corner of my eye. He pulled out his phone and started typing.

"Miles? What are you doing?" I asked in my sweet voice, already having a hunch.

His lips moved to a half grin. "I'm looking for any upcoming plays in Missoula," he said matter-of-factly.

I smiled. "You don't need to take me to see a play." I felt the need to it point out.

His half grin turned into a smile. "Yes, I think I do,"

I snorted as we crossed the street. "I will never be a fan of tragedies, Miles."

"Not all plays are tragedies, Lexie," he countered. "In January, the university is doing a Midsummer's Night Dream." He continued tapping his phone.

"Miles, it's in Missoula," I reminded him.

He smirked. "Yes, which is an hour away," he reminded me. When he was done with his phone, he looked down at me grinning. "It's not a tragedy, and I've already bought the tickets."

I chuckled. The shithead knew me too well. If he had already spent the money, he knew I wouldn't let that ticket go to waste.

"You cheat."

"You started it," he countered.

I shook my head, smiling as I pulled out my beanie. "How are you going to get the guys to go?" I asked, curious now.

He chuckled. "I didn't even bother buying tickets for them. It's not something they'd really try."

I thought about Zeke watching a play and snickered as I pulled my beanie on over my head.

He smothered a grin before looking away.

"What?" I asked.

He looked back, smirking now. "Your cross bones are off center."

I reached up and tried to find the small patch.

"Here, I'll get it." Miles reached over and adjusted my beanie until the patch was at the center of my forehead. "There."

"Thank you, sir," I said in a fake British accent.

His smirk spread into a smile. "Anytime, my lady." His gallant voice always made me smile.

"You are so OCD," I pointed out as we started walking again.

He sighed. "A little, yes," he agreed. "I like things put away, in their place and easy to find when I'm distracted."

I glanced up to see his ears were a tinge of pink.

"I'm the same way," I admitted.

He grinned down at me. "You're not that bad about it,"

I shrugged. We walked for few minutes in comfortable silence.

"How are you doing, Miles?" I asked quietly as I moved to avoid a patch of ice.

"I'm all right," he said, using his smooth, silky voice I loved to hear. "The house is... just quiet."

I bit my bottom lip. Miles' mother hadn't been home since October, and frankly, I was starting to not like her for it. "If you ever need some noise, call me." I smiled up at him while meeting his emerald eyes. "I'm noisy as hell." Then I had an idea. "Or, you can come over to my house and play video games with Rory and me."

He smiled; it was a sad smile. I wrapped my arm around his and rested my head on his shoulder.

"If you need anything, Miles, you know you can call me, right? Anytime." I said seriously.

His other hand went to mine on his arm, he gave my hand a

squeeze then left it there. "I know Lexie." He sighed. "I just don't want to bother anyone."

"You're never a bother, Miles," I reminded him, not so gently. "Definitely not to me." I peeked up at him to see a small half grin on his face. "So, if you want company?"

His warm eyes met mine. "I'll call you," he mumbled, sounding resigned.

I gave him a big smile, making him laugh. It warmed my heart to hear it. It wasn't long after that when his cellphone rang. I let go of him so he could answer it.

"It's Autumn," he told me.

Autumn was Miles' on again-off again girlfriend who lived in Nevada. Since we were in Montana, they took breaks from dating each other. They got back together a month ago.

"Go ahead and head on back." I gestured down the road. "I'm going to walk for a bit more."

Miles looked around the deserted street, frowning. "I can call her back," he offered. "I shouldn't leave you out here alone." His worry was sweet and made me feel all fuzzy inside.

"I'm okay, Miles," I reassured him. "I'll only go another block, then I'll turn back." I headed down the sidewalk away from him. I shooed him back towards Asher's.

"If you're sure..."

"I am, go."

Miles looked like he still didn't like it, but he answered his phone anyway. "Hi, Autumn."

He headed back toward the house. I turned around and kept walking down the street. I kicked snow piles and avoided ice. I was worried about Miles; maybe we needed to get him a pet. What kind of pet would Miles like, though? Something that would keep him company? He was always concentrating on something and losing track of time, so a dog probably wouldn't work. Maybe a cat? They're kind of independent. I wanted to talk to the others about it, though, to see what they thought.

When I judged that the movie would be over, I started heading back. I managed to keep my big secret a secret at least. One of the reasons I didn't watch sappy movies was because they always made me cry. I hated the ones with unhappy endings, too. I'd seen enough of those in real life.

I was walking back towards Asher's street when a chill ran down my neck. I froze. Shit. I looked around for the soul. The chill turned into pain; I spun around to see the fucker behind me. My barriers held against his energy. The old man was dressed in a nice suit; I felt a pressure on my chest. Heart attack probably. I didn't know what to do anymore. I couldn't help him move on. The Veil was shut, and I still didn't know how to open it.

The ghost knew I saw him.

"Can you help me?" he asked.

My chest ached, my head was starting to throb. Maybe I could? I could try?

"Who are you?" I asked.

Then he began talking. Herbert Munich had been a collector of civil war memorabilia. He'd had a full life. He married his high school sweetheart, had four children who gave them nine grandkids. He owned and worked at his antique store for years. After his wife had passed away, he had one of his kids take it over. He understood he was dead. But he didn't understand why he was still here.

Shit. He really didn't have a reason to be here. There was nothing I could do.

I tried to explain. "The Veil was closed by someone. Until I can fix it, everyone's stuck here."

He didn't like that answer. My head was throbbing in time with my pulse now, and the angrier he got, the worse it became. I needed to go, now.

"I'm working on it. I'm sorry." It was all I had to give him.

I stepped around him and headed back towards Asher's block, guilt gnawing at my stomach. Herbert followed. He cursed at me, told me I wasn't doing enough. That I needed to fix it so he could be with his wife again. I felt that pressure in my face and dug a tissue out of my pocket. I was just in time to stop it from hitting my coat. I had no clue what got blood out of wool, and I really didn't want to learn. Herbert's ghost was battering me with energy, more energy than he should have had. I just kept telling him I was working on it. He still cursed me.

When I passed the end of his haunting ground, my stomach was rolling. Every ghost I'd met lately was pissed, and when I told them I couldn't help them, well, they did what Herbert did. They battered their anger at me until I couldn't see straight.

When I reached Asher's house, my nose was still bleeding, my stomach still rolling. I opened the door then hurried through the foyer and up the stairs to the bathroom. I didn't bother to stop to take off my jacket. I stepped into the bathroom and pulled the tissues away; blood started falling again. I cursed and held more tissues to my nose. I used my other hand to unbutton my coat and take it off. My head was throbbing as I sat on the toilet lid and kept pinching my nose shut. The nosebleeds were getting worse as the ghosts got more juice. It was going to start getting dangerous soon. Exactly what I needed right now.

There was a soft knock on the door.

"Lexie? Are you alright?"

"Come on in," I said in a nasally voice.

The door opened, and Miles stepped into the room. He saw the tissues.

"Did you run into a soul?" he asked, gently.

I nodded. "Yeah." I huffed. "I just walked a whole block with this pissed off guy screaming at me to fix the Veil so he could see his wife again." I swallowed hard as a knot of guilt grew in my stomach, it kept getting bigger with every ghost I saw lately.

"I should have insisted that you walk back with me," he mumbled as he came in and sat on the edge of the tub in front of me. His worried eyes ran over my face. "I'm sorry, Lexie."

I shrugged and looked at the floor as I took the tissues away slowly. Only a small trickle this time. I tossed those tissues in the trash and took the toilet paper that Miles handed to me. I put it to my nose.

"Not your fault," I mumbled.

"It's not yours either," he countered.

I sighed. "It's someone's," I said, still in my nasally voice. "I still have no idea where to start."

Miles' mouth pinched down before his eyes met mine. "Lexie, I kind of hired a few graduate students out of several universities."

I raised an eyebrow. Where was he going with this?

"I hired them to research and find anything to do with the Veil or Necromancy," he announced.

My mouth dropped open. My chest instantly felt lighter. He had people out looking for answers? Then I realized what he had said. He hired them. Shit. Guilt slammed down on me hard. I sighed.

"I love the idea Miles, but you don't need to spend money on me," I told him. I didn't want Miles' money, I wanted to see him smile and laugh. Those were the things that mattered to me. I pulled the tissues from my nose, the bleeding had stopped.

His shoulders grew tense. "I've had them looking since October," he admitted quietly.

My eyebrows went up. Wow, the sneaky bastard.

"After we came back from the cemetery I made a few calls and found people who would be able to find what you need. If it exists, they'll find it," he assured me.

I was torn; I didn't want Miles to have to pay for that. But on the other hand, I needed that information as soon as possible. I didn't know what to do.

He saw the indecision in my eyes and gave me a small half smile.

"I'm not calling them off." His voice was firm, taking the guilt away. "Think of it as your Christmas present," he offered.

I don't know what happened next. I was sitting on the toilet lid one second and then the next I was practically in his lap with my arms around his neck. I don't even remember doing it. Miles wrapped his arms around me and squeezed. I really needed a good hug today.

"Thank you, Miles," I whispered against his shirt, my voice cracking.

He rested his chin on my head. "Of course, Lexie."

It wasn't long before I had control of myself again. I let go and sat back on the toilet lid. The sound of the others joking around downstairs floated up the stairs. The movie must have been over.

"I don't think the girlfriends like me," I said, that knot in my gut again.

He frowned. "I think Trisha came with her mind already made up," Miles offered. "She's been sending you glares all night."

I snorted, which hurt my face. Ow.

"I think she's going to try to keep Asher away, not just you, but eventually all of us," Miles added.

I raised an eyebrow at that. "Why do you say that?"

Miles eyes unfocused for a few heartbeats then focused again. "I've noticed some indicators of control issues," he said casually.

I grinned at him. "Yeah, that 'no talking during her movie' shit? What was that about?" Who didn't talk during movies they have already seen a hundred times?

A heavy tread sounded on the stairs.

"I call Zeke," I said instantly.

His eyes unfocused as he listened. "I say, Asher."

We grinned at each other then looked out the bathroom door and waited. Another couple heart beats and Asher came up the stairs into view.

"Damn it," I grumbled.

Miles grinned at me. "I win," he taunted.

I pulled out my wallet and handed him a dollar. "I'm going to figure out how you do that," I warned him, smiling.

Asher was leaning in the door with a puzzled look on his face. I didn't bother explaining our game.

"You okay, Ally?" Asher asked, his eyes running over my face.

"Yeah, just got harassed on the street by a pissed off guy who can't cross-"

Footsteps sounded on the stairs, light ones. I stopped talking and got to my feet. I turned on the water and grabbed a washcloth. "Care if I-"

"Go for it," Asher said before I could even finish.

I smiled my thanks and got the cloth wet. When Trisha stepped onto the second-floor landing, I was just starting to wipe the blood off my face. Asher turned and tried to block her view; he was such a sweetie.

It didn't work.

"Why is there blood?" Trisha asked calmly.

"Bloody nose," I mumbled wiping more blood off my face. She tried to step past Asher, who didn't budge.

"Don't use a washcloth, use toilet paper," Trisha said in disgust.

"I told her she could use the washcloth, Trish, it's fine." Asher's voice was polite, but by the way she reacted, you'd think he'd smacked her. Then she was smiling again.

"Oh, okay. I just wanted to see what was going on," Trisha said sweetly. There was the sound of a small kiss. Then light feet on the stairs again.

Hiding this was going to get annoying. I'd deal--it's what I did. I finished up and folded the washcloth.

"Sorry, Ash."

Asher turned around, still frowning. "Nothing to be sorry for," he told me as he started rubbing the back of his neck. He turned, then headed downstairs.

"That's not a good sign," I mumbled. I tossed the washcloth into the hamper. Miles shrugged.

"Let's go downstairs before I piss someone else off."

"Swear jar," Miles whispered while pointing at me as we left the bathroom.

I chuckled. He smiled. I loved Miles.

I went down the stairs first because, as always, Miles was a gentleman. Everyone was debating the next movie as I pulled my wallet out and dropped another dollar into the jar. The damn thing was almost half full. Zeke was going to be broke soon.

"Lexie?" Zeke asked in his gravelly voice.

I sat down next to the coffee table as I answered. "Just a bloody nose, it's fine." I looked around at the others. "So, what are we watching?"

"We're tied right now. You're the deciding vote," Isaac replied. "Between Hellboy and Along Came Polly."

I winced. "I vote Hellboy."

The guys all cheered. I chuckled at how excited they were. Trisha and Cece sent me a look. I sighed. This wasn't going well. I ignored them and watched the movie.

WE WERE STILL WATCHING Hellboy when my phone rang. I pulled it out and saw that it was Dylan. My eyes met Miles' as I got up. I answered in the kitchen.

"Hey."

"Hey, how's movie night?" Dylan's husky voice rolled through my ear. It was a good voice.

"It's... different. We had to watch a chick flick. And have a swear jar. I'm running out of money."

He laughed.

"How's your night going?" I asked.

Dylan sighed in my ear. "I had to do inventory at the store." He groaned. "I hate inventory."

I smiled. "Yeah, counting is so hard," I teased in a pouty voice to make him laugh.

He chuckled. "I'm seriously going to be counting in my dreams tonight." His voice was muffled, he was probably running his hand over his face; he did that a lot when he was tired. "I wish I could have seen you today," he said, his voice soft.

A heavy weight pressed down on my chest; my stomach knotted. I was sick of this halfway shit.

"I kind of wanted to talk to you about that," I said. My pulse raced as my body tensed. There were a couple heartbeats of silence.

"Oh, yeah?" His voice was neutral; he wasn't giving me anything.

So, I said fuck it and laid it out. "Dylan, I like you. A lot more than I probably should. We've been talking every day since October. I think we hit it off, we have fun just talking to each other, and when we do see each other it's... great." My heart felt like it was going to fly out of my chest. "So, do you want to go out with me?" When he said nothing, I continued. "Cause if not, I'd like to know now. It's time to fish or cut bait." Then I thought about that phrase in the tension. "Me being the bait. That is a horrible saying if you actually think about."

Dylan chuckled.

"But it's accurate," I added. My world paused, I held my breath, and everything around me stilled as I waited for his answer.

"Fish or cut bait?" His husky voice was warm.

My stomach knots had knots. "Yeah."

There was a dull thud then a click. I didn't move for a full minute. He did not just…. I pulled my phone from my ear and saw the truth. The fucker had hung up on me. Almost two months of talking and texting every day and he couldn't even say 'I don't feel that way,' or 'bye'? I stood there, leaning against the kitchen counter, for a good couple of minutes as that sank in. Then it hurt. I fought back tears. I turned to look out the corner windows over the kitchen sink and took deep breaths. It wasn't even that he didn't feel the same way about me; I could understand that. I could deal with that. It was the fucking hanging up without a word that got me. Oh hello, anger, welcome to the party, about fucking time.

My temper pushed back the tears until I could breathe without fighting the tightness in my chest. I'd rather feel angry than hurt, any day. I know I'm supposed to be working on it, but right now, I let myself do what I had to do. I needed to walk back out there to watch movies with my friends and their girlfriends. I couldn't fucking do that if I wanted to fucking cry. Needing a little more motivation, I bit down on my lower lip hard. It pushed the hurt to the back, where it would stay until I was alone to deal with it. I took several deep breaths and found my calm.

I was walking back towards the family room when Cece's voice reached me.

"Why did she get a vote if she wasn't going to watch the movie?"

I had to stop for a fucking moment. I couldn't go in there after hearing that. Not with my temper. I just… needed a minute.

"That was probably Dylan, he usually calls when he gets off work,"

Isaac answered absently. I took deep, calming breaths until my head was clear enough to walk into the family room. I sat back down in my spot and pretended I didn't hear anything. I felt eyes on me. I let out a breath and met Miles' gaze. He raised an eyebrow. I shook my head. He frowned and pulled out his phone. My phone vibrated. I read Miles' text.

Miles: I'm sorry Lexie, if he couldn't see how wonderful you are, than he's too blind for you anyway.

I grinned as I texted back.

Alexis: I agree completely.

Miles grinned then I went back to watching Hellboy. Eventually, I got snacky. I grabbed a small paper bowl and filled it with chips then sat back down. I was quietly munching when Zeke spotted me.

"Lexie, you can't eat chips," Zeke reminded me.

"They're homemade and baked. So, yeah, I can," I snapped. I looked at him and ate another chip in front of him. "See, easy."

"Lexie," Zeke growled.

"Zeke," I growled back.

We suddenly had everyone's attention. I just got dumped without even being in a relationship in the first place, which I'm sure is impossible. But it happened, and I wanted to eat some of the chips I made today. So, yeah, I was going to fight him on this.

"Zeke, she sliced all of them today. Come on," Asher tried to intercede; he saw where this was going.

Some of my fights with Zeke in the last couple of months had been legendary. Yelling and screaming. Hell, I even threw a pillow at him once. Asher didn't want that tonight. I looked back at the movie and tried to ignore him.

"You know what... the doctor said," Zeke tried again.

I sighed deeply and looked him in the eye. "Zeke, man, I love ya, but if you come after my chips today, you will have a fucking fight on your hands," I said, then growled as I pulled my wallet out, pulled out my last single and dropped it in the jar.

Zeke opened his mouth to keep arguing.

"Zeke," Miles warned him with his calm voice.

Zeke blinked then looked at Miles.

"Let it go today," Miles told him firmly.

Zeke frowned at him, then looked back at me, then back to Miles and backed off. I went back to watching the movie.

"What happened with Dylan?" Ethan asked sweetly.

Miles groaned.

"Back off, Snoopy," I warned him.

Isaac burst out laughing at Ethan's new nickname.

"But I'm curious," Ethan insisted.

I rolled my eyes and gave in. The fucker. I looked over at him and gave him my blank face.

"What do you think happened?" I asked looking him in the eye.

I just waited until he got it. His face changed from curious to sympathetic. I looked back at the screen; Hellboy was hitting a monster. I fought the urge to pretend it was Dylan.

"What did he say?" Asher asked gently.

I snorted. "He didn't say anything," I said keeping my voice matter of fact. I just wanted to watch the movie; I stopped fighting it. I put Dylan's head on the monster.

"He had to say something," Isaac asked, joining in.

I had enough; they wanted to know? Fine. I watched Hellboy drop into a subway station.

"He didn't say a word. He hung up," I told them, not taking my eyes off the movie. "I told him how I felt, asked him out and he hung up."

"Damn." Riley hissed.

"Swear jar," Zeke mumbled.

"That asshole," Asher cursed. "I'm sorry, Lexie. I've never seen him treat someone that way."

I nodded. So, it was just me he treated that way. Great. Could today get any worse?

"You still owe the swear jar," I said, my voice was flat.

The other boys chuckled along with Riley.

"You know, Lexie," Riley began, drawing my attention. "You just tell me when and I'll introduce you to three guys who would just love you. And I mean one of them would get on his knees to ask you out."

I smiled. "Sounds good to me. Give me a week, and I'll be up for it," I told her.

She smiled back. "Just tell me when."

I liked Riley.

We all went back to the movie, talking back and forth about nothing, really. Just hanging out. The movie was almost over when the doorbell rang. I was zoning out and didn't notice Asher get up to answer the door. There was the murmur of voices from the foyer. Asher's voice was getting louder. I stopped watching the movie and looked at the archway. What the hell? Zeke got to his feet and peeked out the blinds. He frowned then left the living room. That made me curious. Then Zeke's gravelly voice came from the foyer.

"-off."

It was the end of a sentence. He must have started talking quietly, then got louder. Isaac, Ethan, Miles, and I all looked at each other, puzzled. The twins got to their feet and went to the window behind the couch. They peeked through the blinds.

"Shit," Isaac said.

"Ooohhh, that takes some balls," Ethan said as he started smiling. His smile got bigger.

"Swear jar," Riley chimed.

"What's going on?" I asked.

Isaac was grinning now too. What the hell? I was about to get up when Asher walked into the family room.

"Ally, Dylan's outside," Asher announced. "He wants to talk to you."

I was frozen for a full minute. What the hell? He couldn't see me for the last month, but he could come down now? I snorted and shook my head. Yeah, it fucking figured.

"If you don't want to talk to him, I'll tell him to fuck off," he offered sweetly, already pulling out his wallet and taking out a single. "Hell, Zeke's already said that to him. But he's not budging."

I grew calm; this I could handle. "No, I'll tell him myself." I got up and pulled my wallet out.

"What are you doing?" Miles asked from his side of the coffee table. I pulled out a bill and dropped it into the swear jar.

"Just preparing." I smiled sweetly at them, then tucked my wallet into my back pocket as I turned to walk into the foyer.

"She put in a twenty," Isaac announced. The boys burst out laughing.

I just wanted to get this over with. I saw Zeke standing in the door frame like a huge guard dog. It made me grin as I pulled on my jacket.

"You sure, Ally girl?" Asher asked as he stepped under the archway to the family room, his face worried.

I smiled up and him; he was such a sweetheart. I reached up and gripped his chin lightly between my thumb and forefinger.

"I've got this, sweetie," I assured him. I squeezed his chin once, then let go. I walked up to Zeke's side and touched his arm. He looked down at me, his hard face looking scary for anyone else. His eyes ran over me, becoming a little less stern. He looked like he was debating whether or not to let me talk to Dylan. But it wasn't his decision to make.

"Zeke, I got this," I told him confidently.

He gave a big, deep sigh, sent one last glare out the door, then stepped inside the house. He really didn't like this. My lungs felt tight. I didn't bother to button up my coat; I doubted he'd be here for long anyway. I closed the door behind me then walked out to the middle of the porch to meet him. Bracing myself, I looked up at him.

Dylan was a head taller than me. His dark sapphire eyes met mine, and my heart clenched. His strong chin and angled jaw gave him fuller cheeks. It gave him a boyish charm that made my heart race. His brown hair was shorter than it had been last month. Still a little long on top and sticking up everywhere like he'd been running his fingers through it. His athletic frame was wearing a dark blue snow jacket over black jeans. He was still the hottie I met in October.

"What do you want, Dylan?" I asked calmly as my gut tightened.

He stepped closer, making me look up at his face. He was probably trying to keep the others from eavesdropping. Fine. I didn't want this to be public anyway.

"I need to make something clear to you that, apparently, I didn't on the phone." His warm, husky voice rolled through my ears and ran down my spine. It sparked my temper. I didn't want to feel this way about him, especially now.

"You made things pretty fucking clear when you hung up on me," I snapped at him.

His warm eyes ran over my face as if he was taking in every detail and committing it to memory. The damn butterflies went crazy, the little traitors. When he was done, his eyes met mine again.

"No." He shook his head. "I really didn't." Before I could ask what he was talking about, his fingers lifted my chin; then his lips were on mine. I had half a heartbeat of shock, then I was kissing him back. The world grew fuzzy as my lips moved against his. My stomach did that low, hard flip; my heart was in my throat. My hands went to his chest while his other hand came to my other cheek as his mouth moved with mine. Warmth spread out from my chest, filling me with light until I was sure I had to be glowing. Dylan was kissing me. DYLAN was kissing me. And it was better than I ever imagined. Wait a minute, this was Dylan, the Dylan that hung up on me earlier. I pulled back, breaking the kiss. I stepped back a couple of times then looked up at him, now thoroughly confused.

"You hung up on me. You didn't say a word, you just hung up." I was still trying to get my thoughts together after that kiss. "And now you kiss me?" I had no idea what the hell was going on.

His eyes ran over my face again then came back to my eyes. "Lexie, I didn't hang up on you. I heard you say that you liked me, then I was up and out the door before you even finished your sentence."

My heart raced and melted at the same time. It was an odd feeling.

"I ran to my truck, climbed in, started it, and that's when I remembered I still had you on the phone." He was talking fast, like he didn't think I'd listen to him for long and he wanted to explain everything before that happened. "The last thing I heard was you saying 'fish or cut bait.' I repeated it because hearing your voice say that was fucking cute. I was trying to tell you that I was on my way when I hit that nasty corner by my house. I had to drop the phone, or I was going to run off the road. When I finally managed to get the phone off the floor, the call was over. I thought I had told you I was on my way, and you hung up because you knew I was coming down. I didn't even know you were pissed at me until Asher answered the door and called me an asshole."

I bit the corner of my lower lip. I wanted to believe him, I really did. He came closer, forcing me to look up at him. The butterflies went crazy; my fingers tingled.

"I probably should have called back, but I was still wrapping my head around the fact you like me. I thought you didn't think of me that way."

"Why did you think that?" I asked, my voice soft.

A small smile crossed his lips. His warm eyes ran over my face. "I always started all the flirting," he explained. One of his hands reached out to take mine. "I wanted to see if you were interested or just joking around." His thumb started rubbing the center of my palm. My heart raced from his touch.

"One of my friends told me to stop flirting to see if you kept flirting." He said.

I closed my eyes, that was the stupidest thing ever.

"And I never did." I kept my voice soft, hoping Asher wouldn't hear me.

"Why didn't you?" he whispered.

He used my hand to pull me closer to him, then he wrapped his other arm around my waist under my coat, his fingers spread wide over the small of my back. It sent those warm tingles up and down my body. The rest of the world disappeared as I took a deep breath of sandalwood then opened my eyes. Those dark eyes immediately found mine.

"I didn't expect you to stick around," I admitted quietly. I was still having trouble believing the guys weren't going to bail on me. "I'm not exactly everyone's cup of coffee."

He grinned warmly at me. "So, we were both being stupid," he offered quietly, pulling me closer till I was pressed against him.

I reached up to stroke my fingertips along his jaw as I met his eyes again. "Looks like," I admitted quietly.

He grinned at me before leaning down, his lips going to my ear.

"Lexie," he whispered. "I've been crazy about you since we met." That fuzzy warmth washed through me. He continued. "I thought you didn't want me, and I still couldn't stop calling you."

"I thought you friend-zoned me. And I couldn't stop talking to you," I admitted in a whisper.

"Lexie," his lips brushing my ear as he spoke. "Wanna be my girlfriend?"

I smiled and felt like I could fly. So, naturally, I was a smart-ass. "Sure, I've got nothing better to do." I giggled wickedly.

He groaned painfully at me. He pulled back only enough to kiss me again. It was a soft, tender kiss that made my heart race. He eased back a little then kissed the corner of my mouth. My skin tingled. His lips brushed my cheek where he kissed me again. He made a path up my jaw, and I let him. I loved every kiss, every brush of his lips as he trailed soft kisses to my cheekbone.

"You know, I can't seem to stop kissing you," he mumbled between kisses.

I melted like an ice cube in the sun. I didn't really want him to stop. When he kissed his way back to my lips, I was more than ready for another kiss. His lips took mine again, sending my heart racing. I kissed him back eagerly, his lips moved with mine just as much. Dylan was kissing me like he couldn't get enough of me. I felt the tip of his tongue stroke my bottom lip; sparks ran down my spine. I was about to open my lips when a light began flashing. I growled in frustration. We stopped kissing; I opened my eyes and looked up to see the porch light being turned on and off.

"They are so dead," I stated.

Dylan grinned down at me and pulled me against him, his arms tightening around me. My cheek rested on his chest as I wrapped my arms around his firm waist under his jacket. He felt really good. I was still not quite so sure this was happening. I going to wake up now, right? No? Good. Dylan's lips rested against my forehead.

"I'm sorry I didn't kiss you sooner," he whispered.

"What took you so fucking long?" I whispered back.

He chuckled quietly. "Stupidity," he answered, his voice warm. I smiled. "Lots and lots of stupidity."

I chuckled. The boys started flashing the porch light at us again. We both cursed. The word "swear jar" was yelled from the house.

He groaned. "Is there anything you can do to get them to stop? 'Cause we've got some shit to talk about," he asked, still whispering.

I thought for a moment and grinned. "I believe so." I looked up at him and smiled. "But you'd have to let go of me." His brow drew down, and his eyes unfocused, looking above my head at the house. He didn't let go.

"Dylan?"

His eyes focused again before he looked down at me. "I'm weighing the pros and cons," he admitted. I laughed quietly. He gave a big sigh and let me go. I pulled out my cell phone and texted Zeke.

Alexis: Who is fucking with the lights?

Zeke: The twins.

Alexis: Can you stop them? We're talking out here.

Zeke: Why don't you two come inside, it's cold out there.

"Oh, you little shits," I grumbled.

Dylan stepped back and leaned against the porch rail. "Who?" he asked.

"All of them; they're trying to get us inside so they can hear better," I told him as I texted Zeke back.

Alexis: If you stop them I'll give you five of the curse words I have left. Asher too, if he helps.

Zeke: Done.

I giggled wickedly, and put my phone away. "I just bribed Zeke to get them to stop with the light." I looked up. He was watching me with a little smile on his face. "What?"

"You're just cute," he said, smirking.

I smiled at him. The guy had bad taste in girls.

"We need to figure out our schedules, though," Dylan said. Reality set in. His hands reached out; he took both of mine and pulled me closer so we could keep whispering. The butterflies went crazy. He kept holding my hands.

"If you couldn't get away for a month before, then how are we ever going to see each other?" I asked, keeping my voice low.

"That science project is set up now, so that'll free up some time," he began, his eyes on the house wall, unfocused. "I'll tell Dad that I'm only willing to work three shifts a week. He'll have to hire people immediately; I know a few of my friends from school who could use the cash."

"My Friday night is always free. And I can get my Saturday and Sunday stuff done in the morning and move my research to during the week," I whispered back, mentally going over my schedule.

Dylan grinned down at me. "That works, I can pick shifts that work during the week, or in the mornings on the weekends." He was still whispering; it kept sending those warm shivers down my spine. I tried to ignore it for now.

"What about football?"

"That's over for us; Asher's in the playoffs, remember?" he said as his eyes kept running over my face; he still had that little smile on his lips.

"That's this Saturday; you want to go?" I asked.

That smile grew. "Hell, yeah. That'll make it so we can see each other when school's going on." His eyes came back to mine. "But we're on vacation right now, so, we'll both have a lot more time to see each other. It might not be everyday but-."

"We can switch back and forth on driving, or meet in the middle," I offered.

He gave a soft groan and pulled me until I was pressed against him. "A girl who is willing to compromise, and knows the value of gas." He looked down at me like I was something special. I'd never had anyone look at me that way before. It was... different.

"Bad news, though..."

"You have to go," I guessed.

"If I want to get everything in place so I can see you Friday night, yeah. I need to go." He didn't sound happy about it.

"So, you're coming to game night this week?" I asked, hopeful.

He smiled at me. "Wouldn't miss it." His eyes ran over my face again, then focused on my lips. "But before I go, I need to kiss my girl-friend goodbye."

My stomach did that low, hard flip again. I tilted my chin up as he came down to meet me. His lips were soft and gentle this time. My pulse raced as I moved my lips against his. His palm held my cheek; the butterflies kept going. Dylan was kissing me again. Sweet, cute, funny Dylan. Warmth and happiness filled me until I was sure I was going to be unbearably girly later. He took his time moving his lips over mine, kissing me until I didn't have a thought in my head. Even-tually, he pulled back and took a deep breath, his eyes still on my face.

"Okay, gotta go," he said quietly. I pulled away from him, but he still didn't move. He was looking at me like he couldn't take his eyes off me.

"Dylan..." I reminded him.

He blinked, his cheeks tinting pink. "Okay, I'm going," he grum-bled. "I'll see you later."

He stepped close, leaned down and gave me a quick kiss on the forehead. I smiled.

"Drive safe," I said quietly.

He gave me a wink before he turned and went down the stairs. I waited until he drove down the road to head inside. I paused before opening the door. I took a breath and braced myself. I walked in. I took off my jacket, draping it over the banister then turned around. The family room was a mess. Zeke had Isaac pinned to the floor and was sitting sideways on his butt. Asher had Ethan in an arm lock against the couch. I started laughing.

"That's what happens when you mess with me, boys," I taunted.

Zeke bounced on Isaac. "Say you're sorry," Zeke ordered, still bouncing his big butt on Isaac's back.

"Sorry, Red!" Isaac grunted. "Now get his ass off me!"

"Swear jar!" several of us called at the same time. Trisha didn't seem to think it was funny.

"Don't let them up yet." I pulled out my cell and aimed. "Say don't spy on Lexie!"

The guys just laughed as I took the picture. I immediately sent it to

Dylan, grinning the whole time. The guys let the boys up as the girls fixed the couch cushions. Ethan was practically bouncing on his toes, and he wasn't the only one.

"So, what happened?" Riley all but shouted as she sat back into the wide armchair next to Zeke. Everyone sat down and looked at me expectantly. I sighed and sat down in my spot by the coffee table. I told them about Dylan's mad rush to get here, and why he dropped the phone. The girls awed. My face warmed.

"Oh, my God, Red's blushing!" Isaac shouted. "Get a pic, get a pic!"

I flipped him off.

"So, are you two dating now?" Trisha asked, looking confused.

I thought it was obvious; after all, they had probably watched the whole thing.

"Yeah, we're dating." I couldn't seem to stop smiling. The twins gave out a whoop, and the girls just smiled. Then I looked at the guys. "Now, how much spying did you guys do?"

"None," Isaac said.

"Not a bit," Ethan added.

"I'm pleading the fifth," Asher admitted.

I looked at Zeke. Miles wouldn't have spied but Zeke would. And Zeke never lied.

"Zeke?" I asked directly. He met my eyes and kept his mouth shut. Okay, fine. I looked at his girlfriend.

"Riley, how much watching did they do?" I asked her sweetly.

Riley grinned back at me mischievously. "Oh, they watched the whole thing," Riley ratted them out. The guys groaned while she continued. "When he kissed you the first time, Asher had to stop Zeke from going out there." I looked at Zeke, my question on my face.

"From our angle, it looked like he forced you to kiss him," Zeke admitted, not sorry one bit.

"When Isaac said you were kissing him back, he calmed down," Riley explained as she looked at Zeke with a big smile on her face.

"Zeke," I said. He looked at me. "What would have happened if he touched me and I didn't want him to?"

Zeke rolled his eyes. "You would have kneed him in the balls."

I smiled at him sweetly. "Thanks for looking out for me anyway."

He just gave me that half grin of his.

We all went back to watching the movie. It wasn't long after that when the girls got up to leave, and the guys got up to walk them to their cars. With the sudden free seating, I got up and stole a corner of the sofa. I moved a throw pillow and curled up into the corner. When I was comfy, I went back to watching the movie. Faith and Trisha stalled in the archway.

"Aren't you leaving too, Lexie?" Trisha asked, her voice curious.

I looked up to see her face looking slightly strained, as if she was trying not to do something. I really didn't care right now. If the girls wanted to leave before our usual over time, that was on them. I wanted to watch a good movie with decent body counts.

"Yeah," I looked back at the television. "I just want to watch the last of this," I hedged. I wasn't lying. I did want to watch the rest of this movie, and then the next one before going home. "Nice meeting you girls," I called to them on their way out.

Riley was the only one who said anything back. That wasn't a good sign. I went back to watching the movie with Miles, who chose to stay on the floor. I was tired, but I knew as soon as I went to sleep, a ghost would show up. It had been happening all week, and now I had to deal with the girls not liking me. It wasn't too long before the guys came back in. Isaac plopped onto me.

"Shit, Isaac!" I grunted. The shithead was heavy.

"Oh sorry, Red, didn't see you there." His voice was full of innocence as he slid off me to the middle cushion. Zeke took a wide chair. Ethan sat on the other side of Isaac, and Asher took the other arm chair.

"With you being quiet and all, I figured you went home." Isaac said.

I gave him a half grin and shoved him further off me with my shoulder. Isaac could always cheer me up.

"I don't think the girls like me," I admitted, looking at each of them in turn. They all looked puzzled.

"Riley loves you," Zeke reassured me.

"Oh, I love Riley. She's great."

"Trisha didn't say anything about you to me," Asher said before he looked around at the others. The others shook their heads. Huh.

"Maybe I'm wrong; I had a kind of weird day today," I admitted then looked back at the movie. "Might have thrown me off."

"You started dating Dylan today," Ethan reminded me.

"Yeah, and that's great, but my best friends kept their girlfriends a secret from me. Doesn't exactly make my day," I countered. The guys were quiet as they mulled this over.

"Okay, you have a point," Ethan admitted as he scratched his eyebrow. "We should have shared with you sooner."

"You guys go on and on about how I need to be more open with you, that family doesn't have big secrets." Once I started, I couldn't seem to stop. "A girlfriend is kind of a big secret. Four is an even larger one. You all knew about it; you all met the other girls and made a point not to tell me. That's fucked up."

Okay, yeah. This was what had put me in such a bad mood all afternoon. It hadn't been the shitty painting, it hadn't been Dylan. It had been this. They wanted to know all my shit but kept theirs' a secret. I was tired of it. My heart was heavy as I looked at each of them, well, except Miles. The twins looked like they were in pain. Asher's brow was drawn down. Zeke's face was just blank. They knew I was right. It didn't make me feel any better.

"Is this why you've been quiet most of the night?" Miles asked.

"Yeah," I admitted. "When you guys hide shit like this, it sucks." I wasn't going to say it hurt; they could guess that for themselves.

Isaac got up and dropped on me again. I grunted under his weight. He wrapped his arms and knees around me before resting his chin on my shoulder.

"I'm sorry, Red." Isaac's voice was pouty as he squeezed me. "We didn't mean it like that. You have enough to deal with, and we didn't want to bother you with our shit."

I freed an arm and wrapped it around Isaac's shoulder. "This is the shit you're supposed to talk to me about. It can't be all my shit, all the time. This was you guys not letting me be your friend." Isaac shifted, straddling my hip, taking some of his weight off of me. I guess he wasn't planning on moving anytime soon. He smelled like lemons today. Huh, it was usually limes.

"You're right, Beautiful, we were being shitty friends," Ethan said.

I felt the couch shifting, then Ethan was up and dropping his weight down on my front, pressing me back against the sofa. I grunted under the weight; now I was really getting squished.

"I hate it when she's fucking right," Zeke grumbled. There was the sound of springs moving as someone got up.

"Don't you dare, Zeke!" I warned him. "I'm already being smooshed to death." The twins giggled.

I saw Asher over Ethan's shoulder and braced myself. This was going to hurt. Instead, Asher reached down and yanked Ethan off of me. The relief was instant.

"Oh, thank God." I exhaled in relief.

Asher dropped a laughing Ethan onto the floor and reached for Isaac. Isaac's arms and legs squeezed tight as he clung on like a monkey. I was laughing when Asher yanked him off of me by his belt. I rolled a bit, resting my back against the cushions, thankful that the boys were off of me. That was until Asher sat on the couch edge and leaned back on me. Oh, my fucking God! I smacked him in the back and tried to shove him to the floor.

"Can't... breathe...." I gasped dramatically. Asher pulled up a bit until it was no worse than Isaac had been. His ocean eyes met mine over his shoulder.

"We really didn't mean it like that, Ally. I'm sorry," he said simply

I gave him a small smile to let him know we were good. Vanilla and cinnamon filled my nose. "Just keep me in the loop guys. Okay?" I asked trying not to sound too whiny. "I know I'm a private person-"

"I'll say; getting anything out of you is like pulling teeth," Zeke groused. The others nodded in agreement. I looked over at him and glared.

"And you're just a fountain of information yourself?" I asked sarcastically. "Tell me, Zeke, what color is the couch?" The guys started laughing, as Zeke shook his head with a small grin on his face. I raised an eyebrow, waiting for him to answer.

"Reddish?" he answered uncertainly.

"It's green."

His mouth twitched at me.

"Your being partly color blind is not a huge thing, but it's something you never told me." I looked around the group again. "I'm not the only one who needs to open up around here. You guys all know each other so well. I care about you guys, but you still haven't told me much about yourselves."

They all nodded. They got it.

I smacked Asher's leg. "Now get your heavy ass off me."

Asher smirked and scooted off me to sit on the middle cushion. I sat up and looked at the jar. Thirty-eight bucks. For fucking swearing. I looked up at Asher.

"Can I get my money back from the swear jar now?" I asked seriously. The guys chuckled.

"Go for it," Asher said grinning at me. I gave him a smile, scooted to the edge of the sofa, and grabbed the jar.

"Okay, who had how much?" I asked. They all gave me their numbers as I counted out the money. I handed each of them their stacks, then folded mine and stuck it in my bra. I didn't even think about. The twins started giggling.

I pointed at them. "If you had boobs, you'd do the same thing," I told them honestly. They laughed.

The room felt lighter as I picked up the other stack and held it out to Zeke. "I figured you can give Riley back her money."

Zeke took it and tucked it into his pocket. I sat back.

"Can we please watch a fun movie now?" I begged with a pained look on my face.

"Please?" Isaac begged with me. Miles got up, and the debate began.

"I want a high body count," I demanded. I heard snorts from around the room.

"No chick main character either," Ethan chimed in.

"Lots of swearing," Zeke added.

Miles nodded. "Deadpool it is."

I shot my hands into the air in victory. "Yes!"

The guys laughed at me. Miles put the movie in the Blu-ray.

"This movie might be a bad influence on you, Ally," Asher said as he looked down at me, smiling.

"Well, I don't plan on celebrating International Women's Appreciation Day if that's what you mean." My voice was sweet as I gave them my mischievous grin.

The guys all groaned painfully. That scene always made them wince. I thought it was hilarious.

The movie started, and I was feeling better. The guys understood that they had hurt my feelings, and I didn't actually have to come out and say it. They also understood that I wasn't the only one needing to open up. It brought my happy back.

We finished the movie, and I drove home, washed my face then climbed into bed, smiling. Dylan was my boyfriend. I let myself have one girly giggle, then I rolled over and went to sleep.

CHAPTER 3

EARLY THURSDAY MORNING

*P*ain tore through me, jerking me awake. Still mostly asleep, I scrambled backward, trying to get away from it. Heart slamming, I looked around my bedroom. I reached out to turn on the desk lamp. My hand was shaking so badly that it took me three tries to find the button. The light showed me the soul. It was a man in his mid-twenties; he looked like a construction worker. I couldn't get a good look because it felt like every nerve in my body was firing. My body jerked, going rigid, every muscle clenched. I could barely breathe with him so close. My head throbbed, making my vision blurry. I felt my nose start bleeding. Shit.

"Ba-ck up," I managed to say through the convulsions. The ghost must have heard me because my body went limp. I felt weak, like I'd just run a triathlon or something. I was gasping as I reached for the tissues, my hand missing several times. I was getting my breath back when I brought the tissues to my nose. I felt like I had been beaten with several baseball bats; everything hurt. I fought the urge to whimper and curl into a ball. It took me several minutes to have the strength to sit up.

I finally looked at the soul. He was wearing work pants, a dirty t-shirt and work boots. The only thing missing was the hard hat. His friendly face was drawn, he kept licking his lips.

"Who are you?" My voice was weak as I tried to stay upright. Two ghosts in a few hours was never good thing.

"I'm Carl, Carl Mason. You can see me," he said desperately. "I knew you could. You can help me. Please?" I leaned against the wall, I was still trying to get over the effects of his death memories.

"How the fuck did you die, Carl?" I asked, my voice pained.

He blinked at me a couple of times before answering. "I messed up on the job, did something stupid and electrocuted myself," he admitted. "But what the hell am I still doing here?" I took a deep breath and let it out slowly to give myself time to gather my wits.

"The Veil is shut," I told him in my nasally voice. "Someone has fucked with the way in, and I'm trying to figure out how to fix it. Until then, you're stuck here." I was blunt. I didn't have enough energy for tact. He looked at me like I had just killed his dog. "Carl, I'm trying. I'm trying to find an answer to fix this. You just need to hold on. Okay?"

"You're.... you're a kid, how the hell are you supposed to fix this?" he snapped as he started pacing back and forth across my room.

"I ask myself that every day. But I will. It's just going to take some time." I tried to be comforting but my head was in a vice, and my stomach was starting to roll. "How did you find me anyway?"

He stopped pacing and blinked at me. "The light."

"Huh?"

"From this side, the world is darker. It's always dusk here. I was walking around the lake, there was a bright light in the dark." He looked around the room. "And it's coming from you."

Oh, shit. "So, you just followed it?" This was not good. All the ghosts were ramping up in energy, they were leaving their haunting grounds, and now I was learning I looked like a freakin' beacon? You have got to be fucking kidding me.

"Yeah, there isn't much light on this side," he said.

The pressure grew in my head; my nose bled more. I grabbed more tissues as I felt my barriers shake. "Look Carl. I can't help you right now, but I'm working on it. You can't stay here..." I stopped talking as my stomach lurched. Shit. "You're hurting me."

I jumped from the bed and ran to the bathroom. I made it just in time. I threw up, again and again. When my stomach finally stopped cramping, I leaned against the tub. I wadded up some toilet paper and held it to my nose. Carl didn't come in with me. Thank you, Carl. I sat there, miserable, guilt gnawing at my gut. I knew I needed to reach my center, but every fucking time I tried, I freaked out and climbed back out. Your center is the very core of who you are and what you are. To reach it you had to go through all the significant events in your life. The bad, the good, and the ugly. You'd see it in a way you didn't before. That wasn't always good.

I leaned my head back against the sliding glass door of the shower and just tried to breathe through the pain. I needed to get my beads. They were in my room. I needed to move.

It took me longer than I want to admit to get up and walk slowly into my bedroom. I made it to my desk and opened the drawer. I pulled on my eight onyx beaded bracelets and dropped to my bed. I wasn't conscious long.

THE BLARING ALARM woke me up. I groaned then hit the damn thing. My head was heavy, my body still achy. In short, I felt like shit. I got up and went into the bathroom; I did my usual morning routine without a shower or makeup this time. I was going to be working out; there was no point in doing either now. I put my hair up in a bun and looked in the mirror. My long copper hair was in a mass on the back of my head. My heart shaped face was pretty, at least I thought so, but nothing spectacular. My already pale skin looked even paler this morning. The bags under my eyes were dark. In short, I looked how I felt. My eyes were a mix of dark green and light green, with gold flecks mixed in. At least my eyes were still bright.

I snorted at myself as I went to my bedroom and got ready for my workout. I pulled on my black Capri yoga pants, my black sports bra, and a dark blue tank top. I pulled on my sneakers and headed downstairs.

The great room was empty; not surprising, considering it was before seven in the morning on a Thursday. Rory's house had an open floor plan. The living room, dining room, and kitchen were all in one room. Well, the kitchen had its own alcove on the right side of the house, but otherwise, one big room. I turned the machine on to make a cup of coffee, then I made buttered toast. If it stayed down, I promised myself a real breakfast after the gym. Then a nap at the cemetery. Oh, yeah, a nap, that sounded great. But my barriers held against two ghosts in one day. Yay. I still felt like shit.

I slowly ate my toast and drank my coffee. By the time I was done, I was feeling less foggy. I grabbed my water bottle, keys, cell phone. I pulled on Miles' gray hoodie then my leather jacket and headed out the door. It was butt ass freezing. I ran into my truck and cranked the heater while it warmed up. As soon as I could, I drove to the gym the guys called home.

I hurried inside, cursing myself for not just wearing sweat pants. The gym was made of several huge rooms: a weight room, a mat room, and a room with several MMA octagons. Like I said, huge. I found the guys next to the lockers where members stashed their gear.

"Hey," I mumbled as I walked to my locker. Everyone looked up. Out of the corner of my eye, I saw them all frown.

"You look like shit," Zeke announced.

"You all right, Red?"

"You don't have to work out today if you're sick," Miles pointed out gently.

"You're paler than usual, Beautiful."

"Ally? What happened?"

"I had a double header yesterday, within about eight hours of each other," I told them as I unlocked my locker. The guy a couple lockers down got really interested. He was around our age. Broad shoulders, brown hair, and a cute face. That's all I got when he turned then looked me up and down with a flirty smile on his face. I pulled out my hand wraps and glared at him.

"I was trying to talk about having seizures while being discreet, you dick," I snapped at him. He had a half grin on his face as he went back to putting his gear away. The guys were laughing as he closed his locker before heading out of the gym. I put everything in my locker and slammed it shut. I sat down on the bench and started wrapping my hands. The guys were still eyeing me.

"But good news." I looked up to make sure no one was around. "My barriers held through both. And by the way, don't electrocute yourself; it's the weirdest fucking way to die."

The guys chuckled.

Zeke eyed me. "You sure you're up for this?" Zeke asked doubtfully.

"Bring it, bitch," I challenged him.

Zeke got that grin that I had learned to hate. Oh shit. Could I say I was sorry now? Fuck. Me and my mouth.

"Let's go."

AN HOUR AND A HALF LATER, I hit the mat again. After working out on the bags, the weights, and not to mention the running Zeke always made me do, I was tired. But I wanted to get this damn throw down. I growled in frustration. Hot, sweating, and trying to catch my breath, I sat up to glare at Miles. Sweet Miles was being a dick. Okay, he wasn't. I was the one fucking up, and he was just teaching me.

"Did you see what I did with my hips in that throw?" he asked again for the fifth time.

Okay, now I was getting pissed. "No Miles, I didn't see it. I was too busy being thrown," I pointed out. This wasn't working. I knew what would, but Miles wasn't going to like it.

"Sweetie, I know you aren't all that comfortable touching me, but you're gonna have to let me do this in slow motion. With you putting me in the right position, like Isaac does." It was the fastest way for me to learn. Isaac had the same problem when teaching me; it wasn't until I got into the right position that I understood what he was saying. But since Miles refused to do that, I was still stuck on basic self-defense throws--two months later.

His fingers started tapping out a staccato rhythm against his leg. I just waited. His green eyes met mine without the glasses today. It was strange not seeing him with glasses, but it did show his eyes off more. He nodded. Finally. I got up and stood a couple feet in front of him. He hesitated. I sighed then looked at him over my shoulder. His face was drawn.

"Sweetie, either you put me in position and show me how to do this throw. Or someone else is going to grab me, and I won't be able to do it when I need to."

His eyes flashed from warm to cold. Oh, he didn't like the thought of that. I'd learned over the last couple of months that Miles did get angry, but he always controlled it. I kind of envied him for that ability.

His mouth pressed into a line before he stepped up behind me. "All right, someone grabs you from behind and pins your arms." Miles pressed the front of his body to my back, wrapped his arms around my chest, and locked his hands together. We both ignored the fact his hands were basically locked together over my breasts. "Now you get into the second stance."

I put my feet further apart than shoulder width.

Miles let go of me, his hands went to my hips. "Now, what you're going to do is turn your hips." I turned my hips the way he wanted me to. Miles continued. "But at the same time, you're going to take this leg." One hand went to my upper thigh on my right leg. "You're going to hook it back and around my ankle, but you're crossing behind you to the opposite side. Don't forget to plant it. Otherwise, you're still going to be stuck." He explained. I held on to his shoulder and moved the way his hand made me go. He let go and stood up. "In that position, all you need to do is twist yourself straight, and the guy will drop."

I nodded. "Okay, I think I see what you're saying now," I said, getting back to the starting position.

"Ready?"

"Yep."

Miles grabbed me from behind, pinning my arms. My forearms came up, holding him to me. I instantly dropped into second; turned my hip while hooking my leg back to the opposite side, behind his ankle; planted my foot, then I twisted as I stood up straight. Miles dropped to the mat with a thud.

"Yes!" I threw my arm up in victory. About fucking time!

Miles was smiling as he got up. "Okay, you were right," Miles admitted. "That is the best way to teach you." I just smiled at him.

"Now let's do it again. Get it into your muscle memory."

I nodded.

I continued to drop Miles for another thirty minutes until I really didn't have to think about it anymore.

"Now you're going to do it against Asher." Miles announced.

I raised my eyebrow at that. "But, he's big," I felt the need to point out.

Asher was a head and a half taller than me, not to mention he had way more muscles.

Miles nodded. "Yeah, and you're small. It should work on him, but if it doesn't, I'd like to know now rather than if someone grabs you," Miles said before he looked across the gym and called for Asher. Miles looked back at me. "We'll also need to try it on Zeke; it might work on him too."

Asher came up sweating, his face red.

"Grab her from behind and pin her arms, please." Miles requested.

Asher's brow drew down. "You're still on that throw?" Asher's voice was sharp.

Miles looked uncomfortable. "Yes, it's my fault. I didn't want to grab... places," Miles admitted.

Asher rolled his eyes and came to stand behind me. "All you have to do with her is look at her." Asher looked down at me, I grinned up at him. "And say, 'Ally girl, I'm sorry, but I need to grab places to show you what you need to do.'"

I snickered.

Asher looked back at Miles. "She's not like normal girls, Miles."

Miles glared at Asher. "Yeah, I got that," Miles said, his voice growing colder. "And now, we'll move along faster. So, if you please." He gestured for Asher to get on with it.

I looked forward. Asher grabbed me from behind and locked his arms. I did what Miles taught me. Asher didn't drop, but he did have to let go to keep on his feet. Asher turned back around towards me.

"You're going to have to put more force into that last move, Ally." He gestured for me to turn around again. "Remember it's not me grabbing you, it's some dickhead who's trying to hurt you."

I nodded. Asher grabbed me again. I made the move again only slamming my upper body back against him harder. Asher hit the mat with a big thud. I chuckled. Then I sobered. I looked at Miles, dreading what he was going to say next. Miles grinned. Shit.

"Thanks, Asher; send Zeke please," Miles said. I groaned. Asher was chuckling as he left. I glared at Miles.

"I want to see if it will work for most people. And Zeke's the biggest we have," he pointed out.

I sighed; my body was tired, and now I had to drop Zeke. Ugh.

Zeke came up and looked at Miles.

"Grab her from behind and pin her arms, please." Miles said. Zeke's face became hard, but before he could say anything, Miles cut him off. "Yes, I know, I shouldn't have been so uptight about touching her. Asher already gave me the lecture." Miles' ears were turning pink.

Zeke sighed. He walked up behind me. "I'm grabbing you, Lexie. Sorry if I touch anything," Zeke warned me.

I had a feeling it was more to show Miles than to actually warn me. I bit back a laugh. Miles was never going to hear the end of this.

Zeke grabbed me and locked his arms. I did the move with as much force as I had with Asher. Zeke only rocked on his feet, a little.

"Fuck," I grumbled. I looked up at him upside down. "Why are you so fucking huge?"

He smirked down at me. He loosened his arms and looked down at my stance.

"Okay, I think with someone this much bigger than you, you'll have to move your hips more to hook and plant. You're going to want your knee behind mine." He looked over at Miles. "Think that'll work."

Miles looked thoughtful. "It should if she can move that far," Miles said. "Try it; if not, we need to know."

"Ready?" Zeke looked down at me.

I nodded and looked straight ahead. Zeke tightened his arms around me. I did the move the way Zeke suggested, except I couldn't get my leg that far.

"We forgot I have short legs and I can't rotate 360 on my spine," I announced.

Zeke snorted. He let go and stepped back. Zeke's eyes ran over my body, assessing. It wasn't flirting, he was just trying to figure out how to get me out of this hold. Zeke shook his head.

"Lexie, you're not going to be able to throw me. The size difference is just too much," Zeke said then looked at Miles. "Miles can manage it sometimes, and he's had years of training."

Miles nodded, agreeing with Zeke.

"Well, then what do I do if someone your size grabs me?" I asked. I really wanted to know here. 'Cause the idea of not being able to get out of a hold was scary as hell.

Zeke looked back at me. "Your best bet is going to be going for damage," Zeke said. "Turn around." I turned.

Zeke grabbed me again. "Now don't actually do this to me, because I like my groin and feet." I snorted. "You're going to hit me with the back of your head." I moved my head back and lightly made contact. "Now you're going to sink down a bit and lift your arms like a chicken." I did as he said. "Now step to the side." I did. "Drive your elbow into my stomach."

I did, making sure to go slow and not actually hit him. His hold loosened.

"Now, don't do this: you would bring your fist down into the guy's groin." Zeke instructed.

"Okay, I hit you." I'd rather just say it anyway. This was Zeke. His arms dropped.

"Now, don't do this either: slam the heel of your foot down on my foot; the instep is the best spot," he told me. I tapped his foot with mine. Zeke was now doubled over and on one knee, showing me where my attacker would be at that point. He looked up at me. "And run like hell. Get in a public space, scream, whatever you have to do to draw attention to you."

I nodded, chewing on the corner of my bottom lip.

"I read about one woman who hit parked cars on a deserted city street to set off the alarms, it got everyone's attention," Miles added.

Zeke got to his feet, frowning at me. "Your best chance with someone my size is to run and not get caught," Zeke admitted.

I nodded, not liking it one bit.

"There are a couple throws from the front we can teach you for someone my size, maybe, but a grab from behind-"

"There's not much I can do," I finished for him.

"Besides what I just showed you, not really. Except for screaming like hell," Zeke said simply. That didn't make me feel any better. He crooked his finger. "Let's run through it again. And keep skipping the groin and the foot." I gave him tense smile and stood in front of him again.

We ran through it again and again, until Zeke was sure I had it down. The guys even talked about borrowing the suit from the self-defense class so I could practice making the hits, but no one was volunteering to wear the suit. Miles eventually called Isaac over so I could try the throw on him. He dropped like a rock. In the end, I got it down. I was walking back to the lockers with the guys when the world spun. I stopped walking.

"Whoa," I mumbled as I closed my eyes.

"Ally, you okay?" Asher asked as a hand went to my shoulder. I waited till the dizziness passed to open my eyes. All five of the boys were watching me.

"Just a dizzy spell," I told them as I started walking again.

"Did you eat breakfast this morning?" Zeke demanded in his 'answer me now voice.'

"I threw my guts up at three this morning. I had a piece of toast and some coffee," I admitted. "If it stayed down I was going to eat something after our workout."

"Well, let's hit the diner," Isaac suggested.

Everyone agreed. I just smiled.

SOON ENOUGH, we were all tucked into a booth at the town's only diner. It was still early for Saturday in Spring Mountain, so it was almost empty. I looked over the menu and decided on eggs, bacon, and a pancake. One awesome thing about working out so much was that I got to eat a lot.

"So, Lexie, what are you getting?" Zeke asked.

I glared at him. "I'm getting something I want to eat," I snapped. I was really getting tired of him watching everything I ate. In fact, it was starting to piss me off.

Zeke looked at me from across the table. "Lexie, you know you-"

"Yeah, I know, Zeke. But since you've been on my ass, I've lost over 10 fucking pounds, dropped a cup size, and my clothes don't fit," I growled at him. "I have to go shopping this afternoon." The guys looked at me, their confusion written all over their faces.

"Don't most girls want to be tiny?" Miles asked.

The guys groaned. I ignored the insult and smiled at him. He didn't mean it that way; it was Miles.

"Yeah, sweetie, but most girls don't suddenly need that extra weight in case of burnout," I pointed out quietly. I looked over at Zeke, who was frowning. "I didn't have a lot of padding to begin with Zeke, and right now I need to put some weight back on."

"I guess you do look thin," he admitted. "I just didn't notice it until you said something."

I nodded. "I'm losing fat, but I'm gaining muscle. Except I kinda need that fat."

"Just don't go crazy with the junk," he grumbled. Okay, that was it.

"Okay Zeke, I'll make you a deal," I offered. The others smiled; they saw where this was going. "I'll continue to eat a balanced menu, but with a bit more fat added so I can gain some weight and my C's back."

Zeke nodded, obviously not knowing where this was going.

"If you do the same. You eat junk, I get to eat junk. I eat junk, you get to eat junk."

He looked at me like he was trying to figure out if I was joking. When he realized I wasn't, he nodded. "Okay, deal," Zeke agreed. The other guys were smirking.

"So, I'll be having eggs, bacon, and a pancake. That means you will be having the same, just add as much protein as you need." Zeke's eyes went wide as he realized what my healthy diet meant. Then I added, "and no, you don't get to add to the carbs."

The guys burst out laughing at the look on Zeke's face. I smiled sweetly at him. His gaze turned challenging.

"All right, Lexie, it's on," he said, clearly meaning it.

I smirked. Zeke was going to fold in three days. The guy liked his cheeseburgers and fries.

We started talking about the football game on Saturday. The wait- ress came over and everyone ordered. I got a hot chocolate. When Zeke lifted an eyebrow, I told him he could have a candy bar in exchange. He smiled at me. This was going to get interesting.

When breakfast came, we were talking about game night. I was eating a mouth full of pancake when my cell vibrated. I pulled my phone out of the pocket of Miles' hoodie and checked it.

Dylan: Morning Sunshine, how was the workout?

I smiled as I texted him back.

Alexis: Good, finally dropped Miles, Isaac, and Asher. Learned there is no way I'll ever throw Zeke, at least not from a grab from behind me.

I took a bite of bacon as he texted back.

Dylan: LOL, if you ever could throw Zeke, I want it recorded.

I grinned.

Alexis: You got it, how's your morning?

I checked in on the guys' conversation, it'd moved on to plans with their girlfriends today. I was eating more pancake when my cell vibrated again.

Dylan: Nice, I slept in until three minutes ago.

Alexis: Yeah, rub it in.

Dylan: Lol. Do you think I could get you to myself for a couple hours on game night? Like, have dinner before?

I smiled, the butterflies going crazy.

"Hey, Ash." I looked up and met his eyes across the table. "Do you care if I skip out on making snacks this week? Dylan wants to go to dinner before game night."

Asher's mouth was full, but he waved his hand at me and nodded.

"Thank you, sweetie."

He winked at me.

Alexis: Definitely.

Dylan: Can't wait... now I have to get out of this comfy bed.

Alexis: Okay, now you're really rubbing it in. ttyl

Dylan sent me a kiss emoji. I smiled and sent one back then put my phone back in my pocket and got back to eating breakfast. When the food was gone, Miles looked across the table at me.

"Lexie, you have meditation today, right?" Miles asked, as if he didn't already know.

"Yeah," I muttered, my mood suddenly not so bright.

"What's going on, Beautiful?" Ethan asked from next to me.

I sighed. I had to be honest with them. I needed some help with this; I needed someone to remind me why I was doing this. "You remember how when you're getting to your center, you see the big events in your life, the ones that had a big impact on you?" I asked the group.

They all nodded. Miles' eyes were full of understanding; he knew where I was going with this.

"I don't want to see Mary Summers; I don't want to see it from a new point of view," I admitted, looking at the table. My stomach knotted around my breakfast. "It was bad enough with the first view." Ethan's arm went around me. I leaned my head on his shoulder.

"Lexie, what happens if you don't reach your center?" Miles asked.

"I can't do that thing I need to. But with that place closed, it doesn't even matter. They can't go on their way," I said discretely.

"What if someone comes at you the way the last one did, but worse?" Miles asked gently.

I would be in deep shit, or I'd have to kill another soul. I nodded at him, letting him know I understood.

"You still need to be able to do it, even before that place is open," Miles reminded me.

"Besides," Isaac began, smiling at me from his end of the table. "I've never known you to back down from a challenge."

I smirked at that. A challenge, huh. Thinking of it that way just might make this easier.

"Alright," I said, looking around the table. "I'll hit my center today." Then a thought hit me. "I might be a blubbering mess after," I warned them.

They chuckled.

Asher met my eyes. "I think you'll be better than you think," Asher offered. I smiled at him. I hoped he was right.

"Come over to my house; you can use the conservatory and that tub you love after you reach your center," Miles offered.

I smiled. Miles knew how to motivate me. "Ooh, bribery. I like it."

The guys burst out laughing.

IT WASN'T LONG after that when we split up. I went home, got a change of clothes, and my mp3 player. Rory knew all about the awesome tub at Miles' house, and since he always assumed Miles' mom was home, he never blinked twice if I ran over for a soak. I was hoping to keep it that way.

I drove over to Miles' house and drove up to the circular driveway. The house was freaking huge; three stories of gray stone looming over a hill of snow. I grabbed my bag and headed into the house. I didn't even bother knocking; no one did at Miles' house.

"I'm here!" I shouted. Since I had no clue where he was.

"Family room!"

I went and dropped my bag in the master bedroom downstairs, though Miles just called it my room now. I grabbed my mp3 and headed down the long hall to the family room. The family room had two blue couches, a big screen TV, and several games systems set up. Miles' mother had mostly left this room untouched. Miles was sitting on the sofa playing a shooting game with a headset on. I hopped over the back of the sofa and plopped down next to him.

"What are you playing?" I asked.

"I'm playing Destiny with Autumn," he said absently.

"Hi, Autumn!" I called from my spot.

Miles smiled. "She says, 'Hi back. Now be quiet. Miles is supposed to be doing damage.'" Miles repeated Autumn almost verbatim. I chuckled. If I ever got to meet Autumn, I was pretty sure I'd love her. I left him to it and headed into the conservatory.

The conservatory was huge, with a twenty-foot glass ceiling. The glass room was filled with every color and kind of flower you could imagine. Vines were even climbing up the columns. I walked down the path and found the patio chair I usually used. It was right next to the in-ground fountain with four frog water spouts. The sound of water was soothing.

My gut knotted, my pulse raced. I needed to do this. I needed to get to my center. Otherwise, I was fucked. I took deep, calming breaths as I sat down and put on my headphones. I could do this, it would suck, but I got this. Meet the challenge, Lexie. I was going to do this. Fuck, I was going to do this. I hit play on the meditation recording that Ethan had made for me.

"Take deep, slow breaths." Ethan's voice was low and smooth from the recording. His voice filled my ears slowly, softly till it was all I could hear. "Focus on feeling your body breathing, the air coming in through your nose. Your lungs filling with air. Feel yourself exhale."

I did as he said; no one could resist that voice of his. Ethan's voice played in my ears, giving me instructions; I listened and followed. The world disappeared. There was only Ethan's voice. When my mind was completely blank, free of emotion and thought, I knew I was where I needed to be. The next recording in the list started. Ethan began again, this time giving me instructions on how to reach my center.

"Feel yourself relaxing, sinking deeper into your mind."

I relaxed my hold on everything, my body, my stress, all the pressure I felt to get this right. I just let it go and sank down inside myself.

"You're going to where your instinct is, Beautiful."

I knew where I was going, I'd walked the path a lot over the last couple months. I sank further.

"That's where your center is. That is what you need to find."

I was closer; I could feel it. I felt stronger, more me. Images flashed through my mind, not all of them good, not all of them bad. The big moments in my life.

Seeing my first ghost, Claire saving me, Claire protecting me.

Dad. I saw Dad reading me The Hobbit before bedtime; a wave of love burst over me. Then I saw his casket. Sadness filled me as I fell deeper. I knew what was coming; I'd been here before.

I saw myself being alone at night, trying to understand why Mom wanted to go out instead of staying with me. I saw how I tried every day to make things better for my mother, how every day she blew me off. The first time my mother called me a demon child, I had been fourteen, and she'd been pissed that the pantry was empty.

I watched as Jacob Noon tried to pin me down in the park, his hand going up my skirt as I said no. For the first time, I didn't flinch as I watched myself fight him off, driving my knee into his groin then pushing him off me. I watched the white-hot rage in my eyes as I walked to the Blazer. I watched myself pick up the short crowbar. I didn't hesitate; I didn't think. Then I watched myself smash that crowbar across his face, over and over. When he was unconscious, I watched myself pull my cell phone out, call the police and an ambulance. For the first time, I accepted this; I had a dark side. I always knew it. But knowing and accepting were two different things. I had a dark side, and I needed to control it. What I did that night wasn't right, but it wasn't entirely wrong either. For the first time since that night, I was at peace with it. I didn't fight as I sank lower.

I saw the color of my world leach away until there was barely any color at all. I watched us move from place to place, never settling down. The color kept disappearing from my world. Then we were in LA. I knew what was coming. I watched as my mother yanked me from my bed and dropped me to the floor. I winced as I remembered the pain. I pushed the memory away and tried to dive past it. I didn't want to see this, didn't want to feel this again. But my center wouldn't let me. I had to watch. I watched as my mother beat me, kicked me, and hit me. I watched as I screamed and cursed her, calling her names right back as she stomped me into the floor. I watched as I struck out with a foot, knocking her back from me. I didn't remember that part, that I had fought back. I watched as it went on and on. I watched as the cops broke open the door and yanked her out. I watched as I got to my feet and walked out the door to the police car. I walked out of there; I didn't remember that. That changed something. I don't know how to explain it, except that something inside me shifted with this new knowledge. I felt more like me, the real me. I sank deeper.

I watched as I met Isaac and his laughing eyes. Then Ethan and Miles. Then Asher and even Zeke. As I watched our conversations, I noticed the color coming back. The world was alive again, not completely, but getting there. The color grew the more I laughed with them. The more time I spent with them. I started to feel again; I hadn't realized how numb I had become until now. Serena had been right. I had been so close to cutting myself off from everyone. I watched myself talking to Miles while lying on the dock. He was telling me that just because relationships didn't last, that didn't mean they weren't worth having. Of course, he used the stars as a metaphor, but that's what he told me. I saw how he watched me out of the corner of his eye when I had to stop myself from crying. He had known. I sank deeper.

I watched myself telling Asher my dream of becoming a tattoo artist so he'd admit what he'd really wanted to do with his life. I sank deeper.

I watched myself talking to Zeke at the garage where he worked. He was telling me he couldn't trust himself around me. I watched as my shaking hands pulled off my sweater and told him to look at my back. I didn't remember my hands shaking. And I saw something I hadn't seen before, that I didn't even realize until now. When someone I cared about was hurting, I gave them everything and anything I had to make them not feel alone. If standing naked and showing them my own scars made them feel even a little better, a little less alone, I did it. And it amazed me. I sank deeper.

I watched myself getting jumped by the ghost of Mary Summers. I watched all the guys freak out as Zeke brought my face up so I could tell him what to do. I saw the panic and fear on everyone's face as I went limp. I watched them drive me home and get me in the shower. They took off my sweater and jeans, just like Rory told them to. I watched as they rubbed salt over my skin. I watched their faces as I woke up. Their relief made my heart ache. Then I watched them take turns holding me in the shower. Zeke passed me off to Asher when he got too hot. Asher stopped only to take off his shoes. When Asher got too hot, he handed me off to Isaac. Isaac didn't even bother taking off his shoes. Then they were wrapping towels around me and carrying me to Rory's bed. Everyone one of them had been pale. I sank deeper.

I watched myself being hugged by each of them after I woke up; I saw the relief on their faces. I saw how they cared about me. How they wanted to.... just be there for me. The way I was for them. It finally fully sank in; they cared just as much about me as I did them. I was still a bit dazed by this as I sank deeper.

I saw myself as I pressed gauze against Zeke's hand. I watched as I refused to let up on the pressure. That's when I noticed it. There was a connection. A shining golden thread that went from me to him. It wasn't there all the time, but it was then. I sank lower.

I saw myself at the crash site, pressing on Emily Hann's abdominal wound to stop the bleeding. She was starting to give up. I turned to her, and I saw it again. That golden thread of light wrapped around Emily Hann's wrist, holding her soul to me, and from me, to her body. I watched as her soul tried to move on, and the thread pulled taunt. I watched in disbelief as I pulled her back and held her till she could climb back into her body. What the...? I sank deeper.

I watched myself yank Isaac out of the party at the Dotson's. I watched myself order Isaac to get it out in a better way. I saw the look on Isaac's face that I hadn't then. He looked lost; he hadn't known what he was doing that night. My chest ached. I needed to help, some-how; I needed to help him. I sank deeper.

I knew what was coming. I felt almost completely like me again. I hadn't felt that way since before I got jumped. I watched as I walked toward Mary Summers' soul in my cousin Tara's body. I watched as I threw her out of me. Then I watched as the world disappeared and we entered the Veil. I saw that rocky ledge above the pit of black. The boiling clouds in the sky with lightning and green smoke. But all my attention was on Mary Summers. My heart burned as I watched her scramble for a hold on the stone, only for her to slip off the edge. I saw myself reaching for her. I felt like my heart was being crushed as I watched myself try to pull her back. Then the feeling was gone; I don't know how, but I knew I needed to see without emotion. I needed to see the truth of it. I watched as I pulled against the suction of the pit. I watched as she began to fade in my hands.

That's when I saw it.

I couldn't believe it; the whole scene stopped as if I had hit pause on a movie. I looked closer at Mary Summers. The energy had stripped her of her mind, destroyed who she was. I could see it. She was rotted from the inside out. But not completely. There was still a sliver of her in there. And I saw it. The scene began moving again in slow motion. I watched Mary Summers disappearing. Then I saw something new. She was saying something. The sound came on in stereo at high volume. The wind was howling, but I heard it. She said, 'Thank you.' I knew somewhere my body was crying, but it didn't matter. I watched Mary Summers die and thank me for it. Dazed, I sank deeper.

Light exploded behind my eyes, bright and golden. Then I was standing on a white plain with a golden lit sky, and across from me was me. It was me down to the last detail, even the odd eyes and the way I tilted my head when I was pissed.

"Are you going to listen now?" the other me asked in my voice.

"I didn't know I wasn't," I told her honestly.

She smiled sweetly. Then smacked me upside the head.

"Ow!" It actually hurt.

She smirked at me. "You know the answer to a lot of things, Alexis, but your head gets in the way," she told me. "You need to start listening."

"Yeah, I'm getting that," I admitted.

She half grinned at me. "You need to follow your instinct when it comes to your abilities. Stop thinking there is a set of instructions somewhere. Because there isn't."

I sighed. Shit.

"You need practice with souls, Alexis."

"I don't want to fuck up like that again." My voice was desperate, and I hated it.

She smiled at me. "Don't salt and burn bodies, and you won't. You can't hurt the dead less than that."

There was movement over my other self's shoulder. Another me was walking towards us from farther away. I looked back at the other me and had a hunch.

"You're not me."

The imposter me smiled. "No, I'm not. But this was the best form to take to tell you what I had to." She looked over her shoulder. "Your True Self is coming, and you'll have to face her in order to reach your center." She looked back to me. "If you have any questions, ask them now."

"How do I link with the Veil and force a ghost to cross? Will that even still work?"

She smiled. "You grab them, come here, and think of the Veil. But it'll take time for you to build the link. It'll take work, and it'll hurt. So, don't start with a soul," she warned. "But once it's there, it'll become easier with every use. Steadier."

She tilted her head to the side. It was weird seeing myself do that. "You can't force a soul to cross, you can only get them to the Veil. Most souls can find the Veil-"

"Only someone's fucked with it, and it's closed," I pointed out.

She nodded. "But that someone can't keep you out," she countered. "Or any soul you take with you."

Holy shit. I could still get them to cross even before I opened the Veil! The true me was coming closer.

"How do I grab ahold of a soul?"

She smiled at me. "You've already done it. You've done it with your friend Zeke; you did it with that woman in the car," she said cryptically.

I wanted to hit myself in the face. Which felt weird.

"The gold thread?" I asked.

She nodded, smiling. "You held Emily Hann's soul to her body, don't you remember thinking 'I could let her go now'?"

I nodded.

She smiled. "That feeling in your chest when you were talking to her, telling her to stay. That is the thread. It's how it forms. That's how you grab them. It's pure will. And you need to exercise it to make it stronger." She looked over her shoulder. "And now I have to go."

"Who are you? Am I going to see you again?"

She smirked. "Probably, and it's not who I am so much as what I am."

She started walking away. I was going to ask what she was but my True Self walked by the imposter me. This was so fucking weird. I watched as my True Self came to me. Her hair was different. The left side was back in braids along her scalp, making it looked shaved. Five braids from her ear to the top of her head were each dyed a separate color. The rest of her hair was still the copper I had. She wore a black t-shirt, black leather pants, and boots. Black and bronze scrolling letters were tattooed down the outside of her body in a single line, from the sides of her neck to her wrists. For some reason, I was sure it had a purpose. A ring was on her ring finger on her left hand, but it was black, and there was something different about it. I looked at her face; she looked to be in her early to mid-twenties. I watched her examining me just as much as I examined her. Her eyes met mine, and she smiled.

"Let me guess. You just moved to Spring Mountain," she said, her voice sounding different to me, a bit rougher.

"Two months ago," I said.

She smiled, her eyes warming. "An interesting time." Her smile grew. "I'm your True Self, Alexis. I'm everything you are and everything you will ever be. To reach your center you have to go through me." She tilted her head and looked over my shoulder. "Or more like, I'll show you who you are. 'Cause the other way just sounds dirty if you think about it."

I snorted at her. She smiled.

"So, I'm still a smartass, huh?" I observed.

My True Self snorted. "Always."

"Can you tell me something?" I asked.

She looked like she was considering it. Then her eyes focused back to me. "Maybe."

Good enough for me. I knew I should be feeling my heart race, but all I felt was calm. I didn't question it; I just ran with it. "Do I end up happy?"

She smiled my big happy smile. The one I rarely ever used.

"You can be," she said. Then the smile faded a bit. "But it's up to you how your story goes. Happiness isn't just going to fall on your doorstep. You're gonna have to bust your ass for it."

I got that.

"What about the guys? Will they still be around?" I asked before I even realized it.

"I'm not a fortune teller, I'm you," she said, smiling that big smile again. "But... follow your heart, no matter what normal people say. In fact, throw normal out the window. Then you'll be fine." Then her eyes narrowed on me. "And deal with your fear of abandonment. It's annoying as fuck!"

I snorted.

Her eyes went up above us. Her smiled disappeared. "Yeah, yeah, I hear ya." She looked back to me. "I'm getting bitched at for answering questions," she explained.

I raised an eyebrow. Who the hell could be bitching at her? Or me? This was confusing.

"Will I see you again?"

"No, but after this, you won't need to." Her eyes went over my shoulder as they unfocused. "Well, if you somehow lose your center again, then, yeah, you'll see me again." Her eyes ran over my face, her eyes sympathetic. "You've been lost since Mary Summers, Lexie; it's time to come home."

I took a deep breath and nodded. She held her hands out to me, palms up. I put my hands in hers. She stepped closer.

"Now, this is the weird part," she warned me. She leaned forward and pressed her forehead against mine. I instinctively closed my eyes. That's when it happened. She showed me. I was stripped naked and in the light. Every fault, every flaw, everything I was. It was all laid out before me. I saw it all.

I am Alexis Luanna Delaney. I have an anger problem; a tendency towards violence. I am terrified of people leaving me. I'm terrified I'll be just like my mother. I am impulsive and reckless at times. I tend to be a perfectionist. And I am a huge smart ass. But I also love deeply, passionately. I am kind and generous. I am protective, not only of those I love but of those that don't or can't defend themselves. If you come at me and those I love, you better bring an army, because I will tear you down where you stand. I am a shitty cousin, an alright niece. And I am a more than decent daughter. But through all my faults, flaws, and traits, I couldn't find the word murderer. But I found a different one, one I didn't expect. I knew it all, felt it in my heart and soul. This was my truth. This was who I am. And I liked her.

I felt a hard click. The light was blinding, then it was back to the way it was before. I felt solid. Whole. I felt like I could stand against anything. The white and gold world was empty again. But I knew I could fill it if I wanted to.

"Okay, now how do I-" I closed my eyes and opened them. The world swam; there were swirls of green and other colors. "-get back?"

I closed my eyes till my head stopped feeling dizzy. I opened my eyes and looked around at all the plants. It took me a couple of minutes to remember where I was. Miles' house, the conservatory, right. The sun was still streaming through the glass ceiling. In a daze, I got up and went back into the house. My mind was going over everything as I walked down the hallway. I didn't deserve the shit my mother did to me. Mary Summers.... that word. I kept going around and around. I was so lost I didn't hear my name. A blur jumped in front of me, forcing me to stop.

Miles' worried eyes ran over my face. "Lexie? Are you alright?" he asked, his voice calm. I nodded. He looked more worried. "I'm not going to believe you until you say something."

"I did it," I managed, my head still running around in circles. I blinked and forced myself to focus on Miles. "I reached my center." His eyebrows went up.

"It's just a lot to absorb right now. I'm... I'm gonna take a bath and think about this."

He nodded, his face concerned again. When I didn't move, he took my arm. "Alright, come on." His voice was that soft and silky one that I loved hearing.

He walked me down the hall and into the master bedroom. He picked up my bag and led me into the bathroom. When he let go of me, I sat on the edge of the tub, still thinking, still confused. When I didn't move, he must have started my bathwater because the sound of water filled the room. I was still running around in circles in my head.

Miles was back in front of me. "Lexie, do you want to use your rosemary bath salt?"

I looked at him and focused. I nodded. Miles disappeared, and I went back to going in circles in my head. I was a good daughter to my mother; why did she beat the shit out of me? The water shut off. I smelled rosemary.

Miles was back, kneeling in front of me. "Lexie, if you don't focus for me I'm sticking you in the tub with your clothes on and staying right here," he warned gently.

I blinked at him. "Huh?"

His eyes ran over my face again, then he seemed to make up his mind about something. I was still lost in my head as he took my shoes and socks off. Then I was up in Miles' arms. That woke me up a bit. Then I was in hot bath water up to my neck. It felt good. I sat up and wrapped my arms around my knees. Why would she have beaten me if I had been a good daughter? And Mary Summers... Did this mean...?

And that word... I needed to focus on one thought at a time. Think Lexie. Focus.

Miles was at the side of the tub, his chin resting on his arms. He was watching me. "What happened, Lexie?" he asked softly.

"There was so much information. I saw all the big moments in my life so far." I swallowed, trying to focus.

"You guys were there. You guys brought the color back. You guys brought me back." I felt tears falling down my face, and I didn't care.

"Once I got past when Jacob tried to rape me, once I got past my Mother beating me, everything had no color. You guys brought the color back." I blinked, I wasn't saying what I wanted to say.

"Then I saw the Veil and Mary Summers. But this time I couldn't feel anything. I was calm." Tears fell faster; I forced myself to keep talking. This was helping. Miles could help me make sense of it.

"At the end, when I was holding on to her, everything paused. And I saw what the extra energy had done to her. It had rotted her out, but there was still a sliver of her left." I looked at Miles and his calm eyes.

"Then everything moved again. And I heard her say something that I didn't hear last time." I swallowed hard and looked at him. "She said 'Thank you.'"

Miles blinked, his face stunned.

"She was suffering from all that energy. It was destroying her already. In the end, she wanted to go." I explained. Then there was the other thing, that word. But I wasn't going to tell him that now, not until... later.

"I met me, my true self. And she showed me everything I am. Every flaw, fault, and trait I had. And not one of them... I was expecting to be a murderer," I said simply.

It fully sank in. I didn't really murder Mary Summers. I just put her out of her misery. But I still killed her.... There was more about that, but there was the other thing first.

"That's a good thing, Lexie," Miles said; his voice was soothing as he brushed my hair out of my face.

I nodded, a little more aware. "Then there was the other thing I didn't expect." I looked at Miles and just asked. "Why does someone beat the shit out of their kid, if they didn't do anything wrong?" I blinked hard and focused on his face.

Miles licked his lips before meeting my eyes and answering. "Lexie, your mother is ill. She didn't abuse you because you did something wrong, she abused you because she was a drunk who did drugs. Don't let her make you think it was your fault."

For some reason when he said that it made perfect sense. It finally sank into my heart. "I knew that, in my head, I knew that..."

"But in your heart, it's another matter," he said softly. "You owe that woman nothing. Don't let her take up any more room in your head or heart."

I nodded. He was right. The circle of thoughts slowed down. It felt like a huge weight had been lifted, one that I didn't even know I was carrying. I looked around me and realized where I was.

"Miles, I'm in the tub," I pointed out. "I'm in the tub, in my clothes." I looked back at him and started laughing.

Miles grinned and chuckled. "You wanted a bath, but I was worried about leaving you alone." He gestured at my clothes. "Hence the clothes."

I looked up at Miles and smiled. Then it hit me. "Miles."

He raised an eyebrow at me.

"I reached my center," I told him, beaming, excitement washing over me. I got on my knees in the tub and grabbed his shoulders. "I found my center!"

I was giddy with relief and happiness. I felt light and airy, better than I had in weeks. Which is why I did what I did next. I grabbed Miles by the arms and pulled him into the tub with me. He splashed down next to me then came up sputtering. Water sloshed over the side of the tub. I just kept laughing as I hugged him tight. Miles was laughing at me as I clung to him like a monkey.

"Do you know what that means?" I pulled back to look at him.

He wiped the water off his glasses. "You're closer to linking with the Veil now?" he offered, still laughing at me, still looking at me like I was nuts.

I nodded. "It also means I can take souls to the Veil." I was so excited I didn't even care that he was confused. "I can get them into the Veil so they can cross! Even before I fix the Veil. If I can get the link to the Veil going, we won't have to have another Mary Summers."

Now he got it. His face lit up as he smiled at me. "You're sure about that?" he asked, of course, a little skeptical.

I nodded emphatically and splashed him in the face with water. Miles just laughed and splashed me back. A water fight ensued. The tub was half empty by the time we called a truce. Then I realized I had pulled Miles into the tub. I looked over at him and started laughing again.

"Sorry, I don't know why I pulled you in," I admitted, unable to stop laughing.

Miles just smiled at me. "Because you're Lexie and you do unexpected things," he offered.

I tilted my head to the side and thought about it. Yep, that was accurate. "Yeah, pretty much," I admitted.

He chuckled.

Then another thought hit me. "Hey, what time is it anyway?"

Miles checked his watch. "It's about eleven forty-five." He sighed. "We still have lunch at Asher's today."

I nodded and smacked his shoulder. "Okay, get out, I want my bath," I said sweetly, still with a big smile on my face.

He started laughing again and shook his head. "We don't have time for your bath; we'll be late," he reminded me.

I shrugged. "I say we be late; those girls are annoying. Well, except Riley, and she's not going to be there," I declared, even going so far as to point a finger in the air.

Miles chuckled as he reached into his back pocket. He pulled out his cell phone. I burst out laughing.

"I just keep killing your phones." I couldn't stop giggling.

Miles tapped the screen and showed me it was still working. "Waterproof remember?" he said.

That made me laugh even more. I realized I needed to get out also if I was going to get out of my wet clothes. I hit the plug in the tub then climbed out, slipping on the floor then landing on my side. I didn't care; I was still laughing about the phone. I was so lightheaded with relief that I couldn't stop. Miles tried to climb out but slipped back in.

"You okay?" I called, still laughing.

"Great." His dry voice echoed from the tub.

It sent me into another giggle fit. Miles did get out and managed to keep his feet under him. When he was steady, he held up his phone. "I'll call the guys and tell them to start lunch without us."

"Don't tell them! I want to tell them!" I shot at him.

He smiled. "And pull them into the tub, got it," he countered, still chuckling as he worked his phone on his way out the door. I smiled to myself and looked at the mess we made. Thank God Miles was rich. He had lots of towels.

CHAPTER 4

THURSDAY AFTERNOON

*I*t was fifteen minutes before we were on the road to Asher's. After cleaning up the bathroom, I settled for a quick shower because I really wanted to go tell the guys the news! We weren't murderers, well, not really! How often did you get to say that to people? Okay, well you could all the time if you hadn't, but in this case, it was awesome. I still felt awful about Mary Summers, but it wasn't the heart crushing guilt I had before.

I was wearing my usual blue jeans, my black V-neck sweater, and my gym sneakers. Thank you, Miles, for saving them. Miles drove because I was bouncing around like a fucking rabbit on speed. At least that is what he said, without the cursing, and he was probably right. He ended up having to bring my wool jacket out to the car with him because I had forgotten it inside. I slipped the damn thing on while Miles drove, chuckling at me almost the whole way.

When Miles pulled up to Asher's, he kept the doors locked, and didn't let me out until he finished parking. Apparently, my hands were shaking, and I couldn't work the fucking button. Then I was out and running across the snow; I slipped and dropped on my ass. Miles kept laughing at me. I just got up and ran up the steps. I shoved open the door and ran in. I saw a big guy in the foyer with nothing in his arms.

"Hey!" I shouted, getting his attention. Then I jumped and wrapped my arms around his neck. Asher grunted as I hit his chest; his arms went around me instantly.

He stumbled back but managed to keep us upright. "Ally! What the hell?" His voice was so surprised that I started giggling again. I pulled my head back so I could see him and smiled big.

"Swear jar!" I practically shouted. "I have big news!" I beamed at him. He looked at me like I was nuts. There was laughing behind me. I looked from where I was dangling on Asher to see Miles come into the house.

"Are you drunk?" Trisha asked, almost yelling. I looked over to find her pissed off in the family room.

I kept smiling. "Nope!" I spotted Zeke and the twins in the family room with the girls. I pointed at the boys; Asher's arms around my waist kept me off the ground. "Boys! Kitchen! Now!" I shouted, smiling. The guys looked worried but got to their feet anyway. I looked up at Asher. "You too! Either put me down or carry me in there. Your choice." I started giggling again.

The others were standing around us now, looking at me like I was crazy. It made me keep giggling. Asher looked behind me, I imagine, to Miles. "Is it safe to put her down?" Asher asked seriously.

Miles started chuckling again. "If I were you, I'd carry her in there and put her on the kitchen island. And keep her away from sharp objects right now."

I looked over my shoulder to see Miles' face was bright red and he could barely talk by the end of his sentence.

I looked back up at Asher, beaming. "Pick one! Let's go!"

"Here, give her to me. Your girlfriend is about to pitch a fit," Zeke said from behind me.

Asher and Zeke did some weird switch thing, and I was in Zeke's arms, one around my back the other under my knees. I wrapped my arms around his neck and smiled up at him.

"Hi, big, tall and grumpy one!" I greeted him cheerfully. I couldn't stop smiling.

Zeke was shaking his head as he carried me into the kitchen. The others followed. Miles tried to cover for me with the girls. He said something about an extreme relief reaction. I didn't care. Zeke carried me into the kitchen.

"Someone want to move the knives," Isaac suggested.

I spotted Ethan moving the knife block off the island and away from my reach. I didn't care; I just wanted to tell them the news! Zeke put me on the kitchen island and backed up. Isaac came up and put his hands on my legs, anchoring me there. I was trying to bounce, and he was stopping me. I smacked his hands; he looked at me and smacked my hands back. A smacking war began. Asher pulled Isaac away, and Zeke's hands went to my legs, stopping me from bouncing. Zeke was trying to stop laughing as he looked down at me, but it wasn't working.

"Okay... okay, someone talk to her." Zeke couldn't stop laughing at me trying to bounce and the look on my face.

I looked at the others and saw they all were having the same problem. So, I just told them.

"I reached my center." I made a huge effort not to shout.

Everyone looked at me, surprised. I just kept bouncing as much as Zeke's hands would allow. Then they started talking at once.

"About time," Zeke said.

"Good job, Red."

"Ally, that's great."

"Beautiful, why are you bouncing around like a rabbit?" Ethan asked.

I forced myself to focus. "That's not all." I forced myself to stop bouncing and focused on keeping my voice low. "I found out how to move souls into the Veil, even with it shut off." I smiled big and started bouncing again. Everyone's jaws dropped.

"Are you fucking kidding, Red?" Isaac asked, his voice full of disbelief.

"Nope! There will never have to be another Mary Summers."

The guys all made sounds of relief and hugged me. I was still giggling when they let me go. I was about to continue when the kitchen door burst open.

"What is wrong with you?! You come in, jump on my boyfriend, and now you're all holed up in the kitchen?" Trisha snapped.

Asher turned around and took his girlfriend's arm.

"Trish, Lexie just got some great health news. It's private. Just please go back out there and be patient," Asher said in a rush with his rich voice.

Trisha glared at me and left. Miles came into the kitchen to stand to the left of the island. Asher turned back, and I was smiling again.

"Fuck, Lexie, if you say there's more..." Isaac groaned.

"There's more!"

My face was starting to hurt from smiling, so I stopped. I stopped bouncing too. I gestured for them to come closer. They all leaned in.

"To reach my center I had to see the whole Mary Summers thing again, right?"

They all listened closely.

"It was like a movie this time; I was calm as I watched both of us on that ledge. Then it paused. I saw what the energy did to her. She was like a rotted log inside. Except for a sliver." I looked at them and felt tears welling in my eyes.

"Don't you dare fucking cry," Zeke growled.

I fought them back then shot a look at him. "Then the movie started again in slow motion. And I heard her say something I didn't hear that night." I looked at them and smiled a smile of pure relief. "She said 'Thank you.'"

Everyone's faces showed varying levels of shock, then the relief poured in. I smiled, unable to stop now.

"Seriously? You're not fucking with us? Just to make us feel better?" Ethan asked, his eyes storming.

"Seriously. The energy was wiping her out already; we just put her out of her misery."

They all stared at me, each of them stunned.

"We... still killed her... and we'll always carry that. But she didn't want to exist like that anymore. It was more... assisted suicide?" I didn't know if it was the right name for it or not. But it was what I had.

There were a lot of loud sounds of relief. I just smiled up at them, suddenly exhausted. The guys started looking at each other, then they started laughing. The world began to spin, so I laid down on my side.

"Whoa, whoa! Ally, are you okay?" Asher asked, catching the others' attention. Everyone stopped laughing. I liked my face against the cold tile.

"I'm suddenly very tired," I said, my voice matter-of-fact.

The guys burst out laughing. Miles came around the island; he smiled gently as he looked down at me.

"I can imagine, you've been rather manic since you came out of that state of shock," Miles explained.

I smiled sweetly at Miles. "Thank you for taking care of me, Miles," I mumbled, tempted to go to sleep right here.

"Anytime, Lexie." He looked at the guys. "Let's get her sitting up and some coffee in her, otherwise she's going to pass out."

Hands pulled me up. My face was smacked a bit. I opened my eyes to see Ethan in front of me.

"Hi Beautiful, stay with us. We got coffee coming."

I nodded, reached out, and poked the tip of his nose.

"Boop." I snickered.

Ethan burst out laughing. "Okay, someone else take her. I can't..."

Big hands grabbed me, and I leaned against a broad chest. I looked up and smiled.

"Don't boop my nose," Zeke ordered me.

So naturally, I reached up and did just that. "Boop."

I started laughing, and I wasn't the only one. Even Zeke was laughing at me, his face turning red. It was probably just from relief, but I liked to think I was just that funny. But he still held me up.

"I booped your nose, what ya gonna do, tough guy?" I smiled up at him.

"Lexie..." Zeke began.

I snickered. "You love that I give you shit, and you know it," I said in a cutesy voice.

Zeke smiled down at me as he shook his head. "Yeah, I do," he muttered.

Isaac came up beside him with coffee.

Zeke took the mug. "You've got coffee," Zeke tempted me. "Just the way you like it, cream and sugar."

I smiled and reached for it. My hands were shaking. That was weird. Miles took the mug from Zeke and put it in my hand. He didn't let go as he helped me start drinking.

"Why is she shaking like that?" Zeke asked, his voice growing hard.

Miles let me keep drinking the coffee, it was lukewarm, and I wanted more.

"She was out of it for about half an hour, it was almost like shock. I ended up sticking her in the tub," Miles said absently.

The guys looked at him, frowning. Miles didn't notice.

I stopped drinking long enough to defend him. "I was still dressed, pervs," I shot at them then drained the mug of coffee, my hands no longer shaking. The guys stopped glaring at Miles.

"More coffee please." I asked.

It was like magic, and another mug was in front of me. If only it happened like this all the time. I giggled at myself. I drank this one slower and started to wake up. The guys kept asking Miles questions. Miles answered them vaguely. He didn't tell them exactly what I had said; it was too private.

I was halfway through my second cup of coffee when I blinked hard and looked around. "Oh, fuck. I'm starving." The guys laughed at me. Then I realized how crazy I was acting. I winced. "Sorry Ash, I didn't even realize that was you."

Asher snorted. "It's okay, Ally girl; I understand now," Asher said before he looked at Miles. "What are we going to tell the girls?"

I winced again. Oh, this was going to be bad.

"I told them that she was in the middle of an extreme relief reaction," Miles said. "You said it was medical news, so let's stick with that." I raised my hand while drinking and everyone waited till I was done.

"Tell them the cover; I have a seizure disorder, and we just learned I'm not dying from complications," I offered cheerfully before drinking again.

"That'll work." Miles grinned. I smiled back. The guys nodded in agreement.

"Okay, I'll go tell them," Asher said; he pointed to Miles. "Can you..."

Miles nodded. "I'll take care of her until she's normal, well, as normal as she gets," Miles said. I snorted into my coffee. Miles smirked as he continued, "Isaac is making her a sandwich as we speak."

Asher smiled then pulled me into a hug. "Great news, Ally girl," Asher whispered to me.

Then he went to do damage control. I looked around and saw a bowl of chips. I grabbed a couple. Zeke didn't even bitch. Yay! The others filed out. Zeke looked me over before giving me a shoulder squeeze and heading into the family room. Ethan hugged me and kissed my temple. I felt loved. Then Isaac brought me a sandwich, and I felt really loved.

"You're the best, Cookie Monster," I said before diving in.

Isaac and Miles watched as I finished that sandwich in under three minutes. Isaac was laughing by the end. I was starting to feel better. I kept munching on some chips while I waited till Miles said I was good. Isaac stayed with us.

"So, you put her in the tub, still in her clothes," Isaac said with a big grin. Miles shrugged.

"He took off my shoes," I pointed out while I grabbed another chip. "Then when I came out of it, I got it into my head to yank him into the tub." I giggled as I looked at Miles. Isaac burst out laughing. Then I added, "he had his cell phone on him too."

Miles was smiling at me and shaking his head.

"So, the waterproof phone paid off?" Isaac asked, smirking.

Miles nodded. Isaac was still laughing as he headed into the family room. I kept eating chips till I was full. Then I looked at Miles.

"Sorry Miles," I said, realizing how odd that must have been for him.

"For?"

"Yanking you into the tub. I was just so happy and wanted to have fun," I tried to explain.

Miles smiled at me, his emerald eyes softening. "Lexie, you weren't the only one filled with relief," He pointed out. Huh, I guess he was right.

"Oh, well, sorry about your shoes," I tried again.

He sighed. "I've got more shoes, Lexie," he said patiently.

"You make it hard to apologize to you," I pointed out.

He grinned. "Only when there is nothing to apologize for," he countered.

I shrugged, giving up, and waited. Though Miles wouldn't let me drink any more coffee, he did sneak me one of Asher's homemade chocolate chip cookies. I winked at him before eating it. He just shook his head, still grinning at me. Miles figured I was safe enough to sit alone for a bit and ran upstairs to go to the bathroom. Trisha came in eventually and glared at me. I figured I should apologize.

"Sorry about that Trisha, I was just really happy," I offered.

She nodded as she eyed me. "Asher said something about good news?" she asked as if she couldn't remember. She was checking our story.

"Yeah, my seizure disorder." I threw my arms up in the air. "I'm not dying!" I gave her a big smile. She was still eyeing me. So, I tried again. "To be honest, I didn't even know it was Asher. I saw a big dude with empty arms and jumped." I laughed at myself. "I bet I looked nuts."

She smiled. It wasn't friendly. "Yeah, you did." Trisha's voice was sharp, and not so pleasant. I tilted my head at her. "Don't touch my boyfriend again."

I raised an eyebrow at her. Was she fucking serious? "Um, it wasn't like that. Asher's my friend, and I had just gotten awesome news," I pointed out, trying to be nice.

Her eyes narrowed at me. Miles was coming down the hall behind her.

"I understand that," she began, her voice softening as her face became pleasant. I didn't buy it for a second. "But I didn't appreciate you jumping on Asher." Miles stopped inside the kitchen doorway.

"I understand that, which is why I apologized," I said carefully. What was with this chick? Yeah, it probably didn't look good, but if she didn't trust Asher, then that was her own problem. "I hug the guys all the time, they're family."

Her eyes narrowed at me. "That is going to change," Trisha said confidently. I raised an eyebrow at her.

"There will be no more hugging and no more touching between you and Asher." She took a breath. "A lot of things will be changing now that I'm here, and his relationship with you is only one of them."

Part of me wanted to laugh her off, but the other part, the part I tried to keep locked down, got nervous. Stop it, Lexie, stop putting doubt in your head. The guys weren't going anywhere. But that other part of me was a stubborn bitch.

Trisha turned and froze. Miles looked at her coldly. I'd never seen him look at a girl that way before.

"What else are you going to change around here?" Miles asked calmly in his cold voice.

Trisha stood up straight, her shoulders back, but kept her mouth shut.

He continued, "You might want to ask Asher how he feels about it before you start making ridiculous demands." Miles walked around her and came into the kitchen. He went to the cookie jar.

Trisha's shoulders grew tense.

It sounded like a threat, but knowing Miles, it wasn't meant that way. He was merely giving her advice. But Trisha looked pissed as she glared at Miles' back and opened her mouth. I leaned into her view of him. I gave her my "dead face" and shook my head. I might be trying to get along with her, but if she messed with Miles, I would tear her down, loudly. She seemed to think better of it; she turned around and walked back to the family room.

Miles came to stand next to me and handed me a cookie. I hit my cookie against his, then we both ate our sneak cookies.

But that damn part of me wouldn't go back to sleep.

MILES LET me leave the kitchen eight minutes later. I had a headache, and I wanted a nap, but otherwise, I was back to happy. Well, except for that one word I found, but I'd figure it out later. I went to sit on the floor and winced.

"Hey, can someone throw me a pillow? I fell on my ass in the snow outside," I said.

"Swear jar!" Isaac shouted as he tossed me a pillow.

I reached for my wallet and realized I didn't have it. "I'm going to have to owe you, I must have left my wallet at Miles' house." I leaned to the side and put the pillow under my butt. Ahh, instant relief.

"And your cell phone and your keys and your socks," Miles mumbled as he came in and sat next to me. I pulled my jean leg up and saw he was right. I giggled and dropped my pant leg.

"Why were you at Miles' house?" Cece asked with an odd, subtle note to her voice.

"Uh, because he's awesome," I pointed out like it was obvious.

Miles chuckled. I bumped into his shoulder, then he bumped into mine. We went back to watching some TV show.

It wasn't long before someone's cell rang. Asher answered it. I was trying to remember what I said to Miles while I was in the tub when Asher called to me.

"Ally girl."

I turned around and looked at him.

He tossed me his phone. "Dylan's looking for you."

"Shit."

"Swear jar!" Ethan shot at me.

I snickered. "I still don't have my wallet, guys," I pointed out before getting to my feet and heading into the kitchen.

"Hey, you."

"Hey, what happened to your phone?" Dylan's voice rolled over my ear and made me smile.

"Oh, I kinda got really excited and left it at Miles' house," I admitted. I realized I was going to have to tell Dylan the cover story. Otherwise, Trisha might. I hopped up on the counter in the kitchen.

"What did you get that excited over?" he asked.

I winced. This wasn't going to be easy.

"Well, um. I kind of have this seizure disorder," I told him, wishing I didn't have to. "And I had some test results come in while I was at Miles' house. Good news. I'm not dying." I tried to play it off as a joke. It fell flat.

"What? You... huh?" Dylan sounded shocked.

"The doctor thought I might have some complications but I don't; so, I'm all good," I reassured him. "I got the good news, I got a little manic, and Miles drove me out to Asher's because I was bouncing around like a rabbit apparently. I jumped on Asher, surprising the hell out of him, by the way. And pissed off his girlfriend in the process."

When he didn't say anything, I continued. "Then I ordered the guys into the kitchen and told them the good news, then I kinda dropped. They gave me coffee, food and I'm fine again." I got nothing but silence. "How's your day going?"

"Lexie..."

I winced, his voice was strained.

"You..." He went quiet.

My stomach knotted.

"Run that by me again." His voice was hard. Shit.

"Which part?" I asked, cringing.

"All of it," he said, his words clipped. Okay, this was not going well.

"I have a rare seizure disorder," I began again. "My doctor thought I might have been having some complications. Ran some tests; tests came back clean. I'm fine." He said nothing, so I kept going. "Miles took me over to tell the guys because I was bouncing around like a rabbit. I jumped on Asher and pissed off his girlfriend in the process. That's about it."

He was quiet long enough that I was getting worried.

"Dylan?"

"I'm here." His voice thicker than usual; it worried me. "Are you okay?"

"Yeah, I'm fine." I assured him. I swallowed hard. "Are you okay?"

He snorted. "I..." His voice was strained. "I just..."

I winced; he sounded like he was trying to hold something back. There was the sound of a bell.

"I have to get back to work. I'll... I'll talk to you later." He hung up on me.

I sat on the counter for a couple of minutes, running his voice back through my mind. He didn't take the cover story well; in fact, he sounded upset about it. All over a lie. Shit. I needed to make sure he was okay because he didn't sound it. My mind made up, I hopped off the counter and walked into the family room to hand Asher his phone.

"How's Dylan?" Asher asked, putting his phone away.

"I actually don't know," I admitted. I didn't bother sitting down. "I think he was upset."

Asher's eyes went wide.

I looked to Miles and Zeke. "Can one of you drop me back off at my truck? I need to head up to Dulcet."

Both Miles and Zeke got to their feet.

"I was going home soon anyway; I've got a game date with Autumn," Miles offered.

Zeke sat back down.

We said goodbye to the others and headed back to Miles' house. I told him how Dylan reacted, and he agreed that I should go see him. I picked up my stuff and hit the highway. I had to go shopping today; I could do that just as easily in Dulcet as I could in Northridge. Besides, Tara had mentioned a couple stores that she liked there, and Tara did know her clothes.

The drive to Dulcet was boring but pretty with all the green pines and white snow. It wasn't long before I was pulling up to Miller Hardware, just off Main St., in Dulcet. I'd never been to the store, but it was easy to find on Google. I parked, got out, and hopped up on the curb. I didn't like bothering Dylan at work, but I needed to know that he was all right. The more I kept running his voice through my head, the more I worried.

As I entered, the counter was to my immediate left with a guy around my age behind it. The aisles weren't cramped; everything was neat and clean. In short, it was a hardware store. I looked at the guy behind the counter. He had sandy blonde hair, blue eyes, and a nice face. But he wasn't Dylan. His blue eyes ran over me as a smile grew on his face; the effect was creepy.

"Welcome to Miller Hardware. If you need anything, let me know," he said as his eyes ran over me again.

I raised an eyebrow; that irked me. I decided to mess with him. I looked at his name tag on his green apron. "You can help me, Luke," I said sweetly.

His smile grew bigger. "Anything you need, gorgeous." His voice went soft. He probably thought it was his sexy voice. It wasn't.

"I'm looking for a hottie. Tall, blue eyes." I waited for a beat while he smiled. "His name's Dylan. Can you tell me where to find him?"

"I'm guessing you're Lexie, the new girlfriend?" Luke's voice sounded relieved.

I nodded.

"Good, maybe you can do something with him. He's been bitchy since I got here."

I winced as my stomach knotted worse. "Yeah, sorry, that's probably my fault," I admitted. "Where is he?"

Luke pointed toward the back of the store.

"He's stocking down the far-right aisle, just follow the cursing," Luke said.

I sighed and headed to the aisle. Dylan was mumbling under his breath, cursing and slamming things. I walked down the aisle, watching as he kept muttering while he stocked hinges. He was frowning, his shoulders tense. I bit my lip as I got closer.

"Hey," I said hesitantly. Dylan's sapphire eyes ran over me, his jaw clenched. My stomach knotted some more.

"What are you doing here?" he asked, his husky voice rough. "I thought you were going to Northridge today?" He crossed his arms over his chest, his eyes meeting mine.

"I was worried about you." My voice was soft, my pulse picking up as I stepped closer. "You didn't sound okay on the phone."

He looked away from me to the shelves, his jaw clenching and unclenching. It was only a moment before he turned back to me, his hand running through his hair. "Luke, watch the store," Dylan called loudly.

"Got it."

Dylan stuck his hands in his jean pockets as he turned. "Come on, we can talk in the office." My heart ached with every step we took to the back of the store. His body was almost rigid as he led me through a door that read "employees only."

He was going to dump me. I knew it. He didn't want a girlfriend with some weird health problem, and he was going to dump me. All over a fucking lie. It figured.

He led me down a dark hall then held open the door to a cluttered office. I stepped inside and walked into the middle of the small office. The door closed. I turned around to ask if he was all right, but I never got a word out.

He bent down and lifted me by my legs, his hands just under my butt. I had to grab his shoulders to keep my balance; I instantly wrapped my legs around his waist. His lips found mine as my back hit the wall. The world went fuzzy as I kissed him back, clinging to him as his mouth moved against mine. My hands went to his jaw. His chest and hips pinned me to the wall. My stomach did that low hard flip as his body pressed completely against mine. I gasped at the feel of him as warmth poured through me. One of his hands moved to cup my face, the other sliding to my butt, his fingers kneading. My lips opened under his; he slipped in and left me scrambling for thought. It was a hard, desperate kiss, and with what little thought I had left, I realized I had scared the shit out of him.

I was just trying to keep up with his mouth when the kissed changed; he slowed down. His mouth became gentler, softer until, eventually, he was only brushing his lips against mine. When he pulled back a little, we were both breathing heavily. My back was still pinned to the wall, my legs around his waist. My body was still flush against his, and his body was very happy to be there. It kept my heart racing, my body humming. I opened my eyes to look up at him; his eyes were a little wild as they met mine. I slipped my arms around his neck and shifted, bringing my chest against his. His hand left my face to slip between my back and the wall. He buried his face against my throat, holding me tight.

He was acting like I had just triggered some issue he had. Like Zeke with his guys-hitting-girls thing. I understood that, but I just didn't know what this was about. So, I just stayed where I was, in his arms, pressed against him, holding him back and breathing in sandalwood. He'd let me go when he was ready. It was a while. He took a deep breath and let it out slowly. He lifted his head to look down at me, his eyes full of shadows.

"Dylan, are you okay?" I whispered.

He sighed deeply as he rested his forehead against mine.

"I've been freaking out since I got off the phone with you," he admitted before taking a deep breath. "My mom died from complications from a simple fucking surgery." His husky voice was rough, making my chest tight. My hand moved to the back of his neck, fingers massaging. "So, when you said complications from your seizure thing. I kind of lost it." He admitted.

Shit. My luck was legendary. "I'm sorry, I didn't mean to trigger you like that." I kept my voice soft and soothing.

He pulled back; he looked at me with an eyebrow raised. "Trigger?"

"Yeah, it's a specific event that caused trauma; physical or emotional, it doesn't matter. It brings up what you felt when that event happened," I tried to explain. "Like when that guy pushed me at Vegabond. That triggered Zeke, and you know what happened there." His eyebrow dropped, his eyes resting on my face. "Have you ever had a reaction like this before?" I asked gently. He shook his head, his eyes unfocused. "Everyone has them, honey. At least everyone I know. Well, Zeke, Miles, and I do. I don't really know about the others."

His eyes were focused again and running over my face. "You have a trigger?" he asked, his voice full of doubt.

I smiled gently at him and nodded. "Yeah, you want to see me flip out? Make me lay on my stomach; big emotional reaction. Almost took Zeke's head off once," I told him matter-of-factly.

He grinned at that. It eased the tightness in my chest. He took a deep breath and let it out.

"I acted crazy, didn't I?" he asked, cringing as he waited for my answer. He looked so cute like that. I smiled gently at him.

"Well, hon, you did practically mount your girlfriend of two days, against the wall, in the office at work," I pointed out, whispering. "And you still haven't put me down yet."

He groaned, closing his eyes for a few seconds. "I'm sorry, Sunshine, I..." He looked down to see my legs still around his waist, his arms around me, and his body still pinning me to the wall. "Shit."

He didn't put me down. Instead, he pulled me away from the wall. I held on as he walked across the small office to set me on the tall desk. He didn't move too far away from me; his hips stayed between my knees. His hands began running up and down the outside of my legs. I didn't think he was even aware he was doing it.

He tilted his head back, his eyes closed. "I was just going to kiss you...."

"Hey," I said my voice soft. He looked back down at me. "It's okay, I get it. You needed to feel that I was okay." His eyes were still shadowed, and I didn't like it. "And that's what you needed right then."

"I didn't mean to pin you to the wall like that," he said as his hand ran through his hair.

"I know," I said.

His eyes met mine again. "I'm so sorry, Sunshine." He reached out and cupped the side of my neck, his thumb just in front of my ear. I liked that he kept touching me, it was like he couldn't stop himself.

"Dylan, hon, I get it," I said honestly, my voice gentle. My voice dropped down to a whisper. "But that needs to not happen again for a while."

He nodded. "I completely agree with you," he said adamantly. He leaned in and gave me a quick soft kiss on the lips before he pulled back so I could close my legs. Then he held my thighs just above my knees, his eyes on my face. "Now, tell me about this seizure disorder."

Oh shit.

For the next half-hour, I wove a tale of bullshit that anyone would be proud of. I used the real seizure disorder as my frame and explained that I didn't usually have shaking seizures, but I did get bloody noses and get sick from it occasionally. He asked questions, and I gave him answers from the website Miles had shown me. I even managed to convince him my beads were for a pressure point that helped prevent seizures. It was disturbing how good I was at lying to Dylan.

"Okay, so what if you're out with me and you have a seizure?" he asked, his hands rubbing along the outside of my legs again.

I thought about how to answer. All the guys now had Lexie kits, but they were filled with nausea meds, salt, and salted holy water. They kept them in their cars and their book bags. Maybe we could give him one and tell him it was medicine? I needed to think about it.

"It depends on how serious it is. If I have a bloody nose, I just need tissues and probably a walk. If I have a bloody nose and I'm throwing up, leave me alone until I'm done. It'll be awhile to get that nosebleed to stop." Then I hesitated at the third level. "If I'm with you, and I drop like a rock, make sure I have my bracelets on and call the guys or Rory." He gave me a look. I added, "they've been through it before. They know what to look for and what to do. Mostly it's getting me home to Rory."

His eyes narrowed on me. "And if Rory isn't there?" he asked immediately.

Damn. He was too clever. "Let the guys take care of me. They know what to do." I shrugged, I wasn't going into it any more than that. He saw that I wasn't willing to tell him more. He nodded, his face worried. I reached up and cupped his cheek with my hand. "Hey," I said softly. His hand covered mine, pressing it against his cheek. "I'm okay, no complications. Fit as a fiddle. Which is a strange saying if you think about it. I mean a fiddle lays around all day, how could it be fit?"

Dylan chuckled; the sound made me smile.

"I'm not going anywhere. I'm too stubborn." Then I smirked. "Besides, who else is going to give Zeke shit?" He smiled down at me. "Now, I have a question for you."

He raised an eyebrow.

"Why do you keep calling me Sunshine?" I asked.

His face looked pained as he began rubbing his neck. "I've got to get back to work...." He began, starting to back up.

"Oh, no you don't!" I snagged his arm and pulled him back to me. "You got a whole bunch of my stuff today. You can tell me this one other thing."

He looked down at me. "It's kind of corny," he admitted, his cheeks turning pink.

I perked up. "Even better." I smiled up at him.

He sighed then leaned into me until his mouth was next to my ear. "Because before you came around, my life wasn't so great," he whispered, sending hot shivers down my spine. "It was dull, dark and full of just stuff I had to do." I bit my lip feeling my face warming. He wasn't done. "Then you came along and lit everything back up. Like sunshine."

Those butterflies went crazy as my face burned.

He pulled back a bit to look down at my face. "You are red," he said, smiling.

"That wasn't corny, that was romantic and sweet," I told him, squirming.

He smiled at me. "And now you're uncomfortable," he observed. "That aversion to romance thing again?"

"Yeah, it's a bitch," I admitted, sliding off the desk to stand on the floor.

He smiled. His eyes ran over my face. "Well, we'll work on it."

The way he said it sent warm tingles everywhere. He leaned down again and kissed me gently until I pressed harder against his lips. He made a small noise in the back of his throat. Sparks ran through me as he pressed back. He took my bottom lip between his, nipping at it before kissing me again. I made a small noise. My arms moved around his neck; his arm went around my back. Dylan, my Dylan, was kissing me like I was the only person in his world. He felt so damn good like this. I couldn't think as his mouth kept moving with mine.

A loud knock on the door brought the world back hard, reminding me where we were. Dylan groaned deeply against my mouth. I knew exactly how he felt. I made a small growl of my own. We both eased back till our lips were barely brushing. His forehead rested against mine as we both tried to catch our breath.

"Don't go anywhere," he whispered, his husky voice rough.

"Wasn't planning on it," I countered. He pulled back to kiss my forehead; we let go of each other so he could answer the door.

"What?" he bit out. I leaned against the desk and tried to remember what had just happened. All I could think was... I wanted more. I took a breath and let it out. Down, body, baaad body.

"The other guys are here to do their paperwork," Luke shot back. "Remember, you wanted to hire them."

"Fuck," Dylan cursed. "Okay, just... I'll bring the paperwork out in a couple minutes."

"Uh-huh," Luke taunted in a knowing voice.

I grinned. Yeah, we were making out. I'd own it. Dylan closed the door on Luke then turned back to me.

"You have to get back to work," I said for him.

His face looked pained as he walked back to me. "Yeah, it's my friends." He took my hands in his. "I'm hiring them to take over my shifts so I can see you more."

I grinned up at him; him working less really sounded great to me. "It's okay. I need to go anyway. I need clothes that don't fall off," I admitted, looking up to meet his eyes. "I was just worried about you."

He grinned as he pulled me into his arms. I slid my arms around his hard waist, resting my cheek on his chest. I took a deep breath of sandalwood. He held me tight, his face in my hair as he inhaled deeply.

"You're okay, though, right?" he whispered into my hair.

I nodded. "Yeah, I'm okay. No problems," I assured him. I lifted my head so I could see his face. "You okay?"

"Much better now that I saw you and really know you're alright." His eyes ran over my face. "But before we head out there..."

He leaned down to brush his lips against mine. Butterflies took off as he kissed me gently, his hands moving to cup my face. Warmth filled me fast, taking my breath away. He kissed me softly, sweetly, until I forgot my own name. When he pulled back, his eyes were more than warm on my face.

"Just needed to do that one more time."

"Um… yeah… thought… smart ass comment." I blinked up at him, dazed from his kiss.

He snickered as he stroked his thumb over my cheekbone before dropping his hands from my face. "We need to go," he grumbled, sounding resigned before he ran his hand through his hair. He stepped back so I could move away from the desk. "Want to meet the guys?"

"Sure."

He grinned as we headed for the door. I was stepping out into the hall when he cursed.

"Shit, the paperwork," he muttered.

I looked back in the door to see him opening a file cabinet.

"You forgot the paperwork?" I asked, laughing.

Dylan's cheeks tinged pink. "Not my fault you're distracting," he shot back.

I snickered.

"Fuck, I need copies. Hold on, Sunshine."

I was leaning against the doorframe, watching him make copies, when the door at the end of the hallway opened.

"Dylan! Come on, we still have shit to go over!" A guy shouted as he walked into the hallway.

He was about the same height as Dylan with dark hair buzzed close to his scalp. The guy had broad shoulders and muscles to fill it out. He was almost to me when he looked up; he stopped walking when he spotted me. He wasn't bad looking. His nice jaw and great cheekbones made him good looking, but I knew a lot of good looking guys. My bar was set pretty high.

"Hey, I'm Aaron; are you coming to work here too?" His voice was a nice rough one, not like Zeke's but enough to hint at it. His brown eyes ran over my body, a smile spreading across his face. I was about to tell him who I was when he continued. "Because if you are, I would not mind one freaking bit."

That sparked my temper. "Why is that?" I asked innocently.

His eyes moved to my face, finally. The copier stopped.

"Because we'd be spending a few shifts a week together; we could get to know each other."

He started walking closer. This was one of Dylan's friends? Wow.

I smiled sweetly up at him. "Never gonna happen." My voice was still sweet. "I like guys who aren't dicks."

I felt eyes on me. Dylan must have heard us.

"Oh, I'll grow on you." He gave me a nice bad boy smile. I could see how a girl might fall for it. Fortunately, I could smell bullshit from a mile away.

"So, you're what? Like a barnacle? You latch on and don't let go?" I asked dryly. "Not real appealing in a boyfriend." Aaron's smile disappeared. Dylan walked into the doorway.

"Hey, Aaron." Dylan's hard voice drew Aaron's attention away from looking me over again.

"Hey, everyone's waiting out there." Aaron's gaze went back to me. "What's your name?"

"Lexie," I answered.

"My girlfriend," Dylan followed up. Aaron looked back to Dylan, his brows going up.

"That you're trying to hit on," Dylan added.

Aaron's mouth made an o shape. He looked back at me, his cheeks turning pink.

"Sorry, I didn't know," Aaron said politely.

"Do you come on to girls like that a lot?" I asked, not willing to let him get away without a little more embarrassment.

"Um..." Aaron rubbed the back of his neck, his face starting to turn red.

"'Cause you lost me the second you looked at my body before my face," I told him matter-of-factly. Dylan smirked then leaned against the door frame, content to watch the show. "You always start with the face. You're an asshole otherwise." Aaron was looking uncomfortable.

But I wasn't done. "Second, you introduce yourself like you did. It was polite, and it would work." Aaron was practically squirming now.

"Third, you don't immediately jump to hitting on a girl. But if you want to, try complimenting her. Like, 'wow, you have beautiful eyes. Or a great smile, and I just had to come over and talk to you.'" Aaron's face was beet red. I kept going. "And never say you grow on a girl; that's creepy as fuck."

He was looking to Dylan for a rescue, but Dylan was quietly laughing at Aaron.

"Want to start over?" I offered.

Aaron looked at me like he was drowning and I was throwing him a life preserver. "Yes, please," Aaron said gratefully.

I smiled. "Hi, I'm Lexie, Dylan's girlfriend," I offered politely.

Aaron took a deep breath and let it out. "Hi Lexie, I'm Aaron, one of Dylan's friends," he replied politely.

"It's nice to meet you." I looked over at Dylan, whose face was red. "Do any more of your friends hit on girls like that? 'Cause we can just send 'em back here one by one and I'll teach them on how to hit on a girl."

This time even Aaron chuckled. Dylan managed to get control of himself.

"Can we?" he begged, sliding his arm around me, his hand settling on my hip.

I gave him a big smile then checked the time on my phone. I sighed. "Not today, I still need to buy clothes then get back before Rory realizes I came here and not to Northridge," I grumbled.

Dylan gave me a squeeze and kissed my forehead. "That works, I think I'd rather have Aaron let the others know about you a bit before you really hang out with us." Dylan smiled down at me.

"Oh, yeah, I'll warn them," Aaron said adamantly.

"Or don't. Think of the fun." I snickered. Aaron laughed as he headed back down the small hallway, Dylan held my hand as we followed. We walked down an aisle toward a group of guys who were talking at the counter. Aaron moved a bit further away from me as we walked out of the aisle. I sent him a 'really' look. He smirked at me.

"Everyone, this is Lexie," Dylan announced. Everyone looked at me. "My girlfriend."

"Hey." I kept it simple.

There was a chorus of "heys" and "hi." I felt several pairs of eyes running over me.

"Don't hit on her," Aaron warned. "It won't go well."

I raised an eyebrow at him. "Well, if you were good at flirting, I wouldn't have given you so much shit," I pointed out, grinning.

Dylan started laughing; the others chuckled. One of the guys tilted his head. He was a head taller than me, short styled blond hair streaked with lighter blond highlights. His green eyes were smiling as he eyed me with a smile on his cute face. He was wearing a green button-down untucked over dark blue jeans and sneakers. His wool pea coat did nothing to hide his muscular frame.

"She gave Aaron shit; I like her," Green-eyed boy declared with a big smile.

Dylan snorted as he put his hand on my lower back. "Lexie, this is Jake; he's Asher's rival for the best Quarterback rating in the area." Dylan smiled down at me.

I eyed Jake. "Really?" I sounded doubtful. "His QB rating is at one hundred, what's yours?"

"A hundred," Jake said grinning.

"Impressive."

He bowed his head slightly.

"You know football?" one of the guys asked.

He was a head taller than me; his dark hair was streaked with purple and spiked. He had an average face, with a nose ring, eyebrow stud, and lip ring. He was wearing all black.

"Sunshine, this is Derrick." Dylan pointed to emo boy. "He's a grumpy shit."

I looked up at Dylan. "Zeke bad?" I asked seriously.

Dylan grinned down at me. "No." I snorted and waved a hand dismissively.

Dylan chuckled as he looked at Derrick. "Yeah, she knows football. Stats, plays, all of it."

I winked at Derrick. He smirked.

"Wait, Zeke? Blackthorn?" I looked up at the tallest guy. He was a head and half taller than me, his black hair was short on top and shorter on the sides. Even though it was winter, he had a tan, or it was his natural skin color; I didn't know. But he had lovely green eyes that he ran over me suspiciously.

"Lexie, this is Thomas," Dylan introduced me. Thomas's eyes narrowed on me.

"Yep, big, tall, and grumpy Zeke," I confirmed, wondering why he had that look on his face.

"You're friends with Blackthorn?" Thomas asked again.

His question got on my nerves. "Yeah, and you're friends with Dylan," I pointed out. I had no clue what that look was about.

Luke snapped his fingers. "That's why you're so familiar," Luke announced from behind the counter.

Everyone turned to look at him.

He pointed at me while looking at Thomas. "She was there the night Blackthorn beat the shit out of Markus."

Eyes moved back to me.

I grinned. "How is Markus by the way?" I asked sweetly. "Is he eating solid foods yet?"

Dylan snickered. Everyone but Dylan looked horrified. I guess I needed to explain. "Markus grabbed my ass, pinned me to the bar and wouldn't back off. So, I pushed him away from me." The guys all reacted slightly. Some blinked, a couple frowned. "He pushed me back; I hit the bar and the floor. Then Zeke hit him. A lot." Dylan was getting his laughing under control; his friends were frowning.

"The guys are a bit protective of Lexie," Dylan explained, smiling down at me.

I rolled my eyes. "Over protective, nosey, gossipy, naggy...." I grumbled.

Dylan chuckled.

"The guys?" Aaron asked eyebrow raised.

"Yeah," I sighed, here came the questions. "All my friends are guys."

All of Dylan's friends exchanged looks. I rolled my eyes and looked up at Dylan.

"I'm going to leave you with those questions because I get them enough as it is."

Dylan snorted. I was about to say goodbye when my phone rang. I pulled it out and checked the ID. I grumbled. I looked up at Dylan, wincing. "It's Isaac."

He grinned. "Answer on speaker," Dylan insisted. I looked at him like he was nuts; his friends were right there. "It'll make my day."

I sighed and sent an apologetic look to his friends before answering. "Hey."

"Are you done yet? We need food." Isaac's honey-like voice flowed through the speaker on my phone.

"Then get it yourselves. I haven't even gone shopping yet," I said bluntly.

"Zeke says skip it. We're hungry," Isaac countered.

"I'm not skipping shopping; it's Zeke's fucking fault I need to, so you bitches can just starve," I snapped at him. "Order a pizza."

Jake looked over at Dylan. "Why's it Zeke's fault she needs to go shopping?" Jake asked Dylan quietly.

"Hold on, I love listening to this," Dylan said, waving him off.

"We're at Miles' and he doesn't do delivery," Isaac reminded me.

"Neither do I, get off your heavy ass and go get food," I countered, rolling my eyes.

Dylan burst out laughing.

"Am I on speaker?" Isaac asked carefully.

"Yep." I snickered.

"Red," he shot at me.

"Cookie Monster," I shot back.

A couple of the others were chuckling now too.

"Dylan there?"

"Yeah, I'm here, Isaac," Dylan said cheerfully. "Sorry, I love hearing her give you guys shit."

"Glad to amuse," Isaac said cheerfully. "Dylan, did you know your girlfriend sings in the shower? Off key, and loudly." Everyone else on this side burst out laughing.

"You fucker," I growled. I wanted to rip his head off.

I motioned at Dylan to give me his phone. Dylan was snickering as we switched phones. Isaac was laughing his ass off. I quickly sent a text to get even with Isaac.

"Yeah, laugh it up asshole," I said sweetly as he was calming down. I got a text back and smiled. "You might want to be aware of where Zeke is right now, though." Dylan was snickering again.

"What are you talk-...fuck!" There was the sound of yelling and running. "Lexie, that's fucking mean!"

"Run, Isaac, run," I taunted.

"Shit!" I laughed my ass off as there was yelling in the background. "Call him off!"

"No, you need the fucking cardio."

"Red! Call him off!" Isaac was breathing heavy.

"No, you fucking embarrassed me in front of Dylan and his friends. Now you're going to pay for it," I told him smugly as I traded phones with Dylan again.

"I'm sorry! You weren't even off key! I swear!" Isaac was running out of breath, I wondered why.

"Are the others helping Zeke?" I asked sweetly, sure I was right.

"Yeah!" Isaac snapped. I burst out laughing along with everyone on this side.

"Red... come on..." There was the sound of bodies hitting, then a big thud hitting the floor. I winced as I heard Isaac grunt under someone's weight, cursing followed along with my guys laughing. Someone picked up the phone.

"Still there, Ally?" Asher's rich voice made me smile.

"Yep. Who got him?" I asked with a big smile on my face.

Asher chuckled. "We ran him out, Zeke took him down." I started laughing as he continued. "Zeke is currently sitting on him as he lectures Isaac about embarrassing you."

"Can I get a photo?"

Asher chuckled. "Of course, Ally girl, give me a sec."

I looked up to see Dylan's face was red, and a couple of the others still chuckling. Thomas just kept staring at me, like he was trying to figure me out. I ignored it. I got the photo Asher sent. Isaac was stretched out on the floor, his face red. Zeke was leaning on his upper back, his hip on the floor. It didn't take much of Zeke's body weight to hold you down, the guy was a giant. I burst out laughing as I showed Dylan and the others. Everyone chuckled.

"Did you get it?" Asher asked.

"Yes, thank you," I said in my sweet voice. "Did Zeke really want me to skip shopping?"

"Not that I heard." Asher sounded certain.

I grinned. "Can you hand the phone to him, please?" I asked, still using my sweet voice.

"You got it." Asher was talking away from the phone as the phone switched hands.

"What?" Zeke's gravelly voice shot through the speaker.

"Did you tell Isaac to tell me to skip shopping to get food for you guys?" I didn't bother with my sweet voice, it never worked on Zeke anyway.

"No, I fucking didn't," Zeke growled. His voice sounded further away. "You told Lexie that I said to skip getting clothes? You. Fuck. Shit."

Isaac was in deep shit now.

Zeke's voice came back, and it was his nice tone that he used with me every once in a while. "I'll take care of this, Lexie."

"Thank you, Zeke."

"No problem; go do that girly shit," he ordered. I heard Isaac yelling he was sorry in the background, begging me not to let Zeke handle it.

"No killing, no maiming," I reminded him.

"Fine, take all my fun away," he grunted back.

I smiled as he hung up. I put the phone in my pocket. Dylan pulled me to his side, hugging me.

"Oh, that just made my week." Dylan kissed my temple, still laughing.

"Why is it Zeke's fault you have to go shopping?" Jake asked, an eyebrow raised.

I sighed. "I have a rare seizure disorder. Zeke got on my ass about my diet." I lifted the shoulder of my shirt to show how big it was now. "With all my hobbies, I lost too much weight, and now my clothes don't fit," I said absently as I checked the time. Shit. I was going to be late. "I've got to go." I went on my toes and kissed Dylan's cheek then headed for the door.

"Drive safe," Dylan called to me.

I turned and answered while I walked backward. "No, I'm going to drive dangerously and against traffic," I shot back with my shit-eating grin.

"There's my smart ass," Dylan said, smiling. I winked at him before turning around to open the door. I waved at Dylan's friends.

"Nice meeting you guys."

Then I was out the door. Before the door closed, I heard one of the guys ask for my phone number. I snorted as I hurried to my Blazer. I needed to get shopping done fast.

In the end, I ended up having more fun than I thought I would; without Rory, I didn't feel so awkward. He gave me a limit, and I stuck way below that. Besides, I was planning on gaining some weight back, so I didn't buy much. By the time I was done, I didn't have time to go home; I was supposed to meet the guys at Miles' house. And I really wanted a good soak. I was climbing into my Blazer when I texted the guys, asking if they still wanted me to pick up burgers. They sent their orders. They still hadn't gone out for food, the lazy shits.

I WAS SOAKING in the jacuzzi tub at Miles' house, enjoying my girly time. The guys had already started a game when I showed up with the burgers from the Frosty Freeze in town. I had eaten fast so I could have time in the tub. This tub was magic. I enjoyed the water jets between my shoulder blades the most; the ones for my feet weren't bad either. Though, the hot water to my neck was always a huge bonus. There I was, soaking, when my phone rang. I picked it up off the side of the tub and smiled. It was Dylan. I shut off the jets then answered it.

"Hey, you, aren't you supposed to still be at work?"

"I'm still here," his husky voice groused. "I'm trying to teach these idiots how to do everything as fast as possible. It's not going great." He sighed. "I needed to hear a voice of reason to tell me not to kill them."

I burst out laughing. "And... and... you called me?" I managed through the laughing.

Dylan started chuckling too.

When we both calmed down, he answered, "Okay, maybe I needed a reminder why I shouldn't kill them."

I smiled as warmth filled my chest. "Because if you kill them, you won't get to see me much," I reminded him.

Dylan groaned. "You're right, no killing tonight. A beating?"

"No beating anyone up," I countered.

He chuckled. "Fine. I'll just... repeat myself 'till I'm insane," he grumbled. Poor guy.

"How's the game going? Is Miles cleaning up?" he asked.

I snickered. "Yeah, I think so." Before he could ask, I changed the subject. "So, did your friends think I was nuts?"

Dylan snorted. "Nuts? No. You... left an impression."

The way he said it made me want to know more.

"And that impression was?" I asked.

He chuckled the eagerness in my voice. "A couple of them instantly liked you, one of them called dibs on your phone number if we break up, and one of them thinks you're a bit scary."

I started laughing. "I'm like half everyone's size," I pointed out.

He chuckled. "That's why it's funny as hell."

I could hear the smile in Dylan's voice. There was another voice in the background.

"Hold on a sec, Sunshine." I heard that other voice talking. "Yeah, I'm talking to her."

The other voice was talking again. "I'm not giving her your number, Thomas. Fuck off and go stock shit."

I snorted. I was going to have to keep an eye on Thomas when I hung out with Dylan's friends.

"I'm back."

"Thomas is badgering you, huh?" I couldn't seem to stop smiling.

"Yeah, the shit," Dylan grumbled. "If he asks for your number again, I'm going to clock him."

"Nah, let me do it."

He chuckled. "No, he'd probably love it." Dylan sounded serious.

I smiled.

"Is something wrong with your phone, babe? I keep hearing an echo."

I bit the corner of my lower lip as I heard him tell someone else how to restock the nails. I shouldn't tell him; he was surrounded by his friends. But my twisted side was saying, 'He's surrounded by his friends, torture him a little.' Yeah, my twisted side usually won.

"Remember that first text I sent you on game day?" I asked sweetly.

There was silence for a few heartbeats. Someone else was talking next to him.

"Yeah. I remember." His voice was careful, and a little rougher.

I had to stop myself from giggling wickedly. "You kind of caught me soaking in the tub again," I admitted smiling.

"Lexie..." His voice sounded pained. "Damn it..."

I snickered.

"You're..." There was another voice in the background. "No... I'll... just.... hang on, guys."

I started giggling silently.

"You don't need to fucking know why my face is red, Derrick."

I burst out laughing, not even hiding it now.

"Yeah, laugh it up, Sunshine."

Voices started asking questions. "Lexie! What did you say to him?" Jake shouted from the background.

I couldn't stop laughing.

"None of your fucking business!" Dylan shot at the guys. I heard hoots and hollers coming from the guys.

I just kept laughing.

"Keep laughing, Lexie, and I'll tell them why I'm red," he threatened.

My laughing didn't stop. He was so bluffing.

"Go ahead, tell your friends that your girlfriend is in the tub on the phone. I dare ya." I snickered back to him. "I'm sure Thomas will love it."

He growled in my ear, sending me off on another round of laughing.

"Don't tempt me," he grumbled.

I couldn't stop smiling. I kept hearing other voices in the background.

"I'm not telling you guys shit. Fuck off."

I was snickering now. The sound of voices was getting quieter. He must have been walking away.

"You know what I'm going to ask, Sunshine."

"No bubbles," I answered. I had just embarrassed him in front of his friends. I could give him that. "But there are these water jets that are cool. It's like my own private hot tub."

"Lexie...." he groaned.

"Well, if you hear an echo don't ask," I pointed out.

He snorted. "Now at even a hint of an echo, I'm asking," he assured me.

I smiled. "Then you can't blame me for telling the truth," I countered.

He growled. "Okay, I need to focus on something other than my naked girlfriend, in the tub, on the phone with me," he grumbled. There was silence for a few heartbeats. "Fuck, I'm drawing a blank here."

I started laughing again.

"Wait. Schedules. I need to see when I have days off coming up," he said.

"Sounds like a good diversion." I waited a couple of beats. "Or we could just get off the phone and talk later tonight."

"Nope, I wanna talk now," he said adamantly.

"So, you don't want to talk later?" I teased him.

"Yeah, I want to talk later, but I really want to talk now, too."

I giggled again. When I calmed down, I answered him.

"Okay." I decided to give him a break.

He grumbled under his breath.

"What's wrong?" I asked.

He sighed. "I'm trying to remember what we talked about last night, but I just keep thinking about you in the tub."

"We both agreed to get our shit done in the morning on the weekends, and to keep Friday night open too," I said patiently. Me being in the tub was messing with him more than I thought it would.

"And, I'd take shifts during the week. It's coming back." He chuckled as I heard typing.

"What are you doing?" I asked suspiciously.

"I'm scheduling my shifts for the next couple months before anyone else can," he admitted.

I snorted. "You sneaky bastard."

"You know it."

"How about that science project of yours?" I reminded him.

I didn't really understand what it was, except that it was for a scholarship. Dylan tried to explain it to me once, but there was so much technical jargon that I couldn't follow.

"I'll check on it tomorrow morning. It doesn't really need anything else right now." His voice was warm and soft, sending those shivers down my spine. "I'm making sure I have a lot more time now-" There was the sound of a crash in the background. He groaned. "That is if my friends don't destroy the store first."

I chuckled.

"I have to go, Sunshine."

"Alright, I'll talk to you later."

"Before you go…. hair, up or down?" His voice sounded like he was smiling.

I rolled my eyes, smiling. "Up."

He groaned. "Thanks, babe."

"Bye." I hung up the phone, smiling.

I finished my bath and dried off. I pulled on my now too-big jeans, my grommet belt, a black long-sleeved shirt, and my usual boots. The guys were cleaning up the board game when I came in, humming a song stuck in my head.

"Red, there's ice cream in the kitchen for sundaes," Isaac told me before taking a bite from his bowl.

"Hell yeah, now that's what I'm talking about," I said in my happy voice.

Zeke grinned as I headed for the kitchen. That song was really in my head now; I was singing quietly as I pulled down a bowl. I was singing the chorus when I opened the fridge and found three different kinds of ice cream. I grabbed the chocolate and strawberry. I wasn't paying attention as I kept singing, scooping up my ice cream and adding some whip cream on top. I hit the chorus again as I was putting away the ice cream.

When I shut the door, Ethan was there. I jumped. "Make some noise, Snoopy!" I shouted as my heart rate started to return to normal.

Ethan had a big grin on his face. "Why didn't you tell me you can sing?" he asked suspiciously.

I sighed as I went back to pick up my ice cream. "Everyone can sing, not everyone can do it well," I pointed out before taking a bite of sugary deliciousness.

Ethan's grin turned into a smile. "But you can."

I rolled my eyes. "Not really," I countered before heading toward the living room.

There were hurrying footsteps, then my ice cream was out of my hand.

"Snoopy! Give me back my ice cream."

Ethan stepped back from me, his mischievous smile on his face. "Sing one song for me, and I'll give it back."

"Asher! Ethan took my ice cream!" I shouted, looking for back up.

I couldn't hurt Ethan, not with his back the way it was. Ethan shot me a smug look. Asher walked into the hallway.

"Give her back her ice cream," Asher told him directly.

Ethan held up a finger. "I will if she sings one song for me; you've heard her voice," Ethan said seriously. "You know she's good."

I scoffed at him. The guy was nuts. Asher looked over at me, a small smile on his face.

"You are good," Asher betrayed me. I glared at him. Asher gave me a big smile. "It's not going to kill you, Ally."

I sighed. I didn't think I sounded that great. Fuck it, I'd do it for my ice cream. And it might be fun. I shot a look at a beaming Ethan.

"Fine, but I'm not singing in front of everyone," I grumbled.

"We'll use the music room," Ethan said smugly before he turned and headed down the hallway.

There was a music room? I grumbled as I followed. Asher went back into the living room, not that he wouldn't hear me anyway. Ethan led me to the doors across from the dining room.

The room was practically lined with books, making it look more like a library than a music room. Only instead of comfy chairs, there was a piano, a guitar, a cello and a violin case. Miles didn't play an instrument. Did he? Ethan set the bowl on top of the piano and picked up an acoustic guitar.

"Take the piano bench, Beautiful."

I grumbled the whole time I walked across the room. Ethan pulled up a stool and got situated. He checked the tuning on the acoustic guitar before looking back at me.

"You were singing I Will Not Bow by Breaking Benjamin, right?"

I eyed him. "Yes."

Ethan's eyes were lit up, and his smile was killer. Don't let him sucker you, Lexie.

"My band just happens to know that one. So..." He strummed the first notes. "Show me what you got," he challenged.

I narrowed my eyes at him. Oh, it was on. I watched as he started playing. When Ethan played, it was all I could focus on. Then I started singing the way the song always sounded to me. It wasn't the same as the band's; after all, I'm a girl. But I sang the best I could. I wasn't nervous or worried I was off key. I just sang, my eyes on Ethan's hands playing the guitar. Then the song was over, and all the nerves came back. I sounded awful, I was probably off key the whole song, and I probably fucked up the lyrics too.

"Okay, there happy?" I mumbled, looking at the piano. I grabbed my ice cream and took a big bite.

"Very. Lexie, you can sing." Ethan's voice sounded impressed.

I looked at him like he was nuts. "Everyone can sing-"

"Lexie, you sing great. Did you ever have any voice lessons?" he asked, resting his arm on the guitar.

I snorted. "I was lucky to get a cupcake on my birthday, Snoopy," I said matter-of-factly before taking another bite of ice cream.

He was quiet for a couple of heartbeats. "So, no one ever taught you how to stay in key? Or to read music?" He sounded like he didn't believe me.

I looked at him and shook my head. I swallowed my ice cream. "That bad, huh?" I asked, mostly joking.

His eyes went wide. "No, that good. You were in key the whole time," he began, his eyes narrowed on me. "How do you know what key to stay in?"

"I sing it the way it sounds to me." I shrugged.

I didn't understand what he was getting so excited over. I took another bite of my ice cream. Ethan did something with his phone and set it down.

"Sing one song with me, Beautiful," Ethan asked. I looked at him like he was nuts. "Please, I'll smuggle you some of Asher's cookies tomorrow."

Okay, Ethan knew how to bribe me.

"What song?" I asked, resigned.

"Do you know Broken by Seether?"

I nodded.

"My band has been practicing that for a few weeks," he said.

"It's a duet, Ethan," I reminded him.

He smirked at me. "I'll take the guy's part. Do you remember it that well?" he asked, his eyes running over my face.

I narrowed my eyes at him. "Yeah, I do," I admitted reluctantly.

"Then it won't be a problem."

He started strumming. Then he sang his part. His smoky voice rolled over my ears and down my spine. Again, I forgot about feeling nervous; I forgot about thinking I was going to suck. When it was time to join in, I did. Again, I sang the song the way it always sounded to me. I didn't know if I was off key, or what, but right now, with Ethan, I didn't care. Ethan didn't correct me; he just kept playing. Then he was joining in again. Then we sang together till the end. He was smiling at me as he finished the last notes.

"Lexie, that was fucking awesome." He met my eyes. "I need to borrow you."

I went still. "What?"

"My band has been looking for a girl who has a voice that works with that song for the last few weeks," Ethan began. I raised both my eyebrows. "It's why we haven't performed that song. I need you to sing this song with my band this Saturday."

My heart clenched. "Oh hell no," I said emphatically as I picked up my ice cream and headed for the door.

"Lexie, please."

"No, nope, nada, no way," I told him on my way out the door and into the hall. "Get your girlfriend to do it!"

Ethan's footsteps were hurrying to catch up. "She doesn't have the kind of voice we need, and she can't hit the notes you can." Ethan stepped up to my side as I headed down the hallway. "Lexie, this would help us so much."

"I don't sing, Ethan," I pointed out.

"You do, and you're damn good at it. And with practice, you can be fucking amazing," he countered as we stepped into the living room.

The guys all looked up as I ignored Ethan. I sat down next to Isaac and focused on eating my ice cream.

"Asher, you heard her, right?" Ethan asked animatedly.

I ignored them.

"Of course, I did," Asher answered like it was obvious.

"Then tell her how she sounded," Ethan pleaded.

I glared at Ethan. Asher looked over at me, grinning.

"You did sound pretty great," Asher admitted. I glared at Asher.

"What's going on?" Isaac asked, leaning back on the couch.

My mouth was full, so I couldn't stop Ethan.

"I need Lexie to sing with us at Vegabond this weekend," Ethan announced.

I snorted and kept looking at my bowl.

"That's extremely short notice, Ethan," Miles pointed out.

"I know, but she doesn't need much coaching. She knows the song. All she needs is a little practice with the band for this one song." Ethan was getting excited, I loved when he did that but couldn't he do it about something else?

"Get your girlfriend, or one of her friends," I mumbled before taking another bite.

Ethan came over to me and got on his knees in front of me.

"Lexie, the Manager at Vegabond says we need more range if we're going to keep playing there. You jumping in once in a while would give us that range, without going into pop songs."

His eyes were begging me. My gut knotted.

"I've never sung in front of people, Ethan. I'd probably blow it anyway," I reminded him.

Ethan shook his head. "No, you won't. You already have the song down. You just need more volume and to use your diaphragm more," Ethan explained feverishly. "Lexie, I'm not asking you to join the band. Just help us keep being able to play at Vegabond."

I shook my head. "Ethan, I suck. You need to find someone else," I insisted.

Ethan pulled out his phone, stood up and backed away. "Oh, yeah?" Ethan looked at the guys. "Listen to this, guys."

My heart dropped. "You didn't," I said quietly, as the first notes of Broken played over the speaker.

Oh, my God. I was going to kill the little shit. I couldn't believe it as Ethan's voice came through the phone, smoky and clear. Then mine joined him. It wasn't bad, I'd admit, but no fucking way was I going to do this. I peeked at the guys to see Zeke had a small smirk on his face, Isaac had an eyebrow raised, Asher was just listening, and Miles looked like he was concentrating. I went back to glaring at Ethan. I wanted blood. When the song was over, he looked down at me, his smiling fading.

"Someone's phone is going in the pool," I growled at him. When I went to get up, Isaac draped himself over me, pinning me to the couch. "Isaac off!"

Ethan moved behind the other couch, doing something else with his phone.

"Red, that was awesome," Isaac said, fighting against me as I tried to shove him off me. "You should totally do this!" I tried to give him a big shove, but the shit head stayed put.

"Lexie." Miles' voice grabbed my attention. I looked over Isaac to see Miles with a small smile on his face. "You sounded amazing."

I snorted and kept trying to move Isaac off me. "You guys are sweet, totally lying but sweet." I tried one more time to get Isaac to move, but the shit head was heavy. I cursed at him.

"Lexie." Zeke's voice got my attention. I looked up at him. His face was serious as he met my eyes. "That sounded great. Ethan says you can do this, and I believe him."

I stopped trying to push Isaac off me. Zeke never lied. He hated it. He'd rather be considered an asshole than a liar. If he said I sounded great, I sounded great. I closed my eyes, groaned, and laid my head back on the couch. Okay, maybe I could sing. But in front of people?

"I highly doubt your band is going to go for it." I tried to find any reason I could to make him not ask this of me.

"Already sent them the audio." Ethan's voice was smug. "They want you at practice tomorrow night."

I made a loud groan. I thought about what made me not want to do this. What if I embarrassed myself? What if I choked? What if, what if, what if. I was scared. And I didn't like it. Fuck. I covered my face with my hands as I tried to come to a decision. The guys kept talking about how well I sang, and about how I didn't always have to do it. Just try it once and decide later. What it all came down to was this: was I up to the challenge? I grinned into my hands. Okay, I could do this. Once. I dropped my hands and looked up at Ethan.

"Fine, you asshole," I shot at Ethan. Before he could celebrate, I held up a finger. "I'll go to your stupid practice. If it works, we'll go from there."

Isaac got off me as Ethan walked toward me, his striking face beaming. He hugged me tight.

"Beautiful, you are amazing! You have no idea how much we need to keep this venue!"

Ethan seemed so happy, that it made me smile. Apparently, this did mean a lot to him. I just hoped it wouldn't be a mistake.

Hanging out ended for me right there. Ethan dragged me back into the music room and started teaching me on how to use my diaphragm to project my voice and hit the higher notes. I bitched the whole time. Then he ran me through the song again; this time stopping to help me hit the note, then when I reached it, we would start the song over. By the time I'd run through it once without messing up, I was tired. Ethan said no more tonight; he didn't want to make me hoarse.

After that, I said goodnight to the guys and headed home. I pulled up to Rory's, still not believing what was I going to do. Maybe Rory would tell me no.

I WAS STILL GRUMBLING an hour later when I carried my shopping bags into my bedroom. Rory didn't say no. Instead, he wanted to show up to watch. I begged him not to; he said no. I, at least, got him to agree not to record the whole train wreck.

I had finished putting my new clothes away when I remembered thinking about giving Dylan a Lexie kit. I started a group message with the guys.

Alexis: Hey, got a sec?

It wasn't long before my phone was vibrating.

Zeke: What?

Ethan: Always.

Isaac: Yep.

Miles: Yes.

Asher: Yeah.

I smiled at their responses.

Alexis: Dylan was triggered this afternoon. It had to do with his mom. Now he thinks I've got a seizure disorder. I was thinking of giving him a Lexie kit to help him deal, and just telling him it's medicine. Thoughts?

There were a few minutes of quiet.

Asher: That would help him feel better about the whole thing.

Zeke: Isn't it too soon?

Ethan: No, they've been talking for two months. They were practically dating already, now it's just official.

Isaac: I agree with Snoopy. LOL

Miles: That is a good idea, Lexie, you can say you can't tell him the names of the medicine because it's part of a drug trial.

Alexis: Okay vote: yes or no.

Asher: Yes

Ethan: Yes

Isaac: Yes

Miles: Yes

Zeke: No

Alexis: Majority rules.

Zeke: If this comes back to kick you in the teeth I'm never going to let you guys forget this.

I snickered.

Alexis: I'm not giving him one today, Zeke. I was thinking next week unless shit ramps up around here.

Zeke: Oh, then yeah.

I rolled my eyes and put my phone down. I was still grousing about singing when Dylan called around eleven. I wasn't in the best mood when I answered the phone.

"Hey." My voice wasn't exactly cheerful.

"Hey Sunshine, how was board game night? Did you manage to beat Miles yet?"

Dylan's warm, husky voice made me smile. I sighed. "No, our game night turned into something completely different."

I went on to tell him about Ethan begging me to sing with the band for one song to make the Manager at Vegabond happy. How my shit head friends talked me into it. Dylan was laughing by the end. I rolled my eyes.

"Not funny, it's going to be a disaster," I grumbled, covering my eyes with one hand.

His laughing finally slowed down.

"Oh... oh, Lexie, if Ethan says you'll do great, then you'll probably do great," Dylan reassured me. "That guy knows his shit. I can barely understand him when he talks about music."

I snorted. "And Rory wants to come. Did I mention that?" I countered.

Dylan snorted. "Of course he does, he loves you."

I growled.

"When is this supposed to happen?"

"Saturday night," I grumbled.

"This Saturday?" His voice was surprised.

"Yeah. This Saturday."

"Shit." His voice was full of doubt.

"Yes, join me in the panic, won't you?" My voice was thick with sarcasm.

Dylan chuckled. "Sunshine, it's going to be okay. Ethan would never put you up to something that would embarrass you. Okay... not publicly anyway." Okay, he made a good point. "Besides, I'll be there, and if something happens, I'll kick his ass."

I snorted. "You'll get what's left of him after I get done," I warned him, smiling.

He snickered in my ear. "Lexie, it'll be great. You'll go have fun, then you'll decide if you're willing to keep doing it," he reminded me.

I grumbled, then changed the subject. "So, how did teaching the guys go?" Dylan groaned in my ear; it made me smile.

"Not great, a couple of them got everything down. Those two I can start immediately, the others... it's going to be a bitch."

"I'm sorry, honey, maybe you should stay on Saturday just to make sure-"

"No way, I'm going to watch you sing, Sunshine. So are the guys." He sounded like he was smiling again.

"The guys, too?" I grumbled.

"Yep."

I groaned, covering my eyes with one hand again. Dylan was laughing. I groaned wordlessly. He kept laughing. We talked for an hour that night. Mostly about stuff that didn't really matter. But I climbed into bed with a smile on my face.

I COULDN'T SLEEP. Something was nagging at the back of my mind. I grumbled as I rolled over, punching my pillow into shape. I felt like I was forgetting something. Like I left something unfinished, something big.

Giving up on sleep, I rolled onto my back and tried to figure it out. I ran over my day in my head. Carl, then the gym, breakfast, then Miles', I reached my center and then... My stomach dropped. Then the tub. What did I tell Miles? I tried to remember, but it was all a little too blurry. I covered my face with my hands. I had been rambling like an idiot, about everything. Did I tell him about the park? Oh, no. No, no, no. He didn't need to know that, no one needed to know that.

I took a deep, calming breath. This was Miles. If anyone could keep a secret, it was him. Besides, I didn't even know if I had said anything about it. It didn't help. I had to know what I said to him.

I looked at the clock: 2:13 am. Knowing Miles, since it was vacation, he might be awake and working on some programming. I grabbed my phone and hesitated. What the hell was I going to say? "Hey, did I tell you about the guy who tried to rape me?" I snorted at myself. No way was I going to ask that. I chewed on the corner of my lip as I figured out what I was going to say.

Eventually, I sent Miles a text message.

Alexis: Hey, you awake?

It wasn't long before Miles responded.

Miles: Yes. As usual, I'm laying here trying unsuccessfully to sleep.

I sighed. Miles always had a hard time getting to sleep, unless he was exhausted. He usually worked on a project until he was ready to pass out. I asked him about it once. He only said, "It's too quiet."

Alexis: When I was out of it today, did I say anything weird?

I waited, my stomach knotting.

Miles: What do you mean by weird?

I took a deep breath and let it out slowly. I was going to have to ask.

Alexis: Did I tell you anything that I hadn't before?

There was a minute of tense silence as I waited. Miles tended to write a message, read it again and then rewrite so he wouldn't offend me. It took a while.

Miles: Yes.

Shit. I bit my lip as I asked.

Alexis: What did I tell you?

It wasn't long for his reply.

Miles: You told me about Jacob and what he tried to do.

My face grew hot instantly. Why the fuck did I tell him that? I covered my eyes with one hand and tried not to panic. I never intended to tell anyone about that. Even my mother didn't know. My phone vibrated.

Miles: Lexie? Are you alright?

Biting the corner of my bottom lip, I answered him.

Alexis: Don't tell anyone, please?

Miles: Of course not. Are you alright?

I took a shaking breath before I replied.

Alexis: Yeah, I just didn't plan on telling anyone that.

Miles: You never told anyone?

My face had cooled off by the time I texted back.

Alexis: Just the cops.

Miles: Why didn't you? After something like that, anyone would need some help coping.

I thought about it. Then told him the truth.

Alexis: I didn't have anyone that would have cared.

There were a few heartbeats of quiet before my phone vibrated.

Miles: You do now.

My heart melted. Sweet Miles.

Miles: Do you have flash backs from it? Do you have a trigger we need to be aware of?

I smiled at my phone. Miles was always looking to help in some way.

Alexis: No flashbacks, no triggers. He didn't hit me or anything.

There were a couple of heartbeats of quiet as Miles texted back.

Miles: Did you press charges?

Alexis: No. I broke his jaw. He could have pressed charges on me too, but it's on record.

Miles: It's the least he deserved. It wasn't your fault, you know that, don't you?

I smiled at my phone.

Alexis: Yeah, I do.

Miles: Do you want to talk about it?

I paused and thought about it.

Alexis: Not really.

Miles: If you ever want to, I'll be here.

Alexis: Thank you, Miles.

Miles: You're welcome, Lexie.

CHAPTER 5

FRIDAY MORNING

I was still in bed when my phone rang in the morning. I groaned. It was my Friday, and I was on vacation! Sleeping in was a requirement! Besides, I didn't get much sleep between nightmares.

I answered the phone. "You're evil," I grumbled.

Asher's rich baritone chuckled in my ear. "Still in bed, huh?" he said way too cheerfully.

I rubbed the sleep from my eyes. "Yeah, and I want to stay here," I mumbled.

He snorted. "Yeah, not happening. Everyone else backed out of snack detail today. I need your help," he said, again, way too cheerfully for the morning.

I groaned. "Zeke?" I offered.

"Working."

"Isaac?" I tried again.

"Training."

"Ethan?"

"Band practice; he said to tell you he'd call when they are ready for you," he countered.

"Miles?"

"On a long phone call to Autumn; something's going on there." His voice told me he was smiling.

I couldn't help it, I whimpered. Asher had no mercy.

"I'll give you cookies," he offered.

I was suddenly awake and interested. "And breakfast?" I asked, trying to up the ante.

He chuckled. "And breakfast," he agreed.

I smiled. "Are we doing jammies?" I asked seriously. I did not want to get dressed.

"I'm already up for the day, but you can do jammies," Asher told me.

I thought about it. "Jammies it is. See ya in five," I said before hanging up.

I groaned as I got out of bed and put on my sneakers. I didn't even bother with socks. I did stop long enough to put on a bra. I grabbed my phone and keys and headed downstairs. Since it was Friday morning, I saw no one as I got my jacket and pulled it on. I was at Asher's door a few minutes later. I didn't bother to knock. I just barged in.

"Ash! Where you at?" I shouted before I even thought about it.

"Kitchen, making your breakfast!" he shouted back.

I smiled as I took off my jacket. I even toed off my shoes. I headed into the kitchen and found the usual pre-get-together snack chaos. Asher was wearing one of his blue long-sleeved shirts and tan cargo pants today. His hair was still wet from the shower. Didn't he ever sleep in? I went to get the mandolin out and set it up.

"So, what's for breakfast?" I asked as I washed my hands.

"It's that scramble you like: eggs, sausage, bacon, and cheese," Asher told me as he moved the eggs around.

"Oh, yum." I went back to the mandolin and started slicing the potatoes. "If the girls are coming tonight, why aren't they here making snacks too?" I asked, being careful of my fingers.

"They're guests," Asher said.

I grinned "And I'm family."

"Yeah, Mom had a big rule about guests not having to help clean up, cook, or anything," he said as he shut off the stove.

"What about the other guys?"

Asher smiled as he grabbed a plate and dumped my breakfast onto it. "They became family real quick," he admitted. I chuckled. Asher was still smiling as he handed me my plate and fork. I jumped up onto the kitchen island and started eating. I decided to ask something I had been wondering about.

"You don't really talk about her much," I probed a bit. I didn't want to ask if it would bother him. Asher never even paused as he mixed the seasoning for the chips.

"You never really asked, Ally. Except for that one time at that party." He sighed. "And I was too buzzed to be able to talk about it." He looked over his shoulder at me, his ocean eyes meeting mine. "Are you asking?"

I nodded, my mouth full.

Asher took a deep breath and went back to work. "She was amazing; she gave up her career to have us. She always called Dad out on his bullshit," he began. My heart ached as he spoke, I could hear how much he missed her in his voice. "Every summer she dealt with all of us here all the time. And she always had stuff for us to do. Water balloons, water guns, cooking, baking, even building that awful tree house out back every year. She always had us moving and learning new things." I watched his shoulders grew tense. "Our house was the most stable house out of all the guys, so everyone stayed here all the time. Especially Zeke."

I finished eating and put my plate down. I knew Zeke had a horrible home life before he moved in with his Aunt Sylvia, I just didn't know the details.

"She was pretty much everyone's mom. So, when she was diagnosed with cancer, we all took the hit." He stopped talking to take a deep breath. My stomach knotted. Okay, I shouldn't have asked. I was an asshole. Before I could stop him, he kept going. "We were all fifteen, and my dad was already checking out. So, we took care of her during her chemo. The guys, me, and Jessica." His voice had turned thick and shaky.

I didn't think. I was off the counter and across the room in a second. I wrapped my arms around his waist and hugged him from behind. He put down the knife and turned around. He wrapped his arms around my shoulders and squeezed.

"You don't have to-"

"It's good to talk about it; I haven't in a while." Asher took a deep breath before continuing. I just rested my cheek against his chest and listened. "So, there all of us were, taking care of her. And we knew she wasn't doing so well. The only thing she'd ever eat was Maria's soup, that's the twins' mom. The guys got me the recipe. I still know it backward and forwards."

Tears started falling down my face. I couldn't help it. When someone you cared about was hurting, you hurt too.

"I went in one morning with her breakfast and found her. She had passed away in her sleep. The funeral was a week later. And Dad disappeared after we turned sixteen. He shows up for a week, every three months or so." Asher's hand moved to the back of my neck. He brushed against my cheek. He went still. "Ally, are you crying?"

I sniffed and tried to use my most normal voice. "Me, cry? Never." It didn't work.

He snorted. "I'm tall enough to see your face, you liar," he said. His voice was still thick, so I knew he was holding back tears too.

"Nah, you put too many peppers in the eggs. This is just a reaction," I countered as I got control of myself.

He snorted. The tightness in my chest eased. "I didn't put any peppers in the eggs," he pointed out, his voice almost back to normal.

I barked a laugh. "Now who's the liar?" I shot back.

We both chuckled. He was still holding onto me, so I didn't let go.

"I didn't mean to ruin your morning," I said quietly.

"You asked about her, Ally, not how she died," he pointed out. One of his hands ran through my hair, playing with it. "I guess I just needed to talk to someone about it. Jessica refuses to."

I gave him another squeeze before letting go. I looked up at him. His eyes were full of shadows that had I put there.

"You can talk to me anytime, Ash," I told him honestly.

He gave me a half grin. "I will," he promised.

I took a deep breath and stepped further away. "Now that I've upset us both," I said as I clapped my hands together. "What else can I ruin?"

Asher burst out laughing as I picked up my plate. He was working again by the time I finished washing it. We were quiet until we were done.

We were in the living room talking about games to play with 11 people and were having trouble coming up with them. We finally resorted to looking up party games on our phones.

"Truth or dare," Asher said, still looking at his phone.

"You asking, or the game?" I asked. I looked up to see him smirk.

"The game."

"Oh, no, no, no. With our group? You'd have to increase your house insurance," I told him honestly. He chuckled.

My eyes went to the pictures on the wall. They had bothered me since the first time I came over. I knew I probably shouldn't, but I was going to ask.

"Ash, this is probably a bad question after this morning, but-" Asher looked up from his phone. "Where are the pictures of your mom?"

He blinked.

I rushed to explain. "I see your dad, your sister, and you. But never your mom."

Asher's jaw locked, then he swallowed hard. "Dad took them down and refused to let us put them back up," he said, his voice was hard.

My mouth dropped. That fucking dick head. "Ash, do you want them back up?"

"Yeah." His voice was quiet.

"Then put them back up," I told him. I didn't care if I was crossing a line here. If Ash wanted the photos up, then he should have them up. Even if I had to do it myself.

"It's Dad's house." He sounded like he was repeating his father.

I snorted. "Your Dad is here, what, a month out of the year?"

He nodded, his jaw unlocking.

"This isn't his house, Ash. Yeah, he pays for it and for everything else. But you're the one who pays the mortgage, you're the one who pays the bills. I've seen you do it." I met his warm eyes with mine. "This is your house. If you want the photos up, put them up." I shrugged looking at the pictures still up on the walls. "If he comes back, take them down. When he leaves, put them back up." I couldn't seem to shut up today. "Ash, you like making other people happy."

He swallowed hard.

"You do it in a thousand little ways. Cooking is the most obvious example I can think of right now." I licked my lips, sure he was going to be mad. "I just, want you to make sure you're happy too."

He was quiet for a while. I was starting to think I should apologize.

"I'll think about it," he said, his eyes unfocused.

I gave him a small smile and went back to looking for party games.

"I haven't seen any photos of your dad," he said.

I went still, my heart dropped as pain tore through me.

"No one's been in your bedroom. So, I'm assuming that's where they are."

It took everything I had to look up from my phone and give him a sad smile. "I don't have any," I said.

He blinked, his face became confused.

I explained through my tightening throat. "Mom refused to take any of our photos with us when we lost the house. She wouldn't even let me take a picture of him." I was still pissed about that, but it was what it was. "That fucking bitch." I sniffed, looking back down at my phone, fighting back tears. "They're probably in a landfill somewhere."

"I'm sorry, Ally," he said, his voice soft.

"Not your fault. It's hers." I shrugged. "It is what it is."

"Okay, maybe we should stop talking today. We keep making each other cry," Asher pointed out.

I laughed, looking back up at him, the tightness in my throat easing. "Yeah, maybe we should." I chuckled as I got to my feet. "We just can't seem to stop."

I went into the foyer and pulled my shoes on. I was pulling on my jacket when he walked into the foyer. I looked up at him and smiled. "I promise, tonight I will not make you cry."

He smiled. "I promise, tonight I will not make you cry," he repeated back to me.

I gave him a long hug and headed home.

The house was empty when I came in and sat on the couch. My stomach was knotted up from my conversations with Asher. I really didn't mean to upset him. I was still grousing to myself when my cell phone rang. It was Dylan.

"Hey."

"Hey Sunshine, you busy?" Dylan's husky voice rolled through my ear. It made me smile and instantly feel better.

"Nope, just got back from Asher's. Everyone else bailed on snack making, so I had to help." I took a deep breath. "What's going on?"

"I just wanted to nail down a time to pick you up tonight," he said. My stomach knotted. Pick me up? Here? With Rory? Shit.

"Um, if you do that, you'll have to meet my Uncle Rory," I pointed out hesitantly.

"Yeah, I figured." He didn't sound worried. He didn't get it.

"He's a cop and overprotective and always armed," I told him honestly.

He went quiet. Now he was getting it. He cleared his throat.

"I'm going to have to meet him sometime, might as well get it over with," he offered. He didn't sound so confident now.

I smiled. "Okay, how about six?"

"Six it is; just send me your address."

There was a bell sound.

"Shit, customers, gotta go." He hung up quickly.

I smiled and texted him my address. I had an actual, real date tonight. The butterflies went crazy. How was I going to tell Rory?

I GOT a text from Ethan telling me to be ready by one; he was going to pick me up. The bastard was on time for the first time in his life. I grumbled the whole way as Ethan drove me out to the house of their drummer. Apparently, their practice space was in the garage.

"Beautiful, you're going to do fine," Ethan assured me again.

"I'm going to crash and burn, and you know it," I grumbled back.

He burst out laughing. I flipped him off. He just laughed harder. Ethan drove into a weed lined alley, then parked behind an old beat up van. My stomach was in knots as we got out of the car and headed towards the sound of the occasional drum beat. Ethan took my hand and pulled me with him up to an open garage door. Ethan's two band mates looked up from what they were doing to watch us walk in.

"Guys, this is Lexie; she's going to save our asses," Ethan announced confidently.

I snorted and looked at him like he was crazy. "More likely crash and burn, destroying your band's chance at keeping the venue," I countered, my voice snippy.

Both guys chuckled. The guy sitting behind the drums smiled at me. "If we don't try, we'll lose the venue anyway, and it won't matter," drummer boy pointed out in a deep, smooth voice.

Well, when he put it like that, it didn't sound so bad. Drummer boy was kind of cute, in a big, burly way. He had brown hair, buzzed close to his scalp, nice gray eyes, and a nice grin. But what drew my attention was the horseshoe shaped ring through the septum of his nose and an eyebrow stud. It actually didn't take away from his face. Instead, it seemed to add to it. Drummer boy's eyes ran over me quickly before looking away. Then he stood up; he was a head and a half taller than me, and he had wide shoulders and a wide chest.

"I'm Ryan. It's nice to meet you, Lexie," he said, holding out his hand. I shook his hand, smiling up at him. "Ethan has told us almost nothing about you."

I snorted. "Nice to meet you too." I smiled. "And that is actually comforting."

Ryan chuckled with a killer grin on his face, as he sat back down behind the drums.

The bass player stepped up. He was a head taller than me with thick, curly light brown hair and hazel eyes. He was lean with wide shoulders.

"I'm Oliver." He smiled. He had a great smile and a fucking dimple. Dimples were so cute.

I shook his hand. "It's nice to meet you."

"We really appreciate this," Oliver said sweetly. "We really don't have the stomach for pop songs."

I chuckled. "Don't thank me yet. You haven't heard me sing," I grumbled.

Ethan walked back over with his acoustic guitar plugged into an amp as he blew a raspberry at me. "Knock it off, Beautiful, you'll be great." He strummed a few chords. I flipped him off. Ryan smiled, trying not to laugh.

"Did you warm up like I told you?" Ethan asked.

I rolled my eyes. "Yeah," I grumbled, frowning at him.

Ethan ignored the look on my face and went to the microphone on the stand. He crooked his finger at me. I walked over, regretting that I had even thought to agree to this.

"Okay, we practice like we would be on stage." Ethan pointed out the garage door to the alley. "That's the crowd. This is where you're going to stand." Ethan reached out and turned on the microphone. "On stage, we have one for vocals, so we're sharing. When we sing together, you take that side and I'll take this one." I nodded. He gave me an encouraging smile before looking at the guys. "Let's start with Broken."

The others agreed. I took a deep breath and focused on ignoring everything but Ethan. Ethan started playing, singing into the microphone. Everything else dropped away. Then I joined in with Ethan; I sang the way I knew, with Ethan's corrections from the night before. Soon Oliver and Ryan were playing. Then Ethan joined me again. At some point, Ethan switched to his electric guitar, and we continued to sing until the end. Then there was a heartbeat of silence as I cringed.

"Damn Lexie." Ryan's voice had me turning around. He had that grin back on his face, his warm gray eyes were on me. "That was perfect."

I rolled my eyes. "So, you're delusional too?" I asked dryly.

They all burst out laughing. I crossed my arms over my chest, feeling my oversized sweater slip down my shoulder. Ryan's eyes met mine.

"Do you know any other songs?" he asked, smiling.

I groaned. They were insane.

"She does I Will Not Bow pretty well. We should be able to get that one down fast," Ethan offered.

Wait. What?

"Whoa, I thought the deal was one song, Ethan," I pointed out.

Ethan shrugged. "One might not be enough; we might need a few to convince the manager." He winced.

I glared at him. "You shit head," I bit out.

"Sorry, Beautiful."

"You're dead," I stated simply.

Ethan nodded, cringing now. "But, will you do it?" he asked, his eyes begging.

I growled at him before leaning my head back so I could glare at the rafters.

"I can learn a song fast, so, what do you guys know?" I grumbled.

Ethan all but tackled me. I didn't hug him back. The shit head had lied to me.

"How many are we talking?"

I brought my head back down so I could see the guys. Oliver was beaming, Ethan was glowing, and Ryan had that grin on his face again.

We sat down over the next hour and went over what songs they knew, which ones I knew, what they could learn in the next two days. Thankfully, I already knew a good number of their songs. I did suggest some more girly songs that had a nice edge to them. They agreed it was probably a good idea.

We got back into position and practiced. And practiced. We ran through the list of songs that I was going to do Saturday night. Ethan only had to correct me twice. The others found that rather impressive. While we were taking a break, gravel crunched in the alley. I turned to watch Isaac and Miles walk into the garage. My stomach knotted. Miles looked apologetic. I glared at Ethan.

"You need to get used to singing in front of people, Beautiful," Ethan explained before taking a drink of water. "Isn't it better that it's them and not strangers?"

I flipped Ethan off.

"I'll buy you jewelry," Ethan offered.

I narrowed my eyes at him. "You still owe me jewelry, you ass," I shot back.

Ethan thought about that for a moment. "Oh shit, I do." He cringed.

I nodded as Ryan and Oliver snickered.

"Come on Lexie, it's not that bad. You're going to do great," Ryan offered sweetly.

I sighed, took another drink, then we got back to work while Miles and Isaac sat in old folding chairs in front of us. I missed my cue on Broken. We had to start over. I hit my cue but missed the next one. I cursed and glared at Ethan.

"Relax, Beautiful. It's Miles and Isaac, you know them," Ethan tried to sooth me.

I shot him a look.

"Let's try a different song for now." Ethan suggested.

I nodded. We tried I Will Not Bow. I looked at the floor of the garage and hit my cue. I looked up and missed my second. I cursed as everyone stopped again. Asher and Zeke walked up to join the other two. I shot daggers at Ethan. He cringed.

"Lexie," Ryan called to me.

I turned around to look at him. His eyes were understanding.

"I had the same problem playing in front of people. When you look at the crowd your mind goes blank, right?"

I nodded, hating that I was letting them down like this.

Ryan gave me a small smile. "When you start to sing, close your eyes. I played our first three gigs that way."

I raised an eyebrow at that. He saw my question.

"I practiced a lot with my eyes closed," he explained.

"All right, I'll give it a shot," I grumbled.

I closed my eyes and listened to the music. It let me concentrate on the music and my voice. I made it through the song. Then the next, and the next. As long as I kept my eyes closed, I could sing in front of people. Then we ran into a problem. On Broken, we needed to share the microphone.

"It's a duet," Oliver chimed in. We all looked at him. "Keep your eyes on each other. It might give the girls the drama they crave. You know, 'will they or won't they' shit."

I shrugged, willing to give it a shot. So, when we sang Broken, Ethan and I kept our eyes on each other. I was able to hit every cue, pitch, and note. By the end of the song, my voice was getting rough. Ethan called my practice over.

"We need you Saturday night; go home drink some tea; no shouting, even at Zeke," Ethan advised me as he pulled his guitar strap off his shoulder. "We'll have you on stage for a song, then hop off for a couple, then back on." Ethan looked at the others. "How does that sound?"

"With her songs, we could just go in a row," Ryan suggested as he and Oliver came to stand in a circle. "They line up well."

"But she doesn't have the stamina to flow from one to the next," Ethan pointed out.

Ryan thought about it then nodded.

"I still think you're all nuts," I felt the need to point out.

They chuckled.

"We're not as crazy as we seem," Ryan reassured me.

I snorted. I didn't buy that one bit. The guys agreed on the set list. I was to sing four songs tomorrow night. This was fucking nuts. I said bye to them and headed out to the others. Isaac swept me up in a big hug, taking my feet off the ground.

"Red, that was fucking awesome!" Isaac said, squeezing me.

I hugged him back and rolled my eyes. "We'll see about that," I rasped then swallowed hard as Isaac put me down.

"Ally, that really was great," Asher reassured me. I gave him a small smile. I couldn't help but feel that something bad was going to happen. I shrugged, not wanting to use my raspy voice.

"Lexie, if you'd like, I'll give you a ride home," Miles offered. "The others are probably going to practice for a bit more."

I nodded. He gave me a sweet smile. I waved to the others and got into Miles' car. On the way home, I expected him to want to talk to me about Jacob and that night in the park. When he didn't bring it up, I relaxed. Instead, he told me I really did sound amazing, better than some of the other woman singers that had performed at Vegabond in the past. I really wanted to believe him. When he dropped me off, I made sure to drink some tea, and I tried to be optimistic, but I still felt disaster coming.

CHAPTER 6

FRIDAY NIGHT

"*L*exie! Your date is here!"

Rory's shout made me jump. Thank God I was done with my makeup.

"One sec, I'm just grabbing my wallet!" I shouted back.

I tucked my wallet into my back pocket and my cell phone into my bra. I considered the mirror. The boot-cut blue jeans hugged my curves. The green long-sleeved Henley brought out my eyes, and the two buttons undone gave me enough cleavage for me to be happy and Rory not to have a fit. My hair was down and everywhere as usual. I had kept my makeup light since we were hitting Asher's later. I grabbed my keys and jacket, then headed downstairs.

My gut knotted. Oh yeah, Rory was going to meet Dylan. My chest grew tight as I stepped off the stairs.

Dylan looked just as cute as usual. He was wearing a black long-sleeve shirt, dark blue jeans, and his blue snow jacket. He didn't even bother with his hair. I liked that about him.

"I love that you don't get all girly when you go on a date," Dylan told me, smiling.

I smiled. I looked at Rory as I put on my jacket. My Uncle Rory was tall and still in shape even though he was in his forties. His copper hair was cut short to his head. His attractive face was frowning at Dylan, his brown eyes apprising.

"Rory, this is my boyfriend, Dylan," I introduced them, my voice slightly rough still.

Rory's eyes narrowed on Dylan. Before he could start in on the questions, I added, "Asher is the one who introduced us." Rory's face relaxed as he held his hand out to Dylan. Dylan shook it. It was all very manly.

"Nice to meet you, sir," Dylan said respectfully.

"You too. Now, where are you going?" Rory asked, his eyes going to me.

"We're going to have dinner, then hit game night with the guys. Be back at the usual time?" I asked hopefully.

"Will Zeke be there?" Rory asked, his voice deadpan.

I smiled. "Of course."

Rory nodded. "Okay, see you then."

Rory turned and headed into the kitchen, dismissing us. I rolled my eyes as we headed for the door. When we were outside, Dylan let out a long breath.

"When you said he was a cop, I expected the third degree," he admitted, taking my hand as we headed for his truck.

I grinned. "He already ran your name through the system, twice, and the fact that Asher introduced us didn't hurt any either. Plus, Zeke will be there," I explained.

He chuckled.

I let go of his hand and went to the passenger side of the old truck while he went to the driver's side.

"All right, Sunshine, where are we going?"

"The best burger joint in town," I said, smiling.

He chuckled as he pulled onto the road. "And how's that gonna go with the whole food deal with Zeke?"

"He'll thank me. He's a big burger guy," I promised.

I gave him directions to the Frosty Freeze that Zeke swore had the best burgers in town. It was a small cinder block building with a few tables inside and several picnic tables outside. Inside was full.

"Ooh, looks like we're outside tonight."

We hopped out and got in line. Dylan's arm went around my waist as he stepped up behind me to read the menu. I smiled to myself. It was strange to only be dating him three days and not feel uncomfortable about him touching me so much. That had never happened before in my entire dating history. Especially not after that night in the park.

When it was our turn to order, we stepped up. We both ended up with double bacon cheeseburgers and fries. I even ordered Zeke's favorite. I paid since Dylan drove, and we took our number, then moved with the other people waiting.

"Why'd you order a second burger?" Dylan asked, wrapping his arm around me again; this time I leaned back against his chest. "I know you can't eat that much."

"It's Zeke's 'stop bitching' gift," I told him, looking up at him. He smiled down at me. "If I don't bring him one he won't shut up all night."

He chuckled.

"So, how was your day?" I asked.

He sighed. "Boring. And longer than it should have been." He leaned down and whispered in my ear, "I was kind of excited to see you."

I smiled as his husky voice ran down my spine. I looked up at him over my shoulder.

"How was yours?" he asked quietly.

"Had an emotional talk with Asher this morning, *so* didn't mean to. Had band practice with Ethan, and I think they're insane," I began. He chuckled. "Otherwise, the same. Excited to see you." Then I realized something. "Oh God, we're that couple."

He burst out laughing, his arms tightening around me. "No, that couple is sickening. They do that baby talk and shit," he said. "We just curse a lot." I laughed. "So, how was band practice?" he asked.

I groaned. "It was going great until the guys showed up to watch," I said before I looked up at him, wincing. "I messed up a bit after that."

He gave my waist a squeeze. "Turns out I need to sing with my eyes closed, or staring at Ethan," I grumbled.

"It probably takes practice, Sunshine; you'll get the hang of it," he assured me before kissing the top of my head.

"If their spot in the band rotation weren't in trouble, I wouldn't even think of doing this." I muttered.

"You have a big heart," he whispered down to me as he took a deep breath, his nose in my hair.

"I'm starting to believe you," I grumbled. He sniggered.

Our number was up, and Dylan let go of me to get it. We went to the empty picnic tables and sat down at one. As we ate, we talked about everything; it was our usual. I asked about his photography. He asked about my art projects. He told me about one of his friends trying to snowboard off the roof of his house; it did not go well for him. I told him about Zeke chasing Isaac through Miles' house after a nasty prank involving paint that left Zeke covered.

We had finished with our burgers, and I was still working on my fries, when he became quiet for the first time tonight. I looked up at him; he was watching me with a thoughtful look on his face.

"What?" I asked before eating another fry.

He seemed to decide something.

He scooted closer, till his thigh was touching mine. "Lexie, why are you living with Rory?" he asked, his voice quiet.

My gut knotted, and my body grew tense. It was Dylan, and I was starting to feel like I could talk to him about anything. I took a breath.

"Last October, my mother came home high and drunk," I began as I looked down at the asphalt of the parking lot. "She yanked me out of bed and beat the shit out of me."

He went still next to me. This wasn't as hard as I thought it would be. I looked up at his face to see him frowning, his eyes cold. He did not like this story. "Cops came. I went to the hospital. Rory agreed to custody, and I was up here two days later. The next day I was back in school."

"Wait, so you were all bruised up when we met?" he asked, confused. I nodded.

"My entire back was black, blue, and purple. Even had some red thrown it," I said matter-of-factly.

He closed his eyes, his jaw clenching. "So, when Markus-"

"Oh yeah, that hurt like a bitch," I admitted emphatically before eating another fry.

"Did the guys know?" he asked quietly.

"They found out later that week." I shrugged and looked at him again. His eyes were running over my face.

"Are you okay?" he asked, his voice was that low husky one that I was starting to love.

I nodded, realizing that I wasn't lying. "I wasn't for a while. But I got some perspective recently, and now I know it wasn't my fault. It was all on her." I smiled, then met his eyes. "So, yeah. I'm okay. Well, except for my trigger. Which isn't much of a problem."

His arm wrapped around my shoulders, bringing me against him. He kissed the top of my head. A feeling of being loved washed over me. Whoa, it was way too soon for that. Damn it.

"So, what happened to your mother?" he whispered against my hair.

I took a deep breath and let it out slowly. "She's in rehab right now, but once she gets out, the DA's office will be pressing charges. The trial will probably be this summer or next fall." I hadn't even told the guys that yet. Why did I feel this way about Dylan already? You need to slow down, Lexie. You can't feel this way so soon.

Dylan exhaled hard. "Fuck, Sunshine, why doesn't this feel like a first date?" he asked, his voice rough. Apparently, we'd been thinking along the same lines.

"We've only been together for three days, and we're talking about shit that I wouldn't talk about until at least the third week," he grumbled.

I snorted. I knew exactly how he felt.

Then he added, "I keep touching you without even thinking about it, and I don't usually get that comfortable with someone for at least a month."

"You too, huh?" I asked as I grinned up at him. He looked just as

144

bewildered as I felt. "Ethan said something yesterday that made some sense to me." I offered.

"Please, any insight, because this is-"

"Fucking weird, right?" I offered.

He nodded emphatically.

I explained, "Ethan said we were already basically dating for the last two months, only now it's official."

He thought about that. He blinked then looked down at me, his eyes warm. "That makes sense," he said simply. He took a deep breath and looked at me. "Sunshine, I'm an affectionate guy, and I don't always think about it. At least not with someone I care about. All my old girlfriends got used to it slowly over time, but you're getting all of it at once."

"Dylan." I smiled gently at him. "I'm kind of in the same boat here. I've realized I'm a cuddler and I'm usually not that comfortable with a new person for at least a month. But with you I already am."

"Fucking weird, right?" he asked emphatically. I nodded, my smile getting bigger as he continued. "Just know that if I touch you and you don't want me to. Or don't like it or-"

"I'll tell you really quick," I said immediately. "I didn't hesitate yesterday. Well, that wasn't really not liking it, it was more 'too soon, too soon.'"

He smiled down at me. "Thank you, Sunshine." He sighed and looked around the parking lot. "So, what did we just decide?" He looked back down at me, his brow furrowed.

I snickered. "We just said fuck it. We're cuddlers. So, we're going with it," I summed up.

He nodded. "That's what I thought, just checking."

I burst out laughing, and he wasn't too far behind. We were so weird.

IT WASN'T LONG before the snow started to fall, and we walked to Dylan's truck. We hopped in and headed over to Asher's. I saw the girls' cars as we parked down the street. I grumbled.

"What?" he asked, shutting off the truck.

I gestured at Trisha's car. "Trisha's a bitch. She told me things are going to change in the group, specifically my relationship with Asher." I shook my head. I didn't want to believe it could happen. But that stupid little part of me was still annoying as hell.

"Tell Asher."

I shook my head again. "He likes her, and it's not going to work anyway." At least, I hoped it wasn't. "So what if she doesn't like me. I won't cry over that," I said as I unhooked my seatbelt.

"Sunshine." Dylan's voice was patient as I looked over at him. "It doesn't matter if she likes you. It only matters if she's nice to you. If she can't do that, then Asher will dump her ass faster than you can blink."

"He likes her, and I don't want to fuck that up," I told him honestly. He had an odd look on his face. "What?"

He smiled at me then crooked his finger at me. "Come here. I need to tell you something."

I highly doubted that, but I slid on the bench seat a bit closer. His fingers held my chin, his thumb just below my bottom lip. The butter-flies started flapping. He leaned closer and brought his lips to mine. My heart slammed in my chest as I brushed my lips against his. It was a sweet, soft kiss that made my stomach flip. When he pulled back, he didn't go far. His eyes ran over my face as he grinned at me.

"You have a big heart, Sunshine." His voice was that husky, low one that ran down my spine. Shit. I felt my face turning pink. "And I love making you blush like that."

"You don't know how you're making me blush like that," I pointed out.

"I think I'm narrowing it down." He smirked at me.

"Shit," I said with feeling.

Dylan laughed at me as he let go of my chin. We got out of the truck. I made sure to grab Zeke's 'stop bitching' gift. I almost slipped on the snow as I tried to get to the shoveled walk but Dylan saved me with his hand on my arm.

"Thanks, I'm always slipping in the snow."

He just shook his head and smiled as I reached the sidewalk. Dylan took my hand as we headed down the street towards Asher's. He was telling me a joke when I felt a chill down the back of my neck. My heart dropped as my lungs grew tight. I felt my wrist, and realized I'd forgotten my beads at home. Fuck. I tried to look around without making Dylan suspicious. I spotted him. It was fucking Herbert. Shit. He was striding towards me, looking pissed off. We reached Asher's house. I had to make a decision.

"Oh," I pulled out my cell phone and pretended I had a call. "It's Rory." I looked at Dylan. "Go on in; I'll just be a minute." He looked around the block; I did too, except I saw Herbert and he didn't.

"I'll wait for you," Dylan offered. My heart melted and then clenched as Herbert got closer. I handed him Zeke's food.

"No, hon, it's cold; go on in. It'll probably only be a second."

He nodded reluctantly and headed up the stairs. I acted like I answered the phone.

"Hey, Rory."

I watched Dylan walk into the house and turned around. Herbert was only a few feet from me. I kept my phone to my ear. "Look, Herbert, I've found a way to move you on; I just need more time to set it up," I told him quickly.

His eyes grew bright. I felt another chill go down my neck. Are you fucking kidding me? I looked down the street to see Carl Mason striding towards us. What, were they forming gangs now? My body jerked as he came too close. I backed up and held my hand up. "Carl, I just told him, now I'm telling you. I found a way to get you to move on, but it's going to take some time to set up."

I grunted in pain as I felt both their deaths at once. My head was throbbing now, with both of them standing there. I stepped back again. They stepped forward. Fuck! "I can help, I just need to link to the Veil now."

That seemed to register. I stepped back again. This was fucking insane! My head throbbed, and my face ached. I had tissues out before blood hit my lip. I was thankful my barriers held against both of them, or I'd be super sick. As it was, my stomach was rolling.

"You will be the first ones to cross, just give me time," I promised them.

They both backed off. My stomach gave another hard roll. Oh shit. I turned and ran in the house. I didn't bother closing the door before I was running up the stairs and into the open bathroom door. I heard my name being called, but I didn't care. I dropped to my knees in front of the toilet, ready to puke. Feet sounded on the staircase. I focused on breathing through the pain and nausea. My head was throbbing in time to my pulse, my nose still bleeding and stomach still rolling, but I didn't throw up, not yet at least.

"Lexie?" Dylan's worried voice rolled over my ears.

Oh God, don't let me puke in front of my boyfriend. Warm hands pulled my hair away from my face as I kept breathing.

"I'm fine. I just..." I clamped my mouth shut as another roll went through my stomach. I felt blood soaking through the tissues, I grabbed more from my pocket and added them to the wad. The hands in my hair disappeared. Water was running somewhere in the room. There were more footsteps on the staircase. My hair moved again, and a wet washcloth was placed on my neck. Oh, that felt good. It helped. "A minute, just..." I kept breathing; this nausea wasn't going away.

"One or two?" Asher asked from the doorway.

"Two, not puking yet." I groaned, my head still throbbing.

Asher opened the medicine cabinet.

I was fucking miserable. I focused on breathing.

"What does she need?" Dylan's voice was growing hard.

I wanted to touch him to tell him it was okay, but another wave of nausea rolled over me.

"This is an Ally kit; well, everyone else calls it a Lexie kit." Asher's voice was next to us. I held out my hand, waiting. I listened to the wrapper then felt the tablet in my hand, popped it in my mouth, and started chewing. It tasted like cherries. I held my hand out again.

"Really?" Asher asked, his voice surprised.

I nodded, still not opening my eyes. A wrapper tore, I felt the tablet and popped it into my mouth. The taste of cherries increased.

My stomach was starting to stop cramping. While I waited for it to stop, I listened to Asher explain the kit.

"We have these everywhere: in our cars, in our book bags, and in every bathroom in everyone's house."

I took a deep breath as my head pain finally started to ease. My stomach had stopped cramping, so I sat on my butt and rested my back against the tub.

"What I gave her are nausea tablets. Today she needed two, she usually only needs one. Everything else in here is from a couple new drug trials, so she can't tell you the names. Confidentiality was part of the contract to get her into those trials. However, the white crystalline medicine stuff is for if she drops to the ground. So is this not so clear, watery liquid. We have two in case someone breaks one." Asher explained.

I took a deep breath and was finally not so miserable.

"If she drops like a rock, and blood is pouring from her nose, that's a three. You open a vial and pour it into her mouth. She'll go limp, and she'll be out. But the part where damage can happen will be over. Then you call Rory or one of us," Asher explained matter-of-factly.

I never knew that Asher could lie so well. My head was hurting less, so I lifted my head and opened my eyes a bit. The light hurt my eyes, but I knew it would get better.

"If she's running somewhere, it's usually a two. A one is-"

"A nosebleed," Dylan said.

"Right, if it's a two, she's usually sick before anyone gets in here. The nausea tablets are for after her stomach is empty and still cramping. Today, she's nauseous but not puking. And for a two, that's damn good."

I gave him a thumbs up and opened my eyes again. The light hurt less. Asher snorted. "When she moves off her knees by the toilet, she's always done puking. She's dealing with head pain now, and light hurts her eyes. And when she starts opening her eyes like that..." I blinked owlishly at the tiled floor while ignoring them. "That means the pain is almost gone and she's just got the nosebleed left."

I watched out of the corner of my eye as Asher eyed Dylan, who was watching me.

"You guys have it down to a system. How often does this happen?" Dylan's voice was demanding.

Asher ignored it. "Ones happen every other day I think, Ally?" I held up my thumb.

"Yeah, every other day. They aren't a big deal and usually go away in ten minutes or less. Two's have been more often than normal lately, but it's tapering off, I think. But it has been three days since her last one."

"What about threes?" Dylan's hand was running up and down my back. It felt really comforting right now.

"We've only seen one." Asher began, his voice serious. "And that's the only reason we even know about any of it. It happened at school, and she managed to tell us to call Rory. Rory had us get her home and told us what to do to take care of her. Never call an ambulance. Her disorder is so rare that most doctors can't identify it in an emergency room. Basically, if she goes to the hospital, she will die." Asher closed the kit and moved to the medicine cabinet. "She was talking about giving you a kit yesterday. And I think it's a good idea."

I pulled the tissue from my nose and only felt a trickle. I tossed the tissue in the toilet and grabbed more toilet paper. I held the smaller wad to my nose.

The light wasn't killing me anymore, so I looked over and watched Asher hold out a new kit to Dylan. "I mean if you're gonna stick around?"

I looked back at the floor and tried to remember to breathe. Asher just flat out asked if this was going to scare Dylan off. Wow.

Dylan scoffed and took the kit. "She can't get rid of me that easily, Asher," Dylan countered.

I fought the urge to smile. My face still fucking hurt. I heard Asher snort as he headed out the bathroom door. I checked my nose; it had finally stopped bleeding.

"I wouldn't blame you, you know," I muttered, tossing the tissue in the toilet. I got to my feet, not looking at him, and quickly used the washcloth on my neck to wash my nose, mouth, and chin with soap. I didn't see any blood there, but I washed anyway. I rinsed quickly and used a hand towel to dry.

"If you bailed, I mean." I turned around and looked up at him. He had been standing behind me as I washed. His eyes ran over my face.

"I'm not going anywhere, Sunshine," he said simply. His husky voice was serious. "Now, how soon can I kiss you after one of these?"

I looked at him like he was crazy. "I just had blood on my face," I pointed out.

He shook his head. "No, actually, you didn't. You're really quick with those tissues," he said, smiling. He leaned down and gave me a soft, quick kiss that made my insides melt. I looked at him, trying to wrap my head around it. I just had a bloody nose, yeah, I didn't get blood on my face, but he just kissed me anyway.

"You're nuts," I said, smiling.

Dylan smirked at me. "Maybe a little," he admitted. He took my hand and led me down the stairs.

"Why did my boyfriend have to go up and take care of her?" Trisha's voice carried from the family room. Dylan stopped walking, and so did I.

"She's probably just some drama queen with a stomach ache," Faith added. My jaw dropped. Dylan went still in front of me. That probably wasn't good. I reached out and touched his shoulder. He looked at me, his mouth in a tight line. I gave him a small smile and slipped by him on the staircase. He let go of my hand so I could pass him.

"Oh, she's probably bulimic. You see how thin she is?" Cece joined in. Wow, the shy one was a bitch too. I took a deep breath and made noise on the stairs as I went down. Dylan was right behind me. I stopped to put down my jacket and tuck my cell into my back pocket. I walked into the family room and saw three of the girls. I smiled at them.

"Hey, girls." I looked over at Trisha. "Trisha, sorry for borrowing Asher. I was having a seizure, and he knew where my kit was." Trisha's eyes flashed at me. I continued to explain. "But that shouldn't happen anymore. Asher explained my kit to Dylan, so next time he can take care of me." I gave them a smile. They all smiled back.

"Oh good, your boyfriend should know how to take care of you. Especially if you have health problems. I mean, you can't keep asking the other guys to take care of you, right?" Trisha said too sweetly.

I felt it like a hit to the gut. Wow, I didn't expect that to hurt. Dylan's hand went to my lower back. I looked up at him over my shoulder. His face was pleasant, but his eyes were cold.

"Let's get you some tea, babe," he offered sweetly. I gave him a small smile and went with him. He nudged me ahead of him towards the kitchen.

"Ignore them," I whispered.

"I don't see how Asher doesn't hear them," he whispered back.

"He's not paying attention," I offered. "If they get to where I can't deal with it, then I'll just avoid them or something."

He grunted quietly.

I opened the door and stepped into the kitchen. Everyone else was standing around with mugs. I saw Zeke finishing off his burger. Riley was laughing at the look of joy on his face. I had to admit, I started laughing too. Zeke spotted me and smiled with his full mouth closed.

"What are you guys doing in here?" I asked.

"Cece's a vegetarian and Zeke wanted to eat his burger," Isaac said, like that should make sense.

"Did he try to make her eat his burger?" I asked, not quite believing this. Isaac shook his head.

"Then why did he have to go in the kitchen? It's her issue; she should have gone in the kitchen," I pointed out.

"I agree with Lexie on that one," Riley said. I winked at her.

Zeke finally finished eating. "Not that I'm complaining, but why the burger?" Zeke asked, wiping his mouth with a napkin.

I smiled. "Because I had one for dinner," I said. He narrowed his eyes at me. "And you just ate it, so you can't bitch at me all night!" I smiled cutely.

Everyone laughed.

"Okay, you got me this time," Zeke admitted begrudgingly.

Miles poured a couple of mugs and handed them to us. Ooh, cocoa. I was happy.

Zeke clapped his hands. "Okay, let's play."

We all filed out into the family room. The others already had claimed the couches, so it looked like we were on the floor. Asher paused, then went back out into the foyer and opened the closet under the stairs. He pulled out a few bean bag chairs. He tossed one to Dylan.

"I figure you two can share," Asher smirked at us before he threw another to Miles.

Isaac volunteered for him and Cece to be one of the couples on the floor. Cece looked surprised.

Dylan found a good spot near the couch corner; he put the bean bag at an angle then sat down. He elbowed it and shifted till he got it in the position he wanted. I thought it was funny. Then he leaned back in the bag, his legs open, and crooked his finger at me. I smiled at him. "Come here, Sunshine."

I went over and sat in front of him, but before I could slide back, Dylan snagged me around the waist and pulled me between his legs. He bent his knees and tugged me to lay back on him. I laid back against his chest; he wrapped one arm around me, his palm warm on my stomach. His other hand took mine, his fingers playing with mine. His body acted like a chair for me, a very comfy, warm, sexy chair. I set my mug to the side, then laid my head back against his chest.

"You're lucky that slide didn't give me splinters on my ass," I told him plainly. He laughed in my ear.

"Swear jar," Isaac called out. I sat up and realized I couldn't grab my wallet without groping Dylan. Before I could slide forward, fingers were in my back pocket, and then my wallet was in Dylan's hand, over my shoulder. I grinned. It was like he had read my mind. I opened my wallet and took out two twenties. I put my wallet to the side. I laid back down onto Dylan and held the money up to Ethan. Ethan then put it in the jar for me.

"There, that's forty for both Dylan and me," I announced. The guys chuckled as Dylan got me back in the same position.

"That's my girl," he whispered into my ear before he kissed my temple. I smiled.

"Okay, that's weird," Asher announced. I looked up at him. He was sitting in a wide armchair with Trisha in his lap. "Someone's hugging Ally and kissing on her." Asher shook his head as if to get rid of the image.

"Yeah, that's what it has been like every night with you guys. It's weird seeing your friends all kissy," I countered, not moving an inch. "Suck it up."

The guys chuckled. Dylan gave me a squeeze, and we all began arguing over the first video game to play. Trisha, Faith, and Cece weren't helping. They kept saying they wanted to watch a romantic movie. I groaned.

Cece's eyes flashed at me. "You have a boyfriend, and you still don't want to watch a love story?" Cece's voice had an edge of snide to it.

Stay calm, Lexie.

I looked at her and said with a straight face, "I will not eat them in a house, I will not eat them with a mouse, I will not eat them in a box, I will not eat them with a fox. I will not eat them here or there, I will not eat them anywhere."

The guys burst out laughing. They laughed so hard it took them awhile to calm down. Isaac was wiping tears from his eyes.

"Ah, ah, ah man, Red just quoted Dr. Seuss!" Isaac's face was bright red.

I had to sit up because Dylan was shaking me so much.

"In an argument," Ethan added.

"And totally won," Asher chimed in.

Dylan had stopped laughing enough for me to lay back against his chest again. He wrapped his arms around me and squeezed me tight.

"I'm so keeping you," Dylan whispered into my ear.

I smiled and squeezed his arm back. "Sounds good to me," I whispered back.

When everyone calmed down again, I reminded them. "This was supposed to be game night, guys."

"We can play truth or dare," Trisha offered.

"Nothing but trouble comes from that game, especially with guys and girls," I warned them.

"What if we set rules?" Miles offered.

I raised my hand. "I dare you all *not* to play this game," I said seriously. Dylan chuckled in my ear. It made me smile.

Trisha's eyes narrowed on me. "What? Are you scared, Lexie?" Trisha asked, smirking.

I looked her in the eye and gave her my blank, 'don't fuck with me' face. "You really want to play this game?" I asked, making my voice warm but with an edge of ice to it. I kept eye contact with her, refusing to blink first.

"Do it, Sunshine," Dylan whispered in my ear.

My shit eating grin moved across my face. Trisha must have realized I wasn't fucking around because she flinched.

"She does have a point, though," Trisha said, failing at nonchalance. "Nothing good ever comes from it."

Asher looked from me to Trisha, trying to figure out what just happened. I winked at him. I figured I should offer an olive branch.

"Okay, how about one girly movie. But, it has to have a happy ending. No tragic crap," I suggested to the girls.

They all looked at each other, then nodded. Riley, however, was eyeing Trisha like she'd never seen her before. The girls put a movie on, and I laid my head back on Dylan's chest.

"Too big a heart, Sunshine," Dylan whispered to me.

I smiled. "Yeah, but I want my friends happy too," I whispered back. Dylan kissed my hair and snuggled back against me. I was playing with Dylan's fingers through most of the movie; we even played thumb war. We ended up whispering back and forth through most of the film. We were both bored, but we entertained ourselves well enough. When the movie was over, I sighed in relief.

"Can we please play a game?" I begged pitifully. There were a couple of chuckles.

"I have a bunch of board games in the closet upstairs," Asher announced. He got up and walked across the room. He stopped in front of me. "Come on, Ally, you can help carry."

I looked up at him. His face was serious. Why would he need help carrying a few boxes? I eyed him then held my arms up towards him.

"Up," I grumbled.

He looked at me like I was nuts. "I am not picking you up from the floor," Asher said, almost laughing.

I snickered. "No, I meant pull me up, you shit," I told him, smiling.

"Swear jar!" Isaac shouted. Asher grabbed my hands and pulled me to my feet quickly.

"She's still got 18 left," Dylan pointed out.

I followed Asher out of the family room and up the stairs. When we reached the landing, he turned to me.

"What was with that stare down between you and Trisha?" he asked, his voice quiet.

I knew it. He didn't need help; he wanted to grill me.

"Girl drama," I hedged. "Don't worry about it, we'll work it out eventually." He ran his eyes over my face, trying to see if I was lying. I just gave him my mischievous grin. He snorted and shook his head.

"That fucking smile," he mumbled.

"Swear jar," I shot back. He chuckled as we went the hall closet. He opened the door and started looking through the board games. My eyes were on the folded American flag wrapped in plastic and tucked into a clear spot on the shelf.

"Asher? What's with the flag?" I asked softly. He went still.

"That's Mom's," he said as he went back to looking through games. "She was an Army Drill Sergeant before she quit to have us."

"They have cases for those now, you know?" I looked down at him, feeling like I was crossing a line somewhere. He was pulling out a couple of games boxes.

"Yeah, Dad always said he'd get one specially made. But he never did," Asher said, straightening back up. He handed me a couple of board games. I caught his gaze.

"Your dad is a dick," I said honestly.

He smirked at me. "Pretty much. Come on. Let's see if we can have a game night."

We carried the games downstairs. Trisha glared at me as we came in. I put the games on the coffee table. Everyone shifted around. Dylan brought the bean bag closer, sat on it, and then I sat between his legs in front of him again. We debated on what game to play. It took a while, but we agreed on Scrabble with teams. Miles didn't have a team, which worked because he would probably win anyway.

We were halfway through the game, and I had just finished putting down our word, when my cell phone vibrated. Dylan caught his breath then let it out slowly behind me. He leaned forward, his lips going to my ear.

"Sunshine, you really need to move your phone," he whispered.

My stomach did that flip. I caught his meaning quickly. I leaned forward, pulling away from him a bit. His fingers went to my back pocket and pulled my phone out. I sat back to where I started. I turned a bit at the waist to look back at him. His eyes were warm on my face as I mouthed sorry. He winked at me as he handed me my phone. I turned back around and tried not to brush up against him for a bit.

I checked my phone. It wasn't a text. It was an email, from an email address I'd never seen. I tossed it into the trash and tucked my phone into my bra.

I went back to the game we were losing. It didn't help that Dylan's hand was on my hip. My shirt had come up a bit when I reached for a letter; now his thumb was making circles on my skin, just above my jeans. It really didn't help my concentration. In the end, Miles won-- not a big surprise. We were cleaning up the game when I remembered tomorrow was Asher's football game.

"Hey, we need to figure out rides and shit for tomorrow," I reminded everyone.

"Swear jar," Ethan shot out.

"I still have four." I stuck my tongue out at him. Ethan made a face back.

"And we need to figure out what we're doing after," Faith pointed out.

Everyone started offering suggestions.

"Well, we're playing at Vegabond tomorrow night," Ethan reminded everyone. He grinned over at me. "Lexie's helping out, so that's where we'll be." I wrinkled my nose at him. Faith looked at me then back to Ethan, her face confused.

"What do you mean she's helping you out?" Faith's voice was neutral with an edge to it.

Ethan looked over at her and grinned. "Remember, the manager wants us to have more range?"

Faith nodded, still frowning.

"Lexie's singing with us tomorrow night to help us keep our spot."

Faith's eyebrows went up; her mouth opened a bit. "Oh," Faith said. She looked at me, her eyes almost glaring. "I didn't know you could sing, Lexie."

"Everyone can sing," I grumbled. "Not everyone can sing well." The guys chuckled.

"Red sounded great today. You never even went off key," Isaac offered sweetly.

"And that's all by ear," Ethan pointed out. "She doesn't even know how to read music." Faith's eyes snapped to me as Ethan continued, "She seriously must have perfect hearing."

"I do, remember?" I reminded him of when Rory insisted that I see every type of doctor possible the first month I was here. He had been worried because I hadn't seen a doctor in years.

"No wonder you're an audiophile," Ethan smirked at me. I flipped him off.

"Wait, what did you call her?" Dylan leaned forward. His arm around me tensed.

I answered quickly, "Audiophile, I love music." I shrugged; it was no big deal. His arm relaxed around my waist.

"Yeah, and particular kinds of voices," Ethan pointed out. He looked at Dylan, smiling. "She's so freaking picky about sound that it's weird sometimes." I knew he was referring to the meditation guide he'd downloaded for me.

"Hey, that guide guy had an accent that I couldn't place, and his voice was on the high side. It was like a knife to my ear," I defended myself adamantly. "*Sorry* if I have sensitive ears."

The guys laughed.

"Yeah, I'll give you that. That's why I didn't complain when I re-recorded it for you," Ethan grumbled.

Faith's eyes shot to me. "You re-recorded what for her?" Faith asked.

Ethan was busy cleaning up tiles. "Just a meditation guide she needed; she couldn't stand the guy's voice," Ethan told her absently. I was putting more tiles in the bag when I caught the stink eye.

"But you like Ethan's voice?" Faith asked pointedly.

I paused and realized how that might have sounded to a girlfriend. "Ethan's got an amazing voice." Then I acted like something just occurred to me. "But I guess any of the guys' voices would have worked. Well, except Zeke's."

"Thanks, Lexie." Zeke smirked at me. I shot him a look.

"In fact, Miles voice would probably have been the better one to use." I pointed at Miles. He nodded; he saw what I was doing and went with it. "He has a very calm, soothing voice when he wants to."

Ethan swallowed hard. He must have just realized how it sounded. "I thought of that. He was busy playing games with Autumn that day." Ethan was lying through his teeth, and the guys all knew it. But it was to keep the peace, so everyone went with it.

"Is everyone coming to Vegabond?" I changed the subject. "Because you really don't have to." The girls seemed to think about it, then they started smiling.

"That sounds fun," Trisha admitted. The other girls nodded.

"Now, let's figure out rides to Northridge." I reminded them.

In the end, I was taking Faith, Ethan, and Miles to Northridge, and Zeke was going to take Riley, Isaac, Cece, and Trisha. Asher was driving himself up to Northridge early in the morning. And Dylan was going to meet us there. It was less of a drive for him.

We called it a night early since Asher did have a playoff game in the morning. Dylan and I cleaned up with the guys before heading out. It was snowing lightly when Dylan and I walked to his truck, holding hands.

"So, did you have fun tonight?" I asked, wondering.

He smiled down at me. "I was with you, and you always make me laugh," he said. "So, yeah, I had fun. But those guys were watching me like a hawk all night."

"Really?" I hadn't noticed the guys watching us. Then again, I was kind of blissfully happy with him just being here.

"Yeah, during the movie, anytime I moved, at least one of them would look over," he said.

I raised an eyebrow. "Is that why you started tapping your knee, then my shoulder…"

He gave me a mischievous smile as he began snickering. "Yeah, I was messing with them," he admitted.

I chuckled. "Give them some time, and they'll back off," I said, hoping I wasn't lying. "If they don't. I'll have a chat with them."

"What about you? Did you have fun?" he asked.

I looked up at him thoughtfully. "I had fun with you. I had fun with Riley, and I had fun with the guys." I had to be honest.

"It's getting to the point where you can't hang out with them anymore, isn't it?" he asked, his voice sympathetic.

I sighed. I hated to admit it, but he was right. "Yeah, I think so. The three of them just jump on anything that shows I know the guys." I shook my head, I didn't understand it.

"Well, the re-recording thing is a little weird, but once you explained why, it didn't seem so bad," he offered.

I stopped, so he stopped. I looked up at him. "Does it bother you? The re-recording for my meditation guide?" My stomach knotted as he ran his gaze over my face.

"No, not really." He stepped closer and leaned down until his lips were near my ear. "But Ethan did basically tell me why you've been blushing," he said in that husky low voice that ran down my spine and to my toes.

I felt my face grow warm. "Shit," I said with feeling.

Dylan chuckled as he straightened and smiled down at me.

"This is not a game we are going to play," I declared. Dylan tugged my hand to get me walking again.

"Maybe," he hedged.

I groaned painfully. My face was still burning by the time we reached the truck.

"You are really embarrassed about this," he said, chuckling.

How was I going to explain that he couldn't use that voice on me in public without telling him why? Shit, I couldn't. I shouldn't be embarrassed about this. Everybody had a thing that hit their switch. It was perfectly natural.

"Okay, let me explain it this way," I began as my face began cooling off. We stopped by the passenger door to the truck. "Everyone has a thing, that just does something for them." I swallowed hard. "I like certain types of voices." I forced myself to look up at his handsome face.

He had a half grin again; his eyes had gone from warm to molten. My stomach did a low hard flip at that look on his face. "That's not being an audiophile, Sunshine; that's something else," he said, smirking at me.

"Well, I also like music so, I just clumped it together." Then I narrowed my eyes at him. "And how do you know?"

His cheeks started to turn pink. "You know that soft low voice you use sometimes?" he said, looking everywhere else but at me.

"Uh-huh." My smile was growing by the second.

He cleared his throat. "Yeah, it does the same thing," he admitted, his face now completely red. "I don't know if it's just the sound, or if it's you, but it's the same effect."

I ran my eyes over him. "I use that voice all the time on the phone," I reminded him, grinning.

His eyes met mine. "I know," he said emphatically. "You need to stop."

I snorted. "I only told you so you wouldn't use that voice in public. I didn't ask for your button pusher," I pointed out.

He sighed. "You were embarrassed I knew yours, so it seemed fair to tell you mine." His color was going back to normal.

"Thank you, honey," I said in that low, soft voice.

He took a breath and closed his eyes. "Lexie, that's just mean," he said, his voice pained.

I snickered. "You've been doing that to me all night,"

He chuckled. "Yeah, I guess I have," he admitted begrudgingly.

He reached out, took my hands and pulled me into a hug. I wrapped my arms around his waist as he wrapped his arms around my shoulders. I rested my cheek on his chest.

"I had an idea about tomorrow," he said, hesitating.

"Oh?"

"I was thinking that instead of you having to drive back down here, then back to Dulcet. Why don't you just come up after the game? It's a shorter drive, and I'll show you around town and introduce you to my friends." He suggested. I pulled back a bit and smiled up at him. I really liked the idea except...

"I have to drive Ethan, Miles, and Faith tomorrow," I reminded him.

He nodded. "And after the game, Asher can take them home," he countered.

I thought about it. It would work in theory.

"I can ask if Asher's okay with that, and I'll have to ask Rory," I said, hoping they'd say yes. Then I thought of something else. I looked up at him, biting the corner of my lip. "I'll probably want to take a shower before heading out to Vegabond."

He smiled down at me, a light dancing in his eyes. "You, naked, in my house." He let out a breath. "Yeah, I'm okay with that." I chuckled quietly at that. He smiled down at me. "There are three bathrooms in my house. You can use the one connected to my bedroom, and I'll use the guest bathroom." His smile was warm as his eyes ran over my face. "There's even a lock on both doors if you're concerned about it."

That wasn't it.

"I'm not worried about you walking in. I just wanted to warn you that I'll want to take a shower," I explained. "Some people are weird about things like that, and I just wanted to make sure you didn't have a problem with it."

"Oh, so you weren't worried I'd try and take advantage of you being naked?" he asked playfully. I snorted. He smiled. "Don't worry, Sunshine. I have no problems with you being naked in my shower." I snickered and shook my head at him. "Or anywhere else around me." He kept grinning at me.

I just smiled up at him. There was nothing else I could do. Snow started falling faster. I looked up and giggled as it hit my face.

"Hold on a second," Dylan said. When he let go, I looked at him as he pulled his cellphone out of his pocket. "Lexie, pull your hood up a bit." I did as he said, not really knowing what kind of photo he was trying to take. "Now, do that thing girls do. Their face is kind of down, and they look up with those big eyes. And don't smile." I did the face he was talking about and waited. "Damn, I'm good." He smiled, looking at his phone. "Let me get one with a smile."

"Same face?" I asked, not really sure what he wanted.

"No, just be you." I promptly flipped off the camera. I heard a click as he chuckled. "Come on. Less pissed off you." I rolled my eyes and tilted my head a bit to the side. Then I gave him a smile like he wanted. I heard a click. He checked his phone and smiled.

"Are you going to show me the photos or what?" I asked, really wanting to see them.

He came over and stood next to me. He flipped back to the first one. My red hair looked amazing on my black coat, and with the hood, it looked great. The snow on my jacket and behind me looked beautiful and went with my porcelain skin. My eyes looked bright green in the snow. It was really an amazing photo.

"Wow. What filter did you use?" I asked before he swiped to the next one.

He chuckled. "I didn't use one, Sunshine. That's all you."

My mouth dropped open. I saw the photo of me flipping off the camera. Then the next one with me smiling. They all looked great. For the first time in my life, I felt beautiful. It was way weird. "I think these are the best photos I've ever had taken," I told him, impressed. "Can you send them to me?"

"Definitely," he said, putting his phone away.

I pulled out my cellphone.

His smile disappeared. "No."

I nodded. "Fair's fair," I told him, going to the camera section. "I'm not nearly as good as you, but I still want a photo."

He shook his head. I started pouting. He cursed, and I knew I had won.

"Fine," he grumbled before he stuck his hands in his pockets and gave me his half grin that I was coming to love.

I took the picture and figured I'd tortured him enough.

"See, it only hurt for a second," I teased.

He snorted.

I went back to his side and showed him the photo. It was a damn good picture. With the snow falling and his blue jacket bringing out his eyes. I think it showed who he was. I smiled.

"I like it."

"That's pretty good, send it to me," he admitted. He kissed the top of my head. "Come on. It's cold out here." He opened my door and helped me into the truck before running to the other side. He banged twice on the hood before he climbed in and started the truck waiting for it to warm up.

"What was with hitting the hood?" I asked.

"Oh, um. Sometimes outside cats like to crawl onto an engine while it's warm so if you don't bang on the hood, then you might start the motor with cats on it," he explained. I winced. "Yeah, pretty much." But he hit the hood to scare the cats away. My heart grew warm.

"Let me text Asher and see if he'll take the others home tomorrow." I pulled out my cellphone and texted him.

Alexis: Hey, do you think after the game you could take Ethan, Faith and Miles home? Dylan asked me to go to Dulcet to meet his friends.

I didn't have long to wait; hell, I watched Asher heading up the porch now.

Asher: Yeah, no problem.

Alexis: Thank you.

"Well, Asher's in," I said, looking over at Dylan.

His eyes were warm again, running over my face.

"What?"

He gave me a half grin then reached out and brushed a strand of hair from my cheek.

"You're just... beautiful." His voice was that husky low one that ran down my spine. But I didn't think it was on purpose this time. I smiled at him, heart racing.

"You're kinda cute yourself, honey," I pointed out.

His cheeks started to turn pink. I smiled at him. He leaned over to me, and his lips brushed mine only for a moment before pressing down. My mouth moved with his as everything turned fuzzy. The kiss moved deeper, still soft and slow. My heart raced as his hand cupped my jaw. I loved that he did that every time we kissed. I floated in a world of warmth and feeling until we both pulled back. I opened my eyes and smiled at him. His thumb traced my cheekbone, sending those butterflies flying.

"I wanted to get a proper goodbye kiss before I took you home. I don't think I can kiss you like that at your door," he admitted grinning.

I smirked. "I would not suggest it," I admitted. He smiled.

The heater was finally warming up the cab of the old truck. Dylan drove me home then walked me to my door. We hugged briefly; he kissed my forehead and waited until I got inside to head back to the truck. The whole thing left me feeling beautiful and like I meant something to him. It was a new feeling. I locked the door and turned to find Rory at the front window by the TV. I raised an eyebrow.

"Like you expected anything else," Rory shot at me.

I chuckled.

"How'd it go?"

I smiled. "It was different," I hedged, still thinking about the way Dylan made me feel tonight.

"Good different or bad different?"

"Good different," I said quietly. I looked back at Rory. "I ran into two ghosts at the same time tonight. They had joined up to try to bully me into helping them cross."

Rory frowned.

"I told them I had a way," I continued, "and that I just needed time to set it up. They backed off."

"Were you sick?"

"Nosebleed, head pain, and major nausea but I didn't puke. So, my barriers are holding stronger now."

Rory jerked his chin toward the door. "How'd he take it?"

I smiled, remembering him sitting next to me on the bathroom floor holding my hair back. "He thinks it's a seizure disorder," I admitted. "He has a kit now, though, and thinks it's medicine from some drug trials."

Rory shook his head. "You sure about that kid?" he asked. "If you care about him, you'll need to tell him."

"We've been talking for two months, but only dating a few days Rory. I'm going to wait a while."

He nodded. He knew it was my decision; he'd respect it.

"By the way, Rory, can I head to Dulcet after the football game tomorrow? Dylan wants to introduce me to his friends, and then I have to go sing tomorrow night." I gave him my sweet begging smile.

He frowned at me. "His parents going to be home?"

"His dad should be. His mom passed," I answered instantly.

Rory sighed and nodded.

I ran to him and threw my arms around him. "Thank you! Thank you!"

He gave me a squeeze back. I ran upstairs and got ready for bed. I was almost asleep when I realized that that was the first time I'd hugged Rory since I was eight. Huh. I rolled over and fell asleep.

CHAPTER 7

SATURDAY MORNING

I woke up almost screaming three times that night; I got maybe four hours of sleep. Zeke wasn't going to be happy; the shit head could always tell how little sleep I've had. So, when my alarm went off, I wasn't thrilled. I groaned as I rolled out of bed. I wanted to kill Asher for getting to the playoffs; no one should be up this early on a Saturday.

I went into the bathroom, took a shower, and did my usual morning routine. I went back into my bedroom and got dressed. I pulled on black bootcut jeans, a black cami and my hunter green oversized sweater that reached my hips. This one had a regular neckline, so I wasn't too worried about it sliding off my shoulder as much as I was of light getting in and making it see through. I used my usual leave in conditioner and old hair dryer to dry my hair into its long curly mass. I had learned back in November what happened if you walked outside with wet hair in winter around here. Not fun. I did my usual light makeup and pulled my boots on. Then I realized I was going to have to take a bag with me. I grabbed my book bag and put my clothes I wanted to wear tonight into the bag, including everything I'd need to get the look I wanted. I used my rosemary oil and slipped that in the bag too. I also made a point of putting my bracelets in my pocket. I still needed to build my shields up, but I wanted the backup. I was zipping up my little bathroom bag to put in my bag when my phone vibrated. I finished with my stuff and picked it up.

Dylan had sent me the pictures he took last night, and they still made me feel beautiful. Then he texted me.

Dylan: Morning, Sunshine, see you soon.

I smiled at that and wanted to send him a heart emoji, but I hesitated. Was this too early for a heart emoji? Nah, I'd send him a pink one; besides, I loved my photos.

Alexis: See you soon.

I put my phone in my pocket, got my wallet, my keys, my bag and headed downstairs. I quickly ate breakfast and pulled on my wool jacket. I grabbed my bag and headed out. It took a while for my Blazer to heat up but when it did, I blasted the heater. I drove over to the twins' house where everyone was going to meet. I left my bag in the car and hurried up to the door. Since I'd never been inside, I knocked.

It wasn't long before a woman answered. She had lovely brown skin, the boys' beautiful chocolate eyes, and thick black hair. She looked like she was in her late forties, and she still looked fit. She was also still in her jammies which made me love her instantly. When she saw me, her eyes lit up.

"You must be Lexie." Her voice was smooth and sweet to my ears. I bet she had a killer singing voice.

"Yeah, you must be Maria," I said, smiling.

She smiled at me and waved me inside. "Guilty as charged, honey." She closed the door behind me then turned to me, still smiling. "The terrors aren't up yet."

I rolled my eyes. Everyone was going to be here in like, ten minutes.

Her eyes narrowed at me playfully. "I understand you and Ethan have a prank war going?"

I grinned and nodded.

She smiled mischievously; it was the same smile the boys got when they were up to no good. "Okay, here're your choices. A pitcher of water, ice, or start plucking on his guitars. Anyone of those will wake his butt up fast." I snickered. I loved this woman.

"I'll take ice water," I offered, getting excited.

"Ooh. Good choice. Come on."

She led me through the house, which oddly had the same layout as Asher's. She pulled a pitcher down and passed it to me. I went to the fridge and filled it a quarter of the way with ice. Maria was giggling to herself as she filled her own pitcher with ice and water. I couldn't help giggling too. When we were ready, we tiptoed upstairs. I was practically bouncing with happiness when we reached the boys' doors.

"Okay, go in and on the count of six dunk 'em."

I looked at her smiling. "You are my favorite mom ever," I whispered emphatically.

She snickered, and we both opened the doors. I counted off in my head as I tiptoed over the clothes on Ethan's floor. I didn't bother to look around; I didn't have time. I was next to Ethan's bed. He was stretched out wearing his gray sweats, shirtless, and dead to the world. On six, I poured. Ethan jerked awake.

"¡Mierda! That's fucking cold Ma!" Ethan shouted as he woke up.

The same was coming from Isaac's room.

"Morning lazy bones! Get your ass up!" I managed, laughing my ass off.

Ethan pushed his wet hair out of his face and glared at me. I backed up a step, but it wasn't far enough. Ethan dove off the bed, tackling me to the floor. I grunted as I landed with his weight on top of me.

"Think that's funny, Lexie? Huh!" he shouted as I kept laughing. He wrung his hair out at my face.

"Hell yeah!" I shouted back, still laughing my ass off. Ethan realized the water didn't bother me, so he went for my ribs. Oh shit! I dropped the pitcher and tried to shove him off me, but he had me pinned. His fingers tickled along my sides, making me jump. I couldn't stop laughing now.

"Give up? Huh?" he taunted as he kept tickling me.

I could barely breathe. "Maria! Help!" I yelled for backup as he continued to tickle me.

Feet moved across the floor. I looked up. Maria was walking in with a frown on her face.

"Ethan, déjala en paz en este instante!" Maria shouted at Ethan in Spanish.

Ethan jerked off me immediately; I just laid there still laughing.

"Tu no golpeas así a una niña!"

I had no clue what she was saying; I would have asked if I wasn't still laughing my ass off.

"But she..." Ethan pointed at his bed and his wet body.

Maria started laughing. "I told her to. You brats are late. Your friends will be here any minute." Maria looked down at me, smiling. "I got your back, sweetie."

I burst out laughing again as she left the room. When I could breathe, I sat up. "I love your Mom," I told him, smiling.

He glared and pointed at the door. "Out! I need to get dressed," he snapped.

I got up and went out into the hall, closing the door behind me. Isaac's door was also closed. I was about to go downstairs when I felt that chill down my neck, but it was more like a finger. A ghost who had been dead for some time. I looked around and saw another bedroom door open.

There she was. She had to have been six years old. Long black hair in a braid down her back, big brown eyes. Sweet, beautiful face. She was wearing dirty jeans, a pink sweatshirt, and sneakers. She watched me curiously. My barriers were holding, so I walked closer. I felt a sharp pain in my chest, not an aching. A stabbing pain; it told me of trauma.

"You can see me?" she asked. Her voice was sweet and curious. I nodded. "Then can you help me? I'm stuck here."

I looked around to make sure that Maria wasn't around. I stepped closer to her so that I could whisper. The pain increased, and my head began to throb. I stopped.

"The Veil is shut right now," I told her gently, and she frowned.

"But I do have a way to help you move on. It's going to take some time to set up. Can you hold onto yourself with all the energy running around?"

She blinked up at me and smiled. "Yeah, no problem. I don't like that energy stuff anyway. I only use my energy to mess with Eth and Izzy."

My heart dropped. Oh, God. Please, no.

"Who are you?" My head gave a painful throb, and I didn't care. I pulled out my tissues and didn't move.

"I'm Sophia. They always called me Sophie."

My chest clenched tight. No, no, no, no.

"How do you know them?" I asked softly.

She blinked at me. "They're my older brothers."

I couldn't breathe; my lungs seized. Fuck me. I forced myself to take a deep breath.

"You can take your time. Eth pulled me back here, and I'm kinda mad at him about that. So, I keep knocking over his guitars." She smiled sweetly at me.

I took a good look at her. There was no sign of extra juice whatsoever. She was just her.

I nodded. "As long as you stay you. Okay? If you decide that you want to go, break one of his guitars, and I'll hear about it. Sound good?" I offered, my mind stunned.

I couldn't tell him right now. I needed to process this. My head was starting to throb with my pulse. I reached into my pocket and started pulling on my bracelets as fast as possible. The pain began to ease. Sophie just watched me.

"Okay, if I'm tired of being here and bugging Eth, I'll break one of his guitars," she agreed. "Then you'll help me cross?"

I nodded, my stomach knotted. "I'll work my ass off to make sure I'm ready by then, honey," I promised. I didn't care how much it hurt; I was going to get that link going as fast as possible. I couldn't just leave the twins' little sister to the energy floating around.

She nodded. "Okay, thank you." She turned back around and walked back into the guest room. I closed the door. My head in chaos,

I found the bathroom at the top of the stairs and waited until my nose stopped bleeding. I was just changing the tissues when the door opened, and Ethan came up short. He was wearing black jeans and a black thermal. And his silver rings and earrings as always. His eyes ran over me.

"Oh yeah, I forgot to warn you. We think we have a ghost," Ethan said, cringing.

I gave him a small smile as I changed tissues. "It's okay. I already met the soul." I sure as hell wasn't going to tell him it was his little sister he'd never told me about. And I sure as hell wasn't going to tell him it was his fault that she was here. He went to the sink and grabbed a red toothbrush.

"What are we talking about here? Good? Bad?" he asked as he put toothpaste on the brush.

I swallowed hard and checked my nose. It had stopped. I tossed the tissues.

"Completely fine. The soul isn't dangerous, just playful," I hedged. Until I had that link up, I couldn't tell him.

"Hmm." He went about brushing his teeth.

"How's my face?" I asked, hoping to change the topic. He looked over his shoulder and frowned around his toothbrush. He spit into the sink quickly.

"You're white as a fucking ghost, Beautiful; you sure you're okay?" he asked, his voice worried.

I nodded. "Yeah, just tell me if I have any blood on my face." I needed to step away from him just to process this.

His eyes ran over my face. "No, you're good," he reassured me.

I smiled as I slid past him to go down stairs. I slowed on the stairs and took deep breaths. Holy fucking shit! I needed to talk to someone! But who the fuck could I tell? Miles! I instantly thought of Miles. I pulled out my cell phone and went out the front door to call him. It turned out I didn't have to. Miles and Faith were walking up the path to the house. Fuck. I waited, shifting from foot to foot as they reached the porch.

"Miles, I need to talk to you. Now," I said bluntly. His eyes ran over me; his brow drawing down. Faith looked at me suspiciously. I gestured inside.

"The boys are up and should be down any minute," I offered as I grabbed Miles' arm and dragged him down the porch steps and halfway across the lawn.

"Lexie, are you alright?" he asked softly. When I didn't answer, he seemed to remember something. "Oh, did you see the ghost in the house? Ethan was supposed to warn you."

I stopped walking and looked around to make sure no one was around. Then I stepped close and looked up at him.

"It's Sophie," I said through clenched teeth. His eyes went wide, his face pale. "The ghost is Sophia."

"Oh, fu-dge," Miles almost cursed. I blinked at him in surprise. Hell, I figured if Miles was ever going to curse, now was the time.

"Yeah, that's where I am right now." I looked back at the house, then back at him. "I didn't even know they had a sister." I took a panicked breath and let it out. My chest was tight, making it harder to breathe. "But she's fucking with Ethan because, guess what? He pulled her back here." I ran a hand through my hair, not knowing what the fuck to do.

Miles reached out and grabbed my arms gently, stopping me from rocking from foot to foot.

"Okay, is that extra energy that's running around affecting her?" he asked in his calm, controlled voice.

I swallowed hard and shook my head. "No, she's fine." I took a breath and tried to calm down. "She was just herself, no extra energy." I took another deep, calming breath. "I told her I could help her cross, but it's going to take a while to set it up."

"And how did she take that?" His voice was still that controlled calm.

I seemed to be the only one freaking out now.

"She's said it was okay. That she wanted to mess with Ethan some more." I swallowed hard through the lump in my throat. "She said when she was ready she'd break one of Ethan's guitars." I knew what I had to do. My mind started to settle. My heart began slowing down. "I need that link going as fast as possible."

Miles nodded; even he looked whiter than usual. "I think so," he agreed. His emerald eyes ran over my face before meeting mine again. "Don't tell them."

"Wasn't gonna."

"I hate to ask this, but, just to be sure." Miles' face was pained. "What did she call the twins?"

I understood completely; I didn't want to believe it either. "Eth and Izzy."

"Shi.... mm."

I raised an eyebrow. Miles was almost a potty mouth today. His eyes unfocused as he was thinking. I used the time to calm down and ease the tightness in my chest. Then Miles was back, his eyes focused again.

"Take today off, Lexie, she's okay. Start working tomorrow after breakfast at my house."

I hated the idea. "That's their baby sister," I pointed out, not really believing what he had said. "I can't leave her to rot out like Mary Summers."

He looked down at me with his patient face. "Lexie, is she in pain?" he asked gently.

"No. She was hanging out in one of the bedrooms," I admitted.

"Is she in trouble?"

I took a deep breath and let it out slowly. "No, she's just her," I said, begrudgingly.

He gave me a small, understanding smile. "Then there is no reason for you to have to drop everything and immediately start working on the link to the Veil," he said in his soothing, silky voice. The knots in my stomach started to fade away. "You've been working hard already. If you drop from exhaustion, then it will take longer to get you back to work. You need to have some fun today."

That knot of guilt that had been growing since the Veil closed gave me a big kick. How could I have fun when there were souls like Sophia around that needed help?

"But..." I looked back at the house, torn between what I wanted to do and what I should.

"Lexie, she's safe right now." Miles took my chin between his fingers and forced me to meet his eyes through his glasses again. "If you don't take care of yourself, you won't be able to help anyone."

I sighed, giving in. He was right. There was really nothing I absolutely had to do today. Sophia wasn't in trouble; I needed to have a day off with my friends. I hated when Miles was right.

"Fine," I grumbled.

He gave me a half grin and let go of my chin. Then it hit me. I had just dumped this whole mess on Miles. I was the world's worst friend.

"Miles, I'm sorry."

He raised a questioning eyebrow at me.

"I needed to talk to someone about this, and well, you're you." I tried to explain.

His eyes met mine as he grinned at me. "It's all right, Lexie." His voice was still that smooth, silky one. "I'm always here if you need to talk about anything. Besides, I'd rather know what's going on than be in the dark. Plus, you'll have another set of ears for any broken guitar stories."

I smiled up at him, grateful to have him in my life. Then I hugged him hard. He chuckled as he wrapped his arms around me and hugged me back.

"Don't worry. You'll start tomorrow. It's not selfish to take care of yourself," he reassured me.

I nodded into his shoulder. When I pulled back, I felt a hundred pounds lighter. I'd start tomorrow and work my ass off. When I was ready, we turned to head to the house. Faith was watching us from the front window. Great, what now? I took a deep breath as we went inside. Just make it through today Lexie, you can do this. We walked into the foyer where Faith eyed us.

"You look upset, Lexie, something going on?" Faith asked, looking from Miles to me. I smiled nicely at her.

"I just needed some advice from Miles," I hedged. "He's great with advice." She raised an eyebrow at me doubtfully. Right now, I didn't care.

I walked into the family room and sat on the couch with Maria.

"You *seriously* are my favorite mom ever," I told her honestly.

She chuckled. "Well, you raise twins who are hell bent on creating havoc, you get a sense of humor." She smiled at me. It was a warm smile.

I smiled back. The front door opened, and the others walked in. It got noisy in a hurry; then we were all loaded up and out the door.

IT TOOK fifteen minutes of negotiating on the music to decide what to listen to, but we managed. About that time, my phone vibrated.

I pulled it out of my pocket and handed it to Miles. "Can you check that for me, hon?" I never messed with my phone and drove.

Miles took it and checked it. "It's from Dylan. He says, 'Text me when you get there, I'll meet you at the gate,'" Miles announced.

"Just tell him okay, please," I said, concentrating on driving. Then a thought occurred. "And that it's you."

Miles had a small grin as he did as I asked. It was a couple of minutes later when Miles caught my attention again. "Lexie? Who took these pictures?" Miles asked, holding up my phone.

I looked over and saw the photos Dylan took last night. I smiled. "Dylan took those last night, and I loved them, so he sent them to me," I explained.

"These are some great photos, Lexie," Miles said.

"Let me see." Ethan broke off talking to Faith and leaned forward. Miles did something with my phone. Ethan's phone vibrated. "Wow," Ethan said emphatically. My face grew warm.

"Faith check these out."

"I was majorly surprised too. I thought he used some kind of filter," I admitted.

"No, this was just the right place at the right time," Ethan mumbled. "I'm sending these to the guys."

"Snoopy!" I snapped.

"Oh, come on, we all need a photo for contacts. And these are damn good pictures," Ethan shot back. I sighed. He was right; they were damn good photos. I ignored Ethan and his texting frenzy for the rest of the drive.

I pulled into the parking lot of the Northridge High school and parked. I took my phone back from Miles and climbed out. It was freezing today, so I pulled out my skull scarf and wrapped it around my neck. I pulled out my gloves and beanie too. I looked in the side mirror to make sure the skull and crossbones were centered. Then I texted Dylan. Faith was watching me.

"I love that scarf," Faith announced.

I smiled at her. "Thanks, it was a present. I have no idea where Miles picked it up."

I decided to leave Ethan out of the sentence altogether, and he didn't protest. We met the guys on the way towards the gate. There were whistles and hoots. I rolled my eyes.

"Nice photos, Red." Isaac smiled at me.

"They looked good," Zeke offered.

Riley smacked his chest and looked at me. "They looked fucking fantastic, and you had this hot goth but not goth thing going. And the snow was perfect," Riley assured me.

My face was on fire. "Thanks, guys, but Dylan's the one who took them," I felt the need to point out.

Riley rolled her eyes and left Zeke's side. She wrapped her arm around mine as we headed for the gate. "Sweetie, you looked beautiful. Not a lot of people get one photo like that in their lives let alone three," Riley pointed out. "So just enjoy it."

"Okay, I'll go with that," I grumbled.

Riley laughed. I paid at the gate and started looking through the crowd for Dylan. I didn't have to look long; Dylan found me. We were standing in a circle waiting for him when I heard my name.

"Lexie!" I turned towards Dylan's voice and tried to search the crowd. But with my height, it wasn't possible.

"He's coming over," Riley told me.

I really wish I had a bit of her height. Dylan came out of the crowd and made a beeline for me. He was wearing dark blue jeans and a black snow jacket. I smiled as the butterflies went crazy.

Riley leaned down to whisper in my ear, "Girl, that boy has got it bad."

My face grew warm. Just as she stood up straight, Dylan reached me. He leaned down and surprised me with a soft kiss that scrambled my brain. When he pulled back a little, one of his hands was cupping the side of my neck, his thumb in front of my ear again. His sparkling eyes met mine.

"Hi, Sunshine," he whispered.

"Hi. How'd you find me?" I asked as I smiled up at him.

"Easy, I looked for Zeke."

I chuckled.

He stood up straight then looked at the others. "Hey, guys." He greeted the others. Everyone said hi. "If you guys want to choose your seats, now's the time; they're filling up fast."

Zeke headed out, and the rest of us followed. I held on to Dylan's hand, trusting him to keep us with the others. We ended up to the right side of the field on Spring Mountain's side. We sat halfway up the bleachers. Zeke, Riley, Ethan, Faith, and Trisha sat on the upper row. On the lower row, it was Cece, Isaac, Miles, me, and then Dylan. Dylan planted his feet on the row in front of us and kept my hand in his. It sent that warm feeling through me again. Shit.

His sapphire eyes met mine. "Did you get the photos this morning?" he asked, his eyes running over my face.

I was about to answer when Isaac did for me. "Oh, yeah, we all did." Isaac snickered.

Dylan raised an eyebrow at me.

"Blame Miles. He had my phone while I was driving," I told him. "He sent them to Ethan and of course-"

"Ethan sent them to everybody," he guessed. He shrugged. "They were good pictures, Sunshine."

"Good? Those were fucking great," Riley said, making me smile. "Seriously, every girl needs a good photo like that."

Dylan looked turned a little and looked at her over his shoulder.

"Thanks, what did you think about the one with her flipping off the camera?" he asked.

I just rolled my eyes.

"That was my favorite," Riley admitted.

His cheeks turned a tinge pink as he looked back to me.

I smiled at him. "I really do love them," I admitted, not caring if I sounded girly.

"Then do you mind helping me practice once in a while? All of my friends are sick of getting their pictures taken," he asked. I nodded. "Great, we can do that today."

"I thought you wanted me to hang out with your friends today?" I reminded him.

"We can do both. The guys can stop by in the afternoon and hang out," he offered.

"Okay, but if you want more practice, then I'm pretty sure we can get Riley to show up early and get some photos of her."

"Yes, please. Pretty please," Riley begged from behind us.

"Lexie, what did you just do?" Zeke growled at me.

I looked back at him and smirked. His frown was very much in place. I laughed at the look on his face.

Riley smacked Zeke's arm. "No one said you had to get your photo taken," Riley pointed out. Zeke's face relaxed with relief.

I turned back to Dylan; he had a big smile on his face. "That would be great, just bring any clothes you want to wear in the pictures. I really like highlighting a single aspect of someone. Well, last night I got two. Sunshine's hair and eyes." My butterflies went crazy. His eyes were warm as they met mine before he continued, "So, bring something that brings out your hair color or your eye color. Like black, gray but no white. I was thinking outside shots today."

I looked back at Riley, who was beaming. "I'm so in," Riley said, clearly excited. "How early do you want me in Dulcet?"

"I'd say two and a half hours before dark. That last hour before dark is one of the best times to get some great lighting." Dylan said as he rubbed the back of his neck. "Afterward, you can just hang with us at my house." He looked at Zeke. "You too, of course." I hid a smile. Dylan was a smart guy.

Zeke looked at Riley. My twisted side came out to play. I leaned over and staged whispered to Riley, "Pout, seriously. Do it."

Zeke looked at me, his face furious. "Damn it, Lexie," he snapped. I snickered. The other guys started laughing.

Riley looked at me. "Is that how to get what I want?" Riley asked laughing.

I grinned. "It only works once, and then he'll run like hell if you ever try it again," I warned her. Zeke was still glaring at me. I smiled sweetly back. He was shaking his head at me still not happy.

"You want to play it like that?" Zeke asked, his voice hard. He looked at Dylan. My heart dropped. He wouldn't... "Ask her how much sleep she got last night. Then ask her why." My mouth dropped open.

"You shit, that was two!"

The guys kept laughing at us.

"Lexie?" Dylan asked.

I cringed before looking at him. He had a suspicious look on his face. I smiled tensely.

"What is he talking about?" His voice was getting harder, his shoulders tense.

Thanks, Zeke.

"Zeke, just made that sound really bad," I told him. "I have bad dreams every night, so I don't get a lot of sleep. Last night, I got *maybe* four hours of sleep."

His body relaxed, though his eyes stayed worried. "How the hell do you manage like that?" he asked, his eyes running over my face.

I shrugged. "Lots of caffeine. Work my ass off at the gym, and rock climbing?" I offered. "I usually get more sleep on those nights than any other."

"Sunshine, you don't have to come over today. You can just go home and get some sleep," he offered making my heart melt. He was so fucking sweet.

I looked at him like he was nuts. "Fuck no, I'd rather hang out with you."

He snorted, then smiled at me. "Do you need some coffee?" he asked sweetly. I rolled my eyes up and looked away. He laughed then gave my hand a squeeze. He let go of my hand as he got up.

"I can go get my own coffee," I pointed out, just then realizing what he was doing.

"Stay here, Sunshine, or you'll get lost in the crowd," he said before heading down the aisle.

When he was out of sight, I turned and punched Zeke in the arm, hard. "You shit head!" Zeke rubbed his arm as the guys laughed. "You just made my boyfriend think I was cheating on him."

Zeke winced. "Shit, I didn't think about how that sounded," he admitted. "Sorry."

"And you ratted out two of mine." I pointed out, still a little pissed.

Zeke sighed, then gestured towards Riley. "Go ahead." Zeke's gravelly voice was resigned.

I looked at Riley and smiled. "Your boyfriend is partly color blind," I told her happily. Her eyebrows went up as she looked at Zeke.

"Really?" Riley asked, her voice surprised.

He nodded. "For the first month we were talking, I thought your hair was blue," he admitted not even embarrassed about it.

Riley laughed. "Oh, that's so cute," Riley said still chuckling.

Zeke looked back at me. "Even now?"

"Even," I smiled and turned back around, happy that balance had been restored.

Everyone started talking about the game. It wasn't long before Dylan was back with coffee. I took it from him, smiling. "Ooh, best boyfriend ever!"

He chuckled as he sat back down next to me. "Cream and sugar, I have more in my pocket if I didn't add enough," he offered.

"Okay, that's sexy as hell," I admitted, smiling. The girls actually laughed for once. Dylan just smiled at me as I took a sip. "Oh, that's good."

Dylan reached over and wrapped his hand around the inside of my thigh, just above the bend in my knee. My stomach did a flip, and my body tingled as his thumb rubbed on my jeans. I peeked up at him; he was talking to Miles about something I hadn't heard. But as usual, he seemed not to realize he was touching me. I smiled to myself and took a drink of my coffee. It was a bit later, when I slid my arm around his to rest my hand on his forearm, that he realized it. I watched out of the corner of my eye as he looked down and went still, finally noticing where his hand was. I gave his forearm a squeeze, telling him it was okay, as the teams ran out onto the field. His hand squeezed my thigh back, sending my body into tingles again. It felt good. I was suddenly very glad that Riley and Zeke were coming up to get photos done. They'd help me behave.

The game started, and it wasn't going so well for our team. Asher kept taking hits from the same linebacker on Northridge's team. After a particularly nasty hit late in the second quarter, I noticed it. Every third play the offense made, one of Asher's fullbacks would let someone slip through almost untouched.

"Anyone else see that?" I asked the group.

Dylan's hand around my leg squeezed. "What, the hit?" Dylan asked.

"No, every third play, number forty-eight lets the same fucking linebacker through," I told him, watching the next play get a first down.

"You sure about that, Lexie?" Ethan asked.

I gestured towards the game. "Watch him on the third play, I might be wrong, but I don't think so," I said, still distracted. Everyone watched for it. And sure enough, on the third play, Asher went down hard. I winced.

"Shit, she's right," Zeke said.

"He's relying too much on his fullbacks, with him that deep in the pocket. He needs to fucking back out or have the fucker replaced," I said, still not really caring if I sounded like an overprotective, crazy girl.

Dylan's hand on my thigh squeezed firmly. "Okay, now that is sexy as hell," Dylan said with feeling. The guys burst out laughing. I looked at him and smiled. The clock ran down with only Northridge scoring. It was half-time.

I pulled out my cellphone. "Will Asher check his phone at half-time?" I asked the guys.

"No, they'll be going over the next half," Miles answered me.

I cursed and got up.

Dylan stood up too. "Whoa, Sunshine. What are you doing?" he asked, his eyes running over my face.

"I'm gonna go fucking tell him." I went to walk around him.

He stopped me with his hands on my shoulders. "How about I go tell him? That way you aren't walking into the guys' locker room," Dylan offered.

"Good point," I admitted. "Tell him I said not to be the nice guy on this; this isn't about winning a fucking game. It's about keeping his ass out of the hospital."

Dylan smirked at me. "Got it." Dylan turned and hurried down the aisle and towards the locker room.

I was worried about Asher, but I'd admit I also took the opportunity to ogle my boyfriend's butt. I smiled to myself as I sat down again. I felt eyes on me. I turned to find Trisha glaring at me. Oh, fuck off. I stopped myself from saying it, barely. This jealous, possessive thing she had going on was getting real, fucking old.

The guys all decided to make a snack run while it was half-time.

"Zeke." I looked up at him over my shoulder. "If you get me nachos, you can have nachos. And I'll buy." I smiled sweetly.

He didn't even hesitate. "Done."

I snickered as I pulled out my wallet and gave him a twenty. This food deal was working out great. I'd have those pounds back soon enough. "Can you also grab Dylan a large soda?"

"Yeah." Zeke agreed, then the guys disappeared into the crowd.

"How do you eat like that and stay so thin?" Cece asked.

I turned and looked up at her. "I work out with the guys at the MMA center three times a week for a few hours, and I have rock climbing lessons with Asher another three days a week," I offered. "Plus, Zeke was really on my ass about my diet because of the whole seizure thing. I am starving for junk food." Riley laughed, and Faith smiled. Faith could smile; that was progress. Cece didn't look like she believed me. I really didn't care. But I did get an idea.

I looked at Riley. "Do you have any idea what to get Zeke for Christmas? Cause I'm drawing a blank." Riley thought about it and shook her head. I cursed.

"You know what, we should go shopping together for him, two perspectives are better than one," Riley offered.

"Done. Give me your phone number." Riley laughed as we exchanged phone numbers. The other girls were oddly quiet. I was about to turn around when I noticed Faith and Trisha making faces at each other and tilting their heads towards me. I turned and pretended not to notice.

There was a sigh. "Lexie, we're all kind of drawing blanks on what to get the guys for Christmas," Faith began. I turned around on the bench and looked at her. "I was wondering if you could help us out?" Was she fucking kidding? After the shit they'd been saying about me? I knew I was going to help but, damn it. I sure as hell wasn't giving them my ideas for presents; it took me long enough to come up with them.

"Yeah, um." I thought for a second over what I had heard over the last few weeks. "For Ethan, he was talking about stone guitar picks a couple of weeks ago. They're supposed to make a different sound or something. And for Isaac..." I thought about it, and then I remembered his hand wraps were shit. "He needs new hand wraps; go with Meister hand wraps. He said they make the best." I looked to Trisha, who was waiting patiently. Fuck. "And Asher..." I smiled. "An advanced cooking techniques book. He's been wanting to up his cooking but is having trouble with a few of the trickier techniques." They all nodded.

"Thanks," Faith said.

I gave them a smile.

"No, problem." I turned back around. Maybe now they would finally realize I wasn't after their guys. I could only hope.

It wasn't long before Dylan came back through the crowd. He

came over to me and kissed my forehead. "Asher said to give you that," Dylan announced before sitting down. "He also says 'Thank you for saving my ass.'"

I snorted. Dylan's hand wrapped around the inside of my thigh again, just above my knee. This time I was sure he knew he was doing it; I went all tingly again.

"He was too busy getting hit to notice the pattern," he said.

"Are they taking the guy out?" I asked. I really wanted to know that fucker wasn't out there anymore.

Dylan nodded. "Yeah, Asher's refusing to go on the field with him still on the line." He smiled at me and gave my leg a squeeze. "But seriously, you talking football is sexy as hell."

I smiled as I wrapped my arm around his again. "I try."

"So, how long have you two been dating again?" Trisha's voice came from behind us. We both looked over our shoulders at her.

"Um, four days," I offered after counting in my head.

"Officially at least," Dylan added. "We were already kind of dating for the last two months. We were both just waiting for the other one to make a move."

I smiled and looked at him; we had both been chicken shit.

"Wow, you guys move fast," Trisha said in a snide tone. "I mean, his hand is between your legs in public, Lexie. Isn't that a little much?"

Riley cursed behind me. That was it. I was done. Dylan's face went cold; I mouthed the words 'I got this' before looking back up at Trisha and her smug face. "First, his hand is on my knee. Second, I've known Dylan two months, Trisha. And we've only kissed and cuddled a bit." I met her eyes with my dead stare. "You've known Asher two weeks. I've seen you two making out on movie night; I've seen him grabbing your ass, and sneaking little gropes elsewhere." I looked at her chest, just to clarify. Her smirk disappeared as her face turned red. "A blanket only hides so much in a dark, crowded room. So, get off your fucking high horse." Riley burst out laughing as I turned back around to watch the halftime show. Dylan squeezed my thigh.

"Okay, that was really sexy," he whispered out of the side of his mouth. I snorted and squeezed his arm back.

I didn't know if she would have had a comeback or not because the guys came back with food. Zeke handed me a cardboard container of nachos. Zeke also handed Dylan a soda.

"Thank you, Zeke," I said smiling up at him.

"No problem, Lexie."

Everyone started talking again, except Trisha. She remained strangely quiet. I didn't really care; after tonight, I was going to avoid her like the plague. It was getting harder and harder not to smack the shit out of her. I shared my nachos with Dylan, and he shared his soda with me as we watched the second half. Asher didn't get hit nearly as much, but the damage had already been done. We lost. The crowd started moving; we all stayed put. We had to wait for Asher anyway. I told Zeke that Riley and I were going shopping for his Christmas presents together and his face looked so pained I started laughing.

When the crowd had thinned out enough, everyone got up and picked up their trash. We climbed down the stairs and threw it away on our way to wait for Asher near the gate.

As we were waiting, Dylan wrapped his arm around my waist. I leaned back against him happily as we talked to the others. Asher was taking longer than usual today. I looked up at Dylan. "Hon, you can go ahead and head to your house. I just want to see that Asher's okay before I leave," I offered.

"I didn't drive today, a friend of a friend of mine was coming to the game, so I got a ride with him." His husky voice was soft, making me smile.

"Oh, that works."

Ethan looked at me, a sly smile on his face. "Aren't you driving us home?" Ethan asked, an eyebrow raised. Oh, yeah. I'd forgotten to tell them.

"Actually, no. You guys are going with Asher," I answered. "I am going up to Dulcet to spend the day with Dylan and his friends before tonight." Ethan gave me a knowing look. I narrowed my eyes at him and stepped away from Dylan to smack him upside the head. "Bad Ethan!" I chided. The guys and Riley laughed. Ethan just snickered.

"Hey!"

Everyone turned to see Asher walking towards us, freshly show-ered and in his usual clothes. He had his gear bag over his shoulder.

Trisha smiled a big smile and hurried to him. "You did awesome, baby!" Trisha gushed before going on her toes to kiss him. I rolled my eyes.

"Thanks honey, just give me a sec," Asher said sweetly as she let go of him. He dropped his bag and headed towards me. He looked at Dylan. "I'm hugging your girlfriend, man. Sorry, but I gotta." Dylan chuckled and stepped back as Asher swooped me up in a big hug. My feet were off the ground, and my hands went to his shoulders as he squeezed me hard. "You so saved my ass, Ally girl." His rich baritone rolled through my ears like hot chocolate.

"Can't...... breathe..." I gasped out dramatically. Asher laughed in my ear and loosed his hold a bit. I leaned back and looked down at him. "You trust your fullbacks way too much. Get your ass out of the pocket once in a while."

The guys burst out laughing.

"That's what the coach was calling today," he pointed out; he gave me another squeeze before putting me down.

I eyed him. He looked okay for the beating he took today. "You feeling all right? You took a lot of hits," I asked.

He smiled down at me. "Football's over, I'm happy," Asher told me simply. I smiled back. That's all I needed to hear. He went back to pick up his bag. I noticed Trisha glaring at me, her arms crossed over her chest. No one was looking so I gave her an 'are you serious' look and flipped her off. Dylan had a sudden coughing fit that covered his laughing. I stopped giving her the bird then looked to the others.

"Okay, guys. I'll see you, Ethan, at Vegabond around seven. Riley and Zeke, we'll see you soon," I announced to the group.

The guys said 'bye', and so did Riley. Dylan grabbed my hand, and we headed out to my truck.

When we were out of earshot, Dylan started chuckling. "Sunshine, I love it when you tell her off," Dylan said as we walked through the parking lot.

"I've had it. I've been nice," I began, my voice showing how irritated I was. "They all asked what to get the guys for Christmas, and I gave them some damn good ideas. Right before you showed back up."

"It's like any affection Asher shows you, she takes it personally," he said. "Like it's a slight against her."

I nodded. "And I'm sick of it." I looked up at him. "After tonight, I'm done talking to Trisha. If she's going to be somewhere, I'm not."

Dylan smiled down at me. "Well, that will give you more time to see me," he pointed out cheerfully.

I smiled. "Very true." We reached my Blazer when a thought occurred. "You didn't mind Asher hugging me, did you?"

He snorted. "Sunshine, he was taking a beating out there," he said simply. "If it bothered me I would have said so."

I went on my toes and gave him a quick, soft kiss then dropped back to my feet, smiling. "That's one of the things I really like about you," I said, my voice going soft.

His arms came around me, pulling me to him. His eyes were warm as they ran over my face. "So, what else do you really like about me?" he asked, grinning.

I wrapped my arms around his neck and leaned against him. "I really like your eyes, your laugh and..." I smirked and met his eyes. "You have a great ass."

He burst out laughing. "Just when I think you're going to be all romantic and shit, you say something like that." He shook his head, smiling down at me.

I smiled up at him. "That's me, the moment killer," I admitted without shame. He leaned down and kissed me. My heart raced as his lips touched mine. It was a simple, chaste kiss. But I felt it all the way down to my toes.

He pulled back and smiled at me. "Let's get out of here."

I totally agreed, I didn't want to run into Trisha any more than I already had to today. I hopped in my side and started the truck. Dylan got in on his side. We were out of the parking lot and heading to Dulcet in a couple of minutes. My heart was racing. I was going to spend the entire day with Dylan.

CHAPTER 8

SATURDAY AFTERNOON

*W*hen we reached Dulcet, Dylan had me drive around so he could show me a couple of places. He showed me the high school, the theater and, most importantly, the best burger joint in town. We picked up lunch and headed over to Dylan's house. On the way, I saw the sharp corner that Dylan had told me about, and I cringed just looking at it. We pulled up to a beautiful two-story house, with dark gray shingles and neutral goldish siding. With the light hitting it, the color reminded me of the gold some leaves got in the fall. I parked the truck where he told me to, grabbed my bag and hopped out. My pulse picked up as Dylan unlocked the front door. I was going to see Dylan's house. This was so weird.

I followed Dylan into the foyer; the wooden stairs were in a u-shape on the left. Dylan led me straight ahead into a big living room. The ceiling went up to the second story, with exposed cedar beams. The back wall was all large windows looking out onto the woods beyond. There was a big TV hanging on the right on the gray stone wall, a cedar coffee table, and end tables. And a big, brown leather couch and recliner. The whole place reminded me of a ski lodge. A really nice ski lodge.

Dylan put the food down on the coffee table. "Have a seat, Sunshine, and I'll get some napkins and ketchup."

I dropped my bag by the couch as I watched him walk across the room to large glass-paned double doors. I could see a kitchen and dining table through them. I took off my jacket and laid it on the arm of the sofa. I sat down. The sofa was different. The cushions were wider than a regular couch; if I were to sit back against the cushions, my feet would be off the floor. Huh. I ended up looking at the ceiling in the corners of the room and had a question.

I was eating one of my fries when he came back in with the napkins and ketchup. He sat down next to me and was quiet for the first time since I'd met him. His shoulders were tense.

"I've got a question," I announced in my cutesy voice. He looked over at me, his body still tense. I pointed to the ceiling. "How the fuck do you dust the ceiling?"

He burst out laughing.

"No, seriously," I said as I looked up at the high ceiling and tried to figure it out. "Do you have like a mop on a pole or something?"

"It's like a dust mop on a pole, yeah," he admitted, his cheeks a little pink. His shoulders relaxed again, and he was smiling.

"Thank you for answering, because that was going to bug the hell out of me all day," I admitted, reaching for my burger. He started laughing again. I took a napkin and took a bite of my cheeseburger. I was instantly in heaven. When I finished that bite, I looked over at him. "Okay, you win the burger joint contest. This is the best burger ever."

He swallowed the food in his mouth. "They use local, grass-fed beef. They even make their own buns. Remind me to tell Zeke about it later," he said. He picked up the remote and turned on the large television. "What do you want to watch, Sunshine?"

I was shrugging when I saw a movie just starting. "Ooh. Zombieland!" I said excitedly.

He chuckled. He put it on. "I love that when you have to pick between a chick flick or a horror movie, you choose the one with the most gore." He smiled over at me. I shrugged. "Why is that?"

I sighed and watched the movie. "Well, a lot of chick flicks aren't realistic. I mean, it doesn't take two days to fall in love with someone. That's just being attracted to each other. And it sure as hell takes longer than two days to trust another person. No trust, no love." I thought of something then added, "Well, okay, maybe if you both had perfect families, perfect childhoods, and never been hurt by someone, it could happen. But no one has that."

"But a zombie apocalypse is more realistic?" he asked.

I laughed as I looked over at him. He was smiling at me with warm eyes.

I decided to go with it. "Yes, yes, it is." I took a bite of my burger as he laughed at me.

We finished lunch and put our trash in the take-out bag. Dylan went and threw it away. "Care if I take off my shoes?" I shouted.

"Go for it."

I quickly pulled off my shoes and socks then curled up in the corner of the couch, my knees to my chest. I had a belly full of food, and I was happy just being here with Dylan. When Dylan came back, I moved under his arm and moved closer. With the wide couch, I ended up curled up with my head on his shoulder. His arm was over my shoulder and resting on my hip from the angle I was lying against him. My bent knees were resting against his leg. I felt him kiss the top of my head and smiled. That feeling of being loved and appreciated washed over me again. And for once, I didn't fight it. If this is how I felt about Dylan, then this was how I felt about him. I just wasn't going to tell him. I went back to watching Woody Harrelson beat the crap out of some zombies.

My eyes went to the photos on the wall. There was a woman with Dylan's blue eyes smiling in a family portrait. She had been pretty. "Dylan?"

"Yeah, Sunshine?" His was voice distracted, like his head had been somewhere else.

"I have a question, but I don't want you to answer if you don't feel like it." His body grew tense against me.

"Okay?"

"Why don't you talk about your family?" I asked, keeping my voice soft.

His arm flexed around me before his thumb began running up my side to my ribs then back down again. I wasn't sure he was even aware he was doing it. He was quiet for a few heartbeats. Then he took a deep breath. "Because there isn't much of one left." His voice was matter-of-fact. "Mom was kind of the drive that kept us going. She made sure we did Christmas right, New Years. Thanksgiving was a big one. My family is pretty small. Mom and Dad never had siblings, and all my Grandparents are gone."

"So, it's just you and your dad?" He nodded against my hair.

"Yep. We get along really well, but it's just us."

"Do you still do Christmas and Thanksgiving?" I asked, hesitating a bit. I didn't want to hit a sore topic.

"We do for her. We do the tree and the gifts. Then we sit around and watch action movies all day." His voice was getting tight.

I needed to change the subject. "So, I guess I'll have to give you your present late then." I used my aw-shucks voice. His body shook against me as he chuckled.

"You're getting me a present?" His voice was changing back to his normal husky one. I looked up at him; he was grinning down at me.

"Ooh yeah," I said, drawing the words out. "Everyone is getting a present this year. Even Tara, if I ever see her."

"You can always come up on Christmas; having another person around would be nice." He kissed the top of my head. "Besides, you're funny as hell."

I looked up at him. "Oh, so you only want me here for my entertainment value?" I shot up at him, smiling. He groaned painfully as he smiled. I snickered.

"No, I wouldn't mind seeing my Sunshine on Christmas either," he admitted, his cheeks tinting pink.

I thought about it. I could probably manage it. "I have Rory and Tara in the morning, then the guys at Miles' house." I looked up at him. "Sorry, no girlfriends or boyfriends allowed. Miles is really private."

"I get that."

"But I'm free for the afternoon and on, though. And I'll bring gory-ass horror movies to combat the Christmas overload," I offered, smiling.

He chuckled, his eyes warm on my face. "Sounds good to me, Sunshine."

I went back to resting my head on his chest. Then it hit me. "Shit. I still haven't done any of my shopping," I groaned. He snickered. "What do you want for Christmas?"

He was quiet for a bit. "You know what I really want?" His voice was soft and quiet. I looked up to see his eyes unfocused on the stone wall.

"What, honey?" I kept my voice soft.

"I want my mom's Christmas cookies. She used to make all these different kinds." I smiled. "I've tried to make them, but I always did something wrong."

"Like what?"

He smiled. "One year, I used the wrong kind of oil and made both of us sick," he admitted.

I smiled. His smile started to disappear. I didn't want to see that.

"Do you still have the recipes?"

He looked down at me, his eyes warm running over my face. "You don't have to, Sunshine. It's enough that you'll be here." The honesty in his voice gave me that warm fuzzy feeling again.

I gave him a small smile and repeated myself. "Do you still have the recipes?"

His eyes ran over my face again, gentle and soft. He nodded.

"Will it bother your dad if I try to make them?" I really didn't want to try to make it better and only make it worse. I'd learned over my life to ask first.

"No, he's missed them too." His voice was thick again.

My heart ached. Okay, I couldn't take it. I shifted onto my knees next to him, wrapped my arms loosely around his neck and leaned against him. He gave me a sad smile, his eyes shining as he wrapped his arms around me.

"I'm all right, Sunshine," he whispered to me. "I just... miss her. It's been two years, and I still expect to see her every time I get up in the morning."

"Missing her isn't going to go away, but it gets easier over time." My voice was soft and quiet. "Looking for.... her. It goes away with time."

He pulled me closer so he could bury his face against my throat. I wrapped a hand around the back of his neck, fingers massaging. I didn't know how else to help but to tell him what I knew about losing Dad.

"It took me three and a half years before I stopped expecting to see Dad when I got home." I took a breath. "Then I cried because I didn't expect to see him anymore. I felt guilty about it."

His arms shifted then tightened around me. He lifted me and moved me over, so I was sitting in his lap, one knee on each side of his hips. My chest pressed against his as his arms moved back to hugging me, his face still in the crook of my neck.

"It really sucks around the holidays." His lips brushed against my skin as he whispered.

"It helps to do something to show you remember them," I offered gently; it was the only advice I had. It was the only thing I had found that helped. "Maybe talk to your dad about doing something special for her this year."

He took a shaky breath. "We do the tree for her."

"But it's not enough, is it? Does it help? Do you feel better after doing the tree?"

He sniffed. "No, it feels like a fucking reminder that we lost her," he admitted. Wet drops landed on my skin. My heart clenched. I moved my fingers through his hair at the base of his neck.

"Then it's not helping. It's hurting. The tree isn't working anymore." I gave him everything I knew from my experience. "You need to do something new, baby. Something that you haven't done before. Something that leaves you feeling better about her memory, and not just the loss of her." I just couldn't seem to shut up today. I cursed myself as tears ran down my face for him.

"That's a good idea, Sunshine." His voice was thick, his breathing shaky.

So, I just held him. I didn't know what else to do, so I did what I did with anyone I cared about; I cried with him. He held me like that for some time. When his breathing steadied, and his grip eased, I did the only thing I could think of; I tried to make him laugh.

"I should just not be allowed to talk to people," I said, only half joking. He snorted. "I made Asher cry, like, yesterday. Then he made me cry, and then we decided we shouldn't talk to each other anymore. Because we kept making each other cry." I sniffed, trying to be quiet about it.

Dylan's arm around me tightened as he was wiping his face. Then he lifted his head and looked up at me; his eyes were melting as they met mine. "Sunshine..." I tried to look anywhere else, but his hands cradled my face, his thumbs wiping my cheeks, forcing me to look him in the eye. "Why are you crying?" he asked, his voice soft and so gentle it made my heart skip a beat.

"Me? Cry? No. This is just a reaction to your cologne; yeah, I'm allergic to it. You need to change it immediately." I patted his chest and tried to move.

His hands went to my arms, his grip holding me still. "No bullshit with me, Lexie." His voice was soft, but his eyes were firm as he looked at me. "Why are you crying?"

I sighed. "When someone I care about is in pain or cries, I cry too," I answered quietly.

One of his hands moved to my throat, his thumb stroking along my jaw. His eyes were soft and warm when he pulled me down so his lips could brush against mine. Then he was kissing me, slowly, sweetly. His lips moved over mine, making my heart race; that warmth poured through me. With his hand on my neck, it felt so good I made a small noise in the back of my throat. His lips pressed harder against mine, taking my breath away. His lips took my lower lip, and he nipped it with his teeth before diving back in to kiss me again.

My stomach did that low, hard flip as the kiss changed. His mouth moved hungrily over mine; that was fine. I was kissing him the same way. I barely parted my lips before he was there. He dipped in and drove any thought I had away. There was only Dylan, his mouth on mine and the warmth running through me. I only knew I needed to keep kissing him. Had to keep kissing him. Need drove me to kiss him desperately. I shifted against him. I couldn't help it; the way he kissed me made me want to move. He moaned against my mouth, his arm crushing me against him. He felt so amazing that I didn't want to stop. My mind washed away on a wave of pure feeling; that warmth started growing hotter. We were both breathing heavy, but neither one of us seemed to care. He kissed me deeper, harder. My hips moved again; I was barely aware of it. He made a noise in the back of his throat, his hand sliding down to the small of my back, leaving sparks along my spine. The world was fuzzy, and all I knew was Dylan, his kiss, his touch...

Then a phone rang. The sound brought us both back to earth. We both eased back from the kiss. He kissed me softly one more time before he pulled away. His hands moved to my hips as I leaned back from him, my hands resting on his chest. I was trying to remember how to breathe as he shifted against me to reach his back pocket. I caught my breath as he pressed against me, sparks shot through me. His hand on my hip squeezed, letting me know that he had heard me. He pulled his phone out as I tried to focus.

He swallowed hard before answering. "Yeah?" His voice sounded normal, and I didn't know how since he was breathing just as heavily as I was. His eyes ran over my face, still full of heat.

I focused on brushing my hair out of my face before I thought about how that look made me instantly want to kiss him again. Cool down Lexie, pull back. What the fuck just happened? Oh, I knew what had just happened, but I was trying to remember how it started. My mind was still scattered and fuzzy, making it hard to think. I leaned against him, my forehead dropping to his shoulder as I focused on trying to get my brain working again. His arm slipped around me, his hand slowly running up and down my back.

"Dad, no." Dylan's voice was sharp. "I'm not coming in; call Mason." My heart sank, he was going to have to go to work. I gave a quiet growl in frustration. "Dad, I'm out with Lexie. She came up from Spring Mountain today. Remember, I told you about it last night?" Dylan's voice grew softer when he said my name; it wasn't by much, but I heard it. I smiled into his shirt. "Yeah, call Mason; he needs the cash to fix his stereo system." He sighed. "Okay, bye."

Dylan hung up the phone and dropped it onto the couch. His kissed my shoulder before moving my hair away from my face. "Sorry about that, Sunshine." I snorted. I owed Dylan's dad a huge thank you. Otherwise, we might have gone too far and not even noticed it. Or cared. I probably wouldn't have cared... until later. Dylan just seemed to have that effect on me.

"Don't worry about it," I mumbled, enjoying his hand in my hair. His nose stroked along my ear.

"You okay?" he whispered softly.

I snorted. "Yeah, peachy." I sat up and went still, the shifting he did to get to his phone had kept him pressed against me. Hot shivers ran through me. I made a point not to move for him. "Your dad has incredible timing."

He snorted. "Doesn't he?" he asked sarcastically. I chuckled. He reached up and brushed more hair from my face as his eyes narrowed on mine. "So, you cry when other people cry." He smiled warmly at me.

"Yeah," I said suspiciously.

"Is that why you don't watch tragic romance movies?" he guessed, his eyes lighting up. "They make you cry."

Shit. I smacked his chest and pointed at him. "You will take my secret to the grave, and beyond," I told him firmly. "Or I'll... do something to get even." I really had nothing prepared, no idea how to blackmail him. I was really at his mercy here, and I didn't like it.

He smiled warmly at me. "You really do have a big heart."

I rolled my eyes. I was getting tired of hearing that. I did not. I was a mean bitch who would rip off your head if I had to. Okay, I knew that wasn't entirely true, but fuck. It would be so much easier if it were.

"Promise me." I hated how girly that plea was, but I wasn't letting him out of this without a promise. He started laughing. "Fuck this. I'm leaving. Nope, not waiting around for that bombshell." I went to move off his lap.

Dylan's arms snagged me around the waist and kept me where I was. Then his hands shifted down to my hips. I glared at him. His laughing was fading away now. His warm, sparkling eyes met mine. "I promise I'll never tell anyone, ever, that tragic love stories make you cry," he assured me.

I narrowed my eyes at him. "Or write it down, or record it in any fashion?" I wanted to be a hundred percent on this.

He smiled at me. "Or write it down, or record it in any fashion. I promise." His eyes were running over my face again. I was starting to wonder if I had ketchup or something on me.

"Okay. You can live," I grumbled as I rested my hands back on his chest.

He snickered. "Thank you, merciful one."

I snorted as I smiled at him. I looked at his handsome face, those cute cheeks, that jaw. Ugh. "You're too cute for your own good," I told him, shaking my head.

His eyebrows rose. "Oh, I'm too cute? Lexie…" He paused, smiling up at me. "I see you, and all I can think is 'What is this beautiful girl doing with me? And how am I gonna keep her?'" My face warmed and tried to fight it. Yeah, it was no good. "I love making you blush like that."

I rolled my eyes and went to climb off his lap. He gave my hips as squeeze before letting go. I moved back to my spot next to him, with his arm around me, and my head on his chest, again. The movie was almost over.

His lips rested on top of my head. He took a deep breath. "Mmm… rosemary. I love that smell."

I smiled. "You like the rosemary, huh?"

He snorted into my hair. His arm gave me a squeeze. "I think it has more to do with the person wearing it, Sunshine," he mumbled before kissing my hair. He had a point.

"That must be true; I never liked sandalwood till I met you," I admitted, keeping my eyes on the movie as my face warmed again. He laughed quietly. We cuddled in comfortable silence as we watched the rest of the film, then the next one that came on after. I was just happy to be with him. With his body heat and his arm around me, I started to drift to sleep. I didn't think to fight it.

"Sunshine?" he whispered against my hair.

"Hmm?" I was half asleep already.

"Do you trust me?" His soft husky voice had an edge of uncertainty.

I smiled sleepily. "Yep," I mumbled rubbing my cheek against his chest. I was still half asleep when I asked him. "You trust me?"

"Yeah."

I smiled happily and fell deeper into sleep.

THE SOUND of a door slamming shut jerked me awake. I opened my eyes and looked around. What the...? I saw the TV, the windows. I was at Dylan's. I looked next to me to find Dylan stretching and blinking hard, trying to wake up too. Heavy footsteps came into the living room.

"Dylan!" Thomas' voice had me really opening my eyes to see him walking out of the foyer. "You've got your hot girlfriend alone in your house, and you took a nap?" Dylan's body tensed next to me. I flipped Thomas off just as the others walked into the living room. The others chuckled.

"If my girl's exhausted? Yeah," Dylan shot back before getting to his feet. I scooted over to take his spot as he headed for Thomas.

Jake slipped around the guys then plopped down next to me, putting his feet on the coffee table.

Jake looked at me, smiling. "Hey cutie, now tell me honestly. Is Asher as hot in person as he looks on the field?" My eyebrows went up at the unexpected question. Before I could answer, Dylan had Thomas in a headlock and was pulling him towards the kitchen.

"Remember that rule about girlfriends?" Dylan growled as he pulled the larger guy toward the kitchen.

"Fuck! Shit!" Thomas cursed as he tried to get out of the headlock. Derrick, Aaron, and Luke went to help pull him towards the kitchen. "I forgot! I'm sorry!"

The others were laughing their asses off. I looked at Jake, who was grinning.

"Thomas checked you out, then called you hot," he explained, smiling. "You check out your friend's girl then talk about it, you get dunked."

"What's so bad about that? It's water," I asked, not seeing the punishment.

Jake chuckled. "It's outside in the rain barrel." I burst out laughing as he added, "Waist deep."

"I'll take two! Option two!" Thomas was yelling from the kitchen.

I looked at Jake, who was still snickering. "What's option two?" I asked, smiling.

"You get to punch or kick him," Jake said simply.

I started laughing. As I tried to control myself, the boys were talking in the kitchen.

"Are you sure you want option two?" Dylan asked carefully.

My face was red as I kept cracking up. Jake looked at me questioningly.

"I train in MMA fighting," I told him before laughing again

Jake's eyes went wide before he got to his feet fast. "Take one, man! Trust me! Take one!" Jake shouted into the kitchen, laughing. Dylan cursed.

"Why?" Thomas' voice was hesitant.

I got to my feet and followed Jake to the kitchen.

The guys had the back door open with Thomas almost out the door. "Why do I want one?" Thomas repeated.

I gave him a big smile before looking at Dylan who gave me a half grin.

"You never told them what my hobbies were, did you, baby?"

Dylan shook his head. "Nope," Dylan said, grinning.

I chuckled.

Thomas kept looking between the two of us. "What hobbies?" Thomas asked, his voice worried.

I looked at him and smiled sweetly. "I train with the guys in Mixed Martial Arts."

Everyone but Thomas and Dylan burst out laughing. Thomas went a little pale. I just kept smiling sweetly.

"So, she knows how to throw a punch and make it hurt," Dylan pointed out.

"Or a kick," I said helpfully.

Thomas' eyes went out to the snow outside then back to me. His eyes narrowed. "Where would you hit me?" Thomas asked suspiciously.

"I'd probably give it over to Dylan," I admitted. "He's the one pissed at you."

Thomas looked at Dylan, frowning. "No balls hit?" Thomas offered hopefully.

Dylan glared at him. "No balls hit," Dylan agreed.

Thomas sighed then nodded. The guys let go of him and backed away. Dylan actually grinned as Thomas braced himself. Dylan stood in front of him, cocked his fist back and swung. The sound of flesh striking flesh was loud. Thomas spun and caught himself on the counter. He hissed, then cursed through the pain.

Dylan's face was dark as he stepped up next to Thomas. "You say something like that to her again, and I'll kick your ass," he growled under his breath as he rubbed his knuckles.

I raised an eyebrow. Jake took my arm and pulled me back into the great room.

"He was really pissed off," I mumbled. I hadn't really expected Dylan to be that angry about it.

"Yeah, Dylan has a bit of a temper." Jake snickered. "Thomas had a choice, and he chose the punch."

I shook my head. I would have taken the dunking. I sat back down with Jake next to me.

"So, about Asher. Tell me."

I snorted. "Yes, he's very yummy," I admitted then pointed at him. "I said nothing."

He snickered as he leaned back on the couch, putting his feet up on the coffee table again. "Can you get me some pics? Please?" he begged with big eyes.

I snickered. "No, how would..." Then I thought about it. Summer was coming in a few months. "Can you wait 'till summer?"

Jake's face lit up. "Hell yeah."

I giggled as I nodded. "I'll hook you up, sweetie," I agreed. We fist bumped.

"Yes!" Then he was looking at me. "Now, how about Isaac?"

I burst out laughing. "You get one picture," I told him, smiling. "Pick a guy."

He sighed. "I don't know; Asher's hot, but I usually go for the tall, lean ones," he admitted.

I snorted. "Then that's Miles." I looked over the couch to make sure the guys were still in the kitchen then turned back around. "He's ripped too."

Jake's green eyes went wide. "Really?" Jake said, smiling.

"State swim champion," I told him. Jake made an appreciative face. "He doesn't look it, I know."

Jake raised both eyebrows hopefully. "Tell me he's gay," he begged.

I chuckled. "Nope. Sorry."

He groaned painfully. "That's why I hate these towns. Not a lot of gay guy options." He sighed. "Especially if you're not flamboyantly gay. It's hard for the ones in the closet to tell without a sign over my head."

I wrapped my arm around his. "Sorry, sweetie, but I'll keep my eye out," I offered.

Jake smiled at me. "Okay, I'm keeping you," he declared before shouting. "In the event of a breakup, I get Lexie!" The guys in the kitchen laughed. I smiled. I decided I was going to keep Jake too.

"Do you have trouble with the football team? Being gay and all?" I asked, curious about it.

He snorted. "Nah; it was an issue at first, then I told them all they are too ugly for my taste." I snickered. "Hasn't been a problem since. But I do make a point not to shower with them after a game; that would make them too uncomfortable." His eyes narrowed on me. "So, all your friends are guys?" I nodded. "You know, I think that means you're supposed to be a lesbian." I burst out laughing. Jake just waited for an answer.

I shook my head. "Nope, I think guys are hot." I gestured with my hand towards the kitchen. "Particularly that one."

"Ew," Jake said as he cringed.

"He's got a great ass," I defended my guy.

"Ew, stop it. That's Dylan," Jake pointed out, his voice pained. "I've known him since we were kids." I just smiled at him. "So, why guys?"

I sighed. "Because if they are pissed at you, they tell you. There isn't that guessing game. I'm not really good with subtle," I said honestly.

He nodded. "Yeah, I don't get that either," he admitted.

I smiled at him. I was so keeping Jake. I narrowed my eyes at him. "Do you like shopping?"

OVER THE NEXT THREE HOURS, I got to know Dylan's friends. Even Thomas with a fresh black eye. Derrick was a musician, classical piano, who just got into Juilliard. Aaron was a wrestler for the high school team. Luke loved books, which I understood completely. Thomas was into carpentry. And Jake. My favorite was Jake. Jake was a writer or planning to be one. I immediately asked to read some of his stories, and he emailed me a couple from his phone. The big quarterback wasn't very effeminate, but he did know his clothes. He was now my designated shopping buddy. I had a feeling shopping would be more fun with him than with Tara. I mentioned Winter Formal coming up, and he demanded that we switch phone numbers. He was going to help me find a dress perfect for me. I was *so* keeping Jake. Try and stop me.

We were busy playing a racing game against the others when the doorbell rang. Dylan got up to answer. I was focused on fucking up

Aaron's lead. I finally nudged him to spin out when there was a bark.

"Lexie!" I looked up to see Zeke and Riley standing near the end of the couch.

I shot him a look, then went back to trying to get past the others. "What?!" I shot back.

"Did you get a nap?" Zeke growled.

"Fuck you, I'm not two," I countered. The guys chuckled around me as Dylan sat back down next to me.

"She got about two hours before everyone came over," Dylan assured Zeke. I rolled my eyes as I kept pushing Aaron off the track.

"Lexie! Come on!" Aaron groaned.

"No! You won the last five, and it's time someone else got to." I grinned as I kept knocking him off the track.

"You're not going to win like that," Aaron warned me.

I snickered. "Not trying to," I countered. Aaron cursed. I chuckled as Thomas sped past us and across the finish line first. I threw my arms up in victory. "Yes!" The guys burst out laughing.

"Okay, she's just adorable," Jake said, smiling.

"I'm not adorable; I'm an annoying bitch with a huge attitude problem," I reminded him.

"You're that too," Zeke groused. The guys watched us. I looked over at Zeke and stuck my tongue out at him. He smirked.

"Pot, kettle, black. Ring a bell, tall and oh so grumpy one?" I shot back matter-of-factly. Zeke chuckled along with everyone else. I looked up at Riley. "Can you please remove the stick from Zeke's ass, and beat him with it?" The guys burst out laughing, and even Riley laughed at that one.

"Okay guys, it's time for photos," Dylan announced. All Dylan's friends jumped up and made a run for the door. Jake paused to hug me and tell me he'd talk to me later before he ran after the others. I laughed the whole time.

I looked at Dylan. "They really are tired of having their photos taken," I said, a bit surprised.

Dylan nodded, smiling at me. "Yeah, they are," he admitted.

"I guess I should go wash my face and do my makeup again," I groused. I looked up at Dylan. "Where's your bathroom?"

He smirked at me. "I'll show you two." Dylan got to his feet and held out his hand; I took it, and he pulled me to my feet. I stopped to grab my bag, Riley picked up hers, and we followed Dylan upstairs.

There were only three doors on this floor. Dylan stopped and opened the one on the right. "This is the hall bathroom." Then he walked directly across from it and opened the other. "Here's my bedroom; there's a bathroom inside to the left." He looked inside and paused. "Shit, hold on. Let me put some stuff away," he mumbled as he hurried inside.

That made me curious, so I peeked through the door. He had just put a book away high on a black shelf; then he went around the room, picking up clothes here and there. He didn't want me to see his room a mess. It was kind of adorable. I leaned out of the doorway and waited. Riley raised an eyebrow at me. I gave her a 'what' look. We both giggled.

"Okay, come on in."

I walked into his now clean room and looked around. All his furniture was black. From the wall of built-in bookshelves that were packed with books to the long built in desk that ran below them. Even his dresser, bed, and nightstand were black. I was kind of jealous of his room. He had a double bed with a dark blue comforter, which he was now making as fast as possible.

I looked to Riley. "Okay, what does it say about me that I'm jealous of my boyfriend's bedroom?" I asked, only half kidding. Dylan chuckled as he finished making the bed.

Riley looked around, smiling. "What does it say about me when *I'm* jealous of your boyfriend's bedroom?" she asked me back. I hemmed and hawed. Dylan went to his laptop and closed it before turning back to us.

"I'm going to say it's normal for both of us," I offered.

Riley nodded. "Sounds good to me," Riley agreed. We both smiled.

I turned to Dylan. "Want to double check the bathroom?" I asked, half kidding.

He was still for a second. Then he headed to the closed bathroom door. We burst out laughing. "Hey, I'm trying to be nice here," Dylan shot out at us.

I calmed down first. "I know honey, but it's your room. You live in it, and it's going to get messy," I pointed out, going to his bed and dropping my bag onto it. Riley followed.

"Is yours?" he countered.

I sighed. "Well, you can't really count my room as normal," I hedged, opening my bag and looking for my makeup kit.

"Why's that?" he asked, coming back into the bedroom with a couple shirts and towels that he threw into the hamper.

I was still looking for my makeup when I answered, not really thinking about it. "Because it's the first bedroom I've had since my mother lost the house." I finally just started pulling shit out of my bag. Please tell me I packed it.

"Sunshine, what do you mean?" Dylan's soft voice grabbed my attention. I looked up to find him frowning at me.

"We lived in a travel trailer," I told him, going back to what I was doing. "One bedroom. I slept on the pullout bed for five years. I'm used to cleaning up after myself." I pulled out my hair dryer and put it to the side, then I realized it was quiet. I looked up to see them both staring at me strangely. "What?" I ran over what I just said in my head. Oh, fuck. "Guys, it was what it was." They were looking at me with fucking pity. I hated that. "The only weird thing was how happy and excited I was to have a bedroom door when I got to Rory's." Riley snorted. Dylan grinned at me. I finally found my makeup kit. "Of course, the makeup was on the bottom," I grumbled. Riley was pulling out her clothes.

"All right, I'll leave you girls to do... whatever it is you girls do," he announced. Before he left, he gave me a soft, quick kiss that made me catch my breath. He closed the door behind him.

I exhaled hard. "That boy can fucking kiss." I didn't care if I said it out loud.

Riley giggled. "How's it going with him?" She asked, smiling. I felt my face turning red. Her eyes got big. "Oh spill, I need to hear this."

I made my own quiet giggle. "We're doing great, but we have a slight problem." I looked at her and told her honestly. "The chemistry, oh my God."

Riley's eyes grew wide. "Oh, it's like that huh?" She grinned.

I nodded. "Yeah, so I'm going to end up not kissing him as much I want to. Or as long as I want to. We just kinda keep going..." I couldn't seem to stop smiling. This was so weird to me. I looked at her. "Please don't leave us alone in this house again."

Riley burst out laughing and nodded. "You can always try what I do," she offered. "Don't shave your legs or under your arms, so you have to behave."

I thought about that. "Does it work?"

She nodded. "Zeke is one hell of a kisser." Riley blushed. I cringed. "Sorry, I know he's your friend."

"It's fine. It's just... Zeke," I said, looking at my clothes. I was trying to decide if I was going to change into my Vegabond clothes or not when Riley got my attention.

"Okay, I have to ask," Riley began. I looked up at her. "I know you're not into Zeke, alright." I rose an eyebrow at her. "I'm not asking for those bitches either. But, all your friends are hot. Do you even see that? Does it even occur to you?"

I took a deep breath. I had admitted it to Jake; I could tell her the truth too. "Okay, I'll tell you the truth, but don't tell any of the guys, or those bitches they're dating."

"Promise," Riley assured me.

"Yes, I see how hot they are. I see how good looking the guys are. I frequently enjoy the eye candy. And I often have to force myself to look away when one of them has no shirt on." My face burned. "But honestly, there has never been that spark that you feel towards someone you want to date. No butterflies and no racing heartbeat that tells you to go for it." I shrugged. "I have to have those if I'm going to try to date someone. I have a hard enough time opening up to people as it is, so if I'm going to open up, it's going to be with someone who makes my heart race."

"And if that changes one day?" Riley asked, smirking.

"Just on my side?" She nodded. "I'd keep my mouth shut and wait it out," I told her adamantly.

She chuckled. "And if it's not just on your side?"

I thought about it. "Oh man, then I'd probably fall so hard and so fast that the thud would be heard for miles," I admitted. She laughed. "They are great guys. And I do care about them. Just not that way."

"Unless something changes the way you look at them," Riley pointed out.

I groaned. "My boyfriend is downstairs, and he gets my sense of humor like no one I've ever met. He's sweet, fucking hot, and he doesn't get upset when I don't act like other girls. In fact, he loves it," I told her honestly. "Right now, I'm trying hard not to fall for him too soon."

Riley snorted. "Oh honey, Dylan has already taken that fall," she said in a knowing voice.

Huh? What? What is she talking about? "Why do you say that?" I asked carefully, my heart racing.

She smirked at me. "The way he looks at you when you're not looking," Riley said bluntly.

Oh hell, no. I needed more. "Keep talking, woman," I demanded.

She snickered. "Lexie, he looks at you like you're the only girl in the world." She smiled when my mouth dropped open. "When he was coming through the crowd today, his face was drawn and actually kind of sad. Then he saw you, his eyes lit up, and he had that smile." Warmth filled my chest, and it was starting to make me worried about the cause. "And it didn't stop, not until Trisha pulled that shit."

"Fuck."

She raised an eyebrow at me.

"I'm not good with the love stuff," I explained.

"Better get used to it, honey, cause that boy has it bad for you," Riley said earnestly.

I made a slight panicked sound as I took my makeup kit and went into the small bathroom. Riley was laughing as I closed the door. I used the hand soap to wash my face, and patted my face dry with the clean hand towel. I reapplied my make up as I went over what Riley was saying. Did Dylan really fall in love with me already? The butterflies were going crazy. Did I love him? Or was this hormones because he's a good kisser and…. no. He makes me laugh too much for it to be that. Shit. I took a deep breath as I started my eyeliner. I liked him a whole lot. Seeing him made my day better. Hell, talking with him on the phone did that. But did I love him? Or was I just not there yet? Okay, let's try this from a different side. I started on my eyeshadow. If Dylan disappeared tomorrow would I be devastated? No. But I would have a hard time. I sighed. That told me everything I needed to know. I wasn't in love with him yet, but I was fucking getting there. Shit. I finished up my makeup and brushed my hair. That was about all I was willing to do for practice photos. I headed back into the bathroom to see Riley had changed her clothes.

"Bathroom's all yours," I announced.

"Thanks." She picked up her makeup and headed into the bathroom. I decided to snoop and looked at Dylan's book shelves. There were several pee-wee football trophies, a few academic awards, and tons of books on just about every subject I could imagine. I smiled. I was dating a closet nerd. Awesome. I giggled to myself. Okay, I was done snooping. "I'm heading downstairs. I'll close the door behind me," I told Riley.

"Okay."

I headed out into the hall and closed the door behind me. I came downstairs to find the guys in the living room. Dylan was going through a camera bag. Zeke was sitting in the recliner.

"Riley's almost ready, I think," I said, walking in and sitting next to Dylan. "What'cha doing?"

He smiled without looking up from the bag. "I am going through my camera bag to make sure I have enough memory cards for today," he said absently.

I figured I'd leave him alone, so I didn't distract him. I grabbed my shoes and socks and started pulling them on.

"I'm not ignoring you, Sunshine. I'm just thinking."

I looked up at him from tying my shoes. He was watching the screen on the back of the camera.

"I... didn't think you were," I told him honestly before going back to tie my boots. "I just figured you were concentrating." I sat back up and curled up in the corner.

Zeke snorted.

"What?" I asked not getting the joke.

"Dylan, Lexie is the most reasonable girl I've ever met. She's not going to get mad if you're busy," Zeke said, smirking.

I rolled my eyes at him.

Dylan had a half grin on his face. "That's one of the things I like most about her," he admitted, still distracted. "Yeah, I need to get a few fresh memory cards." He set the camera down on the coffee table and got up.

"Can I look at your photos?" I asked sweetly.

Dylan picked up the camera and handed it to me. "Just don't delete anything," he said before going to another part of the house.

I looked at the screen and started snooping happily. I found the portraits, and he was amazing. Some were posed, but the great ones were when the person didn't know they were being photographed. One girl was sitting on a bench; her blue eyes were sad as she looked off to the left side of the frame. I didn't know why, but I didn't think she knew he was still taking pictures or had started. I flipped to the next one; it was a forest landscape. There were a lot of nature photos, and they were kind of cool. I flipped through them. They were all taken in the fall. I found a group photo and smiled. Dylan was standing with Derrick in a headlock under his arm. I smiled as I kept looking. There was another photo with an interesting rock formation. I went to the next one.

"What do you think?"

I jumped, clutching the camera in both hands, so I didn't drop it. I looked up at Dylan who was smirking down at me.

"Make some noise, man," I said loudly. He chuckled. "I like some of your nature photographs, but I think you really have a knack for portraits. You don't get the stiff, posed ones; everyone I've seen looked comfortable and natural." His eyes warmed as they met mine. "But that's just me, and I don't know anything about photography so-" He bent down and kissed me gently. My pulse kicked up a notch. Then he was standing back up with his camera in his hands, that grin still on his face. I just smiled at him as he moved back to his bag. I watched as he put three more memory cards into the bag. "How many photos are you planning on taking there, hon?"

He smiled. "With you here? As many as I can get away with," he admitted, putting his camera in his bag and zipping it closed. The butterflies just didn't stop. He looked up and met my eyes; then he winked at me. Shit, I was going to be in trouble soon. Thankfully, Riley came downstairs then to save me from embarrassing myself.

"I'm ready to go," Riley announced.

Oh, thank God.

WE WERE at a park next to a river. Everything was covered in snow. So, naturally, I threw a snowball at Zeke; I got him on the back of the neck. He glared at me and went to make his own.

"No snowballs until the photos are done," Dylan declared.

I stuck my tongue out at Zeke. Zeke smirked and started making snowballs. Oh shit, I didn't think that through. Maybe I could hide behind Riley. I looked over to her. She was smirking as she nodded. I hurried over to her side. I wasn't going too far from her until the photos were done. Then I'd hide behind her.

"Okay, who's going first?"

I pointed at Riley. "I already have awesome photos; do hers," I suggested.

Zeke snickered. "That means you have to move away from her, Lexie," Zeke pointed out.

I looked up at Riley. "Group photos?"

Everyone burst out laughing. I sighed, accepting my fate as I walked over to wait with Zeke. We watched and walked a bit back from the others as Dylan found a spot he liked and started talking to Riley as he snapped photos occasionally.

Riley looked a little tense. Her posture was rigid. He began asking her about what she was passionate about, what she loved to do. Riley apparently was big into snowboarding. I watched as Dylan asked her questions about it and asked her to tell him what she loved about it. Riley started to relax. As she relaxed, her eyes glowed, and she had a beautiful smile as she kept talking about snowboarding.

"Huh." Zeke made a noise.

I looked up at him. "What?"

Zeke tilted his chin at Dylan. "He's good, did you see what he did?" he asked.

I smiled. "Yep, got her talking so she'd relax."

"And got her talking about her favorite thing in the world. She always lights up like a Christmas tree when she talks about snowboarding," he said.

"And speaking of Christmas trees, we're still decorating Miles' house on Monday, right?" I asked, looking around the deserted park. There wasn't much to see; the whole place was covered in thick snow.

"Yeah, Miles just wants family only." Zeke was frowning. He looked down to me. "He's been acting off the last few days; did you notice anything?"

I nodded. "He almost cursed in front me today. Twice," I offered.

Both Zeke's eyebrows went sky high. "That's not good," he said, frowning again.

"If you guys show up an hour late, I might be able to find out why," I offered. I could usually get Miles to talk; I just had to be a little girly.

"Okay, I'll tell the others to give you an hour," he agreed.

We went back to watching. Dylan was clicking more photos; every once in a while, he'd tell Riley to turn this way or make a certain kind of face. I smiled. I had a feeling they were going to be great photos. I went snooping.

"What are you getting Riley for Christmas?" I asked him.

Zeke sighed. "I have no clue," he admitted. "What do girls like?"

"Has she mentioned anything she wanted to try or needed to replace?"

Zeke thought about that. Then he nodded. "Snowboarding gloves; she's been tearing hers up."

"There you go; sneak measure her hand in yours, then go shopping while it's fresh." I smiled as Dylan got a good shot of Riley standing in front of a snow bank.

"Good idea, Lexie."

I eyed him. Yeah, I was going to ask again. "I'm going shopping with Riley for your presents." Zeke turned to look at me, one eyebrow arched. "Can you give me an idea? Something you'd like from her, at least?"

Zeke's eyes unfocused as he thought about it. Then he was back. "Wool socks." His voice was completely serious.

"You want socks?" I couldn't believe that was his answer.

He nodded. "Wool socks in my size are hard to find, and I'm always in the garage. There isn't much heat in there," he said, looking back out at the others. Well, when he said it like that, it made sense.

"What size?"

"14 ½."

"Damn Zeke. You got some big feet." I smiled as I teased him.

He snorted. "I'm a big guy, Lexie. Big feet are part of the package." He pointed out. "What are you getting Dylan?"

"You know his mom died, right?" I looked up at Zeke, and he nodded. "She made these awesome cookies at Christmas. I'm going to try and use her recipes for him and his dad." My stomach knotted as I really thought about it. What if I fucked them up? It'd be funny, but Dylan still wouldn't have those cookies back.

"You don't know how to bake do you?" Zeke asked, smirking at me.

"Not a bit," I admitted. Zeke burst out laughing. I couldn't help but chuckle too. I was so screwed. "Think Asher would help?"

"I think he's going to need to." He snickered.

I sighed. He was probably right, but now I had an idea for Zeke's present. My mind went to my other hard-to-buy-for guy. "Any idea what I can get Miles?" I asked. Zeke gave me a look, so I explained. "I'm seriously drawing a blank. He has tons of shirts with equations on them so I can't get him one of those, and he can buy anything he wants."

"What do you get someone who has everything?" he asked, giving me a half smile. I nodded. He thought about it for a bit. Then he smirked and looked down at me again. "Get him something you can't buy." I raised an eyebrow at that. "You're an artist, Lexie," he reminded me. "And you've never given anything you've made to any of us before." He had a point.

I just… I was never happy with the finished piece. I always needed to start over again. Then an idea formed. I smiled. "Thanks, Zeke, I think I know exactly what I'm going to make him." As I thought about it, I liked the idea even more.

"It's not cookies, is it?" he asked dryly.

I snorted a laugh and playfully glared at him. Did Zeke just make a joke? Wow. That was a first. "No." I watched Dylan making Riley laugh and snapped more pictures. "I don't know why I offered. I'm just going fuck them up," I groused.

Zeke's reached over and wrapped his hand around the back of my neck, his fingers massaging. I always loved when he did that; affection from Zeke was rare. "You have a big heart, Baby," he whispered.

I rolled my eyes. "No, I don't. I'm a mean, cranky bitch who will rip someone's head off without a thought," I countered vehemently. He burst out laughing as he looked down at me.

"You're that too," he admitted, still laughing. I just smiled up at him and waited till he was done. By then Dylan was done with Riley's photos and was waving me over. I shook my head, my stomach in knots.

"Nope, I'm good," I yelled to him. Dylan wanting to take my picture made me feel… nervous and warm all at the same time. It was a weird feeling.

"So, we can have a snowball fight now?" Zeke asked mischievously.

"On second thought, who can't use more photos?" I said nonchalantly as I moved through the snow towards Dylan. Zeke's booming laugh taunted me. I passed Riley on her way to Zeke.

"Your guy is sweet," she whispered to me.

"I managed to get a gift idea out of Zeke," I whispered back. "It's all yours."

Her eyes lit up. "You are the best," she whispered before turning and heading to Zeke.

I walked up to Dylan and smiled awkwardly. He grinned down at me. "Okay, let's do this," I said nervously.

Dylan's eyes ran over me. "I've got a different spot in mind for you. It wouldn't have worked for Riley, but it will for you."

He took my hand and led me to another path and further into the park. We walked until we came to a spot next to the river surrounded by thin birch trees. We walked off the path. Dylan positioned me where he wanted me; standing in the trees with the river to the right.

"Okay, I want to take a couple with your hood up like last night."

I reached back and flipped my hood up like it was last night. He pulled some of my hair forward so that it was lying against the black coat. This was so strange. I hadn't really had my picture taken in the last five years, well, except last night.

He smiled and stepped back a couple of steps. "Okay, Sunshine, give me that same look from last night." He smiled as he brought up the camera. I did as he asked. And he started clicking away. "Sunshine, tell me about why you want to be a tattoo artist."

I gave him a warm smile; I knew what he was doing, and I went with it. "People have a lot of big important events in their lives. Some good, some bad, some ugly. I like that you can have something in your skin permanently to show that it happened, to represent it." I stopped posing, looked at the river, and I ignored the clicking. "It's like showing everyone this is who I am, this is what shaped me, and I'm not going to hide it. So, fuck off." He smiled behind his camera. "And when it's a painful event, you can put something on your body that reminds you that you lived through it, you survived it. You are still here. And that means there is hope." I smiled as I remembered something Zeke once told me. "Some days just being alive is the best you get, but there's always tomorrow." When he didn't give me any instructions, I just kept talking. "The hope that tomorrow will be a better day." I shrugged, my hood fell off. I went to put it back.

"Leave it, Sunshine. I have enough of those. Keep telling me why you like tattooing." His voice was that soft husky one that made the butterflies go crazy.

"Then you have memorial tattoos. The fact that someone affected you so much that you put a permanent reminder of them on your body is.... beautiful." I looked down at the snow and leaned against one of the pole like trees. "Pretty much, it's the idea that everyone has shit inside that they deal with. But someone has the guts to put it out there where everyone can see and judge." I looked at him. "That's amazing to me. Someone is showing themselves that way, and not caring what others think about it."

"I thought you don't care what other people think about you?" he asked, moving to the right, getting another angle, taking more photos.

I looked down at the snow. "I don't. But sometimes it crops up. Like with the guy's girlfriends. I wanted to get along with them, and that made me care what they thought." I sighed. "Then it turned out they were bitches, and I didn't give a shit again." I bit the corner of my bottom lip as I thought about it. "I know I should care, but I only really care about what the people I care about think of me," I admitted. Why was I telling him this? I already knew that answer. Because he was Dylan, and I felt like I could tell him anything. I watched him taking pictures of me.

"Stop looking at the camera, Sunshine," he chided me playfully.

I smiled. "What else am I supposed to do? Just stand here?" I asked seriously, wanting to know. This was so weird to me.

"How about you tell me about your dad?"

My chest tightened a bit. I swallowed hard. Did I want to talk about this? I don't know. I didn't mind talking about certain things. "He was a firefighter in Albuquerque, New Mexico. He read me The Hobbit at bedtime, then The Rings trilogy, Twenty-thousand Leagues Under the Sea, and so many others, I can't even remember them all. But since he was a firefighter, he couldn't be home every night." I smiled, looking out at the snow as I remembered him. "So, on the nights he couldn't be home, he'd call and read to me over the phone. A chapter a night, unless there was a cliffhanger; then he knew I'd never get to sleep without knowing what happened." Dylan kept clicking away. "He was always making me laugh. There wasn't a day that went by that I didn't crack up at something he did." I remembered something I loved about him. "He didn't care that I wasn't like normal little girls; that I wasn't into playing with dolls or playing dress up. Mom hated that about me. She was always trying to force me into a dress or to care about my hair." I snorted as I remembered Dad's response. "Mom would say, 'She needs to learn how to be a lady.' Dad would just look at her and say, 'There is more than one way to be a lady.' Mom wanted a little princess, and Dad just wanted me the way I was."

"What if you had been a princess girl?" Dylan asked, bringing my attention back to the present.

I smiled. "He would have played dress up with me and had tea parties," I said honestly. "That's just the way he was." I chuckled, remembering my eighth birthday. "Dad always asked me what I wanted. Did I want to learn to paint? Did I want dance classes?" I looked down at the snow, smiling. "For my eighth birthday, Mom wanted to invite all the girls from school over for a slumber party. Dad looked at me and asked me what I wanted to do that Saturday. I told him paintball, laser tag, and go carts."

Dylan chuckled, drawing my attention back to him. He was still clicking away. "And what happened on your birthday?" he asked smiling.

I laughed. "Mom and Dad compromised. Mom invited the whole class, even though most of them thought I was weird. And we all played laser tag and go carts." I looked up at Dylan. "Dad saved the paintball for the next day. He didn't trust that I wouldn't shoot a couple of the kids more than once." Dylan laughed. I smiled at him. "He wasn't wrong."

Dylan slowly sobered. "How did he die, Lexie?" he asked gently.

My chest burned immediately. "He was at a fire, and he was passing a three-year-old out the second story window to the guys on the ladder when the floor above caved in." Why did I answer that? I took a deep breath. "A massive support beam hit him in the head; he died instantly." I remembered walking through the ruins of that house and looking for his soul, just in case. I didn't want him stuck here. I still don't know if I was happy or sad that I didn't see him.

Okay, I needed a lighter topic, or I was going to cry. "Oh, and the other reason I like tattooing is because it's awesome; you're putting art onto someone that they will carry for the rest of their lives. It's kind of cool if you think about it." He lowered the camera and smiled at me. "Got enough?"

"Yeah, I got enough." He came over to me and tilted my chin up with his fingers. His sapphire eyes ran over my face. Then he leaned down and brushed his lips against mine. He didn't press down; he didn't come any closer. He just kissed me softly, gently. I melted like a puddle at his feet. He pulled back and smiled at me. "Sorry, I asked about your dad. It's just that you have this look you get when you think about something sad. I wanted to get a photo of it."

I raised an eyebrow. He hit buttons on the camera then stepped next to me to show me. I was looking to the left side of the picture, my hair blazing against the trees and jacket. My eyes were soft, sad; my mouth neither smiling or frowning. The whole picture screamed of loss. That this person had lost someone, and it still ached. It was an amazing picture; sad but amazing.

I looked up at him and smiled. "You are really good," I told him honestly.

He narrowed his eyes at me suspiciously. "You're not mad?"

"Nah, it got you what you needed," I said before looking around; it was getting dark. "Time to head back."

"Yeah, you might want to make some snowballs first," Dylan reminded me.

Shit, Zeke was going to kill me.

IN THE END, Riley ended up freezing, Zeke wasn't that bad off, and Dylan was covered. I, however, got away with just my sweater getting hit and ice down my back from Zeke. By the time we reached Dylan's house, Riley and Dylan were shivering. They ran upstairs to take showers and change into dry clothes. I ordered pizza and salad from the local pizza joint. Riley was quick in the shower and came downstairs in her clothes for Vegabond. I left the money with them and headed upstairs. My mind on other things, I went into Dylan's room, shut the door and pulled off my soaked sweater.

"Uh, Sunshine?" I jumped and turned to see Dylan sitting in his chair in the corner by his desk, wearing only black jeans. My eyes ran over him, my heart pounding in my chest. The guy had muscle. He wasn't as bulky as Asher. It was more like he had muscles from using them than from working out. The butterflies went crazy. His eyes were running over me, looking at me just as much as I was him. His eyes were warm when they met mine. "You really need to look around before you start taking your clothes off."

"I thought you were in the other bathroom," I admitted, going to my stuff on the bed. It wasn't like I was naked, I still had my jeans on and my cami.

"I was; I forgot a shirt," he said; his voice was soft. I looked over my shoulder to see his eyes running over me again. "I saw Riley leave, then I thought I'd put the photos onto the computer and got distracted."

I felt that flip low in my belly. The look on his face made my body grow warm. Shit. That damn chemistry. I tried to distract myself. But I was looking at his chest again and wondering what all that skin would feel like. Oh fuck, Lexie, move. I turned back to find my bathroom stuff fast. Shit, my stuff had gotten mixed up with Riley's.

"Sorry, I'll just…. um… get my stuff and…." I couldn't seem to form a sentence. I just kept my eyes on what I was doing. I stopped and took a deep breath then let it out slow. Find your bathroom stuff, and move. I needed to stay calm and not think about Dylan shirtless.

That's when he stepped behind me. I went still, my heart was racing as his hands went to my waist. I focused on breathing. After crying with him, and talking about my Dad, I really wanted to be close. To be held. But right now wasn't the time. I kept reminding myself of that as one of his hands slid across the front of my waist, his palm spreading wide over my stomach. I closed my eyes as my body leaned back against him, feeling his skin on mine. This was too soon.

This was not the time... Zeke and Riley were downstairs... I kept going over the reasons to grab a shirt and run into the bathroom. His body heat warmed my skin, making me want to just press myself against him. Okay, Lexie, move. Come on, move. No, don't let him do that... his lips brushed against my ear. My stomach flipped low and hard. Come on, body, help me out here.

I was about to move when he finally spoke.

"Sunshine..." His husky voice was soft and low.

It sent hot shivers down my spine to my toes. My body tingled.

Fuck it. I turned in his arms and kissed him. The room disappeared as he kissed me back, his lips moving with mine. My arms went around his neck; his hands were on my back, his fingers running over my skin. My chest smashed against his. My pulse was in my ears as the kiss changed. He swept in and took everything I had to give. He kissed me hungrily, desperately. His hands ran down my back to my butt, his fingers kneading. I made a soft sound against his mouth. This was Dylan, sweet, sexy, funny Dylan who just seemed to get me. Who made me feel beautiful just by looking at me. I kept kissing him; I couldn't seem to stop. And I really didn't want to.

His hands shifted, and he lifted me with his hands on my butt. Instinctively, I wrapped my legs around his waist. His hands slid to my thighs, holding me up as he moved. The world spun, then I something soft was under me, and all I could think was yeah, that works. His body pressed me into the mattress. His hips pressing against mine, my legs fell to the sides as he took some of his weight onto his elbows. I couldn't think as his tongue danced with mine. I, I needed to stop this. Right? Yeah, maybe. I, I needed to think. I pulled my mouth back from his. His lips moved to my cheek, leaving sweet, light kisses up my jaw. He made a path to my ear. It felt really fucking good. I was still trying to catch my breath when he reached my neck. Oh, shit. His lips brushed over that spot, an inch or so below my ear. My body moved against his, unable to stop myself from grinding against him. He growled against my throat, his hard body pressing flush against me. One of his hands ran up my side to my ribs. I groaned as he grazed that spot with teeth.

He was torturing me. I wanted to get even, make him as crazy as he was making me. I turned my head, my lips finding his neck. He growled against my throat, his hips moving against me, moving his hard groin against me. Sparks ran through me; my skin grew hot. Then he bit down on that spot. I made an eager noise as lightning shot through my body, my hips moving against his. I couldn't help it, the way he made my body feel made me need to move. His mouth was on mine again, pushing everything away, every thought, every worry. They were gone as long as he kept kissing me. He went back to my neck, that same fucking spot. Every nerve I had was alive and tingling. His mouth left hot kisses over my collar bone. His hand move to my shoulder, his fingers pulling my straps out of the way of his lips.

Alarm bells went off. I was suddenly aware where I was, what I was doing, and that I had only known Dylan for two months, and I'd been dating Dylan for only four fucking days. My body still wanted to keep going, but I knew we had to stop.

"Dylan...." I said, but my voice was too quiet. I swallowed hard and tried again. "Dylan... stop..." I managed between heavy breaths. Dylan stopped moving, his breath fanning out over the skin at my shoulder, his body tense. I couldn't move. If I moved, it wouldn't be to get further away from him. I held myself still as I tried to relearn to breathe.

"Sunshine.... don't move..." he managed between deep breaths. He must be having the same problem. "Please..."

"I was going.... to tell you... the same thing." I was getting my breath back, my mind was coming back, but my body still didn't want me to stop. Oh, this sucked. I needed a freezing cold shower. Neither one of us moved while we both struggled to get control back. I knew when he was okay. His body relaxed against me again.

"You good?" he asked, his voice was gentle and soft.

"Yeah," I whispered back. He didn't move off me, in fact, he lowered more of his weight onto me. His face was in the crook of my neck. I wrapped my arms around him, one hand playing with the hair at the back of his neck. It felt really good. Not strip-me-naked-now good. But good. His hips were still against mine; I still felt him there. It kept my heart racing.

"Just let me feel you for a bit, Sunshine," he whispered softly against my throat. "I'm not-"

"I know..." He just wanted to hold me like this a little longer. I knew how he felt. I felt the same way. He lifted his head and looked down at my face. His sapphire eyes were still shining with heat as they ran over my face. One of his hands came up to my face, his thumb running over my cheek bone. The look on his face took my breath away. He was looking at me like I was precious to him. Heat flooded my chest again, hard and fast.

"I only meant to kiss you once, Lexie, I..." he whispered to me, those beautiful eyes on mine. "I should have fucking left the second you came in."

I gave him a gentle smile. "I kissed you, remember?" I whispered back. "I should have put my sweater right back on."

"So, we were both stupid." He smiled down at me.

I smiled back. "We seem to do that a lot," I observed. He nodded. But I had another problem right now. "Hon, you're squishing me." He lifted his weight off me immediately, and laid down on his side next to me. My body missed the press of him instantly. Baaad body. I rolled to my side to face him, my fingers playing across his chest. He didn't seem to mind. His fingers were stroking my arm.

He swallowed hard, his eyes worried. "Lexie, are you okay with what just happened?" he whispered softly.

"I was right there with you. It's just..."

"Too fast. I know." He took a breath and let it out. "When it comes to you, all my thinking seems to go out the door," he whispered back.

I smiled at him, sure I was glowing. "Is that good or bad?" I asked, only half joking.

He exhaled hard. "Both?" he offered. I laughed softly. He didn't sound so sure about his answer. His eyes ran over my face, and his expression turned serious as he met my eyes again. "Sunshine, I don't want to go too fast with you," he whispered softly. "Anytime I've gone that fast with someone, it never went well. It never lasted long. And I really want you to stick around."

My heart melted and clenched in my chest all at the same time. "And I really want to stick around," I admitted to him.

He smiled a big smile again, making me feel light. My fingers found a scar on his chest; my fingers ran over it, memorizing the funny shape. His warm eyes stayed on mine; he took a deep breath and let it out slowly. His hand left my arm and caught mine against his chest, stopping my fingers.

I needed to distract myself. "So, maybe we need some rules."

"Like, no bedrooms alone?" he offered sincerely.

"Yeah, or house." I licked my lips and added. "And no voice in private."

He smiled. "Yeah, that's a good one." His eyes narrowed on mine. "Phone's fair game, though."

I smiled and laughed at how serious he sounded about that. Then I narrowed my eyes on his. "On the phone," I agreed. "No running around shirtless for you unless it's summer." His eyebrows went up, and he smirked at me. "Oh, don't give me that look," I shot at him. "You didn't put a shirt on for a reason."

He snickered, his cheeks tinting pink. "Okay, I'll admit to that one."

When he didn't get up to put a shirt on, I gave him a look. "Effective immediately," I said in my serious voice. "You're killing me here."

He gave me a big smile. He leaned in and kissed my cheek. It was the only safe place right now. He got off the bed and walked to his dresser. Dylan grabbed a dark blue Henley and pulled it on. I admit it; I was biting my lip as I watched the muscles in his back move. My boyfriend; I have ogling rights. He turned back around, his face full of mischief.

"Okay, no tank top thingies." He pointed his finger at my cami and moved it up and down. "You normally don't show a lot of skin. This is like..." He exhaled, his eyes running over my body. "Like fucking Christmas and Hanukkah, all wrapped into one."

I snickered before getting off the bed and finding my wet sweater. I quickly pulled it back on. "Okay, fair enough," I admitted as I turned back towards him, pulling my hair out of my sweater. "But what are you going to do in summer when I go swimming?"

He closed his eyes and groaned. "Suffer," he answered painfully.

I chuckled. I was enjoying our little game. "No closed-doors when we're alone," I shot back. He nodded, grinning at me. I walked over and opened the door wide then walked back.

He was smiling now. "No skirts." His voice was deadly serious. "Not for a while, Sunshine." His voice told me not to argue.

"Really?" I put a contemplating tone in my voice.

His smile disappeared.

"Lexie... I'm serious."

I nodded, smiling. He raised an eyebrow, waiting for my turn.

"No... against the wall kissing," I offered.

He shook his head immediately. "Uh-uh. That's a dating staple; you can't take that away," he said seriously, stepping closer to me.

I caved; I did like against the wall kissing. "My heart wasn't really set on that one anyway," I admitted. He smiled again. "How about... Oh! I got one." I looked up at him and stepped a little closer. "We'll probably be going to parties together. Only one of us drinks at a time."

He nodded. "That's a damn good one," he admitted, stepping closer to me again. "And at parties, we stick to public places."

I nodded. "Good one," I said.

He reached out and cupped my neck again, his thumb in front of my ear. I looked into those warm blue eyes; he had a strange grin on his face.

"Think that'll work?" I asked.

"Maybe. Then again..." he whispered before he leaned down and brushed his lips across mine. That warmth spread through me again. With the gentle, sweet way he kissed me, I felt cherished at that moment. He pulled back, a soft smile on his face. "Go take your shower, and I'll head downstairs." He didn't move. One of us had to, and I didn't want it to be me. But I nutted up and stepped away. I was very aware of him watching me as I picked up my stuff and walked into the bathroom. I made a point of locking the door. It seemed the only smart thing to do right then.

CHAPTER 9

SATURDAY NIGHT

*B*y the time I came downstairs, the pizza had already been delivered, and everyone else had already eaten. I brought my bag down with me; I didn't think going back into Dylan's room was a good idea for now. I was wearing bootcut blue jeans, my grommet belt and a V-neck black, short sleeve shirt that Ethan suggested I wear. My hair was dried into its usual curly mass. Ethan had told me to wear darker makeup for under the lights, so my eyes were heavily shadowed and lined with black. Otherwise, it was my normal. Except for my neck. I had a bite mark and a couple of hickeys that were visible after my shower. Thankfully, I had concealer in my makeup kit. It was almost time to head out to Vegabond for the sound check, so I ate quickly, and then we headed off. Zeke took Riley. Dylan drove me.

It was almost dark when we parked, and I had just slid out when Dylan walked around the truck. Those eyes met mine as he gave me his half grin. The butterflies weren't there so much as just replaced by warmth flooding me. I smiled back before I locked my door, then shut it. Dylan immediately took my hand and pulled me close.

He leaned down to whisper in my ear, "You look beautiful tonight."

My pulse picked up. I felt my face grow warm. I tilted my head up, so my lips were at his ear. I went with completely honest. "That shirt really shows off your eyes," I whispered back, feeling completely corny as hell. I pulled back to see his cheeks were tinted pink. Good. "Okay, now we're that couple," I said, slightly disgusted with us. He laughed as Zeke and Riley joined us. We all started walking toward the bar.

"Why are we here so early?" Zeke grumbled.

"Sound check." I sighed. "They have to see how my voice works with the equipment here and make adjustments if needed. Basically, it's practice before the show." Dylan wrapped his arm around my shoulders.

"We get a preview!" Riley said cheerfully. I groaned as we neared the door.

"I'm sure it's going to be great, Sunshine."

"You'll hear for yourself in a few minutes," Zeke offered.

I flipped him off over my shoulder. Not because he pissed me off, but because I was just that nervous about this. We walked into the almost empty bar and headed across the dance floor. Ryan was talking to Oliver when he spotted me.

"Hey, Lexie! Just in time; get up here," Ryan called to me before yelling for Ethan off stage. I groaned as I left the others, climbed the steps, and walked through the backstage curtain.

Ethan was pulling on his guitar when his eyes ran over my face, he smiled. "Perfect eyes, Beautiful. You've got a dark, pissed off look going."

I snorted at him as I took off my coat. "That's not the makeup, Snoopy. That's just me," I said dryly. He chuckled as I hung my jacket on a hook. I followed him out onto the stage with the others. I growled as I saw the others standing near the back of the dance floor. I wanted to kill Ethan. One of the usual bartenders was off stage on the other side at a big electronic board with a lot of sliders and buttons.

Ethan looked over at me. "Did you warm up?"

"Yeah, before I left Dylan's," I replied.

Ethan nodded. "Okay, here's what's going on." He pointed to the bartender. "All of our sound goes through that mixer board. Kevin over there, is going to adjust instruments and vocals to get the best mix possible so that the vocals can be heard over the drums and other instruments." I nodded. "Don't piss Kevin off or we're screwed." Kevin chuckled. I grinned. "We already got my settings into the mixer, and now we need yours. So, we're just doing your songs right now." I groaned. Ethan chuckled. "Before you come out, I'll introduce you as a guest singer, and we'll start." I nodded as he moved away from the microphone.

I closed my eyes like Ryan had told me to as the first notes of Angel's Fall played. Then I sang, keeping my eyes closed. I made sure to follow Ethan's corrections.

When we were done, I opened my eyes to find Ethan grinning. "Oh yeah, this is going to work. You sound even better over a speaker, Beautiful."

I rolled my eyes at him.

The next half hour we ran through my song list. The only time I opened my eyes was during Broken. In the end, Ethan turned to Kevin. "You need anymore?"

The tall, bulky blonde man shook his head. "Nah, she's easier to mix than you, man," Kevin said as he grinned. I sighed. "I'll switch settings as she walks on stage. Don't hurry out. It'll take a couple of seconds." I nodded.

I still couldn't believe I was doing this. We got off stage as people started coming into the bar. My stomach was in knots as I started pacing backstage.

Ethan smiled at me. "Lexie, relax, we have an hour before we start."

I sat down in one of the folding chairs near the open back doors.

"You are going to sound great, don't worry so much," Ryan assured me. I gave him a tight smile.

My phone vibrated. I pulled it out of my pocket and checked.

Dylan: You sounded amazing, Sunshine. Riley wants to come backstage for a bit. Are you guys busy?

I looked around at the band and saw they were just talking, waiting for the crowd to fill in.

Alexis: Nope, come on back. Killing time.

It wasn't long before the curtain was pushed aside. Riley, Zeke, and Dylan walked over.

"Lexie, you sounded great," Riley all but gushed.

I groaned. "So, you're deaf too?" I grumbled. Everyone burst out laughing. Everyone started talking about nothing. But as the noise from the bar grew louder, my stomach knotted more and more. Dylan held my hand and gave me a squeeze. I looked up at him, wanting to run away as fast as possible.

He smiled down at me before leaning over to whisper in my ear. "You sounded beautiful. Ethan wouldn't let you do this if you were going to stink."

I took a deep breath and let it out slowly. "Not what I'm worried about," I grumbled. "I'm scared I'm going to let them down." Dylan's warm eyes ran over my face, an odd grin on his lips. "What?" The grin became a smile.

"Nothing, Sunshine." He lifted my hand and kissed my knuckles. It was sweet. I took another deep breath and let it out slowly.

Ethan checked his phone. "About that time," Ethan announced. Zeke and Riley headed back out to the front of the bar. Dylan gave me a hug and a kiss on the temple before heading out. I turned to see Ryan looking away from Dylan and me. Ethan started pacing and spinning his rings. The others stood back and watched.

I leaned over to Oliver. "What's he doing?" I whispered.

"His pre-show freak-out," Oliver said. "He does it every time."

I watched as long as I could, but it was actually painful to watch. As Ethan went to pass me again, I snagged his arm, pulling him to a halt. He looked at me; his eyes a little panicked. I tugged his arm, leading him out the back doors and into the snow. I turned back to him and looked him in the eye. "Why are you freaking out?" I asked bluntly.

Ethan bounced on his toes. "Because I don't want to fuck up." He shot back at me like it was obvious. "I don't want to suck and destroy the fan base we've managed to create."

"Ethan," I began, making my voice calm and soothing. His chocolate eyes met mine. "You are an amazing singer. You have a panty-dropping voice." He snorted. "You know these sets inside and out, right?" He nodded. "You've practiced your ass off the last two weeks, right?" He nodded. I gave him an understanding smile. "Add that to your voice, that can make a girl squirm by the way, and you seriously can't fuck it up." His shoulders relaxed a bit. "You want this?"

"Yeah."

"Then get out there, and bust your ass to give them a good show," I told him emphatically.

He smiled down at me, calm again. He nodded. "You're right. I got this," he said with confidence.

Now that he was calm, I wanted to puke. "The only one here who's likely to fuck this up is me." I took a deep breath. "You guys are fucking nuts bringing me into this."

Ethan's eyes went wide before he wrapped his arm around me and brought me to his side. "Lexie, you have an amazing voice," he reassured me gently. "It's a mix between Amy Lee and Lizzy Hale. I've never heard anything like it." I looked up at him like he was insane. "Lexie, would I ever embarrass you in public?"

"I'm not worried about being embarrassed, Ethan," I snapped, running my hand through my hair. "I'm worried about letting you down."

He snorted. "No way. You'd never let me down."

He was right. I hated to admit it, but he was. I nodded. We headed back inside to join the others.

Oliver raised an eyebrow. "Done with the freak-out already?" Oliver asked, his voice surprised.

"That's a record," Ryan added, smiling at us.

"Lexie has a way of telling you when you're being an idiot," Ethan admitted.

"Yeah, I knock you over the head with the truth, repeatedly," I admitted.

Everyone chuckled. Ethan, Oliver, and Ryan put their hands in the center. I wasn't paying attention until Ryan snagged my hand and put it in the center too.

"Let's go out there and kicks some ass!" Ethan said. They bobbed their hands then threw them up, shouting 'Under Fire.' I watched as they headed out on stage. Ethan winked at me before he walked out. The crowd cheered. Oh, God. They were fucking insane.

I paced backstage, taking deep breaths to keep myself calm. What the hell were they thinking, asking me to do this? They were crazy! I couldn't let them down, but... fuck! The first song ended a lot sooner than I would have liked.

"Now, I'd like to introduce our guest singer. She'll be popping on and off stage to help us out for the night. Let's have a big round of applause for Lexie! Ethan's voice ran through the speakers. There was applause. FUCK! I headed out, keeping my eyes on Ethan as my heart raced. Ethan winked at me before stepping away from the microphone.

"I can't believe you're making me do this," I grumbled. The crowd burst out laughing. Shit.

Ethan was smiling as he stepped closer so the microphone would pick him up. "They can hear you, Lexie."

I looked up at him, my eyes narrowed. "And now they all know you're an ass that guilts your friends into doing shit they don't want to," I pointed out matter-of-factly. I might as well. They all heard me anyway. The crowd burst out laughing. Ethan was chuckling as he stepped back.

I closed my eyes as the first notes of Angel's Fall played. Then I sang; I sang the song the way it always sounded to me. I focused on nothing but the music and hitting the right notes. My heart stopped racing as I tapped my foot to the beat. Then the last notes were played and I stepped back and finally opened my eyes. The fucking bar was full. My stomach instantly knotted. I turned and headed backstage. Oliver gave me a wink. Apparently, I wasn't awful.

Once I was off the stage, I took a deep breath. Holy shit, that was scary as fuck. Then the adrenaline rushed kicked in. It was kinda fun too. I paced back and forth through the next two songs. Then it was my turn again. I headed back out on stage, keeping my eyes on Ethan. I took my spot on the other side of the microphone as they started playing Broken. Ethan kept his eyes on my face and sang. I kept mine on his. I couldn't do this any other way. Then my verse came, and I was singing. The rest of the bar faded away; there was just us, singing together.

When the song came to an end, I turned and walked off stage again. I paced backstage, not needing to take deep breaths this time. The longer we went without someone yelling out 'you suck,' the better I was feeling about all this. I waited for another two songs. Then it was my turn again. I headed out, feeling a little more comfortable about this. Ethan was smirking at me. I shot him a look. The crowd chuckled. This time I had to talk to the crowd. I kept my eyes closed.

"This is a new one for the boys that I blackmailed them into learning because, let's face it, there is only so much screaming a girl can take."

There were laughs through the crowd. The boys started to play Darkside. This song was hard for me. I had to hold notes for a while, perfectly. I blocked everything out but the music and my voice. When it was over, I was so relieved; I hadn't fucked up. As I headed off stage, Ryan was grinning at me. Guess it sounded good.

I went back to my pacing off stage. One more song and it was the loudest. It required a good yell at the end. I took a big drink of water as I waited for the next two songs to end. Then I was up again. I took a deep breath and headed out to the microphone. I closed my eyes again as the first electronic notes of Numb played through the speakers. Then I started to sing. I loved this song; it reminded me of my relationship with my mother. It required backup vocals, but instead of Ethan, it was Ryan who backed me up with his deep, smooth voice working alongside mine. It was a song that needed everything you had. I thought of my mother and gave it everything. This song pushed my range, which is why we left it for the end of my songs. So, when I had to yell, I hit it just right then dropped my voice right back down to where it needed to be. The last notes of the song played out, and that was it for me. I took a deep breath in relief.

"That's it for Lexie tonight. Wasn't she great!" Ethan's voice rang through the crowd, and there was applause and several hoots from voices I knew. I finally looked at the crowd and was happy I had kept my eyes closed tonight. The place was packed. I gave them a wave then headed off stage. "We'll be taking a short break, see you in fifteen."

When I made it backstage, I dropped into a chair, almost limp with relief. The guys came off stage and laughed at me.

"You did great, Lexie," Oliver assured me as he opened a bottle of water.

I didn't know about great, but I thought I managed not to embarrass them. "Thanks, Oli." Oliver grinned at his nickname.

Ryan stood across from me with that killer grin on his face. "You need to join the band, Lexie, seriously."

I snorted. "Oh no. Not happening." I shook my head. "I'm just helping you guys out." My voice was getting raspy. I took a drink of water.

"Go to the bar and ask for some tea," Ethan said, pushing his sweaty hair back from his face. "Otherwise you'll lose your voice." I nodded then got to my feet. Ethan pulled me into a sweaty hug. "Thank you so much, Beautiful."

I hugged him back. "No problem, I'm just going to bitch about it for a bit," I grumbled. "And you owe me lots of jewelry."

He chuckled as he let go. I told them to kick ass on the next set, grabbed my coat, then headed out to the front of the bar. I had just stepped off the steps when Dylan popped out of the crowd.

Smiling, he hugged me tight. "Sunshine, that was incredible," he whispered in my ear.

I squeezed him back. "I didn't suck?" I asked, my voice uncertain. I hated how girly I sounded right then.

He chuckled. "You killed it, babe." The knots in my stomach loosened. I pulled back a bit to see if he was joking; he just leaned down and gave me a quick soft kiss that made my heart race. "Come on, everyone's waiting."

Club music came on over the speakers. I got on my toes so I could reach Dylan's ear. "I have to get some tea first or I'm going to lose my voice."

He nodded, took my hand, and led me through the crowd, to the bar. I ordered my tea as Dylan told me what he'd heard people saying about my singing. So far, it was all positive. Then he hesitated. My tea came in a big paper cup; I added honey.

"What?" My voice was quickly disappearing. I started sipping, the heat soothing on my throat.

Dylan gave me a tense smile. "The three bitches were making fun of your voice when the guys weren't listening." He shrugged, looking apologetic. "I wanted to warn you."

I snorted. "I don't care what they think. They're bitches," I croaked. Shit. I focused on drinking my tea.

He grinned at me. "Well, they're pissing off my friends. Jake has already told them to stop bitching."

I snorted. Jake was awesome.

"They're probably going to find another spot to hang out," he said. "But everyone is waiting for you first."

I nodded. "We can join them if you want?" I offered.

He grinned at me. "If it gets too bad, yeah," he agreed before leading me back through the crowd toward the back wall of the bar. When we stepped out of the crowd, I saw that everyone had put four tables together to form one long one. There was enough room for everyone to have their own seat. Though two of the three bitches were on their boyfriends' laps. Everyone said 'hi.'

Jake jumped up and all but tackled me. "You killed it sweetness!"

Jake squeezed me tight, and I hugged him back, laughing. I couldn't help it. "Thanks, hon."

He pulled back, his eyes running over my face. "Your makeup is starting to smear." I reached into my pocket and handed him some tissues. He lifted my chin and started fixing it. I just let him. I didn't have a mirror, and I trusted him not to make me look worse. When he was done, he leaned in. "If those bitches keep trying to tear into you, I'm going to pay someone to drop colorful drinks on those nice white shirts." I snorted. It was so weird to hear the big jock talk about ruining a girl's clothes. Jake moved back to his spot so that the others could see me.

Isaac picked me up in a big hug. I grunted as he squished me. "You did great, Red!"

I smiled as he put me down. "Thanks, Cookie Monster."

He grinned big before heading back to his seat where Cece was. I put my coat on the back of an empty chair between Miles and Dylan.

"Ally, you were wonderful." Asher got my attention from across the table. I wrinkled my nose at him, and he chuckled.

"Lexie, that was great," Thomas called from down the table. I sent him a smile.

"It sounded awesome," Derrick added.

"Even I know that sounded good," Aaron said.

"Thanks, guys. You're too sweet."

I had just sat down between Miles and Dylan when Faith chimed in. "Well, she did go off key a couple of times."

Derrick snorted. "No, she didn't,"

"How would you know?" Faith shot back, eyeing him.

"He's been accepted to Juilliard, for the year after next," I explained smugly. "They're holding a spot specifically for him. I think that means he knows a shit ton about music."

Faith glared at me before whispering to Cece next to her. I ignored her and looked over at Dylan's friends. "So, what trouble have I missed?"

Aaron chuckled. "Jake almost got his ass kicked by some big guy," Aaron said, smiling.

I looked over at Jake from across the table; he was laughing. "What happened?" I asked, dying to know.

"A guy thought I was hitting on his sister," Jake told me. "I had to tell him I was more interested in him than her." We all chuckled.

"You should have seen his face." Derrick grinned down the table. "What he actually said was, 'I was trying to get to know her so I could find out if I should ask for your number.'"

I burst out laughing.

Jake looked like he didn't regret a thing. "Hey, I got a phone number," Jake pointed out smugly. "I'm ahead of all of you, except for Dylan."

"Shit, he's right." Thomas got up and looked around the bar. He grinned. "And there is Sara." He looked around at us. "Someone wingman me?"

Jake sighed. "You're going to need my help," Jake warned him, getting to his feet. "You about as smooth as sandpaper."

I chuckled as they headed off to get Thomas a phone number. Aaron, Luke, and Derrick were in a discussion about something I couldn't hear, and the guys were talking to their girls. I looked up at Miles; he looked tenser than usual, almost rigid.

"How was your afternoon?" I asked as Dylan's hand found mine under the table. I put his hand on my knee. I didn't know why but I wanted my hands free around these bitches.

Miles shrugged. "The usual. I played games with Autumn," he said, his voice stiff.

He didn't sound like himself. I racked my brain, trying to figure out what could put him in this gloomy mood. There wasn't much on the list. I bumped my shoulder into his; he grinned and bumped his shoulder into mine. I smiled back. Dylan leaned over and asked what games he played today. He must have noticed something off about Miles too.

While they talked, I looked around the table. Faith's eyes darted from me to Miles and back again. What was her problem now? No, I didn't care.

When there was a lull in Miles' and Dylan's conversation, I slipped in. "Miles, you want to come get a drink with Dylan and me? I'll buy." I smiled sweetly up at him. He nodded immediately. Yeah, something was wrong.

I went to get up, but Dylan stopped me and leaned in. "You go, see if you can get him to talk; I'll see if the bitches have something to say here." It was right then and there that I felt it. I was really falling for this guy. It was terrifying and exciting all at the same time. I nodded and got up. He winked at me before I turned around.

I wrapped my arm around Miles' as we headed to the bar. My head was going crazy, shit, shit, shit. No, no, I couldn't. Maybe it was just because I was grateful, and I was mixing up the feelings. Yep, that was it. I wasn't falling in love because that would mean actual feelings and real... feelings. I pushed that all out of my head as we reached the bar. I ordered two sodas, and Miles ordered another.

After I had paid, I turned and looked him in the eye. "Spill. You're jumpy; what's up?"

Miles sighed. "Faith, on the car ride home, kept giving me these weird looks," Miles began, pushing his glasses back up on his nose. "Then when we split up at the twins' house, she cornered me." I wanted to hit the bitch. I took a deep breath and kept my calm. "She kept asking me questions about you and me," he continued. I raised an eyebrow. "She wanted to know where we hung out, what we did. She even wanted to know where I lived." That was weird. "During the whole drive home, she was also making these snide little comments about you and I being so close."

I got it then. I rolled my eyes. "She thinks we're screwing around behind Dylan's back," I said as I shook my head.

Miles nodded. "That is the conclusion I came to, also." He took a drink of his soda before continuing. "I have a feeling the three of them have decided to try to get rid of you and are looking for anything they can use."

"That'll be funny as hell, watching them scramble and find nothing." I snickered.

Miles chuckled, then he sobered. "They can make problems for you and Dylan," he pointed out. I laughed at that. Yeah, I wasn't too worried about that. Miles raised an eyebrow at me.

"Dylan knows all about what's going on. Hell, he's seen more than you, sweetie. You just got caught in the ricochet." His eyes were worried. "Don't worry, Miles, after tonight I'll be avoiding those three like the plague."

"I think I'll join you," he admitted dryly.

I smiled. "Are you getting along with Dylan's friends?" I asked, changing the subject.

He nodded. "Had an interesting discussion with Derrick about the piano, and why he chose it," he said cheerfully. "It made me hate the piano less."

I raised an eyebrow at him. "You play the piano?"

His ears turned a light shade of pink. "Yes, I play several instruments. My mother insisted on it," he told me. I smiled up at him. "No, I will not play for you," he shut me down before I could ask.

I gave him a half-hearted pout then moved on. "Well, if it gets too bad tonight, we'll split off to sit with Dylan's friends. Sound like a plan?" Miles nodded, still frowning. "Cheer up. This is going to be my only night off until I manage that link. So, please just have fun." He gave me a real smile. The one that showed just how handsome he really was. "You're dancing with me tonight; I know you can, so you have to." His eyes went wide. "Yes! My last night of freedom until I get that link up. Think of it as my last request?"

He sighed. "Who told you I know how to dance?"

I gave him a big smile knowing I had won. "Ethan; who else? That guy can't keep a secret if his life depended on it," I said as if it was obvious. Miles burst out laughing.

I pulled out my phone and texted Dylan.

Alexis: Faith thinks I'm screwing Miles behind your back. Just a heads up.

Dylan: Lmao, I got that. She's prying into our relationship and pissing off my friends in the process. Want me to tell her anything fun?

I snickered and looked up at Miles.

"Faith is questioning Dylan about our relationship. What's the kinkiest thing you've ever heard? Cause I need something to tell her," I said excitedly.

Miles burst out laughing, his ears turning pink. "No. I'm not going there with you, Lexie," he said adamantly.

I snickered and texted Dylan back.

Alexis: Tell her something freaky and watch her face.

Dylan: Best girlfriend ever, thank you!

I chuckled. That feeling washed over me again, fuck. I swallowed hard and put my phone away. "Ready to go back? We could just find you a hottie to charm, so you don't have to go back?" I offered.

Miles looked like he was considering it. "No, I'll be alright. Besides, she was after you, not me," he pointed out.

I nodded. Good point.

I grabbed my two sodas and Miles grabbed his. His hand went to my wrist to help get me through the crowd. It had become a family ritual whenever we were in a crowd. The closest one held my hand, so they didn't lose me. When we reached the table, he let go, and of course, Faith noticed. Dylan's mouth was drawn into a tight line; his eyes were hard as he kept his gaze on the table. Aaron's fists were clenched on the table, his knuckles white. Derrick and Luke were glaring at the girls. It made my stomach knot; what had those bitches been saying? I put my soda down and touched Dylan's shoulder. He looked up at me. His eyes instantly softened as he smiled at me. The knots disappeared; he was just pissed at one of the girls. I handed him his glass and leaned down to whisper in his ear.

"Do you need to get away?"

"If I don't, I might ask you to hit those bitches," he whispered back.

I smiled. I stood up straight and nodded. I looked over at Miles. "Miles, can you watch our stuff please?" I tilted my head towards Dylan.

Miles' eyes darted to him then back to me. "Of course, Lexie."

"We'll join you," Derrick offered as he got up, glaring at the three bitches. Aaron and Luke followed. Dylan stood up and wrapped an arm around my lower back. He all but shoved me away from the table. We stopped walking on the dance floor; Aaron, Luke, and Derrick followed us.

"What the hell is with those bitches?" Aaron asked, his face hard. "'Cause with the way they're going after you, I'd think you had killed their kittens or some shit."

I shook my head. "I'm a girl that's friends with their guys. Apparently, that's enough to make someone hate me," I explained tiredly. I didn't understand it myself.

Luke shook his head. "Sorry Lexie, but we can't sit with your friends, not with those girls there," Luke said apologetically. "Derrick's real close to calling them on their shit. And I'm not far behind."

I gave them a smile. "I understand; I'm sorry guys," I felt awful about this. "If they keep this shit up, we'll be joining you guys tonight."

"They have the heaters on out on the patio. There should be some tables free," Derrick offered. The guys nodded.

Luke sent out a text to the others. Then he looked up at me. "Sorry, Lexie," Luke said again.

"Hey, I get it. I'm pretty close to joining you," I reminded them. They smiled at us then disappeared into the crowd. The band changed to a slow song. My arms went loosely around Dylan's neck as we started dancing.

He leaned down to whisper in my ear, "Those guys are fucking oblivious to what's going on. They're just sitting there talking to each other and not listening to what their girls are saying."

"Boobs, they are powerful things, honey," I pointed out, hoping for a smile.

Dylan snickered as he pulled back to look down at me.

"Faith cornered Miles today, and I'm having a hard time not knocking the bitch's teeth out," I said sweetly. I sighed. "I want the guys happy, but the girls are making it impossible for me or Miles to be around anymore."

Dylan leaned down and pressed his cheek against mine so we could talk better. "You need to tell the guys, Sunshine. They wouldn't tolerate this bullshit." His voice was getting hard again. He really was angry.

I wrapped one hand around the back of his neck, my fingers massaging. He sighed a small moan into my ear. I grinned; his neck was really tense. "I'm just going to avoid them from now on." He grunted at me, but I was still massaging his neck, so it wasn't a hard grunt. "It'll be fine, I've got a lot of work on my project coming up, and I won't have time to see everyone anyway. I'll arrange to see the guys at Miles' house, where none of the girlfriends are welcome. And I'll see you as much as I can till school starts..."

Then I realized a problem with my plan. They all went to our high school. Shit.

"Then what? You're going to avoid your friends all the time?" he asked, sounding even more pissed. "You can't do that, Sunshine, and you shouldn't have to."

I nodded. He was right. But I wanted the guys to be happy more than I wanted to kick the girls' asses. And there was that other part of me that was still nagging at me. Telling me that they'd choose the girls. My stomach knotted as I tried to push that back.

"I'll figure something out before then." I was lying through my teeth. I was just going to go back to taking their bullshit. But this time I was going to fire back. I wasn't their fucking punching bag.

Dylan kissed my temple and kept his cheek against my hair. I just wanted to enjoy my last night out for a couple of weeks. I closed my eyes and danced with my boyfriend. When the music changed up, I smiled up at him hopefully. He kept an arm around my waist and danced with me. I liked dancing with Dylan; if we got too close, it wasn't a problem. I could just dance and not worry about anything. I moved to the beat and enjoyed myself. Then my cell vibrated in my bra. I pulled it out. It was Miles.

Miles: The guys went to get drinks; a little assistance would be appreciated.

I cursed and stopped dancing. I showed the text to Dylan, who nodded and gestured for me to go. I hurried back through the crowd. When I got to the table, Faith, Trisha, and Cece were all asking Miles questions. He just sat there, his mouth shut, staring at the table. I could see how tense he was from where I stood.

"So, have you ever slept with a girl, Miles?" Faith asked. It was clear how much she was enjoying watching Miles blush.

My temper ignited. I stepped out of the crowd. Miles turned to me, his face cold, his eyes like ice. Miles was pissed and probably felt like he couldn't do anything about it because they were girls. Okay, that was it. I walked over and slammed my hand into the middle of the table to get the bitches' attention. The table shook, glasses rattled. "You girls leave Miles alone. I'm done playing nice. Miles is too much of a gentleman to tell you when you're being bitches, but I'm not. Come after me all you want. But you mess with Miles, and we'll have a problem," I growled at them. They glared at me, but they stopped talking to Miles, and that's what I had wanted.

I looked back to Miles. "Come on, sweetie, let's hang out with some non-bitches." Miles smirked as he got up, taking his drink with him. I grabbed my coat and Dylan's. He followed me like my taller shadow until we met Dylan on the way to the dance floor. "We're hanging with your friends tonight." Dylan gave me a small smile then took his jacket from me. He took my hand and led us through the crowd out to the side patio. Though the tall, stainless steel heaters made the area much warmer, you still needed your jacket. But it didn't feel like you would freeze to death. Dylan's friends were the only group on the patio. They waved us over.

"That didn't take long." Derrick grinned at me.

I snorted. "You don't fuck with my family." I held up my finger and thumb with only a quarter inch separating them. "I was this close to playing smack-a-bitch." The guys chuckled as Miles, Dylan and I pulled up seats. "Miles is too polite to tell them off, so we came over."

"How the hell do your friends not see that?" Aaron asked, frowning.

I shrugged. "Not paying attention." It was the only answer I had.

Aaron snorted.

"That's fucking ridiculous," Thomas announced.

I nodded.

Then we changed subjects. We talked about what video games were coming out, who got who's phone number. We just had a good time and laughed. Dylan and Thomas made a run for hot drinks while we continued talking. I was listening to a funny story from Aaron when my cell vibrated. I pulled it out and checked it.

Asher: Where are you? Did you leave already?

Alexis: Just hanging out with Dylan's friends. He hangs out with you guys all the time, so I'm hanging out with his.

I was laughing at the how the story ended when my phone vibrated again.

Asher: We'll join you. Where are you? Zeke's getting pissy.

I cursed and looked around at the guys.

"We're about to be found, boys," I grumbled. "Zeke's getting worried about not seeing me."

Dylan and Thomas walked up to hand out drinks. "Tell them. If they come out here, maybe they'll hear their girls talking to you," Dylan offered.

I looked at the others. "You guys okay with that? I can always go back in," I offered. They all snorted.

"Bring those bitches out here," Derrick insisted. I smiled.

Alexis: Out on side patio, we have it to ourselves.

"Okay, they're coming." I looked over at Miles to see his blank face. I winked at him; he grinned at me. It wasn't long before the doors opened and they all came out.

"This is much better than inside, why didn't we think of this?" Asher asked, smiling.

"Because it's freezing, that's why," Trisha complained.

Asher pointed out a chair right next to the heater. "That should work for you, Trish." Asher and Trisha went to sit down as the others grabbed chairs and sat in a big circle. Faith sat next to Miles, smirking at me. I sent her back my 'don't fuck with me' face. I met Miles' eyes and got up; he bit back a smile as we switched places. Dylan's friends chuckled while my friends looked confused. Everyone started talking about nothing really.

When all my guys were distracted, I looked at Faith and smiled. "I warned you once to leave Miles alone," I whispered quietly. Faith's eyes burned as she glared at me. "This is the second warning. Don't fuck with him, or I'll fuck you up. There will not be a third warning." I went back to looking across the circle. Dylan grinned and winked at me. Asher looked at me with narrowed eyes before going back to his conversation with Jake over football stats. Everyone started to relax and really get into the conversation.

My guys, including Miles and Riley, got up to make a drink run for everyone. Derrick, Luke, and Thomas made a run for us. I knew it was going to start. I waited till the guys were inside before I got up and headed back toward Dylan. Dylan got up and scooted down a chair, taking Miles' chair. I took Dylan's, and Luke even scooted his chair down so he could put one for Miles between us. I smiled gratefully at him as the guys chuckled.

The girls shared looks. Here we go.

Trisha looked over at me grinning. "So, you're fucking all of Dylan's friends now too?" Trisha asked sweetly.

I burst out laughing and had trouble stopping. "Sorry, it's just... how many people do you think I'm fucking now?" I asked, still laughing. The guys were tense; they must not have realized how bad it was going to get.

Trisha shot me a look. "I don't care, just keep your hands off of mine," Trisha warned me.

Dylan was shaking his head next to me. I winked at him, letting him know I was okay. "You need to see a shrink about your trust issues," I told her honestly. "'Cause if you don't trust Asher, then why are you with him?"

Trisha sent me a death glare. Ooh, I'm shaking. I smiled to myself.

"We all know she's screwing Miles," Faith announced. "It's obvious to anyone paying attention."

I rolled my eyes. "Or, we're friends who hug," I shot back sarcastically. I was done playing nice. I looked over at Dylan's friends. "Did the definition of sex change when I wasn't paying attention? Is a hug, fucking now?" The guys started laughing. I smiled, keeping my eyes on Faith. "I hugged Jake today, does that mean I screwed him too?"

"That'd make my Grandpa happy," Jake said, still laughing. I snorted, as the other guys chuckled. "He always wanted me to be straight. And you are very cute."

I smiled at Jake. "Thank you, sweetie," I said in my cutesy voice. Jake winked at me.

"You know the boys don't need you anymore, right? They don't need some trailer trash piece of tail. They have classy girls now," Cece said smugly. Wow. These bitches were really going for it tonight.

My hands were starting to shake. I looked back at them with an eyebrow raised. "I only see bitches here, not a classy girl in sight," I told her bluntly. They got offended. Oh, darn. I feel so bad. I was going to need to leave; I couldn't sit here and listen to these bitches.

"You realize you just called yourself a bitch, right?" Trisha pointed out.

"Nah, she's a slut just like Jessica says," Faith chimed in. Cece just chuckled.

I calmly looked at them, my nails biting into my palms. "Yeah, I called myself a bitch too. Because I know me. I'm a cranky, pissed off little bitch who will fuck you up if you mess with my family," I said with complete honesty.

Trisha eyed me with a sly grin on her face. "What family? Your mom's in rehab and your dad is dead," Trisha said in a snotty tone. I went still as that hit me hard. "Hell, your dad probably died in a crack house somewhere."

A red-hot wave of rage poured over me. I was up and striding towards her immediately. I was going to pound my fist into that bitch's face. Trisha's eyes went wide as she scrambled out of her chair, backing away. I was almost on her when an arm snagged around my waist. I smelled sandalwood, so I didn't try to break free.

"That's it! Sunshine, we're out of here!" Dylan's voice was cold. He was pissed, too.

I pulled at his arm. I wanted that bitch's blood. Dylan lifted me off my feet and carried me back, away from Trisha. Aaron and Thomas stepped between the girls and us. As if from far away, a door open and my name was yelled. "Oh, no, I'm not done. I'm going to bash her face into a fucking table!" I shouted. "Then I'm going to break her fucking nose!" The guys were coming back outside, their jaws dropping. I struggled against Dylan.

He put my feet back on the ground and wrapped his other arm around my upper chest, pinning my back to his chest. "I would love to see that, babe, but the shit stain isn't worth the bruised knuckles," he countered. He had managed to get me back to the other side of the circle. He stopped pulling me then and just simply held me. With all of Dylan's friends standing between Trisha and me, I took a breath. "Come on, Sunshine, let's leave the bitches to explain this shit."

There was chaos on the patio, the two groups of guys were yelling at each other. I took a deep breath and nodded. He kept an arm around my waist as he pulled me off the patio and towards the parking lot. It was probably a good idea. I was fucking shaking to hit someone. I caught sight of Trisha's pale face and wide eyes. Yeah, piss yourself, you bitch. Dylan gave me a pull, forcing me to turn away and move toward the parking lot. Asher was shouting my name. I kept walking or else I'd be going at Trisha again. I heard Aaron telling Asher to leave us alone, to let us go. Dylan's friends kept my guys from coming after us.

Dylan kept a firm hold on me as we walked through the parking lot. He didn't let go of me until we reached his truck, and then it was only to get me in on the driver's side. Still furious, I scooted over the bench seat as he climbed in behind me. Dylan started the truck and pulled out of his spot, going well over what was smart in a parking lot. He peeled out onto the highway. I was shaking I wanted to hit Trisha so bad. I took deep breaths, trying to calm down.

"Put your seatbelt on, babe." Dylan's voice wasn't as hard as it had been at the bar. I did as he said.

When I was calmer, at least enough to talk, I broke the silence. "Should have let me hit her," I said, my voice still angry.

He snorted. "Really wanted to, Sunshine. But this way is better; now they're going to lie to the guys, and you're going to tell them the truth. It'll be done." His voice was still angry.

I didn't really want to tell the guys the truth. I just wanted to tell them it was girl drama and that I couldn't hang out with the girls anymore. I didn't want to make them choose. When I was silent, Dylan must have guessed what I was thinking.

"You are telling them, right?"

I looked out the window. That small part of me wasn't so small anymore. It was a big tight knot in my chest.

He cursed long and loud. He pulled off the highway into a scenic overlook and parked the truck. He turned to me, one arm along the back of the of the seat. His face was hard, his eyes burning as he frowned at me. "God damn it, Lexie, you need to tell them," he all but shouted at me. "This bullshit needs to stop."

I really didn't want to have this conversation right then; I was still boiling from earlier, and that fear was too fucking close right now. "It's my fucking decision," I snapped. He needed to stop. He needed him to let me figure this out. I needed him to stop pushing.

"And it's the wrong fucking one," he snapped back.

I was starting to shake again, only this time it wasn't from anger. I jerked my seatbelt off me and opened the door as fear poured through me. "I want them happy, and those bitches make them happy!" I jumped out of the truck and slammed the door. Dylan cursed. I stepped onto the curb and took a couple of steps before his door slammed. I turned to meet him. My phone vibrated in my bra; I ignored it.

He strode towards me, his face furious. "Do you understand what those bitches are going to do?" he asked, his voice low and hard. "They are going to say you went after them for no reason." His hand was shaking as he pointed at me. "And you're what? Not going to defend yourself? You're going to let the guys think those bitches are telling the truth?"

"I haven't thought that far ahead," I shot back, pushing my hair out of my face. The fucking wind on the overlook was throwing it every-where. "I don't know what the fuck to do, Dylan!" I finally just gath-ered my hair in and held it in one hand. "I want them happy, and the bitches make them happy. Fucking Isaac's been after Cece for two years! Ethan never really clicked with any of his girls, and now he has one he does click with! Asher... fuck! He deserves someone who thinks he hung the fucking moon. They all do. So, what the fuck am I supposed to do?" My eyes filled. I wasn't yelling anymore; I couldn't, my chest felt tight, and I was really at a fucking loss. I was stuck.

And in the back of my mind that nagging fear wouldn't disappear. The one where they would choose the girls over me. It was bigger than before, big enough now that I couldn't ignore it anymore. I knew I shouldn't think it, or even worry about it. But everything in my life so far told me that this was going to happen. My phone vibrated again.

"So you're, what? Going to keep taking their shit?" Dylan scoffed. He walked closer, his face a weird mixture of horrified and pissed off.

"You're just going to let them pound on you? Just grin and take it?" He shook his head. He came closer, forcing me to look up at him. "Lexie, you can't sacrifice your happiness for other people's." His voice wasn't angry now; it was almost gentle. "You're fucking happiness matters; you fucking matter. To those guys, and to me."

Tears fell down my face. I hated it because he was fucking right. The guys wouldn't want me dealing with this bullshit. But what if...?

The heat in his eyes melted away. He reached out and cupped my face in his hands, his thumbs wiping my tears away. "You don't take shit, Lexie." He leaned closer. "It's one of the things I love about you." My heart slammed in my chest for a different reason, but I didn't have time to examine it right now. "My Sunshine doesn't take shit."

All my anger was gone. I hated that he was right. I needed to tell them, but I really didn't want to. Because then they'd have to choose. "You're right," I admitted, "I won't take their shit." I reached up and held onto his forearm, my thumb rubbing circles on his skin. I needed someone to tell me I was wrong. That what everything in my life was telling me to expect was wrong. That the guys would stay.

My voice was thick and small when I asked, "But, what if they don't pick me?"

Understanding filled his eyes; he pulled me closer until I was in his arms and against his chest. I pressed my face into his shirt and took deep breaths.

"Sunshine." His voice was gentle as he brought a hand up to hold the back of my neck, his fingers massaging. "Those guys love you," he whispered down to me. My phone vibrated again. I swallowed hard, trying to listen. "When Asher gave me your number, he told me he'd been answering questions about me to the others until late the night before. They fucking voted on it." I snorted at that. The tightness was easing in my chest. "When I'm around, they've started taking turns watching me with you."

Huh? I lifted my head from his chest and looked up at him. "What?"

His warm eyes met mine as he half grinned at me. His fingers brushed my hair out of my face. "There're those beautiful eyes," he mumbled under his breath. Before I could process it, he was talking again. "Anytime I touch you around them, at least one of them watches me for a couple of minutes. I think it's one of the reasons those girls have an issue with you," he admitted, his thumb stroking over my cheekbone. "They think their boyfriends are watching you, not me."

I didn't know that. I knew they did it on game night but... I closed my eyes, took a deep breath, and listened to what he was saying. I really fucking needed to hear it tonight.

"They care about you. My phone has been going off since we left the bar and I'm damn sure that it's them calling."

I snorted at the tone in his voice, half amused, half irritated.

He kept looking into my eyes as he continued. "Lexie." His voice was quiet. "You trust those guys to take care of you when you have a seizure, right?"

"Yeah." My voice was soft and quiet, but it was loud enough on the overlook for him to hear me.

"You trust them with your life," he pointed out gently. "And from what I've seen, they would trust you with theirs." I thought about that. He was probably right. The guys were nuts that way. "Do you really think they would throw all that away for some girls?"

When he put it that way, it sounded ridiculous. But it really didn't feel ridiculous. He was right, though; how could I trust them to keep me alive but not trust them to stay with me? It wasn't logical; it was fear. Bone deep, horrible fear that had no basis in the real world.

"Well, if you're going to bring logic into it," I grumbled.

He smiled down at me. He pulled me in against him, opening his jacket to wrap around me. I rested my cheek on his chest and listened to his heart beating. His fingers kept kneading at the back of my neck.

"Sunshine, was that the only reason you haven't told them?" Dylan asked gently.

"No. I want them happy," I explained honestly. "I just have this nagging fear in the back of my mind that just kept getting bigger." I took a breath before continuing. "Everything in my life has taught me that people leave. That I have too many problems to deal with and they leave. Always," I explained, hoping I didn't sound pathetic. "I just really needed to hear you tell me that I was wrong."

He gently kissed the top of my head. "You need to tell them, honey," he whispered softly to me.

"Hell, your friends probably already told them," I grumbled.

He snorted. "No, they would have kept their mouths shut. Jake might have called the girls bitches, but that's about it."

I sighed. Great. "Just… give me a couple of days to think of something else besides just telling them." His body grew tense against me. "I don't want to take away someone else's happiness if I don't have to."

"Are you sure that's not that scared part of you talking?" he asked, his voice soft again. I pulled back enough so I could look up at his face. His sapphire eyes ran over me, then focused on my eyes.

"Yeah, I'm sure."

His hand on my neck moved to cup my face, his thumb ran over my cheekbone making warm shivers run through me.

"You make too much sense not to tell them some of it at least."

He sighed deeply. "Too big a heart, Sunshine." His voice was resigned. "Okay. A couple of days. But if the guys ask me what's going on, I'm telling them the fucking truth. I'm not going to watch you take those hits anymore, babe."

It was my turn to sigh. "Okay. Deal." My phone vibrated again. I closed my eyes and took a deep breath. I realized I had just yelled at Dylan because of a stupid issue of mine. "I'm sorry, Dylan…" I began, my voice pained. My phone vibrated again.

"That's what I'm here for, Sunshine," Dylan began. I opened my eyes to see his half grin, his eyes still soft on my face. "You need me, and I'm here. I need you, and you're there. That's how it works." I gave him a small smile. "Well, that's how it's supposed to work. I've never found someone who kept their side of the bargain before."

I snorted. "Me either," I admitted.

He raised an eyebrow at me. "Feel better?"

"Yeah."

He gave me that half grin. "Good," he whispered before leaning down and kissing me gently, thoroughly. It wasn't a long one, but it still made my toes curl and my body warm. When he pulled back, he didn't go far. He rubbed his nose along mine, making me smile again. "Let's get you back in the truck, it's cold out here."

Now that I was calm again, I realized how cold I was. My fingers were numb, and I had goosebumps all over. "Ooh, it's fucking freezing."

"Come on, Sunshine." Dylan kept me at his side as he tried to block the wind for me. It was one of the sweetest things anyone had ever done for me.

I grinned to myself as he opened the door and gave me a boost into the seat. Then he shut the door and hurried around the truck. When he got in, he started the engine and blasted the heater. I put my fingers on the heating vent to warm them when my phone vibrated again. I growled and pulled the damn thing out of my bra.

"Those guys are going to give me a fucking tumor if they keep calling," I snapped and put the phone on the seat.

"Don't fucking keep it in your bra," Dylan countered. I started laughing. I don't know why, but Dylan telling me that was funny to me.

While I was laughing and getting warm, Dylan picked up my phone and read my texts to me. "Red, what the hell happened? Lexie, answer your fucking phone. Beautiful, talk to me. Call me back Ally, why did Jake call our girlfriends bitches? Can you tell me what happened? The girl's story is ridiculous." I groaned. Dylan looked at me. "You're not going to get a couple of days, Sunshine; they want to know what happened now." He handed me back my phone.

I bit the corner of my bottom lip. "We're having breakfast tomorrow. I can probably put them off till then," I thought aloud. "I don't have time to figure this out." I closed my eyes and tilted my head back. The vinyl squeaked as Dylan moved. His hand took mine and gave me a tug towards him. I leaned against his chest, his arms wrapped around me. It sent another wave of emotion through me, and I didn't bother to fight it or even identify it.

"I know you don't want to do this, but if they treat you like this; those girls aren't good enough for them." Dylan had a point.

I leaned back and looked up at him. "You just gotta keep being right tonight, don't you?"

He grinned. "Just remember, I'm always right," he said, his voice cocky.

My eyebrows went up. "And you just lost your winning streak," I countered. He laughed softly as I smiled at him. "So, your phone's been blowing up too?"

"Yeah, my left ass cheek is numb from the vibrating," he said matter-of-factly.

I laughed as I texted the boys back in a group message.

Alexis: I will talk to you guys about it tomorrow at breakfast.

I was telling Dylan what I sent when my phone blew up again.

Zeke: NOW Lexie!

Asher: Where are you? We'll come to you.

Ethan: What happened?

Isaac: I agree with Asher. Where are you?"

Miles: Are you alright?

I groaned and handed the phone to Dylan. He grinned. He did something, then gave me mine back. He leaned forward and pulled his out of his back pocket.

"What did you do?" I asked suspiciously.

He gave me that half grin of his. "I added myself to the group message. I'll deal with the guys," he said as he typed out a message.

I smiled as I looked at my phone to watch the show.

Dylan: I've got Sunshine, she's calmed down and fine.

Zeke: WHY wasn't she calm in the first place?

Ethan: What fucking happened?

Asher: Where are you?

Isaac: I want Red!

Miles: A calm Lexie doesn't mean she's okay.

I snickered. This was rather funny to watch when I wasn't the one trying to handle the boys.

Dylan: She wants to talk to you about it tomorrow. She's sitting with me in my truck with the heater on, and she's okay.

"Oh, you just opened a can of worms." I snickered.

Dylan looked at his phone like it was an alien as it blew up again.

Zeke: I want proof and why was she cold to begin with?

Isaac: I'm with Zeke, a pic, phone call or I'm sending Zeke after you two.

Ethan: Agreed! Send a pic of her, and we'll believe you.

Zeke: You can't sic me on people, you're not Lexie. But yeah, I will hunt you two down.

Asher: That sounds reasonable, a pic works.

Zeke: Why was she cold?

Miles: I'm sorry, Dylan, but majority rules. Send a pic, please.

I was laughing my ass off. Dylan looked very much out of his element. "Oh, honey, you can't give them any info or they jump on it," I offered, trying not to laugh again.

Dylan shook his head in disbelief. "Are they like this all the time?" he asked, looking over at me.

I smiled gently. "Yeah, that's my guys." My voice was warm as he messed with his phone.

"They want a pic," Dylan mumbled as he held up his phone. "Smile, Sunshine." I flipped the camera off, with my smart-ass grin on my face. Dylan laughed and sent it to the boys.

The phones blew up again.

Ethan: Does anyone recognize where they are?

Isaac: That better be a new fucking pic, man.

Miles: It is, that's what she was wearing tonight.

Isaac: How can you tell? She wears the same stuff all the time.

Zeke: They're in a parking lot somewhere, start driving.

Asher: Can't. I'm stuck here, with the girls all of you ditched looking for Ally.

Ethan: And I've got another fucking set.

Miles: By the way ,Dylan, I met your dad. He's very nice. Didn't mean to wake him up, though.

I was laughing my ass off again. I couldn't help it. Dylan was in way over his head.

"Would you like me to show you how it's done?" I asked smugly.

Dylan looked at me like I was crazy. "You can make them stop?" he asked not really believing me. I nodded. "Please, make them stop."

I snickered and texted the boys.

Alexis: ENOUGH. I am perfectly fine. I will talk to you all about this tomorrow at breakfast and not a minute sooner. Zeke, don't fucking come looking for me or I'll rip your head off. I'm with Dylan. I'm safe. I'll text you guys to tell you when I get home. Does everyone understand?

"That's going to work?" Dylan asked.

Our phones blew up.

Isaac: I'm happy.

Asher: Okay, Ally.

Ethan: Alright.

Miles: We'll see you tomorrow. Please make sure you are awake enough to drive.

Zeke: Fine. I'll stop looking. Drive safe and watch out for black ice tonight.

Alexis: You guys drive safe too.

"Okay, how did you do that?" he asked, impressed.

I smiled. "Each of them worries about something different with me. You have to hit them all at once and make it clear you're not fucking around." I shrugged. "I figured it out about a month ago; it has saved me lots of phone time."

Dylan chuckled. Then he sighed. "We need to head back if you're going to get back before curfew," he grumbled as he put his cell phone away.

"Thank you, Dylan." My voice was soft and quiet. "For, well, being you."

He smiled at me, reached over, and rubbed the top of my thigh. "Anytime, Sunshine." His voice was soft again, making another wave of emotion run through me. I was getting more comfortable with that feeling. Shit.

Dylan buckled in. I put my phone away and did the same. He drove us back to his house. I was putting my bag in the truck when he said he'd be right back. I turned the truck on and turned on the heater. He was back a couple of minutes later, carrying something. I opened the door to get out, but his hand on my thigh stopped me. He put a big book in my lap. It was an old binder that said 'Recipes.' There were several pages loose that stuck out at odd angles. His mom's recipes. I had completely forgotten about the cookies.

I met his eyes, my heart filling with that warmth again. "You sure?" I asked gently.

His warm eyes met mine. "Yeah, just be careful with it; we've kind of destroyed it."

He smiled at me. I leaned down, and he tilted his head up a bit. I kissed him softly, moving my lips over his gently, trying to tell him how I felt without actually having to say it. His teeth did that nipping thing that sent sparks through me. When I pulled back, I knew I was in trouble.

"Drive safe, Sunshine. Don't worry about tomorrow morning. It'll all work out." I nodded, letting him know I heard him.

"I'll see you on Christmas." I winked at him and put the book carefully in my bag. He waited outside till I drove off. My heart was still racing a couple of blocks down the road.

After I got to Rory's, I texted in the group message that I was home and fine. I got a lot of smile emoji's back and a kiss one from Dylan. I sent one back. Isaac told us to stop making out in front of them on the phone. It made me smile.

I went to bed, but I didn't sleep. In fact, I didn't sleep at all. What the fuck was I going to do? Dylan was right; I should tell the guys what their girls were really like. But the girls made them happy, and I wanted them happy. But I didn't want to be around the girls. I went around and around all night until I had a vague idea. If I could manage it, the question of who they would choose wouldn't need to be answered at all. I hoped.

CHAPTER 10

SUNDAY MORNING

$\mathcal{J}$ got out of bed around eight and did my usual morning routine. I had dark bags under my eyes. Great. At least the marks on my neck weren't so bad today. I still used concealer to cover them; I didn't bother with the bags. I pulled my hair back into a loose braid and dressed for meditation. My true self said building the link was going to hurt, so I dressed with that in mind. I wore my usual blue jeans and my oversized gray sweater. It was loose, comfortable, and reached my mid-thigh. I picked up my belt and tried to decide if I needed it. These were new jeans, so no. But did I want to wear it? I pulled it on and looked in the mirror, eh. I pulled it off and looked again. I was about to put it back on again when I realized what I was doing. I cursed. I was stalling. I pulled on my jacket, got my keys, mp3, and cell phone then headed downstairs. I waved bye to Rory as I headed out the door.

It was Sunday; I always had breakfast with the guys on Sunday. As I drove to Miles' house, my gut knotted. They were going to want answers. How was I going to avoid giving them? Just play last night off as girl drama? Would they really buy that? I had the other idea, and I knew I was going to do that, but I was trying to do it without telling them the details. Oh, this was going to be tricky. My body was tense

255

as I punched in the combo to Miles' gate and drove up to the circular driveway. Just my luck that everyone was here on time for once. I shut off the truck with shaking hands. I could do this; I could get them to go with my plan without details. Right? Right. I took a deep breath and let it out. Maybe I should call Dylan. Get a pep talk? I groaned at myself. I was stalling again.

I opened the door and forced myself out of the truck. The walk to Miles' door was the longest walk of my life. I opened it and walked into the foyer. I swallowed hard as I closed the door.

"I'm here!" I shouted.

"Living room!" the guys shouted back. Wow, guess I didn't have to shout. I took off my jacket and left it on the banister as usual.

Taking a deep breath, I walked into the living room. They were all there waiting for me. It was a weird time to notice that Miles had moved the furniture again. The brown leather couches were facing each other again across the coffee table. You're stalling, Lexie. I forced myself to look at them. Ethan was sitting on the arm of the far side of the left couch his feet on the cushion, his elbows on his knees. Zeke was sitting on the high stone hearth of the fireplace. Asher was at the far side of the right sofa; Miles was in the corner closest to me. And Isaac was pacing, his hands laced behind his head. Every one of them were waiting, patiently.

So, naturally, I was a smart ass. "So, where's the firing squad? Am I getting voted off the island? Am I the weakest link?" I was letting my mouth run because they all just kept watching me. No one laughed. That small fear from last night came back. Lexie, come on. You can do this. I sighed and sat down in the corner of the left sofa. "Well, I thought it was funny," I mumbled. My stomach knotted even more.

"Ally, what happened last night?" Asher asked, his eyes on my face.

I smiled sweetly, my pulse picking up. "How'd everyone sleep last night? Good? I slept great," I lied enthusiastically. I didn't know what I was trying to do, but the tightness in my chest was making it harder to tell them. I could do this, right? Yeah. I could do this.

"You didn't sleep last night," Zeke bit out, his words clipped. "I can tell by the bags under your eyes; now answer the fucking question."

I sighed. Maybe I should have gotten that pep talk from Dylan. Too late now.

Okay, fine. Here goes. "Let's call it girl drama," I offered.

"Girl drama? You went after my girlfriend," Asher reminded me.

I shrugged. "Extreme girl drama?" I tried again, my voice uncertain. Everyone frowned at me. That pressure was back in my chest.

"The girls said they were just talking to you when you lost your temper over nothing and went after Trisha," Miles told me calmly. "Dylan's friends wouldn't say anything." I met his eyes; he had a small smile on his face. He knew they were lying.

I had to come clean, a bit. "Okay, look. Your girls and I don't get along, except Riley. We get along great." I fought the need to bite my lip. "So, I'm not going to be able to hang out with them anymore." Everyone, except Miles, looked at me like I was speaking another language.

"I won't be hanging out with them either," Miles added, and the guys looked at him the same way.

"Why? What happened?" Ethan asked, his eyes storming.

I swallowed hard around the knot forming. "I don't want to fuck things up between you guys and your girls," I admitted. "I want you guys happy, and if they make you happy, then I don't want to get in the way of it." There, that was all I was giving them. Every one of them was to some degree looking at me like I was insane. I needed them to take this answer and not ask. Please. Please, guys. I don't want to make you choose.

"So, you're not telling us what happened to make you go after Trisha?" Miles asked gently.

I nodded, my stomach still aching.

"Screw this," Asher bit out. He pulled out his cell phone and started hitting buttons. "If you won't fucking tell us then I'm calling someone who will." Before I could say anything, Asher's phone was on speaker and ringing. It was answered almost immediately.

"Yeah?" Dylan's husky voice came out of the phone.

My heart dropped; my lungs were instantly tight. I closed my eyes. Fuck.

"Lexie's not telling us shit, what happened last night?" Asher demanded, his voice hard.

I bit my lip, trying to think fast. I wasn't fast enough.

"Those girls have been bitches to her all fucking week, man," Dylan announced, his voice still pissed from last night.

Everyone's face showed surprise, well, except for Miles. His face was just blank. I groaned and curled up in my corner of the couch.

"What?" Asher's voice was full of surprise.

"Yeah, Trisha, Cece, and fucking Faith," Dylan kept talking.

Fuck.

"Dylan..." I groaned painfully.

He realized he was on speaker. "Sorry, Sunshine, but I'm not watching this anymore." He didn't sound sorry at all. His mind was made up. I buried my face in my hands again and tried reminding myself that the guys weren't going anywhere. "They started off being sneaky, and then they stopped trying to hide it at all. Cece thinks Lexie's trailer trash; Faith thinks she's screwing Miles behind my back. And fucking Trisha thinks she's trying to screw you, Asher." I groaned against my hands.

"Seriously? Trisha said that last night?" Asher asked, his voice still stunned.

Dylan scoffed. "She's been saying shit like that all fucking week. Anytime you showed Lexie any kind of affection; she tore into my girl. Anytime that it showed that Lexie knew you better than she did, she tore into her. She even threatened that she was going to cut Lexie out of your life."

Asher's mouth was open in shock.

I tried to explain why I didn't say anything. "Asher I didn't think-"

"No! You had your chance to talk, so sit there while we find out what the fuck has been going on!" Zeke shouted at me. His eyes burned as he glared at me. I'd never seen him this mad at me before. I kept my mouth shut as my heart pounded in my chest.

"Zeke! Don't talk to her like that!" Dylan's voice was hard and cold. "Not over this. You haven't heard everything yet."

Zeke's jaw clenched as he glared at the phone.

"What has Faith been saying?" Ethan asked, his voice boiling.

"Faith believes the shit that Jessica has been spreading around," Dylan answered, his voice still hard. "Then yesterday she started in on Miles, asking all sorts of shit about Lexie and their friendship."

The guys shot a look at Miles. "That's the only thing I knew that was going on, except the threatening thing. Those girls kept asking me very invasive questions," Miles admitted. "Until Lexie told them to... well, leave me alone last night."

"Was that how the fight started?" Isaac asked as he walked to stand next to Asher. I bit my lip. Oh, this was going to be bad. I took a quiet deep breath. Come on Lexie, fucking nut up. I hated this feeling.

"No, Sunshine walked away from that with Miles. That's when we went outside with my friends." Dylan snorted. "My friends saw this shit in one night, and you guys still didn't have a fucking clue."

"What started the fight?" Zeke growled.

"As soon as you guys were out of range they started in on her. They went fishing." Dylan's voice was hard. "They went looking for a reaction, and they fucking got one."

"Give us details man," Ethan shot at the phone.

"Trisha started with accusing Lexie of fucking all my friends."

I winced. Oh yeah, this was going to be bad.

"Then she accused her of trying to steal you, Asher."

"What did Faith say?" Ethan asked, his voice boiling.

"Faith accused her of fucking Miles. Lexie, of course, was a smart ass and asked if hugging was the new fucking."

Isaac snorted.

"Then Cece told her that you guys didn't need a piece of trailer trash tail around now that you had classy girls."

Isaac growled in Spanish under his breath as he started pacing again. I had only ever heard Isaac speak Spanish when he was really pissed off. It didn't bode well for me.

"Oh, it gets better." Dylan's voice was still cold. "My girl, being who she is, told them she only saw bitches there."

Ethan smiled; he still looked pissed, but he at least smiled.

"Then Faith chimed in with that Jessica bullshit. And then Trisha, this fucking bitch…"

I looked to Miles, but he didn't seem to have a problem with Dylan calling the girls names right then.

"She said that Lexie didn't have any family and that her dad probably died in a crack house." The room was dead quiet. "That's when Sunshine went at her."

Zeke looked over at me, his eyes on fire.

"Trisha doesn't even curse…" Asher said, probably trying to wrap his head around this.

"Oh, yeah she does," I said emphatically.

Everyone was silent for a minute.

"My girl's been trying to take that shit, just so you guys wouldn't have to dump the girls you cared about," Dylan ratted me out again.

He was so getting burnt cookies for Christmas. Okay, no he wasn't, but I liked the idea.

"I just can't fucking watch it anymore," Dylan admitted.

The guys were quiet for a minute, processing everything. My gut knotted tighter. They were going to choose. I took a deep breath and braced myself, just in case. Yeah, it was stupid, and I had no real reasoning for it. But fear didn't always listen to reason.

"Well, Faith's going out the fucking door," Ethan announced.

Isaac was frowning as he nodded. "So is Cece," Isaac bit out.

"Trisha is… it's way fucking over," Asher announced.

I let out the breath I had been holding. The tightness in my chest was disappearing; my stomach unknotted. That fear was shoved back into the dark corner it lived in, and I went limp in my corner of the couch for a full five seconds. Then I was looking around at the guys. My heart ached all over again; they liked these girls.

"It doesn't have to go like that…" I began.

Everyone looked at me like I was nuts.

"Ally, they can't talk to you that way," Asher snapped at me.

"If they won't even try to get along with you, then they are fucking gone," Isaac joined in.

"I'm with them," Ethan said; his voice was adamant.

That feeling of being loved washed through me. I really did love these bastards. So, I had to try to make this work. "Okay, I know that, you know that. But do they know that?" They looked at me with confusion written all over their faces. "You like these girls, right?" I looked at Ethan. "Ethan, do you have more in common with Faith than your other girlfriends?"

"Yeah," Ethan admitted.

I looked at Asher. "How'd you feel about Trisha before you heard this shit?" I didn't ask; I demanded an answer.

"I liked her," Asher admitted.

I looked to Isaac. "Cookie Monster, you've been after this girl a long time. You finally got her. Don't you want to keep dating her?"

Isaac glared at me. "If she refuses to be nice to you, she can fuck off," Isaac snapped at me.

I took a deep, smooth breath and decided to tell them my idea.

"Those girls don't know that you guys would choose me over them," I pointed out. "Make it clear to them." The guys looked at me, obviously wondering where I was going with this. "I'm going to be real busy for a couple weeks with... that project. So, I won't hang out with you guys and the girls." Isaac was already shaking his head. "We'll still hang out without them. We'll just schedule some friend time. It won't be forever, just like a week? Enough time for it to sink in that I'm not the replaceable one here." They were listening, at least. "And that they can't treat Miles the way they have been. Then we can all try again before school starts. We'll go out and do something as a group. If they can't handle it, then you'll have my blessing to dump the shit out of them."

The guys were quiet, mulling it over. However, my boyfriend wasn't.

"Too big a heart, Sunshine." Dylan's voice rang through the room. The guys nodded, agreeing with him.

"You're really willing to give them another shot? After this shit?" Ethan asked, his brow drawn low. He didn't look like he believed me.

"Yeah. I'll let it go, for you guys. I want you happy," I told them sincerely.

All their faces softened as they looked at me.

"You're too fucking good to them, Red," Isaac announced. The others nodded.

"What about you, Miles?" Asher asked.

Miles' shoulders moved as he let out a big breath. "If they can be polite, I'll let it go also. But those three will never be welcome here at the house." Miles pushed his glasses back up his nose.

"Let's make it real fucking clear to those girls that the only reason we're not dumping their asses now, is that Red's willing to give them a second chance. Miles too." Isaac announced.

"Ooh, I'm gonna," Ethan said, voice boiling.

"I'm going to make it real clear," Asher agreed, still fuming.

"Dylan?" I called sweetly.

"Still here, Sunshine."

"You're getting burnt cookies for Christmas," I informed him, smiling.

He chuckled. "Worth it," he chimed. I chuckled quietly.

"Thanks, Dylan," Asher said, lifting the phone.

"More than happy to stop this shit," he said. "I'll call you later, Sunshine."

"Ooh, you're gonna," I told him, mimicking Ethan. The twins and Dylan chuckled.

"Bye." Dylan hung up.

Then everyone looked at me. I was still in deep shit. I gave them a smile, hoping to ease some of the tension. It didn't work. "Okay, I should have said something sooner," I admitted grumpily.

"You fucking think?" Zeke snapped at me.

"How did we not see this?" Isaac asked the group.

"How the hell did I not hear any of this?" Asher asked, sounding angry at himself now.

"They have boobs, and you weren't paying attention," I offered sweetly. "Boobs are powerful things, guys." Most of them chuckled at that. "I'm sorry," I said honestly. "I just wanted you guys happy."

Ethan moved off the arm of the couch and walked on the cushions over to me. He dropped his weight on me. His arms and knees wrapped around me. "We're not gonna be happy if you're not happy, Beautiful," Ethan pointed out, his face in my hair.

I smiled at that. Then Isaac walked towards me.

"Oh, not again," I groaned.

Isaac snickered as he dropped down in my lap like a kid, his arms around my neck and his brother. "We care about you, Red, but don't be that stupid again." Isaac's voice was serious.

I rolled my eyes. I agreed with him, but I wasn't going to admit it to him. That would just create a monster.

"You're family, Lexie." Asher's rich voice had me looking to him. His ocean eyes settled on mine. "Our family always comes first."

I nodded, letting him know I heard him. They really meant it. They cared about me and weren't going to leave me. I needed to accept that and stop poking at it. That warm feeling ran through me, threatening to choke me. I needed to change the subject before I cried.

"Okay, squishing small girl," I pointed out. The boys refused to budge. I looked at Zeke. "Help?"

Zeke shook his head. "You deserve this one," he told me.

I sighed, then came up with a better idea. "Boys, there is food in the kitchen for breakfast," I pointed out in a sing-song voice.

Both the twins' heads came up, then they were shoving themselves off me and headingto the kitchen. Asher and Miles burst out laughing. Everyone got up to follow but Zeke. He was coming around the coffee table toward me. Oh, shit. He took my arm gently and pulled me with him into the foyer.

"Zeke…" Miles' voice called.

"Just having a talk," Zeke shot over his shoulder; his voice was grumpier than usual.

He grabbed my jacket, handed it to me and pulled me outside with him. Fuck, it was cold! I quickly started pulling on my coat. How the fuck wasn't he freezing? His body heat began rising off his broad shoulders in steam. How could he stand it?

When he had me out of Asher's hearing range, he stopped and pulled me closer. There was going to be yelling I was sure of it. His ice-blue eyes met mine; his face hard.

"From now on," he began, his voice low and quiet. "Anyone fucking messes with you, I want to know." I raised my eyebrows at that. Seriously? "Dylan said those girls kept tearing into you. What did they say?"

Oh, yeah. He was pissed. His shoulders were rigid, his voice was telling me not even to try to get out of this. This wasn't Zeke's overprotective shit; this sounded like it was nearing a trigger. But... that didn't make sense. They were girls.

I didn't try to figure it out; I just answered him. "The usual, that I was a slut, that I was trying to bang all of you." I shrugged, not knowing what else to tell him. So, I summed up. "They basically tried to make me feel like a piece of shit, or... like I was nothing."

His eyes were burning as they ran over my face. "Did they?"

I scowled at him. "Fuck no, they just pissed me off." The corner of his mouth twitched. I pulled my jacket closed and crossed my arms over my chest from the cold. "Zeke, I can't tell you whenever someone messes with me. That's not..." I didn't know what word to use, a waste of time? Normal? A huge time suck? "Realistic." Yeah, that sounded reasonable.

His eyes narrowed on mine. "You're on probation." His voice was hard.

I went still. Probation? "Huh? What the hell does that mean?"

He took a deep breath and let it out slowly, his jaw was still clenched. "Those bitches were tearing into you. You didn't tell us." His voice was a low growl I'd never heard before. "You didn't tell me." My chest burned as I realized what not telling him did. I hurt him. Shit. "You didn't trust us. Because of that, I'm not trusting you right now."

I didn't know what to do. I didn't know how to fix this. I reached up and put my hand on his chest to try to... I don't know. His eyes never left my face as he reached up and held my hand there.

"Zeke, I didn't mean to…. I'm sorry…." I tried to apologize, but he gave my hand a squeeze. I shut up.

"You've got a fucking month," he said, his voice a little softer. "You will tell me every fucking day if someone messes with you. You will tell me what they said, and you will tell me who."

"For a month?" I asked, cringing.

"For a month."

"Then... you'll trust me again?" I hated to ask, but I wanted to understand.

He sighed deeply as he looked over my shoulder at the front door. "Yeah." His eyes were back on mine. "You tell me everything for a month, and I'll trust you again. Every insult, every fucking dirty look, every catcall. I want to know." He wasn't growling anymore; his voice was back to his normal gravelly one.

I took a deep breath and let it out. A month. Once we got back to school, I was going to have to keep a list or something. "Okay," I agreed. "A month." I could do that if it would make Zeke trust me again. I looked up at him, guilt gnawing at my stomach. "I'll tell you everything."

"Come on, let's get some breakfast before the twins eat it all," he said, his shoulders relaxing again.

I turned and walked with him back inside, feeling awful. I really hadn't meant to hurt Zeke. I didn't even think the guys would see it that way. But probation? What the hell was that? His big hand went to the back of my neck, his fingers kneading. He must not be that mad at me, not if he was touching me. When we got inside, his hand dropped. I took off my coat and left it on the banister. I walked into the kitchen just in time to hear Zeke.

"Lexie's on probation," he announced to everyone as he was pouring a cup of coffee. The guys laughed. Isaac was practically giddy. Apparently, this was something Zeke had done before. It made me feel a little better about it. This wasn't the first time he'd done it.

"Well, it's majorly official now. You're family," Asher said, smiling. "How long did you get?"

"A month," I admitted. The guys started laughing again.

"You got in trouble," Isaac taunted me as he filled his plate with food.

I rolled my eyes and got my breakfast.

"A month isn't bad, Beautiful." Ethan caught my attention as he loaded up a few melon slices. "Isaac once got three."

I chuckled at that before I turned to Isaac. "What did you do?"

Isaac shook his head. "The rule about probation is, you never have to tell why," Isaac said in a knowing voice.

"The fucker stole my Jeep," Zeke informed me.

My jaw dropped as I looked at Isaac. He just shrugged, looking like he didn't regret it one bit.

"Do you have a death wish?" I asked, suddenly feeling even better about this whole thing. The guys laughed. I looked over at Zeke, who was grinning. "What did he have to do?"

Zeke gave me his big smile, the one with teeth. Those were rare. "Every time he got in a car he had to send me a text of whose car it was, where he was going and when he'd be home."

I winced. Every time? For three months? That would get old fast. But Zeke wasn't done.

"And if he was driving, he had to send me a picture of the license plate to prove it was theirs."

I looked over at Isaac. "Never did that again, did you?" I asked, smirking.

Isaac was chuckling as he answered. "Hell no. I ask for permission just to get in that thing now."

I snickered.

"What did you end up with, Beautiful?" Ethan asked, putting eggs on his plate.

"I have to tell Zeke if someone messes with me at all, every day," I grumbled.

The guys all burst out laughing. Except for Zeke; he just drank his coffee. I shook my head and looked at all of them. They were crazy. No wonder I fit in.

IT WAS ALMOST AN HOUR LATER, and I had just finished off my second cup of coffee. The guys were still telling me about their own probation stories. I was finishing my piece of toast when someone's cell rang. Asher pulled his phone out and frowned. He sent it to voice mail before reaching for another slice of melon. Then another phone rang. Ethan pulled his out and sent it to voice mail too. I was smirking now.

"So, what is everyone doing today?" Miles asked just before another cell phone rang. I shook my head. Isaac pulled out his phone and sent it to voice mail.

"I was going to hang out with Trisha, but now I think I need to cool off before I see her," Asher admitted, rubbing the back of his neck.

"Same here, I'm going to have it out with Faith. But not yet. Maybe this afternoon," Ethan added.

"Oh, I'm getting on the phone with Cece after breakfast, and we're having it out," Isaac said plainly.

"You know you're all welcome to hide out here," Miles reminded them.

The guys nodded.

"Sounds good to me," Ethan said

"Yeah, friend time sounds good right now," Asher admitted.

"After my call, I'll be free the rest of the day," Isaac added. "There's no way I can look at her today."

"I've got to meet Riley at two for a movie, but I'm free till then." Zeke shrugged as he looked around the group. "What about you, Lexie?"

I met his eyes across the coffee table. "Well, I'm working on building that link to the Veil today. I'm expecting a lot of pain," I admitted. I looked around the group at them. "So, probably me in the fetal position looking pathetic the rest of the day." The guys suddenly looked worried. Oh yeah, I didn't tell them that part.

"Then I'm not going anywhere," Ethan announced. "I can talk to Faith on the phone just as easily here."

"That's my plan," Isaac pointed out.

"It's probably better if I don't see Trisha during that conversation anyway," Asher agreed.

"I can cancel with Riley; she'll be fine with it," Zeke said as he pulled out his phone.

"Zeke, don't bail on Riley," I told him. "The other's will be here. I'll be fine."

His brow drew down as he eyed me. "You sure?" he asked uncertainly.

"Yeah, it's going to be kind of boring anyway," I said giving him a small smile. "I'll be in my little trance, and that'll be all you guys see." At least that was what I hoped.

"Okay." Zeke put his phone away.

Cell phones went off again. I snorted as the guys sent the girls to voicemail again.

"I got ten that they are all together and trying to figure out what I told you," I offered. They shook their heads. No one would take my bet.

"I can push your rock climbing lesson to tomorrow if you need, Ally," Asher offered.

"I already have one tomorrow," I reminded him.

"Okay, Tuesday," Asher tried again.

"Fighting training," Isaac answered.

I decided to end this before it continued. "We can do two in one day, or we'll have to make it up Friday if I can't make it today, it's the only free day," I told him.

Asher frowned. "Your schedule is really packed, Ally," Asher said.

I gave him a small smile. "Yeah, luckily Dylan lives in another town." I shrugged. "It'll ease up after I get the link going. It should... okay, I'm really hoping here." The guys chuckled.

My cell phone rang. I looked at the screen. "Uh, who's number is 555-7424?" I asked the group.

Ethan cursed. "That's Faith; how the hell did she get your number?" Ethan groused.

"Ever leave your phone with her?" I asked.

He frowned and looked pissed all over again.

"Should I answer?"

The guys nodded.

"On speaker, don't let her know we're listening," Zeke said in his 'I'm not really asking' voice.

I answered on speaker. "Hello."

"Are the guys with you?" Faith's voice was sharp and pissed off.

"Yeah, they're out in the kitchen right now, we're doing our usual Sunday breakfast thing. How'd you get my number?"

"Off Ethan's phone," she said it like it was obvious and normal. "I'm coming to your house. I need to talk to him."

"Be my guest; we're not there," I said, keeping my voice pleasant. "And how the fuck do you know where I live?"

"Then where are you?" she demanded, ignoring my question. Ethan was shaking his head already. I gestured for him to be quiet. "We're at Miles' house; it's our friend-only zone," I said, keeping my voice pleasant.

"Tell me where he lives; I want to talk to Ethan," Faith demanded.

"Miles doesn't want any of you to know where he lives, so, no," I told her just as clearly. "Call Ethan's phone if you want to talk to him."

"I don't give a fuck what that nerd wants; next time I see him, I'll chew him out over it. But right now, I'm dealing with you," she snapped at me, her voice full of attitude.

I became pissed off calm. "I warned you twice and told you there will not be a third," I told her, keeping my voice calm. "Now if you so much as come near Miles, I'll fuck you up." The guys smirked; Ethan just looked furious. He gestured for me to hand him the phone. I handed the phone over.

"Bring it on, bitch," Faith shot at me.

"What the fuck, Faith?" Ethan spoke at the phone. The phone went quiet. I expected Ethan to get up and walk away to talk to her, but he stayed put.

"Ethan, that was so out of context that it's crazy," Faith's voice changed to her sweet one. "You don't know what that bitch has been saying to me on the phone."

"Yeah, I do, I was sitting here listening the whole fucking time," he countered.

"Honey, I-"

"I also know all about the shit from this week now too," Ethan snapped.

"She's lying-" Faith tried.

"She didn't tell us. Dylan did." He snorted. "And here's the real fucked up part. Lexie is the one who just sat here, convincing us guys to give you girls another chance."

"Really?" Faith's voice was hopeful.

Ethan licked his lips and pressed them together hard. "Yeah. And you just fucking blew yours. No one treats my family that way. We're over." He hung up the phone. I noticed his hands shaking.

I pulled out my mp3. "Ethan," I called. He looked at me. I tossed it to him.

He gave me a tight half-smile and handed me my phone back. "I'll be down in the workout room," Ethan announced before getting up and heading into the long hallway. It was quiet for a while.

Then I had to ask. "Where's the workout room?"

The guys burst out laughing. I just waited for an answer. When they finally calmed down, they told me about the hidden staircase in the kitchen to the basement. I thought they were messing with me until Isaac took me in there and showed me. The door just looked like another fucking pantry. Apparently downstairs was just as big as upstairs. There was a workout room, a theater for movies, a sauna, and a few other rooms that Miles never even bothered to use.

I walked back into the living room and looked at Miles. "Can I move in?" I asked, only half kidding. Miles laughed and smiled. It was the best smile of the morning.

IT WASN'T LONG before the guys went to play video games, and I went to the conservatory. I went to my chair and sat down. I had never tried this without the guide, but I was sure I had the steps memorized by now. I took a deep breath and closed my eyes. I let every thought go, every worry, every emotion go and just sank. I went a lot faster. I didn't so much as sink as fall this time. The images of my life flashed by so quickly that I didn't even know which were which.

Then I was there. The white plain and golden sky stretched out above it. I looked at the white plain and the white sand. It was peaceful here; it was me. I took a breath and tried to picture the Veil. I was pulled hard across the white sand. Before I could get scared, I stopped. I was standing on a ledge. The ledge stretched out to the sides so far, I could barely see the curve of the edge of my center. Out across from the ledge was a field of black with stars scattered across it, like diamonds over black velvet.

Out in that space, I saw the Veil. It was like an island. Just floating there, but something was… I needed more light. As soon as I thought it, the blackness pulled away, like a sunrise over a mountain. I finally saw the Veil for what it was. I looked above me and saw the golden sky change to the dusk of dawn; it had texture, like fabric being pulled and pleated. I followed it out to the Veil. The closer the fabric of the world got to the Veil, the more it folded over on itself to attach to that island out there. I looked over the edge and saw the same below. The fabric was pulled and pleated below, just as it was above. This side connected to the bottom of the Veil. The Veil really was just a portal to two different sides.

Now, how the hell do I get out there?

Maybe if I made a bridge? I tried to create a large stone block out of a memory, nothing important, just something I wouldn't miss. The block appeared in front of me. I pictured where I wanted it to go. It moved to the ledge and pressed against the edge. Then I let go. The stone dropped like, well, a stone. Pain burned through my head, making me wobble on my feet. Fuck. Okay, that hurt! And I suddenly couldn't remember what my third-grade teacher's name was. Okay, so don't use memories because that fucking hurts.

The other me, or the person who was pretending to be me, had said making the link would hurt, but something told me that wasn't what she was talking about. So, I needed to figure out what else would hurt. I looked over the edge and decided no jumping. Pacing along the ledge, I looked out over the stretch of sky, trying to think of a way over. A balloon? No. A rope bridge? Attached to what, Lexie?

That other me, the pretender me, had said that a lot of my gift was instinctual. I had to get out of my own way to figure this out. I closed my eyes and took a few deep breaths. I cleared my mind again. Then looked out over to the Veil. Walk. I froze. It was the first thing to pop into my head. I frowned; it couldn't be that simple. Could it? Oh fuck, I was going to wake up with amnesia or something. I should be shaking. I should be feeling my heart racing. But I didn't. I was afraid, but I didn't feel the physical effects of fear. It was really unnerving.

I had a fleeting thought of sending my love to the guys. Then I was sliding my foot out over the ledge. My foot met with resistance, so I pushed. Pain lanced through my head, taking my breath from me. I stepped back. When I could see straight, I looked down. The ledge had extended out over the field of stars. Yeah, walk. Pushing against the fabric of the world hurt like hell. Well, the pretender me had been right. This was going to hurt a lot. I walked back up to where the ledge had extended. I put my hands up in front of me, a little farther apart than my shoulders. If I was opening a way, then I was going to have it be big enough for me to get through. I took a couple of deep breaths. I rested my hands against that invisible wall in front of me. Then slid my foot and pushed with my arms at the same time. Pain washed over me as every nerve I had was lit on fire. I grunted through my teeth as the wall moved back, and I took a step out. Sharp knife points dragged along every nerve in my body as I kept pushing. I was grunting, yelling, screaming, as I pushed and pushed.

Making a new pathway in the fabric of the world required pain, sacrifice. Everything had a fucking price. I thought about Sophia when I wanted to stop. I thought about how I would have to tell Ethan I couldn't help her cross. The knife points along my nerves became blades. My vision doubled, and I still pushed. I kept pushing and pushing. Step after step until the world began to flash around me. I was too exhausted to keep going right now, my body hurting too much; my center was yanking me back. I looked across and saw I had only made it about a third of the way across. Fuck. I felt myself get yanked back and thrown upwards.

MY HEAD EXPLODED; my body felt like it was trying to kill itself. I kept my eyes closed, the light coming through my eyelids felt like daggers already. My body was jerking and shaking; I had no control. There was cold stone under my face, and even that hurt. Every nerve was burning slowly at high heat. My stomach rolled with the agony racking my body. My weight on the stone hurt, my clothes even hurt. I kept taking shaking, jerking breaths. I don't know how long I was laying there. But I very slowly became aware of the wetness on my face, of the sound of water. I needed help. I could barely fucking move.

"Ash... Ash," I tried to call for him. Even he probably couldn't hear me right now. Any other way? Cell phone... did I have...? I tried to think through the bone-deep pain. I concentrated on finding my arm. It was on the stone tile in front of me. I focused everything I had on moving it. It only moved a bit. My body seized up in agony. Fuck, fuck, fuck. Oh, fuck me, why? I was drowning in a sea of agony for I don't know how long. When it finally broke, and I could think again, I realized if I moved I was going to be in agony.

So, I had to make someone hear me. Oh, Ash, please still be here. I swallowed hard, braced myself and tried to scream. "Ash!" My body seized up, my back bowing, my fingertips scraping along the stone. The world turned into hell as my body tried to drive me mad with my muscles locking and staying locked. It went on and on. When it finally broke, I was still gasping. Muscles were still locked up. Fuck it. I was going to lay here till I died. I didn't even get higher than my quiet voice. There was no way Asher was going to hear me.

I just laid there and focused on taking complete breaths. It was sometime later, in a haze of pain, that there was a noise. I came to the surface more, still shaking, muscles still locked up. I whimpered. It was the only noise I could make right now. Footsteps were moving over stone. Oh, please keep coming this way... please. I was still whimpering, and I didn't care, as long as someone found me.

"Red?" Isaac's voice was hesitant. Oh, thank God. Isaac's footsteps came closer. "Red!" Oh, he saw me. The relief was so great I thought I was going to pass out. Isaac's handsome face was over me, his blue hair the most beautiful color I've ever seen. "What's wrong?" Isaac touched my shoulders. I cried out in pain as his touch sent a wave of agony through me. His hands moved off me immediately. His amber eyes were wide. "Gotta get you some help."

"Don't leave," I whispered. I just wanted him here. I didn't care if there was nothing he could do, I just needed him to stay.

His chocolate eyes met mine. "I'm not going anywhere." He sat up and looked over towards the door. "Guys! Get your asses in here! Lexie's down!" he bellowed. Then he was back, his hand gently taking mine. He slowly uncurled my fingers and slipped his hand in mine. Large feet were running towards us; then I knew I was surrounded because of the cursing. I couldn't see anyone, only Isaac. "Don't touch her!" Isaac snapped. "I barely fucking touched her, and she practically screamed."

Wintergreen tickled my nose.

"Lexie, you need to tell us what's wrong." Miles' soothing voice made me want to cry.

I took several deep breaths and tried. "Locked up." It was all I could manage through my nerves that were still firing. There was shuffling, and Isaac's hand went away. Miles was in Isaac's spot. His green eyes were worried as they ran over me. I could hear the others trying to figure out what was wrong.

"Blink twice for yes, once for no," Miles said calmly. I blinked twice. "Good, are your muscles locked up?" I blinked twice. His brow came down. "Can you move" I blinked three times. "If you move, will it hurt a lot?" I blinked twice. He frowned. "Okay, Lexie, I need to touch you to feel what's wrong. I think I have an idea, but I need to be sure. It'll probably hurt."

I didn't care anymore. I blinked twice and closed my eyes. Miles gently touch my arms. Pain ran through them taking my breath away. His fingers dug into the muscle. I whimpered, it hurt so fucking bad I started crying. There was a scuffle, cursing, Zeke's angry voice. I focused on not making any more noise. Zeke couldn't take it. Miles stopped touching me. I lay in a haze of agony for a bit. Then someone was wiping gently at my face. I opened my eyes to see Isaac with one of Zeke's handkerchiefs, trying to clean the blood off my face.

Miles was gone. I could hear him, though. "-get here now. Bring

everything you have for severe dehydration. She's locked up tight."
There was a pause. "I don't care about the cost, just get here!" I'd never
heard Miles' voice like that. It was strange.

"Dehydration? Are you fucking with us?" Isaac asked, not taking
his eyes off my face as he kept gently cleaning the blood off. I knew I
should probably be scared, but right then I was too exhausted to feel
anything.

"Her muscles are locked up tight; that's severe dehydration. Except
for the blood, which is the norm for her anyway." Miles' voice was
strained. "We need to move her, and it's going to hurt, a lot."

"Get out of here Zeke." Asher's voice was hard.

"Oh no, we're not fucking moving her," Zeke growled. "Wait for
the doc, get her an IV, and when her muscles unlock, then we'll
move her."

"Zeke outside," Miles ordered his voice firm. "We need to move
her to the closest couch now, and then we can say she's been sick."

"If the doctor sees her like this he's going to have questions we
can't fucking answer," Ethan pointed out.

"Ask her if she wants to be moved!" Zeke shouted; his voice had an
edge of panic.

"Lexie, did you hear what's going on?" Isaac asked. I blinked twice.
"Good, do you want us to move you?" I thought about it then blinked
three times. Isaac frowned. "What do three blinks mean?"

"It's yes and no," Miles answered for me.

"Are you willing to be moved?" Isaac tried again. I blinked twice.
"But it's gonna hurt like a bitch?" I blinked twice. Isaac looked up at
the others. "She says move her, Zeke."

Zeke cursed a string of inventive curses even I had never heard.

"Go wait outside for the doctor," Miles told him, his voice cold.
Zeke was cursing the whole way out the door. "Now, who's going to
move her and risk getting killed by Zeke?"

"I've got her," Isaac said instantly. "I can run Zeke around in circles
if I have to."

"Asher, go watch Zeke. You might have to block him," Miles
warned him. Big feet walked off.

"Now, how are we doing this? Fast, no stopping?" Ethan asked the group. "Or move, stop, move? Cause either way it's going to hurt like hell."

"Lexie, blink once for move-stop-move, twice for fast and no stopping?" Isaac asked me. I closed my eyes and thought about it. Draw it out? Or get it all over with at once? Fuck it. I opened my eyes and met Isaac's worried eyes. I blinked twice. He went pale.

Then I tried to talk through shaking. "Gag," I barely managed. Isaac's brow furrowed.

"She wants us to gag her, so if she screams, Zeke won't hear her," Miles explained. "It's a good idea. Ethan, go grab a clean hand towel from the bathroom."

"Are we seriously fucking doing this? Gagging Lexie?" Ethan asked, his voice thick and boiling.

"We have no choice right now. Move!" Miles shot back.

Footsteps ran off. Isaac finished cleaning my face. His face was still pale and drawn. Ethan was back soon. Isaac took the hand towel and rolled it lengthwise. He almost looked like he was going to be sick.

"All right, sweetie, open up." Isaac's voice was resigned. I tried, but I was still shaking. He sighed and took hold of my jaw and force my mouth open enough for him to stick the middle of the towel between my teeth. "I'm so sorry about this, Lexie, please don't fucking hate me after this." I winked at him, he snorted. "Take a few deep breaths, Red, then I'm going to move you fast and keep going." I winked again.

I took several deep breaths. Then Isaac did exactly what he said he'd do. He rolled me on my back and my world exploded. I tried not to scream as he picked me up in his arms. My entire body shook worse as I sank under a tsunami of agony ripping through me. I couldn't stop myself from screaming as we moved, then the world went blissfully black.

CHAPTER 11

SUNDAY AFTERNOON

I woke slowly. My body wasn't hurting. Why wasn't it hurting? My body wasn't locked up anymore, but I still couldn't move. Or maybe I wasn't willing to. I floated near the surface of consciousness and tried to decide if I was going to go back to sleep or wake up.

"Need to change the bag." Zeke's voice was hard. Oh, that's not good. Someone was moving. I smelled wintergreen.

"Third banana bag, this has to be a new record," Miles' voice muttered.

"What did the doc give her again?" Asher's voice was strained too. Oh, I didn't like that.

"He gave her a muscle relaxer and some pain medication that might make her loopy. The banana bags are to replace liquids, vitamins, and minerals. She's getting everything she needs back," Miles assured them.

"Rory wasn't happy," Ethan said.

Oh shit, they called Rory. I was in trouble. Maybe I should just go back to sleep.

"We explained what she told us. I thought Rory was up to date on everything," Isaac mumbled.

"At least he agreed not to move her right now," Asher offered.

"But she's in deep shit when she gets up," Zeke pointed out.

Ugh… please pain meds, make me loopy, so I don't have to think about Rory. But no, I just kept floating there.

"How long has she been out?" Ethan asked.

"About three and a half hours," Isaac answered.

"What about your date with Riley?" Asher asked.

"I told Riley that Lexie had a bad seizure, that I…. not until I see she's awake and okay." Zeke's voice was rougher than usual.

Oh, tough guy. I needed to wake up. He had to go on that date with Riley.

"What did you tell Dylan?" Zeke asked.

Oh shit. Yeah. I needed to wake up. I started swimming to the surface.

"Told him the same, and that's she's out cold right now. He's stuck at work, but he's been texting every twenty minutes," Asher said. "I wouldn't be surprised if he tried to show up; if he knew where we were and all."

Oh no, no. I felt like shit. Looked like crap. I didn't need Dylan to show up right now.

"Honestly, Asher, how long do you think he's going to hold out if shit like this keeps happening?" Zeke asked.

I stopped swimming; I kinda wanted to know, myself.

"Right now, I'd say he's sticking. He cares about her. But he hasn't seen her sick like this yet. So…" Asher answered.

I started swimming to the surface again.

"Well if he won't, he doesn't deserve her." Ethan's voice was quiet. "She fucking kept taking shit from those girls, *just* because we liked them." Ethan's voice sounded baffled.

"Crazy Red."

"I may be crazy, but you're the ones who picked me." I groaned. "What does that say about you?" The room filled with the sound of my guys laughing. I opened my eyes to see them all there, around the bedroom Miles had called mine for the last couple of months. I was confused. "I thought we were going to the couch?" The world seemed fuzzy. Maybe the drugs were helping. That was okay. I could do with fuzzy right now.

Miles moved off the wall to stand next to me. His fingers found my pulse in my wrist as he was looked down at his watch. "You were unconscious before we even got you out of the conservatory; I figured going a little further wouldn't matter," Miles explained gently.

I smiled sleepily. "Good call, sir," I said in a funny voice. Miles smirked. "What fucking time is it?"

"It's around four in the afternoon," Isaac answered me. "I found you around one."

"Lexie, what happened?" Asher asked as he got out of his chair and came to the end of the bed.

I sighed. "I was fucking stupid," I admitted it freely. "It took me a bit to figure it out, but then I was, well, pushing against the fabric of this world to create a new pathway. And everything comes with a fucking price." I snorted at myself, finally lifting my head off the pillow. I blinked hard again. "This price was pain, lots and lots of pain. Even before I came out of it." I don't know why I said that; I didn't mean to say that. It must be those drugs Miles had been talking about.

"So, you overdid it making the link... and..." Asher stopped. "Ally, help me out here, why did you wake up this dehydrated?"

I yawned big and blinked hard. "Um, maybe, making the link is like physically pushing against a movable wall," I offered, giving it a shot at explaining it. "You can move it, but that doesn't mean you aren't going to feel it the next day." At least that's what I thought happened.

"So, you exerted a lot of energy. And you got dehydrated like if you were doing physical work." Miles said, putting it together for me.

"Ding ding," I stated in another funny voice. "You are correct, sir." There were small chuckles around the room. "At least I think that's what happened, but I don't fuckin' know." I blinked hard again, trying to get a little clearer headed. "I'm sorry, guys. I really didn't know that was going to happen."

"As long as you're all right, Ally."

"You're not doing that shit alone anymore," Zeke growled.

"We know, Red."

"You scared us, Beautiful."

I smiled at them and looked at Isaac. "So, did Zeke try to kill you?" I asked, still fuzzy.

"No, the gag idea worked," Isaac grumbled.

"You gagged her?" Zeke growled.

I made an uh-oh face and giggled.

"It was her idea, Zeke." Miles' voice was firm. "Even in that much pain, she was worried about you killing whoever moved her."

Zeke took a deep breath and let it out. He needed a hug, but right now I had to use the bathroom badly. And I was starving. I didn't want them thinking they had to hang around when they had other shit they had to do.

"Okay, I'm fine guys," I announced pushing the blankets off me. I went to put my feet on the floor, and all five of them rushed me. "Down boys!" I snapped then giggled at myself.

Miles leaned down, lifted my eyelid, and checked my eyes. "She's loopy," Miles announced.

I giggled. "Loopy and starving." I looked up at Miles. "Is that going to be your nickname for me now? Loopy?"

Miles grinned at me and brushed my hair out of my face. I smiled warmly back. "No, I'm just worried about you getting up," Miles said. "We don't need you falling."

"Well, I'm going to the bathroom," I announced. "And no one is following me in there." I giggled. The twins chuckled at the voice I was using.

Miles' eyes ran over me, then he sighed. He reached down to my arm and unhooked me from the IV, but left the needle in place. Then he held his hands out palm up. "Let's see how you stand before we make any decisions," Miles offered.

I raised an eyebrow and shook my head. "Nope, no, nada. No one is going in with me," I told him firmly, or as firmly loopy me could manage.

"Lexie, let's get you standing first." Miles' tone told me not to argue. I didn't like hearing that from Miles. From Zeke, I was used to it. Miles, no.

I sighed deeply and put my hands in his, then I stood up. The world spun for a minute, and I felt a bit drunk. "Whoa, okay, give me a minute," I mumbled to myself. I kept blinking as I waited for the world to right itself. By the time the world stopped moving, I was leaning against Miles' chest, with my forehead on his shoulder. "Okay, world not spinning. Let's try this again." I straightened slowly. When the world didn't spin, I gave a thumbs up. Miles slowly let go of me, ready to catch me. It wasn't necessary; I was good. "I got this."

Miles didn't move. "Walk first, and then I'll back off,"

I made a face at him. Then I took a step. I was okay. I took another, and another. I really needed to pee. "Miles, I'm good. Now move before I go through you," I warned before I sidestepped him and hurried into the bathroom. I shut the door and hurried, a little shaky, to the sink. I turned on the water full blast. I didn't need Asher hearing me.

When I was done, I was much happier. I just finished washing my hands when a wave of dizziness washed over me. Shit. I leaned against the counter and hoped this was the drugs. I eyed the distance to the door. Too far. I needed a ride. I giggled to myself. "Zeke," I called. The door opened almost immediately. His striking blue eyes found me leaning against the counter and the wall.

He didn't need to be told what was wrong, he just walked over and steadied me. "Can you make it? Or not?" he demanded.

"I want a taxi," I said in my sweet voice with a smile, trying to make a joke of it. He chuckled quietly. His eyes softened as he bent down and lifted me. One arm wrapped just under my butt, the other across my back and my face burrowed into his neck. My arms wrapped around his shoulders. I took a deep breath of leather and engine grease. It was my favorite hug ever. He was walking. "You needed a hug anyway," I mumbled into his neck.

"Why's that, Baby?" We must be alone; otherwise, he never called me that. Well, that one time he did, but I was dying at the time. It didn't count.

"I hurt you, pissed you off. I scared you. Then the guys had to hurt me to move me. You really don't like that," I mumbled, my forehead against the warmth of his neck. His big warm hand ran up and down my back.

"Baby..." Zeke's voice was soft, or soft for Zeke that is. "I'm fine, don't worry so much about me."

He moved me with his arms. Then I was looking up at him. How'd he do that? Did I black out? Zeke put me down on the bed and slid his arms out from under me. I snagged a hand and tugged him down to my level. He knelt, his face near mine.

"I worry about all of you. Get fucking used to it," I told him matter-of-factly. Then I touched his nose. "Boop." I snickered.

He smiled at me, not with teeth but almost. "Are you really okay?" he asked in that soft voice he used with me sometimes. His eyes ran over my face, looking for a lie.

"Yeah, just feeling weak and dizzy," I grumbled. "I don't like it." I narrowed my eyes at him. "Don't you have a date?"

He blinked at me. "Yeah," he said quietly as he reached down and pulled the blankets up to cover me. "But I was worried about you so..." Zeke trailed off as he met my eyes again. Those beautiful eyes were full of shadows that I had put there.

I didn't like it. I booped his nose again. "Go. I'm fine. See your girl," I ordered. Riley could probably cheer him up, right? "Have lots of fun." I snuggled down on my side, facing him. There was a flicker of something in his eyes, then it was gone before I was sure of what I saw. It must be the drugs.

His eyes ran over me again. "You sure?"

"Yep," I said in my silly voice. "There are four other dudes here. I think they got me covered. Unless they all left."

Zeke smirked down at me. "Asher is making you something to eat. Isaac is cleaning up in the conservatory. Ethan is telling Rory you're awake and okay. Miles is talking to the doctor," he informed me.

"See, covered. Go."

Zeke took my hand off the top of his and held it. His thumb started rubbing on the back of my hand. He looked like he was making his decision. Then he made a strange half sigh, half growl noise. "If you're sure you're fine?" he asked, his voice full of doubt.

I took my hand from his and pointed towards the door. "Go. And say 'hi' to Riley for me," I ordered him in my silly voice. He gave me a strained half smile before getting to his feet and leaving the room. I was starting to think about trying to get up again when I smelled food.

"Ally, I have cheesy food," Asher called sweetly. I sat up slowly; I was dizzy again, but only for a second. Then I was reaching for the cheeseburger he was handing me. I took a big bite. Oh, heaven, it even had bacon. When I finished chewing, he was sitting on the side of the bed, facing me and grinning.

"How did you get this by Zeke?" I asked before taking another bite.

Asher chuckled softly. "He doesn't care what you eat right now as long as you eat," he pointed out.

I finished chewing my bite. "Thanks, Ash. Sorry about all this, again," I said, feeling guilty.

His brow drew down, his eyes narrowing at me. "What about?"

"I keep having problems, and you guys keep having to clean them up." I shrugged. "It's not really fair to you guys." Then I realized what I was saying what I was thinking. "What did the doc give me? Truth serum? No, I shouldn't talk anymore." I took a big bite of my burger as Asher chuckled at me. I needed to stop thinking about this.

"Ally, you take on our problems too," Asher pointed out.

I raised an eyebrow at him. What problems? I didn't notice any problems.

Asher grinned, his ocean eyes ran over my face. "You don't see our problems at all do you?" I gave him my blank face as I kept chewing. He smiled, shaking his head. He reached out and tried to brush the hair off my face; his fingers got stuck. I made a noise. "Damn, Ally."

I finished that bite. "I'm a mess right now, and my hair is usually a mess so...." I grumbled putting my burger down and reaching up to untangle his fingers.

"Where's your brush?"

"At home, where all my shit is," I pointed out sarcastically in a silly voice, picking up my burger again. Ooh cheesy goodness.

Asher got off the bed and went into the bathroom. I didn't even care what he was doing; I had an excellent burger, and I was only half done. Asher came back to the side of the bed.

"Scoot up, Ally girl, I'm going to brush that out before it gets so bad you have to cut it."

I wasn't paying attention; he told me to scoot, so I scooted up. I was chewing another bite when Asher sat behind me. His hands went into my hair, and I got confused. Was he brushing my hair? Huh? Did guys do that? But it seemed guys did indeed do that because that's what Asher did while I ate. He held a section of my hair and combed out the knots before going higher in that section. It was surprisingly comforting. When I finished eating, I wiped the grease off my fingers and mouth with the napkin and just sat there as he brushed my hair. I noticed he wasn't yanking my hair at all.

"How do you know how to do this?" I asked. "Brushing long hair without it hurting, I mean."

"I have a sister, Ally. When Mom was sick, I'd brush Jessica's hair for her. Then Mom would instruct me on how to do basic girl hair-styles," he told me quietly. "Mom didn't have the strength to do it anymore, so I was her hands for her."

My heart melted into my feet. "You are an amazing guy, Ash," I mumbled as the brush ran through my hair.

He snorted. "Not really." He said it so quietly that I almost didn't hear it

"Yeah, you are." Then I used my bossy voice. "And don't argue with the drugged girl. We get mean." He chuckled. Then I thought about it. "Okay, maybe not mean. But we get snuggly, and you wouldn't want to see that."

Asher laughed behind me. It made me grin a little. He put the brush down, and then his hands were in my hair doing something; I couldn't tell. Then his hands were on my shoulders, giving me a squeeze.

"Okay, what did you do?" All I could feel was the mass wasn't heavy on my back.

"A not-so-messy braid. It's not a French, but it will hold a lot better than those you've been doing," he said, getting off the bed behind me.

I blinked up at him. "Do you still do your sister's hair?" I asked, not really knowing why.

His eyes narrowed on me. "No, I don't think she'd appreciate it," he admitted, picking up my napkin and throwing it in the trash.

"You should offer." I don't know what was running my mouth today, but it was weird. "If your mom used to do it, then you did with her..." I snuggled down in the bed. "If I had a mom like that, I'd like to remember her. Maybe it will help her remember your mom a bit more." Then I realized what I was saying. What was with me today? "Or not. It might just be the drugs talking."

Asher's eyes ran over my face, his face almost frowning.

"Thank you for fixing my hair, Ash."

He grinned down at me. "Anytime, Ally girl." He turned and headed out the door.

Isaac almost ran into him trying to come in. "Tag in?" Isaac said in his excited voice. Asher chuckled and smacked him on the shoulder. Isaac threw his arms up in victory as he came in. He didn't bother to stand next to the bed. He just jumped on and crawled up until he sat next to me with his back against the headboard. I rolled onto my back, so I could look at him.

"Hey, Cookie Monster." My voice wasn't so cheerful now, and the world was starting to feel less fuzzy. My body was starting to ache a bit. Isaac smiled down at me, but it didn't reach his eyes. "What's wrong?"

"I don't like that we had to move you like that, Red," Isaac began. "And the whole shit with the gag... I..." He sighed.

"It's not your fault," I told him. "I told you to. And you had to listen." When he went to argue, I cut him off. "Would you have moved me if I said no?"

"God no," Isaac said adamantly.

"See, not your choice," I pointed out. "It was mine. Besides, I was knocked out pretty quick."

Isaac shook his head. "Not quick enough for me," he grumbled. "Carrying you when you were screaming was a fucking nightmare."

It probably was. Thankfully, I didn't remember that much of it. But Isaac did.

"You want cuddles?" I asked sweetly. I wanted to make him feel better and touching someone always did that for the twins.

He grinned down at me. "Zeke might kill me if I touch you again today," he warned me.

I smirked at him. "He's gone; I sent him out to see Riley."

He chuckled quietly. Then shook his head. "You're hurting, Red; you don't need to be trying to make me feel better."

"Painkillers are still working, snuggle now or lose the chance," I said in my sing-song voice.

He snickered at me, then scooted down till he was leaning back against the pillows. I scooted over and snuggled up to his side with my head resting on his shoulder. His arms wrapped around me. He smelled like oranges today. I just laid there and let him hold me. It wasn't couple cuddling; it was friend cuddling. It was comforting, warm and safe. That was what we needed right then. After some time, my mind cleared up a bit more, and I realized we were both dating people. Oops. "Know what?"

"Hmm?" He sounded half asleep.

"Your girlfriend and my boyfriend would have a shit fit over this," I pointed out.

I felt him shrug.

"Don't care; you're Red. Rules don't really count for you," he mumbled, his face burying in my hair.

I smiled at that. "Why's that?"

"'Cause you're Red, it's what you do. You break all the rules, and it always comes out good," Isaac muttered, yeah, he was half asleep.

"I don't break all the rules."

He snorted into my hair. "No, but you sure as hell bend them." He sounded awake again. "How many girls cuddle with their guy friends to make them feel better? Even though you're dating Dylan, you're still snuggling with me because I feel like I tortured you today."

"I'm just that lovable," I grumbled at him, not entirely happy with my answer.

He snickered and gave me a squeeze. "Yes, yes you are," he said in an irritating, cutesy voice. I poked him in the ribs. "Ow. Not fair, I can't get you back right now."

I snickered.

It wasn't long before Ethan walked in, a cellphone to his ear. "Yeah, yeah, hold your fucking horses, woman," Ethan snapped into the phone. He spotted us cuddling, and it didn't surprise him a bit. "Your fucking girlfriend is on the phone and won't stop bitching till she talks to you."

Isaac sighed. "Time for that conversation then." Isaac's smooth voice went lower. He still sounded pissed at Cece. I moved so he could move. Isaac rolled to the other side of the bed and got up. He took his phone from Ethan, who passed him to climb onto the bed with me.

"Cuddle time!" he cheered as he plopped down next to me. I smiled while I cuddled into him as I had done with Isaac. His warm arm went around me, giving me a squeeze. "How are you feeling, Beautiful?"

"Okay." My voice was small as I went back over what Isaac had said. A deep ache was starting to set in. "Ethan, do you think I break all the rules?"

He snorted through his nose. "Oh yeah, that's you, Beautiful." He sounded confident.

I frowned. "Is that a good thing or a bad thing?" I really had no idea.

Ethan seemed to think about it. "It can be both," he began, his smoky voice quiet. "It can be good, like just now with my brother. He's been tearing himself up over having to hurt you, and the gag really bothered him." His hand moved from my arm and ran over my hair. "You knew it, and you cuddled him to make him feel better. Most girls wouldn't cuddle a guy just to make them feel better unless they were dating him."

So, I was weird? Heh, fuck it. I'd own it. "And the bad?"

He was quiet for a bit. "You have a temper, and sometimes you're a little violent," he said gently. "So, when you break those rules, it's not so good. Like going after Trisha."

I pulled back and looked up at him like he was nuts.

"Let me finish," he said.

I frowned and laid back down.

"Did she hit you? Did she try to hurt you?"

"No."

"But you went after her to hurt her," he pointed out. I chewed my bottom lip. "What she said was completely fucked up. But she didn't offer any physical violence, and you went after her."

I hated to admit it, but he was right. Fuck. No matter how pissed off I got, I shouldn't have gone after her like that.

"You might have a point...."

"Some rules you can break, and it's fine. But others you can't."

I wondered where he heard that. "Did Miles tell you that?" I asked suspiciously.

He sighed into my hair. "Yeah, a few years ago," he admitted. "I was having a hard time, so Miles put a few rules in place for me to follow. It helped me with my anger issues." I snorted. "What?"

"Everyone of us has anger issues, well, except Asher," I pointed out, smirking.

Ethan chuckled. "Yeah, you're right about that, Beautiful," he agreed and put his arm back around me. It hurt, but I didn't say anything. Not yet.

"I'm sorry about Faith," I whispered.

"I'm not," Ethan began. "She's been a bit jealous since the beginning. It was just little things, but I thought 'hey, that means she likes me.'" He shrugged. "She got pissed if I even talked to another girl. Then she got in my phone for your number; she knows where you live and all that crap about you and Miles." He kissed my forehead. "It wasn't all you, Beautiful. There were problems already."

"Well, now I don't feel so bad." I winced as the meds really stopped working.

Ethan went still. "Beautiful?" he called, his voice worried.

I rolled off him to my other side and curled up. My entire body was aching. I felt like I had the world's worst Charlie horse, but it was every muscle in my body. I focused on breathing and not whimpering like a bitch.

"Miles!" Ethan shouted, his hand lightly went to my arm. When I didn't smack him away, he started to stroke down my arm gently.

"Lexie?" Miles' voice came from the doorway. Then he was there, kneeling by the bed. His emerald eyes were running over me. I kept focusing on breathing. Miles' hand moved Ethan's off me so he could feel my arm. "She's locking up again." Miles got to his feet, took my arm with the line still in it, and hooked me back up to the banana bag.

"What do we do?" Ethan wasn't on the bed anymore; he was standing next to Miles. His fingers were spinning his rings.

"We give her a second dose of muscle relaxers," Miles told him calmly as he walked over to the table by the bathroom. I was so focused on breathing that I barely noticed when someone else came in the room.

"What's wrong?" Asher's voice came from the doorway. I just kept breathing.

Miles returned to the bed with a small needleless syringe in his hand. His hands were steady as he connected with one of the ports and began injecting me with the medication. "She just needs another dose of muscle relaxers right now," Miles explained, still calm as he focused on what he was doing.

"Are you sure that's the right dose?" Ethan's voice was strained. There was the sound of running feet.

"What's up?" Isaac's voice was breathless as he came in.

"Just giving her a second dose of meds," Miles repeated himself. "The doctor drew them up himself, said she might need them through tonight and told me how far apart to keep them," Miles reassured them. "She was due about fifteen minutes ago; I didn't want to give her anything if she didn't need it." Miles finished injecting the medicine and tossed the syringe in the trash. "Technically she doesn't need the muscle relaxers, but the doctor said that after being seized up like that for so long, her muscles are going to want to go back to that for a while. I thought this would be better than pain meds." Miles squatted back down so he could look at my face. "You should be feeling better pretty soon, Lexie. This stuff won't make you loopy like the pain meds."

I gave him a thumbs up. He gave me a gentle smile. I reached out and held his hand. His thumb rubbed back and forth on the back of my hand. He didn't seem inclined to go anywhere. Gradually over the next few minutes, my body eased up. When I relaxed into the mattress, Miles smiled. "Better?"

"Yeah," I groaned.

Asher came into my line of vision, a cell phone to his ear.

"She's fine now. Miles gave her the second dose she needed," Asher said. It was probably Rory. I looked at Miles.

"So, I'm crashing here?"

Miles nodded. "Yes. Rory is not happy with you by the way," Miles informed me. I didn't really care right now. "You didn't tell him about linking to the Veil?"

"No, I should have but I just..." I trailed off. I don't really know why I didn't. Too busy? Didn't want to bother him? "It must have slipped my mind."

"You have been really busy," Miles admitted. "Rory brought you a bag of clothes."

I gave him a small smile. "Thank you for taking care of me," I said sincerely. "You seem to end up doing it a lot."

His eyes softened. "I don't mind, Lexie. You're pretty easy to take care of," he said gently.

I narrowed my eyes at him playfully. "Did you just call me easy?"

His eyes went wide; his mouth dropped open. There was real panic there for a second. I snickered at the face he was making.

When he realized I was joking, he shook his head at me. "You are feeling better," Miles observed, smiling his big smile now.

"Yeah, I feel almost normal. The shit kicked out of me normal, but normal. Can I get up? Move around? Please?" I begged.

"Yes, you can. You just have to take the IV pole with you," he said. "I want you to finish that bag and another before unhooking you again." I made a face but didn't care. I let Miles go, he moved away, and I sat up. My muscles still hurt but weren't tight as a guitar string anymore.

"We're still decorating tomorrow, right?" I asked hopefully. Decorating Miles' house was going to be fun. I had ideas for that moose head in the living room. Ethan chuckled at me, as he finally stopped spinning his rings.

"That's the plan," Miles said cheerfully. Something flickered in his eyes. It was there, then it was gone just as fast. Zeke had said Miles had been acting off lately. I wanted to get to the bottom of it. Just not today. I'd find out tomorrow.

I noticed Asher still talking on the phone. Huh. Okay. Miles, Asher, and Isaac headed back out of the room, leaving me with Ethan.

I waited until they were down the hall before speaking up. "Think you can help sneak my ass into the kitchen? I'm dying for some fucking chips," I whispered to him.

Ethan chuckled at me. Then, of course, he went with me to make sure I didn't fall on my butt. We raided the kitchen and took our haul into the empty family room. Ethan threw on a movie while I opened a bag of barbecue chips and went to town. Ethan even gave me the throw off the back of one of the chairs so it would look like I was still resting. I curled up in the corner of the sofa. Ethan, my partner in crime, laid down on the couch with his head on a pillow on my bent legs. It was ten minutes later when Miles found us.

"When did you guys come in here?" Miles asked as he came around the couch.

"As soon as I could convince Ethan to go with me," I admitted before putting another chip into my mouth.

"It took, like, a minute." Ethan snickered. I joined him.

Miles came over to me and handed me a glass of water and a couple of pills. I raised an eyebrow. "It's ibuprofen. It'll help with pain," Miles explained.

"Thank you, Miles," I said in my sweet voice. I took the pills and set the glass down.

Miles sat on the other edge of the couch near Ethan's feet as he looked through the horde and pulled out a couple of cupcakes. My mind was going over my schedule for the next few days. I was going to have to make some changes.

"Well, if you guys are serious about being with me while I work on the link to the Veil, then I'll need someone in the morning and then someone at night."

"Lexie, that sounds exhausting. Why are you setting that pace?" Ethan asked, leaning over and going through the snacks on the coffee table. My eyes met Miles'. Ethan laid back down.

"I have some souls that want to move on, and the fuckers are starting to team up to find me," I told him. I wasn't lying; it had happened. It just wasn't the whole truth.

Ethan looked up at me, frowning. "When did that happen?"

Oh yeah, I didn't tell them. "Game night. Two of them came at me outside Asher's." Again, it wasn't a lie.

"You think it's going to happen more often until you start passing souls on?" Ethan said, his eyes storming. "They're trying to bully you into helping them. That's fucked up."

I sighed. "Ethan, they are stuck here. One of them wants to see his wife again, and the other just wants to move on," I tried to explain. "With all that extra energy running around I'd be a little desperate to get out of here too."

Ethan seemed to understand that.

We went back to watching the movie but were interrupted by Asher. "When did you move?" Asher asked, his eyes flashing; he had his phone to his ear again.

I pointed at Ethan. "His fault; I was just the innocent luggage," I said immediately. Ethan glared up at me, promising retaliation. "Plus, snacks."

"Yeah, like I believe that." His eyes ran over me again, still worried. "You have any trouble getting out here?"

"Nope, dizziness was from lack of sugar I think." I pointed at all the wrappers and food still on the coffee table. "Since Zeke's not here, we're pigging out. Wanna join? You know you want to." Asher chuckled, his face and eyes relaxing to normal. I heard Miles quietly laughing behind me. I smiled sweetly at Asher.

"I found her. She snuck out of bed and raided the kitchen with Ethan. She's back to normal," Asher said into the phone. "Hold on."

Asher held out what was apparently my phone, to me. "Dylan. He's been texting every twenty minutes, worried about you."

I winced and took the phone. "Hey, you," I said cheerfully.

"Are you okay?" Dylan's husky voice was strained.

"I'm good now. I passed out for a bit and woke up starving. I'm now eating all the junk food in Miles' house. Don't tell Zeke," I answered, smiling. "How are you doing?"

He sighed deeply. "Much better, now that I know you're okay. What happened?" His voice was starting to get back to his usual husky sound.

"I had a seizure when I was alone. Isaac found me, yelled for the others," I began. Isaac walked in and frowned at me on the couch, then looked at Asher.

Asher shrugged. "She seems fine."

Isaac appeared to relax a bit. I reached forward and threw him a candy bar. He caught it and smiled. I knew how to make Isaac happy. Oh wait... that sounded wrong.

"And the guys picked me up, tucked me into bed, and watched me till I woke up," I added. "I only hurt a little, and I took some over--the--counter stuff for that."

"Sunshine…" He trailed off; he didn't sound so good. My stomach knotted.

I tapped Ethan's shoulder, and he moved so I could get up. I left the family room. He was going to dump me now; it just figured. My chest ached as I thought about asking Asher to take Dylan back his mom's recipes. He wouldn't mind. I was mentally preparing for it when he sighed.

"I'm just so fucking glad to hear your voice right now."

That threw me for a loop. He wasn't dumping me? Huh?

"I've been fucking worrying about you and trying to work, but I got nothing done. I just kept stopping myself from calling Asher every five minutes."

The knots went away; that tightness disappeared. Warmth flooded my chest then the rest of my body.

"I thought you were dumping me," I told him honestly.

He snorted. "No, you're stuck with me, Sunshine."

I smiled, feeling completely relieved. Then I wanted to play. "Good," I said in my soft low voice that he loved. "I kinda want to keep ya around."

I heard him take a deep breath and hold it. "Woman..." I snickered. "You really want to play that game?" His husky voice went low.

Hot shivers ran over my spine. I took a breath and let it out. Okay, I wasn't ready to play. Not yet.

"Truce?" I offered.

He chuckled. "I miss you," he said, his normal husky voice rolling through my ear.

That warmth flooded me again. "I miss you too." I sighed. "I'll be seeing you in three days, and I need to finish my shopping, bake your cookies, work on my project twice a day, and still do MMA training and rock climbing."

"That's a lot. Maybe it's a good thing you live in another town," he offered. "That way, when I do see you, you're not running off to do something else."

"That's one way to think about it." I smiled. "But the good news is, once I'm done with this project, I'll be done with it."

"So, you'll have more time." His voice was happy again. "Okay, I guess I can sacrifice not seeing you for a few days if it means I get to see you more often later." I chuckled. "So, tell me what happened with the other girls?"

"Well, I only know about Faith," I told him. "She called my phone, the number she stole off Ethan's phone by the way, and was a bitch. Ethan dumped her right there."

"Good." He stated. "I have those photos on the computer now, so give me your email, and I'll send the really good ones to you. And you can get them to Riley."

I gave him my email. "So, what are you doing the rest of the day?"

He sighed. "Catching up on all the shit I was trying to do when I was worried about you," he grumbled.

I winced. "Sorry, Dylan. I-"

"That came out wrong, Sunshine," he reassured me. "I'm just a bit turned around now, and I need to figure out where I left off. It's nothing huge. I just... don't want to do it now." He was grumbling.

I chuckled. "If you don't do it, does it mean I can't see you on Christmas?" I asked sweetly.

"No."

"Is it essential to the store?"

"No..."

"Is it life or death?" I asked sarcastically.

He sighed. "No, but it is scholarship related. So, I need to get it done." He sounded resigned. "I'll talk to you tomorrow, Sunshine. I'm glad you're okay."

"Bye, honey." I hung up, went back into the family room and took my spot back. Ethan laid back down on my legs and passed me some chocolate. I smiled and ate it. I was so not telling Zeke about tonight.

CHAPTER 12

THE DAY THAT NEVER ENDS

*I*t wasn't long after that when Miles took me off fluids but left in the IV needle so he could give me my last dose of muscle relaxers before bed. When he was done, he carefully took out the needle. It stung, but that was about it. It was late when I said goodnight to Miles and went to my bedroom. I looked through my stuff and saw I had everything I needed for tomorrow's lesson plus another outfit for shopping. Go Rory! I changed into my jammies, and I slipped into bed.

I was having a nightmare; Sophia was rotting right in front of me, and the twins were yelling at me to do something, when that chill down my neck. I woke up fast and groaned as I turned on the light. A woman was standing inside the bedroom door. Her blonde hair was up in a French twist, her skirt suit perfectly pressed. I felt the press of something around my throat. I looked closer at her neck. Rope burns. She'd killed herself and not too long ago. Fuck. Suicides were a fucking mess, no offense to the people who did it. But when a suicide dies, that soul sticks around for a while. Simply because they didn't understand what they did, why they still existed. I took a deep breath and reminded myself to be patient.

"I see you," I said simply. The woman looked at me, her blue eyes sharp. She started to walk toward me. "No, no, no… don't come any closer." I scooted back, just to be sure. She froze. "I really don't need your death memories right now." My throat was burning just from that step she had taken already. "Backup, please." The woman's brow drew low as she stepped back, her head held high. "Thank you. Who are you?"

"I am Jennifer McClain." Her eyes looked around the room, searching for something. "I was following a light, and now it's disappeared. Do you know anything about it?" Her voice was very cultured and polite. It was an interesting change.

"Jennifer-"

"Mrs. McClain if you please." Her voice was crisp but still polite.

I gave her a polite smile. "Mrs. McClain. That's me." She looked at me, confused, so I hurried to explain. "The Veil is shut, and I'm your only way in right now." She blinked at me, her mouth pressed into a thin line. "I'm trying to link to the Veil so that I can cross souls over. But I haven't been able to finish the link." I took a deep breath and let it out. "I can't help you cross over yet. I'm going to be busting my ass every morning and night. But it's going to take time. I need you to hold on to who you are." She looked dignifiedly upset, if that was even a thing.

"This is unacceptable," she stated simply, her head still held high "I demand you take me now."

My head was starting to throb.

Oh fucking, come on. "Did you not hear what I said? I can't. Until I get that link connected, I can't help you." I took a breath and tried again. My pulse was throbbing in my ears. "I will help you cross, but the link does not exist yet."

She drew her suit coat around her and gave me a piercing look. "Then get to it. I have somewhere to be," she demanded, then stood there with an expectant look on her face. "Come on, get to it."

Oh, for crying out loud… you've got to be kidding me.

"It's going to take days, Mrs. McClain." I tried to be very clear. "I'm going to work hard, but if I burn myself out, you will have no way into the Veil." Pressure built in my face. I grabbed tissues from the nightstand and put them to my nose. Come on, lady. "You can't stay here, Mrs. McClain. You're just going to end up making me sick."

"I'm not leaving until you help me cross," she announced.

Are you fucking kidding me? You fucking bitch.

"If you make me sick, I will not be able to build that link," I managed through clenched teeth.

"That is your problem, not mine or my husband's," she told me calmly. I felt that chill down my neck again. FUCK! I dove for the bracelets on the nightstand and yanked them on as fast as I could. My head stopped throbbing as another ghost came through my door. The man, who I assumed was Mr. McClain, had a bullet hole in his head. Oh, thank God I wasn't feeling that.

"Hello, dear," Mrs. McClain greeted him in a monotone voice.

"Darling," Mr. McClain said back to her. Mr. McClain was a portly man who had very clear disdain on his face as he looked around my room. "Have you found the light yet?" His voice was very cultured, almost feminine in its sound.

"Yes, apparently, it's this young girl here." Mrs. McClain gestured towards me. "She says she can help us cross, but she can't right now." Mrs. McClain's distaste was clear.

I was really getting sick of these two already. Mr. McClain glared at me. And if he didn't have a mustache that resembled a walrus', then it might have been intimidating.

"What I said was, I am working on a way to link to the Veil so I can help souls like you cross," I tried to explain again. "The link takes time to build, and I haven't finished it yet."

He didn't like that at all.

"Well get to it, young lady. Chop, chop," he demanded. "We don't have all day."

Okay, that's it. "Look, you have all the fucking time in the world," I said bluntly with a polite smile on my face. I was tired; I needed some fucking sleep, and these fuckers weren't getting it. "You're dead. Your immediate concerns are not that life threatening. However, if I kill myself trying to finish the link, I can honestly tell you that you will be stuck here for eternity."

They didn't like hearing that. They immediately began talking, telling me why I needed to do things their way. It went on and on. I said fuck it, walked into the dark hallway, and the fucking souls followed. I went to the kitchen and got a tub of salt. I went back to my room and spread it across the floor so that they couldn't enter. I was going to get some fucking sleep. I shut my door and laid down in bed.

Only I didn't get any sleep. The fucking McClain's stood at my door all night shouting about why I should help them immediately and be grateful for it. I wrapped the pillow around my head and tried to shut them out. It didn't work. They were at my door all night shouting at me. By the time dawn came, they finally ran out of energy and were shot back to their haunting grounds. Oh, my fucking God. I didn't bother trying to go to sleep, because I had to get up and go to rock climbing, then work on the link to the Veil, then go shopping with Riley.

I had a full fucking day on no sleep for forty-eight hours. Coffee. I needed coffee. I got dressed in my climbing lesson clothes: black capri yoga pants, sports bra, green tank top. My body was still aching from yesterday. I pulled on my shoes like a zombie and went into the kitchen. I made the coffee maker start and waited. I couldn't believe how fucking tired I was. Like nightmares weren't enough to mess with the little sleep I managed, now I had stuck up ghosts keeping me awake. I laughed at how strange that sounded.

The coffee was ready. I tossed a couple of ice cubes in and watched them melt. Then I started chugging. I was done quickly. Okay, coffee drive through. Espresso shots. I got this. I waited till the coffee kicked in a bit and got my gears turning before heading out. I got a small coffee that had five shots of espresso. The barista thought I was insane. Yeah, it tasted shitty, but I fucking needed that caffeine. I drank as fast as I could without burning myself.

I was still drinking when I walked into the climbing center. Asher was at the counter next to... Trisha. Just fucking great. I took a big drink. I was starting to wish my coffee was Irish. I walked to the counter as I finished my coffee and threw it in the trash.

Asher's eyes grew wide. "Ally? You okay?" His voice was sharp with worry. Wow, I must have looked like I felt.

"Peachy," I lied. "I had a double last night that wouldn't go away. It just kept going on and on and on. Until dawn."

"Wow," he said, his eyebrows up.

"Yep. I've had a lot of coffee this morning."

Asher nodded. "Okay. How's the filter?" he asked, meaning the filter between my brain and mouth.

"Barely there, and not looking good right now," I warned him honestly.

He nodded, getting my meaning. He turned to Trisha. "Trisha, I know you wanted to apologize to Ally, but today is not the day," he told her seriously. Her brown eyes darted from him to me and back again.

Then I remembered what Ethan had said. Fuck. I was tired enough maybe that'd make it easier. "Trisha, I do have something to say to you." Asher turned, almost cringing. Trisha looked like she was bracing herself. "I should not have gone after you that way. You didn't try to hurt me physically, and I went at you. So, I'm sorry I did that. I've learned recently I really need to control my violent tendencies." I took a breath and let it out. I looked at Asher's shocked face; it was a match for Trisha's.

"Did that coffee have a little extra something?" Asher asked seriously.

I snorted. "I wish. No, Ethan just told me I broke a rule that shouldn't be broken. You don't throw the first punch. You just throw the last." I thought about that a second. "Or something like that. I'm paraphrasing on zero sleep here, man."

He nodded, understanding.

He looked to Trisha who still looked like a stunned fish. "Trish, I'll talk to you later," Asher said. She looked up at him, smiled, then walked away and out the door. I let out a big breath.

"For the first time in my life, I need a drink," I groaned, rubbing my eyes.

"That was…. shit. Ally…."

I looked up at him. He was staring at me like he'd never seen me before. I usually would have thought about that, but right now, I didn't have the extra brain power.

"Hardest fucking thing ever," I told him honestly. "Now let's get going; I still have Veil crap and shopping with Riley before we decorate Miles' house." Asher nodded and got my shoes. I looked up at the climbing walls. Please don't let me do anything too stupid. I had no clue who I was asking. I went and put on my shoes.

AN HOUR AND A HALF LATER, Asher lowered me to the mats. Today was shitty already.

"Well, at least you got practice falling today," Asher offered. I groaned. "Ally, you need to get some sleep."

I started taking off my harness. "Yeah, I'll get some tonight. I don't have time to take a nap right now." I growled at myself. Too much fucking stuff right now. "I need that link up asap." I had to stop messing with the buckles. I took a breath and tried again. They unsnapped immediately this time. I stepped out of the harness and handed it to Asher.

"What's the rush with the link?" he asked as we walked over to the benches so I could take my shoes off. I focused on that. I didn't want to tell Asher, but with the way I felt, I would if he pushed.

"Ally?"

I sighed and looked up at him. "There is a very specific soul I need to be ready to move on," I said in a deadpan voice. Then I went back to taking off the shoes. I put them on the bench and started to pull mine back on.

"Are you going to tell me who?"

I shook my head as I tied my shoes.

"Ally, I don't think you should be driving right now."

I snorted at that. I didn't have a choice. "Is there coffee here?"

He shook his head.

"Well, that's where I'm headed now," I told him. "Then I'm going to shower, get more coffee, then go to Miles' house, then get even more coffee and meet Riley to shop for everyone." I sighed, already tired. "I don't have another time to do it. Tomorrow we're doing Dylan's cookies. Tonight's Miles' house, and another project he's helping me with, then Veil work again." I got up and grabbed my coat.

"Ally, I'm still worried about you driving," Asher said, stopping me from heading to the doors.

I sighed. "Can you leave work and drive me right now?"

"No."

"Then don't worry about it, 'cause there isn't anything you can do," I pointed out. "I'm headed straight out to grab more coffee, and then after my shower, more coffee." I looked at the clock on the wall. "But I need to go now." I stepped around him and out the door. "See ya, Ash," I called over my shoulder.

ONE COLD SHOWER and two small coffees with five espresso shots each, and I was at Miles' house. I walked in the front door, shut it, and walked into the living room and dropped my coat on one of the couches.

"I'm back!" I shouted. Wow, even my shout sounded tired.

"Kitchen!" Miles shouted back. I walked into the hall and peeked my head in. Miles was at the breakfast counter, his hair still wet from his shower.

"Hey, I'm going to go get working." I was about to walk off when he called for me.

"Lexie!"

I stopped and turned back.

Miles' eyes were wide as they ran over me. "Are you alright?"

I rolled my eyes. "I had two fucking ghosts at that bedroom door all night bitching at me and telling me to kill myself to link to the Veil immediately." His eyebrows rose. "They left around dawn. I'm coffee fueled and don't have time to stop right now." I turned around and headed down the hall.

"Lexie." Miles was using his lecture tone; I moved faster. I didn't have time today.

His footsteps sped up. I gave up. The booger had longer legs and was faster. He moved in front of me, forcing me to stop. "You need some sleep," he pointed out, adjusting his glasses.

"I know."

"But you're not going to stop to get any sleep?" he guessed.

"You are correct, sir," I shot back as I stepped around him and opened the conservatory door.

"You're going to hurt yourself like this," he warned me.

"Okay, I'll just stop and let Sophia rot out like Mary Summers," I shot over my shoulder, walking towards my meditation spot. It was harsh, but that's what was at stake here.

"She didn't have any extra energy. That's what you said," he said logically.

I got to my chair and sat down. "That was Saturday. Today is Monday. I haven't seen her today," I countered. "I'm not going to let the twins' little sister end up like that."

Miles' eyes ran over my face; he saw I wasn't going to give on this. "All right." Miles sat down on the bench to the right of me. I took a deep breath, closed my eyes, and cleared my mind.

I dropped fast today; maybe it was because I was tired and didn't resist, but I was at my center almost instantly. I looked around the white plain and didn't waste time. I thought of the Veil, and I was shot across the plain to the link pathway I had started yesterday. The bridge was still there. Yay. Now let's get the fuck to work.

I didn't know what it was about today, but I changed my tactic. I pressed my palms together and pushed forward like a blade. My arms spread the fabric of the world for me. It still hurt and felt like knives on every nerve in my body, but I was moving faster. I was opening as much as I could safely do today, and quite frankly the fabric of the world needed to get the fuck out of my way. After I thought that, the resistance became lighter, the pain a bit less. It still hurt more than anything in my life. But it was a bit less. I pushed and stepped until I first felt like I should stop. I pulled back, my vision swimming. I was taking deep breaths as I looked out at how much distance I had left. Fuck. I still had a long way to cross. I wanted to push forward but I couldn't. I didn't want a repeat of yesterday. Even though the nap would be nice. Okay, time to get out. I was yanked back and thrown upwards.

MY HEAD WAS THROBBING, my nose pouring when I came back. Just the usual. I pinched my nose closed and waited for my head to stop throbbing. My body was shaking, but not nearly as bad as yesterday. Okay, I could do this. Couple times a day, I'd have that bridge built in no time. I checked the time on my phone. I had thirty minutes to recover, get coffee, change my shirt and meet Riley. Okay. I could do this.

I looked up. Miles, Zeke, and Isaac were watching me. Shit. Miles had ratted me out. I glared at him. He shrugged. I guess I didn't give him a choice. Miles handed me tissues. I held them to my nose.

"Red, you're white as a fucking ghost," Isaac announced.

"What's new?" I countered. Isaac snorted.

Zeke was frowning at me. "You need some sleep, Lexie." He was using his 'do what I say' voice. Yeah, no, not today. Don't have time sorry. I snickered at myself. I pulled the tissues back and saw that the nosebleed was slowing.

"What I need is a clean shirt, a small coffee with five espresso shots, and to get going," I said honestly. I got to my feet and went still as the world tilted. I waited it out with my eyes closed, my hand on the chair for balance. When it passed, I opened my eyes. Miles was next to me, his face concerned. "I'm good. Gotta go."

I weaved between the guys and headed for the master bedroom; I had a shirt there still. The guys followed like giant wardens.

"Lexie! How long has it been since you slept?" Isaac asked me.

"Over forty-eight hours now, not counting the three and half of unconscious time," I called back as I walked down the long hallway to the other side of the house.

"That's not good Lexie, your barriers-" Zeke began.

I interrupted by shaking my wrist above my head. "Not a problem right now." I took the tissue off my face. It had stopped. Yay. I walked into the bedroom and went to the bag I had left there. I opened it and found a black shirt.

"You can't be driving like this," Miles tried again.

I chuckled at that. I didn't know why, but I did. I walked into the bathroom and began washing the blood off my face.

"You're going to get someone killed, if not you." Miles' voice was calm and soothing.

I tried to ignore it as I dried my face with a towel then looked in the mirror. The guys were right. I was pale as a fucking ghost. Huh. I never thought I could get any whiter. The bags under my eyes were dark. And as a redhead, they always looked worse. They were a mix of brown, pink, and a little red that almost looked like faded bruises. Yeah, I looked like shit. Who cared?

"Guys I'm fine; I'll be picking up more coffee, and I'll get lots of sleep tonight. Right now, I don't have time," I told them. I didn't think they were in the bathroom with me, so I just pulled my shirt off.

"Whoa."

"Shit!"

"Lexie!" Zeke barked.

I was already pulling my other shirt on. "Didn't think you followed me in here," I said honestly. "Besides, I'm wearing a bra." I grabbed my bloody shirt and went to walk past them. Miles' back was still turned, Isaac's eyes were closed, and Zeke just looked pissed.

Zeke grabbed my arm and yanked me to a halt. His blue eyes were on fire as he glared at me. It didn't really work today. "You need sleep," he said again in his deep, gravelly voice.

"I know. I'll get some tonight," I said mimicking him. I yanked my arm out of his hand and walked out of the bathroom. I dropped my shirt into my bag and headed out into the hallway.

Zeke moved to block me. "You are not driving." He said it like it was a fact.

I glared at him. "Then invent the self-driving car," I shot back, still mocking his voice.

He blinked, and I was around him heading to the kitchen. I went to Miles' one cup coffee thing and hit the button for espresso. The guys were talking in the hall like old biddies at a swap meet. I snickered at the image. I went to the freezer pulled out some ice and dumped that into the mug. By the time it was ready, it was lukewarm. I shot that back quick then went to the sink and washed my cup. I was headed back to the living room for my coat when Isaac stepped in front of me.

"Sorry, Red, I can't let you," Isaac said, smiling.

I narrowed my eyes at him. "You really want to do this?" I asked seriously. Isaac raised an eyebrow at me and smirked. He figured he'd win. In a fair fight, yeah. But I didn't fight fair.

Zeke was on the phone with someone, and I didn't really care who, I had things to do.

"You think you can take me, Red?" Isaac asked, his voice cocky. I checked my phone for the time. I had fifteen minutes. To get past Isaac, I needed two. I reached out, snagged his ear and pulled him down to my height.

"Oh fuck, fuck. Red, damn it! That's cheating!" Isaac was shouting, his face grimacing in pain. Miles, who was standing to my left, started laughing.

"You are a head taller than me, and outweigh me by around fifty pounds," I pointed out calmly. "You bet your ass I'm gonna cheat." Zeke was chuckling now. Isaac was still cursing. "Are you going to move now?"

"Yes! Yes! Fuck, Red!" Isaac shouted. I pulled him to the side and let go. He straightened, his hand going to his ear as he backed out of range. I was already picking up my coat and heading for the door. Big feet moved over the floorboards. Oh, come on.

Zeke jumped in front of the door, his hands out. "You're not driving," he said again.

I wanted to scream. "I need to get this shopping done today. Ash's gift is time sensitive, and so is Miles' so move it, Tough Guy, or I'll call your girlfriend and apologize to her for kicking you in the balls." I was tired of this, and I needed more coffee.

"Lexie, I'm not saying you're not going." Zeke's voice was more patient than I had ever heard it before.

"You can't drive me; we're buying your presents, and I'm still buying everyone else's," I pointed out. There was a knock on the door. I'd never seen Zeke's face looked so relieved. Zeke opened the door, and Riley walked in. Her eyes went wide when she saw me.

"Wow, you do look like shit," Riley said.

I snickered. No one said hello anymore.

"I'm driving you, bitch; let's go," she told me.

I raised an eyebrow and turned to look at Miles. I pointed at him, then pointed at Riley. Miles let Riley know where he lived.

Miles shrugged as he stepped closer, his emerald eyes running over my face. "I don't mind Riley knowing if it means you're not driving today," Miles explained to me gently.

I sighed. "You really didn't have to do that, Miles," I groaned, feeling awful, guilt slamming into me hard.

He snorted at me. "Yes, I really did, Lexie," Miles said calmly. "I don't want you driving. This fixes it." I must have been scaring him. Shit.

I sighed. "I'm sorry," I told him tiredly.

He gave me a half grin. "I'm not."

"Great, now let's get going before the stupid mall gets even more packed today," Riley suggested.

I sighed then turned to follow Riley out the door. "I need coffee."

ANOTHER SMALL COFFEE with five espresso shots, and we were at the mall in Northridge. Riley and I had already taken care of most of our lists. The cheery Christmas music, though, was threatening my sanity.

"Okay, Ash's will be ready in half an hour. Who's left?" I asked Riley.

"Zeke; what did he say he wanted?" Riley asked, tucking her list into her pocket. I gave her a small smile.

"He wants wool socks." Riley eyed me. "He works in the garage all the time, and there isn't a heater in there."

"Okay, that makes sense," Riley admitted. "Do you know what size?"

"14 ½."

"Okay, wool socks it is." We headed into another department store; this one had some industrial and construction workers' clothing along with the everyday stuff. We were combing the racks for Zeke's size when Riley caught my attention. "So, why haven't you slept in two days?" Riley asked, her voice distracted.

I snorted. Because ghosts are assholes lately and I have nightmares that will turn your hair white. "Nightmares one night and two seizures last night." I went for the half lie. I found a pair in his size. "Ah-ha! I got a pair. How many did you want?"

"Three at least; he'll probably layer them," Riley said, still looking.

We spent the next hour looking through the wool socks, and in the end, we found four pairs in his size. We were thrilled. While we were there, I made a point to pick up my gift for Zeke. They were cold weather mechanic's gloves, specifically designed to be easy to work in and keep his hands warm. Riley and I high fived. We headed back out and picked up Asher's present. I hoped he didn't hate it. It was the only thing I could think of. We were heading out when Riley pulled me to a stop at the food court.

"Have you eaten today?" Riley asked.

I had to stop and think about it. Shit. "No, actually. Fuck. Let's eat."

Riley laughed at me. I ended up getting orange chicken with veggies and rice. Riley got some pizza from another place.

"Okay, if you don't want to answer this, don't," Riley began. I put some chicken in my mouth and chewed as I waited. "What's it like living with seizures?"

I gave her a big smile as I swallowed my bite. "So fucking fun," I said sarcastically. Riley laughed. "It's basically preparing every day to deal with bloody noses, puking, and possible brain damage." Well, when I thought about it like that, it sucked. "At least no day is boring." Riley didn't laugh.

"That really sucks, Lexie," she said sweetly. I liked Riley.

I nodded. "Pretty much," I agreed.

"So, how do the guys fit in?" she asked. I grew tense, expecting a Trisha question. "When you go down, they all fall out of contact with everyone. I mean, Zeke even canceled a date yesterday." Then she seemed to realize how she sounded. "Which I don't care about, I'm just wondering… well. You seem to play it off like it's nothing. But the guys, they act like you're almost dying each time. I guess what I'm asking is, which is the right reaction?" .

I sighed and thought about it. I knew I made light of my ghost issues, but what other choice did I have? It wasn't like I could flip a switch and turn this shit off.

"Okay. Let me explain it this way," I began. "This is my everyday life. I have no choice. It's going to happen, and I'm going to have to deal with it. So, I make jokes and make fun of it." I took a deep breath and admitted to Riley what I'd never admitted to anyone else, "Because deep down, I know any seizure I have can turn into a three. My worst level, brain damaging level. I could become a vegetable or just die." I swallowed hard. "With this kind of disorder, if I go to the hospital, the doctors will kill me simply because it's so rare that they don't know how to handle it or even recognize it." Riley's eyes went wide. "Because of that, I have to have people around me who end up dropping everything because I'm having a seizure. They end up having to take care of me and watch me until I wake up." I snorted, my chest growing tight as those dark thoughts came out of their corner. "I disrupt their lives, their relationships and any kind of normal around me." I hated it. I really fucking hated it. I pretended that I was okay with it, that I could handle it. But deep down, I hated that I needed this much fucking help. I didn't realize I was crying till a tear hit my hand.

"Lexie…" Riley's face looked, I don't know, full of sympathy?

I grabbed my napkin and wiped my face off and tried to push my emotions back behind that door where they belonged.

"Those guys care about you."

I scoffed as I wiped my face again. "Yeah, and I care about them, but what does that get them? Their lives disrupted, constant worry, and Lexie kits everywhere," I said quietly. My chest ached.

"Lexie, they get you. And if they didn't think the price was worth it, they would have bailed already," Riley pointed out.

She had a point.

But I still had that nagging doubt in the back of my head. Maybe I should just wear my beads the rest of my life? Wait. What the fuck? I sighed deeply. My brain was fried. I knew that the guys didn't want to leave me. You're just fucking tired, and you know what happens when you get like this. You get depressed and all gloomy. I wasn't crying anymore.

I shook my head. "Sorry, you're right. I'm just exhausted, and when that happens... actual thought goes out the window," I admitted to her.

"That's okay, hon; it's okay to feel that way sometimes." Riley smiled at me. "Just don't let it sink you."

I nodded; she was right. Fuck. Zeke had great taste in girls.

I sighed, I needed coffee soon. "If you're done, let's get some coffee and get out of here. The music is driving me mad," I said seriously. Riley agreed. We threw our stuff away and got into Riley's car. I figured we'd hit a drive through coffee place, but Riley just drove onto the highway. I eyed her suspiciously.

"We were going to get coffee," I pointed out. Riley smirked at me. Shit. "Okay, how much did they pay you?"

She laughed. "Nothing, honey; Zeke just said to get the shopping done fast and not let you have any coffee after." She was still smirking at me.

"That's fucked up," I declared.

She snickered. "No, this is the guys getting you to sleep for your own good," she lectured.

I groaned. Fuck! "I seriously don't have time to sleep today; we're supposed to decorate Miles' house," I grumbled. The drive was starting to make me sleepy.

"Zeke said to tell you that you guys will decorate tomorrow," Riley reassured me.

"Can't; I have cookies to bake tomorrow," I countered.

"Zeke said to tell you that you guys can do both and that the guys will help," Riley said patiently.

I groaned, she had turned the fucking heater on, and the damn car was nice and toasty. I tried to roll down the window, but she'd enabled the child locks.

"You're so fucking mean, Riley," I grumbled. "And you were my favorite." Riley just laughed at me.

I MADE IT TO MILES' house, barely. As soon as she stopped the car, I was out into the cold, waking up fast. I even took off my jacket, just to keep myself awake. Riley was laughing her ass off.

"So, fucking mean!" I shot at her. Riley just kept laughing. We walked around her car, and I got the gifts I bought for the boys and put them in the back of the Blazer under my sleeping bag. I glared at her after. "What's next? You gonna put me in a headlock? Knock me out with something?"

Riley was smiling as she shook her head. "Nope, my job was just no coffee, try to get you to sleep on the drive and bring you back here," she admitted.

"Okay, thanks for shopping, hon; except for the attempted forcing of sleep, it was fun," I called over my shoulder. Riley was still laughing as she got into her car.

I had to blink hard as I opened the door and walked into the house. I slammed the door behind me and yelled, "You guys are assholes!" I heard nothing back. The shitheads were hiding. That's fine, hide.

I put my jacket on the banister before I headed into the kitchen and made a beeline for the coffee maker. Arms wrapped around me. I did one of the moves that Miles had taught me, and whoever grabbed me dropped to the floor, groaning. I turned to find Ethan on the floor, and the others were blocking the exits. It was a fucking trap.

"No! No! Hell no!" I shouted at them. Not really thinking, I tried to dodge between them. Isaac grabbed my legs and Zeke my arms. They lifted me into the air. I fought against their hold, kicking and cursing at them. "You fucking assholes! Put me down!" I kept swearing at them. They kept their grip.

"Lexie, this is for your own good," Zeke told me calmly.

"Fuck you!" I screamed at him.

I managed to get a hand free and swung a fist at the back of his knee. He cursed as I made contact; he almost went down but managed to right himself. Barely. Adrenaline pumping, I looked down my body and kicked hard at Isaac. Isaac wasn't ready and dropped me. There was cursing. I scrambled up and tried to break Zeke's hold on me, but the fucker somehow got his arms over my upper body, pinning my arms against me with my back solidly against his chest. I stomped down on his foot. He cursed.

"Where the fuck is he?" Zeke grunted. I tried to break away like Zeke taught me, but the way Zeke was holding me made it impossible. Asher grabbed my legs around my knees, pinning my legs against his chest. I kept thrashing as they carried me down the hall and into the family room. I tried head butting Zeke, but the fucker was too high.

"He should be here any minute," Asher grunted as I used my whole body to try to shove him away and jerk back. Nothing I was doing was working. They just kept hanging on.

"Just keep fighting, Beautiful, you'll be out in no time." Ethan came in groaning. "And when the fuck did she learn that move?"

"Do you have any idea how fucked up this is? Five guys holding down one girl?" I shouted at them as I kicked out.

"Yeah, we do," Asher grunted.

"But we're just trying to get you to sleep," Zeke pointed out. I was getting tired, my legs getting heavy.

I kept cursing at them. "I hate you fuckers!"

"We love you too, Ally," Asher taunted back.

"Okay, bring her down," Zeke said.

I kept trying to kick free, but the assholes had too good of a hold on me. Then Zeke was sitting on the couch with me in his lap, still pinned to his chest. Asher was kneeling on the floor still holding my legs, only now by my ankles. I got my second wind. I jerked against Zeke's arms and slammed back against him. I tried to get one foot free, but Asher's grip was solid.

I kept cursing. "I'm going to take each of your fucking presents back!" I tried to bounce and hit Zeke in the groin, but the bastard had a grip of steel. My adrenaline was running out.

"Aw, you don't mean that Red," Isaac said.

"Yeah, I fucking do!"

The doorbell rang.

"About fucking time," Zeke growled as I tried again to bash him in the face with the back of my head. Only this time when my head went back and hit his chest, I didn't want to pick it back up. I just kept yelling as I kicked weakly with my feet; I was getting tired. But I could run my mouth.

"No means no, you fuck heads!" I shouted weakly, trying again to break free.

"Oh, that sounded bad," Asher warned, looking up at Zeke.

"Yeah. We might need a little help with him," Zeke replied to Asher. I kicked out again, feeling my limbs turn to lead. I was out of breath; I couldn't fight anymore. I needed a break.

"What the fuck are you guys doing?" A husky voice shouted. I knew that voice, and it was really pissed off.

"Dylan man..." Isaac began moving around the couch, out of my sight. Asher was distracted, so I tried a kick. I barely moved him.

"Let me go, you shits." I wasn't screaming now. I was barely yelling.

"Get the fuck off my girl!" Dylan's voice was boiling.

Good, maybe he could get them to let go. There was a scuffle somewhere to the right.

"We're just trying to get her to sleep!" Ethan shouted before moving the wood and glass coffee table back and away from the couches.

Dylan and Isaac came into view to my right. Isaac was keeping Dylan from reaching us, but Dylan was making him work for it.

"Don't believe them. They are lying assholes who took away my coffee!" I called out.

Asher and Zeke chuckled.

I jerked forward against his arms and only ended up hurting myself. "Yeah, laugh it up, assholes. I'm going to... I... don't... ow... I hate you fuckers." I was suddenly out of breath again.

"Dylan! Look at her!" Isaac's voice rang through the room. "Stop for a second and fucking look at her!"

Dylan stopped trying to get past Isaac and looked over at me.

"You guys fucking suck... wait till... I'll tell Maria... she's going to..." My head fell back against Zeke's chest, and this time I didn't pick it back up. "I... hate... you..." My eyes closed. I just needed to rest for a second. Then I'd make them let go.

"She's been up for two fucking days straight. And a seizure knocking her out for a few hours doesn't count as sleep." Isaac's voice filled the room again.

I tried my legs again, and I wasn't even sure I moved them.

"The last time she slept was that nap at your house," Zeke spoke up behind me, his voice vibrating through me.

I tried to jerk to the side, but it didn't work. I didn't want to sleep. I had stuff to do...

"She's been downing coffee all day, a small coffee with five espresso shots each. She's had four already," Miles chimed in.

"Spying... ass... hats..." I mumbled. Zeke's body heat was making it hard to stay awake. "Zeke... please... don't make me..." I whimpered. I didn't want to see it again. The room went silent.

"Why don't you want to sleep, Lexie?" Miles asked, his voice was soft, but it still brought me closer to the surface. The rotted-out image of Sophia and the twins screaming filled my head.

"... dreams... bad, bad, bad..." I whimpered, not really hearing myself.

Someone cursed.

"That's why Dylan's here, Ally." Asher's voice was reassuring.

"Dylan, she has bad nightmares." Ethan started talking, it brought me closer to the surface again.

"Yeah! I know! That doesn't mean you have to fucking hold her down!" Dylan still sounded pissed.

Good, get 'em off me... I didn't want to...

"No, Dylan, we're talking waking-up-screaming nightmares," Asher said from my feet. Was he still there? I tried to move my feet. I only managed a knee. "She never sleeps more than a couple of hours at a time now."

"She's out! Stop touching her!" Dylan's voice was hard.

"If we do that she'll be screaming in... what's the record for after letting her go?" Ethan's voice went through the room.

"Ten minutes tops." Miles' voice was calm.

"She'll be screaming in ten minutes." Isaac chimed in. "The only way we've found for her get any sound sleep is for someone to be touching her."

"A shoulder, a hand on the back. Fuck, even holding her hand will work," Zeke said, his voice quiet. I was sinking deeper, but I didn't want to go. I whimpered and tried to move. "Ah, Lexie, come on. Stop fighting it." Zeke's voice sounded pained.

"I hate that fucking sound," Ethan grumbled.

"Zeke, get your fucking hands off my girl, man," Dylan growled loudly.

"I'm not fucking hurting her," Zeke growled back.

"Dylan!" Asher's voice grew hard. "We have a solution, but it's not going to be here until Christmas. And right now, someone's got to hold her while she sleeps today and it's either going to be you or one of us. So, which is it?"

"What do you fucking think my answer's gonna be?" Dylan snapped. "Now stop fucking pinning her down!"

"Then get over here and take her so we can fucking let go," Zeke snapped back.

It pulled me back to the surface. I whimpered and tried to move again.

"Lexie, Dylan's going to help you sleep now." Miles' voice was soothing.

I stopped fighting. Dylan? Okay, I'd go with that. You guys suck right now anyway...

"Is that okay with you, Ally?"

"Sandalwood..." I mumbled more than half asleep. I wanted my sandalwood.

"Sandalwood?" Asher's voice was confused.

"It's my fucking soap," Dylan bit out. "Get the fuck out of my way, Turner."

Footsteps came closer. The hands on my ankles let go. The weight across my chest eased up but didn't go away. "Let me get her shoes." Hands moved over my feet.

"I know you're pissed at us man, but soft hands," Isaac warned.

Something came off my feet.

"Don't even fucking talk to me about soft hands right now," Dylan warned, his voice still furious. "Let go of her, Zeke."

The weight across my chest lifted. An arm gently wrapped around my back, another under my knees, and then I was lifted. I met a warm hard chest. I smelled sandalwood. I rubbed my cheek against the warm.

"Are you alright, Zeke?" Miles asked.

"She almost took me down with that knee hit," he groaned. "She nailed my instep perfectly."

I wanted more sandalwood. I reached up, wrapped my arm around his neck, and shifted in his arms until I was closer to the smell. Something inside me relaxed.

"Sunshine." Dylan's soft voice washed over me, soothing me. I smiled; I loved that sound.

"Take the couch." Miles' voice was still calm. "Ethan grab that throw." I was moved again, barely conscious. I was sitting on someone again, their arms around me were nice, not holding me down anymore. Something soft covered me. I sighed as everything really started to fade away.

"I've got you, Sunshine..."

I WOKE UP WARM, safe, and surrounded by the scent of sandalwood. It reminded me of Dylan. I smiled, still half asleep. I was on my side, my head on someone's chest, my leg wrapped around one of theirs. I didn't care. Someone's arms were around my back, a hand in my hair. The other was on my shoulder. The sound of a heartbeat was loud against my ear. It was soothing. I wanted to go back to sleep. What woke me up?

"Do you need a break?" Asher's voice was whispering.

"None of you are fucking touching her right now," a husky voice snapped quietly. "Not until I can get that image out of my head."

"We hated doing it," Asher's voice whispered again. "But she wouldn't stop to sleep."

"I don't care." Dylan's voice was still quiet. "Five big guys against your girl, Asher, with her screaming to be let go. Fucking imagine walking in on that."

It was quiet, I started to sink again.

"Yeah, I get that."

"Just... give me more time to cool off." He sounded so angry.

Footsteps walked away. I slid my hand up his chest and wrapped my hand around his neck, my fingers moving.

"Sunshine?"

I started to sink again. Lips touched my forehead, and the world disappeared.

I woke up still surrounded by the smell of sandalwood. It reminded me of Dylan and made my heart warm. I was snuggled, comfortable, and safe. I took my time waking up. As I did, I noticed I was still in the same position as earlier. It was very comfy. His deep even breathing told me he was asleep. That was okay; I was thinking of going back to sleep too. I just floated there for a while, half asleep, half awake. Complete peaceful, sleepy laziness. Then his breathing changed. He took a deep breath. His arms moved off me as he stretched out. When he was done, both arms wrapped back around me. A hand cupped my face, a thumb stroking my cheekbone. Isaac and Ethan never really did that. Only... then I remembered what had happened. The guys grabbing me, holding me and forcing me to stop. Dylan had shown up angry because they wouldn't let me go. Then everything was a blur. I didn't even bother opening my eyes; it was too much effort right now.

"Dylan?" I mumbled against his chest. "That you?"

"Yeah, Sunshine. It's me." His husky voice was soft as he whispered to me.

I smiled. "Good; otherwise one of the guys were playing a joke, and I was gonna kill someone." He made a sleepy, quiet chuckle. I shifted against him, moving a bit higher on his chest until my nose hit his neck. His hand went to my knee at his waist now. Then he began rubbing up and down my leg, from knee to hip and back again.

"The guys cuddle you a lot?" He still sounded half asleep too.

"Depends on how bad the dreams are. The twins take the hit." I tilted my head down and kissed the base of his neck. "This much better."

"That's a little much for me, Sunshine." He sounded like he was waking up more.

"I'll stop," I mumbled back.

"Thank you." He kissed my forehead. Then he rested his cheek there. "How many times a night do you wake up?"

I was waking up now too. I still didn't want to open my eyes.

I sighed. "Three or four. Depends on how long I have to sleep," I admitted, not really whispering anymore.

"What do you dream about?" he asked gently.

"Bad stuff. Lately, things I'm afraid of happening," I hedged as I stretched, then moved back to the same position and opened my eyes. The family room was dim with only one lamp on. "What time is it?"

Dylan reached down to the floor and picked up his phone. "7:43," he said, then put the phone back on the floor. He shifted out from under me, moving to his side, so he was facing me. He scooted down a bit, so his face was even with mine, his body pressing me a bit into the cushions on the back of the couch, his arm still around my back. "Lexie?" Those sapphire eyes ran over my face. His brow drew down, his mouth pressed into a tight line. "How many times have they pinned you till you fell asleep?" His voice had gone firm. He really hadn't liked that. His free hand brushed my hair from my face.

"First time," I answered honestly as I looked into those beautiful eyes.

His face relaxed. "Really?"

"Yeah. First time ever."

He leaned over and kissed my forehead. Then he relaxed again, still looking at my face.

"You really didn't like that," I stated.

He snorted hard. His eyes grew stormy. "I got a call from Asher that I needed to get down here for you. Miles answers the door; I hear you screaming no. I got past Miles and ran in, following your voice." His voice was getting hard again, his mouth pressing to a thin line. "Then I see two big fuckers holding down my much smaller girlfriend." I winced at what he described. Yeah, that sounded terrible. "I get why now, but they didn't have to fucking use Asher and Zeke."

I snorted. He looked at me questioningly. "They didn't start with Asher and Zeke," I told him honestly. He raised an eyebrow at me. I smiled. "I was at the coffee machine when Ethan grabbed me. I dropped him to the ground before I even knew who it was." He was smiling now, clearly enjoying this story. "Then Isaac and Zeke had me; I broke away from Isaac, almost knocked Zeke on his ass. In the end, Asher and Zeke were the only ones who could hold on to me."

He burst out laughing. I snickered myself. I was rather proud of that. He gave me a squeeze.

When he stopped laughing, I had to ask. "How angry are you at the guys?"

He sighed. "I was really mad at first." He ran his fingers through his hair, sending it in every direction. "Seeing them hold you down just...." He took a breath. "I understand they needed to get you to sleep. But it's the way they did it that really pisses me off."

I had to come clean. "Well, to be honest, I was being a bit of a bitch at the time," I admitted. I thought about how I had talked to Miles and changing my shirt in front of the guys. Yeah, I wasn't telling Dylan that one.

Dylan snorted. "Still, I don't like the way they did it," he repeated.

I sighed and moved my face closer to his. "But it did get you down here," I whispered soft and low. His eyes grew warm. My heart filled with warmth at the way he looked at me, making me feel beautiful all over again. "And I did get the best sleep I've had in a long time because of you."

He leaned closer, his lips almost brushing mine, but not quite. "That is true." His husky voice was low and soft, sending those warm shivers down my spine.

I closed the distance and kissed him. My heart raced as his lips moved with mine. His hand went to my cheek, and my toes curled. That warmth in my chest spilled through me, filling me till I felt like I was glowing. The world disappeared; there was just me kissing Dylan. The guy who made me feel beautiful, who always made me smile. My Dylan.

His lips opened, and this time I swept in, claiming everything I could. He groaned deep in his chest, making my stomach do that low hard flip. His hand moved around my back, pulling me against him as his mouth dancing with mine. I slid one hand up his chest to wrap around the back of his neck. His hand slid down my spine, leaving a trail of sparks behind. Every thought I had disappeared. His hand moved to my butt, and he pulled me against him. Sparks ran through my body; my breathing grew heavy. He was kissing me now. His mouth taking mine just as I had his.

I knew this wasn't going anywhere here, so I just enjoyed kissing him, feeling him touching me as I touched him. My chest filled with... yeah. That emotion I never talked about, as I kept kissing him. His hand ran down my leg and pulled my knee up to hook around his hip. His body flush against mine. He felt really good like that. My body was melting, I was sure of it. Our kiss changed, turning hungry as his hand ran back up my thigh to my butt, his fingers digging in. His teeth nipped my bottom lip before he kissed me again, the kiss turning desperate. I was making little sounds in the back of my throat, and I didn't care. As long as he kept kissing me, I didn't care about anything. His hand moved back up my spine, his arm pulling me so my chest was smashed against his. Why did he feel so fucking good?

From far away, voices came from the hallway. He eased back from our kiss, his forehead resting against mine. Both of us were trying to catch our breath.

He swallowed hard. "Sunshine, I-"

The voices in the hall got louder.

"You don't need to check on them, Zeke. They're still asleep."

Asher's voice brought the world crashing back immediately. I opened my eyes. Dylan pulled back, eyes open as he was listening to what Asher was saying.

"If they weren't, I'd hear it."

I cringed. Yep, he knew we were awake and what we were doing. Shit!

"It doesn't hurt for me to check," Zeke pointed out.

"It does if you wake her up," Asher countered. "Let her sleep. I can hear if anything is going on in there. Just leave her alone right now."

I bit my bottom lip. Asher was running interference. Best friend ever!

"Yeah, I guess you're right," Zeke grumbled. Heavy footsteps moved back down the hall, away from the family room.

"Thank you, Ash," I whispered. Asher whistled softly as they walked away from the family room door. Dylan started laughing quietly, and I couldn't help but laugh too. That was a close call. When I finally stopped, I looked up at him. "You can't be mad at Ash now. He so saved our asses."

Dylan starting chuckling again. "Yeah, I guess not." His eyes were sparkling when they met mine. "You and your fucking five big brothers." I chuckled, relaxing again. He smiled at me, his hand cupping my face again.

"You love it, and you know it," I teased, smiling at him.

His eyes ran over my face, making my heart flutter. "Yeah, I know." He sighed. His hand ran over my shoulder, down my back, over my hip, and to my knee. "I need to calm down, Sunshine," he whispered, his eyes meeting mine. "And you feel way too good like this."

I winked at him and moved my leg off his hip. He gave a deep suffering sigh, kissed my cheek then did a strange turn and sit up move, so he was sitting on the couch edge normally. I shifted so that I was lying on my back more, stealing his spot.

"I'm sorry you had to come down." I was starting to feel guilty for how much he ended up driving down here.

"I'm not," he said, turning a bit, so he was facing me. "I got to see you, cuddle you, and even kiss you." I grinned at him. "That's a good day in my book."

I chuckled softly.

I reached over and took his hand. I started playing with his fingers, and he just let me. I loved that about him. Hell, I… I stopped myself before I even thought the words. Too soon Lexie, and you probably actually don't. You're just caught up in how cute he is, how funny he is, and how sweet. And the fact he's a good kisser. Yeah, that list wasn't helping. I pushed the list out of my head for now.

"What did you have to skip to come down?" I asked suspiciously.

He gave me a half smile. "Just checking on my science project. I can do it later tonight," he admitted. "What are you doing tomorrow?" He reached out with his other hand and pushed more hair out of my face as he grinned.

I smiled back. "We're decorating Miles' house, and I'm baking your cookies." And working on another present for him. But I wasn't going to tell him that.

"So, you're really going to bake the cookies?"

I nodded.

His smile grew bigger. "Thank you, Sunshine. Even if they don't turn out, like mine never do. Thank you."

I winked at him. He cringed. I knew that face.

"You need to go," I said, not even having to ask.

"Yeah, the hour drive is a bitch," he grumbled then stood up, and I followed.

"I'll walk you to the door," I mumbled.

Dylan's arm went around my shoulders, pulling me against his side. My hand went up and held his hand on my shoulder.

"What are your plans for Wednesday?" he asked as we headed into the hall.

"We have our first official friends only get together at Ash's house," I told him. "I'd invite you, but-"

"It's friends only, I know." Dylan looked around the hallway. "I got in here, though. That's something."

I smiled then got worried. "Uh, Dylan. Miles is really private..." I began. He looked down at me as we walked past the dining room. "So, can you not tell anyone where he lives?"

He smirked at me. "You mean certain bitches I wish you'd punched?" I nodded. He smiled. "No problem, Sunshine."

We reached the living room where, Zeke, Asher, Isaac, and Miles were playing a board game.

"How much trouble are we in?" Asher asked, his voice worried.

"Are you really taking our Christmas presents back?" Isaac joined in, smiling.

I smiled at them. "No. I've forgiven you, but you still have to appease Dylan," I warned as we stopped by the coffee table. Dylan snickered evilly, and I snorted. The guys just shook their heads.

"It'll be okay," Dylan told them. "Next time, just call me; I'll come down and talk to her."

I rolled my eyes. Dylan made me sound like a hysterical girl from the 1700's. The guys saw it and snickered.

"I'll see you guys later," Dylan said.

I walked Dylan to the door and gave him a very quiet, soft kiss before he left. I was grinning like a mad woman when I walked back into the living room. Then I remembered how I had spoken to Miles today. The grin went away. I went over and sat next to Miles then promptly leaned against his shoulder and hugged him.

"I'm sorry I was a bitch today, Miles."

His brow furrowed as he looked at me like I was nuts. "You weren't. You were just very blunt," he assured me before looking back at the game board. "And rather unaware that we were in the room with you."

I cringed at that. "Yeah, sorry, honey," I said softly.

His cheeks tinted pink. "I'll survive," he reassured me.

I snickered, and he gave me a shy smile. Asher looked at us, confused.

"Okay, what did I miss?" Asher asked. No one said a word.

THAT NIGHT, BEFORE LEAVING MILES' house, I got another bit of the link built. If I could keep this rate up, I'd have it done in a few days. I went to bed that night, and the ghosts finally stayed away. I woke up three times, two of the dreams were of Sophia rotting like Mary Summers.

CHAPTER 13

TUESDAY MORNING

$\mathcal{T}$he next morning, after my morning Veil session, during which I more than made up for the shitty job I did yesterday, I was feeling like a bad ass as I put the finishing touches on the moose head over the fireplace in Miles' living room. Miles had answered a call from Autumn and was somewhere else in the house. When I was done, I was giggling as I climbed down. I took the end of the lights and plugged it into the extension cord. The colorful lights I had strung around the antlers of the moose head lit up. With the lights on and the red Santa hat on the moose's head, it looked great. I loved it. Yeah, I knew it was a dead animal. But it was Christmas; even the dead could have some fun. I put the plug down and went back to going through a box of decorations. I kept looking up and giggling to myself. Miles' mom would probably make him take it down. It didn't really say classy Christmas. But I wanted the guys to see it before then.

I was stringing lights on the huge front windows, well, the ones I could reach with a ladder at least when Miles came back in.

"Lexie, what...?"

I turned and watched as Miles started laughing his ass off. I smiled a big smile as I watched his face light up. He'd get close to stopping, then he'd look at the moose and start up again. I sat on the top of the ladder and watched him laugh. Miles had a good rich laugh that always caught my ear. So, I just sat and smiled as he tried to get control again. When he managed to stop laughing, his face had changed from pink to red, and his eyes were watering. It made my week to make him laugh like that.

"Oh, Lexie," he said, wiping his eyes. "I really needed that today."

"I thought so, you've been quiet today, even for you," I pointed out, moving to stand on the ladder again. The ladder wobbled.

"Lexie!"

I managed to save my ass from falling off the ladder, barely.

"Okay, get down." Miles' voice was calm but firm.

I looked down to find Miles holding the ladder still. Damn, he moved fast. I was going to argue, but the look in his eye told me not the bother.

I sighed and started climbing down. The shit head. When I was near the floor, he let go of the ladder and stepped back. I stepped onto the ground, then looked up at him. "I still have lights to string ya know," I pointed out. He gave me a half smile as he adjusted his glasses.

"I'll take care of it, or one of the guys will," he assured me before going back to one of the boxes of decorations. "There's enough stuff here to keep you busy with both of your feet on the floor."

I felt like being a smart-ass. So, I lifted one foot and hopped over to the boxes. He laughed again. I put my foot on the floor and dug into the box. There were a lot of tree ornaments.

"Are you getting a tree? Cause it's getting close," I asked.

"The guys are picking one up now," he said.

I gasped in mock outrage. "Without us! Those bastards!" I said dramatically.

Miles chuckled at my antics. "The girls are with them, and they're dropping them off before bringing the tree here."

Miles' eyes were warm now, making me happy again. When I got here, he had his blank face on. I was glad I could get his smile back.

"Is that why you did the antlers? You didn't think we were getting a tree?" he asked, his voice was full of suppressed laughter.

I smiled. "No," I admitted. "I've wanted to do something to Gus since I saw him."

Miles raised an eyebrow. "Gus?"

I gave him my big smile, the one I rarely ever used. "Yep, I named the bugger." Miles laughed again, his smile staying around this time. I looked up at the moose and sighed. "Your mom is going to make me take it down, isn't she?" I looked back at him to find him frowning as he watched me. "It doesn't exactly say classy Christmas. She'll probably hate it, right?"

Miles looked away as he started pulling out tree ornaments, his shoulders grew tense. "She's not coming back." He spoke so quietly I almost didn't hear him. It took me a minute to understand. She wasn't coming back for Christmas? What the fuck? What kind of mom left their kid alone on Christmas?

"Is she stuck somewhere and can't fly because of weather or something?" I asked gently, hoping he'd say yes.

His face became drawn, his mouth a thin line. "No."

I stopped looking through the boxes. My stomach knotted. That fucking bitch was choosing to leave Miles alone on Christmas!

"When is she showing up?" I asked, my voice not hiding how I felt very well. I had just pulled out a nutcracker when he answered.

"She's not."

I went still. I looked up at him, not quite believing what I had heard. Oh, this was fucking unbelievable. "She's not coming home for Christmas at all?" I asked, my voice showing what I really thought about that.

Miles' posture became rigid. "She's not coming back period," he muttered.

My heart dropped. He didn't just say... I reached out and grabbed his forearm, stopping him from pulling something from the box. He went still and waited. He kept his eyes on the box.

"She's not coming back, *at all?*" I asked, my voice hard.

He swallowed hard. "Yeah." His voice was rough. Then he gently slid his arm from me and went back to pulling stuff out.

Oh, no, no, no. He wasn't just going to say that like it was nothing. My heart ached as I watched him. He was back to his drawn, tense look he'd had on this morning. No, no, I couldn't take it. I dropped the nutcracker into the box and walked around the coffee table. I all but tackled Miles as I hugged him. He didn't move for a couple of heartbeats; then his arms were around me too. I held him tight, not knowing what to say besides calling her every name I knew. But Miles would hate that. His grip on me tightened. Miles' hugs were usually quick, loose arms and a squeeze. But he was holding on to me like a kid with his favorite teddy bear.

"I'm alright, Lexie." His voice was slightly shaking. He was so not fucking fine.

"No, you're not; you've been off for a few days now," I whispered, my cheek against his collarbone. "No one would be okay after that, Miles, so don't bullshit me."

One of his arms moved, his hand went to cup my neck, his thumb resting in front of my ear. His cheek rested against my forehead. He took a deep, shuddering breath. I squeezed him tighter.

"She's just, not coming back," he whispered, his voice thick. "She says there are too many bad memories here for her."

I wanted to rip that bitch apart. Yeah, her husband beat the shit out of her here, but this was her kid. Her kid who saved her fucking ass!

"Like there aren't any for you?" I countered, pissed as hell. He took another deep breath and let it out. It fanned across my face. I didn't care; he always smelled like wintergreen to me anyway.

"It's not the same-"

"Bullshit. It is the same. You watched it happen. You heard it all the time, and you saved her ass," I pointed out, my anger starting to show. "Not having the balls to come home to your son after that is fucked up." I took a deep breath to calm down, but I kept talking. "Yeah, she got beat up. Yeah, it was horrifying. But you're her son. You should fucking come before everything else right now, at least till you're eighteen. And especially at Christmas." Tears fell into my hair, and my heart broke. I kept hanging on to him. He had to know. "Miles, your mom is fucked up. This isn't your fault." His breath caught then was let out slow. "You deserve so much more than this shit." His arms tightened around me almost painfully; I didn't say anything about it.

Over the next half hour or so, I kept talking; he just listened, tears falling into my hair. I thought I managed to hide my crying, but I wasn't sure. Probably not. It was Miles. He noticed everything. I told him everything he already knew but needed to hear. That it was okay to be pissed at her. That it was okay to feel the way he did. That it wasn't his fault. I said that last one a lot. But the most important thing I told him was at the end. I promised him he wasn't going to be alone. That he was stuck with me, with us, trampling all over his house at odd hours, making huge messes then running off when it came time to clean it up. He snorted. That was better, but I wanted more. I reminded him of Zeke's snoring, Isaac's pranks, and I may have mentioned a few ideas I had to get the twins back good. But they involved remodeling certain parts of the house. He finally chuckled.

Eventually, his hold loosened and he pulled back. His hands went up to wipe his face. I kept my eyes on his chest until his arms came back down. Then I peeked up at him.

His red eyes narrowed on me. "Lexie..." His voice was that soft silky timbre I loved to hear. He reached out and wiped my face for me too. "Why?"

I sighed deeply. Why did the guys always ask that fucking question? "Because I'm a girl, that's why," I explained, making him laugh. I pointed up at him and glared threateningly. "Tell no one." He laughed a good, real laugh. It was the best sound in the world to me. I smiled as I wiped my face. I wanted to hear it again. "So, we can keep Gus lit up like a tree?" I asked in my cutesy voice. He burst out laughing; I smiled my big smile as he kept going.

When he was done, he looked down at me with warm eyes, and an expression that screamed 'I don't know what to do with you.' "Yes, we can keep him lit up." His voice was his silky timber that always soothed something inside me.

I threw my hands in the air in victory. "Yes!" He chuckled again. I stopped then looked at him seriously. "How about smores? Can we make smores?"

His big smile was back. "Lexie, we can do whatever you want," he said sweetly.

I smiled mischievously. "Okay, then I'll need a paintball gun, paintballs of course, and permission to hunt Ethan through the house."

Miles burst out laughing again; it went on and on. Whenever he was close to stopping, he'd look at my eager face and start up again. By the time, he was done, the shadows in his eyes had almost disappeared. I still wanted to kill his mom. I thought about the Gucci pumps in the closet in 'my' bedroom and all those designer clothes. I'd need a good pair of scissors...

BY THE TIME the guys showed up with the tree, I had been looking for the scissors for ten minutes. And doing that while not telling Miles why wasn't working very well. When I finally gave in and told him, he just smiled down at me. Then he showed me where the good scissors were. Miles went to help put the tree up, while I went into Miles' mom's room.

I opened that huge fucking closet and went to town. I tore that place up. I cut up her designer clothes, broke the heels off several of the shoes, yanked off several straps for those strappy heels. I was concentrating on ripping the seam on the sleeve of a particularly elegant suit jacket when Zeke and Isaac found me. Zeke's eyes went wide, Isaac's jaw dropped.

"Shit, Red!" Isaac's voice was loud. "Miles is going to kill you."

I snorted. "No, he won't," I said distracted. I was concentrating on snipping only enough thread in the seam so I could tear the fucker off. I had been finding it oddly satisfying. "He gave me the scissors." There was a full minute of silence in which the only sound was me tearing that sleeve off. Aaah. That felt great.

"His mom is going to kill him," Zeke said as he was looking around the closet.

I snorted again as I reached for another designer shoe. "No, she won't." I tried to cut the shoe, but the scissors weren't so sharp anymore. Damn it. "Anyone have a pocket knife? I have shoes to destroy," I asked looking up at them. They looked at me like I was crazy.

"Red, when she gets back and-"

"She's not coming back," I told him, my voice matter-of-fact. The guys went still.

"You mean for Christmas, right?" Isaac asked slowly.

"No," I said calmly, even though I was wanting to tear into more of her clothes. "She's left Miles here. And decided that she doesn't need to come back to be with her son, ever," I snapped the last part of the sentence. Isaac cursed and strode out of the closet, muttering under his breath. I went back to trying to cut the leather on the shoe. Zeke squatted down in front of me, getting my attention.

His face was hard as he pulled out his pocket knife and opened it. He held it out to me hilt first. "Go to town, Baby." His gravelly voice was hard, even for him. I smiled happily, took the knife and did just that.

With Zeke's knife, it was so much easier. I even managed to get Zeke to break off a few heels I couldn't manage myself. We sat in the closet and Zeke watched me destroy hundreds of thousands of dollars' worth of clothes. I didn't think of donating them to charity until it was too late. Shit. That would have been more productive. Oh well. Maybe we'd do that with what was left over. When I was done, well, for now. There really were a lot of clothes. I gave Zeke his now duller knife back. When I mentioned getting it sharpened, he just smirked at me and told me it was fine. I smiled back and told him I was planning to borrow it again, and he shouldn't have to pay for it. He was still laughing when Ethan, Asher, and Isaac walked into the closet. They all looked rather shocked at the carnage. I just sat among all that devastation and smiled sweetly.

"Now, there's an image I'll never get out of my head." Isaac shook his head.

I snickered before looking at Ethan and Asher. "Do you guys know?" I asked.

Asher's eyes narrowed on me. "Know what? Why you tore up Miles' mom's clothes? No."

I looked at Zeke and Isaac. "Can you guys go keep Miles company, so he doesn't come looking for everyone, please?" I asked. Zeke nodded and got up. Isaac and Zeke walked out of the closet. I looked up at the guys. "Miles' mom bailed on him." Asher's face became drawn, and Ethan's mouth dropped open. "She's not coming back. Ever." I swallowed hard as I remembered the way he'd clung to me. "We need to hang out here a lot more. I know we have since vacation, but I also mean when school starts." The guys nodded. "I promised him he wouldn't be alone. I know we can't keep that for everything but-"

"We got it, Ally." Asher's voice was firm. His fists were clenched, his knuckles white.

"Yeah, we can do that," Ethan added. His dark eyes storming. "He can spend the night at our house for Christmas Eve. Hell, Mom's got presents for him anyway."

"I'll take New Year's," Asher said.

Ethan nodded. "We'll figure it out," Ethan reassured me. "But we can keep that promise, Beautiful."

I smiled up at them, all the guys were so amazing. They didn't hesitate to jump in when one of us were in trouble. I loved these big bastards. "Thanks guys." I held up the scissors. "Want a turn?"

CHAPTER 14

CHRISTMAS EVE

I was walking up Asher's front walk the next day, thinking about this morning's Veil session. I was still trying to get to the damn Veil, but I was about three-quarters of the way. The closer I got to the Veil, the thicker the fabric of the world seemed to be. It was taking more time than I liked. It was frustrating.

That's when it hit me, or two things hit me. One in the chest and the other on my shoulder. I looked up and spotted the twins running around the house, giggling like maniacs. Okay, guys, it's on. I ran after them, scooping up snowballs on the run. I got Isaac in the back and Ethan in the butt before they reached their stockpile. Those little fuckers! I dove behind the picnic table and started making snowballs as fast as I could. A snowball came over the table and landed on my back near my collar. Mother...! The ice slipped under my coat. I stood up and started throwing. I nailed Isaac in the chest once, then the face a second time. Then I dropped back down under my cover, laughing my ass off.

"Not cool, Red!" Isaac shouted.

"You started it!" I shouted back, making more snowballs. Isaac started laughing. Snowballs started flying over the table. Fuck! I kept getting hit. I scooted down, looking for a better spot. The backyard was empty of any other cover except for the tree, and that was no good. Shit. Then I had a thought; where was Ethan?

I barely heard the crunch of snow a second before water poured down on my head. I was instantly soaked through and freezing. "Oh, you fuckers!" I gasped as the cold air and water stole most of my body heat. I was shivering hard, my teeth chattering instantly. The twins were laughing hysterically.

"What? Don't like the ice water, Beautiful?" Ethan taunted.

I got to my feet, shaking down to my bones. "You were ins-s-s-s-side y-y-you f-f-fuckers-s-s," I managed to say as I shivered hard, hurrying toward the house. I needed to get inside fast, or this was going to be bad.

The back door opened, and Zeke looked outside. "What's going on now?" Zeke called.

I couldn't answer; my teeth were chattering too much. The twins were still laughing. I reached the back porch before Zeke got a good look at me. His eyes went wide as he saw my wet hair and the ice starting to form on my coat. "Lexie, get in here!" he barked, opening the screen door and moving onto the porch, waiting for me. His eyes ran over me; his face grew hard. "They fucking soaked you?"

I nodded as I finally reached him. He grabbed my arm and pushed me into the house.

The house was hot, like a summer day, and I knew that wasn't right. Asher usually kept it around sixty-eight. I stopped a few feet in the door, not wanting to track water through the house.

Zeke turned me towards him roughly and bent down to look at my face. "Your fucking lips are turning blue." His hands went to the buttons on my jacket. I couldn't help; my hands felt frozen. "Asher!" he bellowed as he opened my coat now stiff with ice. The air made me shiver even worse, and I cursed. Footsteps ran this way.

"What's going...." Asher's voice trailed off. "What the hell happened?"

Zeke was pulling my jacket off one arm when he looked towards the kitchen door. "We have to get her warm now," he snapped.

Asher moved to stand in front of me, his hands pulling off my gloves. I knew I should be scared right now, but I was just too fucking cold to care. Zeke stopped trying to be gentle. He jerked the jacket off my other arm. "We need to get her out of these clothes and into something dry."

Asher ran back down the hallway. Zeke bent down and untied my shoes. I leaned against his shoulder, shaking as he yanked them off my frozen feet along with my socks. By the time I stood up again, Asher had come back with a blanket and towels. Asher wrapped the blanket around my shoulders; it covered me completely and pooled on the floor.

Asher leaned down into my sightline and grabbed my chin, making sure he had my attention. "Ally, honey, you need to take your clothes off," he said calmly in a firm voice. "Either you do it, or we'll do it for you. But the wet clothes have to come off now."

I nodded. My stiff fingers went to my jeans. I barely managed to unbutton them, and it took time.

Zeke cursed. "Lexie, you need to move faster. Your temperature's still dropping."

I couldn't fucking move faster. "C-c-c-c-can't," I managed through chattering teeth.

Asher's eyes went to Zeke over my shoulder then back to me. "Sorry, Ally, but we need to get the wet clothes off." I nodded that I understood. He put the blanket down. His hands went to my jeans, and Zeke's went to my shirt. My shirt came off over my head fast; the hot air hit my skin, then Zeke had a towel around my shoulders and was hurrying around us and into the laundry room. I crossed my arms over my chest, not out of some sense of modesty. I was just that fucking cold. The back door opened as Asher was peeling my wet jeans down my hips.

"What the fuck?" Isaac's voice shot through the room. I was too fucking cold to care. Besides, my important parts were still covered. Zeke strode back into the kitchen, his face furious.

"Get the fuck out!" Zeke shouted as he strode back towards us, his burning eyes as he glared the twins. "She's hypothermic, you fucking idiots!" The twins cursed and the back door closed. Asher got my soaked jeans down my legs. I had a weird thought of being thankful I had shaved my legs today. I lifted one foot then the other, and the jeans hit the tile with a wet plop. Zeke's arms came around me, holding a large black shirt in his hands in front of me. Asher and Zeke helped me slide my arms in and slip it on. It was huge and reached my knees. Asher grabbed my chin again as Zeke pulled my hair out of the shirt.

"Ally, can you get the rest?" Asher asked bluntly. I tried to move my fingers, but they still felt frozen still. Asher saw what I was doing and felt my fingers. "Shit, her hands are stiff. Zeke, unhook her bra. She should be able to get the rest off then."

"Sorry, Lexie," Zeke whispered before pulling the back of the shirt up and exposing my back to the air. I was still freezing, and just that made me shiver harder. Zeke's hands were at my back; my bra unhooked. Zeke dropped the shirt and made sure it covered me again. I pulled my arms into the shirt and pulled the bra off and dropped it to the floor. I moved my hands to my panties.

Asher realized what I was doing. "Zeke, hold the shirt down." Asher knelt and held the hem in the front, while Zeke did the same in the back, and I moved a bit faster knowing that I wasn't going to flash someone.

"This is the weirdest fucking day ever," Zeke grumbled.

Asher chuckled. "Yeah, stripping Ally naked in the kitchen. Not exactly on our list of things to do today," Asher joked as I shimmied my panties down my hips and then my legs. Teeth still chattering, I kicked them to the pile of wet clothes. I slid my arms back through the sleeves, crossed them over my chest and kept shaking. Asher grabbed the blanket and wrapped it around me. Zeke again pulled my still soaked hair out.

"The electric blanket is in the family room, already on. I'll make her something warm to drink," Asher said looking over my shoulder and stepping back. Zeke scooped me up in his arms, blanket and all. He was like a freaking furnace. I pressed myself closer because he felt so warm. He hurried into the family room and put me on the couch.

Zeke wrapped the blanket around me. It felt scorching. I hissed at how hot it felt. Zeke heard and checked the controller

"It's only at a one," he said gently, squatting down in front of me. His worried eyes ran over my face. "It feels like that because you're so cold." He pulled my hair out of the blanket and used the towel he'd brought to keep soaking up the water in my hair. His jaw was still clenched as his hands worked. The whole time, he was cursing under his breath about the twins, how he was going to kill them, and in all the many ways. If I weren't still so cold, I would have agreed. The shaking was down to shivers when Asher came in carrying a mug.

"Ally, can you hold this?" Asher asked. I nodded and took the mug. It felt like my hands were burning. I hissed. Asher took it back and felt the side. "It's warm, honey. You're just cold." He handed it back to me, and I didn't bitch this time.

I took a small sip and felt it go all the way down. Oh, it was warm. Thank God. Asher disappeared back into the kitchen. Zeke didn't budge until the shivering was almost gone. He took a deep breath and let it out, his shoulders relaxing.

He brushed some hair away from my face, his fingers still feeling hot to me. "Lucky it was my laundry day, huh?" Zeke said with that half grin of his. I snorted and smiled.

"Y-yeah, who knew you had a dress," I shot back my teeth finally not chattering anymore.

He grinned at that, relief flooding his face. Then his anger was back. "I'm going to kill the twins now," he told me his voice matter-of-fact before standing up. I snagged his hand before he could leave. The blanket fell off my shoulder, and I shivered immediately. Zeke reached down and wrapped it back around me. "You don't want me to kill them?"

I shook my head and grinned. "Call Maria." He gave me a big smile, with teeth. Those smiles were few and far between. "Or blackmail."

He snickered. "I like the way you think, Lexie." He ran his fingers through his hair, grabbed the controller for the TV and sat next to me. "You pick."

Zeke scrolled through the menu, and I saw what I wanted. "Pacific Rim."

Zeke chuckled as he put it on. "Monsters vs. Robots, why am I not surprised?" he mumbled.

I smiled over at him. "Because it's great," I pointed out, my body no longer shivering. I was still fucking cold, just not shivering. "And it's not robots; it's machines. Human run, so not a robot."

His eyes ran over me again, his face relaxed a bit more. "You're getting some color back," he said.

I snorted. "What little I have." He snorted. He reached over felt my hands then turned the controller on the blanket to a four. "By the way, just to obey the rules of my probation." I looked up at him. "The twins messed with me."

He shook his head, his jaw clenching. "No shit. What the fuck were they thinking? They know how cold it is outside." His voice was hard again.

"They weren't."

"They do that a lot," he grumbled.

I nodded. The little shits went too far today. Something occurred to me. I chuckled at myself.

"What?"

"I'm just glad I'm not girly enough to be embarrassed when I need to be stripped down by my guy friends in an emergency," I said, grinning. He chuckled. Then something else occurred to me. "Now imagine if Miles had been here." We both burst out laughing, yeah it was probably from relief, but I liked to think I was just that funny. We were still laughing when Asher came back into the family room. He raised an eyebrow at us. We didn't fill him in. When we calmed down enough, Asher used an ear thingy to check my temperature. I was almost normal again.

He handed me a pair of folded sweats. "Your clothes are in the dryer, but I thought you'd like some pants," he said sweetly.

I looked up at him adoringly. "Thank you."

He gave me a small grin then looked at Zeke. "Ready to kill the twins? Cause I am," Asher asked his voice growing firm.

Zeke smirked evilly. "Oh yeah, get those fuckers in here." Zeke got up, and they both went into the kitchen. I took the opportunity to get out of the blanket; I shivered almost immediately. I was just sliding a foot into the sweats when the front door opened. Shit. I hurried and slipped my other leg in.

"I'm here." Miles' voice came from the foyer. Shit, shit, shit. I pulled the sweatpants up just in time for Miles to walk in and see me finish pulling them on. Miles froze. There was no point in turning around this time; I was tying the drawstring. "Lexie..." He closed his eyes, his face turning red. "Why are you always naked?" he asked, exasperated.

I finished tying the knot and dropped Zeke's shirt. Wondering what exactly he saw, I pointed at him. "Not my fault this time," I insisted. Zeke's shouting came from the kitchen. Miles looked towards the kitchen then back at me. "The twins soaked me with a bucket of water outside. I ran in. Asher and Zeke had to strip me down because my lips were turning blue." I sat down and wrapped the electric blanket around me, trying to look a bit pathetic. "They got me warm, and in one of Zeke's giant shirts; my clothes are in the dryer, and Asher just brought me sweats. They just went in to yell at the twins, and I was just pulling them on." I explained quickly, then felt compelled to add, "Sorry." There was more yelling from the kitchen.

Miles' face became blank, his eyes cold. "They poured water over you? Outside?" he asked, his voice chilling. I nodded, biting the corner of my lower lip. His mouth became a tight line. "Excuse me." Miles put down the video games he had brought then strode into the foyer and towards the kitchen. Uh-oh.

Zeke was explosive scary when he was mad; Miles was the opposite. Cold as ice, completely controlled. I really didn't want to be the twins right now. The yelling stopped in the kitchen. I figured Miles was talking. He never yelled; that was its own kind of scary. I watched the movie as the guys had a talk about not almost killing me in the kitchen. At least, that's what I assumed. It was awhile before the kitchen door open. Ethan strode in with Isaac right behind him. They were both pale.

"Red, we are so sorry," Isaac started as he stood in front of the TV, his hands threaded behind his head.

Ethan was by the end of the coffee table. "We were just trying to get your coat, and make it hard to take off," Ethan admitted. "We way over did it." Ethan was spinning one of his rings.

"We thought you were just being over dramatic when you ran inside," Isaac said. "You're always talking about how cold it is here."

"Then, when we saw you in the kitchen, it took us a couple of seconds to understand what we were seeing," Ethan continued.

"Then Zeke was yelling at us. And then we realized what happened," Isaac finished.

"We are so sorry. We really didn't mean for it to go that far," Ethan added. I looked at them both. Their faces looked pained. Their eyes were full of guilt. They really didn't mean to soak me through. I sighed. They really needed to learn to think first.

"No more buckets of water unless it's summer," I told them and used my I'm not joking voice. They agreed immediately. "And I'm so fucking holding this over your heads. We're talking blackmail." They both winced.

Then Isaac shrugged. "We deserve it," Isaac admitted. Ethan nodded.

"Now move, Cookie Monster, your ass is blocking an epic fight."

The twins smiled then came and sat next to me, one on either side. The other guys came in not long after. Asher pulled out the bean bags, and the guys all sat down.

It wasn't long until we were talking about what video games to play. There was a particular dungeon crawler game that I liked playing with the boys. Diablo... something. I didn't remember the name but I knew it was fun to play with the guys, and I wanted to finish the storyline. I had my demon hunter, big surprise, right? And everyone else had their characters on screen too. Then we started playing.

APPARENTLY, when your clothes were soaked, they took a really long time to dry. Asher said this last run through on high should do it. It was fine. Zeke's shirt was big enough that you couldn't tell I wasn't wearing a bra, well, unless you looked closely. And Asher's sweats were comfy. So, I didn't really care that it took three hours to get my clothes almost dry.

"Zeke, man, you're killing me here. Will one of you tanks grab these little bastards." I was diving away from the little annoying monsters and shooting for all I was worth, but they were eating me alive.

"I've got you, Lexie," Miles said, moving his paladin across the screen and shouting. He drew all the monsters off me.

"Thank you, sweetie."

"Your welcome," he answered. "Now do some damage."

I grinned as I shot multiple arrows through the horde of monsters. The fight was over soon; we were close to the end of the game when the front door opened. I was focused on the movie inside the game. Diablo was teleporting us to him. Yes! I'd wanted to own this bitch for weeks.

"Hello!" Two girls' voices rang from the foyer. I was focused on the opening fight video that I had been waiting weeks to see. I'd even been good and hadn't looked it up on YouTube.

"What the…?" Asher said, turning toward the archway.

"What the hell is this?" a shrill scream ricocheted through the family room. I looked away from the screen long enough to see Trisha with a glass baking dish in her hands. And her pissed off face. Then I was back to looking at the screen.

"Fuck! What did he say?" I asked, worried I had missed something vital.

"He said we're going to die," Ethan summarized for me. I snickered as the fight began. I was trying to concentrate, but Trisha was screaming and making it difficult.

"What the hell is she doing here?" Trisha screamed.

I assumed she meant me. I just focused on dodging the cage trying to crash down on my character. Asher's character stopped moving as he got up to deal with Trisha. Shit! We needed that damage.

"It's friend's day," Asher reminded her. "Lexie's our friend."

"You said guy's day, not Lexie day," Trisha snapped back.

I kept trying to do damage as the guys acted like tanks, and Isaac healed everyone.

"I said friend's day; you said guy's day," Asher told her gently.

I would have shouted it, but he wasn't me.

"I didn't hear friend day," Cece's voice piped up. Isaac cursed under his breath but kept playing. "Isaac, what's going on?"

"We're hanging out with Lexie as was our arrangement, without you girls," Isaac told her bluntly, not bothering to look at her. His voice was about as happy with her as I was right now.

"And what the fuck is she wearing?" Trisha snapped.

"Swear jar," I stage whispered sarcastically as I dodged the cage again. Everyone but Asher, Trisha, and Cece laughed.

"Lexie, don't even start with me! You're in my boyfriend's house, wearing his sweats." Trisha sounded pissed. Ooh. I was shaking. No! Fuck. I took a big hit.

"Shit! Isaac save my ass here," I shouted.

"Recharging, you're on your own," Isaac shot back. I used one of my few remaining health potions and tried to keep my character out of reach.

"Why is she wearing your sweats? And whose shirt is that?" Trisha demanded.

"Mine, so stop bitching," Zeke shot at her, not taking his eyes off the screen.

I snickered; so did the twins. Trisha made an offended noise.

"This isn't funny, Isaac! She's not even wearing a bra," Cece yelled.

"Isaac, tell your girlfriend to stop checking me out," I said seriously.

He laughed. Cece got pissed.

"Why is she wearing your pants and not wearing a bra, Asher?" Trisha's voice got higher.

I winced. It felt like a knife in my ear. Distracted, I took another bad hit.

"Shit! Isaac?"

"Got you, Red." Isaac healed me for almost all my health.

"Thank you."

"Asher!"

"The twins soaked her outside as a joke, and they went too far. By the time she got inside, she was turning blue," he explained patiently. "She needed something to wear so we could put her clothes in the dryer."

"That's all she's wearing!" Trisha's voice was becoming shrill.

Miles' shoulders grew tense; his ears were starting to turn pink. I didn't like that.

"Asher, your girl's asking about my underwear, man. You sure these two aren't interested in me?" I asked seriously.

Zeke, the twins, and Miles laughed. Miles' ears turned back to normal; his shoulders relaxed a bit. That was better. I peeked at the archway to see Asher trying not to laugh. We were making progress killing Diablo, but it was slow. We needed Asher back.

"This is not funny!" Trisha snapped, sounding furious.

"What was I supposed to do? Let her freeze to death?" Asher's voice was getting harder. Trisha was pissing him off.

"She's supposed to wear her own clothes." Trisha said it like it was obvious.

"Which were soaked through by the water and turning to ice," I pointed out, getting annoyed myself.

"Stay the fuck out of this, Lexie!" Trisha shouted.

"Okay, pause it," I said. I was done with Trisha. Someone hit pause. I looked over at Trisha; she was so angry her cheeks were red. And I really didn't care. "You're mad I'm wearing Asher's sweats, right?" I asked.

Ethan grinned. He knew me well enough to see where I was going.

"No shit," Trisha snapped back.

I nodded, a bit pissed off myself now. I stood up. "Miles," I warned. Miles closed his eyes with a half grin on his face. I quickly untied the knot, put the shirt back down to my knees and began shimmying the sweats down my legs. When they dropped, I reached back, held onto the bottom of the shirt like you would a short skirt and picked the pants off the floor. Zeke and the twins were laughing their asses off. "You can look now, sweetie." Miles opened his eyes but respectfully kept his gaze elsewhere. I folded the sweats carefully, then tossed them to Trisha. "There, now only Riley has the right to bitch." I made sure the shirt was under me and sat back down. Zeke was in the wide chair and tossed me the throw off the back, still laughing his ass off. I draped the throw across my legs. I looked at Trisha. Her mouth was gaping. Asher was openly smiling now.

"You are not going to sit around here in only a shirt!" Trisha screamed.

I sighed dramatically. "I can't make you happy, Trisha; you don't like me with pants, you don't like me pantless. I'm kinda out of options here," I pointed out sarcastically. Her voice was giving me a headache. This time all the boys laughed. When they quieted down, she started again.

"I want you in your own clothes!" she snapped.

"I do too," Cece joined in. "I don't appreciate this at all."

"I do too. But my clothes were soaked, and it's freezing outside," I said slowly, as if I was speaking to a particularly stupid kid. "They are in the dryer so I can wear them again."

"Then you should have gone home," Cece shot back.

I looked at her like she was nuts.

"Cece, she was fucking turning blue," Isaac shot at his girlfriend. "She was already hypothermic when she got in the house."

Cece shut up. I was starting to think she wished they had just left me outside to freeze.

"What are you girls doing here?" Zeke asked bluntly. "It's friend's day; you shouldn't even be here."

I loved Zeke. The girls ignored the question.

"Your girlfriend would have a problem with this too, Zeke," Trisha shot across the room.

It sounded like a threat to me. I had to fight a smile. Oh, this was gonna be good.

Zeke put his controller down and pulled out his cell phone. "Let's find out." Zeke smirked and hit a couple buttons. The room was quiet as the phone rang on speaker.

"Hey, cutie."

"Riley, you're on speaker," he began. "Trisha's having a fit over Lexie sitting around in one of my shirts. It reaches her knees, which is longer than the skirt Trisha is currently wearing." I snickered as Trisha's face became red. "She threatened me that you wouldn't like it either, so I figured I'd just tell you now."

"What happened?" Riley's voice was concerned.

I loved Riley.

"There was an incident involving the twins, a snowball fight, and water. Her clothes are in the dryer," he explained simply.

Riley sighed. "I don't give a shit if she's sitting around in your shirt. As long as she's okay," Riley said emphatically.

I looked at Zeke. "Zeke, awesome girlfriend pull," I said, my hand going up. He smirked and high fived me. Riley laughed her ass off. So did the guys.

"Thanks for clearing that up, Riley." Zeke said.

"Talk to you later."

Zeke hung up the phone and looked at Trisha with a blank face. "Now that that question has been answered. How about mine? What are you two doing here?"

"We made you guys dinner and brought it over. We thought our boyfriends would be happy to see us," Trisha explained. Her eyes ran over me as her lip curled. "I didn't expect Lexie to be sitting around practically naked."

Miles went still; he was angry. Shit.

"Lexie would never sit around practically naked," Ethan shot back, defending me. "She's too modest for that."

"Yeah, that photo on the big screen was real modest," Cece shot back.

Isaac went still beside me.

"Oh, stupid move," I whispered to no one, cringing.

I turned to Isaac, he was glaring at his girlfriend. He handed me his controller and got up. He walked into the foyer and gestured for her to go with him out front. He was scary quiet, at least for Isaac. Cece went out the front door; Isaac followed. I winced as the door closed.

"Zeke-"

"On it." Zeke was already up and going to the window. He looked out the blinds.

"If she-"

"I'll tell you," Zeke assured me.

If that bitch hit Isaac, panties or no panties, I'd rip her apart.

"What? You're spying now?" Trisha demanded an answer.

I had no patience left for her. "No, Zeke's watching to see if Cece hits Isaac when he dumps her," I told her plainly. "If she does, I'm kicking her ass."

"You are fucking insane!" Trisha turned to Asher, who was frowning at Trisha. "Do you see how crazy she is?"

"Yeah. It's crazy to want to protect your friend from someone they can't hit back," Asher snapped at her. "Insane, right?"

Trisha seemed to realize she had fucked up.

In the silence, the dryer dinged. I hopped up and dropped the throw on the couch. "Yay! I get pants still warm from the dryer," I said in my excited, cute voice. The guys chuckled. I moved past Ethan then hurried past Trisha and Asher. I was almost in the kitchen when I added, "I'm changing in the laundry room, just warning ya!" Several male voices acknowledged that they had heard me and didn't care.

I hurried into the laundry room, really excited to have pants again. I closed the door behind me and opened the dryer. They were dry! I pulled my clothes out and started getting dressed. When I was done, I folded Zeke's shirt and put it in his basket of folded laundry.

I headed back to the kitchen but pulled up short by the pantry. Asher and Trisha were in the kitchen. I listened shamelessly.

"I don't like you hanging out with Lexie without me." Trisha still sounded pissed off.

"She is one of my friends, Trisha. You need to accept that," he said patiently, though I heard the strain in his voice.

"I don't want to," she snapped back.

"We had an agreement that we would have time with Ally without you girls while you got used to her," Asher pointed out. His patience had run out. His voice grew hard. "You just came into my house, on our time, without knocking and stood there yelling at one of my friends."

"The others do it all the time." Trisha sounded hurt.

I winced.

"They are family; they have keys, Trisha. You aren't there yet." He was honest and tried to say it gently. I'd give him that. "You came over when you knew you weren't supposed to be here, then you were rude to Ally."

"She was rude to me too."

"You were screaming at her. She made jokes to lighten the tension you were creating. Then you made Miles uncomfortable. So, yeah, she made a joke at your expense so Miles would feel better." His voice became hard, his words clipped. "You need to get over your issues with her."

"Or what?" Trisha snapped. "You'll dump me?"

I winced, bad move, Trisha.

"Maybe I didn't make it clear before," he said, his voice still hard. "If it comes down to you or Ally. It's going to be Ally."

I winced. Ouch. Yeah, a part of me loved it. I couldn't help it; the bitch had been rude.

"Trisha, I think we can be something good when Ally isn't around, but when she is, you turn into someone else. And I can't stand that girl. It's time for you to decide. Get over your issues with her, or we're finished." I bit my lower lip. Big tension was in that room. "Take the night to think it over and call me tomorrow. But right now, I would appreciate it if you took Cece and left."

The room was so quiet I thought they had left, but then I remembered the kitchen door hadn't squeaked.

"I will talk to you tomorrow." Trisha's voice sounded like she was holding back tears.

I rolled my eyes. The door squeaked, then the front door shut.

"Ally."

I winced. I peeked around the pantry doorway. Asher was standing there with an eyebrow raised, hands on his hips.

"Busted," I whispered to myself. I came into the kitchen and squirmed. "Sorry, I kinda got stuck."

He looked at me then at the door, his hand rubbing his neck. "That wasn't by accident."

I raised an eyebrow.

Asher looked back at me. "I wanted you to listen so you can tell me if I was too harsh with her."

Oh, I wasn't in trouble. Yay! "I get that," I admitted. I walked over to him and hopped up on the island. He turned and looked at me. "Do you think you were too harsh?" I asked carefully. He gave me an irritated look. I held up my hands. "I'm still going to tell you my opinion. But I want to hear what you think first."

He sighed and rubbed his neck some more. "Honestly, no." He came over to lean against the counter next to me, crossing his arms over his muscled chest. "I thought I made it clear before, and she had said I did. But then she pulled this. So, I wanted to make it very clear this time." He took a breath and let it out. "I don't think I was too harsh. But I'm not sure." He looked at me, waiting.

I sighed. "I don't think you were too harsh on her," I began. "I think you made your boundaries clear, like not walking in without knocking. You told her how you felt about this situation, how you felt about her, and told her flat out that if she can't get over her issue, then it won't work." I leaned over and rested my chin on his shoulder while I looked at him. He sighed. "I think she was expecting you to cave and you didn't. I think now she's going to have to actually think about this and give you a real answer."

He leaned his head over and touched mine.

"Thanks, Ally girl." His voice sounded relieved.

"No problem, Ash."

He sighed then pushed away from the counter. "Okay, let's go kill Diablo," he said with a smile.

I smiled and hopped down. We went into the family room and joined the others.

It took a couple tries, but we made Diablo our bitch. It made my day.

SEVERAL HOURS LATER, we were watching a car movie that Zeke liked when a phone rang. Asher reached into his back pocket and pulled out mine.

"It's yours, Ally." He tossed it to me. I got up and headed to the foyer.

"How did your phone survive?" Ethan asked before I left the room.

"I upgraded to waterproof a couple weeks ago; I got to keep the same number," I called over my shoulder as I stepped into the foyer. I answered, not checking the caller id; I was sure it was Dylan anyway. "Hello."

"Lexie?"

My heart dropped; my stomach knotted. I instantly wanted to puke. I swallowed hard.

"Sugar, are you there?" My mother's voice rang in my ear.

I started shaking; I was instantly pissed off. I opened the front door and walked out onto the porch. I don't remember if I slammed the door behind me or shut it.

"How the fuck are you calling me?" My voice was hard and low.

"Tomorrow's Christmas, Lexie; the rehab faculty here are letting me call to wish you Merry Christmas," she said like it was perfectly fine.

"Yeah, and does the faculty know you beat the shit out of me?" I growled into the phone. She wasn't allowed to contact me, and she fucking knew it.

"Lexie, now, I understand you're angry. I would be too. I was drunk and high as a kite," she started explaining.

I pulled the phone away and began recording the conversation. Then I brought it back to my ear.

"-I'm really sorry about it, I really don't know what happened."

"I'll tell you what happened. I was asleep, you came in, threw me

349

on the floor, and beat the shit out of me. That's what fucking happened," I growled into the phone.

"Lexie, don't you use that language with me," she snapped.

I laughed, anger burning in my belly. "Oh, you're going to be a mother now? Not when I was paying the bills on a part-time job so we could eat while you were drunk all the time? Not when you were high? Not when you kept calling me a demon child? But you're going to be one now?"

"Lexie! You need to listen to reason-"

"Why? So, you can tell me how I shouldn't press charges?" I snapped. "That's what this is about, isn't it? You found out after rehab you're being charged with a felony."

"Lexie, I do not appreciate you speaking to me this way. You know you have problems, and you know you're not the most stable person."

I went still, I realized I wasn't the only one recording this conversation. She wanted to play? Fine. "That wasn't the first time you hit me." I made sure my voice was clear enough for both recordings. "And you fucking know it. Whenever I couldn't make enough money for food, you hit me. Whenever you couldn't get drunk, you hit me. Calling me names was your way of saying hello."

"Alexis!" Oh, she was pissed now. Good. "I only ever disciplined you when you cursed at me."

I snorted at that lie. "You're so full of shit your eyes should be brown." I was done. "Just so you're aware. I've been recording this too. I'll be sending this recording, in its entirety, to the LA District Attorney's office. Enjoy jail." I hung up the phone with shaking hands.

But man, that fucking felt good. For about five seconds. Then the nausea came back, and the knots in my gut. I wrapped one arm around my stomach and covered my mouth with the other. I focused on taking deep breaths. That fucking bitch. I ignored the tears running down my face and kept breathing. A coat was put on my shoulders; it was mine. I closed my eyes. Of course. "How long?"

"Since 'Oh you're going to be a mother now?'" Asher's voice was quiet.

"You didn't even hear the door open," Miles' calm voice added. I sighed.

Isaac and Ethan came around to hug me. I smiled as I was squished between them. I really needed the weird twin hug tonight.

"How did that feel?" Zeke asked as he stepped up next to us, his gaze on the snow in the front yard.

"Good, for about five seconds." The twins let go of me and stepped back. "Now I want to puke." The rest of the guys came around and filled in the circle.

"When's the trial?" Zeke asked, still looking out at the snow

"This summer, or fall." I sighed.

"Do you have to testify?" Miles asked in that soothing voice. All those jagged edges inside me smoothed out, and my stomach unknotted. Miles always did that to me.

"Depends. If they have a strong case, which they should, then no." I took a deep breath and added. "If they don't think they do, they will probably offer her a fucking deal for a smaller sentence. Or if the DA is particularly pissed off, there will be a trial, and then I'd have to testify." I used my phone to email the entire voice recording to the DA's email in LA. The guy had been nice and wanted to know if she ever contacted me. I gave my name, a short explanation, and the recording.

"Do you want to go even if you don't testify?" Ethan asked.

I thought about it before answering. "A part of me does. I want to see her face when they convict. But another part me doesn't. I don't want to see the photos, listen to the excuses. And if they don't convict, I don't know what I might do if I was there," I told them honestly.

"When the time comes, if you want to go, we'll go with you." Zeke's voice was soft as he spoke. He was still looking at the snow. I noticed his shoulders were tense. I pushed it out of my mind.

"We'll see when the time comes, what the DA's chances are." I looked around at them. They were amazing. My family was amazing. "I love you guys." It was out before I even thought about it. Oh shit. "That sounded-"

"We love you too." They all said at once. It was so weird that they looked at each other and laughed. I smiled and laughed too. I was about to suggest we head in when that chill went down my neck, only it was like a blade now. I slapped my hand to my neck and hissed.

"Ally?"

I looked past the guys and saw them. And I meant them. Herbert and the McClains had apparently met and had a chat. They were all coming across the street, and I had left my beads at home. "Oh, you've got to fucking be kidding me," I said my heart racing. "Kit, now." Asher ran past me into the house.

"How many?" Miles asked, his voice cold.

"Oh, three, and they are pissed off." I swallowed hard as pain racked me, they had reached the curb. "Anyone got a charm? Beads? I'm kinda caught with my pants down here."

Ethan yanked his onyx ring off his finger and handed it to me. I slipped it onto my thumb. Isaac gave me his bracelet. I was putting that on while Zeke pulled off his necklace and put it over my head. Normally I wouldn't take what they had, but the dead weren't after them. They were coming for me. They were on the grass. Oh, fuck. Miles held out his necklace. I grabbed it.

"Um, guys, inside or back. Take a pick but fucking move." My voice was getting strained as their pain rushed over me. It wasn't as bad as it could have been but it was still enough to make me double over. The boys moved behind me, not seeing what I saw.

Miles mumbled something about salt and ran into the house. Yeah, that would be great. But the fuckers could stay till dawn. I had to deal with them if I wanted to go home. My stomach rolled as they reached the steps to the porch. Today was not the day to fuck with me like this. Not after talking to my bitch of a mother. I walked to meet them at the top of the steps. I felt them against my barriers, pushing.

"Back the fuck off," I snapped at them with feeling. They were pushed back several steps. My nose started bleeding, and I pinched it closed. Tissues appeared over my shoulder. I took them and used them instead. The ghosts were shaken; they didn't understand what I had just done. "I am working as fast as I can to get the link going," I reminded them in a strained voice as my head started throbbing.

"You aren't working hard enough!" Mrs. McClain shouted. Pressure built in my head.

"It doesn't help when you fuckers keep me up at night, so I can't rest." I looked at each of them. "I am not going to burn myself out for you."

"Salt, Lexie," Miles' voice said from behind me. A big salt shaker was handed over my shoulder. I took it and unscrewed the top as the world started to waver. I wasn't going to get jumped today. No. Tomorrow was Christmas, and these fuckers could just back off. Big talk coming from the girl who wanted to puke her guts out right then. But still. I put a few pinches in my mouth, even tucked some salt into my pockets.

The ghosts glared at me. Their energy hit me hard, but with the charms, they couldn't touch me. That didn't mean they couldn't tear my barriers apart. Pain tore through my head as they kept shredding. My mind was starting to feel raw. Oh, you fuckers. I was pissed.

"I said no!" I shoved them back several more feet. I took deep breaths as I followed them. I was done with this shit. I walked down the stairs. Yeah, my body was in agony, but I wasn't going to take this anymore. I had that hard feeling in my chest, and I was fucking going to use it. "I've told you and told you. I'm busting my ass for you fuckers, and all you want is faster, faster," I snapped. With each word, I pushed them back further. Their eyes grew wide, their mouths gaping. Wetness began running down my ears, and down my neck. "I get that you're impatient, but I'm not going to die for the dead." With that, I shoved them out into the street. "The time where my family dies for you shits is over." They backed off, glaring at me as they backed away.

I held on until they were out of sight. Then I wobbled. My hand went to the trunk of a car. I bent over and threw up. Repeatedly. Someone got my hair out of the way, and someone else steadied me as I was sick again and again. I felt like I was puking up my toenails. I wanted to pass out, but something told me that wasn't going to happen today. Oh, those fuckers ruined Christmas Eve.

Eventually, I stopped puking, and the guys gave me some nausea tablets. It took four today. My eyesight was still fading in and out with my pulse, and I was kind of out of it. Miles carried me back into the house and set me on the couch. I closed my eyes to try and deal with the pain in my head. I was still holding tissues to my nose, and my eyes were still streaming from being sick.

When the bleeding finally stopped and the pain had eased, I opened my eyes to find Miles sitting on the coffee table in front of me. The others were spread around the room, waiting. I knew what that must have looked like to them. Me yelling at nothing they could see. I wished I could show them sometimes, just let them know I wasn't crazy. Miles saw my eyes open.

His gaze narrowed on me. "Lexie, you were bleeding from your ears," Miles said gently, his voice worried.

I nodded. "Yeah, that happens with long exposure to the dead. Hell, if they stayed long enough, I'd be deaf for a couple of days. But in this case, it was three with upped energy. They haven't started to rot, but they're drinking the Kool-Aid now." I shook my hand showing them their charms. "These kept them out, but they just tore the shit out of my barriers." I looked at each of them "Okay, how crazy did I look?" They all looked at each other.

"Um, Lexie," Isaac began. "When you shouted at them, telling them to back off. They kind of... shimmered."

I looked around the room at them, wondering if he was joking. "You mean...?"

"We saw them, a couple times, just for a split second," Miles explained with a straight face. My mouth dropped open. I blinked at them. The guys chuckled; it wasn't often they got to surprise me in this area.

I had to ask. "Okay, did you guys get a good look?" They all nodded. "Gotta ask. What did they look like?"

"One guy was big, had a nasty walrus mustache," Ethan began.

"There was one woman, very put together," Asher added.

"Yeah, she looked like she had a stick up her ass," Isaac continued.

"There was an older guy, very rich looking," Zeke kept it going.

"The McClains were there." Miles shocked us all to silence. Miles gaze met mine.

"You know who they are?" I asked quietly.

He nodded. "Jennifer McClain and Henry McClain. My father was friends with Henry. I saw in the paper that they died a few days ago, murder-suicide," Miles explained. "But, they died in Aspen. Not here."

I was still trying to wrap my head around the fact that they had seen them, let alone Miles being able to identify them. Oh, the world was spinning again. I rested my head in my hands and took deep breaths.

"Beautiful?"

"Oh, for the first time in my life, I just might faint." My voice sounded as shocked as I felt. They had fucking seen them. "You fucking saw them." I took a deep breath. "You fucking saw them, enough to describe them. You fucking saw them."

"I think we broke Red," Isaac stage whispered. The guys chuckled.

When I could, I looked up at them. I knew they had believed me before about the dead, hell, they even saw Mary Summers. But they had seen those fuckers out there, even for just a second. It was the most amazing feeling in the world. They saw them too. My eyes filled as I looked at each of them. They fucking saw them. All I could say was, "Best fucking Christmas present ever."

A COUPLE OF HOURS LATER, I was feeling better. When it was around nine, my reminder on my phone went off. I had somewhere to be.

"I'm headed out guys," I announced as I got to my feet from the couch. The guys looked at me with either surprised looks or confused ones. Yeah, it was weird for me to be the first one to leave; I never usually did. I ignored the looks as I walked into the foyer and started pulling on my coat. I heard all of them getting up; it made me smile. I turned to see them standing in a semi-circle behind me. All of them looking for some sign that something was wrong. "Guys, I just have something I need to do," I reassured them. "I'll see you all tomorrow." That seemed to make them stop worrying. I gave each of them a hug and kissed each twin on the cheek. Everyone said goodbye, and I headed out to my Blazer.

When the truck finally warmed up, I headed out to the small church on Rose Drive. The Catholic church wasn't huge, but for a town this small, it didn't need to be. The parking lot was almost empty; the Christmas Eve service was just over. I only knew that because I had looked it up earlier today. No, I wasn't Catholic. But Mary Summers was. I climbed out and headed for the door. The church was built with gray stone. The stained glass was beautiful, especially lit up from the inside. I stepped into a small foyer with a double door made of dark wood. I looked around the foyer and didn't find what I was looking for. So, I opened one of the doors and walked into the church's empty main chapel. It wasn't as fancy or elaborate as the ones in LA. It was simple, no frills, no elaborate decorations. It seemed right that way. I found what I was looking for. I pulled off my jacket, my scarf and walked down the side of the church to the alcove there. The statues of Jesus and Mary were at the back of the alcove. I'd never gone to church in my life, but you didn't grow up seeing the dead without looking at a bunch of different religions. In front of the statues and surrounding them were large stands filled with votive candles in little, red glass candle holders. Not a lot of them were lit tonight.

I put my coat down on the edge of a pew before walking into the alcove. I pulled out the cash I brought to help the church pay for the candles and put it in the small box there marked 'donations.' I thought about Mary Summers, pictured her face as I picked up a couple of matches. I lit one for Mary Summers. She had loved this church, had loved singing here. Then I lit one for Dad. It was my Christmas Eve tradition. Every year, I'd go to a church somewhere and light a candle for him. It wasn't always a Catholic church, but they did make it much easier to do. A door opened as I shook out the match and put it into the small sand-filled bowl the other matches were in.

I thought about Dad and how much I still missed him. The rest of the year I never thought about it. If I did, I'd push it away and focus on something else. But tonight, I could. Tonight, I let myself miss him. I let myself feel how much. Tonight, I could cry over it. I stepped out of the alcove, sat down in the pew across from it and cried. It wasn't sobbing crying, just tears running down my face crying. I remembered his face, the way he always smelled like wood smoke even when he wasn't working. I remembered him reading to me, then when I was old enough, reading to him. I remembered how he'd make chocolate chip pancakes every Christmas morning. How he'd always be the first one up, and then he'd be jumping on my bed like a kid yelling, 'It's Christmas! Lexie! Get up!'

I was wiping my face when someone sat next to me. I took a breath of wintergreen. I looked up, not surprised to see Miles next to me, his gaze on the back of the pew in front of us. I let out a small breathy laugh that barely made any sound. "Did you all follow me?" I asked in a whisper. "Or just you?"

Miles' emerald eyes met mine. "Just me." He kept his voice quiet. I gave him a half smile. "I didn't know you were religious."

I looked at the back of the pew in front of us as I answered. "I'm not." I wiped my face again now that my crying was stopping. "It's just my tradition for Dad."

"You light a candle for him." His voice was the silky smooth one that calmed me.

"Every year." I swallowed hard. "I light a candle for him, sit down and let myself do what I never do the rest of the year."

"You mourn him."

I smiled at his word choice. "I cry. Yeah." My voice was still quiet. "Do you want me to-"

"No," I assured him. "It nice not being alone this year."

Miles reached over and took my hand. It was the first time he'd ever done that. It was always me grabbing his hand.

"This year you lit two," he said softly.

I nodded. "One for Dad; one for Mary." His hand gave mine a gentle squeeze. I pointed over my shoulder and up towards the choir loft without even having to look behind me. "She sang in the choir up there. The second spot in from the left, first row." Guilt ate at me. I knew she had been suffering from all that energy. I knew that she was glad to go in the end. That knowledge didn't take away all the guilt that I had over killing her soul. Nothing was going to take it away completely.

We were quiet for a couple of minutes. He didn't seem to know what to say, so I just started talking. "I started doing this the Christmas after Dad died. Mom was drunk, so I went for a walk and saw a Catholic church open." I looked over at Miles to see if he was bored. He was listening with his gaze on the back of the pew in front of us. "I got curious and went inside. I saw the candles and lit one for him." I took a breath and let it out. "Then I cried my eyes out." I smiled sadly, looking back towards the front of the church. "I've been doing it every Christmas Eve since."

"Does it help?"

I nodded. "Yeah. I cry less every year. And it helps to do something that shows I remember him." I shrugged. "It's probably not what the candles are for, but it's what I use them for."

Miles pulled out his phone and started doing something. I knew what he was doing. It was Miles. He was looking up what the candles were for. I watched his face as he looked for the answer. He had a little wrinkle between his eyebrows when he was concentrating as he was now. It made me smile; it was a small one, but it was there.

"That is exactly what they are there for, Lexie." He looked up and met my eyes. "To pray for someone."

My smile got bigger. "It's good to know I'm not fucking up some candle thing I didn't know about," I admitted honestly.

His expression changed, his smile disappeared and his eyes unfocused. It was his thinking face. "Lexie, I know this is your tradition," he began slowly, his usual speed when he was trying to say something without offending someone. He was thinking over each word. "But some of the others might benefit from this also." I looked back towards the altar. I hadn't thought about that. This was just something I did. But it did sound like something Asher would like. "Would you mind if I invited them out here? To light some candles?" His voice was pained. "If not, it's okay. I'd understand. It's extremely personal."

I smiled gently. Miles never asked anything for himself, it was always for someone else. It was one of the things I loved about him.

"If you think it would help."

He gave my hand a squeeze before letting go. He got up and walked to the foyer to make the calls. I went back to thinking about Dad and Mary Summers. I didn't cry again; my crying was done for this year. I focused on the good things about Mary Summers, and the good times with my Dad.

It wasn't too long before the doors opened again. Heavy footsteps moved along the wood floor. I figured it was Asher and didn't bother to turn around. The footsteps walked into the alcove. I kept looking at the front of the church; he didn't need me watching him. Then I got a whiff of engine grease. Stunned, I looked over to see Zeke lighting two candles and blowing out the match. I looked back to the front of the church, not wanting him to know I was watching. Zeke's footsteps came towards me. I slid over in the pew to make room. He sat down next to me with his hands on his legs. It was a few heartbeats before he said anything.

"Now what?" he asked gruffly.

"I think about my dad," I said quietly. "And let myself feel how much I miss him. I usually don't-"

"Let yourself during the rest of the year," Zeke finished for me, his gravelly voice quiet. "I do that too."

I didn't say anything. There was nothing that needed to be said. I just reached over and held his hand like Miles did for me. Zeke's fingers gave me a squeeze.

Over the next fifteen minutes, I listened to Zeke's breathing change from a few shaky breaths to deep, calming ones, then back to normal. I didn't know if he cried; I didn't look at him. I held his hand and gave him what privacy I could.

"Every year?" he asked softly.

"Yeah."

"It helps?"

"It helps me to do something to show I remember." I shrugged. "It's my thing."

He gave my fingers a squeeze. "It's better than anything I've come up with," he said gently. I leaned my temple against his arm, just below his shoulder. We sat in silence for a few minutes before he leaned down and kiss the top of my head. "Thank you, Baby."

"Anytime, Tough Guy."

The back doors opened again. Big footsteps moved across the floor; this time it had to be Asher. We both stayed put while Asher lit his candle. When he came out of the alcove, Zeke gave my hand a squeeze before he let go and got to his feet. Zeke met Asher at the side of the pew.

"Did one for Alice too," Zeke muttered to Asher, his gaze over Asher's shoulder. Asher nodded. Zeke turned away and headed out.

Asher took Zeke's spot next to me. I knew Alice was Asher's mom's name. I understood Zeke doing that; the woman had practically raised all the guys, but both of Zeke's parents were dead. Why did he only light two? I pushed the thought away; there was no point in wondering about it right now. Asher was staring at the altar up front.

"What do I do now?" Asher's rich voice was quiet.

I reached over and took his hand. "Now, you think about your mom." I kept my voice quiet and gentle. "And let yourself feel how you feel." There was quiet; then I had to admit something. "I usually end up crying, but that's just me." He gave my hand a squeeze, I squeezed back and kept my gaze ahead of me.

Asher did the same thing Zeke did. He stayed quiet, only his breathing let me know what he was thinking about. And just like with Zeke, I gave him what privacy I could. I just kept holding his hand. When his hand clamped down on mine, I peeked at him. His gaze was on the floor and tears were running down his face. He was taking deep shaking breaths, but the tears weren't stopping. Everything in me ached for him. It had been only two years; his loss was much fresher than Zeke's or mine. I remembered how hard that second Christmas without Dad had been. I leaned against his shoulder and hugged his arm with my free hand. I didn't know what else to do. Eventually, when he was ready, the tears stopped falling. I just kept holding on to him. When he sniffed, I pulled some tissues out of my pocket and handed them to him without a word. I kept my eyes on the front of the church and waited. Eventually, he took a deep breath and let it out slowly.

"Thanks, Ally." His voice was a thick. "This actually helps."

"Anytime, Ash," I whispered back.

"Miles said you lit two?"

"Dad and Mary Summers." I sighed. "Someone should remember her." It wasn't long after that when Asher got up and left the church.

I was half expecting the twins to show up. But it was Miles that came and sat next to me again. "No twins?"

"No. They both still feel guilty over Sophia," Miles answered quietly. "It was a car wreck; Maria was driving. But still..."

"Knowing in your head and knowing in your heart are two different things," I finished for him.

Miles gave me a small smile. "Yes. They really are." He was quiet for a few heartbeats. "Are you alright?"

I nodded. "Yeah." I looked at him and gave him a small half grin. "Next year, we can all come as a group." Miles cringed. "What?"

"I staggered Zeke and Asher for a reason. Neither one of them will talk with any of the others around. It's why I stayed in the foyer," he explained. It made sense.

"Maybe one day, years from now, when everyone is more healed up," I offered. He nodded.

I sat with Miles a little longer before I was ready to go. I gave him a hug goodbye and headed home. I didn't think about telling Rory about my tradition until I was in bed. Next year. Next year I'd bring Rory too.

CHAPTER 15

CHRISTMAS DAY

*O*n Christmas morning, I had a small Christmas with Rory. We made chocolate chip pancakes and opened the presents we had gotten each other. I gave him a remote-control drone that he immediately started playing with, and he gave me a certificate for painting the Blazer. I knew what he was doing, but I loved it anyway. Tara wasn't there; she was coming in the afternoon. I left her present on the tree: a gift certificate to the spa in Northridge she'd been wanting to go to for months. Rory helped me pay for it, thankfully. Otherwise, I wouldn't have been able to buy presents for the guys. When we were done, there were still presents under the tree.

I looked and smiled. "Rory?"

"What?" he answered from the kitchen. He was busy making cocoa.

"Did you get the guys presents?" I asked with a big smile. I turned to watch him come back out of the kitchen with two mugs.

"Maybe." He had his shit eating grin on his face.

I took my mug and sat back down in my corner of the sofa. "I saw their names, Rory," I pointed out. "That's not a maybe."

Rory snorted at me. "Yeah, I got them presents," he admitted openly. "Those boys are good kids. And none of them has a dad worth a fucking damn." He looked over at me and shrugged. "There are some things that a father gives their son that no one should miss out on."

My eyes filled at his reasoning, my heart warming as I smiled at him. "Thank you, Rory."

He narrowed his eyes at me. "You didn't get any extra presents," he shot at me playfully.

I laughed, and my eyes stopped filling. "They'll really appreciate it." I pulled my cell phone out of my bra. "Want me to have them come over to open them?"

Rory grinned at me and shook his head. "Next year; this year I want you to take them with you to Miles' house." I nodded. Next year the boys would have to come over. I smiled. I realized I that wasn't expecting them to leave me anymore. It was progress on my shit.

I spent the rest of the morning with Rory, watching Christmas movies on television. Around noon, I bundled on blue jeans and a purple thermal. I loaded up the gifts from Rory into the back of my car and headed to Miles' house. I walked in the front door, closing it behind me.

"I'm here!" I shouted before taking off my coat. I heard something, a weird noise. It was too far away to figure it out, so I decided to ignore it.

"Living room!" the guys called back. I smiled and walked into the living room. Everyone was already there; the twins were even still in jammies.

I frowned at them. "What the fuck! We could have done jammies?" I asked, annoyed at the twins. "I got dressed, you fuckers."

The guys chuckled. I just sighed.

I made a face at them before going around the group and hugging each of them; everyone got a kiss on the cheek today. Zeke didn't bother getting up from this side of the left couch. He gave me a quick squeeze and didn't seem to mind the kiss to his cheek. Asher got off the far end of the left couch and gave me a good hug, not minding the kiss either. Miles got off the hearth to get his hug, his ears turned pink from his kiss on the cheek. Then I looked at the twins, still in their jammies. I smirked before I rushed over and jumped into Isaac's lap; he laughed as I gave him his peck. Then I shifted and did a fall turn into Ethan's lap. He gave me a kiss back. Everyone was laughing at me as I stayed in Ethan's arms and looked at everyone.

"So, are we doing presents or what?" I asked. They all smiled and got up. I climbed off Ethan. Everyone was picking up their presents when I had to stop Ethan. "Ethan, your present is heavier than it looks," I warned him. His eyebrow went up before he picked it up. When everyone was done stacking, we sat down. I sat between the twins; the others were back in their spots. Then we all looked at each other.

"Go!" Miles said. Everyone laughed as we started opening presents.

"Oh, Ash!" I looked up, remembering his present. Asher looked up at me. "Open mine last."

He smirked. "You might want to do the same thing," Asher warned. I raised an eyebrow, curious now. But I didn't ask.

I opened Zeke's present; it was my own Leatherman multi-tool. Sweetness. "Zeke, this is awesome. Thank you, sweetie!" I didn't bother looking up.

"Now you can stop borrowing mine," Zeke mumbled loudly. I snorted as I reached for another package.

"Beautiful, what the...?" I looked over at Ethan. He'd just opened the box full of music composing paper. I bit my lip, wondering if he liked it. I had ordered as much as I could; it was one thousand pages. The stack was four inches thick. "Did you buy out the store?" He looked at me, smiling.

I snickered. "Nope, online shopping at its best. The mailman did not like me that day."

Ethan laughed, still smiling big. He leaned over and hugged me. "Thank you, Beautiful," he whispered to me.

I smiled, happy he liked it. "You're welcome, Snoopy," I whispered back. He gave me a squeeze before letting go.

I went back the gift in my lap. I tore into the wrapping. My mouth dropped open. It was the most awesome purse I'd ever seen. The black leather was slashed to show the red fabric underneath, making it look like dragon scales. This was the kind of purse I would use. "Miles! Holy shit, where did you find this?!" I looked over at him.

He pushed up his glasses and smiled. "I found it online; I thought you might like it," he said simply. "Look inside." I raised an eyebrow and opened the purse; inside was a black flowy scarf. I pulled it out and smiled a big smile. It had, written in white, different equations, some chemistry, some math I couldn't even recognize. It looked like a chalkboard, and I loved it.

I got up and climbed over the back of the couch; then I was on Miles, hugging the shit out of him. "I love them! Thank you so much!" The guys were laughing at me as I gave Miles another kiss on the cheek, his face turned red again.

"You're welcome, Lexie," he mumbled as I gave him another squeeze. I let him go and climbed back into my spot. I put the scarf back in the bag so I wouldn't lose it.

"Red." I looked over at Isaac, who had just opened my gift to him; he was smiling. They were new fighting shorts, with black and white Asian symbols up the side. "These are perfect, my old ones weren't fitting anymore."

I snorted. "I know, I've seen more of your ass than I need to," I shot at him. The guys started laughing.

He leaned over and gave me a hug. "Thank you, Lexie," he whispered before giving me a kiss on the cheek.

"You're welcome, hon." I went back to opening my next present. It was an iPod shuffle. "Ethan..." I said, smiling.

He snickered. "Your mp3 sounded like shit," Ethan said, pointing at the shuffle. "This will sound much better, not perfect but better."

I gave him a big hug. "Thank you so much, Snoopy," I whispered.

He gave me a big squeeze. "You're welcome." He pulled back and smirked. "I gotta take care of those ears of yours. Besides, I'm also taking you shopping for some jewelry. I owe you." I chuckled.

I was reaching for another package when Miles got to his feet and went to the big rectangular gift leaning against the corner of the fireplace. I bit my lip.

"Lexie?" Miles asked, his voice curious.

My stomach knotted. "Just open it quick, before I decide it's not good enough," I shot at him, my voice pained. Everyone stopped and looked up. I was biting my lip when he started pulling off the paper. There was a big weight on my chest. I watched as he stepped back and looked at the huge canvas.

I had painted the Andromeda galaxy. The best I could anyway. I managed the swirls of gasses, but it was the colors that were a bitch. There was a specific pinky purple that I had absolutely hated mixing by the end. There were lots of violets, orange, white and lots of dark. I figured I couldn't fuck up dark. Then trying to get the positions of the stars right had been a huge pain in the ass. But I tried; I'm sure a few stars were missing, but I tried. I held my breath as he looked it over. Oh, please don't hate it, please don't hate it.

"This is amazing, Lexie." Miles' voice was an odd mix of impressed and surprised. He liked it? Was it accurate? I really wanted to know, but I was afraid to ask. Have some balls Lexie.

I took a breath. "So, you like it?" I asked painfully.

He looked back at me, a stunned look on his face. "I freaking love it," he said emphatically.

"Oh, thank God." I exhaled, my body going limp. The guys laughed at me.

"It's beautiful. And amazingly accurate," he said, looking at the canvas again.

"Oh good. I was afraid I left out something important," I admitted.

Miles shook his head. "You got all the major stars, the colors, and even the tilt right," he assured me before coming over. Isaac moved so Miles could hug me. "Thank you so much, I love it."

I admit I clung to him a little in relief. "You're welcome, sweetie."

Then Miles let go and went back to his pile. I was reaching for another package when I got hit with a ball of paper. I looked up to find Zeke glaring at me.

"You went over the limit we set," he accused me.

I gave him my innocent face. "I have no idea what you're talking about," I said, picking up another package.

He frowned at me. "Lexie, I know what these gloves cost. You went over," he said in his grumpy voice.

"I got them on sale," I lied through my teeth. His eyes narrowed at me. I kept my face neutral.

"You're a bad liar, Lexie," he told me.

I narrowed my eyes at him. "You want to talk about going over the limit?" I challenged him. I held up the Leatherman he bought me. "I know for a fact this was over the limit." The guys burst out laughing. Then I looked at each of them. "So far, all of you have gone over the limit," I pointed out. The guys all tried to look innocent. I wasn't buying it. I pointed at Zeke. "So, no bitching." He smirked and shook his head at me. "Will they work? They are supposed to have excellent dexterity."

He sighed and nodded. "They are perfect. Thank you," he said sweetly, well, as sweet as Zeke got anyway.

"What did she get you?" Isaac asked.

Zeke held up the gloves. "Mechanic gloves, so I can work in the garage and not freeze my hands off," Zeke replied.

"Oooh, good gift Red." Isaac sounded impressed.

"You're welcome, Zeke." I smiled at him and reached for another present. It was Isaac's. To be honest, I expected it to explode or something. I opened it, and my mouth dropped open. It was a pair of MMA sparring gloves. The gloves were padded over the knuckles, the short fingers left the last joints of your fingers open so you could grapple. "Isaac?" I asked, looking over at him.

Isaac looked up and smiled. "Yeah, Red. You start sparring after New Year's," he told me excitedly.

I leaned over and gave him a big hug. "Thank you, sweetie." I kissed his cheek and pulled back. Then I eyed him. "I'm not sparring with you, am I?"

He burst out laughing. "No, Zeke would kill me. There's a girl just starting, and she needs a sparring partner too. The trainers set it up," he assured me. I smiled and put them in my new purse.

Then there was Asher's gift. "Okay, Ash, it's time for yours," I warned him.

"Hold on, I want to open yours first," Asher told me.

Those knots were back, and it made me want to puke. As I watched him pull off the paper; my chest grew tight and heavy. Oh, it was probably a bad idea. I should have gotten him something else. SHIT! I bit my lip and waited for him to get mad and tell me I had crossed the line or something. When Asher finally had the box open, he went still. I stopped breathing.

"Ally…"

Oh, I'm sorry, I'm sorry. I was out of line. I'm an idiot. My hands were shaking as he looked in the box. I bit the corner of my bottom lip hard. A few heartbeats later and he was looking up at me. His eyes were bright as he put the box down and walked around the coffee table. Oh, he's pissed. He's gonna kill me. He was going to strangle me. Instead, he knelt in front of me and pulled me into his arms. Oh, he wasn't mad! Yay! Relief swept through me as I hugged him back. He took several deep breaths. I just held on tight and fought to keep from shaking.

"Thank you, Ally," he whispered to me. "She would have loved it."

I bit the inside of my cheek to stop myself from crying. "I didn't know if-"

"It's perfect," he reassured me, giving me a big squeeze.

"What the hell did she get you?" Ethan asked, getting up off the couch. Asher didn't say anything; he just kept hugging me.

"Oh, that was real fucking scary," I admitted, the shaking slowing down. He chuckled as he pulled back.

"Whoa." Ethan's voice drew everyone's attention.

Asher looked at me. "How did you get the dates?" Asher asked.

"What?" Zeke asked, leaning over to look in the box.

"Miles, of course." I smiled at him.

"Fuck, that took balls." Zeke's voice was impressed.

"Okay, tell us what it is," Isaac demanded from next to me. Both Asher and I started laughing.

Asher looked at Isaac. "It's a box. For Mom's flag," he said, his voice a little thick. Then he eyed me. "Custom made from what I could tell."

"I don't know what you're talking about," I said innocently. Asher leaned forward and kissed my forehead. Then got up and went back to his spot.

"I think Lexie won the best present giver game today," Isaac announced.

Asher sat down with a smirk on his face. "Let's not call it yet," Asher suggested, leaning forward, resting his elbows on his knees. I raised an eyebrow at him. Hmmm, intrigue.

I started opening mine; everyone was watching now. It was a plain white box. I was scared to open it. I shoved the fear away and took the lid off. My heart slammed in my chest; my throat closed. Tears immediately started to fill my eyes. Dad's face looked up at me. He was in his dress blues, and it looked like an official portrait, but it was him. I sat stunned for a few heartbeats. My heart bursting, I put the box on the coffee table and got up, tears already running down my face as I moved around the table. I practically tackled Asher as I hugged him around his neck. He lifted me to sit sideways in his lap and squeezed me tight. He rested his cheek on the top of my head. I couldn't say anything.

"What is it?" Miles asked in his calm voice.

"A photo," Isaac said, confused.

"Of her dad," Asher answered for me, I was still crying too much to answer. He kept holding me tight as I cried into his shoulder. "Her mom left all that stuff behind when they lost the house. She wouldn't let her take anything."

"Shit," Ethan said softly.

"How?" I asked my voice tight and cracking.

"Rory," Asher said. "He got me in touch with your dad's old fire house. I told them what happened and they sent that out overnight."

"Thank you, thank you so fucking much." I was still crying, but it was slowing down. I could cry later if I needed too but right now I needed to stop. "You have no idea…"

"You're welcome, Ally girl," he whispered with another squeeze.

"Okay, Asher wins the best present giver game," Isaac announced. Everyone laughed, even me.

When I had more control, I pulled back and wiped my face. I

gestured toward the photo on the table without looking at it. "Could someone put the lid back on?" I asked desperately. "Or I'm not going to stop crying." Someone moved, tissue paper crinkled.

"It's on, Beautiful."

I nodded and climbed out of Asher's lap.

Miles handed me tissues as I passed. I laughed and took the whole fucking box with me back to my seat. I wiped my nose with a tissue as the guys kept watching me. "Stop staring," I snapped weakly at them. They all chuckled. Everyone was done with presents, so we picked up the paper and threw it into the fireplace. I reminded Miles to move the painting before lighting it.

"So, where are you hanging your Lexie original?" Ethan asked.

"Bedroom, right above my desk," Miles answered instantly. I smiled. I was so happy he liked it. Everyone was talking while the paper burned down to ashes. I was about to tell them about Rory's gifts when the guys all looked at each other with smirks. That couldn't be good.

"What?" I asked. "Don't tell me you guys all ate Dylan's cookies." The guys laughed.

"No, we didn't eat his cookies," Asher reassured me.

"We got you another present, from all of us," Miles announced.

I raised an eyebrow and got excited. "I get to hunt Ethan through the house with a paintball gun?" I asked, really hoping this was what was happening. Everyone burst out laughing.

"Why me?" Ethan asked, still laughing.

"Okay, Isaac too," I agreed with fake frustration.

"What the...?" Isaac trailed off, just shaking his head. I smiled at him.

"No, it's not that," Asher said. "Though that would be awesome to watch."

Miles looked over at Zeke. "Zeke?"

Zeke got up and headed upstairs.

"My present is upstairs?" I asked suspiciously. The guys just grinned at me, not giving me a hint. It was a couple of minutes before Zeke yelled to us.

"Coming down the stairs!"

"Lexie, close your eyes," Miles ordered me. I eyed him, then did as I was told. Zeke started down the stairs. My heart was racing. What did they do? It was obviously unwrapped, so what the hell was it? I bit the corner of my bottom lip, trying not to peek. Zeke's footsteps come into the living room.

"Seriously guys, if it's something weird...." I warned them.

"You'd love it anyway, and you know it," Ethan said. I nodded. Yeah, he was probably right. Zeke's footsteps stopped in front of me. Butterflies were in my stomach. Let me look!

"Okay, Lexie. Open your eyes." Zeke told me.

I hesitated. "If someone's ass is in my face, I will punch you," I warned them. The guys laughed.

"Lexie, just fucking open your eyes." Zeke's voice was still laughing.

I opened my eyes and looked up. At first, I didn't see it. The color almost completely blended in with Zeke's shirt. Then I saw it. It was a big puppy. My jaw dropped. The puppy was black, with short hair, a wrinkly little face, and it had skin folds here and there. The puppy was laying on Zeke's arm, looking perfectly content to stay there. Its long legs were dangling around Zeke's forearm.

"Holy shit." I couldn't help it, it was so fucking cute. And not your average cute. Weird cute. The folds on his little face told me he was going to be a little funny looking. I loved him instantly. The guys were laughing at me. "You guys got me a fucking puppy?" The puppy heard me; it opened its eyes and blinked at me with light blue eyes. He reached out from Zeke to sniff at me, its tail starting to wag. Zeke smirked as he handed it to me. I took the little guy and rested him against my body. "Hi, baby," I cooed. Yeah, I fucking cooed at the puppy. The guys burst out laughing again. The puppy's butt was in my hand as it sat on my stomach, it's front feet standing on my chest. It went on a sniffing spree. "Rory's gonna kill you guys," I said in a sweet voice as the puppy sniffed my cheek. The guys laughed again.

"Rory already knows," Miles assured me. "We got permission first."

I peeked at the puppy's junk. It was a boy. "Oh, my fucking God, you guys." I couldn't believe this. He was sniffing my neck now. "What kind is he?"

Zeke went back to his spot as everyone kept watching me with the puppy. "Neapolitan Mastiff," Zeke answered.

I looked up at the word mastiff. The puppy gave me lick on my neck, making me laugh. Then he snuggled down on my chest, looking very content. "Mastiff? As in that huge fucking dog?" I asked, wondering if he was messing with me. The guys started laughing again. I ignored that as I petted the puppy's head.

"Yeah, he's going to be a big guy," Asher answered.

"I saw his dad; he was a huge fucker," Zeke admitted. My eyebrows went up. He pointed at the now sleeping puppy. "And that little shithead is a cuddler; he seriously was hogging my pillow all last night."

I laughed at the image of Zeke struggling to sleep with a puppy in his face. It was awesome. "I don't care about the cuddling, but how big are we talking here?" It was starting to sound like this dog would be giant. The guys snickered.

Zeke stood up. "His dad went to here." Zeke put his hand at his hip. My mouth dropped. The dog's head was going to reach my belly button? Holy shit. "He also weighed around 180 to 190 pounds."

This dog was going to outweigh me. Fuck. Miles saw my face.

"He might not get that big; genetics are funny. But he should be around your hip when fully grown," Miles explained calmly.

"I'm gonna need a bigger bed," I said honestly. The guys burst out laughing. The puppy just kept sleeping on me. He was like a big ball of love. "This guy's going to outweigh me?" I was kind of worried about it.

Zeke gave me a grin. "Lexie, with training he will be easy to manage," Zeke assured me. "I'll work with you to train him. When we're done, he can be at a full run and will come to a dead stop on command."

"And walks?" I asked, because this guy was going to be yanking me everywhere.

He smiled. "I'll help you leash train him; that's all part of it," Zeke reassured me.

Okay, I felt better about it. Of course, it helped that he was so fucking cute.

"Why did you guys get me a dog?" I asked, smiling down at the puppy, who was stretching out across my chest.

"I had an idea," Miles began, drawing my attention away from the puppy. "That if a dog slept next to you, you wouldn't have so much trouble sleeping at Rory's. That he would work like the twins."

"I'm still getting my fucking cuddles, dog or no dog," Isaac said, sounding grumpy. The guys chuckled.

"That is brilliant, Miles." I was majorly impressed. I started thinking up names. He was so fucking adorable. "Thank you, so much. I love him."

"No problem, Red."

"Of course, Beautiful."

"Glad you like him, Ally."

"You're welcome, Lexie," Miles said sweetly.

"You owe me a pillow," Zeke told me.

I snickered. "What, did he pee on it?" I asked, smiling.

"No, he fucking ate it." Zeke's face was dead serious.

I burst out laughing, accidentally waking up the dog. He lifted his head and moved till he was against my throat then snuggled back down.

"I'll get you a new one tomorrow," I assured him. Zeke didn't really seem to care. His eyes went to Miles, and he tilted his head towards me. Was there more? "Okay, what's up?"

"Well, there's a reason why you got this breed of dog," Miles began.

I smiled. "Because it's a guard dog and it'll be huge?" I asked like it was obvious. "Zeke was involved so I figure he'd pick the most protective animal on the planet." The guys snickered. Zeke looked completely unrepentant about his protective streak.

"No, but that was a factor he insisted on," Miles admitted. He pointed to the puppy. "There's an interesting bit of history with this breed. The myths about them are that they were originally called hellhounds. That they guarded the gates of the underworld, keeping souls where they needed to be." My eyebrows went up. "The whole

Cerberus guarding the gates of the underworld myth was supposedly a Neapolitan Mastiff."

"But with three heads," I pointed out.

Miles smiled at me. "Yes, so I thought there must be a reason the myth came about." He leaned forward a bit, bracing an arm on his knee. "I did some more digging and found that this breed is believed to keep the souls of the dead away." My jaw dropped. Was he serious? "And there was a bit about keeping away evil, but I wasn't focusing on that."

"So, you guys think this little guy can keep the ghosts and nightmares away so I can sleep," I said, just wanting to be clear. The guys nodded.

"If lore and mythology have any bit of truth in it at all, then yes," Miles answered.

I blinked at them, stunned. If this worked... even if only the nightmares stopped, then it would be amazing. I could get a full night's sleep all the time. I wouldn't have such a big coffee budget.

"Total game changer," I said, amazed at the idea. The guys chuckled. I looked down at my puppy and realized what he really meant. I could actually sleep. "You, buddy, got a big job description on your little head. Physical guard dog, spiritual guard dog, and nightmare guard dog all in one," I said to the puppy in a cute voice.

"This is the most girly we've ever seen you, Red," Isaac said, sounding stunned.

I looked up at him and shot him a look. "Fuck off." The guys laughed.

"And she's back," Isaac said, smiling. I smiled at him.

"Thank you so much, guys. He's amazing. Even if he just helps with nightmares, it'll be awesome," I told them earnestly. Then something occurred to me. "Wait a minute. Is this why Rory got all of you to help put up the backyard fence before the ground froze?" The guys smiled.

"Yes. That was part of the deal," Miles said. "You don't need to worry about food or anything tonight; Rory has it all hidden in his bedroom."

"Along with chew toys; we made sure to get the kind without squeakers," Asher added. "Not to mention, a crate."

I scoffed at that. "I'm not crating him," I said bluntly.

"It doesn't hurt the dog to crate him, Ally," Asher pointed out.

I shot him an 'are you nuts' look. "Dogs shouldn't be cooped up in a fucking crate; they should be able to go anywhere in their area that they want to at any time. Would you like to be forced to sit in one spot for hours? No. You wouldn't. So, no crate," I told him, slightly ranting.

Asher shook his head and looked to Zeke. "Will you tell her that crating is okay?" Asher asked Zeke.

Zeke looked at me then back to Asher. "I'm with her on this one," Zeke said. "I don't crate my dogs; those guys run around all they want, and it keeps them healthy and happy." I raised an eyebrow. Zeke had dogs? How did I not know this? Asher threw his hands up in defeat.

I decided to change the subject. "Okay, we need names," I announced.

"How about Cerberus?" Isaac offered. I winced.

"Dogs will understand two syllable names. Go any higher, and he won't know who you're talking to," Zeke informed us. I didn't know that.

"I like the idea of a mythology name, though," I pointed out. I tried to remember what I knew about Greek and Roman mythology.

"Aries?" Miles offered.

"Pluto. I'm not saying mythology, I mean the cartoon dog," Isaac offered. I smiled; that wasn't bad. The guys went around till I got one that was perfect.

"Hades." I looked up at them. "Hades, God of the Underworld." The guys all smiled.

"Okay, that's a bad ass name," Ethan said to everyone.

I looked down at the puppy. "Are you a Hades?" I asked him. The puppy woke up and looked at me. "Hades?" His little tail started to wag. I smiled. "Hades it is." The puppy started licking my face excitedly. I smiled and kept him away from my mouth. "Okay, no more kisses," I told him. I pulled my head away, and he stopped then looked at me with his head tilted. I smiled. "You're going to be trouble, aren't you?" I mumbled. The guys snickered at me. Hades laid back down on my chest, apparently ready to continue his nap. I decided it was time for Rory to surprise them.

"By the way." Everyone looked at me. "Rory got you guys presents too; they are in the back of the Blazer." They all went still; every one of them looked stunned, like a fish on land. All wide eyed and gaping. I snickered. "Come out and get them cause I'm not carrying." I carried a sleeping Hades with me as I headed out to the foyer and pulled my jacket on. I heard the guys following. I made a point to keep Hades under my coat where he'd stay warm. I opened the back of the Blazer, and I gestured at the packages. "I got a puppy, so, you guys carry them in." The guys were quiet as they picked up the big boxes that had each of their names on them.

Miles hesitated; he looked uncomfortable. "Why did he get any of us a present?" Miles asked. The others stopped heading in and turned back toward us. They must have wanted to know too. It broke my heart that he had to ask.

I gave him a gentle smile. "He basically told me... you guys are great. Your dads are dicks, and there are gifts that you guys shouldn't miss out on." I had to bite the tip of my tongue to stop my eyes from filling again. Rory was pretty amazing.

Miles' face was blank, his body tense. It was his 'I'm controlling an emotion' stance. He always went still when he didn't know what to do. He swallowed hard. "Do... we... get him a gift now?" he asked, looking confused. "Should we...?"

I smiled at him. "If you want to." He looked like he was struggling with something and the others weren't moving either. "He wasn't looking to-"

"I know," Miles assured me. "Rory's not like that. It's... just-"

"It's new," Ethan answered for him.

I looked over at the others; each of them seemed to be deep in thought. It made my heart ache. So, I was a smart ass. "Guys, he could have filled the boxes with stuff that pops out and scares the shit out of you. This is Rory we're talking about." That had them chuckling and moving again.

The prank war had extended to Rory after a month or so. Ethan accidentally got him instead of me with a stink bomb. Rory soon retaliated by replacing the cream filling in Oreos with toothpaste. It was funny as hell.

Miles picked up his box and gave me a small smile before heading in. I closed the back of the Blazer and hurried in behind them. I wanted to know what Rory got them; the curiosity was killing me. Everyone got back in their spots as I was taking off my jacket. The boys were all looking at each other and Rory's gifts like they were going to bite. I needed to make this easier for them.

I hurried back in with Hades, smiling. "Come on, come on. Open them! I wanna see," I said in my excited kid voice. The guys chuckled as I slipped past Ethan and sat in my spot again. "Come on! The suspense is killing me." I raised a finger. "But if there is a live snake somewhere, I'm climbing one of you like a tree." They guys burst out laughing. Yeah, I wasn't joking about that. I'd take my puppy with me too.

The guys started opening their boxes, and I visibly cringed, looking like I expected an explosion. The twins kept laughing at me. I peeked over into the boxes and realized they didn't get just one present. Rory had filled the boxes with stuff. The room was quiet as they looked in their boxes; they all seemed to be frozen again.

"Any live snakes? Spiders? Scorpions? Seriously tell me here." I pulled my feet up onto the couch and moved to sit on the back of it, clutching Hades to me like I was expecting crawling stuff any second. The guys looked at me and burst out laughing. The tension in the room disappeared, and the guys started pulling out their presents from Rory.

"Nothing alive, Lexie." Miles' voice had me looking at him. He had that half grin on his face. He knew what I was doing and appreciated it. I winked at him. Miles' half grin turned to a smile before he was going through his box too. I slid down back into my spot between the twins. Hades was still asleep.

I watched Ethan pull out a black leather wallet. "Okay, this is awesome." Ethan was smiling.

"It's a wallet." I didn't get it.

Ethan leaned over, opened it, and pointed at the slots in the wallet. "It's a wallet with pick slots," he explained, still smiling. "This baby can hold twelve. I bitched about losing picks to Rory like, a month ago."

I smiled. Good one Rory. "Okay, that's pretty cool," I admitted. Ethan shook his head and went back to looking through his box.

"Hey, Red, where are your sneakers?" Isaac asked. I looked over to see him with his mischievous grin on his face again.

"Why?" I asked suspiciously.

"Rory got me a custom sneaker kit." He looked back over at me with a big smile. "There's paint to use on your sneakers." That sounded pretty cool. "I want to test it out."

"No, use it on your own shit," I said, smiling. "But if you want, I'll help you with the artwork?"

"Yay!" He did a little dance in his spot and kept digging through his box.

"Ally..." I looked over to see Asher holding a smaller box. It looked like a set of knives.

"Did he get bad knives?" I winced, hoping that wasn't the case.

Asher shook his head, his face looking stunned. "Oh no. He... he got me some of the best knives in the world." Asher looked up at me.

"What did he get you?" Ethan asked, looking up from his box.

"A full Wusthof set of knives." Asher still looked like he couldn't believe it.

I smiled at him. "He knows you love cooking, Ash," I gently reminded him. Asher nodded slowly, still looking at the box. I watched him pull a post it off the front. Miles started laughing. I looked over to see him chuckling at a poster he'd unrolled. "Miles?"

Miles looked over at me, still laughing. "On this one, there was a note attached. It said, 'To help you keep up with Lexie.'" I raised an eyebrow at that. "It's a flow chart of Shakespearean insults." He smiled at me. "So, I can insult someone without cursing." Everyone burst out laughing. Oh, that was perfect. I was looking over Isaac's shoulder when Zeke spoke up.

"Lexie.... your uncle." Zeke's voice sounded weird. I looked over to see him holding a black, full face motorcycle helmet.

I flinched, expecting something wrong. "What, sweetie?"

Zeke looked up at me, his face just as stunned as Asher's was. "This..." He stopped and looked back down at the helmet in his hands. "This is a Shoei RF-1200 helmet. It's one of the best helmets on the market." His voice was a little rougher than his usual gravelly one, but it was so subtle I doubted the others heard it. He pulled a yellow post-it note off the face of the helmet. "And on it is a note saying 'If me or any of my friends on the force ever see you not wearing a helmet again, I'm going to ticket you every day for the rest of your life. Ask Lexie if I'm kidding.'" Everyone else burst out laughing but Zeke and me. He still looked stunned.

I didn't know what to say except the obvious. "He wants you safe, Tough Guy." He looked at me, still not quite believing it. "And he's not kidding; he will do that." Zeke was still shaking his head, looking like he was still trying to understand something, when Ethan caught my attention.

"Holy mother..."

I looked over to see him looking at a piece of paper.

I shifted Hades and leaned over but couldn't make it out. "Okay, what is it?" I asked, smiling. Rory was a damn good gift giver. Watching the boys open their presents from him was like a present just for me. It was fun.

"Rory bought me a Fender Mexican Strat." His face was shocked. "It's waiting for me to pick up at the music shop in town." Ethan looked at me; his mouth was moving, but nothing came out.

I gave him a smile and bumped his shoulder with mine. "He knows you're good, Snoopy." Ethan looked back down at the paper in his hands like he expected it to disappear. I could tell by his expression that the guitar must have been good or really good. I didn't know.

"Lexie..." Miles' voice had me looking to him. He was looking at a piece of paper too.

"Yeah?" I was dying to know what Rory got Miles.

Miles looked up at me with a stunned look on his face. "Rory bought me a telescope. It'll be here tomorrow." He looked at me with a curiously.

"I might have told him you wanted to be an Astrophysicist," I admitted, smiling. "He's trying to encourage you, honey." Miles looked back down at the paper with his 'I'm dealing with an emotion' face. "Is it a-."

"No, it's..." Miles stopped me, not even looking up. His voice was quiet. "It's perfect." His voice was thick.

I was about to get up to hug him when Isaac let out a hoot. Hades woke up and let out a small woof. Then he settled back down on my neck. Isaac was doing a dance in his spot.

"Rory is awesome!" Isaac yelled, pulling out a bag of a new set of MMA pads. "And the note says, 'Stop getting your head kicked in.'" Everyone burst out laughing, even Isaac.

The guys kept emptying their boxes. Everyone seemed to get a lot of little things that they'd like too. A new wallet chain for Zeke, galaxy lollipops for Miles, a gadget that Ethan was thrilled about; he said it was a pick cutter. Free guitar picks for life. Isaac got silly stuff that he was happy to instantly start playing with. Asher got something called a Gray Kunz spoon; it was used for plating or something.

"Anyone else get a shaving kit?" Zeke asked suspiciously. All the guys said some variation of yes.

"You guys got shaving kits?" Was that a guy thing? They all nodded.

"Yeah, and they're the old-fashioned kind," Ethan said, picking his up and handing it to me. I held Hades in one arm and looked in the leather case. There was a shaving mug, a brush, a soap disk, a safety razor, a small bottle of scentless after shave, extra blades, and instructions on how to shave with a safety razor.

"Why would he give you old fashioned ones?"

"His note said that it gives a closer, better shave," Asher answered for everyone. "That it takes longer, but it's worth it to not have to shave every day."

"I think he meant that bit about me," Zeke admitted, smirking. I snorted. Yeah, Zeke didn't like shaving all the time.

WHEN THE DEAD COME A KNOCKIN'

I thought about that. "Shit. I need to find one for myself." The guys chuckled. Yeah, I wasn't joking. I never could find a razor worth a damn.

Each of their boxes had things specifically for them, but there were things that all of them got, like the shaving kits. They all also each received a nice dress watch, cufflinks, tie clips, and a shoe polish kit. According to Rory, these were all things guys needed. I had no fucking clue. Then there were the things that were for each of them. Ethan got a tuner for his new guitar that he'd been wanting. He was so happy he did his own dance when he pulled it out of the box. Miles got a bioluminescent globe thing. It was a plastic ball almost filled with water, but when you moved it, the plankton in it glowed blue. Miles loved it instantly. Isaac's favorite was a smartphone projector box. You used your phone to watch a movie, and it projected it onto the wall. It was cool. Asher got a subscription to receive a box of artisan ingredients every month for a year; he was really excited about that. Zeke got a gift certificate to go overhaul his protective riding gear. Gloves, boots, and even a new jacket with inserts for armor. Rory also demanded that Zeke pick up several pairs of motorcycle jeans too. Apparently, they made jeans now that hade Kevlar worked into the fabric so if you crashed, your skin wasn't scraped off by the asphalt. Ouch. I needed to hug Rory when I got home.

But in every one of the boxes, there was what looked like a letter to each of them. Ethan started reading his before everyone was done looking through the boxes. I noticed after a couple of seconds that he stopped and put it back in the envelope. When Asher went to open his, Ethan coughed, catching his attention. I pretended not to notice him mouthing the words 'not here.' Whenever one of them started opening their letter, Ethan would do the same thing: get their attention and tell them to wait. I wasn't going to ask, but I really wanted to.

In the end, all the guys were shocked by Rory's gifts. I couldn't stop smiling. The guys started talking about gift ideas for Rory. I suggested yard work hours. The guys snickered, but Zeke looked like he was considering it.

While the guys were still talking, Hades woke up and was ready to play. Zeke brought down the toys he'd left with him upstairs. While everyone else started a board game, Zeke was teaching me what not to do when playing with a puppy. He told me you weren't supposed to let them bite on your hands. I had no clue. Zeke also told me how to use positive reinforcement to get the obedience you wanted.

"Especially with house training, you can't do the whole 'rub their noses in it' shit. That creates fear in the dog, and a dog that fears you might obey, but he won't trust you as much," Zeke said as he held the end of a rope while Hades yanked on the other end. "It'll take longer, and there will be more mess, but in the end, it's better for the bond."

I smiled to myself. "Okay, lots of treats and positive attention," I agreed. I was willing to follow anything he said right now. I had no fucking clue how to take care of a dog.

I put Hades on a leash and took him out back to see if he needed to go. My coat pocket was full of treats like Zeke had suggested. The back yard was covered in snow, and I was worried about whether Hades' short hair would keep him warm enough. I watched him carefully to make sure he didn't start shivering. While I was out there, I took a couple photos of Hades to show to Dylan. Shit! Dylan! I was supposed to head up there this afternoon. Could I take Hades? Fuck! I waited a few more minutes outside as Hades peed on a bush. When he was done, I gave him a treat and some love. His tail was wagging like helicopter blades. We came back in and headed into the living room.

"Okay, dog question," I asked. Zeke looked up from the game. "I'm supposed to leave to see Dylan in twenty minutes. It's an hour away. Do I take him?"

Zeke's eyes were unfocused for only a couple of seconds. "If someone else were going with you, I'd say yeah. But he's a puppy, and he's going to want to explore the Blazer while you're driving," Zeke explained. "I wouldn't if I were you." Shit. I was afraid he was going to say that. "Lexie, don't worry. I'll take him back to my house, and you can pick him up on your way home." My eyebrows went up. Zeke's house? I'd never seen Zeke's house.

"Really? I get to see your house?" I asked, smiling.

He rolled his eyes. "I do have a house, Lexie; it's where I sleep," he pointed out, being a smart ass. I wrinkled my nose at him. "Besides, you'll have to start socializing him with people and dogs. And I'm your only friend with dogs." He made a good point.

"You don't mind?" I didn't want to put him out.

He didn't even look up from the game. "Not a bit; it's kinda fun to have a puppy around again," Zeke answered absently. My heart melted a bit right there.

I leaned over and gave him a side hug. "You're the best."

He smirked and patted my back. "You might want to stop your dog from eating your new purse," Zeke said not even looking up from the game. I turned and found Hades gnawing on the bag strap. Oh shit.

I hurried over and took it from him. "No," I told him firmly. He looked at me with a tilted head.

"Now give him something he can chew on," Zeke called from the table. I grabbed one of the chewing bones and held it out to Hades. Hades sniffed it then took it and began gnawing. "Now you give him a treat and tell him he's a good dog." I did what Zeke said. Hades ate his treat and went back to chewing on the rawhide. "You'll have to do that a lot, Lexie. It's repetitive and all the time, but in the end, it's pretty fucking worth it."

"I'm going to end up calling you a lot," I warned him.

He snickered. "Just not after midnight or before eight in the morning," he shot back. I just smiled.

Then it was time for me to go. I didn't want to leave my puppy. The guys started laughing at me, and that got me out the door with Dylan's presents. Those shit heads.

AN HOUR LATER, my stomach was in knots as I pulled up to Dylan's house. It was around four, and it was going to be dark soon. I texted him I was here and needed help carrying stuff. A minute later he was coming out the front door. He gave me a big smile before he gave me a quick, soft kiss. He pulled back, his eyes warm.

"Merry Christmas, Sunshine."

"Merry Christmas, cutie." I smiled up at him; I couldn't help it. But

I did have a question before I met his dad. "Does your dad care if I curse? 'Cause I might need a swear jar."

He laughed at me. "Sunshine, I curse around him all the time. He won't even notice," he reassured me. That took a big weight off my shoulders.

I turned to the back of the Blazer towards the two stacks of boxes. "Okay, you take one stack. And I'll take the other. Please don't drop them, it was hard enough to make them the first time," I begged him. He smiled and took a stack. I took the other one and the book bag I had stashed in the back.

We closed the back and headed in. My stomach knotted even more as we walked into the foyer. Dylan looked back and gave me a wink. It made me smile. Okay, this wasn't going to be so bad. Right? Dylan led me into the great room. His dad was sitting in the leather recliner. Wow, he looked like an older version of Dylan. Except for his eyes. Dylan's Dad had his hair buzzed down to a short layer on his head, like he just didn't want to deal with it. I envied that guys had that option.

"Dad." Dylan got his attention. "This is Lexie. Lexie, this is my dad, David."

"It's nice to meet you, Mr. Miller." I was on my best behavior. It felt weird.

He waved a dismissive hand. "Just call me Dave, honey," he said with a friendly voice. "So, you're the girl Dylan won't stop talking about?" Dylan's face started to turn red. I looked at him, smirking.

"Dad..." Dylan groaned.

"Oh really?" I asked, smiling. I looked back at David. "What's he been saying?" David started grinning.

"Lexie..." Dylan pleaded.

I looked at Dylan, still smiling. "Sorry, sweetie, you brought me here." I turned back to his dad. "Come on, tell me what he said? Were there details? I bet there were details." Dylan groaned and headed for the kitchen. I held it together until he was in the kitchen; then I started snickering. I looked back at David, who had a big smile. "Oh, that was fun."

David started laughing, his eyes warming. "I think I'm gonna like you," David declared.

I smiled back, then tilted my head at the TV. "Have you guys been drowning in Christmas movies?" I asked.

David nodded. "Yeah, it's overload at this point," he confirmed.

"Well, I did bring some anti-Christmas movies if you're interested."

He raised an eyebrow. "I'm listening,"

I put the boxes down and opened my bag as I walked over to the coffee table. I pulled out several stacks of action movies and bad horror movies that I personally loved. Not to mention the classic comedies: Spaceballs and Monty Python. David whistled. I gestured to the stacks.

"Have at it." I picked up the boxes and eyed David. "Do you want your cookies now?"

His eyebrows went up, and a light came to his eyes. "Have you tried them first?" he asked cautiously.

I snickered. "Yes, and so did everyone helping to bake them. No ill effects," I assured him.

His face lit up. "Then, yeah," he said, smiling big. I walked over and just put the whole stack of boxes in front of him on the coffee table. His eyebrows went up. "That's a lot of cookies."

I snickered. "That's your half." He looked up at me, his eyes wide. "Dylan has his with him in the kitchen." I took a breath and added, "They might not taste the same. But I can tell you my friends wouldn't stop eating them, so they aren't bad." He gave me a smile.

"Hey, Lexie, where'd ya go?" Dylan called.

"I didn't go anywhere; you ditched me," I shot back over my shoulder. David burst out laughing. I smiled and headed into the kitchen. I found him waiting in the doorway. "What do you mean where did I go? You're the one who walked off without me," I pointed out.

"Okay, yeah, I'll admit that." He grinned down at me.

I stepped a little closer. "Let's give your dad a couple of minutes; he's going to try the cookies and if we succeeded..." I whispered. Dylan's eyes warmed on my face. He nodded, took my hand and led me into the kitchen. I took my coat off and hung it on the back of a dining chair and put my bag on the table.

"How many cookies did you make, Sunshine?" he asked, going to the boxes.

I went to the empty counter next to him and hopped up. "We made a whole fucking bunch," I told him honestly. "Your Dad has his half."

Dylan's brows went up, his eyes wide. "Half?" He pointed at the gift boxes full of cookies. "This is half?" he asked in disbelief.

I gave him a big smile. "Yep; that's your half. And there is no sharing," I said, my voice matter of fact. He kept looking at me like I was nuts. "What? We did a test batch of each, and when we realized we got it right, we went crazy."

"The guys helped?" he asked, not quite believing me.

I nodded emphatically. "Oh yeah; without Asher, this would have gone baaad."

He shook his head. "Sunshine, I wasn't talking about a huge number of cookies. I was talking one batch of one cookies." His eyes were running over my face as he smiled.

"Yeah, well. Tough shit." I smirked at him. "I really don't do things halfway."

Dylan opened the top box and saw exactly how full each box was. "Damn, Lexie." I snickered. He closed his eyes and cringed. "I should have gotten you a better present."

I raised an eyebrow at that. "Present?" I asked in a perky voice.

He looked at me and smiled. "Yeah, I got you something. But now I need to upgrade it." His cheeks tinted pink.

"Why?" I asked. "Because I went cookie crazy?" He nodded. I snickered. "Honey, the guys were helping. I expected them to eat a lot more cookies than they did." He burst out laughing. "There's still a few batches at Miles' house, which I'm sure the guys are eating right now." He just kept laughing.

I was waiting him out when my phone vibrated. I pulled it out and checked it while he was calming down.

Zeke: Did Hades take a leak or shit outside when you took him?

Alexis: Yeah, he pissed.

Zeke: K, taking him out again now. Didn't want to stand out there forever for nothing.

Alexis: Would you mind if I picked him up around 9?

Zeke: No, I'll still be awake.

Alexis: Thank you.

I snickered.

"What?" he asked.

"Zeke's taking care of one of the presents the guys got me." I smiled as I brought up Hades' picture and showed him.

Dylan burst out laughing. "They got you a puppy?" he asked, his voice full of disbelief.

"Yep."

He cringed. "I'm screwed, I can't beat a puppy." He was laughing and shaking his head.

I looked at him like he was nuts. "Are you kidding? You're the boyfriend. You make me happy just being you," I said, being completely honest. "I don't even need a fucking present."

His eyes ran over my face. "You really mean that," he said, sounding surprised.

"Yep. Now try your cookies, because the suspense is killing me," I all but whined. He smiled and picked up a cookie.

My stomach knotted, I bit the corner of my lower lip. It was Asher's present all over again. Terrifying. He took a bite and chewed, then froze. Oh God, did someone leave an eggshell in the batter? Did we not use enough sugar? I shouldn't have even tried this. Fuck.

He swallowed his bite and looked at me. His eyes were shiny as they met mine. "Damn Sunshine..." He took a breath. "They're the same."

Relief washed over me, almost making me dizzy. "Don't pause like that!" I smacked his arm. "You scared the shit out of me."

He put his cookie down and moved to stand in front of me. He cupped my jaw in his hands and kissed me. It was a soft, sweet kiss that didn't last long but still took my breath away.

He eased back and met my eyes. "Thank you, so much, Sunshine." His voice was soft and quiet. It was a voice full of feeling. "You have no idea how much this means to me." I felt my face warming and fought the urge to squirm. He saw and smiled. "Aversion to romance?"

"Yeah, a little bit," I said, my voice sounding pained. He chuckled and let me go.

He stayed leaning against the counter between my knees as he reached into his back pocket and pulled out a small box. "Now, it's not a puppy." His voice was nervous, and he handed me the box.

"I already have a puppy, and I've never had a dog in my life. It's scary as hell," I admitted. He laughed.

I tore off the wrapping paper and found a small white box. I opened it and found silver angel wings. They were beautiful. I picked them up. They were part of a necklace. I smiled and pulled the necklace out of the box. The angel wings were different heights on two small chains that connected to the main chain through a loop. The oxidization made the wings really stand out.

"Dylan, this is beautiful." My voice was soft and quiet. No one had ever bought me jewelry before. Hell, I didn't own any. I looked up at him to see his anxious face. "I love it."

His face started to relax. "Really?"

"Yeah, I love it. With both at different heights, it's like two necklaces in one. It's amazing." He let out a big breath. I smiled and crooked my finger at him. He smirked and leaned down so I could kiss him. And I did. Thoroughly. When I eased back, my heart was racing, and his cheeks had turned pink.

"Okay, you really like it." He smiled down at me, his body relaxing.

"Oh, yeah." My eyes ran over his handsome face. "Thank you so much."

His warm eyes met mine. "Your welcome, Sunshine." He reached to my right and opened the cabinet.

"Now I just need lower necklines, and I can wear it." I watched as Dylan paused, then kept grabbing the plate he was going for.

"That works for me," he admitted and I chuckled.

"So, how's your Christmas going?" I asked, watching as he pulled down a plate and glasses.

"It's the usual. Not much going on. Missing Mom." He shrugged then looked at me. "You're making it a lot easier this time."

"Cookies always help." He smirked at me then went to get the fridge. "What?"

When he brought the milk back, he was still smirking, and now also shaking his head. "I wasn't talking about the cookies, Sunshine." His voice was soft as he poured the milk into three glasses.

"Oh." I felt my face heating up again. "Glad I can help? What is the proper response to that?" I asked, feeling completely awkward. He chuckled and looked over at me again. I felt my face turning redder. I looked up at the ceiling and tried to stop blushing. He leaned over and kissed me on the cheek. I needed to distract myself. "I brought lots of movies; they are piled on the coffee table." He chuckled. I rolled my eyes.

"Okay, let's give Dad a few more minutes." He started opening the other boxes and put a mix of cookies on the plate. "How's your Christmas going?"

"Rory and I hung out this morning. Tara wasn't coming until I left." He winced. "Yeah, I got her a certificate to her favorite spa, so maybe that will help smooth things over."

He nodded. "It will, Sunshine. It's just going to take time," he reassured me. I smiled at him. "How are the guys? Why did they get you a puppy of all things?"

My smile got bigger. "It's their solution to my sleeping problem," I explained. "They think if the dog is lying next to me then it might keep the nightmares away."

He thought about that; then he smiled. "Huh, that was the solution they were talking about. The dog," he muttered. I raised an eyebrow. He smiled. "When the guys were forcing you to take a nap, they said they thought they had a solution to the problem, but it wasn't going to be here until Christmas," he told me.

"I do not remember any of that," I said honestly.

He smiled. "You were exhausted, babe," he reassured me. "And you were already almost out." Yeah, he was probably right. "What else did the guys get you?" he asked, putting the plate between us and taking a cookie.

"A Leatherman, sparring gloves, an iPod shuffle. And Miles got me the most awesome purse ever, oh and a scarf." I paused. "Then Asher gave me his present. It was a photo of my Dad."

His eyes went wide. "I thought there weren't any?" he asked, his hand going to the inside of my knee.

"So, did I." I snorted. "Rory got him in touch with the fire house Dad had worked at. They sent his portrait."

His eyebrows were up, his mouth open. "Wow." He sounded stunned. "That was real sweet of him." His eyes narrowed on me. "You cried, didn't you?"

"Oh, like a baby," I admitted. "But that's okay, 'cause awhile later they gave me the puppy." I smiled. It sounded so weird.

He smiled at me. "You really like that puppy." He snickered.

"He's so cute! He's got all these wrinkles. He's gonna be one of those so ugly they're cute dogs," I all but gushed about Hades.

Dylan was still laughing at me when my phone vibrated.

Asher: Trisha agreed to work on her issues. Up for a group thing tomorrow night?

I groaned. Then I looked up at Dylan.

"Can you come to down tomorrow night? Trisha is apparently willing to work on her shit. And we're all going to try to get together without us killing each other," I asked, giving him my pleading face.

He gave me a half grin. "Yeah, but how did this happen?" he asked, frowning. Shit. I forgot to tell him about yesterday.

I texted Asher back.

Alexis: Yeah, we'll come. Let's try somewhere not so loud, though.

I looked up at Dylan and tried to figure out how to explain what had happened. I was about to start talking when my phone vibrated.

Asher: Shooting pool at the bowling alley it is. Tell Dylan he can crash at my house.

"Okay, we're on for tomorrow." I looked up to him. "Asher says you can crash on his couch."

He smiled. "Sounds good; now what happened?" he asked. Oh, he wasn't going to let it go.

Shit. This was going to be a long one.

"So, the guys stripped you down in the kitchen, you were wearing their clothes, and Trisha had a shit fit. Then Asher told her to make a decision," Dylan summed up. His brow was furrowed, his shoulders tight. I figured it was the first part that had him upset. Shit.

"Dylan. My lips were turning blue," I reminded him. He nodded that he heard me. "Asher wrapped a blanket around me so I could try to get the wet clothes off myself, but my fingers could barely bend." I understood why he was upset, but there was nothing else I could have done then but die. "They didn't see anything that wasn't on the big screen," I pointed out.

His eyes snapped to mine. "Wait. They only got your jeans and shirt?" I nodded then remembered something. "What?" Damn, he read my face too well.

"I couldn't unhook my bra, so Zeke unhooked it and pulled the shirt, which was a tent and reached my knees, back down. I got the rest off myself," I said quickly.

He rubbed his eyes with one hand and started laughing. "For crying out loud, Lexie…" He smiled at me. "You had me thinking they took everything off you." He laughed at the horrified look on my face. "I'm okay, Sunshine, if you're okay. And they didn't see everything." I started laughing. "What?"

"Trisha still doesn't know about that." I couldn't stop laughing.

Dylan started laughing too. "Oh, that would be fun to tell her." Dylan's eyes lit up.

I snickered. "I know, but we're trying to play nice for Asher. Hell, Isaac dumped Cece for throwing that big screen shit in my face."

He smiled. "Okay, I'm not going to kill Isaac now."

"Or Ethan. I've got blackmail now, and I intend to use it," I said in my serious voice.

He chuckled. "I guess we've given Dad enough time." His warm eyes ran over my face before settling on my eyes. "The cookies were the best present ever, Sunshine."

I smiled a wicked smile. "That wasn't your present."

His brow furrowed. "It wasn't?" I shook my head. "Then what is?"

I bit my lip trying to decide if I should show him now. Yeah. It would probably be better. I hopped off the counter, went to the table and opened my bag. He followed closely.

"It's kind of a present for you and your dad," I warned him as he stood next to me.

"Okay." His voice was cautious.

I pulled out his mother's recipe book and slid it over to him. He blinked and opened it. The torn parts had been repaired and all the pages were laminated. The whole book was now virtually spill proof or accident proof.

"Sunshine…" He swallowed hard. He looked at me with a new look on his face. I had no clue what it was. His eyes were soft, and there was a small smile on his face. It was a mix between stunned and well, something else.

"It should stop you guys from destroying it anymore, except fire." I looked up at him. "Please keep it away from fire." He smiled before he dove in and caught my lips. It took me a couple of heartbeats to kiss him back. I didn't want to, but I eased back. "That's not your present either."

Now he looked completely stunned. "What else could you have fucking done? Cure cancer over the weekend?" he asked, his sarcasm thick.

I smiled up at him. "No, but…" I opened the recipe book and pointed to a recipe. "Your mom was using cook's shorthand. Only someone who knows tons about cooking could have read it."

"That's why everything always turned out like shit." He laughed as he smiled.

I nodded. "Now, Asher knows a shit ton about cooking. He's the only reason those cookies came out. He gave me a key to reading your mom's recipes." I pointed to it on the inside cover where it was laminated.

"Sunshine... that's fucking..." His face was full of disbelief.

I kind of felt guilty about the next part. "That's not your present either." He ran a hand down his face, his eyes wide. I was driving him crazy. It was kinda fun. "This is your guys' present." I pulled out a new binder. The cover said Miller Family Recipes. I slid it over to him.

He took a breath before reaching out with a slightly shaking hand. He opened it. There was the first recipe from the first page of the other book. Only it was translated so ordinary people could use it. Hell, even I could follow the recipes from this book. He turned the pages, again and again, seeing that he could understand what was there. I bit my lip, waiting, hoping he'd like it.

"How did you... when did you have the time?" he asked me, his eyes shining.

"I don't sleep much," I reminded him. "Besides, since the guys made me take a nap, they helped. Miles is a fast, fucking typer."

Dylan reached out, grabbed my wrist and pulled me to him. He wrapped his arms around me and buried his face into my neck. I hugged him back and just waited till he was good again. "Sunshine..." he whispered, his voice thick.

"Merry Christmas, Dylan," I whispered back.

He took several deep breaths. He lifted his head; then he was kissing me. Warmth flooded from my heart out as he moved his lips against mine. He kissed me slowly and gently till I forgot where we were. I could only hear the pulse in my ears. His hands were on my face again, holding me still while he brushed his lips across mine. Every nerve felt alive when he eased back a little and gazed into my eyes.

"Thank you, Lexie." His eyes were almost glowing sapphire as he ran them over my face then back to my eyes. "You are always constantly surprising me."

"That's my job, to keep you on your toes," I teased, smiling up at him. He gave me that look, the one that made me feel beautiful. It sent shivers down my spine.

"You sure as hell do." He looked at the cookbooks. "I should show-"

"Um, can you wait until I leave?" I asked awkwardly. He looked back to me. "I'll turn fucking bright red and be uncomfortable for a long while," I warned him.

He grinned at me. "Okay, Sunshine, but I'm still telling him it was you."

I shrugged. "As long as I don't have to watch or be there, I'm good," I agreed.

He snorted. "Come on, let's go watch some movies with Dad." I nodded and followed him out into the living room.

We spent the rest of the evening watching movies. I got them to watch Spaceballs, and David laughed his ass off. I liked Dylan's dad. He was kind of fun. I tried to make them both laugh as often as I could. When it was nearing eight, I got my bag and coat. I said goodbye to David, who actually got up and hugged me to thank me for the cookies. Then Dylan walked me out to the Blazer. I started the truck, letting it heat up, and slid out so I could keep talking to Dylan. He pulled me close and rested his forehead on mine.

"Sunshine," he whispered. "You don't even know what you gave us today." He swallowed hard. "We can't have her, but we can have her cooking again." I squeezed my hands on his arms. "You are so fucking amazing, and you don't even know it." My pulse picked up.

"I'm okay." I tried to lighten his mood. He was so serious right now; it was making me nervous.

He lifted his head and looked down at me. "You're so much better than okay," he said. "You have the biggest heart I've ever seen."

"Not always a good thing, sweetie," I reminded him.

He narrowed his eyes at me as he sighed. "Lexie, let me fucking compliment you." His voice was growing harder. I wanted to squirm. He saw it and smiled. He pulled me closer till his lips were at my ear. "You are beautiful, Sunshine, inside and out." It was easier to listen when I didn't have to see his face.

"Thank you." My voice was quiet. I was uncomfortable now. Edgy. I wanted to squirm.

"You're just dying to make a joke or something, aren't you?" I could hear his smile in his voice.

"You have no idea," I shot back emphatically. He chuckled.

He pulled back a little, and he kissed me goodnight. It was another one of his slow and sweet kisses that made my heart race and got my blood moving. It seemed to go on forever, but it still wasn't long enough. When he eased back, he kissed my forehead before letting go. I got in my truck and promised to text when I got home. Then I headed back to Spring Mountain. That feeling had washed over me all night. Anytime he looked at me a certain way; anytime he touched me at all. I was getting there, a lot faster than I thought I would. Damn it.

I PULLED into Zeke's driveway around nine. He apparently lived across town and further out than Miles did. The driveway was graveled, stretching from the road into the trees. I wondered if Zeke and Sylvia ever got snowed in. When I reached the house, I parked next to Zeke's Jeep. The house wasn't as big as Rory's, but I liked the bungalow-cabin crossover look it had, with its gray weathered shingles. There was a big garage to the left; though, it looked newer than the house. I got out and heard dogs barking; there was a lot of barking. How many dogs did Zeke have? I walked over the gravel and stepped up to the simple wrap around porch that had stuff scattered here and there. Snow shovels, a couple of metal buckets, and even a set of snowshoes. I was about to knock when the door opened.

Zeke was looking down at me with a half grin on his face. "Come on, Lexie, move it," he ordered as he walked around me and through a small archway to the immediate right.

The small family room had a big comfy blue sofa on one wall and a yellow armchair to the left, its back flush to the wall. There was a TV on the left wall in a long, white built-in that also had bookshelves. Besides the white wooden end tables, that was all the furniture, except for several dog beds scattered here and there. I took a quick look around. The front door opened directly into a not-so-big area. There was a small dinner table that currently had a laptop and a pile of papers on top of it. There was another walk through on the left; it looked like the kitchen and a hallway straight ahead. The whole house had a beach cottage feel to it. It was so not Zeke. I smiled to myself.

"Yeah, if you don't mind me annoying you," I said as I took my jacket off and found a row of hooks behind the door. That was handy. I hung my coat up. I walked into the family room and saw my puppy sleeping next to Zeke on the middle couch cushion. Zeke gave me a half smile.

"I'm used to it by now, Lexie," he pointed out. I stuck my tongue out at him; he chuckled.

I sat down on the other side of my puppy. "So, did he destroy anything new?"

Zeke smirked as he looked down at the dog. "No, nothing new. He's got his toys to fuck with now." He looked back at the TV. Zeke seemed a bit off. He never talked a whole lot, but now he seemed to be having trouble. His shoulders were tense; his thumb was tapping the remote. He looked nervous. Huh. It was kind of hard for me to believe, but there it was, right in front of me.

"So, Zeke." He looked over at me. "Your house, man..."

He rolled his eyes. "Is cute, I know," he grumbled. I burst out laughing. He just shook his head. "Sylvie likes cute, so she gets cute." He shook his head. "As long as she leaves my room alone, she can do what she wants." I just smiled. I heard another dog barking. Zeke tilted his head, listening. His eyes were unfocused.

"What?" I asked, wondering what he was doing.

He shook his head. "The dogs are just playing," he said matter-of-factly. Then he smirked over at me. "Wanna meet 'em?"

"Hell yeah," I said cheerfully. He smiled and got up. We stopped on the way to grab our coats. "How many do you have anyway?"

He grinned. "Four."

My eyebrows went up. "You have four dogs?" I couldn't quite believe it. I was worried about taking care of one.

He chuckled. "Yeah, we have the space, and when we're not home, they have each other for company," he explained. "They're high-energy dogs, so having each other to play with keeps them happy and calm." I followed him through the left archway, which led to a small kitchen. Zeke opened the back door and stood in the doorway, blocking me. "Just stay in here for a sec; I'll call you out when they calm down to introduce you."

"Gotcha." He flipped the switch on the right wall, and the windows lit up before he stepped outside. He closed the door behind him fast. I heard him call the dogs. Then I heard happy sounds from them.

While I waited, I wondered why Zeke was nervous about having me here. He'd been to my house a hundred times in the last couple months. Then again, this was his house, not mine. It was a little more… personal? The more I thought about it, the more I realized that Zeke was about as private as Miles. He just wasn't vocal about it. If he didn't want to answer a question, he just glared at you or told you to fuck off. Hell, he talked to Riley for two months before asking her out. Huh. I had never noticed that before.

"Lexie, you can come outside now," Zeke called. "Just walk out slow." The way he said that made me curious. What kind of dogs did he have? I opened the door slowly and stepped out just as slowly. Zeke was kneeling in the snow with four huge fucking dogs sitting in front of him. No, not dogs. Fucking wolves.

I froze. "Zeke? What kind of dogs are these?" I asked, keeping my voice calm.

"Wolf hybrids." I could hear the smile in his voice. He didn't turn around; his attention was on the dogs. "They're just skittish of strangers. That's why I want you moving slowly." When I still didn't move, he looked over his shoulder and laughed at me. "Lexie, it's okay. Would I ever make you do anything where you could get hurt?" He had a point.

I closed the door behind me and walked forwards slowly. When I was eight feet from him, one of the dogs started growling. I stopped.

"Kita." Zeke's voice wasn't chastising, more comforting. His hand went out to the big white one on his right. The dog calmed down when he touched it. "Lexie, stay there. I'll send each one over, and they can meet you one at a time."

"Okay." I wasn't moving any closer; the dogs were fucking huge.

Zeke looked at a gray and black dog on his far left. "Kato." The dog looked at Zeke. Zeke pointed at me. "Greet." The dog got to his feet and walked towards me slowly. I held still. "Let him come to you; he'll get there when he's ready. He's going to sniff you a lot, maybe circle you, then sit down in front of you. Don't move till then."

I watched as the big dog, who looked more wolf than anything else, came towards me. He had a loose, smooth walk. His head was down, his blue eyes on me. He came halfway then stopped. He sniffed the air before coming any closer. He was huge. His head reached my fucking waist. Was Hades really going to get this big? Shit. I waited. The dog's fur was streaked with white, black, and gray. His paws were surprisingly wide for such lean legs. Kato walked towards me again; I kept my hands in my pockets of my coat as his nose started sniffing over my legs all the way up to my hips. He liked what he smelled in my right pocket where I still had some of Hades' treats.

Zeke snorted. "You still have those treats, don't you?" I nodded, keeping my eyes on Kato. "Good, when he sits down in front of you slowly pull one out and hold it in your palm. Kato's nipped my fingers trying to get a treat before." I nodded that I heard him.

Kato backed off and eyed me. Then he sat down in front of me. I slowly pulled out a treat and held it out to him in my palm. His tail went crazy. I smiled as he took the treat from me and munched on it.

"Good, Kato." Zeke's voice was positive and full of praise. Kato finished and looked at my pocket then back to my face. I laughed. "Okay, you can touch him now. Just move slowly at first."

I held out my hand and slowly moved it to his head. I went for between his ears. My hand touched his fur; it was coarse and soft all at the same time. Then I scratched. Kato pushed into my hand, forcing it to the back of his neck. I smiled as I scratched there. He shifted and leaned against my legs, his head against my stomach as I scratched. Zeke chuckled.

"He's so soft," I said as I put both my hands into his fur and scratched the hell out of him. I thought Kato's eyes rolled back in his head.

"He's the easiest out of all of them, and now that his scent is on you, it'll make it easier for the others." I looked up to see Zeke look at the next dog. "Nadie." The dog looked at him. Zeke pointed to me. "Greet."

Nadie came towards me a little slower than Kato had. Nadie looked a lot more like a wolf, but she had longer fur than Kato. She was mostly white but had a beautiful tan, brown coloring along her back and tail. Nadie did the same as Kato. Only it took her a bit longer, and she circled me twice. When she sat, I gave her a treat the same way I had Kato. Kato actually whined. I smiled and gave him one too.

"You're going to spoil my dogs, Lexie," Zeke warned me.

I looked up and smiled. "Oh totally; I'm going to spoil them rotten," I told him honestly.

He smiled then looked at the next dog. "Tank." Zeke pointed to me. "Greet. Easy." I raised my eyebrows at the new command.

The big burly dog started towards me. He was fucking huge. His head was probably even with my chest. I stayed still. He looked completely wolf to me, just giant. He was black from snout to tail; his yellow eyes watched me as he came closer. The dog looked like he was on steroids. If I didn't trust Zeke so much, I'd be running to save my ass from this animal.

"Uh, why the new command?" I asked quietly, not moving an inch as Tank came closer.

"Because he's a klutz," Zeke said bluntly. "He's knocked me over by sliding into me a few times. I said easy so he would know to walk slowly and be careful of you." I instantly felt better about Tank.

Tank didn't come too close; he circled me four times, sniffing the air around me from a couple of feet away. Then, when he was ready, he came closer. The other two moved to sit next to me, Kato still leaning on me. Tank sniffed my legs and my chest, which was weird. The fucking dog could stand on his hind legs and be taller than me. He kept sniffing me until he was comfortable. Then he sat down. His head still reached high on my stomach. I slowly gave him his treat, then followed that up with one for each of the others. Zeke snorted. I was so spoiling his dogs.

Zeke got to his feet this time; he had Kita on a leather leash. That made me nervous.

"She's on a leash?" I asked, my eyebrows up.

"She's the newest one," he explained. "She's still adapting, and she's real skittish. I'm not risking your ass to introduce you." That sounded like Zeke. "She's going to do the same thing, but I'll be with her the whole time." I nodded. Zeke had her. He'd keep me from getting hurt. He looked down at Kita and pointed at me. "Kita." His voice was different with her; it was firm but gentler, softer. "Greet." She looked at me then back at him like she wanted to argue.

Then she started to move very slowly. Once Zeke moved with Kita, she seemed to relax a bit and walked a little faster. She was beautiful. She wasn't huge like the others. She had the wolf body, but her face looked all husky to me. Not to mention she was completely snow white, with beautiful blue eyes. It took some time, but she stopped almost three feet from me and sniffed the air. Then she started circling me. Zeke talked to her softly the whole time; I couldn't hear what he was saying, but his tone was encouraging and gentle. Kita kept circling me and the other dogs; she started coming closer. When she was ready, Zeke told Tank to move and walked with her to stand in front of me. She sniffed my legs for a bit. Then she eyed me. Eventually, she sat down. I slowly held out her treat. She sniffed my hand until she was sure of me. Then she gently took it from me.

"You're not going to pet Kita today," Zeke said, his eyes on Kita as I was giving the others their treats too. "This is enough for one day with her." He reached down and unhooked her leash. "Go play guys." They took off like a shot, disappearing into the backyard. Except for Tank. He had taken Kato's spot and was leaning on me. Seeing this, Zeke laughed and looked at me. "You spoiled my dogs, Lexie." I snickered and scratched the back of Tank's head.

"Why is Kita so skittish?" I asked.

He sighed and looked out at the dogs running back through the snow then jumping on each other. "She was a rescue from some fuck head over in Colorado." His face grew hard as he spoke. "The guy starved her, beat the crap out of her. Just fucked her up." He looked back to me. "I've had her for three months now, and I'm only now introducing her to new people. Hell, Sylvie met her a few days ago for the first time."

"Wow, how did you get her if she was in Colorado?" I had never seen this side of Zeke before he was... talking about himself, or at least his dogs.

"There aren't a lot of people out there with enough room for hybrids. Sylvie and I are on a short list on this side of the country that will take in and rehabilitate these guys." He shrugged. "When they're ready, they go to families that we've thoroughly checked out."

My heart warmed. He really was sweet under all the pissed off.

"So, you don't keep any of them?" I asked curiously. That seemed kind of sad, to love on them, work with them and then just let them go. I didn't think I could do that.

"Tank is probably going to stay," he said as he looked down at the huge dog at my side and smirked. "He's funny as hell. If Kita doesn't make any more progress then, yeah, she'll stay too." He looked back out at the dogs. "I can't give her to a family with her this skittish. She still needs special handling." I smiled at Zeke. I didn't know what I expected of Zeke and his dogs, but it sure as hell wasn't this. Zeke was relaxed; the nervousness he had around me earlier was gone.

"What about Kato and Nadie?" I asked, massaging Tank's ears.

He looked back down at me. "Kato is leaving for a family in North Dakota next week. And Nadie will probably be up for adoption in the next month or so."

"Oh. That's sad." Tank shifted against me, and I moved to stay on my feet. "Aren't you going to miss them?"

He shrugged and looked back at the dogs. "Yeah, but we can't help more if we keep them all," he pointed out.

"Good point."

He grinned at me. "Come on. I need to bring the shitheads in, and I can't do that yet with Hades here," he said.

I gave Tank another big scratch before turning and heading back to the house. Inside, I found Hades by the door, whimpering. I immediately picked him up. His tail went crazy, and he licked the hell out of my hand.

"Do you need to go, baby?" I asked him, already heading for the front door.

"He went out thirty minutes ago, that dog..." Zeke began, closing the door behind him and taking off his jacket. I turned around to listen "That dog does not like being alone. I went to the bathroom, and he was scratching at the door the whole minute I was in there." My eyebrows went up in surprise as I looked down at Hades. He was still happy licking my hand. "His breed is known to like to be with their person, but I didn't think it'd be that bad." Shit, I couldn't take him everywhere with me.

"That's fine now, but what am I going to do when school starts?" I asked seriously. "Is there such a thing as puppy daycare?"

He snorted as we headed back to the front of the house. Zeke hung up his coat and headed into the family room. "No, but I called Sylvie, and she says she'll be happy to watch the booger when school starts." Zeke started picking up Hades' toys.

"Seriously?" I hadn't even met Sylvia, and she was willing to watch my puppy? I loved her already.

Zeke straightened. "Yeah, she works nights, so she'll be sleeping, but he's a puppy. He's going to sleep a lot anyway." He shrugged and filled a plastic bag with Hades' toys. "Besides, she fell in love with him yesterday."

"I love your aunt already," I told him. "Just saying."

He chuckled as he handed me the bag. "You just need to pick him up immediately after school; that's the only time she gets free time anymore," he informed me. I nodded. No problem. "Besides, once he's older and knows you're not disappearing on him, he'll be okay staying home eventually." That was a load off my mind.

I looked down at Hades who was still wagging his tail. "Looks like you're going everywhere with me, like one of those annoying Chihuahuas," I told him disdainfully.

Zeke laughed. "I'd suggest putting that crate Rory has in the Blazer. At least until he's not so small anymore." He reached out and scratched Hades' head. Hades immediately moved to lick his finger. He grinned.

"Thank you, Zeke." I looked up at him. "I really appreciate it."

He met my gaze and gave me a half smile. "No problem." He tilted his head towards the door. "Now get him out of here so I can let the terrors in for the night." I snickered and headed out. "Text me when you get home," he shot out before I closed the door. I just rolled my eyes.

I ended up driving with Hades in my lap, which was not easy. I was so putting that crate in here. I got home and brought him in, Rory was in the living room, watching television with Tara.

I smiled as I saw her. "Hey, guys!" I held up Hades against my chest. "Look what followed me home." Rory chuckled, and Tara's eyebrows went up.

"Where did you get a puppy?" she asked without her usual grumpiness. Maybe she really did like her gift.

"The guys," I said as I put Hades down and watched while he started sniffing around. "Where's the stuff I need for him?"

Rory gestured towards his door. "There's a lot. The guys might have gone a little overboard," Rory told me, smiling.

I headed into his room. There was a huge crate that was full of fucking dog toys, dog food, training pads, and a couple of dog bowls. The number of toys the guys had bought was nuts. I pulled everything out of Rory's room. I filled Hades' food bowl and water bowl, to which he ran to immediately and began chowing down. As I figured out where to put everything for now, I told Rory about how the puppy was going to have to go to Zeke's during the day until he understood I wasn't bailing. Tara thought that was funny as hell. She mentioned puppy daycare. I laughed with her.

After I had everything set up downstairs, I took the training pads and another full bowl of food and water up to my room. Then I had to come back down to get Hades. I stopped by Rory before heading up. I thanked him for helping Asher with my gift. He just smiled. Then I told him that he had surprised the hell out of the guys. He fidgeted as his face turned pink. He said the guys already called to thank him. I went upstairs, taking my presents from the guys with me, and went to my room.

I put Hades down and closed the door. I went around and moved anything that might be chewable out of his reach. He ignored me the whole time, very happy with his food dish. I got in my jammies and texted everyone I was home. By the time I was done, Hades was on his back paws, trying to get in my bed. I smiled and lifted him up. I snuggled down in bed and shut off the desk lamp. Hades snuggled up to me, his face lying on my neck. Okay. Here it goes. I went to sleep.

CHAPTER 16

THURSDAY

*T*he sun was already up when I opened my eyes. I felt different. It was... I wanted to get up and move. I wasn't groggy. I wasn't cursing everything under the sun. I had gotten a full fucking night of sleep! Pure happiness filled me.

I had grabbed my phone when my ball of love woke up too. He slid off the bed and started looking around. Oh no. I quickly picked him up, grabbed his treat bag and hurried downstairs. I barely stopped to shove my feet into the galoshes by the back door before I was out and putting Hades down. He looked around the snow and moved to a spot before he took a leak. I checked the time, and my mouth gaped. It was ten in the morning; I had missed my workout, and no one had come to yank me out of bed. I smiled. Hades decided to move to another pristine patch of snow and color that one as well.

I texted the guys.

Alexis: IT WORKED! I slept all night.

It didn't take long before my phone blew up.

Isaac: Awesome, Red!

Asher: How do you feel, Ally?

Ethan: No more eye baggage for Beautiful!

Zeke: Did he eat your pillow too?

Miles: When you didn't show up this morning, we called Rory. He told us you were still sleeping.

I loved my guys. I looked up in time to watch Hades taking a squat. Then I was back on my phone.

Alexis: I feel fucking fantastic! No, he didn't eat my pillow. Tell me what kind you want, Zeke, and I'll pick it up before I see you guys tonight.

Zeke: I want my old pillow, but uneaten.

I snickered at Zeke. I looked up to see Hades was done. I called his name and went over to him. I gave him two treats and gave him some love. Then I picked him up, and we went back inside. I had forgotten my coat, so now I was freezing. I put Hades down inside, and he ran to his food dish. I went back to my phone.

Alexis: Well, I can give you the remains of that pillow, or I can get you a new one. Your choice.

I snickered as I hit send. I went to the kitchen, not even bothering with coffee this morning. I was pouring my cereal when my phone vibrated again.

Zeke: Soft but firm.

I snickered. My dirty side came out to play.

Alexis: I said pillows, Zeke, not boobs.

I hit send. My phone blew up.

Isaac: Nice, Red.

Ethan: LOL

Asher: That so just made my morning.

Miles: Even I thought that was funny.

Zeke: Ha ha, who is it that needs help training her dog?

Alexis: I'll get your pillow. Any particular brand?

I went back to making my breakfast and then started eating. Hades was apparently doing the same. Zeke sent me the name brand of the pillow he preferred. I couldn't blame him; if I were as big as him, I'd be picky about my shit too. I looked around the house and realized I was alone. Then I looked at the couch.

I decided to do some Veil work. I sat down on the couch and got to work. I pushed as much as I could today, but it was still getting harder the closer I got to the Veil. I managed maybe eight feet today before I had to stop. Fuck. I was tired, so I came back up and out.

I OPENED my eyes to the real world again. My nose was bleeding, my head pounding and I was fucking starving. I checked the time; it was one in the afternoon. After my nose had stopped bleeding, I got up to make a sandwich and realized I hadn't let Hades out. I had a mess to clean up. Mental note: Get puppy sitter during Veil link work. I was in the middle of eating when my phone rang. It was Dylan.

"Hey, cutie," I greeted him, smiling.

"Hi, Sunshine. Did you sleep last night?"

I smiled my big happy smile. "Oh yeah. Slept like a fucking rock. I even slept through my alarm and missed my workout this morning."

"Good, I'm glad it worked." He paused. "Though I think I might still need some naps with you."

I chuckled. "How are you doing today?" I asked, eating a chip.

He sighed. "Edgy. I want to get out of here to see you. But I'm stuck here at the store, where it's dead as a doornail," he grumbled.

I smiled. "Sorry, honey, but if it makes you feel better, I'm just playing with Hades and napping anyway," I said, watching Hades chase one of his balls across the floor.

"You named him Hades?"

"Yep, God of the Underworld." He laughed as I ate another chip.

"Oh, that's so you," he said; his voice sounded like he was smiling. "By the way, after you left last night, I told Dad about your presents."

I bit the corner of my bottom lip; my gut knotted instantly. "And?" I prompted when he didn't say anything.

"And he's making Mom's meatloaf tonight." I smiled. "He really loved it, Sunshine."

I felt all warm inside. I was glad I had just gone with it instead of hemming and hawing over it. "I'm glad. I really didn't want to put my nose into your guys' business but-"

"It was the best Christmas we've had since Mom died." He chuckled. "After I showed him the binders, he looked at me and told me to hold onto you because I needed to marry you the minute we turned eighteen."

I burst out laughing, my face turning red.

Oh, wow. Dylan's dad did like me after all. It took a bit before I could stop laughing at that, by then my gut knotted. "Tell me you reminded him we've been dating for like, a week?" I asked. He'd better not even think of fucking asking. I'd hang up immediately and not talk to him again until he got the damn idea out of his head.

Dylan chuckled. "Oh, yeah. I put a stop to that really quick." He waited for a few beats before adding, "He was still mumbling about a ring this morning, though."

"Aw, you're just going to have to keep saying no," I taunted him.

He snickered. "I will, Sunshine; I didn't mean to scare the shit out of you." His voice was soft and teasing.

"You didn't," I lied through my teeth.

He laughed quietly. "Oh yeah, I did. That was hilarious." He wasn't quiet about laughing anymore. "Your voice actually got high pitched."

I winced. "Okay, I'm hanging up." My face was turning red again.

"No, I'm sorry. I'll stop teasing you," he promised. "It was just really cute."

"I'm not cute, Dylan. I'm a pain in the ass," I countered.

"Yeah, a really cute pain in the ass," he mumbled. My face warmed again. "What's the plan tonight anyway? If Trisha's a bitch, did Asher give you permission to start swinging?"

I snorted. That would be great, but I really needed to work on my violent tendencies.

"We're going to the bowling alley. They've got that whole section of just pool tables," I said, watching Hades start sniffing. "Shit, give me a sec." I got up, hurried to him, picked him up and opened the back door. I set him outside while I put on those galoshes again. I stepped outside and shivered a bit. "Sorry, Hades was sniffing around for a leak."

"No worries. So, we're playing pool tonight. I'm pretty good, how about you?" He sounded a bit cocky to me.

I smirked. "No, I'm not that good. Only played a couple of times in

LA," I lied. I had spent a lot of time in a pool hall that let minors in. I didn't have any friends, so I'd play pool by myself. That was kind of sad if I thought about it. I pushed the thought away.

"Well, then we'll have to play a game. I can help if you need it."

I bit my lip to stop myself from laughing. "Sounds good to me." I managed to keep my voice normal. I watched Hades take his leak and look up at me expectantly. I smiled; I gave him his treat and his love, then took him back inside. Dylan was laughing at me. "Shut up," I snapped at him as I closed the door behind me.

"That was the girliest I've ever heard you sound," he pointed out, still chuckling.

I sighed. "It's my puppy. Of course, I'm going to be girly," I countered, still feeling my face warm.

"It's just really cute, Sunshine." He finally stopped laughing. I rolled my eyes.

Hades brought me his rope, and he wanted to play. I sat down on the floor and started playing tug-a-war with my dog.

"Yeah, yeah. The guys thought it was funny as hell too," I admitted.

He snorted. "Do you want me to pick you up tonight? Or do you want to meet there?" I heard him doing something in the background.

"I can meet you there, no point in you having to drive across town and back," I said, distracted by Hades yanking on the rope.

"I love that you value gas." His voice told me he was smiling again.

"Just the kind that goes in the tank, not the other kind," I snickered.

He groaned. "And a fart joke. Sunshine, you're just..."

"Awesome, stupendous, funny as hell?" I offered, smiling.

He chuckled. "All those things, Lexie." His voice had gone soft again.

It made me smile. "Well, I try."

He sighed. There was a bell. "Customers; I'll see you at six, Sunshine." He hung up the phone before I could say anything, which didn't really bother me; he was at work.

I played with Hades until the booger passed out. Rory came home and agreed to dog sit tonight. I explained how I was supposed to be training him. When Rory started protesting about it, I explained Zeke's experience with dogs. Rory's eyebrows went up; then he agreed to do it the way Zeke told me to. I ran upstairs to get ready for our group thing tonight. I hoped it wasn't going to be a disaster.

I WAS STANDING AROUND in my usual black underwear, trying to figure out what to wear. My hair was already done into its thick curly mass, and so was my natural makeup. I really wanted to wear the necklace Dylan gave me tonight. With how long the necklace was, I was going to end up showing a little more cleavage than normal; though, I wasn't going to be hanging out like, well, Trisha. I finally settled on a shirt. I pulled on my blue jeans, black boots, and grommet belt. Then my shirt and necklace. I looked in the mirror. The forest green v neck top was long sleeved and form fitting. The necklace worked beautifully with the shirt, which clung down to my hips. The neckline wasn't plunging; it just showed a bit more cleavage than I usually did and framed the necklace. And with the long sleeves, it wasn't too much.

Yeah, I was a little more modest in how much skin I was showing, but you would be too if you were pale as fucking snow. I kept covered up so I didn't blind people. I made sure to put a hair tie around my wrist; I knew I was going to need it when I kicked Dylan's ass at pool. I grabbed my beads and made sure to put them in my coat pocket. I put on my rosemary oil, got my cell phone and headed downstairs. I said goodbye to Hades and thanked Rory for watching him then headed out. I made a point of picking up the pillow Zeke wanted before I drove to the bowling alley and headed in.

The inside of the bowling alley was warm, so I took off my coat. The place was busy; after all, in this town, there really wasn't much else to do. I headed towards the back section of the building where the pool tables were. I spotted Riley and Zeke in the back-left corner. Zeke was in his usual: black jeans, black long sleeve shirt, motorcycle boots, and wallet chain. Riley looked great tonight in a black and purple plaid that showed off her assets, black leggings, and black knee-high boots. I headed over.

Riley's eyes went wide. "Lexie, is that some cleavage I'm seeing?" Riley asked as I got closer, and my face went red. Zeke rubbed a hand across his eyes.

"Yeah, am I blinding planes yet?" I asked seriously. Riley laughed. I looked at Zeke who still hadn't looked at me. "Zeke, I'm showing less than Riley is. Chill out."

Riley laughed and hugged Zeke. "Honey, her shirt is a fraction of an inch lower in the neckline. You'll live," Riley reassured him. He sighed and looked at me. I stuck my tongue out at him. He snorted, and he relaxed.

"Your pillow is in the Blazer, so grab it before you take off tonight," I told him. Then I looked at Riley. "I've got your photos too," I chimed, smiling. Her face lit up as I pulled out my cellphone. I went to my email and opened the first email address I didn't recognize. It wasn't the photos.

Your voice is like music to my ears- S.A.

It took me a second to realize what I had just read. Then I read it again. Okay, that was weird.

"Did Dylan send you that?" Riley asked as she read over my shoulder.

"No... I think someone has the wrong email address." I backed out of that email and threw it away. Then I opened the next one that had a different email address; this one was Dylan's. I downloaded the photos to my phone. Then I handed her my phone, so Riley could send the pictures she liked to herself. I sat down across from Zeke. "So, are we expecting Trisha to be able to keep her shit together? Or are we taking bets tonight?" I asked, smiling. They both laughed.

Zeke shook his head. "I say no; she's gonna have an issue tonight," Zeke predicted.

"I think so too, but I will be on my best.... okay, least obnoxious behavior," I promised. He raised an eyebrow at me. "To her," I smirked. Riley cracked up. Zeke just shook his head. "I'm going to try. But if she starts shit; I will not put a hand on her. Unless she touches me first." Zeke grinned. Though if she mentioned Dad again, the guys might have to stop me from killing her.

"Then it's war?" he asked.

"Then I'll rip the bitch apart," I admitted.

Zeke chuckled. He gestured with his chin behind me. "The twins are here."

I scooted my chair until the back was against the wall. The twins came in smiling. Ethan was in his usual all black. Isaac was wearing jeans, a gray sweater with blue horizontal stripes and one orange one. He also had a big black eye. They grabbed chairs and brought them over to us.

"What happened to you? Didn't you just get a bunch of safety equipment?" I asked, looking at his swollen eye.

"Wasn't watching my guard during sparring today," Isaac grumbled. "The trainer kept reminding me, but Zeke got fed up with it." I shot a look at Zeke.

He shrugged. "Better he gets a black eye now then another concussion later," Zeke pointed out. Okay, he had a point.

I looked at Ethan. "Remind me not to spar with Zeke," I said to Ethan.

Zeke huffed loudly and shook his head. "Uh-uh, no. You are not sparring with any of us, Lexie. You're going to spar with a girl or not at all," Zeke said in his 'don't fuck with me on this' voice. I gave him a small smile. Riley raised her eyebrow as she eyed Zeke. Did she not know Zeke's trigger? Should I tell her? Or was that meddling?

"I was making a joke, Zeke," I pointed out.

He glared at me. "Not a funny one," he snapped back. I rolled my eyes at him. Riley handed me back my phone.

"Have you seen my puppy yet?" I asked her.

Her eyes went wide. "What puppy?"

"The guys got me a puppy for Christmas." I brought up the photos and showed her.

"Aw, he's fucking adorable," Riley cooed. The guys groaned.

"She's going to be all girly now because of that puppy," Isaac said. I flipped him off and kept talking to Riley. The boys laughed. Soon enough, Zeke and Isaac went to shoot pool while Riley and I talked, with Ethan joining in with gossip. I always found it hilarious that Ethan liked to gossip, but not with the guys.

I asked if anyone wanted a soda then headed up to the concession stand to order a couple. I was on my way back when a guy passed me. Then he came back. He was two heads taller than me, with black hair and lovely brown eyes. He had a sweet face.

"Hi, you're Alexis, right? You moved here a couple of months ago," he asked, his voice friendly and open.

"Yeah, that's me." I had no clue who this guy was. "I'm sorry, I don't know your name."

He smiled. "Of course not; you're the only redhead in school so everyone can recognize you." He began, making a joke of it. "The rest of us are a little harder to recognize. I'm Clay. You actually stole my usual parking spot." Oops. I winced. If he was irked enough to talk to me about it, he could have his spot back. It was just a fucking parking spot.

"I'm sorry," I began. "I'll park in a different spot from now on. Didn't mean to put anyone out."

He looked at me, surprised for a second. "No, no. I wasn't asking for my spot back." He laughed. "There are plenty of open spots in the student lot..." He exhaled and tried again. "I just meant that's how I know you. So, I don't come off creepy, and it's not working, is it?"

I laughed. "It was until you said that," I told him honestly with a smile. He closed his eyes and groaned, then looked back down at me.

"Let me try this again," he said. "Hi, I'm Clay. It's nice to meet you."

I snorted. "Hi, everyone calls me Lexie." I spotted Ethan coming this way, his shit-eating grin in place. That wasn't good. I also noticed Miles had shown up wearing his usual khaki cargo pants and green button down. I looked back up at Clay; I didn't know what this guy wanted. Did he just want to chat or something?

"So, where did you move here from anyway?" Clay asked. I took my eyes off Ethan to look back at Clay.

"Um, LA," I said, mostly worrying about Ethan's grin. "It's freaking freezing here." He laughed. Ethan stepped up and took my soda from me.

"Hey, Beautiful, Zeke says if you pick him up nachos he'll buy you some too," Ethan announced. I raised an eyebrow. Nachos? Sweet. Ethan looked up at Clay. "Hey, Clay Ordin right?"

Clay smirked. "Yeah, you're Ethan Turner. Heard your band playing a couple of weeks ago; you guys are good," Clay said, making Ethan grin.

"Thanks, man," Ethan said before drinking out of my soda. He looked back at me, grinning. "Thanks for the drink, Beautiful." He snickered before trying to take off. I snagged hold of his belt, forcing him to a stop.

"Oh no, you don't, you shit!" I snapped at him. Ethan chuckled and looked over his shoulder at me, smiling. "If you're going back, you're taking Riley's soda. Apparently, I have nachos, and a soda to get now too."

"Fine," Ethan grumbled.

"Then you can send your brother to help carry."

"Sounds good to me." He held his hand out over his shoulder, and I passed the soda to him before letting him go. He walked off, snickering.

Clay raised an eyebrow at me. "I take it you're friends with him," he said.

I sighed. "Yeah, I'm friends with the soda stealing bastard," I said, smiling. Clay chuckled. Ethan had given me the out I needed. "I better go get that food before Zeke gets... grumpier." I snickered to myself. "It was nice meeting you, Clay."

"You too, Lexie; I'll see you around." He gave me a smile and headed off in the direction he was heading before he had stopped. I went back to the concession stand. Isaac showed up just in time to help.

"So, Clay Ordin." Isaac grinned. "What did he want?" Isaac took Zeke's nachos. I took my soda and my nachos. I wasn't trusting one of the twins with my food.

"I apparently stole his parking spot in the student lot," I told him as we headed back towards the others.

Isaac snickered. "He was hitting on you," Isaac teased.

I sighed. "He could have just been trying to get to know the newish girl?" I offered, not really buying it myself.

Isaac snorted. "Doubt it," Isaac said in a sing-song voice. I rolled my eyes as we reached the others. Isaac handed Zeke his nachos; Zeke looked confused.

"Thanks, Lexie," Zeke said in an odd voice.

I glared at Ethan. "You didn't ask for nachos, did you?" I asked Zeke bluntly. I didn't take my eyes off Ethan, who started giggling like a hyena.

"No, but I'll eat them anyway," Zeke admitted. I put my food down and smacked Ethan on the arm. He just laughed harder. "What did I miss?" Zeke asked.

"Clay Ordin was hitting on Lexie." Ethan snickered. Isaac laughed with him.

I rolled my eyes. "He was saying 'hi,'" I explained, looking over to Zeke. "He said I stole his parking spot at school."

Zeke eyed me. "Did he want it back?" Zeke asked.

"No."

The corner of Zeke's lips twitched. "He was hitting on you," Zeke declared. I rolled my eyes and sat down.

"Sorry, Beautiful, but I could see you trying to get away from there," Ethan said. "You couldn't figure out a nice way to say 'go away,' so I gave you one."

I winked at Ethan. "Yeah, you might be right about that," I grumbled. The boys snickered. "What? I have trouble when people are polite. If they are assholes, I know what to say." I ate a chip soaked in cheese. The conversation went on around me as I munched away on fatty, cheesy goodness.

I was almost done with my nachos when Asher and Trisha showed up. Asher was in his dark blue jeans and blue V-neck sweater. Trisha was wearing black leggings and an oversized cream sweater. I became tense instantly. Everyone said 'hi.' Trisha's eyes found me, and she gave me a tight smile. I gave her one back. I was going to try here, for Asher.

Then the pool games began. I threw away my empty nacho container. I was leaning against an empty pool table, watching the game, when Riley made a noise. I looked over at her, and she had a grin on her face.

"Dylan's here," Riley announced.

I smiled and looked over my shoulder. His eyes were on me as he made his way through the crowd. He had a mischievous grin on his face. When he reached me, he swooped in and kissed me. It was quick and sweet, but it still left my heart racing and that warmth rushing through me. He pulled back and smiled at me.

"Sorry, I'm late, Sunshine. Had to take care of something." His warm eyes ran over my face before he looked at the other guys. "Next time, a heads up would be great when she's gone all present crazy, guys!" he shot at the boys. They all chuckled. Asher just smirked. Not one of them felt bad. Dylan looked down at me and slid a hand down my arm to my hand. "I need to steal you for a second." I raised an eyebrow. He grabbed my coat and looked at the guys. "We'll be right back."

Curious, I followed him back through the bowling alley and out the front door. I pulled my jacket on as he led me back to my truck. "Dylan, what are we doing?" I asked, really getting confused now. He pulled me close and smirked at me. He handed me a small black jewelry box. My heart dropped. No, no, no... he was not...

He burst out laughing. "Relax, Sunshine. It's not a ring."

I smacked him on the shoulder. "You cannot tell me that shit your dad said and then hand me a jewelry box, Dylan!" I snapped at him, my heart finally beating again. He doubled over laughing. I was just trying to catch my breath.

He straightened, his face red. "Babe, I'm sorry. I didn't even think of that until I saw your face just now." He was trying to stop laughing at least. I waited, my face burning, till he was done. "I swear I didn't mean to do that to you." I was just thankful I had stopped blushing. I kept glaring at him. He smiled a big smile as he slipped his hands around the back of my neck, under my hair. He unhooked my necklace. "I realized after I saw those cookies that I needed to get you something better," he said, his voice soft and warm. He pulled my angel wing necklace off me.

"Hey, I love that necklace," I pointed out.

He smiled. "I'm not taking it back, Sunshine; I'm upgrading."

"I don't want an upgrade," I reminded him.

He just smiled and tilted his chin towards the box. "Open it."

I sighed and opened the box. Inside was a small gold circular pendant with an A engraved into the front. "Dylan..." I didn't know what to say. It was beautiful. Elegant, timeless and simple enough that I loved it.

"Flip it over." His voice was warm enough to be the tropics.

I flipped over the small pendant that was about the size of my thumbnail. On the back, the words "One in a million" were stamped. My heart slammed in my chest; that feeling of love poured over me. Butterflies went way fucking crazy. I didn't know what to say. I loved it. I loved how he saw me.

I didn't know what to say, so I kissed him. One of his hands went to my face, holding me gently as his mouth moved with mine; the other moved around my waist, holding me to him. I tried to show him how I felt. How much I loved the necklace. How much I loved the way he saw me. How I loved that he always made me laugh. How he always made me feel beautiful. I was teetering on that edge and so fucking close to falling that it was insane. But I couldn't tell him that. So, I just showed him. And during that crazy, hungry kiss in the parking lot, I was pretty sure he understood what I was trying to tell him.

Our kiss came to an end. Dylan eased back enough so he could see me. His sapphire eyes were burning as they ran over my face. I knew what that look on his face was now. He loved me. My heart melted in my chest. At least, I thought he did. Oh, I needed to get myself under control. Ease down, Lexie. Come on, back up the love shit. You've been dating a fucking week. I really didn't care. I just wasn't going to tell him how close I was to loving him.

"You're not mad I upgraded your Christmas present?" he asked, but he wasn't really asking.

I smiled up at him. "No, it's beautiful. Thank you," I whispered quietly to him. I resisted the urge to squirm; it wasn't as hard to as it usually was this time.

"You're welcome, Sunshine." He smiled softly at me. Then he let me go and reached for the necklace. "Now, gimmie. I want to put it on you."

I snorted and handed him the box. He carefully pulled the thin chain out of the box. He gave me the box and gestured for me to turn around. I turned. He brought the necklace down over my head and to my neck. I pulled my hair out of the way so he could hook it. When he was done, he gave the base of my neck a quick kiss before letting go. I smiled as I dropped my hair. The pendant sat right in the middle of my upper chest. It was perfect. I turned around and looked up at him; he was smiling all the way to his eyes.

"Now, are you happy with my present or are you going crazy again tomorrow?" I asked seriously.

He snickered. "I'm happy now," he assured me as he put my angel wings necklace into the box and handed it to me.

I opened the door to the Blazer and put it in the glove box. I closed the door, and we headed back inside. When we reached the guys, Riley eyed my necklace change and smiled big. I mouthed to her that I'd tell her later. She winked at me. No one else seemed to notice the change. I took my coat off and put it on the back of my chair. Dylan claimed the one next to mine.

"Does anyone have next game?" Dylan asked as he sat down next to me, his hand finding mine.

"No," Isaac answered.

Dylan smirked at me, then looked at the guys. "I call it. I was thinking of teaching Lexie how to play," he announced.

I immediately held my finger to my lips. The guys saw and smiled. I dropped my finger back to my lap. "That'd be great, honey." I smiled, doing my best not to laugh my ass off.

"Yeah, Red sucks," Isaac said before turning his back.

"She could use some help." Ethan's voice almost cracked as he took his shot. He missed.

"It's sad, really, how bad she," Asher laid it on thick with a straight face. Then he went off to pick up drinks suddenly.

Zeke just looked at me across the pool table and smirked at me. His eyes were laughing. I winked at him. Riley caught my eye an eyebrow raised. I pulled out my phone and texted her.

Alexis: I'm the best pool player here. Shhh.

Riley checked her messages, smiled, then put her phone away. Zeke and Ethan seemed in a hurry to finish their game. By the time Asher came back with a tray of sodas, Ethan had scratched on the eight ball. Automatic loss.

"Ah, shit," Ethan groaned, though he could barely keep a straight face. He turned to Dylan and me. "Guess you guys are up." We both got up, and I barely managed to control my smirk as I found a good straight cue that was a good length for me. By then, Dylan had racked the balls and was chalking his cue.

"Sunshine, do you want to break?" he asked with his back to the guys. The guys behind him all had to control themselves. Zeke actually put his hand over his mouth, and so did Ethan. Isaac got his camera out and moved for a good shot of the table and Dylan's face. Miles' hand was a fist in front of his mouth. Asher was practically dancing in place. Trisha just had a confused look on her face.

"Sure, that's the shot to break the balls up, right?" I asked, sounding innocent. All the guys had trouble keeping their mouths shut. Isaac was already laughing silently as he filmed. I walked over to the table and chalked the cue. Dylan smiled down the table at me.

"That's right. You want to break them up as much as possible," he said patiently.

I almost felt bad. Almost. I had to bite the tip of my tongue to stop myself from laughing. I pulled my hair back into a ponytail before I moved to my favorite spot to break. I kept my face sweet as I lined up my shot from the corner. I took a breath and made my shot. All the balls scattered over the table. Two fell in the pockets as I leaned against the table and watched Dylan look at the great break I had just done. The guys burst out laughing. Ethan was doubled over, Miles was red, Asher had to sit down, Zeke's face was red, and Isaac was still filming, but his face was red too. When the balls stopped moving, Dylan looked up at me, smiling.

"Is that good honey? I can't tell?" I simpered. I couldn't stop the shit eating grin on my face. The guys kept laughing. Dylan walked around the table to me. His hand went to the back of my neck. He pulled me to him and kissed me. It was a hard, hot kiss that told me he really wasn't mad. In fact, it was quite the opposite.

"Hey, hey! Ease up!" Zeke warned from his spot. "We don't want to see that." Dylan's hand ran down my spine to my lower back before he pulled away. His eyes promised retaliation. I just kept snickering.

"Where did you learn to play?" he asked, still smiling.

"I spent a lot of time in a pool hall in LA," I admitted.

He shot me a challenging look. "Funny; I have a pool table in the basement at my house. And I play a lot," he said, smirking at me.

I raised an eyebrow. "Oh, a challenge. Let's go, big man." I smiled. "I've got solids." He gave me a look that told me he really wanted to kiss me again. I walked around the table to decide my next shot.

"I've got ten on Red!"

"I'll take that," Asher shot back. "I've seen him play."

"I got twenty on Lexie," Zeke shot out.

"You're on, Zeke," Ethan shot back.

Miles just shook his head at the others.

I ignored the guys and focused on playing. I sank two before I didn't have a shot. Naturally, I put the cue ball in the worst position possible for Dylan. He shot me a look; I just smiled innocently. He didn't try to sink a ball. He just put me in a shitty position. I smirked at him. It went on and on like that until it was down to just one each and the eight ball. I had a hard bank shot, but if I pulled it off, I would be in an excellent position for the eight ball. I was aiming when Dylan came over and leaned down to whisper in my ear.

"You don't want to miss this one, Sunshine." His husky voice was that soft and low one that killed me. I stood up straight and leaned back into him.

"Sweetie, do you really want to play who can distract who more right now?" I whispered softly. "Because I have boobs. And I'm not afraid to go stand where you're aiming and lean down a little." I tilted my head back to see his eyebrows had gone up.

He looked down at me. "Fair enough," he admitted. He patted my butt cheek twice then walked away.

I was hard pressed to stop laughing. I took a breath and made my shot. I missed by a fucking hair, but at least he was in a shitty position. Dylan moved around the table. As he was aiming, I looked around the table to see what he was trying to do. The eight ball was between his and his last ball; he didn't have a bank shot. So, what was he doing? Dylan adjusted till he was aiming down on the cue ball. No fucking way. He made his shot. The cue ball jumped over the eight ball and knocked into his. His ball sank into the pocket. He looked up at me, smirking.

"You fucker," was all I could say. He winked at me. I hated to admit it, but that was sexy as hell. I put the cue back in the rack. He had a clear shot; it was over. Sure enough, he sank the eight ball. The guys either groaned or cheered but the losers paid up. Dylan came around the table and wrapped his arm around my waist. "Please tell me you weren't fucking with me this whole time?"

His eyes grew wide. "God no. That was my nothing to lose, save my ass move," he said. "I've managed that shot, like, eight times. And that was in the last month of practice." I instantly felt better. I leaned into him and gave him a quick kiss. He gave me a squeeze then went to put away his cue. I walked over to the guys and shrugged.

"Don't feel bad, Red, it was an amazing game," Isaac reassured me. "And I got it all on film."

I smiled. "Send that to me; I want to see how I fucked up that last shot."

Isaac laughed as he did just that.

Asher got to his feet and pointed at Isaac. "You and me, blue hair," Asher challenged. Isaac snickered, got up, and they started a game. I sat down in my chair as Dylan and Ethan went to pick up another round of drinks. Trisha came over and sat in Dylan's spot.

"That was really good," Trisha said in a polite voice.

I smiled at her. "Thanks, though I'm pissed that his jump shot worked." I shook my head, replaying it again.

"You and Dylan seem to be doing good," Trisha said quietly.

I grew tense. Come on, Lexie. She's trying. "Yeah, we are. He gets me in a way that most people don't," I admitted to her. That was vague enough, right? Trisha gave me a tense smile. Oh, fuck it. I suck at small talk. "Okay, Trisha. Here it is. I want Ash happy, and you make him happy." She blinked at me. "Why don't we try to start over?" I held my hand out. "Hi, I'm Lexie. I'm a smart-ass, a little odd and, when I'm uncomfortable, I make bad jokes."

She was tense when she smiled again. She shook my hand. "Hi Lexie, I'm Trisha. And I can be insecure when it comes to the people I care about." We shook hands.

"Nice to meet you." She smiled then got up when Dylan came back with drinks.

He took his spot and gave me my drink. "What was that about?" Dylan whispered to me.

I smiled. "I think Trisha and I just started over."

His eyebrows went up. "Really?" he asked. I nodded. "Good, I hope it works out that way."

I leaned my chin on his shoulder. "Me too."

IT WAS an hour later when I had to use the restroom. I got up and headed to the closest lady's room. It was at the corner of the building down a small hallway in the back. I was on my way to return to the group when I felt it. That chill down my neck, only it was like a blade. I looked up and saw him. He had long dark hair and dead eyes. Half his face was rotted away. My heart slammed in my chest as he headed my way. I moved back into the bathroom and checked my pockets. I had left my fucking beads in my coat. Shit! The ghost came in through the door.

"I'm working on the way to help you guys cross," I told him bluntly. His head tilted to the side. "It's taking longer than I thought it would, but I'm working on it." He cackled; it was a dry, broken sound. My gut knotted while my chest felt like it was being pulverized. I gasped as he came closer, and I stepped back. My back hit the wall. He kept coming closer. I felt multiple spots on my chest grow more painful, stabbing down into my lungs. His energy poured against my barriers roughly, like the ocean in a storm.

That's when I knew. He didn't want to cross. He wanted to hurt me, as much as possible. Before I could shove him back, he slammed his energy into me, knocking me back. My head hit the wall, and I dropped to the tile, stunned. The world was spinning as my head felt like it was being squeezed in a vice. I tried to move, but I couldn't seem to figure out how to move my arms or legs. It felt like I had been hit in the face; vaguely, I felt blood pouring from my nose. My stomach churned as my forehead rested against the tile.

The fucker didn't want to jump me. He wanted to peel my barrier apart and burn me away. The world faded in and out as his memories ran through my mind. He liked hurting women, loved it. He had done it a lot when he was alive. He slammed his energy against me hard; I felt him punch a hole in my barriers like a physical snap. He poured into my mind. I threw up a small barrier around my mind, forcing his memories to roll over me where they couldn't get to me. All I could feel was the pain, my lungs burning. I barely managed to sit up and grab the waste basket from the stall before I was puking. He tore into my barriers with invisible claws, shredding them. My world exploded, my body felt like it was trying to kill itself. I was jerking and shaking; I couldn't stop it. Every nerve I had felt like a red-hot iron was being laid across them. I dropped back to the tile, my stomach empty.

I focused on each breath as he tore through my mind and poured his sick thoughts into my head. I turned away from the images he was showing me. I didn't want to watch him hurting women, torturing them, killing them. I didn't want to hear them screaming for their lives. If I had to look at it, I'd go insane. There was wetness in my ears then running down my neck. I watched the pool of blood form on the white tile. I cried as my mind was invaded.

There was a noise. Trisha walked into the bathroom. Thank you, thank you. Please. The world wavered as if I was looking up from the bottom of a pool.

"Get… guys…." I barely managed before the ghost locked down on me. I couldn't move, could only breath and watch as Trisha smiled at me.

"Did you really think we could start over, you bitch?" Trisha sneered at me. She got up, smiling as she walked away. That fucking…

The rest of my barriers were blown apart. I gasped as my mind became raw; his energy poured through me like saltwater in an open wound. I could only breathe and watch the puddle of blood grow. I didn't know how long I laid there, but I felt myself disappearing. That barrier I had around myself was thinning. I was watching his memories. I didn't have a choice now. He was everywhere. I couldn't think. I could only breathe, watch, and feel. It felt like acid burning through my brain. I hated it…. please make it stop…. please…

There was a noise.

"Lexie?" I blinked and saw a purple haired girl…. I knew her…. she knew the guys…

"Guys…"

Then the fucker poured more memories into my head. These were really fucked up and horrifying. They ate away at me. I watched as the blood pool keep growing and held on by my nails to the memory of who I was. There was thunder, the ground shook.

"Lexie…" A husky voice spoke.

"Help or get the hell out of the way!" A rich baritone voice was shouting. The tile vibrated.

"Ally!" A hand grabbed me, the world spun, and I was against someone's chest. Lots of hands ran over me, hands I knew, hands I recognized. They were checking my pockets.

"Isaac get her coat!" A gravelly voice barked. "Don't block the door!"

They were here. I closed my eyes. Just hold on, just hold on.

"Anyone got a kit?" A smooth, smoky voice yelled.

"Here," the husky voice said.

The fucker ground down on me. I whimpered as the world started to fade, as I began to fade. No, no, no. Hold on, hold on. Something poured into my mouth; I tasted salt water. The fucker had to pull back a bit; he wasn't trying to possess me, but he had to give me room. The memories eased, just a bit. But it was enough for me to get a hold again.

"She's still fucking awake!" that baritone cursed. Hands were on my head, moving over my ears.

"It looks like last time: prolonged exposure," a silky-smooth voice said. "We need those beads."

"Here! Get 'em on!" a smooth, honey voice said.

The fucker was trying to push down on me again. Hands slipped something on my wrist, and suddenly the bastard was weaker. They kept putting things on me, and he was forced back. The more they put on, the more I was me. And the more I remembered what that soul had done.

"She's fucking crying," the gravel voice... Zeke said.

"That's new." The smoky... Ethan that was Ethan.

"Get Rory on the phone," the smooth... Miles said. "Let's get her face clean. We need to see if the bleeding has stopped."

"Here, use this." Zeke's voice sounded angry. Something wet was wiping my face, but I didn't care. All those poor women. All that pain. That fucker.... what he did to them. I whimpered and tried to curl into whoever held me.

"Ally, come on honey, talk to us." Asher's voice came from above me. I couldn't stop crying. Something wet wiped against my ears, and I didn't care. It was too much. The screams were too much. The sight of those women....

"Hey, Isaac." Rory's friendly voice echoed through the bathroom.

"Rory, we found her in the bathroom with a pool of blood on the floor. Ears and nose were still bleeding. She's still conscious. But she's not talking, just crying," Miles said quickly.

"Are her ears still bleeding?" Rory's voice became hard and clipped.

"No, we've got the bracelets on her now. Nose has stopped too," Isaac answered.

"Then you saved her ass. If she's conscious, it wasn't-"

"Not alone, Rory," Ethan all but shouted.

There was a sigh. "It sounds like an incredibly long one. Don't fucking move her. Not until she tells you to or you'll start the bleeding again, and she'll end up in the emergency room."

"Rory, there's already a lot of fucking blood," Zeke growled.

"Send me a photo."

I started gasping as I remembered the screaming.

"God, Red. Please..." Someone touched my leg.

"Okay, got it. Shit!"

I kept whimpering and sobbing. Asher held me against him, fingers brushing the hair from my face.

"If she starts bleeding again, she'll need the hospital. Do not move her until she tells you to."

"We're in the girl's bathroom, Rory," Miles pointed out.

"I don't give a fuck where you are! Do not move her! Not until she can tell you to. Got it?" Rory's voice was furious.

"Got it," everyone said at once. I was just trying to breathe through the pain and tears.

"Miles, check her eyes," Rory demanded.

Hands were on my face. It hurt. I didn't like it. I whimpered.

"She's dodging," Isaac's voice bit out.

"Someone hold her fucking head! You need to check her eyes," Rory barked.

Zeke cursed. I was still trying not to see when big hands grabbed my face.

"Sorry, Baby," Zeke whispered. Someone touched my eyelids. Light stabbed through my brain I whimpered and jerked against the hands. Then it was over, and I was crying harder than ever. It hurt so fucking much. A big hand smoothed back my hair.

"No bleed," Miles announced. The pain started to roll back bit by bit.

"Good. Don't move her until she's ready, and if someone tries to call an ambulance, call me."

"Got it." The room echoed with voices.

Long fingers wiped my cheeks. I stayed curled up into a chest. The memories were rolling back. I tried to push, but I had nothing to do it with. I could only wait for that filth to leave.

"Ally, come on, sweetie," Asher whispered.

I slowly remembered me. Bit by bit as the sick cloud of the soul's memories began to lift. You are not me; you do not belong here. I am Lexie, I am Lexie, I am Lexie. I kept thinking it over and over. Finally, the sick cloud lifted enough for me to stop sobbing.

"Oh, thank...." Zeke's voice was rough.

"She's still crying," Ethan's voice pointed out.

"But she's not fucking sobbing. I can't take that shit from her," Zeke bit out.

"None of us can take that from her," Isaac pointed out.

"Let's find the janitor's closet." Miles' voice was rough but calm. "Let's get this cleaned up so no one calls the police or an ambulance." Asher began rocking me slowly; a big hand smoothed my hair back, another hand with rings was holding mine, and another was around my ankle. "Riley, will you please-"

"I'll guard the door," Riley offered.

"Thank you." Miles' smooth voice helped soothe me.

"Miles, keep talking," Isaac's voice demanded. "She stops making noises when you talk."

"She said she thinks his voice is soothing," Riley reminded them.

"Lexie, we're here." Miles' silky smooth timbre slid through my ear, easing the ragged torn pieces left in my brain. "We've got you. Rory says you're going to be all right." The voice was closer, right next to my head. He lowered his voice. "It's just going to take some time. We're all here. We're not going anywhere. Take all the time you need to come back to us." Miles kept talking. I couldn't tell what he was saying all the time, but his voice helped. It helped put back the broken pieces of me that were still bleeding inside back in place.

When the last of that sick cloud was gone, and I was me again, my brain felt like it had been set on fire. My body felt like it had slammed through several brick walls, in every direction. I couldn't move, not an inch, not a finger. I felt like death.

"Ouch," I managed very quietly.

"She said 'ouch.'" Asher's voice was filled with relief. Relieved chuckles filled the room. I didn't know why, but I really fucking hurt. I floated in a sea of pain; they couldn't move me yet, not until it didn't feel like I was going to be torn apart.

"Were you in here the whole time?" Zeke asked quietly.

"Yeah..." My voice was barely a sound.

"She said 'yes,'" Asher answered for me.

"Are you ready to move?" Ethan asked. I whimpered at just the idea. "That's a fuck no."

"Was this..." Dylan's voice asked quietly "Was this a three?"

"No," Miles said calmly. "Isaac, Ethan, was she sick?"

"Yeah, she managed to grab a garbage can," Isaac answered from somewhere.

"Then this was a very long two," Miles said, his smooth voice rolling over me. "She's going to need her clothes stash. Dylan, can you get it from her truck?"

"Yeah, yeah, no problem."

"It's behind the driver side seat. It's just a black backpack." Miles' voice was getting colder. "The keys should be in the right-hand pocket of her coat." A door closed.

"He fucking froze," Zeke growled. Calloused fingers wiped my face. Was I still crying? I needed to stop, or Zeke would flip out. "Did you see his face?"

"I saw." Asher's voice was firm, unhappy.

I tried to stop crying. I tried to think of something happy, but I couldn't right now. Any thought hurt my head.

"That doesn't matter right now," Miles said, his voice cold. "We just need to get her cleaned up and out the door when she's ready."

"I propose a motion; if she goes out alone with Dylan, she has to wear her fucking beads." Isaac's voice was boiling.

"No vote needed. Motion passed," Zeke snapped.

"Brother, can you get her hair out of the blood." Ethan's voice wasn't calm. I felt hands moving my hair. The world was slowly coming back.

"Shit, her hair is soaked with it," Isaac bit out.

"There should be some towels in the bag too," Miles' voice said. "We'll need to get her to sit up, or it'll just keep soaking."

"Ally, can we shift you, honey? Just sit up a bit more so we can get your hair out of the puddle?" I thought about it. It took some time; everything fucking hurt.

"Real... slow...." My voice was still weak, barely there.

"We've got to do this slowly. Zeke, take your side and help me, very slowly, sit her up. Miles, get her head. I'll keep her; I'm already covered." Asher's voice was calm, like when I had been freezing. "One, two, three." I was moved very slowly. The world didn't explode. I didn't want to die completely at least; it still sounded really fucking good, though. Then I was almost sitting up and limp in Asher's arms, laying against his chest.

"Ally, are you good there?"

"Uh-huh..."

"She's good," Asher told them. Someone was wiping my face again. And I still didn't give a fuck. I was still twitching; each little jerk threw my body into a sharp pain. Chemical smells burned my nose.

"Lexie, I need to clean your neck." Miles' voice was calm and soothing. I felt something wet on my neck, wiping the blood away. I kept twitching. Hands moved in my hair.

"What's taking him so long?" Miles cold voice was by my head. "Someone pass me some more paper towels, please."

I knew when I finally stopped crying. There were sighs of relief around me.

"Asher, honey, let someone else take her. You're covered in blood." Trisha's voice made my insides jerk; pain exploded through me. I whimpered. Miles started talking softly to me again, something about a rabbit, a turtle, and a fishing trip? I couldn't really understand. But I remembered something. I remembered her.

"Ash..."

"Yeah, Ally?"

"Trish.... left... me..." I had to concentrate to get that many words out. It was fucking hard; my brain felt like pureed meat. But I needed him to know not to trust the bitch, just in case...

Asher's body grew tense against me. Lips brushed my ear. "She saw you on the floor? The blood? And left you here?" he whispered softly.

"Yeah...." My voice was still almost non-existent.

Asher took deep breaths. "Can I hand you to someone?" Asher whispered.

"Slow..."

"Someone take her; I need to fucking handle something." Asher's voice was hard.

"Here, my clothes will hide the blood," Ethan said. There was silence. "Sitting, I can hold her, guys. Come on."

"Slow." Asher's voice was sharp now. Lots of hands were moving me this time, more than two people at least. When they went too fast, I whimpered, and they froze. When I stopped, they moved slower until I smelled Ethan's spicy cologne and my head was on his shoulder.

"Hey, Beautiful, I've got you," Ethan whispered to me.

"Snoopy...."

"She said, 'Snoopy.'" Asher's voice was hard and moving away.

"That's me, honey." Soft lips rested on my forehead. "Your Snoopy."

"You knew she was in here?" Asher's voice threw the room into silence. I struggled to pay attention.

"No, of course not," Trisha lied.

"She just told me you knew she was in here, on the floor, bleeding. And you fucking left her here!" Asher was furious.

"I just thought she was puking up that snack bar food," Trisha said, trying to placate him.

"Yeah, with blood on the floor and coming out her ears." Isaac's voice was boiling.

"Get out of here, Trisha. We are way beyond fucking done. You'll stay the fuck away from me if you know what's good for you." He paused. "No, that's wrong. You'll stay the fuck away from Lexie if you want to avoid a beating from her."

"What's the fucking big deal? She's fine," Trisha snapped, sounding snotty. Curses went around the room.

"What's the big deal?" Asher growled. "You left her here to die. You knew she had a seizure disorder, and you knew it could kill her." Asher's voice was shaking. "Get the fuck out of here! Stay far away from us, or I'll let Lexie kick your ass."

"What is with you guys and this skank?" Trisha shot out. "How many of you is she fucking?"

"Riley, would you-" Isaac began, his voice hard. The sound of a slap rang out. Trisha made a startled sound, then started crying. I wish I saw the hit.

"Get the fuck out!" Riley shouted. A door opened and shut.

"Thank you, Riley." Isaac's voice was sweet now.

"My fucking pleasure," Riley growled back.

Ethan's lips were against my forehead, just resting there. His hand cupped my neck, his thumb in front of my ear. He started humming a quiet song. It helped the pain roll back some more. I could think now. The world was returning.

"Sorry guys... night ruined..." Again, my voice was barely a whisper.

"Screw our night, Ally. You be okay, and it'll be the best night in the world."

"She apologizing?" Isaac asked.

"As usual," Asher answered.

A door opened. "What did I miss?" Dylan's husky voice was back.

"A lot. Where's the bag?" Zeke's voice was hard and sharp. Feet moved across the tile. A bag opened.

"I'll start drying her hair," Dylan said. I heard movement then hands moved in my hair. I didn't care; I was almost ready to go home. I just couldn't fucking move.

"Tell me she brought a loose button up?" Isaac asked. There was a sigh.

"No. Pull over," Miles said. "Lexie, you really need to pack several different shirts."

"Not exactly the time to lecture her, man," Isaac chided.

Ethan just kept humming to me. It was soothing, comforting.

"Okay, taking off or pulling over?" Miles asked everyone.

"How loose is it?" Asher asked. The hands in my hair stopped moving.

"I don't know...." Miles trailed off.

"Riley, come tell us if this shirt will be loose on Lexie." Zeke's voice was hard.

"Not too much. It looks a size bigger, but that's not a lot of extra room." Riley's voice was closer.

"Guys, you don't need to change her shirt. Just cover her with her coat. That should hide everything," Dylan pointed out.

"If blood gets on that coat, she'll be pissed," Isaac pointed out.

"We need a button up, or we're taking off and pulling on," Asher announced. There was silence.

"Miles, what are you doing?" Isaac asked.

"I've got an undershirt on. She can have my button up. Taking her shirt off and pulling on the other one would probably be too much movement for her," Miles said, his voice silky to my ears. "Besides, she loves that coat, and I doubt she'd let me get her a new one."

"Beautiful, we're putting Miles' shirt on you, but we need to shift you. Is that okay right now?" Ethan asked softly. I thought about it.

"Slow... can't move."

"She says do it slow, and she can't help. She can't move." Asher's rich baritone was calm again.

"Ethan, you keep her sitting up. I'll get the shirt on this side. Then we'll switch," Miles said.

"We're moving you a bit now, Lexie. Make a noise if we're going too fast for you," Ethan said gently. Hands were on me, pulling the big shirt on one side and around my back. "Take her, Miles." Gentle hands moved me slowly against another chest. He held me gently but made sure he wasn't going to lose me. Wintergreen filled my nose as hands pulled the shirt onto my other side. The gentle arms stayed around me.

"Isaac, the buttons." Miles' voice wasn't asking.

"I can do-"

"Isaac's already almost done," Zeke said. "Don't worry, Dylan. It's big enough that he's not touching her." When he was done, Miles passed me slowly back to Ethan. The only reason I knew who was moving me was because of their smells. Ethan began humming again, rocking me gently. This time another voice joined in. A similar smooth honey-like voice. The melody was soothing and beautiful with both of them humming.

"Is that...?" Asher stopped himself.

"Yeah, it's the best we got." Ethan's voice had thickened slightly. I doubted anyone else had noticed, but I did.

"Red deserves the best," Isaac mumbled.

I heard sounds of agreement. My guys were sweet, delusional, but sweet. I took a chance and lifted my eyelids a bit. The light was fucking bright. It stabbed through my brain, and I whimpered.

Ethan's arms tightened. "Take your time, Beautiful. We're in no hurry," Ethan whispered down to me.

I wanted to go home; I wanted to stay with them. I opened my eyes again, and this time the light didn't try to kill me. I blinked several times.

"I have never been so happy to see those green eyes in my fucking life. Well, except after that one time," Isaac exhaled, his voice full of relief. I looked around at them as much as I could without moving. Asher's shirt was covered in my blood as he stood against the sinks, his face pained. Zeke was down at my waist; his hand wrapped around one of mine. Miles was across from Ethan, his face carefully blank. Isaac was next to Ethan holding my other hand. I couldn't see Dylan; he must have been behind me.

"Sorry... worry," I said in my barely-there voice.

"Ally, stop apologizing." Asher's voice was still hard but calm. I took stock of how I felt. I was weak as hell, but my body felt more stable. I didn't feel like I would fall apart if they moved me.

"Go... home..."

"She's saying we can leave now," Asher told them.

"Where are we taking her? Rory's?" Ethan's voice was soft above me.

"She's going to have bad nightmares tonight. Hades might not help and fucking Tara's at home," Isaac pointed out.

"Call Rory. See if he'll let us take her tonight." Miles sighed. "He'll come out to check on her anyway."

"Wait, why is her cousin being home-"

"That's something you don't fucking need to know about right now." Zeke snapped at Dylan hard. I gave everything I had to squeeze his hand. I didn't want him upset. Zeke looked to me and met my eyes.

"Calm... down..."

"She said 'calm down,'" Asher said for me. Zeke closed his eyes and took several deep breaths. Then he squeezed my hand; he was working on it.

"Rory, she's ready. Do you want us to bring her home? Or take her to her room at Miles' house?" Isaac's voice filled the room.

"She has a room at your house?" Dylan's asked, his voice filled with doubt.

"All my friends do." Miles' voice was neutral, carefully, coldly neutral.

"Yeah, Miles doesn't mind," Isaac said into the phone.

"Tell him to bring Hades when he comes out," Zeke reminded him. I smiled. It was tiny but there. I wanted my puppy.

"And her emergency overnight bag. Inside her closet, right side," Miles added. Isaac nodded and repeated everything to Rory.

"Okay, who's carrying her out?" Ethan asked the group. There was half a minute of silence.

"I will. I can hide my shirt with her," Asher said, pushing away from the counter. Everyone started moving except Ethan.

"Give me her keys, Dylan." Isaac's voice wasn't asking. Keys jingled. "Rory said Miles' house."

"Okay," Ethan said above me. "Let's put her in the front seat of our car, and we'll put it back, so she doesn't flop around." There were sounds of agreement. Asher squatted down next to us.

"Ready to move, Ally?" Asher asked, his ocean eyes running over me. I slowly winked at him. He gave me half as grin before he reached out and lifted me from Ethan's lap to his chest. If I could have thought, I would have been impressed. But my brain felt muggy. Asher stood, and I groaned. Too fast. My coat covered me. "Ally, do you want me to walk quickly through the bowling alley or slow?" I thought about it. If my eyes were closed, it should be okay.

"... fast..."

"Fast it is," he whispered to me. "Guys, we're moving fast. Don't forget your coats. Ethan-"

"He's already heading to the car." Isaac's voice was calm. "He'll pull up to the doors."

"Okay, let's go. Zeke, are you blocking?" Asher asked.

"What do you think?" Zeke snapped.

"Blocking?" Dylan asked.

"Yeah, it's in case someone tries to stop us from taking her out of somewhere public. It's happened once or twice," Isaac explained.

That was all the talking I heard because Zeke and Asher took me out of the bathroom and into the bowling alley. I closed my eyes as Asher moved fast, Zeke right next to him. That's when I felt it. It was like a branding iron against my neck. I gasped.

"Ally?" I opened my eyes, and my heart dropped. Ghosts were walking through the crowd, lots of them. They spotted me and started towards me. I whimpered and clung weakly to Asher. He shifted me higher so my face could bury in his neck. "Ally, what are you seeing?" he whispered as we moved.

"... dead.... lots... following...." Asher cursed and moved faster. I just closed my eyes. We were almost to the door when someone shouted for us to stop. Zeke broke off to explain our cover story as Asher kept going out the door with me. Cold air hit my skin, but it didn't matter anymore. I was shifted and laid down. I groaned as my stomach protested. I was somewhere warm. Something was buckled.

"Get out of here fast; there's a lot of dead and they're following her," Asher said.

"Shit." Ethan's voice was sharp. A door closed, and we were moving. "Hold on, Beautiful. I'm getting you out of here." His hand took mine. I squeezed. It wasn't much of a squeeze, but he must have felt it because he squeezed back. I just couldn't move, and the world was getting fuzzy. We stayed like that for a while.

I was half out when we stopped. I was unbuckled.

"Ethan, don't even fucking think about it!" Zeke's voice ordered. Car doors shut.

"Then someone hurry up, or I'm taking her in!" Ethan shot back. Several footsteps in the gravel reached us. Then there was silence.

"I've got her." Miles' voice was neutral again. Arms wrapped around me. I smelled wintergreen as I was lifted and held. My cheek rested against a collar bone.

"... winter... green..."

"She said 'wintergreen,'" Asher spoke for me again.

Miles made a 'humph' sound. "Yes, it's me, Lexie." Miles' voice was soft as he moved. "Someone get the door."

"Wintergreen?" Dylan's voice asked.

"I chew a lot of gum when I'm concentrating on something." Miles' voice was cold. I didn't like it.

"Miles..."

"She said 'Miles,'" Asher repeated. "I think she's asking you to calm down."

I felt Miles take a deep breath and let it out slowly. He leaned down to me, his lips brushing my forehead. "Sorry, Angel," he whispered so quietly I was sure I didn't hear him right. "She's half out, let's get her in bed."

"Her hair is still bloody," Dylan warned.

"Then I'll buy new bedding." Miles' voice was hard and cold this time. I really didn't like it. I made a small noise, which seemed to be all I could do right now. Miles laid me down on a soft bed.

"Miles, she really doesn't like that voice right now," Asher warned him. Hands moved over my feet.

"I'm trying, Lexie," Miles whispered to me, his voice soft again. Something came off my feet.

"Dylan, grab her some water. She's going to need some when she wakes up," Asher instructed, his voice calm. I felt myself sinking into sleep.

"Yeah, be right back." Dylan's voice was leaving.

"Don't take forever," Miles mumbled.

"Miles," Asher chided.

"I don't trust him. Not with her like this." Miles' voice was hard and cold again. I didn't even know what he was saying, but I didn't like his voice that way. I wanted my soothing voice back. I tried to move my hand but couldn't.

"I agree." Zeke's voice was hard too. Why were they so mad? I didn't understand. "He froze, and then he just stood there, gaping."

"He's never seen her like this, and he cares about her." Asher's voice was matter-of-fact but strained.

"Then why didn't he ask to carry her? Why did he take so long with the bag?" Ethan asked, his voice boiling. "We gave him every chance to volunteer."

"Why didn't he ask to hold her?" Miles asked coldly. "Why was it me who gave up his shirt? He's wearing a button up too."

"Guys, give him the benefit of the doubt. He's never seen her that way. He was probably freaked out," Asher tried again. "Remember the first time she dropped? How freaked we were?"

"Yeah, but we fucking did something about it," Zeke pointed out.

"Would you have jumped in if there was someone else who knew more about what to do then you did? He doesn't know what to do in this situation. He has never seen it. He'll learn," Asher defended, his voice hard. Their angry voices were bringing me back to the surface. I wanted them to be okay. I needed them okay. But they were upset.

"I don't want him alone with her when she's like this," Zeke said, his voice telling everyone not to argue.

"One of us in the room at all times," Isaac agreed.

"And he stays out of that bed." Miles wasn't asking. "Anyone of us? Fine. Hades? Fine. Not him. Not right now."

"Seconded," Zeke said.

"Third," Ethan agreed.

"Majority rules," Asher agreed. All their voices were hard. I didn't like it. I had to fix it. I made a small noise. "Let's change up our voices guys. She does not like the sound. It's keeping her up." Asher's voice was his rich baritone again.

"I have an idea. Isaac, please run to my room and grab the book off my nightstand," Miles said. Feet ran off. The bed shifted next to me. It was so quiet I almost slipped over to sleep.

"Brought the water. How is she doing?" Dylan asked.

"She'll be fine, she's just going to sleep it off," Asher answered. "We are using soothing voices right now. If she hears an upset one, she tries to wake up and fix it." Zeke grunted in agreement. Something soft covered me. There were running footsteps.

"Here. Your house is too big." Isaac was out of breath.

"Or you aren't in fighting condition yet," Ethan said smugly.

"Ha ha," Isaac shot back sarcastically.

Pages were turning.

"You're reading to her?" Dylan said, his voice surprised.

"She needs to pass out, and she's fighting it," Ethan explained, his voice smooth and smoky again. "If she's awake right now, she's in pain. It's better if she's asleep."

"She's fighting because...?"

"She knows we're upset and she wants to make it better but can't move to do it," Asher answered.

"Classic Lexie," Zeke said. "Rory should be here any minute."

"I'm going to start reading, so quiet or out." Miles' voice wasn't cold, but it wasn't warm either. "Lexie, I'm reading you The Hobbit." His voice was my soothing, silky one again. "In a hole in the ground, there lived a hobbit. Not a nasty, dirty, wet hole, filled with the ends of worms and an oozy smell, nor yet a dry, bare, sandy hole with nothing in it to sit down on or to eat: it was a hobbit-hole, and that means comfort." Miles' voice slid me into sleep as the world faded away.

I WOKE UP HALFWAY, wondering what it was that had pulled me back. There were voices.

"You're leaving?" Isaac whispered.

"I have some work to do back home." Dylan's voice was strained, hard. "That science project is kicking my ass." It was quiet. Lips touched my forehead; I smelled sandalwood. "Stay safe, Sunshine." Then the smell was gone. I didn't understand. I tried to move my hand, but it was on a warm ball of fur. Hades. I gave him a sleepy rub before sinking again.

"He seriously left?" Isaac's voice sounded stunned. I wondered why.

"He doesn't fucking deserve her," Ethan bit out.

"No shit," Isaac said. "Fuck 'em. I'm climbing in." The bed moved, and a warm body lay down behind me. The scent of limes filled my nose. Isaac curled around me and buried his face in my hair at the back of my neck.

"Yeah, fuck him." The bed moved on my right. I smelled spicy cologne.

"Really? We're sandwiching her now?" Isaac whispered sarcastically.

"You're not the only one she scared the shit out of tonight, brother," Ethan whispered back.

"Good point."

Ethan scooted closer, and the puppy protested with a whine. "You're not going anywhere, buddy. I just need to get in here too," Ethan whispered. I felt Ethan close by. Still mostly asleep, I reached over and scooted behind him, cuddling my front to his back. I wrapped my arm around him, my hand over the middle of his chest, my cheek against his back. His warm hand held mine against him.

"Now I have to chase her," Isaac grumbled. Isaac scooted up to my back and maneuvered into his favorite cuddle spot again. Fuzzy warmth washed over me for them. My twins. "What about Hades?"

"He just slipped between my back and her lap, and he's balled up to sleep now," Ethan whispered back. The room went quiet. The boys' body heat and the feel of them cuddling me threw me back into to sleep hard.

CHAPTER 17

FRIDAY

I woke up slowly. I was snuggled and safe. With my eyes still closed, I smelled limes and spice. I smiled; the twins were with me. I was about to slide back into sleep when there was a whine. Hades needed to go out. I opened my eyes and jerked upright. My little ball of black fur was pacing on the bed. I went to move, but Isaac sat up and snagged Hades.

"I'll take him, Red," he said drowsily. He held Hades against his chest and left the bedroom. I lay back down. Ethan rolled over onto his back and reached for me. I moved until I was against his side and rested my head on his chest, still half asleep. He wrapped his arms around me.

"How are you feeling, Beautiful?" Ethan mumbled.

"Pissed off. Tore up," I mumbled back into his shirt.

He snorted. "What happened?"

Images flashed through my mind. "The fucker didn't want to cross," I muttered, my throat growing tight as I remembered. "The bastard liked to hurt women when he was alive. He just wanted to hurt me."

Ethan's body became tense; one of his hands came up and cupped my neck. "What do you mean he hurt women?" Ethan sounded wide awake now.

"He tortured them, raped them, then he killed them." Tears began to run down my face as I remembered the images. Ethan's hold on me tightened. "He was a serial killer from around the forties. Never caught. He was shot in a bar brawl in town; he was just passing through." He shifted onto his side and pulled me in against him. I buried my face in his chest as his arms tightened around me, one hand in my hair. I started shaking.

"You got his memories, didn't you?" he asked gently. I nodded, my throat too tight to say anything. He cursed. "That's why you were crying last night?" I nodded again, inhaling slow and deep then exhaling. Footsteps approached the door. "Get Miles now!" The footsteps ran back down the hall. "Lexie, what you must have seen... fuck." He pressed me against him hard. "I'm here, honey. You're safe; you're home." I just kept crying as he continued whispering to me. Running footsteps came into the room.

"What's wrong?" Miles' voice was breathless.

"Listen to this shit," Ethan announced, still holding me while I cried. Ethan told them everything. Everything I had seen. Well, everything he knew I had seen. He didn't know the worst part.

"I'm calling Riley. I need another favor," Isaac growled.

"If anyone should get to hit that girl, it's Lexie." Miles' voice was cold. I just cried into Ethan's chest as the memories kept pouring through my mind. Miles let out a breath. "Ethan, swap out with me." Even through my tears I could tell the room had gone silent.

"Really?" Ethan's voice was surprised.

"Do it, before I change my mind," Miles warned him.

Ethan's hold on me loosened. "Lexie, Miles is going to take over, honey." His voice was gentle. "He knows how to help better than me."

I nodded that I heard him. I was still seeing all those images. Ethan moved away.

I was taking deep breaths when I smelled wintergreen. Miles was there; he scooted closer but wasn't touching me. He'd never touch me like this without permission. So, I scooted that last inch and pressed my face into his chest. He shifted an arm under my head, and his other around my arm and ribs. A hand went into my hair. His body was rigid until he felt me crying. Then he relaxed against me.

"Tell me what happened, Lexie." His voice was the soft silky one that always worked on me.

"He just stood there, tearing up my barrier." I sniffed and clung to Miles. I kept my voice down at a whisper. I didn't want the others to know this part. "Then he poured his memories in, and it was sick. It was so fucking disgusting, Miles. He made me feel what he was feeling." I had to stop and take a few more gasping breaths. "He was there for so long; I started to fade." Miles' hand stroking my back went still.

"What do you mean fade?" he asked softly.

"I felt myself disappearing. He was trying to make me disappear." I swallowed hard as I remembered how close I had been to losing myself.

"Was he trying to take over?"

"No, he was just doing it for fun," I whispered back through a tight throat. I stopped talking as those images ran in a loop through my head. I really wished I could scrub my mind out. I pushed them back, told them to get out. They weren't mine; I shouldn't have to carry them. But they just stayed, burned there. "Miles, those feelings aren't going away."

"That's not you, Lexie. Just because you remember it. Remember how that... soul felt about it. Doesn't mean you feel that way about it too," he whispered to me, his lips in my hair. "That's not you, Lexie."

I nodded, he was right. I knew he was right.

"It just feels..."

"Like it was you?" he asked gently. I nodded. "Lexie, you are so far away from being that. You don't want to hurt people." I snorted. He sighed. "All right, if they hurt you. Yes, you want to hurt them. But you never go after them first."

"I went after Trisha," I pointed out wiping my face.

"And I heard you apologized for that," he countered. "You realized it wasn't the right thing and you tried to make it right." He rubbed his chin on the top of my hair. "Even with how horrible she was to you. That soul would never have done that."

"The fucking memories…"

"How do you feel about them now? Now that the soul isn't here?" he asked softly. I thought about it. The memories were disgusting, horrifying. Like a slide show for the psychotic.

"I want to puke just thinking about them." The tears were slowing down. "They are probably the sickest things I'll ever see in my life."

Miles squeezed me tight. "Then that is how you feel about them. About what that person did in their life." He stopped rubbing his chin on my hair. "He made you feel the way he felt about it. That's…. sick, invasive and…." He swallowed hard. He was trying not to say a particular word.

So, I gave him another one. "Violating, that's the word you're looking for," I offered, the crying slowing down some more. Miles was making sense, smoothing out all the broken pieces inside me again.

"Yes, it is," he agreed before taking a calming breath. "In fact, there is probably a debate going on right now over whether or not we're going digging tonight."

I snorted. The guys would want to destroy the soul that did this to me. They couldn't get to Trisha, but they could get to that bastard.

"They can't," I said quietly.

"Does that soul really deserve to move on? Does he really deserve to exist?" Miles' voice was growing colder.

"I can't be judge, jury, and executioner," I pointed out. "I'm not God. And I don't know what goes on after this. Maybe you do have to pay for everything you've done wrong. Maybe not. But I can't play God." I wiped my cheeks, moved my face out of his shirt and looked up at him. His eyes were unfocused.

"Do you think there is a God?" he whispered softly.

It was a good question.

I saw souls everywhere, and I'd seen them move on. I'd seen one be destroyed. But… "I don't know," I admitted. "Everything I've seen has been, well, like the world is on autopilot. It's going the way it's set up to go." I sighed. I remembered meeting my true self and her getting bitched at by someone, but I didn't know what that meant. "So, no, not until I see something else that makes it seem like there is someone in charge. No. I don't."

His warm emerald eyes ran over my face, the corner of his mouth lifted. "Fair answer."

"But I really like the idea of assholes and sick fucks getting what's coming to them in the end," I told him honestly. He snorted, and his arms loosened on me. His hand came up to my face, his thumb running over my cheek.

"I do too, Lexie," he said softly.

"Sorry to interrupt." Isaac's voice came from the door. Miles let go of me as we both started to sit up and lean back against the headboard. Isaac was holding a whimpering Hades. My stomach knotted at the sound. "Hades is upset he's not with Red, I think." He walked over to the bed and handed me the still whimpering dog.

"Hades, baby, what's wrong?" I asked, holding him to my chest. I knew he couldn't answer or understand, but I always talked to Hades. It seemed normal to me. His nose came up towards my neck, and he licked me. His eyes and nose went to my face; then the whimpering stopped.

"He stopped. What was that?" I asked them.

"How long was he doing that?" Miles asked, pushing his glasses back up his nose.

"Since I took him out there so you two could talk," Isaac explained. "Last time he saw Red, she was crying."

I looked down at my puppy. He did not like being away from me when I was upset. His big blues eyes ran over my face before he laid down on my chest, his nose going to my neck.

"Looks like if you're upset, we need to keep him with you," Miles said. I nodded. Isaac headed back out the door. "Are you all right, Lexie?"

I took a deep breath and let it out as I took stock. "Yeah, I feel like me again. Gross, sickened out me, but me." I looked up at him. "I just wish there was such a thing as brain bleach."

He gave me a half grin. "That would come in handy," he admitted.

"Maybe there is a way to get rid of them in the Veil? Burn them out or something."

I went still. "Miles, you're a fucking genius." I looked at him.

He raised an eyebrow. "Why this time?"

"There is a way to do that. I found it on accident, but it's a way." Then I remembered how much one memory hurt to get rid of. It hurt like a bitch. I needed to get rid of a lot of fucked up shit. If I managed it, it was going to be awful, and after last night with the guys... "We might need to take a vote."

"Why would we need to vote about this?" His eyes ran over me, the worry back in his eyes.

"'Cause it's going to hurt. A lot. And I don't know what will happen after. If there'll be an after burn or if I'll get locked up again," I answered him honestly. "I don't know what to expect."

Miles took a breath; his eyes ran over me. "I'll get the others."

"No," Asher said firmly. "Hell no." I took a deep breath and reminded myself to be patient. I was still sitting in bed, my back leaning against the headboard. I had Hades laying on my legs, his chin resting on my bent knees. I had started petting him when we began discussing how I could get rid of those memories. He was out cold now.

"Asher." Miles' voice was calm and patient. "You need to listen to what she is saying."

Asher's hand was rubbing the back of his neck, his face drawn. "I know the memories suck, but this is her mind we're talking about," Asher shot back at Miles.

"Those memories..." Miles began, his voice growing colder.

"Are from a serial killer, I know." Asher took a deep breath and looked at me. "Ally, you can't fuck with your memory. You said so yourself, that you don't know what the after effect would be."

I was tired; I had just woken up, and I was already exhausted. All I felt was a numb, heavy weight in my chest.

"Ash." I tried again to be calm and reasonable. "Those memories-"

"Are sick, horrible, and fucked up. But you don't know what will happen after." Asher's voice was firm but shook just a bit. "How can you be sure you won't erase everything? How do you know when you wake up you will remember anything?"

"It doesn't work that way," I tried again to make him understand. "I tested with one memory, and it hurt like a bitch. I have to pick exactly what I'm getting rid of. There is no way I'm going to erase everything."

"That was one memory, Ally. And it hurt a lot. Right? Think about how much you want to dump," he pointed out, his eyes rough. "You were already tortured once last night. Do you really want to go through it again?"

I couldn't take it. "God damn it, Ash!" I shouted. I couldn't believe I was going to have to tell all of them. I met his rough gaze with mine. "You think I would do this just to get rid of some fucking memories?" My hands started shaking.

"Isn't that what you want to do?" Isaac asked from his spot on the end of the bed. I shook my head.

My eyes filled as I told them. "It's not the memories I'm trying to get rid of." My voice was tired, soft, and quiet. "That fucker made me feel the way he did about them." Out of the corner of my eye, I saw Zeke push away from his spot on the wall next to the bathroom door. I kept my eyes on Asher's. "Every murder, every torture, every rape of twenty-two women. I felt how he enjoyed it, how he liked it." The room was dead silent. My stomach rolled, and if I had had anything in my stomach right then, I'd probably be puking. Asher looked like he had taken a hit to the gut. No one else moved. "That's the part I want to get rid of."

"Ally-"

"I can take more fucking nightmares. I can take the sleepless nights and the bitchy fucking dead. But this..." I took a breath as tears started falling. My voice was shaking now. "This I can't take." Zeke moved. "This will break me."

Zeke stepped between Asher and me. "We're not voting this time," Zeke said in his 'don't fuck with me' voice. "She is doing this, Asher. You either help or get the fuck out. But we are not leaving that shit in her." Zeke's back was rigid, his hands were clenched into fists. Asher nodded once. Zeke turned around, came over and sat on the side of the bed. His sky-blue eyes were burning as they met mine. His face was full of more rage than I had ever seen before. He reached out, his hand was shaking as he held my chin, forcing me to keep my eyes on his. "Lexie, you do your thing." His voice was a strange mix of hard and soft. Of command and understanding. "Do what you have to do to get that shit out. Every feeling that fucker had, get it gone." I nodded. "We'll have the doc on standby, and we'll deal with any after effects. But get that shit out of you." His eyes ran over my face then met my eyes again. "You hear me?"

I nodded and took a deep breath. No one in the room objected this time. "I hear ya."

Satisfied, he let go of my chin and reached for Hades. "I'll watch him while you're down." His hands were gentle as he lifted the puppy off my legs.

"Don't spoil him," I mumbled, trying to lighten his mood.

"Oh, I'm spoiling the fuck out of him," he admitted immediately. "Now, do what you have to do."

I nodded.

I closed my eyes and took a deep breath. Then I went down to my center. It was almost as natural as breathing now. I looked around the white sandy plain and smirked. This was going to feel so fucking good. I thought of the edge of my center and was jerked there immediately. I was looking out on that field of stars again. I'd never been so happy to see them in my life. Because Miles had been right. What that soul did to me was.... invasive and violating. I didn't want to remember it. I could get rid of the memories over time, but I wanted those feelings gone now. I needed them gone.

I tried to get them all at once, but I couldn't get a grasp on all of them. I was going to have to do this one victim at a time. I took the worst one. She had been twenty and a waitress. I took the memory of those feelings and formed them into a metal ball. It was black and oozing. But it formed. I checked to make sure I got all his feelings about that woman; I didn't want a single one. I looked at the ball hanging over the edge and dropped it. A searing pain filled my head, dropping me to my knees. It went on for what felt like an eternity. When it finally stopped, I was gasping while on my hands and knees on the ground. Blood was dripping from my nose onto the white sand. I sat back on my butt in the sand and looked out at the field of stars. When I was ready, I looked back at that memory of the waitress. I sighed in relief. All I felt was horror and disgust.

I didn't bother to get up. I went to work on the next memory's feelings. This woman had been a second-grade teacher. She had fire in her. She was cursing the fucker up until he gutted her. I made the sick metal ball again, with its boiling surface. I braced myself and dropped it. Lightning slashed through my head like every brain cell was suddenly trying to escape. My body jerked as I fell to the sand. It didn't last as long as the last one, but it still knocked me on my ass. I opened my eyes to find myself on my back in the sand. Two down, only twenty to go.

I laid in the sand and continued to drop metal balls of that fucker's feelings. I jerked, I convulsed, I screamed, and I bled. I hoped my real body wasn't doing this in front of the guys. I didn't stop, not until the last one was gone. My mind felt torn up, but at least it fucking felt clean again. Or as clean as it could get with those memories still in my head. And right now, I'd take it. I didn't even bother to stand up. I pulled myself out.

I opened my eyes and immediately closed them again. It didn't hurt; I was just so fucking tired. I felt wet on my face and my ears, but I really didn't care. I was just going to fall asleep, but I heard the guys.

"Back... tired... nap..." I mumbled before I started dropping into sleep. I felt a hand give mine a squeeze. I smelled wintergreen. Then everything was gone.

I OPENED my eyes and blinked against the light. I felt so much fucking better. I wasn't at a hundred percent or anything near it, but it was a lot better than where I had been. I double checked my memories. I knew what happened. I remembered that sicko pouring his sick memories and feelings into me. But I didn't feel his feelings about them anymore. Oh, big fucking relief. I sat up and put my feet on the floor. The world spun like a top.

"Whoa," I mumbled as I closed my eyes and waited. Hands were on my shoulders. I got a whiff of vanilla and cinnamon. "Dizzy." I tried to reassure Asher, but I kept my eyes closed. He didn't say anything; he just waited. When the world wasn't moving again, I opened my eyes. Asher was sitting in a chair across from me, his neck red from rubbing and his ocean blue eyes were rough as the sea in a storm.

"Do you remember me, Ally?" he asked, his face pale.

I nodded. "You cook. You have a bitch for a sister, a dick for a dad. And the poor taste to hang out with me." I smirked at him.

He grinned back, but it was strained. "And do you know my name?"

I raised an eyebrow at him. He needed the reassurance. "Your name is Ashley," I said in a sweet voice with my mischievous grin. Asher chuckled then seemed to relax.

"That fucking smile," Asher mumbled, shaking his head.

"Yes, Ash, I remember you." I reached over and patted his knee. I didn't have a lot of comforting in me right now. I looked around the room. The light had shifted from earlier. "How long was I out?"

He sighed deeply with relief. "Four more hours. It's around two right now."

I looked back at him. He had his worried face on again.

"What's wrong Ash?" I asked gently, or as gently as I could manage right now.

His eyes ran over me before going over my shoulder. "Did you get them all?" he asked, his voice strained. Asher was struggling today.

"Yeah, all those feelings are gone." I gave him a small smile. Asher nodded.

"Ally... I didn't..." He paused then met my eyes. "I wouldn't have argued with you if I knew what that-"

"I know, Superman," I assured him. He blinked at me. "I just didn't want to tell anybody about it."

"I'm sorry, Ally."

I nodded that I heard him.

Then his eyes narrowed. "Superman?"

"It's your nickname now." I grinned at him.

He frowned, his eyes confused. "Why Superman?"

I smiled. "Ask me when I'm not so tired," I offered. I really didn't want a long discussion right now.

He gave me a small smile. "Okay," he agreed; then he took a breath. "I'll go make you some food. You haven't eaten all day."

"You are a god among men," I told him seriously. He snorted as he headed out the door. Asher told someone I was up.

Miles walked in, his eyes running over me, his face concerned. "Are you feeling better?" he asked quietly.

"Ooh so fucking better; it was like brain bleach," I told him earnestly and he grinned at me. "Thank you, Miles."

He blinked at me. "For?"

"For climbing in, for the cuddle," I said, trying to make light of it. "I know you're not always comfortable touching me." His cheeks tinted pink. "And I've embarrassed you. I need to learn to shut up sometimes."

"You're welcome, Lexie. I'm probably going to be uncomfortable around you for a few days," he admitted.

Then I remembered something. "No, you won't. Aren't you flying out to Nevada tonight?"

"Yes, I am." His voice was weary.

"What's wrong, sweetie?" I asked gently. It was never that hard for me to get Miles to talk.

"I'm trying to figure out where to take Autumn. Dates aren't a big area of my expertise," he confessed.

I smiled. I had a perfect idea. "How cold is it in Nevada right now at night?" I asked.

Miles pulled out his phone and checked. "Not bad, around fifty-five."

"Okay, here's what you do," I began. "When you rent a car at the airport, get a truck." He raised an eyebrow. "Then when you're taking her out, have the back filled with pillows and blankets." Both of his eyebrows went up, as he started to turn red. So I quickly explained. "Then take her out into the middle of nowhere and go stargazing." His eyebrows dropped as he blinked at me. "The blankets will keep you guys warm, and some hot chocolate and food would be an awesome surprise. Romantic, simple and beautiful."

He smiled at me. "Thank you, Lexie. You just saved me," he said adamantly.

I winked at him. "That's what family does." I sighed. "How's Zeke doing? I noticed he was shaking before I went under."

He nodded. "He had a difficult time until you came out of it and we knew you were okay," he said. "After that, he distracted himself by playing with Hades."

"And is he still pissed at Asher?" I asked, wanting to know what I'd be walking into out there.

"He never was," Miles said. "He just wanted to cut through the diplomacy... stuff and get you what you needed." He paused, his eyes unfocused. "That and he hates that you have those memories. It's difficult for him to accept there is nothing he can do about it."

"Where is he?" I needed to talk to him, let him know it was okay.

Miles frowned. "He won't talk about it," he said carefully. "I only know because I've known him so long."

I smiled. "Well, I'm not going to ask. I'm gonna be subtle," I informed him, getting to my feet. Miles looked at me. He was trying not to laugh. "I can be.... sometimes." He was smirking now. "Shut up, Miles," I grumbled.

"He's in the living room with Hades." Miles was laughing now. I left him to it.

I could be subtle, well, subtle enough that Zeke wouldn't notice. I walked down the long hall and into the living room. Zeke was asleep on the sofa closest to the kitchen; Hades was curled up on his chest. I smirked as I pulled out my phone and took a picture. I was sending a copy to Riley when I heard the guys coming down the hallway. I was still snickering over the photo when the boys came in; it was the only reason that I didn't remember.

I leaned over the sofa a little and touched Zeke's shoulder. "Wake up, Tough Guy." I had barely moved when his hand shot out and wrapped around my wrist. The sound of skin slapping skin echoed through the room. I jumped, my heart in my throat. Someone cursed.

Zeke's fingers squeezed my wrist. "Baby?" he mumbled, his eyes still closed. He was still mostly asleep.

Everything happened fast. The guys surged around the couch. Asher held Zeke down by the shoulders, Miles and Ethan were prying Zeke's hand off my wrist, and Isaac was holding his legs down. Still half asleep, Zeke fought against them and tried to pull me over the back of the sofa. Miles' arm around my waist kept me from going over while Ethan worked on Zeke's grip. Hades jumped to the floor.

"That's Lexie, Zeke!" Ethan shouted. Everyone kept yelling at him that it was me he was grabbing. It was chaos for a minute. Zeke let go of me. Miles instantly lifted me off my feet, he got me away from the couch and out of Zeke's reach.

"I'm awake!" Zeke barked in his deep, gravelly voice. Everyone backed off; Miles put me down and let go. Zeke sat up and put his feet on the floor his hands running over his face. Everyone else relaxed. "Lexie?" His voice was rougher than usual. "Did I hurt you?"

I looked at my wrist; it was red where he grabbed me, but that was probably from the slap. "Nah, I'm all right."

He turned to look at me, his eyes haunted. He crooked his finger at me to come over. I walked around the couch and stood next to him. He took my wrist gently and looked it over. His thumb made a small circle in my palm.

"It was my fault, Zeke. I was distracted by the puppy." He turned my wrist over, examining it again. "I got a great picture of you and Hades taking a nap, though." He looked up me, his face drawn and hard. His eyes were running over my face the same way they had my wrist. "I might have already sent it to Riley." I gave him my shit eating grin.

Everyone walked off, leaving me alone with Zeke. Asher scooped up Hades on his way out.

"Lexie, you can't wake me up. I could have..." He exhaled hard. "I was going to hurt you."

I winced. "I'm sorry, Zeke. I just... forgot," I admitted honestly.

He sighed deeply. He looked at me with a baffled look on his face. "I hurt you, and you apologize to me? Lexie..." He sounded like he was gathering steam.

"But you didn't hurt me," I pointed out. I shook my hand so he'd look at my wrist; the red was already almost gone. "See, you just grabbed me. And I knew I shouldn't have woken you up; this is on me." When he still looked like he was going to argue, I reached out and touched his nose. "Boop." I gave him a big shit-eating grin.

He snorted and shook his head. He was looking at me like he was trying to figure me out. Good luck.

"Lexie..." he began again, fighting a smile.

"Love you," I said in my cutesy voice, still smiling at him. He chuckled this time. Yes! I win.

"Love you too," he grumbled back under his breath.

I shook his hand on mine. "Come on. I'm hungry," I said impatiently. He snorted again and let me go. I headed for the kitchen; Zeke followed. We walked into the kitchen, and Asher pointed to a spot at the breakfast bar. I hopped on a stool and found a big bowl of spaghetti. Ooh. Carbs. I dug in.

"Zeke, there's pesto sauce for you," Asher said as he picked up Hades again.

"Thanks," Zeke mumbled as he got his own bowl and sat down next to me.

Asher was scratching Hades' belly; the dog looked like he was content.

"Did you really take a picture of me sleeping?" Zeke asked, sounding like he was dreading the answer. I snickered, pulled out my phone, and brought up the photo. I showed him. He groaned.

"I already sent it to Riley."

"You're fucking mean," he said under his breath. I snickered. The twins came in and seemed surprised to see Zeke in the kitchen.

"Is Zeke done with his post 'almost hit someone' sulk already?" Ethan asked, coming up to the counter. Isaac went to get a bowl of food. Zeke flipped Ethan off. Ethan chuckled before turning his attention to me. "How are you feeling, Beautiful?"

I finished my bite before answering. "Good, tired but good. Got all that feeling shit out," I said. "Over the next couple weeks, I'll be getting rid of those memories too. I am not holding on to that shit." I mostly said that for Zeke; it was my version of subtle. I rolled noodles around my fork as I mumbled, "I have enough nightmares."

"Sounds like a plan, Red."

I nodded, my mind on other things. While everyone started talking about their plans for the week, I was wondering why my boyfriend wasn't here. "So," I said during a lull in the conversation. "When did Dylan leave?" Every one of them looked, to some degree, pissed off. Asher was frowning; Zeke's face was hard; Isaac's face was drawn, and he was cracking his knuckles; Ethan's face was dark, his eyes storming; Miles' face was blank.

"Around eleven thirty." Ethan's voice was boiling.

"Wow, he made it three hours. That's pretty good," I joked. I didn't know what I expected from Dylan last night, but bailing hadn't even been on the radar.

"He froze, Lexie." Zeke's gravelly voice grabbed my attention. I looked at him, an eyebrow raised. "He was the first in there, and Asher had to shove him out of our way because he froze."

That sucked, but it was a lot of blood. I shrugged. "Last night was freaky, and he's never seen anything close to that," I offered. The guys all exchanged looks. "What?"

"We made a rule last night," Asher said. "If you go out with Dylan alone, you have to wear your beads. No exceptions. Not until we trust him to take care of you."

I went still. "You guys don't trust him to do that?" This was news to me; it made me pause. The boys exchanged looks again.

Zeke met my gaze. "We did; he seemed fine with it. Then he froze last night," Zeke explained. "There were other things last night that made us trust him less with you."

"We all agreed you wouldn't be left alone with him last night," Miles said in his calm voice. I felt like I had taken a hit to the gut.

That…. that was a huge loss of trust. They didn't even trust him alone with me now?

"We wouldn't let him climb in the bed with you either," Isaac added. He met my gaze. His face was serious. "Not with you unconscious like that. Not that he tried."

Shit. What the hell did Dylan do? What could he do to make the guys not trust him this much?

"He sat in a chair next to you, holding your hand, though." Asher grabbed my attention. "He was kind of pale, and he looked like he was thinking hard about something."

"Did he call my phone?" I asked, dreading the answer.

"No," Zeke replied when everyone else hesitated.

Okay. "Did anyone call to tell him I was awake?" I asked.

"We thought we would leave that to you," Ethan said, giving me a half grin.

I snorted. "Okay, where's my phone?" I sighed. Miles pulled my cell from his back pocket and handed it to me. "Thanks, I'll call him before I head home." I looked over at Miles. "When do you have to leave for the airport, hon?"

Miles finished chewing before he answered, "In about a half hour."

"Damn, Miles, you better get ready. We'll clean and lock up." I shooed him.

Miles looked at the others. "You're sure?" Everyone convinced Miles to get moving.

All of us had finished eating by the time Miles brought his suitcase downstairs. I gave him a big hug as we all saw him off. I was going to miss Miles while he was in Nevada. The guys finished cleaning up while I took a shower. Dried blood was a bitch to get out of your hair, by the way. I packed my stuff and loaded up the Blazer. Zeke locked up the house and set the alarm while we all got in our cars. I put Hades in his crate between the two front seats where he could still see me; otherwise, he was grumpy as hell. I called Dylan while the truck warmed up.

"Lexie?" He sounded off, like he had a cold coming or something.

"Hey, cutie, just wanted to let you know I was awake and doing fine," I said in a cheery voice. There was silence on the other end. "Dylan? Hon?" A tightness grew in my chest as I waited to hear his voice.

"Yeah, I'm here." His voice was a little more normal. The tightness eased. "I'm really glad you're okay, Sunshine. That was…"

"Freaky? Yeah, I know. It was freaky even for me," I admitted, hoping to make him feel better. "That's the worst one I've had in months, but I'm fine. You guys took care of me and got me back to Miles' house." There was silence again. Okay. "Are you in the middle of something? You can call me back later if you are."

"Yeah, I'm sorry. I am in the middle of something. I'll call you back tonight, okay?"

"Sounds good. Bye."

"Bye."

I hung up the phone and stared at it. A chill ran through me. That had been…. different. He had definitely freaked out last night. He was probably trying to deal with it by working on that science project again. I put it out of my mind, and when the truck was warm enough, I drove home.

It was around three when I got home. I was just pulling onto my street when that chill ran down my neck. No, not ran; it was more like I took multiple punches down my neck. I had to pull over down the street from the house. Four ghosts were waiting outside Rory's house. How the fuck? Then I spotted Carl and the McClains. There was a new ghost too. And one coming down the road. I couldn't deal with these guys today. And knowing the McClains, they were going to be pissed. I flipped a fast U-turn and got the hell out of there. I was not going to deal with this shit today. I was taking the fucking day off from ghosts.

I racked my mind trying to figure out where to go. Miles' was out, he was on his way to the airport now. Fuck. I could only think of one place, the cemetery. But Hades needed food first. I ran through a drive through and headed for the cemetery. When I got there, I parked in a hidden corner and opened Hades' crate. The little booger made a beeline for the food. I set him on the passenger side seat and fed him his double cheeseburger, without the bun. He ate about half of it, and then he was full. When he was done, I picked him up and moved into the cargo area. I laid out my sleeping bag and slipped in; Hades climbed in and curled up on my stomach.

I called Rory and let him know what was going on. He wasn't happy, but he understood. Then I texted the guys to tell them what was happening.

Alexis: Went home to find ghosts camping outside the house. I turned around, and we are currently hiding out at the cemetery. If you need me, this is where we'll be tonight.

I was petting Hades when my phone vibrated.

Isaac: Need anything?

Ethan: I'll bring you out some books if you want.

Zeke: I'll bring you dinner.

Asher: You sure about that, Ally? Not exactly safe.

Zeke: I was going to check it out when I brought her food.

Asher: Oh, okay. Need anything?

Miles: I'm gone for not even an hour...

I just smiled at them.

Alexis: Food will be appreciated. I have a full charge on my phone, so I can watch movies. I'll be okay. Got Hades and planning to nap.

Miles: Go to my house, you have a key.

I cringed.

Alexis: Big house? Hiding from ghosts? That sounds like a horror movie plot. I won't be okay there without you, Miles. Sorry, sweetie.

Miles: I understand. I don't like it, but I understand.

Isaac: Don't really like it either.

Ethan: If you need anything, call.

Asher: Just let us know you're okay.

Zeke: I'm still checking the place out. See you later.

I snickered at the guys. They were so sweet.

Alexis: Love you too, guys.

I put my phone down and snuggled into my sleeping bag. Time to catch up on years of sleep deprivation.

I JERKED AWAKE. There was a loud bang again. Shit! It was probably a cop. How was I going to explain this? As I was unzipping my sleeping bag, the back tailgate opened. Ethan and Isaac were standing there, smirking at me.

"I think we scared Red!" Isaac announced happily.

"I think you're right." Ethan was smiling too.

"Shit, guys, I thought you were a cop," I grumbled, opening my bag. Hades jumped off me and went to the edge of the tailgate to greet the boys.

"Hey, Hades, aren't you supposed to be her guard dog?" Isaac teased. Hades barked at him. I smiled. "A little late buddy." Isaac picked him up and put him on the ground. "I'll take him for a leak." He started walking, and Hades followed.

Ethan hopped up on the gate with me. "Hey, Beautiful, change your mind yet about Miles' house?" He smirked at me.

I shook my head. "Nope, I don't know how he lives in that house all alone. The place would creep me out," I admitted. "Don't tell him I said that."

Ethan chuckled. "Promise." He showed me the book bag he brought. "We come bringing entertainment. There's a Nintendo DS in here, fully charged, games, and some books. Even a book light and some extra batteries."

"Wow, you guys thought of everything." I took the bag and started digging. "Ooh, Mario Brothers!" I cheered.

Ethan chuckled. "So, you're planning on staying all night?" he asked.

"Yep."

"What if you... ya know...need to take a leak?" he asked seriously.

I snorted. "I'll go to a gas station," I assured him, still smiling. He shrugged.

"Oh, you have to hear this." Ethan began eyeing how far away his brother was. "Cece called today, asking for Isaac to give her another chance."

I raised an eyebrow at that. "Wow," I said impressed. That took guts. "What did he say?"

458

Ethan gave me an 'are you crazy' look. "He told her to fuck off," he said, smiling. "He said he didn't like bitchy liars who treat his family like shit."

"Wow." Ethan nodded at me. "Luckily, Miles didn't hear him."

Ethan snorted. "Miles heard us call them bitches; he just agreed at that point," he pointed out. Then I thought about it. Miles had been there when there was name calling.

"Shit, how did I not notice that?"

He laughed. "When it comes to you, Beautiful, we're all a bit protective," he reminded me. Yeah, he had a point. "How is Dylan doing?"

I sighed. I watched Isaac heading back with Hades running after him, not wanting to respond. "We talked for about two minutes. He said he was in the middle of something and that he'd call me back tonight," I confessed. It hadn't gone well. Ethan bumped his shoulder into mine; I bumped back.

"Lexie, you're kind of awesome. If he gets scared off because of this one thing, then he's not good enough for you," Ethan said, his voice was earnest.

I smiled sadly at him. "I know; doesn't mean it won't hurt," I mumbled, looking up at the clouds rolling in.

"You really like him, huh?" Ethan asked, his voice quiet.

I looked over to watch Isaac play with Hades. "Yeah." I shrugged. "He... this sounds so fucking corny it's not even funny." Ethan's eyes all but lit up. "Can you keep this to yourself?"

"For you? Anything."

"He... is the first guy to... look at me and..." I continued in a mumble, "Make me feel beautiful." I felt my cheeks turn pink.

Ethan snickered at me. "Wait, wait. I call you beautiful all the time," he pointed out.

"Being called beautiful and feeling beautiful are two different things," I explained. "You know you like performing, but you feel it when you're up there."

Ethan thought about that. "Okay, I see your point," Ethan admitted.

"Doesn't mean that I don't love my nickname," I said, just in case he thought I didn't.

He chuckled and smiled at me. "Good, 'cause I'm not changing it."

"Okay, Snoopy," I said pointedly. He groaned. "What, you don't like Snoopy?"

He looked pained. "No, it's fine, I earned it," he grumbled. "Just be on the lookout for another one."

"Okay, you'll have two," I smirked at him. Ethan snorted at me. Isaac was almost back with Hades. "By the way, I think I gave Miles a date idea that is so going to get him laid." Ethan burst out laughing, which I expected, but when he kept laughing, I started to suspect he knew something I didn't.

Isaac reached us and handed me Hades; then he pointed at his brother. "What's with him?" Isaac asked. I shrugged; at this point, I had no clue.

Ethan's face was red as he waved his hand. "Beautiful here gave Miles a date idea that she thinks will get him laid," Ethan said before bursting out laughing again. Isaac joined him. I just waited until they were ready to tell me what was so funny.

Ethan was the first to recover. "Oh, Oh, Lexie, he was going to see Autumn," Ethan explained breathlessly. "Those two go at it like fucking rabbits."

My eyebrows shot up, my jaw dropped, and the boys broke out into another fit of giggles. "Really?" I asked. I couldn't have been more surprised if he'd said Zeke liked wearing dresses. Ethan nodded, still giggling.

"Oh yeah, those two barely see the light of day when they're around each other," Isaac assured me. "Once, she came up here for a week last summer, and we saw them both once. Right after he picked her up."

"Okay, so they enjoy each other; what's up with the on again off again?" I asked, looking from one to the other.

"Well, because of the distance, sometimes Autumn gets interested in someone else," Ethan explained. "She tells Miles and he says, 'Okay, we're not dating.'" He shrugged.

"They have an arrangement: if you're interested in someone else, tell the other person," Isaac began. "They still talk on the phone, still play games together. She's just dating someone else."

"And Miles goes with that?" I asked, not believing it. They both nodded.

"Oh, it's not just her," Isaac said. "He told her... what? Six months ago, he was interested in someone else. They broke up. He dated that chick, they broke up, and, bam, he was back with Autumn. No hard feelings, no jealousy problems."

"They're very honest with each other," Ethan added. Then his brow furrowed. "But, if he was worried about taking her somewhere, then he might be trying to change the arrangement they've had."

"That makes sense," Isaac admitted. "You know Miles. He'd do something romantic and then talk to her about it." My head was still spinning about this side of Miles. I had never actually wondered what Miles... Lexie stop. Don't go there. The guys started talking about games to play in the cemetery. It was obvious they were trying to keep me company.

"Guys, go home. I'm all right."

"We can go get our sleeping bags, and we can all crash in the Blazer," Isaac suggested, looking at his brother.

Ethan cringed. "That would really hurt," he admitted. I raised an eyebrow. Ethan admitting his back hurt was so rare I thought this was the first time I'd ever heard him say anything.

"Has your back been bothering you, sweetie?" I asked as I reached over and ran my hand along his back. His muscles were tight as a rock. "Ethan! What the fuck?" I moved back behind him then scooted up to his back with my legs on the outside of his hips.

"I'm fine; it's fine. Leave it alone," Ethan grumbled. I ignored him. I ran my hands over his back lightly, finding all the incredibly tight spots. He kept protesting, but he didn't move away from me. I started at the top of his back. My hands working out the knots. Ethan groaned and dropped his head forward. He stopped saying he was fine; he stopped talking. He was just making little noises now. Isaac watched, frowning as I worked out several knots in Ethan's upper back, but when I moved lower with the same pressure, he hissed. I eased up, going lightly. He groaned again, his head still hanging.

"Be careful around his spine in the curve of his lower back; that's where the problem is." Isaac's face was drawn as he watched his brother. I started working from the outside in. I'd work the knots out to a point on one side, then go to the other and go to the same point. Then I'd switch. Then I'd repeat. It was when I got right next to his spine in his lower back that I had trouble. I'd switch sides then come back, and it'd be locked up again. So I worked my thumbs up and down the muscle on both sides at the same time. Ethan twitched, jerked, and hissed.

I stopped. "Did that hurt?" I asked, worried about his reaction.

"No, no, Beautiful, it didn't. There are just a lot of nerves right there," Ethan explained. "You just hit them, and I'm currently using them right now." I looked at Isaac over Ethan's shoulder. I gestured for him to turn around. He understood immediately.

He turned and stood directly in front of Ethan. "Lean on my back," Isaac offered. "It'll take the pressure off, and she can get the last of the knots.

"It's fine-"

"Brother, if you say you're fine one more fucking time, I'll knock you out, and then Red will massage that spot," Isaac growled at Ethan. I eyed Isaac. I'd never heard Isaac so forceful. It was weird.

Ethan sighed and leaned forward, practically getting a piggy back without leaving the gate. I went back to work. Ethan still jumped, but it was mostly when I found another knot. There were so many in the area along his spine that I couldn't believe he could stand it. It took a while, but I finished the last one. I ran my hands over his back again, just checking to be sure. I didn't like how tight his back had felt. When I stopped touching him, I was still worried about him.

Ethan sighed then slowly sat up. "Oh, mother..." He stretched his arms and shoulders. Ethan got off the gate and very slowly stretched his lower back.

Isaac caught my eye. He mouthed, 'Thank you.' I winked at him, then went back to watching Ethan.

"Better?" I asked, hoping. I couldn't have made it worse, right? Ethan stood back up slowly and returned to me. He wrapped his arms around me and kissed my forehead before resting his cheek on the top of my head.

"You have the most incredible hands in the world," Ethan said enthusiastically.

I snorted and hugged him back. "Just glad I could help, Snoopy."

He snickered. "Call me Snoopy all you want, Lexie. I don't give a shit," he mumbled to me, squeezing me tight.

"Well, if you need, I can give you back massages during the week so your back doesn't get that tight," I offered. I really didn't want Ethan in that much pain.

Ethan squeezed me again. "Normally I have a massage therapist every week or so, but she's out of town till after the new year. I'm all yours, Beautiful!" I snickered. He pulled back and gave me a big kiss on my cheek. "You are the best, seriously."

I winked at him as Isaac chuckled. "Now go home and do whatever it is you do to baby your back," I ordered.

He smiled down at me. "All right. We're going," Ethan grumbled and let go of me to head towards the car.

Isaac swooped in and gave me a tight hug. "Thank you, Lexie. He's been a grumpy bitch all week at home." I snickered. Isaac kissed my other cheek then ran to the car, since Ethan had started it and was threatening to leave without him. I waved as they took off. They passed Zeke's Jeep on the way in. I snorted. That figured. The sweet little shits were trying to keep me company.

Zeke pulled up, parked, and got out. He handed me a greasy bag that Hades was immediately interested in. "I ate shitty today, your turn," Zeke explained as he dropped onto the tailgate next to me. I snickered and opened the bag. I pulled out a small cheeseburger for Hades and took the bun off for him. He went to town. Zeke smirked as he watched him. "That dog is going to be big."

I pulled out my burger. "Wasn't that the point?"

"Yeah, pretty much," he admitted without any sign of remorse. "So, the twins came out huh?"

463

I shot him a look. "Like you didn't know that already," I said accusingly. He gave me a half grin. Yeah, he knew. "You're a shit."

He snickered. "Your point?" he countered. I snorted.

"Ethan's back was so tight it was like a rock," I said, changing the subject. Zeke frowned. "Gave him a back massage and managed to get the knots out." He lifted an eyebrow. "His massage therapist is apparently out of town."

He nodded. "Thought he was walking funny." He looked back to me. "So, you're giving massages now?"

"Yeah, I guess," I said before I took another bite of my burger.

"Hell, if my shoulder gets any worse I might have to ask," he grumbled.

I raised an eyebrow at him. "Don't you have a girlfriend to do that?" I reminded him.

"Yeah, but..." he trailed off, his gaze going out to the cemetery.

"Are you having trouble with her touching your back?" I asked, eating a fry. He looked down at me, surprised.

Then his eyes narrowed on me. "Who told you about that one?" he asked grumpily. I finished eating my bite before answering.

"Asher, the morning after Vegabond," I answered. "He explained about triggers, so I asked what other triggers you might have so I could avoid them."

He seemed to relax. "That's how you knew to come to me at my side when I was at the door on movie night." He exhaled. "Wondering about that has been bugging the shit out of me." I snorted as I took another bite of my burger. "Yeah, I'm having trouble with her touching my back," he groused as if he hated to admit it.

I finished my bite. "But you think you'll be okay with me touching your back?" I asked gently. "Even though I'm on probation?"

He sighed deeply. "I might not trust you a lot right now, but I know you." His voice was quiet as he looked over the tombstones. "I'll work my way back to trusting you, Lexie. It's just, gonna take some time."

"I know," I grumbled. "In a month."

He snorted. I looked over to see him smirking. "A month isn't that bad. Isaac got three, remember?"

I eyed him. "Was taking your Jeep really that bad?" I asked curious now.

His eyes met mine. "You know that big dent in the passenger side door?"

My mouth dropped open. "No," I said, my voice full of disbelief.

Zeke nodded. "I busted my ass to buy that thing and fix the engine. A month after I got it running right, Isaac took it, and somehow managed to do that." I was speechless. He smirked at me. "He is still working off what it's going to cost to fix it for Sylvie."

"How?"

"Sylvie's big into her flowers, garden, and yard in the spring and summer. Hell, she sells veggies at the farmer's market every Saturday. Isaac's her designated bitch until he's helped us save enough money to fix it," he explained. "He should be done this summer around July."

I eyed him. "So, on the scale of trust-breaking, who's was worse? Mine or Isaac's?"

"Isaac's," he answered instantly. A tightness I wasn't even aware of eased in my chest. His warm eyes ran over my face. "You didn't do it on purpose. You had no idea I would take it like this." He looked out over the darkening graveyard. "Isaac knew how hard I had worked, how many late nights I had put into that Jeep. He knew I'd be pissed off at him. And he did it anyway."

"And after three months?" I asked hopeful.

He grinned at me, eyes running over my face. "I trust him again. That one took some time, but I trust him again," he said simply. I took a deep breath and let it out. We were going to be okay.

"So, you want a back massage?" I asked, changing the subject.

His grin disappeared; he went back to looking at the cemetery. "Not today. It's not bad enough yet that I'm willing to deal with those memories." His voice was his quiet, soft one that I didn't hear that often.

"When you are, give me a call," I offered. Then I had a thought.

"You know you could use a heating pad, or two 'cause you're giant, on your back." He snorted. "Always works for me."

"I'll give that a try." He sighed. "Now if only Riley would back off." I raised an eyebrow. His face was blank. "I need some advice from a girl," he grumbled.

"Hit me," I said before I took another bite of my burger.

"I'm having some issues with Riley," he admitted. "She's nice and all, but she wants answers to questions I don't want to talk about."

"Family questions?" I took a guess.

"Yeah."

"Then just tell her that." He frowned at me. "Tell her that you aren't ready to talk about that with her."

His brow drew down. "Think that will work?"

"If not, she's an insensitive ass. And you know she isn't," I pointed out. Hades came to the end of the gate and tried to get into Zeke's lap. "I think he loves you."

He grinned as he picked up Hades. "He's a good dog," Zeke said, bringing the puppy up to his chest. I watched as my puppy licked scary Zeke's nose. Zeke chuckled as he started petting him. "Our training today was a bust, though."

"Are you sure it was training and not playing?" I asked, smirking at him. Zeke suddenly found the cemetery fascinating. I burst out laughing. "Zeke, you can play with him anytime. Just let me know when you want a play date." I snickered.

He groaned. "Did you just say play date?"

I smiled. "Is he really going to get as big as you said?" I was thinking about my bed and how small it was already.

He nodded. "Yeah, he should." He raised a brow at me. "Do you have room for a bigger bed?"

I groaned. "Not really, but I can sacrifice most of my floor space for no nightmare sleeping," I said before eating a fry.

His eyes narrowed on me. "How small is your room?" he asked. I looked around for a comparison. I couldn't find one.

I hopped off the gate and walked out the width: about eight feet.

"That wide." Then I walked the length: about nine feet. "That long," I said around the food in my mouth. I hopped back onto the tailgate.

"That is not that big," he pointed out.

I snorted. "Only room I've had since my mother lost the house, Zeke," I grumbled. He went still. I pulled out a fry and fed it to Hades.

"Where did you sleep?" His gravelly voice was softer again. He flipped Hades onto his back in his arms and rubbed his belly. Hades' eyes closed in bliss.

"There was a way to turn the dining booth into a bed." I shrugged before reaching over to feed Hades a fry. Zeke stopped rubbing his belly long enough to let him eat it.

"Could have been worse, right?" he offered. Zeke gave me his lip-twitching smile.

I nodded and threw my wrapper into the bag. "That's what I think, but I mentioned it to Dylan and Riley; then I got that look." I cringed, remembering.

Zeke nodded understandingly. "The pitying look?"

"Yeah, I hate that fucking look," I said.

"I know what you mean. Anytime someone learns my parents are dead, I get that fucking look," he grumbled before he shook his head, frowning at the gravel. "Fucking hate it."

"Yeah, it's like, 'I don't know you. I'm a not a child, and I don't want your fucking pity. So, shove it up your ass,'" I said in my sweet voice. He burst out laughing; I saw a smile with teeth. Those were rare from Zeke.

"That describes it perfectly," he said. I chuckled.

It wasn't long after that he was going to meet Riley. But he insisted I climb back in the truck so he could close me in. I did what he asked because there was no reason to fight him on it. After he left, I watched a couple of movies on my phone and then snuggled back down to sleep.

A HARD BANG woke me up. I opened my eyes to see my breath in the air. What the fuck? The back gate opened. Asher was standing there, frowning, with snow falling behind him. His ocean eyes ran over me.

"You're not even wearing your coat, Ally," Asher snapped as he reached across me for it. "Haven't you been paying attention to the weather?"

I was still trying to wake up. "Hmm? What?" I mumbled. Why was he pissed off?

Asher unzipped my bag, took Hades and gave me my coat. "It's going to go below zero tonight. You're not staying here." His voice told me not to argue, and it was fucking freezing. I pulled my coat on as he tucked Hades into his jacket and held him.

"Well, I can't fuckin' go home," I grumbled, half asleep, still pulling on my coat. Apparently, I wasn't moving fast enough for him. He reached out and jerked my coat up onto my shoulder. That woke me up a bit more.

"You're coming home with me; now get in my truck."

I eyed him. I'd never crashed at Asher's house before. I was straightening my coat as I tried to come up with an argument. But with how frozen my face already felt, I decided I wasn't going to argue. Still rather asleep, I nodded.

Asher pulled Hades out of his coat and handed me the big fur ball. I took him, slipped him inside my coat, and closed it. Asher grabbed the bags in the truck and shut the back. The cold was finally waking me up. Snow was falling everywhere, and there were occasional flashes of lightning. What the hell? Asher grabbed my arm and got me moving towards his truck. When I was walking, he let go. It was really coming down. I climbed into the warm truck, shutting the door behind me.

"Why is there lightning while it's snowing?" I asked, completely weirded out.

Asher buckled up and started driving us out of the cemetery. "It's a big storm; it came in around eight," he said. "It's supposed to get to around -10 degrees tonight."

"That I get," I tried again. "I mean the lighting and snow, totally fucking creepy."

He grinned. "This from the girl who sees the dead," he teased.

"Yeah, some things should just not happen together," I grumbled. He chuckled. "Wait, I could have driven the truck."

"Zeke says not tonight," he replied.

I eyed him. "Did Zeke send you out?"

He gave me a half grin. "No, I was already on my way here when he called," he said. "I told him I was almost there then he barked at me about not letting you drive."

I looked out the windshield. It was getting hard to see the road. "I'm not bitching," I agreed. I heard him chuckle. I shifted Hades, who was still in my jacket.

"You're not arguing? Are you feeling okay?" he asked, smirking.

I snorted. "I'm stubborn, not stupid," I countered. He chuckled again. Asher pulled up to his house and parked. "Your sister still isn't home, right?"

"She's still at the spa." He shut off the truck. That's all I needed to hear. I grabbed a bag and was out of the truck fast. I almost slipped on the sidewalk, but Asher grabbed me around the waist and practically lifted me off my feet. "Ally girl, you need a pair of winter boots," he grumbled as he steadied me.

"They have winter boots?" I growled. He snickered as he held onto my arm until I was up the steps and on the porch. He unlocked the door and pushed me inside, with his hand on my back. The house was nice and toasty. I put Hades down and took off my coat. "What time is it anyway?" I put my jacket on the banister.

"Around 10:30," he said as he picked up Hades. "Go ahead and head on up. I'll take Hades out real quick."

"And... where am I heading?" I asked, not sure. Was I sleeping in his dad's room or Jessica's? Both were kind of gross.

"You can take my room, and I'll sleep in Dad's. Just let me grab something to sleep in first," Asher called over his shoulder on his way to the kitchen. That worked for me. By now, everyone knew my issue with sleeping in the bed of someone I didn't know. It creeped me the fuck out.

"I can sleep on the couch, Ash," I reminded him.

He stopped at the back door to look at me. "There are three beds upstairs, Ally. You're not sleeping on the couch."

"Thank you, Ash."

"No problem, Ally girl." He smiled at me before walking out the back door.

I took my overnight bag upstairs. I opened the door on the left side of the bathroom, and no, that was Jessica's. I shut the door and went to the door on the other side of the bathroom. Vanilla and cinnamon tickled my nose. Yep, this was it. I felt around and hit the light switch.

Asher's bedroom walls were white, just like the rest of the house. Only in here there were sports posters on the walls. The room was at least double the size of mine, which wasn't surprising since my room was small. There was a TV on the wall opposite the bed. Asher had a big double bed covered in white sheets. The blue, orange and white comforter was rumpled as if he'd been in bed when he saw the weather report. His nightstand, desk, and dresser were all the same wood: oak, I thought.

I put my bag down on the desk chair and started snooping. I couldn't help it; I was nosey. His desk was covered in cookbooks, cooking technique books, and printed out recipes. I smiled. He was such a foodie. He really needed to go to culinary school after high school. I looked at the shelves. There were a lot of football trophies, even basketball. But those were from years ago; it looked like he had played both for a while. I wonder what happened there. I saw a couple of MVP award plaques on the walls too. I smiled. I wished they were cooking competition awards; was there such a thing? I heard the back door shut downstairs, and I kept snooping. Asher knew me; he knew I was nosey. I looked at his bookshelf and found nothing but cookbooks. Asian, Italian, Mediterranean. He had everything. The room bugged me. It was like two different people were living here. The football guy and the chef. I liked the chef more.

"Being nosey huh?" Asher's voice came from the doorway. I turned to watch him put Hades down on the bed.

"You know it," I said in my cute voice. I went over and sat next to Hades and began petting him. "I'm nosey with all of you."

Asher had a half grin on his face when he went to his dresser. "You're actually not that nosey, Ally," he said as he opened a drawer. "You never go digging, you just see what's there."

I shrugged as Hades climbed into my lap. "That's my nosey," I pointed out. "I don't like to dig into other people's stuff without a damn good reason."

Asher closed a drawer and opened another one. "What would it take for you to go digging?" he asked, pulling out some pajama bottoms.

I sighed and thought about it. "If I thought one of you were doing drugs, had gone missing, or if you asked me to find something." I thought about it again. "Yeah, that's about it." I looked over to see him smirking at me.

"So, what would you do if you found one of us smoking pot or something?" he asked, eyes sparkling with mischief.

I raised an eyebrow. "Before or after I smack the shit out of them?" I asked sweetly. He chuckled and I smiled.

"You have something to sleep in?" he asked.

"I have a shirt," I hedged. Asher turned back to his dresser, dug out a pair of pajama bottoms and tossed them to me. They were blue with Sylvester the cat all over them. I loved them instantly. "Thanks, but you might not get these back," I warned him seriously.

He grinned as he shut the drawer. "I'll be down the hall. 'Night, Ally girl."

"'Night, Ash."

He closed the door behind him. I changed into his drawstring jammy bottoms; I had to roll the waistband over several times, so I wasn't standing on them. I pulled on my black cami. I knew it was winter, but I moved around a lot, and I liked my arms free. I turned off the light and climbed into Asher's bed. I snuggled down with Hades and fell asleep.

CHAPTER 18

EARLY SATURDAY MORNING

I felt the blade in my hand as I ran it along her skin. She had been so easy to take, so trusting. I pressed down and watched the skin cut and bleed. She was covered with them now. I smiled as she whimpered. She was going to pay; the stuck-up bitch was going to beg before the end. My hand moved to my trousers...

I JERKED AWAKE, screaming and still half asleep as I scrambled to get away. My heart was slamming against my ribs as my back hit something hard. I changed directions; I had to get away. No, no, no! I fell and hit the floor hard; I kept scrambling. I had to get away from her! I had to leave! I didn't want to touch her! My back hit a wall, and I stayed there, my chest tight, my body shaking too much to move. I was gasping for air, tears running down my face. I didn't see Asher's room; I was in the basement in Newport where I worked. What the fuck did I do? What did I do? What did I do? I wrapped my arms around myself and rocked. A heavy, tight knot was crushing my chest.

As if from far away, there was a small bark. "Ally!" someone yelling.

It wasn't one of the girls. I closed my eyes; I'm a girl. I'm not him. A door burst open, and I barely noticed. I was still in that basement.

"Ally...."

I'm a girl. I'm not him; I didn't do those things. I'm a girl. It wasn't me; he's the one. I closed my eyes and tried to focus, panic tearing through me. I'm Lexie, I'm Lexie, I'm Lexie. I didn't do that. I didn't hurt them. I kept repeating it over and over.

"Ally."

A hand touched my shoulder. I jumped and moved away till I hit something big and hard. I didn't want him to touch me! He's the one who did it, not me! I rested my forehead against the cold surface and took deep breaths. I'm Lexie, I'm Lexie. I didn't hurt them. I'm a girl; I didn't hurt them that way. I couldn't have. I didn't hurt them.

A dog was whimpering somewhere, and it made my heart hurt.

"Ally, you didn't hurt anyone."

That wasn't his voice. I knew that rich voice. Lexie knew that voice. I knew it. I turned towards it. I'm Lexie, I'm Lexie, I'm Lexie.

"Ally, open your eyes and look at me; see where you are."

Still gasping for air, I opened my eyes, half expecting to see his face. It wasn't him. It was Asher. I knew Asher. I knew those beautiful eyes, that handsome face. I knew him. I looked up at him and felt broken. I was shattered on the floor, and there were only that fucker's memories left. His face changed; his face looked pained, his eyes soft and warm.

Asher reached out, his hands holding my face. "Ally, are you seeing me?"

I nodded, still trying to get those images out of my head, still gasping for breath as I cried. I felt sick, dirty, like I had done something horrible. That wasn't me. I didn't do that. But his hands on my face helped, helped push those images back. My shaking hands dug into his white undershirt and I clung to him. He pulled me against him, his arms tight around me. I buried my face in his chest and tried to breathe.

"I've got you, Ally," he whispered gently.

I wrapped my hands in his shirt and focused on remembering who

I was. I'm Lexie, I'm Lexie, I'm Lexie. I didn't do it. I didn't do it. I'm not a monster. I didn't do that. I didn't hurt them.

"You didn't do anything, Ally. You didn't hurt anyone," Asher started talking, and I listened while my body remembered how to breathe. "You aren't a monster; you're our Ally." His hand ran down the back of my hair. "You love bad monster movies, and you make smart-ass jokes." I nodded; yeah, I did that a lot. "You're an amazing artist, and you're thoughtful and generous. And a hard ass when it comes to telling me to do what I really want, no matter what anyone else thinks." One of his hands buried itself in my hair. "And you'd tear apart anyone who tried to hurt the people you care about." I nodded. Yeah, I would. I wasn't that thing in the basement. I was someone else. I'd never... The images finally fell back into their dark little corner, giving me room to breathe again. I took deep breaths as my pulse started to slow back down.

It was awhile before I really knew I was in Asher's room. Lightning flashes lit up the room every few seconds, giving us light to see.

"Oh, that sucked," I whispered into Asher's shirt. I felt Asher let out a deep breath. I turned to rest my cheek against that space between his shoulder and chest. Hades whined from his spot on the bed.

"No shit." His voice was relieved and strained all at the same time. "Are you okay?" I didn't know how to answer. I shrugged. His hand started rubbing up and down my back. It felt so good right now. "What was that Ally?"

"Nightmare, bad." I finally had my breath back, but I kept clinging to Asher. I wasn't ready to let go. "Forgot who I was, did bad things."

His body became tense against me. "What do you mean, honey?" he asked, his rich voice soft. "I've got her, Hades, calm down." Hades stopped whining.

"It was one of his fucking memories. But when I dream about the dead, it's always me." I took a breath and kept talking. "I'm always the one dying, I'm always the one... hurting other people. He was about to rape one of his victims. I woke up right before he...." My throat closed.

"Shit, Ally." I nodded against his shirt. That about summed it up.

Asher held me tighter. He rested his cheek against my hair. "Can you get rid of the rest of those memories tomorrow? Like you did today?"

"Yeah," I said quietly. Even my voice sounded tired. But I really didn't want to go back to sleep.

"Do that tomorrow, Ally. You can stay here all day and night if you need to. I don't care. I don't want you to think you've... done that again." His voice was hard and panicky.

I moved my hand to the back of his neck, my fingers kneading. My mind was on Sophia; I needed to get the link going for when.... "I have to finish the link. It's already taking too long," I told him wearily.

He went completely still for a couple of heartbeats. Then his hands were hard on my arms, pulling me away from his chest. I looked up. His face was drawn, hard. His ocean eyes were rough as they ran over my face. "The link can wait. This can't." His voice was firm and clipped, telling me not to argue. He didn't understand. I needed to convince him.

"I... I can't," I argued. His eyes raged at me. "People are counting on that link. I can't let them down."

"No soul is worth this, Ally. Can you go through that dream again? Can you stand to think you did that again?" His eyes ran over my face again. "Because I don't think you can."

My eyes filled. He was right. I didn't want to do it again. But... he didn't know... "I don't have a choice." He opened his mouth to protest again, but I cut him off. "It's Sophie." Asher's face went pale, his eyes wide. He exhaled hard as the news hit him. His grip loosened. I rested my hand on the middle of his chest, reminding him I was here. I waited till he got over the shock.

"Are you sure it's her?" he asked quietly, his voice brittle.

"She called the twins, Eth and Izzy."

He looked horrified, his brow drawn together, his mouth open. "She's at their house? She's the ghost that's been...."

"Yeah, she is." I ran my eyes over his face; his mouth had closed, but his eyes were full of shadows. "She's okay right now, no extra energy." I needed him to understand why those memories didn't matter right now. Why this didn't matter right now. "But it doesn't mean that won't change. And I need to be ready when she decides she wants to cross. I'm not leaving her to rot like Mary Summers." Asher ran his hand down his face as he took a deep breath. His eyes went to the wall over my shoulder as he let go of me. I pulled my knees to my chest, wrapped my arms around them and waited. My tired body was begging for me to go to sleep. As I waited for Asher, my head started dropping. I wasn't going to sleep; my body just wanted to lay down.

"Okay." His voice was calm. I looked up and blinked at him. He looked down at me, his eyes determined. "Do the twins know?"

"Fuck no." My voice was still tired. "Miles does." He narrowed his eyes at me. "I had to tell someone; I was freaking the fuck out. I didn't even know they had a sister."

"Yeah, that would be a shock." The tension on his face eased. "How much longer do you think the link will take?"

I thought about it. "If I push it a little more, a couple of days. Maybe."

He nodded, he seemed to come to a decision. "You're right, Ally," he began. "We need that link. We can't leave Sophie here to..." He took a deep breath then let it out slowly. His eyes ran over my face; his face was drawn again. "Until you finish with that link, until you can get those memories out, you're going to be having these nightmares."

"I know," I sighed. "She's just more important to me, Ash."

His eyes were full of understanding as they met mine. "You forgot who you are, Ally." His face became worried. "You thought you were the one..."

I looked down at my knees. I didn't want to remember that part. I didn't think I was going to sleep for a couple of days. "I know." I rubbed my eyes with one hand. I just wanted... I snorted at myself. I wanted to sleep, but I didn't want to go through that again. I felt him brush my hair from my face. I looked up at him. His worried eyes were on me.

"You're going to wake up screaming every night for Sophie," he said slowly. "You're going to think you're the one who hurt those women every night so you can cross her when she's ready."

"It's their sister, Ash." My voice was soft but loud in the quiet of the room. "If she needs to go, I'm going to be ready. I promised her."

His brow drew together as his eyes ran over my face. "Then you're staying here," he declared.

"Huh?"

"You have to do this; I get it." He let out a breath. "But you're not doing it alone. You're staying here until you finish the link, until you get the worst of those memories out." He reached out and cupped my jaw in his hand. "When you can sleep without thinking you're him. Then you can go home." That warm and fuzzy feeling filled me until I thought my heart would burst. My eyes filled as it sank in. Asher wasn't going to let me go through this alone; he wasn't going to let me forget who I was.

I wrapped my hand around his wrist and squeezed. "Ash..." The corner of his mouth raised a bit; then he was pulling me against him, his arms wrapping around me. I hugged him tight, not wanting to let go. My voice was thick when I whispered to him. "Thank you."

He squeezed me tight. "Of course, Ally." I took a deep breath of vanilla and cinnamon. Something inside me relaxed. Exhaustion poured over me. I rested against him, my body not listening to me anymore. Asher caught me. "Ally, you need to sleep, honey."

I shook my head against him. I didn't want to sleep... I didn't want to see it again. "Coffee, I need coffee." My voice was quiet, barely above a whisper. But Asher heard me. He always heard me.

Asher shifted, his arm slipping under my knees. He got to his feet, lifting me against his chest. "No Ally, you need sleep, not coffee." His voice was gentle.

I shook my head as another flash of lightning lit up the room. "Uh-uh. No, nope, nada. I'm not sleepin'," I grumbled as he carried me across the bedroom.

"You're sleeping, Ally."

I shook my head again. "Can't make me."

He snorted. "Did already, Ally girl," he reminded me softly. I snorted. He set me down in the middle of the unmade bed. Before I could even sit up, Asher had laid down next to me and pulled the blankets up to cover both of us. Hades moved up from the foot of the bed to the pillow next to my head.

"I don't wanna..." I grumbled. I heard him chuckling quietly as he shifted on the bed. He wrapped his arm around my waist and pulled me to him. My body fit into the curve of his. My head ended up on his arm with his other arm holding me snug against him.

"Tough shit," he whispered back. He wasn't hiding his laughing now. I grumbled at him. He buried his face into my hair at the back of my neck.

"No sleepy..." I mumbled while my eyes were closing. Asher's body heat was pushing me into sleep. I wanted to sleep... but... dreams... if he got up.... "Ash?"

"I'm not going anywhere, honey," Asher whispered against my neck. Really? He wasn't?

"Promise?" I felt him smile against my skin.

"Promise."

I started to slip into under. I felt a small kiss on the back of my neck, or I thought I did. It didn't matter. I dropped into sleep hard.

I WOKE UP SLOWLY, my body in a strange position. I was almost on my stomach; Asher was still against my back. I tried to move, but I realized I was pinned by Asher's leg between mine, his knee on the mattress. His arm around my ribs, his elbow was bent and his forearm running up the space between my breasts. His hand was spread flat on my upper chest, his fingertips touching my collar bone. His arm held me against his chest. It was the only thing keeping me from laying completely on my stomach, as if, even in his sleep, he was aware of where I was and stopped me from laying on it. It made me feel warm and fuzzy inside.

I was still floating in that half sleep when I realized what else I was feeling against me. Yeah, it was morning. I ignored it and just floated there. A small part of me remembered I had a boyfriend and he wouldn't like this. But it was Asher, kind, talented, wonderful, sexy as hell Asher.

The rules didn't feel like they applied to him, or any of them. Fuck it. The world was quiet, and I was good exactly where I was. I was almost back to sleep when Asher's breathing changed. He took a deep breath and let it out. He rubbed his face on my back, his arm tightening around me. I didn't mind. Then his lower body shifted against me, pressing harder against my butt. Yeah, he was still mostly asleep; otherwise, he would have moved away. I didn't care. At least until he started to pull his arm down my chest; he was probably just trying to roll over, but I still stopped his hand just as the heel of his palm reached the top of my breasts.

"Mmm…" he grumbled.

I woke him up a bit. "Ash," I mumbled into my pillow.

"Hmm?"

"Wake up before you move your hand," I muttered back. His arm went limp. I just held his fingers now, reminding him not to move. Vaguely I knew my breasts were on his forearm, but I didn't care. I was still floating when he woke up a little more, his face moving to my hair.

"Ally?" he mumbled.

"Uh-huh," I muttered, still enjoying the half sleep.

"Thought I smelled rosemary." He rubbed his nose into my hair. I smiled. "You feel good…."

"You too," I mumbled back. "Warm and snuggly…." I was floating back down to sleep when he mumbled something I couldn't hear.

"Hmm?"

"You have a boyfriend… shouldn't cuddle… you," he muttered, not moving an inch.

"Fuck 'em. You guys were here first…. you have cuddle dibs." He snorted and started laughing. I smiled as his laughing started waking me up. I knew when he woke up entirely. His entire body became rigid and still. I just stayed put while he figured it out. He pulled his arm off me and rolled away like I was burning him. That made me smile.

"Ally, I'm sorry," he groaned. Huh?

"What?" I asked, almost completely awake now.

"I didn't mean to grab you like that. I'm sorry, I... knew it was you I just..."

"You didn't grab me, Ash," I grumbled, wanting to go back to sleep.

"But my hand..." His voice almost sounded panicked.

"Your arm was between my boobs when I woke up; your fingers were practically on my neck." I sighed. Giving in to the inevitable, I rolled over to face him. He was sitting up, his back against his headboard, knees bent. One hand was rubbing his neck. "You were actually keeping me from rolling onto my stomach."

He shook his head, his face looking pained. "Ally, I was practically laying on you, and my leg..." He sighed and rested his head back against the headboard.

"Yep, your leg got up close and personal; your point?" I was comfy and wanted to go back to sleep. He looked down at me, looking bewildered. "You were asleep, Ash. It's okay. You didn't do anything," I grumbled. "Freak out later... sleep now." He snorted. I pulled the blankets up over me, and I snuggled down, perfectly happy to stay here.

"Ally, I'm so-"

I pointed at him then opened my eyes and glared. "If you apologize one more fucking time, I'm going to start taking it personally," I warned him. His eyes grew wide as I rolled over to my other side. "Like I'm covered in fucking boils or something," I grumbled. I could practically hear his jaw drop.

"That's not what I-"

"You really know how to make a girl feel pretty, Ash," I grumbled, pulling the blanket over my head.

"Shit.... Ally... I..." He sounded so confused and worried that I started laughing. When he realized I was messing with him, he yanked the blanket down and started going after my ribs. "You are such an evil little shit sometimes!"

I snickered and jerked as he tickled me. "Takes one to know one!" I shot back as I continued smacking his hands away from my sides. When he kept coming at me, I went after his spot, the right side just under his last rib. He smacked my hands back. Then he grabbed my hands and pinned them above my head. I tried to dive away, but I was still laughing too much to move. He moved them to one hand and brought his other hand down to tickle along my ribs again. "No! No! Cheater!" I shouted as I tried to move out from under him.

"That's rich, coming from you!" he shot back. I just snickered up at him. His eyes ran over my face then focused on my lips. He stopped tickling me; his fingers gently traced my ribs. Then his face changed just a bit. He blinked hard several times and pulled back. His eyes were wide. "Uh, truce?"

"Truce! Truce!" I was still laughing my ass off when he let me go to sit at the edge of the bed. I had just got my breath back when Hades whined. I looked over at Asher. "You know, if you're really sorry-"

He snorted. "Nope. After that, I don't feel bad at all," Asher said, smirking. I playfully glared at him. "But I'll take him out anyway." He picked up Hades and headed out the door.

Yes! I didn't have to go out in the snow. But I did have to get up. I groaned deeply then rubbed my eyes with one hand. I needed to talk to Rory, tell him what was going on. I also needed to work on the link and push it more than usual today. I dropped my hand to my side. I didn't want to tell Rory what had happened at the bowling alley, but it looked like I wasn't going to have a choice. I looked at the ceiling. The next few days were going to suck. And poor Asher was going to go through them with me. I got up and started making Asher's bed when something clicked in my brain. Asher had slept next to me last night. He'd never done that before. Hell, it was probably going to be the only way I wasn't waking up screaming all night. Poor guy. The boys always seemed to be taking care of me. I didn't like it.

I finished making the bed before taking my bag into the bathroom and doing my usual routine. I didn't bother getting out of my jammies, but I did pull on a bra and a loose green t-shirt. I dropped my bag off in Asher's room, grabbed my cell phone and went downstairs. I found Asher in the kitchen already getting ready to make breakfast. Hades was drinking out of a water bowl next to the door.

"Are you jammy cooking?" I asked, hopping up on the counter.

He smiled while he worked. "Yeah, I'm jammy cooking today; it doesn't look like we're going anywhere for a while." He looked up from the cutting board to look out the window. "Looks like it was a white out last night. So, the roads won't be clear for hours." He went back to dicing potatoes.

I checked my messages and cringed. I had forgotten to call Rory last night. But apparently, he got ahold of Zeke and found out where I was. I was in trouble. My gut knotted. I needed to tell Rory what was going on. Now was better than later, right? I looked up at Asher, who was still on the potatoes. I had to ask. "Ash?"

"Hmm?" He sounded distracted.

"Are you sure you want me to stay?" He stopped cutting. "I could go to Miles' house; it'll be weird without him, but I can nut up." His shoulders grew tense.

He put the knife down before turning to me, frowning. "And when you wake up screaming and not remembering who you are? What are you going to do then?" he snapped at me. I went still. "You're not getting a choice, Ally. You are staying here until those memories are gone." His voice told me not to argue. It made me feel all warm and fuzzy. I hadn't felt that a lot in my life, but since meeting the guys, I was starting to get used to this feeling.

"Thank you, Ash." His shoulders relaxed as he gave me a half grin and went back to cutting up potatoes. I looked down at my phone; my stomach knotted even worse. I took a deep breath and called Rory.

"Your ass better be at Asher's!" Rory shouted as soon as he answered the phone.

"Yes, my ass is at Asher's; he came out and got me around ten." I took a breath and groveled, "I'm so sorry, Rory. I was out cold when he woke me up. He got me back here fast, and I was up asleep in his sister's room before I even woke up all the way." I lied my ass off. "I just woke up, and I haven't even taken Hades out yet." I just kept on lying. Asher was smirking at me. I stuck my tongue out at him. This was about survival, damn it. Okay, it was about my freedom.

"Next time call! I had cops on the lookout for you until I got a hold of Zeke," Rory growled at me.

I winced and kept groveling. "I'm so sorry Rory."

He sighed. "Just as long as you're okay," he grumbled. "You're staying there until the roads are cleared. Then I want your ass home."

I took a deep breath. "Rory, I can't come home." There was dead silence for several heartbeats. I hopped off the counter and headed for the family room.

"Why?" he sounded scary calm.

"You remember the long exposure the night before last at the bowling alley?" I curled up in a wide chair and waited.

"Yeah, what about it?" Rory's voice was strained.

"Did the guys tell you what kind of soul it was?" I asked, hoping they already explained this part. I bit the corner of my bottom lip, waiting.

"No. What happened, Lexie?" He wasn't asking; he was demanding.

I looked down at my knees, and I told him. I explained who it was, what he did, to who and how many. I told him about yesterday, how I got rid of those disgusting feelings. I told him about the dream, not the last part of it. I couldn't tell him that. It didn't take long.

"Lexie... that's..." I heard him take a deep breath. "That's horrible, and we'll deal with it, but why do you think this means you can't come home?"

I swallowed hard. "Rory, I woke up screaming. I didn't remember who I was. I thought I had done those things. That I was..." My voice was thick as I continued, "The only reason I came out if it was Asher. He helped remind me who I was."

"Shit."

"I can't do that with Tara there, Rory." I swallowed hard. "Asher said I could stay here so that when it happens again, he'll be there again."

"You told me you could dump those memories; you need to do that." Rory's voice was very clear.

"I can, but I can't do that and build the link. And right now, the link is more important," I said, my voice sincere.

"Lexie... tell me why, or you're coming home as soon as the road is clear." Rory's voice was hard and unyielding.

"Because the soul of the twins' little sister is in their house," I explained, my gut still knotted. "And I'm not leaving her here to rot." Rory was quiet so long, I thought he had hung up. Then I heard him moving.

"Shit."

"Yeah, pretty much."

"Okay, Lexie, stay there as long as you need to." Rory's voice was worried. "Get the link done, then get the memories gone. Don't kill yourself to do it, though." I swallowed hard. I should have kept Rory more up to date than this. But there were some things he didn't need to know.

"Thanks, Rory."

"I'll bring you out a bag of clothes. Do you need anything else?"

I thought about it for a second. "Hades' dog food, treats, and some chew toys." I hated having to ask.

"No problem. I'll see you after the roads are plowed."

"Bye." I hung up the phone, a bit of the weight lifting off my shoulders. Rory understanding made things easier, not by much but it helped. I got up and walked back into the kitchen. Hades was eating a small plate of eggs, his tail going crazy. It was cute. Asher was leaning against the counter eating breakfast.

"How'd it go?" he asked as his eyes ran over me.

"He understood why I couldn't come home," I said as I grabbed a plate and began filling it with eggs and fried potatoes. "He doesn't like it, but he understands it." I walked over to the kitchen island across from him and hopped up on the counter. "He's bringing over some stuff after the roads are plowed."

Asher nodded and finished his bite. "I'm glad he understood," he said. I nodded as I started to eat breakfast. "The next week or so is going to suck for you. No reason for him to make it worse."

I looked up from my plate and eyed him. "Us. It's going to suck for us," I reminded him. He smirked at me. "You're the crazy one who volunteered remember?"

He chuckled. "Yeah, I remember." Asher pointed his fork at me.

"But you didn't wake up again last night, so I think with both Hades and me we can keep those dreams away." He took a bite of potato.

"Thanks for taking the hit, Ash."

He shook his head as finished chewing. "Ally, helping you sleep isn't taking a hit." His eyes met mine. "It's just…. cuddling." He gave me a strained smile before looking at Hades, his shoulders tense. He seemed to have something on his mind, so I went back to my breakfast. I was almost done when my phone vibrated. I picked it up to see it was another email from that same email address I didn't know. This time I opened it.

YOUR EYES GLOW with a fire that's hard to quench. – S.A

I SIGHED. Whoever this was had the wrong email. And they were a romantic. I threw the email away and checked my texts. Nothing from Dylan.

"Did Dylan text you?" Asher asked before taking a bite of his toast.

"Nope, no phone call either." I put my phone down on the counter and looked up at him. "I talked to him yesterday for about two minutes. He said he'd call me last night. No call, no text."

Asher frowned. "That's fucked up," he muttered before taking his plate to the sink. Asher wasn't defending Dylan? Asher always defended Dylan or at least offered an alternative. Asher's shoulders had grown tense, his jaw clenching.

I decided to ask the question that I had wanted to since I woke up at Miles' house. "What happened that night that has all of you not trusting him?" I asked quietly. I needed to know.

Asher put his plate in the sink then turned to look at me. His face was serious. "Are you sure you want to know, Ally?" His voice was warning me.

My stomach knotted. "Yeah."

He nodded then moved to stand across from me, leaning against the counter.

"I'll give him this. He was the only one with a kit on him. Ours were in our cars." His voice was carefully neutral, like he was trying to hide what he was feeling. "He was also the one who asked Riley to see if you were all right. We thought you probably had a bloody nose or something." I waited silently. "When Riley came out yelling that you were on the floor in the bathroom, he was up and off like a shot. We were a step behind." He crossed his arms over his chest, which made him look adorable in his Tweetie Bird jammy bottoms. "He got in the door and froze. I had to shove him out of the way." His shadowed ocean eyes met mine. "Ally, you were in a pool of blood and twitching. It scared the shit out of me."

Guilt hit me hard. All because I forgot my fucking bracelets. "I'm sorry, Ash. I didn't mean to scare you," I said, feeling awful about it.

"I know, honey; it was just a nightmare to walk into." He sighed. "I got you mostly off the floor, and we started working on you. Isaac ran for your beads, and Zeke had to yell at Dylan to move from the door. He seemed shocked to the core. Miles sent him out to get your bag, partly to give him something to do. He took a long time getting back." I frowned at that. He knew exactly where my truck was, so what took so long? "When he got back, he did try to get the blood out of your hair. Then it was time to change your shirt. We all know how you love your coat. He suggested that we just cover you with it. Miles suggested a button up. Miles waited thirty seconds for him to volunteer his shirt." Dylan had been wearing a button up that night; he had worn it open over a gray shirt. "Miles gave up his own shirt, and he and Ethan got it on you. Then it was time to pick who was carrying you. We all waited for him to step up. I waited almost a minute before I volunteered." I blinked at what he was describing. Dylan didn't try to carry me? Was it the blood? "Then we got the hell out of there and got you to Miles' house. Same thing again. Ethan looked like he was going to pick you up. Zeke told him no. And we all waited for him to volunteer. Miles' waited fifteen seconds."

"Was I still covered in blood?" I asked my voice quiet.

His eyes ran over my face before he shook his head. "Just your hair at that point and it was still in a ponytail." His voice was calm but firm. "Miles was angry with him on the way in. Dylan asked about you calling Miles wintergreen." I snorted. Yeah, that sounded like me. "Miles was going to put you in bed when Dylan reminded him of the blood covering you. I honestly thought Miles was going to put you down and punch him."

I went still. "Seriously?" I asked, not quite believing it. Calm, controlled Miles?

"Yeah, instead we got Dylan out of the room for a bit, made a few decisions, and sent Isaac for a book in Miles' room." A book? That was new.

"Why a book?"

"You heard us upset and kept fighting to stay conscious, so Miles read to you. Then you finally passed out." His eyes ran over my face; his brow was drawn down. "When he left, the twins wanted to kill him." I raised an eyebrow. "Okay, when I found out, I wanted to kill him."

I gave him a proud smile. "There you go, sweetie, own the rage," I said cheerfully.

He snorted. "That's everything that happened to make us not trust him with you." Asher's brow was still drawn down. "I want to think that it was just all the blood, but... he was freaked, Ally."

I sighed. I knew the guys must have had good reasons not to trust Dylan, and now I knew what they were. "I figured he was freaked." I shrugged, acting like it didn't hurt to know he didn't want to help take care of me. "It is what it is."

Asher gave me a sad half grin before he pushed away from the counter. He took my plate and went back to the sink.

Dylan didn't try to carry me. He didn't even stay. Those weren't good signs.

"If the roads are cleared by tonight, there'll be a big party out at the Henderson's." Asher broke my train of thought. I looked over to see him looking out the window.

"Why?" I asked, curious find out how he would know.

He smirked. "Their parents love skiing; with this snowfall, they'll be out at their cabin as soon as possible." He seemed to think about it.

"More than likely they already are." He looked over at me. "It'll be fun."

I snorted. A party sounded good to me but... "I'd love to, but I need to work on that link tonight too."

"You can do both, just come home early," he offered, his eyes starting to sparkle. "You need some fun, Ally girl." I sighed. He did have a point.

"Okay." I smiled at him. "You've convinced me."

He snickered as he went looking back out the window. "It was real hard too." I snorted. Asher smiled. "Quick, lock the back door!" he suddenly called. I hurried and did just that. Someone tried the knob. Then there was pounding.

"Open up, Asher! We know you got Red!" Isaac shouted.

"Who is it?" I asked in an annoyingly high-pitched voice.

"Beautiful, open up, it's freezing," Ethan begged.

"Maybe I should dump some water on you. It'll be fun!" I smiled as I taunted them. Asher started laughing.

"NO!" They both shouted at the same time.

I started laughing. I looked at Asher. He nodded.

"Say please, bitches!" I called to them.

"Please bitches!" They both shouted. I snickered as I turned the lock and let them in. Isaac and Ethan hurried in and shut the door behind them.

"Whoa." Isaac started pulling his jacket off. "It was a pain in the ass just to get over here." I was still laughing as I hopped up on the kitchen island. Isaac picked up Hades and started petting him.

Ethan had just hung up his coat when he pointed at me then strode towards me. "You are the most awesome woman in the world!" Ethan declared as he came over and hugged me tight.

I hugged him back, surprised. "I know, but why do you think so?" I asked, smirking. The guys chuckled as Ethan kept hugging me.

"Because after you gave me that back massage last night, I had the best night's sleep ever," Ethan said, pulling back. "I haven't slept that well since my massage chick left town."

"Glad to help." I smiled at him. He leaned in and gave me a big kiss on the cheek. Then he stepped back and gave me a sweet, exaggerated smile. "You want another one, don't you?"

He nodded. "Yeah, kinda tweaked myself trying not to fall on the ice out there. I already want to lay down," he admitted. I smiled at him. Ethan at least talking about his back hurting made me happy enough that I'd give him a massage anytime.

"Sure, but you're going to have to share me. And you have to massage my hands first," I said. "They're sore."

"Aha! Already massage cheating on me!" Ethan said with fake outrage.

"Well, sweetie, with hands like these...." I smiled sweetly. The guys chuckled. Ethan reached out and took one of my hands, his fingers massaging hard. I hissed. He stopped. "Lots of bones and stuff, Snoopy, easy." Asher started pouring coffee. Isaac jumped to sit next to me on the kitchen island.

"Sorry, Beautiful," Ethan said as he winced in sympathy. Then he started to work the soft muscle tissue in my palm. It felt damn good. "So, I assume Asher was your massage mistress."

"No mistress. Zeke just warned me that if his shoulder gets worse, he's going to ask."

Ethan froze, the room went silent. Ethan's eyebrows went up. "Zeke," he said slowly, as if to be clear. "Is going to let you touch his back? Zeke Blackthorn?"

"Ezekiel Blackthorn? Our surly giant of the north?" Isaac added as Hades licked his cheek.

"If his shoulder starts hurting worse, I think so," I answered.

Ethan looked impressed. "Never thought Zeke would get over that one," Ethan mumbled.

"He didn't," I admitted. Ethan looked back up at me. "He said he wasn't in enough pain to deal with those memories yet." Ethan's face was still impressed.

"But he said he'd ask?" Isaac asked. I nodded. Asher handed me a cup of coffee. I thanked him and started drinking.

"Wow. We got to get your hands in shape," Ethan said.

I wiggled my hand in his to remind him. "Yeah, so if you want another massage, get massaging yourself." The guys burst out laughing. I closed my eyes and chuckled. Oh, that sounded dirty. There are just some things you couldn't say in a room full of guys.

Ethan finished massaging my hands by the time I was done with my coffee; they felt a lot better. After morning dishes, I had Ethan lay down on the couch. He yanked his shirt off and dropped happily. I took a second to enjoy the eye candy of Ethan without his shirt on. He worked out, but he didn't go nuts about it like Asher, Zeke or even Isaac. But his body still was, well, drool worthy.

"Ethan's stripping," I yelled to the guys, trying to distract myself.

"Yeah, bring lotion!" Ethan added. We both burst out laughing. Asher came in looking at us like we were big weirdos. Isaac just brought the lotion down from the bathroom upstairs. I took it and put some in my hands to warm it up.

"So, what did you do to fuck up my work from yesterday?" I asked as I started rubbing the lotion on his back while finding the tight spots again.

"Almost slipped on the ice on our back porch. I grabbed the rail which tweaked me funny," he complained. "Should have just let myself drop, would have hurt less."

I found the tight areas. It was his lower back again. I started working the knots out on one side then the other. Ethan was making his little noises of happiness, which of course made me smile. Poor guy. When I got to almost his spine, I did the double thumb massage I figured out yesterday. His leg twitched.

"What was that?" I asked while still focusing on what I was doing.

"Sciatic nerve; it runs down from your back, through the butt and down your legs," he answered. "It's annoying as hell when it hurts."

I smiled. "So, you're butt hurt?" I snickered.

Ethan burst out laughing. "That's not wrong," he admitted.

I sighed as I kept working on a particularly stubborn knot. "Ethan, what's wrong with your back?" I asked gently. "I mean, why are you hurting all the time?"

He sighed into the couch cushion. "There was a car wreck about five years ago; it caused a couple vertebrae to slip in my lower back, which pushes on the nerves going to my legs, which causes pain." His voice told me he didn't want to talk about it.

"Ouch." My voice was full of sympathy.

He snorted. "Pretty much."

I didn't ask anymore, but I smirked. "I'm still not rubbing your ass," I said in my serious voice.

He burst out laughing. "I wasn't gonna ask," he shot back while continuing to laugh.

"Just wanted to be clear." I smiled as I felt that knot finally go.

He groaned deeply, his back relaxing now. "Thank you so much, Beautiful."

"No problem, Snoopy." Someone's cell vibrated, I didn't feel it, but I heard it.

Ethan pulled his phone out and checked it. "Hey! Party at the Henderson's tonight!" He rolled over, and I had to force myself not to look at his chest. I grabbed his shirt and threw it at him. "You going with? Should be fun."

I smiled at his mischievous grin. "I'm in if I can come home at a decent time for Veil work."

He smiled. "Any time you want, Beautiful," he reassured me.

"Then sounds good to me; I could use some fun." I got off the edge of the couch and headed for the foyer. "Ash, I'm going to use your room for Veil work!" I shouted into the kitchen. I heard the oven close.

"Damn," Asher cursed. "I just put cookies in the oven."

"I'll take Veil shift!" Ethan volunteered from the couch. I turned to see him finish pulling on his shirt.

"Works for me." I turned back to shout at the kitchen. "Don't let Isaac eat all the cookies!" Asher and Isaac were laughing as I headed upstairs with Ethan following.

I dropped onto Asher's bed and stretched out. Ethan took the other side and did the same. I looked over at him and smiled a small smile. I hated that they had to do this. He winked at me, instantly making me feel better. How did the guys always do that? I put it out of my head, closed my eyes and went to work.

I OPENED my eyes and immediately wished I hadn't. The world was spinning, my head killing me and my stomach rolling. I thought for a second I'd be fine, but then my stomach gave a lurch. I jumped out of bed and rushed to the bathroom. I was already heaving when I hit the tile in front of the toilet. I was immediately sick over and over. Hands held my hair while I wanted to die. A cold cloth went to my neck; it felt really fucking good. I stayed on my knees with my eyes closed, hoping the world would stop spinning soon.

"Okay, Beautiful, take this." Ethan's smoky voice was soothing as he slipped the nausea tablet into my hand. I popped it into my mouth and chewed. I felt like I had a bad stomach flu, in short, like shit. When I could, I held a tissue to my nose. I got to my feet then wobbled. Ethan steadied me as the world kept tilting.

"Tell the room to stop moving, Snoopy," I mumbled, my voice nasally as I made my way along the wall back into the hallway.

Ethan didn't laugh; his grip on my arm tightened as I stumbled against the wall. "Lexie, what the hell? Why did you push it?" he snapped at me as he wrapped an arm around my waist and helped me step away from the wall. The floor continued tilting.

"'Cause I'm the broken bitch that always needs a babysitter," I grumbled as I climbed back into Asher's bed.

"What?"

I couldn't answer; I was already slipping under. A hand brushed the hair out of my face just before everything went black.

CHAPTER 19

SATURDAY AFTERNOON

I woke up still feeling lousy, not like shit, but lousy. I got up and used the bathroom. I made a point to wash the blood off my face. My hair was all over the place, and I was paler than usual. Oh well, the guys had seen worse. I zombie walked downstairs to find all the guys in the family room. Isaac was lying on the floor with a sleeping Hades on his chest; it was adorable.

"Lexie, you look like shit." Zeke's gravelly voice had me looking at him.

"Thanks, Zeke," I grumbled as I stepped around Isaac and sat down between Asher and Ethan on the big couch.

Asher's eyes ran over me. "Let me get you some lunch, Ally. You slept straight through," Asher volunteered.

"You are my favorite," I told him in all honesty, well, right now he was. He was bringing me food. The guys chuckled as Asher headed out to the kitchen. I stole his spot and curled up in the corner of the couch.

"Asher says you're staying here for a few days." Ethan reached over and started playing with my toes. "The ghosts at home that bad?"

My mind went blank. I didn't know what to tell them. I settled for a half lie. "Yeah, they're camped out. I just needed a break from all the

493

bitching." I rubbed my eyes with one hand then started watching the movie. It wasn't long before Asher brought me a big bowl of soup. It smelled familiar. "Is this Maria's soup?"

"Yeah, made at lunch for everyone," Asher said, smiling.

"Ooh, yum." I suddenly had an appetite. I enjoyed the soup; it settled my stomach and gave me warm soup belly. "So, fucking good." I put the bowl on the end table to take in when I got up.

"Rory stopped by and dropped off a bag of clothes and stuff for Hades," Ethan announced.

"I must have been out cold. I expected a lecture," I admitted, relieved. The guys snorted.

"No, we got the lecture." Isaac's voice was still half asleep as he stretched. Hades lifted his head and looked around. When he saw me, he jumped off Isaac and hurried over to me. It was so fucking cute. I picked up my big ball of love and settled him in my lap.

"Why did you guys get the lecture?" I started petting Hades, who settled down on my legs.

"For letting you make yourself sick again," Zeke grumbled as he looked over to me. "You need to knock that shit off, Lexie."

I sighed and just kept petting Hades. "I'll try," I lied. I was going to do it again tonight; I was getting very close to the Veil, and I needed that link up. Sophia needed that link up. My answer seemed to satisfy Zeke. Me looking like shit probably helped too.

My cell phone in my bra rang. I pulled it out and checked the caller id. It was Dylan.

"Should I even answer Dylan's call?" I asked, only half kidding.

"What? He didn't call last night?" Ethan asked from his side of the couch.

"Nope."

Ethan frowned.

"Ask him to the party tonight," Isaac suggested. "We'll see if he's still freaked."

I sighed. I was hoping they would tell me not to answer it.

"Hello."

"Sunshine, I'm sorry I didn't call last night." Dylan's husky voice filled my ear.

Ethan tried to lean across Asher, but Asher slammed his shoulder into Ethan's, forcing him back. I wasn't going to bother moving unless I was getting dumped.

"Yeah, what happened?" I asked, trying not to be pissed. I noticed the TV had gotten quieter and the guys were trying to look like they weren't eavesdropping. Except for Ethan, who had no problem letting me know he's listening. Today, I didn't care.

"I got caught up in what I was doing, and then I passed out," he explained. Though it wasn't much of an explanation. Then again, I'd given him plenty of those myself. I decided to let it go.

"It's okay. I get it." I sighed. "I'm not going to hold it against you."

He chuckled. "How'd you do in the storm last night?" he asked.

"Lightning and snow, freaky as fuck," I grumbled. He burst out laughing. "What? They should not go together, and when it does... damn."

"Yeah, it makes a kind of cool light show," he said.

"No, scary ass light show," I corrected playfully. He snorted. "So, what are your plans for tonight?"

He inhaled then let it out. "I was kind of hoping to see you." His voice didn't have its usual warmth to it. I decided to ignore that for now.

"There's a party out at the Henderson's tonight, wanna go?" I asked, my stomach knotting.

"Yeah, Sunshine, I can take you." His voice sounded weird.

"Are you okay? You sound... off." I had to ask; it was starting to nag at me.

He snorted; it didn't sound like a laugh. "Yeah, I'm okay. Just drained," he began. "I woke up and was half asleep when I remembered I didn't call you last night."

"Thank you for calling, but go back to sleep," I said, not even kidding.

"Half way there, babe. I'll pick you up around eight?"

"Sounds good. I'm staying at Asher's for a few days." I decided to lie. "Tara and I have been tearing into each other, so I'm crashing on his couch till we both cool off."

"Okay, I'll pick you up there. Bye."

"Bye." I hung up the phone. He was just tired; he got into something he was working on. He was okay. But that knot didn't go away. "He didn't ask about me staying here," I told the guys quietly. I looked up to see them sending each other looks. "Not good. Right?"

Zeke nodded. "If you were my girlfriend, there would be a lot of questions," Zeke admitted gently, well, gently for him. I nodded.

"Then again, he and Asher have been friends for years," Ethan pointed out. "He knows Asher wouldn't cross that line."

"Good point," I admitted. The knot still wasn't going away though. The doorbell rang. Asher got up to answer it. My mind went to more important things. "Are there still cookies in the kitchen?"

"Yep. Asher about took Isaac's hand off when he went after yours." Ethan snickered. I smiled, gave Ethan a sleeping Hades, grabbed my bowl, and headed into the kitchen. I was in the foyer when I heard a voice that made me stop dead.

"-I didn't think it was that serious, she told me she was fine." Trisha's voice had my temper boiling instantly. That bitch was here? After what she...? I turned around and saw her outside the front door.

"No. There's your answer, now please leave." Asher's voice was firm and growing harder. I barely noticed it; I only had eyes for Trisha. I put the bowl down and was moving before I knew it. She was the fucking reason it had gotten that bad. She was the fucking reason I thought I had... I was past Asher before he knew I was there. I swung. I caught that bitch in the eye, and she went down. Vaguely I felt the pain in my knuckles but then adrenaline was flowing, and I was on her again.

"You fucking bitch!" I hit her again. "You left me to die!" I screamed as I went to kill her. When I pulled my arm back again, arms wrapped around me, yanking me off her, and pulling me off my feet. I smelled vanilla and cinnamon. "You fucking piece of shit! Do you have any idea what you did!" I tried to reach for her, but Asher pulled me further away from her. "You have any fucking idea what you put me through?" I couldn't seem to stop screaming at her. I wanted more blood. "You fucking spoiled princess! Do you even think about anyone but yourself?"

Trisha was stumbling off the porch, clutching her face. "Fuck you, Lexie!" Trisha shouted back, tears falling down her face. "You fucking ruin everything around you! You destroy everything!" I didn't want to feel the verbal hits, but I did. I fought to break Asher's hold, but I had no opening, no leverage.

"Get the hell out of here!" Asher shouted over my shoulder. I tried to jerk against him and got nowhere. "Don't call, and don't come back!"

She glared at me, holding her bleeding nose. "Be happy with your whore!" Trisha snapped before hurrying down the porch stairs.

"Can't be, the whore's leaving!" I shouted at her. I was raging mad. The guys laughed as she all but ran to her car. I was still shaking. Asher waited until Trisha had driven off before putting me down. I pushed my hair out of my face with a shaking hand. I turned and moved through the still laughing guys to my bag at the foot of the stairs that Rory had brought. I grabbed it and headed upstairs. "I'm taking a shower," I shot down at them. The guys were still laughing as I shut the bathroom door behind me.

I flipped the shower on and focused on getting the water just right. I held it together as I stripped down and stepped into the tub. As I stood under the spray, letting it soak my body and hair, I cried. Trisha was a bitch, yeah. But she wasn't wrong. I fucked up the guys' lives, and I'd screwed up Rory's. I required so much fucking help that the guys always ended up taking care of me. I hated it. Asher was going to have to take care of me for the next fucking week and why? Because I couldn't fucking nut up and deal with this shit. I had to stop asking them for help. I had to stop counting on them to take care of me. What did it get them? Nothing! I stood in the shower and had a small pity party. It didn't take long before I sounded pathetic even to me. Okay, Lexie, remember what Riley said. If they didn't think you were worth it, then they would have bailed already. But you lost control out there, you wailed on her. I broke one of the rules, and it made my gut knot. I needed to do better than this.

I sniffed and took my shower. I used Jessica's shampoo and conditioner. The conditioner surprised me. I checked the bottle and committed the name to memory. It was fucking great. Yeah, I was focusing on something besides the knot in my gut. I finished my shower, dried off and got dressed. I pulled on my black jeans and a loose black boyfriend shirt. I tried to towel dry my hair, but it wasn't working. I wondered if Jessica left a hairdryer here. There was a knock on the door. I was still trying to dry my hair, so I just said, "Come on in."

The door opened. Ethan stood in the doorway, his chocolate eyes running over me; he was frowning.

"You okay, Beautiful?"

I snorted. No, I wasn't, but I'd deal. I had put enough shit on them already. "Fine. Why?" My voice sounded weird even to me. I watched his eyes narrow on me in the mirror as I continued trying to dry my hair.

"Because you just beat the shit out of Trisha, then ran upstairs." His smoky voice was questioning.

I looked down at the sink. "I just... needed time to cool off," I muttered as I hung up my towel and started packing up my stuff. I heard him snort.

"Lexie, you're a bad liar."

I looked up at his reflection in the mirror. His eyes met mine, and they were storming. I looked back down into my bag and found my makeup kit. I pulled it out and went through it, more for something to do than to look for makeup. "Do you need the bathroom?" I asked, still pretending to focus on what I was doing.

"No." His voice was soft. "I wanted to know if Trisha's hits made contact."

I took a deep breath and gave him a reassuring smile in the mirror. "I'm fine, Ethan." I started pulling out the makeup I was going to use. I needed better control over myself. It made my chest tight; I didn't want to talk about it. I didn't want to think about what it meant.

"Then why don't I believe you?" Ethan asked.

I shrugged then focused on putting on my eyeliner, so I didn't have to look at him when I told him. "I lost control when I heard her," I whispered. "Then I was outside, and I was hitting her. I broke a rule."

He sighed. "Lexie, what you did out there? She fucking deserved it." I stopped doing my eyeliner to look at him in the mirror. His chocolate eyes were watching me. "She left you for dead. I think hitting her was the least she deserved."

I braced my hands on the sink, my eyes on the drain. "I lost control," I said softly.

His hand was warm on my lower back as he stepped up next to me at the sink. "Think about the memories you have now, think about the pain you've been in the last couple days because of her." His smoky voice was quiet, soft; it made me want to listen. "You losing control for a minute is understandable." I went still; this didn't sound like Ethan.

I looked up to meet his eyes in the mirror. "Miles tell you to say that?"

He grinned at me. "I told him what I thought was wrong; he told me what to say that would help." He shrugged. "I'm not as good with the emotional shit as he is. I'm... well, I'm wired differently." I chuckled, shaking my head as I looked back down at the sink. He leaned over, resting his chin on my shoulder. "The point is, no one has control all the time. Everyone breaks once in a while. This time it just happened to be Trisha's nose." I snorted and looked in the mirror to see him grinning mischievously. His warm eyes met mine again as his fingers rubbed my lower back. "Don't be too hard on yourself, Beautiful. You're not perfect," he said gently. I nodded, letting him know I had heard him. He gave me a quick kiss on the cheek before leaving the bathroom.

The knots in my stomach were gone. Yeah, I had lost control, but I was only human. Or Necromancer. Was there a difference? I really hoped not. I focused on getting ready for the party.

CHAPTER 20

SATURDAY NIGHT

That night, as I waited for Dylan to pick me up, my stomach was one huge knot. I checked my clothes again for the fifth time. The same black jeans, black V-neck shirt, and boots. I was still wearing the necklace Dylan had given me. It was a big contrast against the black. My makeup was my usual day makeup. I looked at my hair again. Thanks to Jessica's hair dryer, my hair was in a long mass down to almost my waist now. I was going to need a haircut soon. Did I want to do something different? Did I want to for me or because I was nervous about seeing Dylan? Fuck it. I played with the hair tie on my wrist.

I was still contemplating my clothes when there was a knock on the front door. He had showed up. Yay! Those knots tripled over each other. I took a breath and grabbed my coat. I made sure I had everything before I left the family room. My heart was racing as I opened the door. Dylan was standing on the porch. His chestnut hair was rumpled as usual. He was wearing blue jeans and a dark gray thermal under his coat. I noticed the bags under his eyes. My chest ached. Please be okay. Come on Lexie, only one way to find out. Dylan's sapphire eyes warmed up when he saw me, then he smiled. The knots disappeared completely. He was okay. We were okay.

"Hey you," I said, smiling.

"Hey, you ready?" His husky voice rolled through my ear, and I was just happy to hear it.

"Yeah, the guys are already out at the party." I stepped out and locked the door behind me. Zeke had said it wouldn't hurt to leave Hades alone for a few hours; he needed to learn I wasn't disappearing. Dylan took my hand as we headed to his truck. "Did you get any more sleep?"

"Yeah, I passed out. Woke up a few hours ago. Watch the ice, Sunshine," he warned me. I looked down and walked carefully around the ice patch. He held onto me till I got to the passenger side of the truck.

Then he turned me towards him and kissed the hell out of me. My heart raced, butterflies went nuts, and something inside me relaxed. He was kissing me like I was the air he needed to breathe. I kissed him back the same way. It erased every doubt I had, every fear I had about him. No one could kiss you like that and not care about you. When he eased back, we were both out of breath.

His glowing eyes met mine. "Sorry, I really needed that," he whispered.

I smiled up at him. "Me too," I admitted.

He smirked down at me before stepping back. "Come on. We have a party to go to," he said as he opened the door of the truck. I climbed in, and he closed it behind me. That was a first. Dylan hurried around the truck, hitting the hood twice, and climbed it. He didn't even realize he did it. I smiled. Oh, this guy... I took a breath as he drove onto the road. That warm feeling was still running through me. Okay, no drinking tonight, Lexie. I smirked at myself.

Dylan was telling me about his shift at the store yesterday when he pulled up to the Henderson's. They were rich, almost Miles rich. The house was enormous and sprawling. And packed with people already.

"Wow; Ethan said awesome parties but..." Dylan snorted.

"More like epic."

He smiled over at me. "I'm driving, you drinking, Sunshine?"

I thought about it. With those memories running around in my head? Fuck no. "Nah."

He smiled at me. "Come on. The guys are probably waiting," he said. I got out of the truck and slid to the ground. I closed the door and met Dylan at the front. His face was relaxed as he took my hand and we entered the house. The house was huge. There was cedar everywhere: the stairs, the exposed beams. It looked like anywhere they could they put cedar, they did. It was overwhelming.

Dylan led me through the crowd, and I was too short to see if the guys were around. So, when he pulled me into a large room with music playing, I thought the guys were in here. But nope. Dylan took my jacket off and set it down then took his off too. Then he pulled me onto what seemed to be the dance floor. The music was slow and, well, sultry. It reminded me of hot summer nights. Dylan pulled my arms around his neck then wrapped his arms around me. I smiled as he leaned down, his lips going to my ear.

"I just wanted you to myself for a couple more minutes," he whispered in that soft low voice that sent shivers down my spine. "Before your big brothers find us and all."

I snickered. Oh, poor delusional Dylan. I had already spotted Isaac in the doorway of the room out of the corner of my eye. I waved Isaac away; he got the hint and moved on before Dylan saw him. I ran my eyes over his face. His bags were dark, and the lines around his eyes were deeper than usual.

"Honey, are you okay? You look like you haven't slept at all."

His eyes were warm as they ran over my face. "Yeah, babe, I just had some trouble sleeping the other night, and I didn't make up as much as I thought I would today," he mumbled, still looking at me as if he was memorizing me.

"Wanna bail? I'm pretty sure I can find a place for you to take a nap," I offered, smiling.

He gave me a big smile. "No, Sunshine. I don't want to be anywhere else right now," he whispered, pulling me closer until he had me pressed hard against him.

I tightened my arms around his neck. I must have really scared the shit out of him. Fuck. He rested his cheek against mine and danced with me. Another song came on, and it was another slow one. He just kept holding on to me. That warmth washed over me again, filling my heart. I moved one of my hands to the back of his neck and started massaging. He groaned and dropped his head to my shoulder.

"I scared you again, didn't I?" I asked softly. I kept my hand working on his neck, it was like a rock.

"Little bit," he mumbled.

"I'm sorry." I swallowed hard. "That was newish, even for me." He tightened his arms around me; it was almost painful now, but I didn't say anything about it. "That's my new three; my old three is four now." I didn't know what else to say, so I just worked the knots out of his neck.

"Don't worry about it, Sunshine," he said, his face pressing against my neck. "Just let me hold you right now." I nodded.

When I was done with the knots on his neck, he lifted his head and ran an arm up my back, his hand cupping the back of my head. I rested my cheek against his chest. His lips rested on my forehead. I was warm, loved, and smelling sandalwood. I was happy there. This must have been the slow music room because he danced with me, holding me like that for four songs. When he was ready, his arms loosened and he lifted my chin. He gave one of his amazing slow, sweet, chaste kisses that got my blood pumping.

When he eased back, he was smiling. "Okay, let's go find the guys." He sounded so not thrilled.

"If you want to see some of your friends, we can." I thought that was obvious; he hadn't introduced me to his in-town friends yet.

He shook his head. "Most everyone is in Dulcet tonight." He sighed. "I'm all yours." I raised an eyebrow at him and grinned wickedly. He seemed to know where my head was because he chuckled and smiled at me. "Sunshine, don't tempt me tonight."

I winked at him then went to get our coats. I handed him his; he took my hand, and we went out to look for the guys. We found them at a pool table in a game room. I smiled as we reached them. The guys were all standing around, talking to girls and watching the game. I put my coat down and got close enough to look at the table. Isaac was playing some guy. He was around Asher's height, had blond hair and gray eyes. The guy wasn't too bad on the eyes. And he was doing decent on the table.

"Hey, guys," I greeted them, smiling.

"Hey, Lexie," Zeke said.

"Hi, Beautiful."

"Hey, Ally."

"Hey, Red." Isaac's voice was grumpy. He must be stripes. I looked at the table again and got pissed. There was money on the table.

"Isaac, what are you doing?" I snapped at him. Dylan put his coat down and stood behind me; I leaned back against him a little. His hands went to my hips, his thumbs making circles. Isaac looked at me.

"Losing," he grumbled.

Ethan came away from the table to talk to us. "Guy totally sharked him. He was acting drunk, and now he's sober," Ethan whispered, filling us in.

"How much?" I growled low.

"Only thirty bucks." Ethan smiled. "But that'll teach him." Ethan pulled back and went back to watching the game.

I watched the other guy. He wasn't that good. My wicked side came out to play. I leaned back into Dylan. "Want to kick someone's ass at pool? Or should I?" I whispered.

Dylan chuckled softly and looked in my eyes. "You; it'll be so much more fun." I smiled big and gave him a quick kiss. Then I turned back to watch the other guy sink an easy eight ball shot. He raised his arm like it was a huge victory, not thirty bucks. It pissed me off.

"Hey!" I shot at the guy. I walked away from Dylan and towards the table. The guy saw me, then ran his eyes over me before looking at my face. Yeah, an asshole. "Double or nothing." His eyes warmed as he smiled cockily. The guys went still.

"You got it, Red."

"You don't call her Red," Isaac snapped at him. "I call her Red. You can use her name."

The guy's eyebrows went up. Then he looked over at me. "Which is?"

"Lexie. And you are?" I asked sweetly. Yeah, I knew it wasn't fair, but the fucker messed with Isaac. If he hadn't acted drunk to get Isaac to play, I wouldn't care. But he had, so I cared.

"Doyle Barns." He held out his hand over the table.

I reached out and shook it. My hand instantly felt slimy. "Nice to meet you." When I got my hand back, I was hard pressed not to wipe it on my jeans.

"You want to rack or break, Lexie?" His voice grew warm. Was he...? Oh... no.

"I'll break if you don't mind." I batted my eyes at him. Isaac turned away, having a hard time not smiling.

Doyle grinned at me. "No, problem." He went to rack, and I went to find a cue that was right for me. I had just found a good, straight one when Doyle spoke up. "You want some help getting wood?" I went still; the guys went still. Oh, stupid move pal. But he didn't know that.

I turned and smiled sweetly at him. "Oh no, a girl never has trouble finding a good stick to use when she needs it," I countered. Doyle smiled. Dylan chuckled, and Zeke looked like he was going to have a heart attack. Riley and the others just laughed.

"Shit... Lexie..." Zeke grumbled and covered his eyes. I snickered. Doyle didn't notice Zeke.

I chalked my cue, taking my time because this wasn't going to take long. At least, it shouldn't. And if I were wrong, then I would learn something myself. Doyle was waiting. I kept my face sweet as I went to my favorite corner to break. I noticed the guys smiling out of the corner of my eye. I focused on my shot. Then I took it. The balls scattered everywhere, and three went in during the break. I stood and smiled at Doyle. He was frowning at the table. Then he looked up at me, catching on.

"I'll take solids." The guys burst out laughing. Dylan had a big smile on his face. I smirked and moved around the table to a good shot. Doyle kept frowning. And after I sank three more balls, he got pissed.

When I didn't have a shot, I gave him a shitty one. He glared at me and went to try his shot. He missed. I made another shot then another. I called my pocket for the eight ball and made it without scratching.

He cursed. "Are you fucking kidding me?" he growled, glaring at me.

I smiled sweetly as I went to the money pile we both had added to. I picked it up and counted it out. Doyle was still gaping at me when I walked around the table. "Never play pool shark. Because there is always someone bigger and badder than you that will tear you to pieces." I smiled sweetly. "This one just happens to come in a smaller and cuter package than you."

I held up his half of the money to him between two fingers. He wasn't glaring at me anymore. He was grinning. He took his money and counted it.

Then he looked back down at me. "You're giving the rest to Isaac?" he asked.

"Oh, hell no." I snickered. Doyle laughed.

"Red!" Isaac sounded surprised.

I turned and looked at him. "You know better than to do this shit," I shot at him. "I'm keeping your cash." Everyone was laughing now but Isaac, who was grumbling. I kept laughing.

"You single?" Doyle asked, surprising me.

I pointed behind me to Dylan. "Nope."

Doyle looked at Dylan. "Your girl's hot, man." Oh, ew.

I backed away from Doyle, and the guys stopped laughing.

Dylan stayed where he was. "Look all you want," he said, which surprised me. "But touch her and die." Yep, that was more along the line that I was thinking. The guys snickered around the table. Doyle eyed Dylan playfully like he was sizing him up. Yeah, I didn't like that. Neither did the guys. They shifted in their seats.

"I think I can take you," Doyle said jokingly.

Dylan chuckled. "Oh, it wouldn't be me." Dylan tilted his chin to me. "It'd be her."

Doyle gave me a contemplating look. "Hmm."

Oh, double ew. "Yeah," I smiled sweetly. "And if that didn't work..."

I smiled sweetly and pointed to the boys. He turned and froze. Zeke was glaring at him now, popping his knuckles. Riley was watching from her seat, but all the guys had moved forward. Doyle went white. "Every Lexie action figure comes with a boyfriend and four enormous best friends. Well, five, but one of them isn't here tonight," I said sweetly. The guys burst out laughing; even Doyle laughed at that one.

He held his hands up and backed away, smiling. His eyes ran over me one more time. "Damn girl," Doyle mumbled before walking off.

I burst out laughing and looked at the guys. Oh, that was funny. Dylan snagged my hand and pulled me back to him. He wrapped his arm around my waist, and I leaned back against his chest. The guys all sat back down.

"Red, you're giving me my money back, right?" Isaac asked hopefully. I just smiled and shook my head. He grumbled. The guys laughed. I was happy.

It wasn't long before Dylan pulled me away from the guys to dance with me in the slow music room again.

He held me close and whispered in my ear. "So, what are your plans this summer?" he asked. I smiled as I remembered the surfing trip he wanted to take me on. But...

"I was hoping to get a part-time job at the tattoo place in town just to learn about how a shop is run." I shrugged. "They probably won't hire me."

He kissed my cheek. "Then you'll need to show up every day and be a pain in the ass until they do." His voice sounded like he was smiling. I snickered. Yeah, that did sound like something I would do.

"I probably will. I just want my foot in the door." I brushed my lips against his earlobe and heard him catch his breath.

"What about you, honey? Still planning that surfing trip?" I asked softly.

His arms tightened around me. "I'm hoping to, but with the way things are going, I might have to skip this year," he whispered back.

"What's going on?" I asked.

He sighed. "You remember that science project?" he asked, his hand starting to run up and down my back.

"Yeah, for that scholarship," I said. One of his hands moved around the back of my neck and rubbed the muscles there. I dropped my head to his chest instantly.

He snickered. "There are some problems with it," he said, still massaging my neck. "I might have to can the whole thing and start over." I made a moany noise to let him know I'd heard him. His fingers felt like magic. I focused on what he had said.

"I'm sorry. I know you've been busting your ass on it." I didn't know what else to say. I didn't understand it enough to try and help him figure it out. I suddenly wished I was Miles. Or, as smart as Miles at least. I felt his lips on the back of my neck before his fingers let go. I looked back up at him. "I wish there was something I could do to help."

His warm eyes ran over my face as he gave me a small, sad smile. "Me too, Sunshine." He pulled me close again and rested his forehead on mine as he danced with me.

It wasn't long before my cell vibrated. I pulled it out and checked.

Ethan: Your turn. Game room, poker table.

I sighed and looked up at Dylan.

"I need to go take Isaac duty," I grumbled. He raised an eyebrow. "Isaac picks fights when he's drunk, so we watch for the signs then yank him out before it happens." He shook his head and sighed. "Wanna come with?" He nodded.

Before I could walk off, he pulled me back and kissed me. It was a hard, desperate kiss on the dance floor. It felt like our kiss the other night in the parking lot. Just reversed. My body filled with heat as his mouth kept moving on mine. I kissed him back, forgetting where we were. He didn't, thankfully. He eased back and looked down at me.

"Wow." I was trying to get my thinking... thing... moving again after that kiss.

He smiled and chuckled. "Just, needed to do that," he whispered, leaning down and kissing my forehead. I smiled. Okay, boyfriend... amazing kisser. I loved kissing him.

It took me a couple of minutes to get my wits back. I blinked hard and looked around. "Okay, um... yeah... Isaac duty... yeah..." I mumbled before turning away and heading through the crowd. Dylan kept hold of my hand, laughing the whole way.

We joined the poker game with Isaac. Dylan sat across from me, throwing me flirty winks and smiles for the next hour. It kept making me smile. The guy was nuts. Or crazy about me. Was there really a difference anymore? I decided there wasn't. I looked over and saw that Isaac had gone quiet. Not good.

"Cookie Monster, go for a walk," I said firmly as I reached for another card. Isaac looked up at me and met my eyes. I winked at him. He gave me a half grin and nodded. He got up and went to take that walk. Dylan raised an eyebrow at me. I shrugged.

"And if he didn't go?" he asked, smirking.

I smiled. "Then it wouldn't have been a suggestion," I admitted unrepentantly. "I'd make him go, and the guys would be following." Dylan smirked. I picked up my soda and found it empty.

"I'm getting another soda. You want one?" I asked, looking at him across the poker table.

"Yeah, thanks, Sunshine." He gave me a warm smile that warmed me to my toes.

Soda, definitely soda. No beer tonight, not a good idea. I got up and dropped the cans into the trash then went to the big cooler across the room. I pulled out the sodas and was heading back when some guy stepped out of a group of people into my path. I went to walk around, and he moved with me. I looked up smiling, thinking it was an accident. He had short cropped black hair and brown eyes; that was all I got before he leaned in closer to my face until I could smell the tequila on his breath.

"Hey, fire crotch." His words were slurred, but I heard the fucker.

My temper flashed. I pulled back, instantly wanting blood. I dropped the cans, balled my fist, reached back, and clocked the bastard across the face. He went down hard. I wasn't done yet. That fucker was never going to say that to me again. I walked over to him still on the ground, and I kept punching my fist into his face until I heard his nose break. I saw red. I still wasn't done. A big hand grabbed my arm and spun me around. I felt a wide shoulder in my stomach, and suddenly I was upside down. A big hand was on the back of my knee, keeping me on his shoulder. I smelled leather and engine grease.

"Zeke! Put me down! I'm gonna kill that fucker!" I shouted, I started smacking his back and tried kicking to get him to let me go. He didn't even bother answering me. "I'm going to break that fucker's balls!" I shouted, pushing myself up on his back to see the others following. Dylan was checking on the asshole I'd hit.

"Ally, calm down until we get you outside," Asher called to me. I flipped him off. The guys laughed. Oh, laugh it up, shit heads, wait till I was on the ground again.

"Put me the fuck down, Zeke!" I started hitting him in the back with my fist, but I wasn't managing to get much momentum. He didn't seem to feel it at all. The air got cold as Zeke strode outside. I stopped fighting and just hung there. There was no point; the shit head was too strong for me. Isaac joined the others as they followed.

When we were almost across the lawn to the cars, Zeke finally put me down. I immediately tried to go back inside, but the guys had spread out in a line to keep me from getting past them. So, I paced, fuming. Riley was watching from the front porch. I was shaking I was so pissed off.

"What did he do, Lexie?" Zeke barked at me.

I was so angry I answered without thinking. "He called me 'fire crotch,'" I snapped. Zeke's face grew hard, his eyes darkening. He turned and headed back towards the house, furious. Oh no! If I didn't get to kill him, Zeke sure as hell wasn't going to get to. "Riley! Stop him!" I shouted.

"How?" Riley asked, moving to the porch stairs.

"Block him! Grab him! Fuck, kiss him! He's not going to hurt you!"

Zeke had reached the porch. Riley stepped in front of him. Zeke tried to go left; she went left. He tried right; she went right. He glared down at her. She smiled. Zeke's jaw was still clenched when he looked over at me. "You fucking cheat, Lexie!" Zeke shouted.

"No shit!" I shot back sarcastically. "If I don't get to kick his ass then you sure as hell don't!"

Dylan walked out of the house, his face dark as he passed Zeke and

Riley. His eyes were on me as he crossed the lawn. When he got here, the others backed off.

"You got her?" Ethan asked. Dylan nodded, his jaw clenching. The guys went back in the house; they wouldn't go far. When they were out of sight, Dylan turned back to me, his face furious. What the...?

"What the hell, Lexie?" he all but shouted at me. "You broke that guy's nose."

"He called me 'fire crotch,'" I shot back.

His face went blank. "He did?" I nodded. His face relaxed, but his eyes were still storming.

"Yeah, that's why I hit him," I pointed out sarcastically. I stopped pacing and pulled on my coat the guys had brought out with them. I needed to stay outside till my temper cooled off.

"Good," he sighed, sounding tired. "All right, Sunshine, let's get out of here." I nodded.

He took my hand and headed back through the cars to his truck. While we were waiting for the truck to warm up, I texted the guys, letting them know Dylan was taking me home. The drive back to Asher's was quiet, though Dylan kept hold of my hand the whole way. I was too busy feeling the bruises on my knuckles to talk. My fucking right hand hurt. Dylan pulled up to Asher's and shut off the truck. He was still quiet as we went up to the door. Hades was already barking at me. I smiled proudly. That was my fierce little baby.

"You'll finally get to meet Hades." I was still smiling as I unlocked the door.

"That'd be nice." Dylan sounded distracted. Probably worrying about the drive home.

I opened the door, and my black ball of love scrambled to me and jumped up to rest his paws on my knees. "Hey, baby," I said sweetly to him as I bent down to pick him up. He went sniff crazy on my face. Could dogs tell if you'd been kissing someone? I stepped further into the house and turned on the lights. Dylan followed me into the living room. I held Hades against my chest and turned toward Dylan. "Hades, this is Dylan. Don't lick him to death."

Dylan snorted as he looked at my ball of love. "What breed is he?" he asked, smiling as he reached out and petted Hades' head.

"Neapolitan Mastiff," I answered. Dylan stopped petting Hades to look at me with a raised eyebrow. "Apparently, he's going to outweigh me. But Zeke's going to help me train him, so he'll listen when he's that big." Hades whined. "And he needs to go out. Give me a minute."

"No problem." Dylan still sounded distracted.

I put it out of my mind and took Hades out back to do his business. When he was done, he started jumping into little piles of snow and dug until they were destroyed; then he would move onto another pile. I was laughing as I brought him back into the house. I put him down in the kitchen, and he ran to his food bowl. I headed back to the foyer and started taking off my jacket.

"That little bugger apparently hates snow piles. He destroyed three of them and was going for more," I said over my shoulder as I put my jacket on the banister as usual.

"Oh, yeah?" Dylan said absently. I walked back into the living room to find him pacing.

"Yeah," I narrowed my eyes at him. His face was pale. "Are you okay?"

He stopped pacing to look at me. "Lexie, this isn't working."

I went still. Did he just say...? "What?" My heart was already aching, but I just needed to be sure I had heard him right. Because this was a hit I hadn't seen coming.

"The fucking distance is too much, the driving and never seeing each other," he started rambling. I looked at him as my heart clenched tight. He was breaking up with me? He wouldn't look at me as he explained how we would never see each other when school started anyway, so we might as well end it now. It felt like I'd been kicked in the chest. I wrapped my arms around my stomach as if that was going to fucking help. Thankfully, by the time he was done with that speech, I was pissed. Otherwise I would have been crying.

"Bullshit," I called him on it. He finally looked at me again. My eyes were filling anyway. Fuck! "This isn't about distance. It's about what happened at the bowling alley. My seizures." I took a shaky breath as I watched him struggle with how to answer that. I didn't let him. He had spoken, now it was my turn. "You saw how bad they could get. And you flipped the fuck out. Right?" I felt a tear roll down my face, but I didn't look away from him. "Tell me I'm wrong, and I'll believe you." I refused to look away.

"You're not wrong." His voice was quiet. I took a breath through the tightness in my chest. "You just have a lot of problems, Lexie, and I can't take care of you all the time. I've got my own shit going on at home." That felt like a kick to the gut.

I nodded. "I get it." My voice cracked. Fuck. I was so pissed at him; he fucking kept telling me he wasn't going to leave. He kept telling me he was staying. And I had fucking started believing him. And now, one messy thing happened, and he was out the fucking door. I took a breath. "Why did you even come down tonight? When you could have fucking told me this on the phone?"

He swallowed hard. "I wanted one more good memory, before...." His voice was thick now. Like he had something to be fucking upset about. Anger burned through me.

"Well, thank you, for fucking with me all night so you could have a good fucking memory!" I snapped at him. I couldn't fucking believe this. "I just spent all night thinking we were fine, and that I was fal-" I stopped myself. No, he didn't get to hear that. I looked at him again. His face was pained, drawn. "And you were already gone."

His throated worked hard as he swallowed. He looked at the foyer over my shoulder. "It doesn't mean I don't care about yo-"

"That's exactly what it means, Dylan," I told him, my voice almost calm. But inside I was raging. "You're breaking up with me because I have seizures." I scoffed. "And if that is all it took for you to stop caring about me this much, then fuck off." I felt another tear fall, and this time he saw it.

He stepped closer, the lines on his face becoming deeper. "Sunshine-"

"Don't you fucking dare," I growled at him. He closed his eyes then looked down at the floor. He started taking deep breaths. "Don't ever fucking call me that again." I stepped away from him and wiped my face. He needed to leave, and he seemed to know it.

He was walking by me, out to the foyer, when he stopped next to me. "I'm sorry Su... Lexie," he whispered softly, his voice thick. Why was he fucking upset? He was the one doing this. He had probably just realized he hurt me. Dylan wasn't unfeeling... just an asshole.

"Drive safe," I muttered looking down at the wood floor. He closed the front door behind him, and I kept it together until I heard his truck drive off.

I gasped as the pain hit full force. My chest felt like it was on fire, and my stomach was rolling so much I thought I was going to puke. Tears fell down my face, and I couldn't seem to stop them. I sat down on the couch. I just needed a couple of minutes to... I pulled my tissues out and blew my nose. I struggled to get myself under control.

That fucking asshole. He lied to me! He said he'd be there for me. Then to come down here and fucking... pretend all night that things were fine. Then bam! He dumped me, just like that. I snorted. How could someone fucking do that to another person? No wonder he fucking kissed me that way when he first saw me. And every fucking chance he had tonight. He knew he wasn't going to get another one. I pushed the pain back. Yeah, I was going to have to deal with it but not here. Not now.

Right now, I had to go upstairs and work on the link to the Veil. As always, the fucking dead took priority. I sat there until I had control of myself again. It took some time. It wasn't a lot of control, but it was what I had. I picked up Hades and headed upstairs. Tonight, I decided just to cut out the middleman and work in the bathroom. There was no point in going to Asher's room. I was just going to end up in here anyway. I snorted. I always did. I set Hades down and leaned against the tub. I took a breath, closed my eyes, and dropped to my center.

It was quick and easy; I was on the white sandy plain and under that golden sky almost immediately. I looked around at the empty sand. Yeah. That felt about right. I snorted then thought about the Veil. I was whisked to the edge of my center, the link I was building, and the open field of stars. It was beautiful. I walked the bridge till I reached the end of what I had managed. I had a good thirty feet to go. Well, with the way I felt tonight, I didn't give a fuck. I pressed my palms together and pushed against the fabric of the world. Pain tore through me as I pushed, every nerve burning. I growled through my teeth. Today was not the day to fuck with me. I kept moving, ignoring the knives dragging along my nerves. I just pushed and pushed. I couldn't help but think about Dylan and the way he left me. The fucking fake he'd been all night. The lies I had believed. It helped me keep going.

I passed my usual stopping point; then I passed my next. I was a few feet further when I got dizzy, and I stopped pushing. I felt the wetness on my face and knew I had a bloody nose in the real world. Like always. It didn't fucking matter. I looked out over the distance I had left. I had covered a third of the distance left. I had to stop. I closed my eyes and focused. I went back and up.

I OPENED MY EYES, and the world spun. I would have closed them, but my stomach lurched. I moved to the toilet and was sick again and again. I held my own hair back as I emptied everything I had in my stomach and destroyed any desire to eat ever again. My body felt like it had exploded; my vision was fading in and out with my pulse. When I was done puking, I tried to sit up, but the room tilted, and I was back on the tile. Fuck. It felt like the world was on a boat in rough seas. It kept rising and dropping, throwing me from side to side. I closed my eyes and reached for the toilet paper. It took me a few tries. The cold tile felt good against my cheek, so I just stayed there. No point in getting up right now. I couldn't. I just laid there waiting till my nose stopped bleeding. When it was done, I figured I should get up. I could do this on my own after all, right? I snickered at myself as I sat up, and the world spun like a tilt-a-whirl. I held on to the tub and waited for it to stop. It didn't. It kept spinning. Of fucking course. I tried to get to my feet. The world gave a lurch, and I hit the tile again.

Fuck it. I gave up. I stretched out on the tile, enjoying the cold against my face. I'd just stay here and die. Then everyone's problems would be solved. My head kept throbbing; I could hear my pulse in my ears. Stupid fucking Lexie, can't even get your ass to the next room without help. This Necromancy shit was just going to keep coming and coming. It was never going to go away. It was going to drag me down, and I was going to take the boys with me. I felt tears falling and didn't give a shit. They had to fucking sleep next to me so that I could sleep. You broken shit! I'd taken over their lives. I felt something wet on my face. I opened my eyes to the tilting and spinning world to find Hades licking my forehead. I smiled. I'd probably destroy your life too. I closed my eyes again.

Too many problems. I snorted and immediately regretted it. My face felt like I had taken a hit. At least my nose hadn't started bleeding again. Dylan was right. I did have too many fucking issues. My temper and tendency towards violence alone were hard to take. Add in the other bullshit.... No one could handle that shit. Not all the time. It was too much. The guys had to juggle me already. I needed to stop letting them. They needed to stop babysitting me... They needed to enjoy their lives.

I didn't have much time left anyway. Every woman in my family had died before they were thirty. The dead just took over their lives. They either went out being jumped or by committing suicide. Claire hadn't been the first, but she'd be the last. No kids for me. I gave a sick, twisted laugh that echoed off the tile and bounced around the walls. I couldn't even have that. Why the fuck was I bothering with anything? I was seventeen and half, and my life was gone. I didn't stop laughing. I became light headed. That was probably a bad thing, but right then I didn't give a fuck. I just laid on the floor, in pain, and for the first time in my life, I didn't care if anyone found me or not.

I needed to let the guys go. I had to let them go... for them... It was better if I was alone... the guys wouldn't get hurt. They could go back to their regularly scheduled lives. I giggled at that. Regularly scheduled... hehe... normal. They could have normal. While I laid there for however long it was, I ran in dark circles through my head.

Hades started barking. I didn't bother trying to move. I wasn't going anywhere till morning, and it really didn't matter. A door opened. There were voices. A deep, gravelly voice and a rich baritone were talking. I liked the sounds. The tile felt perfect right now. It sucked the heat right out of my body. I liked it. Hades was barking again. I couldn't do anything about it, so I tried to ignore it and the pain still running through my head. I slipped a little further towards the darkness that was pulling me down.

"Hades?" The barking kept going. It was a cute bark. As if from far off, there were footsteps. Whoever it was should stay away, I just destroyed everything anyway. The barking wouldn't stop.

"Lexie!" The floor shook; rough hands grabbed me. I groaned as they pulled me up into big arms. The floor had felt so good, though. Put me back. "Asher!" I felt a light, hesitant tapping on my face; a loud thumping was getting closer. "Wake up, Baby, what's wrong?"

"Floor good," I muttered wishing he'd just leave. Let me stay here. Didn't he know he should stay away?

"What happened?" the rich voice asked.

I knew those voices... Tough Guy and Superman... I snorted.

"I found her on the floor," Tough Guy growled.

I tried to move to go back to the floor. "Tile good. Floor good," I muttered.

Tough Guy changed his grip and wouldn't let me budge.

"Are you drunk?" Superman asked.

I laughed that sick twisted laugh again. I should be... that would probably be good.

"She wasn't drinking," Tough Guy reminded him.

"You guys shouldn't be here... you should go away," I mumbled, unable to do much else.

"She sounds drunk," Superman pointed out. "She was planning Veil work tonight. She must have pushed it too far."

"Better for you guys…. just leave... let me deal... you can have normal…." I muttered with my eyes still closed.

"What the fuck is she saying?" Tough Guy snapped.

I didn't like that. I lifted a limp hand and tried to pat him on the chest, but with my eyes closed, I had bad aim. I hit something, but I didn't know what or cared.

"Leave me here... be happy..." I muttered. "I got this..."

"No, Ally, you really don't." Superman's voice was strained.

"Don't take care of me... I like floor anyway...."

"We're not leaving you on the fucking floor!" Tough Guy spat at me.

I felt arms move around me. I smelled vanilla and cinnamon. Then I was lifted. I didn't want that. "No, no, no.... you go... don't have much time left anyway..." I muttered. "Tick, tick, tick."

"Ally, what are you saying, honey?"

We were moving, and I wanted them to leave. To go on with their lives without me. It was better for them. "Ruin everything..." I grumbled in Superman's arms. "No point... tic, tic, tic."

"What the fuck are you talking about?" Tough Guy growled.

"Stupid broken Lexie...... can't take care of herself... always needs a babysitter..." I grumbled in a weird voice. I was still floating in pain. "... no point...." I felt something soft under me. It felt almost as good as the tile.

"What's no point, Ally?" The arms holding me went away. I missed them, but it was better this way.

"... dragging you down too .... want you happy... alive.... tick, tick, tick," I mumbled. "Half time gone..." I rolled over into the softness and snuggled down. Someone brushed the hair off my face. "No more... babysitter. No more taking care of... you free.... tick, tick, tick."

"Where the hell is this coming from?" Superman wasn't happy.

I giggled into the softness. "Things will get worse... not taking you with me... tick, tick, tick... I'll miss you guys..." I mumbled.

"Lexie, you take on our problems too," Superman said gently.

I snorted; my face hurt. "Wha'... problems?" I mumbled. They snorted. I ignored it. My heart was breaking as the world started fading. "Just.... remember... me..." The world disappeared.

CHAPTER 21

SUNDAY

I woke up still hurting. I opened my eyes, and the light felt like needles to my brain. I closed my eyes a bit, taking the pain. I deserved it. I kept hurting everyone around me. When I could, I opened my eyes further. I was in Asher's room again. I snorted. Yeah, because you can't fucking sleep by yourself, you broken shit. I felt broken. Numb and sad, all at the same time. How did that happen? Numb and sad? I knew Asher was in bed; I could smell his vanilla and cinnamon, feel his hand on my back. I wanted to cuddle with him, have him take this empty feeling away. Have him make it better. I couldn't... wouldn't do that to them anymore. They deserved to be happy. They deserved... normal.

I got up slowly, moved around the bed and picked up my bag. I slipped out the door closing it behind me. He should sleep, he needed it. He spent too much time taking care of me. I went into the bathroom, closing the door behind me. I put my bag down on the toilet lid. I washed my face then used a towel to dry. I remembered laying on the floor in here last night. I remembered coming to my decision. I needed to leave. They shouldn't have to take care of me anymore. I put down the towel and looked in the mirror. My skin was as white as paper, my eyes no longer bright green but dull. I had deep bags under my eyes. I almost looked like a raccoon. I snorted at myself. It didn't fucking matter.

Focusing on one thing at a time, I changed into blue jeans, a black cami, and a pitch black, oversized sweater that almost reached my knees. I pulled on my boots and picked up my stuff. I shouldn't leave a mess for the boys. I snorted at myself again. They'd cleaned up enough of my messes already. I picked up my bag and went downstairs with that numb sadness still filling me. I found Zeke snoring on the couch with a sleeping Hades on his chest. Good. He'd take care of him. He loved dogs. I pulled on my coat then slipped outside, closing the door softly behind me.

The sun was just coming up, and it reminded me of the sky at my center. I went down the steps, cursing myself. Nothing ever reminded me of something normal, not anymore. I headed toward the cemetery. My truck should still be there. I'd go work the link, pass out, then do it again. However long it took, I was getting this shit done. Then the guys could go back to their lives. And I could just deal with my shit. No more calling for help, no more dragging them down with me. They deserved better than to have a life with one foot in the grave. I didn't. I was born here. I would die here. Tick, tick, tick. And that was the way it would always be.

I walked the distance to the cemetery through the snow, not really seeing anything except the path in front of me. My mind was empty, clear of thought. Nothing but the tick, tick, tick of my life clock counting down till I was dead. Half my life was gone. Why the fuck was I making plans? What was the point? The dead were just going to take over.

When I reached the truck, it was covered in snow. It didn't matter. I wasn't going anywhere. The cemetery was covered in a thick blanket of snow too. This was where I was supposed to be, right? With the dead. I unlocked the truck and climbed in the driver's side. I put my bag on the passenger seat. I didn't bother to waste any more time.

I closed my eyes and dropped to my center. That fucking empty white plain greeted me. And I didn't care that it was empty. I thought about the Veil, and I was yanked to the edge of my center. I didn't bother looking at the void. I went to the end of the bridge, pressed my hands together and pushed. Pain filled me where before there was nothing. I cried today as I worked. Every nerve felt like it was scorching, but I kept pushing. I needed to be ready for Sophie. I needed to let the boys go. I needed to fucking stop taking over their lives. I pushed harder. I passed my first stopping point, then my next. When I got dizzy again, I didn't stop. I pushed until my stomach rolled. I checked the distance, everything tilting. I had closed a little more than half the distance left. One more time and I'd be there. The guys would be free of me. I was yanked back and thrown upward.

My body felt like it had exploded. I opened the door and tried to be sick. I had nothing in me, so I dry heaved over and over. My stomach cramped and lurched. It hated me; my body hated me. I didn't blame it. I hated me too right now. When the heaving stopped, I pulled out tissues and opened my eyes. The world spun and tilted. It was like last night, only worse. I used my memory of the Blazer to climb into the back, using the side of the truck to keep me up. By the time I reached my sleeping bag, I wanted to barf again. I didn't. I climbed into my sleeping bag and was out almost immediately.

BANGING BROUGHT me back to the surface, not a lot, just enough to hear and barely understand. A wave of cold washed over my face. I didn't care. I was going to pass out again.

"Lexie, what the fuck do you think you're doing?" Tough Guy's voice was sharp and hard.

"She looks like shit, worse than yesterday." Superman cursed.

I giggled... Superman cursed... warm hands touched my face. I felt tapping on my cheek. I opened my eyes; my eyes burned, and the world spun. I closed them again. "Go away," I grumbled. "I fine..." My head felt raw and sore... everything inside was... big... raw... hurting.

"You are most definitely not fine," Superman snapped. It hurt inside.

"She sounds drunk again," Tough Guy grumbled. "Let's get her back to the house."

"I'll get her. You get the door."

A zipper opened, and it got cold. "Uh-uh... stay here... better for you..."

"Knock that fucking shit off, Lexie!" Tough Guy growled.

I felt the hit inside. I was too raw right now. It was too much. Tears slid down my face.

"Shit," Superman snapped. "You made her cry."

"What the fuck is going on?" Tough Guy growled. "I've said shit like that to her before."

"Zeke, she's exhausted. And for some reason, she just walked two miles in the snow. I don't think there's a lot of thinking happening right now."

Someone's arms pulled me out of the warmth and lifted me. "No, no, no..." I grumbled against a chest that smelled like vanilla. "You go home... I stay. No more... babysitting." Everything went quiet. I started slipping back under.

"Ally, do you want us to stop taking care of you?"

"No point... waste of time... tick, tick, tick..."

"Fuck that," Tough Guy snapped. "You're coming home whether you like it or not. You're going to sleep, and when you wake the fuck up, we're having a family meeting."

"Leave me here... live lives...." I was suddenly laying down somewhere warm. I liked the warmth.

"Why the fuck is she pushing herself this hard?" Tough Guy bit out from somewhere close by.

"Because... there's a particular soul she doesn't want to let down."

"No, no, no...... Superman.... shh...." I groaned and tried to move. A hand went to my shoulder, stopping me. It wasn't hard; the hand was heavy.

"Fuck the soul; she's killing herself," Tough Guy growled.

"It's Sophie."

I made a whimpering, crying noise. "Bad Superman... you told... no cookies for you..." I mumbled. I had tried so hard...

"Sophie?" Tough Guy's voice wavered. My heart hurt.

"Yeah, she's been practically killing herself so she can help her cross when she's ready to." Superman just wouldn't stop talking.

"Fuck!" Tough Guy practically shouted. "That's why she set this pace? For Sophie?"

"Yeah."

"Lexie…" Calloused fingers stroked my face, brushing my hair off my cheek. It felt good. "You can't kill yourself doing this."

"Tick, tick, tick…. doesn't matter… halftime up… in third quarter now…" I mumbled.

"What the fuck is that about?" Tough Guy demanded.

"Let's get her inside and call Rory. He might know," Superman offered.

"No, no, no…. leave here… you go live life… get laid… do fun stuff… I stay." Someone snorted.

"Did she just tell you to go get laid?" Superman burst out laughing.

"Superman… you get stick out of ass…" Tough Guy burst out laughing. I loved that I could make them laugh. But I just wanted them to leave. It was better for them. "No babysitter…" Hands grabbed me gently, then big arms were lifting me.

"No babysitter, got it, Lexie," Tough guy said.

"Not listening…" I grumbled, snuggling into his body heat, smelling leather and engine grease.

"Not one bit."

"Asshole…"

"Bitch," Tough Guy countered.

I smiled. "Shit… head."

"Harpy."

"Point…?" The chest holding me vibrated with laughter. Superman was chuckling from nearby. We were somewhere warm again.

"I'll take her up and put her to bed." Tough Guy sounded like he was smiling. I liked when he smiled.

"I'll start making that soup broth again and tell the others we found her. Zeke?" We stopped moving. "Don't tell the twins."

"No fucking shit," Tough Guy shot back. We started moving again.

"You're going to get some rest, Lexie, and when you wake up, we're all going to talk about this babysitting shit." Tough Guy's gravelly voice was gentle and soft. I loved that sound.

"No babysitting..." I grumbled. "... destroying life..." We stopped moving.

"Do you think you're destroying our lives?"

I started to cry... I didn't want to think about it... Don't make me think about it. I just curled into his chest, my face in his shirt.

"Baby..." His voice was soft and full of understanding. We moved again. I felt softness under me. Oh... okay... this good. Something came off my feet. A hand cleared the hair off my face. "Lexie, we'll talk about this when you wake up." I gave him a raspberry. He chuckled quietly. I snuggled down into the bed; blankets were pulled over me. Lips kissed my temple. Then the world went black.

I woke up slowly to something warm and soft curled into my neck. It was my ball of love. My body hurt but didn't feel like it was going to explode. My stomach muscles ached like I had done too many sit ups. Did Zeke make me work out? I tried to remember. Nope. Dry heaving. Figured. Wait. When did I dry heave? It was all blurry. I remembered a voice telling me to knock it off, probably Zeke. But that was it. Hades got up and looked at me, then whined. He needed to go.

I pushed the blankets off me and went still. Why were my clothes different from last night? Hades whined again. I picked him up and headed downstairs. I felt like I was getting the flu; I hoped that wasn't the case. I found everyone in the living room, well, except Miles. I waved as I headed for the back door. Footsteps hurried towards me.

Ethan stopped me. "I'll take him, Beautiful; go sit down in the family room." Ethan's voice was soft. "We're having a meeting after you get something to eat."

I frowned up at him. A meeting? Meetings were rare and only when something big was going on. Okay. One of the guys must have an announcement or something. I hoped one of them wasn't pregnant. I snorted at myself.

"Okay," I mumbled tiredly as I handed Hades over. I walked in, and conversations stopped. I didn't really notice it. Zeke was in one of the wide armchairs, Asher was on the left side of the big couch, and Isaac was stretched out on the floor. I went to the free corner of the big couch and curled up. I winced.

"Are you hurting, Red?" Isaac asked.

"I think I did some dry heaving, but... I don't really remember," I admitted, laying my head down on the arm of the couch. Asher and Zeke exchanged looks.

"I'm going to get you some soup, Ally." Asher got up, his voice... different. Strained.

"No thank you, I have Veil work. It'll just come back up anyway," I groused. Asher didn't listen; he left for the kitchen.

"You already did your Veil work this morning, Lexie." Zeke's gravelly voice had me turning to him. He was frowning at me. "Don't you remember?" I blinked at him, what was he talking about? I was asleep in bed all morning.

I shook my head slowly. "No, I didn't." Isaac cursed.

"You're more worn out than we thought," Zeke mumbled; his eyes were running over my face. "We'll talk about it after you eat." I cringed. The idea of food did not sound good at all. Asher soon came in with a steaming mug. I cringed again as I took it. It was just broth. My stomach didn't clench like I thought it would.

"Thanks, Ash." I took a sip; it was Maria's recipe. I waited to see how it would settle. The guys just watched me. "Okay. Getting creepy guys," I told them. They all smirked then turned the volume back up on the TV. No one was talking; there was tension in the room, and I didn't know why. Someone must be pissed at someone else. Ethan came back in with Hades and started playing with him on the floor. I finished my soup quickly; I wanted this dealt with so I could get my Veil shit done and pass back out. I had just swallowed the last of my broth when they turned off the TV. I laid my head back down on the arm of the couch. Isaac pulled out his phone and hit buttons while everyone else looked at me. There was ringing. Isaac had put the phone on speaker.

"Hello." Miles' voice came from Isaac's phone.

"Miles, Lexie's up, and we're ready to have the meeting," Isaac announced to the phone.

"All right, just give me a minute." The sound of muffled voices, rustling fabric and movement came from the speaker. It wasn't long before he was back. "All right, put me on speaker." I snorted.

"You already are." Ethan snickered.

Miles was silent for a moment. "Thanks, guys," Miles eventually said, his voice embarrassed. I raised an eyebrow; what was he doing this morning? I snickered. "Lexie, how are you feeling today?"

I was tempted to ask if we interrupted something, but it wasn't enough to make me ask. "Alive." I smiled, thinking myself funny.

"She looks like shit, Miles," Zeke said. I flipped him off.

"How bad?" There was a click. I looked over to see Ethan doing something to his phone. That shit.

"Snoopy..." I groaned.

He smirked. "Sending you a pic now," Ethan announced.

"Lexie, you look like death." Miles' voice was worried. I snickered. Oh that was funny, considering that word I found from my true self. He was very close to the mark.

"When was the last time you slept? You know passing out from Veil work doesn't count as sleep," Zeke demanded.

I tried to think of the answer. It took me a bit. "The night Asher picked me up from the cemetery I guess." The room was quiet.

"Red, that was almost two days ago," Isaac pointed out. I thought about it. I guess it was. I shrugged. Everyone frowned at me.

"Lexie, you did Veil work this morning. Don't you remember?" Zeke asked.

I looked at him like he was nuts. "No, I didn't; I just got up." I gestured vaguely towards the stairs. There was silence again.

"Ally." I lifted my head and looked at Asher on the other side of the couch. His face was strained. "You got up this morning, got dressed, then walked the two miles to the cemetery." My dropped mouth open. "You did Veil work and passed out. Zeke and I found you, and we brought you back."

"Are you serious?" I asked, not wanting to believe it. Asher nodded. I looked at Zeke.

"It fucking happened," Zeke answered without me even asking. Shit. That would explain the clothes. That worried me a bit. It should probably scare me more, but... I wasn't feeling much right now except tired.

"Shit," I said weakly.

"Last night and this morning you overextended yourself. Zeke and Asher both told me you sounded like you were drunk." Miles' voice was calm and soothing.

I raised both eyebrows at that. What did I do? "Did I streak the neighbors?" I asked seriously. The twins chuckled.

"No, but you did talk," Asher answered.

My heart dropped. Did I tell everyone about Sophia? I looked at the twins then back to Asher as I felt the blood run out of my face. Asher shook his head, then tilted his chin towards Zeke. Heart clenching, I looked at Zeke. He gave me a small nod. Fuck. He knew too. Fuck, fuck, fuck. I closed my eyes and rubbed them with one hand.

"Do you remember anything you said last night, Lexie?" Ethan asked gently. I shook my head, not bothering to open my eyes.

"How about this morning?" Isaac asked. I shook my head. The room was quiet.

"Lexie, you said a lot of disjointed things, some were... unsettling." Miles' soothing voice was back, making my gut relax. I didn't even notice that it was knotted.

"The strangest was you talking about halftime being over; that you were in the third quarter now." Asher's rich voice was gentle to my ear.

My heart dropped. I felt myself grow paler; I hadn't even thought that was possible. "That's nothing. Just gibberish," I lied through my teeth as I looked at the coffee table.

"Really?" Zeke's voice was hard. I looked up to see his face had gone dark. "Because it sure as hell didn't sound like nothing this morning."

I shrugged. I wasn't telling them shit about my expiration date.

Zeke seemed to understand it was something, but I wasn't talking. He took a deep breath, shaking his head at me. He was pissed. I didn't care; I still wasn't going to tell him. Zeke looked away from me towards the foyer, his jaw clenched.

"You kept saying something about having to need a babysitter." Asher's voice had me turning to him. "You pretty much kept telling us to stop taking care of you."

"You did that yesterday morning too," Ethan chimed in from the floor. I didn't know how to answer. I felt raw, exposed, and I hated it. But maybe if they knew, they would understand why they needed to stop.

I looked down at the coffee table, took a breath and let it out. "I don't like having to pull you guys out of your lives all the fucking time," I began. "I do it too much."

"What are you saying, Lexie?" Miles asked, his voice careful from the phone.

"You guys are always having to take care of me. Always. If not one day, it'll be the next." My chest grew tight. "I hate it." I took a breath. "I don't like forcing you guys to do this all the fucking time. I don't like that I need this much fucking help. I don't like doing this to you guys. I don't like you guys taking on my shit." I had only hit the surface with Riley. I hadn't meant to go this far, but now that I had, I went with it. They were all looking at me like I had grown an extra head. "You don't need to deal with this shit anymore." I felt like my heart was breaking again, but I refused to let them know. They were all silent.

"Lexie." Miles broke the silence. His voice calm and reasonable. "When I told you about my mother, did you feel like you were taking on my problems?"

I blinked. "No," I answered instantly.

"When I talked to you about my mom, did you feel like you were taking on my issues?" Asher asked from his spot on the couch.

"No." I still didn't see where they were going with this.

"How about when I started a fight at that party?" Isaac asked.

"No."

"How about my freak out at Vegabond?" Ethan asked.

"No."

"How about when I talked to you about Riley?" Zeke asked quietly.

"No."

They all smirked, I imagined Miles was too, but I didn't know.

"Lexie, that's how we feel about you," Miles explained gently. "You take on our problems without even seeing them. Because you don't see them as problems. You see them as a part of who each of us are." I thought about it. I guessed he was right. But Miles wasn't done yet. "You think of Necromancy as a problem, something that is wrong with you, something that needs to be fixed or hidden."

"This thing you can do is a part of you," Isaac continued. "It's part of who you are."

"And it's a good part," Ethan chimed in. "It lets you see things differently than the rest of us."

"You're more compassionate than anyone else because of it, Ally," Asher added from next to me. "You are because you've seen that, deep down, everyone is lost or messed up in some way. And they aren't always what they seem on the outside."

"You're not broken," Zeke bit out. "You don't need to be fixed. You're not defective. You're you." He looked out of the window over my shoulder, his face pained. "And we love you that way." I wanted to smile. He looked so uncomfortable, it was funny as hell. I was still mostly numb, but that was fading fast.

"We don't think of it as taking care of you, Lexie." Miles' voice had me looking down at the coffee table, my throat growing tight. Everything they said was soothing those broken, torn up parts of me that had been there for years. I had lived with them for so long, I couldn't remember a time when I didn't have them. "When you get a nosebleed, or something happens like at the bowling alley. All I think is, 'What can I do to help make this easier on her?'" I felt tears running down my cheeks and tried to reign in my emotions.

"I always think, 'Please don't let it be too bad,'" Isaac admitted.

"I think, 'Tell me one of us is with her,'" Asher added.

"How much damage is there going to be?" Ethan's voice was quiet.

"Let her wake up." Zeke's voice was hard.

"We aren't thinking about what we're missing; we don't think that it's too much," Miles explained patiently. "We're just hoping you're going to be okay."

I swallowed hard. "But you guys drop everything-" I began, my voice thick.

"And that's our fucking choice," Zeke snapped, his voice hard. "Our choices are just that. Ours."

"You have no say in what we choose to do," Ethan said more gently. "If we drop something, then we've decided it can wait."

"And that's on us. Not you," Isaac added.

I wiped my face, keeping my gaze on the coffee table. I swallowed hard. "You... you guys really don't care that you end up taking care of me?" It was hard to believe what they were telling me, but I really, really wanted to.

"What would you do if one of us was sick?" Isaac asked simply.

"I'd take care of you," I answered instantly. The guys all chuckled.

"See," Ethan pointed out.

"You're not sick that often, Ally; you've just been hit a lot lately," Asher added. "You're exhausted, and you're setting a pace you can barely keep." I shot him a look. "And you have a reason."

"But you aren't all there right now, Lexie." Zeke's voice was hard. I looked up to see his worried face. "You set this pace for a reason. And.... it's a fucking good reason. So, just let us fucking take care of you while you deal with this shit."

I looked back down at the coffee table. I was amazed at what they were telling me. "So, you guys really don't care if you're taking care of me? Or dropping everything-?"

"No!" they all shouted at once.

"You're not a burden; you're our Lexie," Miles assured me.

"And you're one of a kind," Ethan added.

"So, you're stuck with us," Isaac continued. I started smiling.

"You're family," Asher said.

"So, fucking get used to it already," Zeke grumbled.

I snorted then chuckled quietly. I looked around the room at each of them. If I had any doubt left that they loved me, at that moment it was gone. And it wasn't coming back. I was so filled with that fuzzy warmth, I thought I'd catch the couch on fire. I nodded, letting them know I'd heard them. I swallowed back that big wave of love washing through me that demanded I hug the crap out of each of them.

"Okay, I hear ya." I cleared my throat. "Now can we please stop talking about feelings like a bunch of girls?" They all burst out laughing. I grinned.

"I'm with her on this one," Zeke announced, his voice pained. Everyone laughed again.

It wasn't long after that when Miles hung up. But not before telling me to take a nap. I rolled my eyes, but Zeke threw the throw at me and glared. So I cuddled into the corner of the couch and fell asleep with the guys talking around me.

I WOKE up to an almost dark room. I opened my eyes to find Asher in the wide armchair next to the couch, watching a cooking show and eating dinner. I took a second just to look at his handsome face; he always seemed so perfect. I smiled to myself. He had been baking; there was a smudge of flour above his left eyebrow. It looked like everyone else had gone home.

"Hey," I said softly.

Asher's ocean eyes moved to my face, and he gave me a small smile. "Hey." He leaned forward, hit mute, and put his plate down before turning towards me. "How are you feeling now?" He reached out and pushed some hair out of my face.

"Like an idiot," I groaned, rubbing the sleep from my eyes. He chuckled. "How crazy did I get this time?"

"Not too bad; you seemed mostly depressed," he told me gently.

I snorted. "Sorry."

"Don't worry about it, Ally. Stay put; let's get some dinner in you before you start working again." I cringed at the idea of food. He noticed it. "It's just broth; it'll be easy coming up." Okay, that didn't sound so bad. Asher went into the kitchen and brought me out a mug of that awesome broth.

"Thanks, Superman."

"No problem, Ally girl." I concentrated on getting the broth down as Asher ate his dinner.

I was halfway done when I had to ask. "So, Zeke knows now? Or did I dream that?"

He snorted. "Yeah, Zeke knows." Asher looked over at me, smirking.

"How much trouble am I in?" I asked, cringing.

"None." My eyebrows went up. "He was glad you kept it quiet. He doesn't think anyone should tell the twins until you have the link up, and you're able to cross souls." Yay! I wasn't in trouble.

"I should reach the Veil tonight," I told him.

His eyebrows went up. "You're that close?" His voice was doubtful.

"Yeah, hopefully this will be the last shitty night for a while." I gave him a smile before drinking again.

His eyes were on me, but unfocused. Then he blinked, and he was focused on my face again. "Ally, why do you call me Superman?" he asked quietly.

"Your handsome good looks," I offered, smiling.

He laughed and shook his head, his cheeks turning pink. Then his eyes were on mine. "No, really. Why do you call me Superman?" He wasn't going to let it go.

I sighed, giving in. "You always expect yourself to be perfect, Ash. Well, except in art class." I gave him a small smile. "You always try to your best. Which is great. But..." I gestured towards him. "You set this impossible standard for yourself and expect yourself to reach it." My mouth was running, and it wasn't stopping. "Like Superman. He wants to protect Earth, right?"

"Yeah."

"But Earth is huge, giant. Full of people." I tried to explain what I meant. "He can't actually protect everyone; he can't be everywhere at once. He can't stop every mugging, every robbery; he can't stop all bad things from happening. But he always feels responsible for everyone's safety. He expects himself to keep everyone safe." His eyes were on my face as I looked down at the couch arm. "You're like that. Except instead of safety, you want everyone happy. And you expect yourself to keep everyone happy." His brow drew down as he looked at Hades in my lap. I tried to explain again. "Your dad wants you to go into the NFL. When I met you, you were planning on doing that. To make him happy." I swallowed hard, sure I was crossing some line somewhere. "You expected yourself to be satisfied with that life, even if you didn't want it. You still expect yourself to be responsible for other's happiness." I took a deep breath. "You're not. Every person is responsible for their own happiness, no one else's." He was quiet for a while. I just drank my broth, hoping he didn't hate me now.

He sighed then met my eyes. "An exceptionally high standard. Sounds familiar," he said as he raised an eyebrow at me.

I smirked at him. "We recognize our own," I said in a knowing voice. Asher chuckled. "Yeah, I do it too. I just…" I couldn't finish my sentence.

"You know where to draw the line," Asher finished for me.

I met his beautiful eyes and smiled gently. "Sometimes," I answered, my voice soft. "I didn't with those girls. But I do when it comes to someone telling me what to do." I shrugged. I was weird; I'd own it. I looked over at him; he seemed to be thinking again. "I won't use it if you don't like it."

He looked up and met my eyes. "Nah, it'll be a good reminder." He gave me a half grin. "You can stop using it when I don't need it anymore."

"You got it." I winked at him.

Then we both finished eating dinner. I stretched out on the couch. I closed my eyes and dropped down to my center. It wasn't long before I was on the white plain with that golden sky again, looking out over the bridge. I walked to the end of the bridge; I had maybe ten feet left. Okay, I got this. I pressed my palms together and pushed. Pain poured through me, knocking my breath from me.

I was so close to the Veil I could almost touch it. I pushed forward, knives pushing into every nerve I had. I was almost there; I gave one last big push and made contact. I stumbled into the Veil and hit the dirt. I laid on my back, gasping for several minutes. Fuck! That hurt! I was so going to pay for that.

"So, you made it?" a familiar voice said.

I sat up and saw a mirror version of me, only standing. I nodded, still taking deep breaths.

"After your first day, I thought you'd quit."

I flipped myself off, which was weird. She laughed, or it--I still wasn't clear what this person was. Finally getting my breath back, I got to my feet. I was at the very edge of the Veil. The sky was still boiling overhead, lightning flashing every few seconds like a storm just waiting to break. I looked around at what was left of the trees, all of them burnt to charcoal. It wasn't supposed to be like this. The whole place felt wrong. I started walking in towards the center. The pretender me walked along with me.

"Why are the trees burnt?" I asked her, looking towards the center.

"The one who did this used the energy in the Veil itself to close it off," she said in my voice. "Now the Veil just keeps reinforcing it."

"So, they don't have to come back to keep the Veil locked. It just does it for them?"

"Exactly." Pretender me had a small half grin on her or my face. I started walking towards the center again, my eyes on the boiling sky; she stayed beside me.

"Why keep the dead out? Is it just for the energy pouring into the physical world?" I asked her, hoping for an answer.

"How should I know? This is your job, not mine," she groused. "The Veil... is not my usual field."

I looked at her, frowning. "Then what is?" Her eyes ran over my face as she kept her mouth shut. I wasn't going to get an answer. "Is there any way you could stop looking like me?" I asked, getting annoyed by it. "It's creepy as fuck." She tilted her head, or my head, grinning. This was confusing.

"I could, but that would take time and energy, I have more important things to do than make you comfortable." She smiled at me.

I snorted as we kept moving. "Fair enough." I turned back and looked across the Veil. The sense of wrong was thick. I gestured towards the sky. "So, what? I just bring a soul now?" I asked.

The other me shook her head. "Before you can do anything, you need to calm The Way," she answered cryptically. I wanted to punch me in the face. It was a weird feeling.

"The Way?"

She pointed up to the boiling clouds. "That is The Way. The way on, up, and out." She looked up, her hair falling back from her face. "Since the Veil has been closed, it's having a bit of a fit." I looked up, watching as the clouds writhed. "To cross souls, you're going to need to calm The Way first."

"How the fuck am I supposed to do that?" I snapped. She gave a smirk. Is that what I looked like when I did that? It was kind of cute.

"Remember when Mary Summers tackled you in the cemetery?" she asked patiently.

My stomach knotted. "Yeah."

"You felt something that night when you hit the ground; do you remember?" Yeah, I fucking remembered. It still made me break into a sweat whenever I thought about it. "You felt the entire cemetery, every one of the dead." I gave her blank face. "How many dead were in that graveyard?"

I hated that I knew the answer. "147."

"You touched the ground while fully open; you felt the dead. Eventually, in the physical world, you'll be able to use that to raise the dead." I felt like I got hit in the gut. Her eyes ran over me. "That, however, is a long way off. But here, you can use the ability to manipulate the Veil. Use it to calm the way."

I looked up at the way and took a deep breath. "How the fuck am I supposed to do that?"

The pretender me snorted. "Meditation, focus, and will," she shot at me. "You meditated in the physical world; now, you're going to do it here. Instead of focusing down, you are going to focus out." She shrugged and looked up at the sky. "You'll have to figure it out from there. Like I said, the Veil isn't usually my field."

I nodded. I was on my own now. I looked at the pretender and asked about the word that had been haunting me since I met my true self. "What's a Reaper?"

The pretender me grinned as she turned back to me, a small light in her eyes. "Caught that, did you?" She took a breath. "Grim Reapers exist, Alexis. They work with lost souls, and…. other situations. Natural Necromancers have Reaper blood." She eyed me. "Some great grandma or great, great however many times grandmother of yours was a Reaper." I felt the blood drain from my face. "Could be very far back; Reaper blood doesn't dilute. But it does stick with the gender of the Reaper." She ran her, or my, eyes over me, the corner of her lips twitching. "A woman is rare. It's usually men." I was trying to wrap my head around this when she started walking off. "Get to work, Alexis; shit's out of balance, and we need it back." She disappeared.

I stood there listening to the dry wind blowing across the stone. A Grim Reaper. Fuck me. I was tired, and I knew I needed to return. I took one long look at The Way before heading back. I had more work to do, it seemed. But not today. I was going to get some sleep. I closed my eyes and was jerked back and thrown upward.

I OPENED my eyes and groaned. I pinched my nose shut then sat up, putting my feet on the floor of Asher's family room. I grabbed the tissues off the coffee table and put them to my nose. My head was pounding, but it wasn't killing me.

"You okay, Ally?" Asher's voice was soft, and I really appreciated it.

"Peachy," I said in a nasally voice. I opened my eyes to see him still sitting in the wide armchair, a cookbook in his lap. "Just… give me a few. I think this will go away." I closed my eyes and focused on breathing. It wasn't too long before my nose stopped bleeding and the headache was down to a dull ache. I leaned back and rested my head on the back of the couch. "I made it to the Veil."

"You don't sound happy about it," he observed. Asher was dead right.

I filled him in on everything that happened. Minus the Reaper part. I needed to keep that to myself for now.

In the end, he just smiled. "Ally, you're a step closer to crossing the dead over. That's a good thing." He was right; I knew he was. I was just already so tired.

"You're right. I know it is," I admitted, smiling. It was progress, progress I needed.

He grinned at me. "We should all go out and celebrate." Asher checked his phone. I was already shaking my head. I wanted to sleep. "It's still early; call Dylan down then we'll go out and do something." My heart ached at Dylan's name.

"I can't do that." I sighed looking down at the coffee table.

"It's not that late," Asher tried again.

I shook my head before meeting his ocean eyes. "Dylan broke up with me last night," I said quietly. Asher looked so shocked that his mouth opened a little.

Then he recovered. "What happened? You guys seemed solid at the party," he asked gently.

I snorted. "Yeah, I thought so too." My heart still ached, but my anger was right there with it. "He pretended all night, so he'd have one more good memory. We got back here, and he dumped me. I didn't even see it coming." I looked down at the table, my voice getting thick. I swallowed hard. "He tried to say it was the distance, but I called him on it. It was the 'seizures.'" I swallowed hard again, keeping my eyes down on the table. "He said I had too many problems for him to deal with." I smiled down at Hades, who had just woken up and was looking to climb into my lap again. I was going to pick him up, but first I reached behind my neck and unhooked the second necklace Dylan had given me. I held it out to Asher.

"Ally, that was a Christmas present," he reminded me.

I nodded. "Yeah, and I don't want it. Not from him. Can you get it back to him, please?" He nodded and held out his hand. I put it in his palm. "He can probably get his money back, but I'm fucking keeping the other one." He snorted as I picked up Hades. "Thanks, Ash."

"Were... did you love him?"

"He made me feel beautiful. You don't get that every day." I was going to cry, and I needed to be alone before that happened. "'Night, Ash," I murmured before getting up and heading upstairs, taking Hades with me. I changed into my jammies and slipped into Asher's bed. Then I cried. Because the answer was yes. I had loved him. Not completely, and it was new, but still. I had loved the fucker just a little.

THE BOYS: ASHER

I couldn't take it anymore. I couldn't just sit here listening to Ally crying upstairs. My gut was a rock as I turned off the TV and got to my feet. I started pacing. I heard her sniff again. She was trying to be quiet about it. But I could hear every sniff, every time she had to catch her breath. A wave of boiling rage ran through me. I threw the TV remote at the wall. That fucking asshole! What the fuck was Dylan fucking thinking? Dumping Ally like that! Lying to her all night! Telling her she had too many fucking problems! I started pacing again as I fought the urge to drive up to Dulcet and beat the shit out of him for every tear she was crying upstairs. That piece of shit! My hands were shaking as I tried rubbing the tension out of my neck, my chest one deep ache.

Seeing Ally cry always fucking killed me. Hearing it wasn't any better. I needed a distraction. Not cooking; I'd probably slice a damn finger off right now. I looked around the family room, trying to find something to fix, clean, anything. My eyes went to the photos on the wall. Ally's voice ran through my mind. 'If you want them up, put them up.' Yeah. Today was the day. To hell with Dad. I walked up the stairs and found the linen closet. Or it had been before Dad went and took down all the photos of Mom. Now it was the picture closet.

I opened the door and started looking through them. I found the one of our fifth birthday. Mom had cake all over her face because instead of eating it, Jessica and I had started throwing. I smiled, remembering how Mom had joined in. I picked up the big box with the good ones, along with the photo of the birthday. I closed the door and started down the stairs. Then I stopped. Mom's flag. I turned around, opened the game closet and pulled it out, still in the plastic. Feeling steadier, more sure, I headed downstairs and put the box on the coffee table. I paused. Ally was talking to Hades, telling him she'd be okay. She'd get over it. She always spoke to Hades. I focused on what I was doing, the only sane thing to do right now. Over the next hour, I put up every photo we had up when Mom died. Not just in the family room. On the stairs, in the upstairs hallway, and I even put a few Jessica would love on her bed. She needed to have them too. It felt right and real damn good.

I went to the table in the foyer and found Ally's Christmas present where I had left it. The triangular box was beautiful. It had a trim of carved flowering vines and leaves. On the front plaque was Mom's name, birth and death dates, and the words 'Devoted Mother.' It really was beautiful. Mom would have loved it. I went back into the family room and opened the back. I pulled out the flag, making sure not to mess up the fold. I put the flag inside and closed the back. I turned it over. It was perfect. Something inside me finally felt done. Finished. This was right. We couldn't just forget Mom, erase her like she didn't exist. We needed to remember... I snorted as Ally's words ran through my head again. Someone should remember, and she was right. How did she always see straight through to the heart of things? Straight through me? How the hell did she do that?

Some things were so simple to her. You want to be a chef, go be a chef. Fuck everyone else's expectations, fuck what they wanted. It was your life, be happy. My fingers ran over the flower carvings on the box as I was lost in thought. What the hell was Dylan thinking? Ally was funny, smart, sweet, and insanely giving. She had worked her ass off to make sure Dylan and his dad could use that cookbook. And all those fucking cookies! Not to mention she fucking apologized to Trisha! Who would do that? She was taking those girls' shit for days only because we liked them and she wanted us to be happy. Who the fuck did that? And if you pissed her off? I grinned as I pictured her face when she realized we were going to make her take a nap. Her eyes had gone wide in surprise then narrowed in challenge. She always liked a challenge. She tried to take us all on, and she almost took out Zeke. I chuckled this time. She had fire and a smart mouth that never failed to make me laugh. I smiled, well, sometimes even her bad jokes were just too awful. But she always gave that strange giggle because she thought it was funny. Whenever those big green eyes flashed with her temper, I had to stop myself from smiling. What the fuck was wrong with Dylan?

I put down Mom's box. I picked up Ally's necklace and looked at it. The initial Dylan had chosen for her was an A. It would have worked from me. I always called her Ally, but everyone else called her Lexie. No one called her Alexis. If he really knew her, he would have gotten an L. I turned over the pendant and went still. 'One in a million' was stamped on the back. I snorted. At least he got that right. Ally was definitely unique. She was beautiful, and that laugh… I went still, finally listening to what I was thinking, had been thinking for a few days. Since before the bowling alley, since she apologized to Trisha.

The image of Ally soaked in my kitchen flashed in my mind. Taking her clothes off like that had been torture. I rubbed my eyes with one hand. I had done my best not to look; she was cold, shaking, shit, she had been turning blue. But I still saw her curves, her tucked in waist and her fucking legs. I groaned at myself. She was petite but had those legs that still somehow managed to look long. I needed to stop thinking about it; my body was more than aware of what I was thinking. And yesterday, waking up wrapped around her. My arm between… I was pressed … and my leg… I laid back against the back of the couch, tilted my head back and groaned painfully. And when I was pissed at myself for touching her like that, she had laughed at me. She made it okay again. Then she smiled up at me with that fucking smile.

I really wanted to just kiss-my heart dropped; I realized what I was thinking. What I was feeling. I liked Ally. My heart raced as it sank in. And not just as a friend. Oh, no, no, you idiot. Asher! What the hell? You know you can't date her! You know... and.... she's... "Shit!"

THE BOYS: MILES

$\mathscr{I}$ shifted in my seat, trying to get comfortable. But it wasn't happening tonight. Autumn had worked her usual magic on me, and every muscle I had was sore. I sighed as I looked out the window of the plane as we waited to taxi out to the runway. I moved my glasses to sit on my head and rubbed my eyes with one hand. Then I just sat there, fingers on the bridge of my nose, leaning my elbow on my armrest, eyes closed. I ran through the conversation with Autumn tonight in my head.

"MILES, BABY, COME BACK TO BED," Autumn's sweet, sultry voice called from the bed. I finished washing my face and used a towel to dry. Autumn needed to slow down, or she was going to kill me. My back was already scratched to hell.

"If I do, we won't talk," I reminded her. That's how the last had round started. I was trying to talk to her about our relationship, then she... distracted me.

"Do we really need to?"

I snorted, hung my head and closed my eyes. How could she keep doing this? We needed to talk. "Yeah, we really do." I kept my eyes off her as I grabbed my pants from the floor and pulled them on.

Autumn was still only wearing the white sheet. Her blonde hair was streaked with pink and blue. Her eyes were an unusual blue. And her face was pretty. I had thought it beautiful at one point, but that was some time ago. That's what I was trying to save here. I leaned against the dresser, out of reach of the foot of the bed. It was the only safe thing to do with Autumn around. I crossed my arms, looked at her face and waited. She pouted, actually pouted. And it wasn't nearly the cutest thing in the world anymore. When she realized I wasn't going to budge, she sat up and wrapped the sheet around her body. A great body, but I was tired of this game.

"Okay, you look serious. Are you pregnant?" she asked seriously. I snorted. Yeah. She made me laugh.

"Autumn, I don't like this arrangement anymore." I needed to be honest. "I want us to be us, full time." She blinked at me; I'd surprised her. That was strange; she usually knew what I was going to say before I said it.

"Why the change?" she asked. Her normal voice told me she was being honest with me now.

I sighed. How could I explain it? There's a girl back home that's driving me crazy, and I'm here hoping you'd date only me so I could maybe stop thinking about her? Yeah, even I knew that would be a stupid thing to say.

"I'm just... tired of the back and forth." I licked my lips.

She raised an eyebrow. "It's Lexie, isn't it?" she asked grinning. Shit, she knew me too well. "How hot is she?"

"No, it's not really about Lexie." It was only a half lie, but I never lied to Autumn; it felt... odd. "She just reminded me of what I want." I tried again. "I want you, all the time. I know the distance stinks, but I can come down for a couple of weekends every month. Or I could fly you up." Her eyes ran over me, seeing entirely too much. I fought the need to start tapping. That would be a dead giveaway.

"Miles, it sounds like you're saying we go full time, or we are over. Am I hearing this right?" she asked quietly. I felt that like a kick to the gut. But she wasn't wrong. This was more difficult to do than I had thought it would be.

"Yes." Her eyes went wide. "Autumn, I can't keep doing this. I want someone full time; I want to be able to call you when stuff happens in my life at any time." I tried to get her to understand. "I want to be able to talk to you and know I'm not going to be calling and interrupting you with some guy. I want to be your guy." Her eyebrows went up in surprise. "I want us back, the way we were before we started this on again off again thing. That's what I'm trying to save here." She blinked, I could see from here that her eyes were filling with tears. Shit.

"So, if I say no, we're done? No talking? No games? Just done?" Her voice started to shake.

I shook my head and came around the bed to sit on the side of the bed facing her. "No, not just done, Auty," I reassured her. "I couldn't do that; you have meant so much to me over the last four years that I could never just cut you out of my life." I reached out and held her cheek in my hand. My chest burned. This felt awful. But I needed her to understand how I was feeling, what I was saying. "If you say no, then this part of us will be done." Her eyes went wide again.

"You mean the dating. We wouldn't date anymore, no more kissing, no more..." She gestured toward the bed. I nodded. "Wow, that's kind of mean... cause this part..." We both laughed. Yeah, this part we were great at. I dropped my hand from her face and held her hand, squeezing it gently.

"You really mean this, don't you?" she asked quietly. I looked at the nightstand and nodded. "What did she remind you of? Because this has been working for years."

I sighed. Was she listening or not? I couldn't tell anymore. "She reminded me what it was like to have someone there, someone who you can call at any time, who would... put up with a lot just to see you happy. She reminded me what it was like to have someone care about me." I couldn't explain it any better than that.

The tears were gone as she nodded. "She reminded you what it was like to have a real girlfriend." Autumn's voice was soft. She understood; she wasn't hurt by it. It just was. "Miles... if we're full-time, that is a lot of traveling. That is a lot of time taken away from other things. I've got softball coming up in the spring; you have swimming. I need that scholarship for college, and I'm not going to let you pay for it." She stopped me before I could even offer. "We have other things we want to do besides get on a plane every other weekend." I nodded slowly. I knew she was right. I just... needed to give it another chance.

"I figured that, Auty," I said, giving her a sad half smile. "Can't blame a guy for trying."

She gave me a teary smile. "I love you, Miles. I always will, but we just haven't been that couple for a long time." She sniffed and smiled at me.

I smiled back, my throat tight. "I love you too. And that's not going to change." My voice was thick. This really freaking sucked. It was done; we were over.

She gave me that sultry smile she knew drove me crazy. "Want to say goodbye the right way?" she asked. I laughed before I kissed the hell out her.

"MR. HUNTINGTON?"

I lifted my head and brought my glasses down so I could see the stewardess. She was in her twenties and had always been very nice over the last three years.

"Please call me Miles, Lucy," I reminded her. "We've been on these flights often enough."

She smiled at me and sighed. "If I did that to your father, I'd get fired," she pointed out.

I smiled. "And I'd just hire you back," I countered.

She chuckled. "The pilot says we're ready; he wanted to make sure you didn't change your mind," Lucy said politely.

I sighed. "Tell him to take off, please. We won't be making this trip anymore," I said politely. Lucy blinked at me. Then she gave me a sympathetic smile and headed towards the front of the plane. I went back to looking out the window. I wasn't watching as the ground fell away. I pulled out my phone to look through my photos. Lexie's face looked up at me, her big green eyes contrasting with everything. It was one of Dylan's photos. I had to hand it to the guy; he knew how to get the right light and a good angle. But the rest was all her.

I sighed. Lexie. Why did I climb in bed with her? I leaned my head back and called myself every name in the book. Idiot was often repeated. I was dealing with... things. Yeah, I slipped up the other night and called her Angel. But she was so out of it I doubt she even heard. I was handling it fine until I was stupid and climbed into bed to hold her. But what else was I going to do? She was crying, she had those fucked up memories that weren't hers, and she... she kept remembering what that psycho felt. Climbing in and holding her was logical; she wasn't getting out of bed, and I was the only one who could have possibly helped at the time.

I needed to forget about it. I needed to forget how she fit perfectly against me. I needed to forget how her skin felt under my fingers. I needed to forget the feeling of her crying against my chest. I needed to forget how it felt when she hugged me while I told her about Mother not coming back. My chest grew tight as I remembered how she had cried with me. Telling me over and over that it wasn't my fault. I needed to forget... how I felt about her. Though, maybe I should remember that. It was what made me realize how far gone my relationship with Autumn was. How far away from an actual relationship we had been in for the last year.

I looked down at Lexie's face again and swiped to the next one. This one was different. I'd seen that face before. It was her 'I'm thinking of sad things' face. Why would you want a picture of that? I swiped to the next one; she was laughing with Zeke. I grinned as I remembered her face as she admitted why she was looking for scissors. She was so furious at Mother for abandoning me. She was angry for me, wanting to tear her to pieces for hurting me. Lexie cared deeply about the people in her life. I'd seen it myself. But it always surprised me when I was included on that list.

I kept looking through my photos. I could deal with this. I could get over these feelings quickly. I'd meet a new girl. There was that brunette in Trig that kept sending me notes. Lexie was dating Dylan, and she was really into him. At least that was what she said the last time they talked about it. Not to mention what Ethan was telling everyone yesterday. I needed to warn her about talking to Ethan when I saw her next. She was dating Dylan, and that would make this a lot easier.

My phone vibrated. I checked my texts. I had missed a lot of them. Asher had sent out a group message without Lexie included. It was a big red flag.

Asher: Ally reached the Veil tonight.

I sighed in relief; a big weight lifted off my chest. She wouldn't have to push herself so hard now; she could get some rest, remove those memories. Lexie was going to be all right.

Isaac: Whoop!

Ethan: Yes!

Zeke: Good, now she can get some fucking sleep.

Asher: Yeah, but there's more work to do in the Veil. I'll let her explain.

Ethan: Where is she? We're heading over.

Isaac: Hell yeah!

Zeke: Let her sleep!

Asher: Not tonight guys.

Isaac: But I want Red...

I snorted.

Asher: Dylan dumped her yesterday, in a real fucked-up way. Did anyone know?

Everything in my world went still. Dylan broke up with Lexie? What the hell happened?

Ethan: I thought they were good.

Isaac: No, what the fuck?

Zeke: How did he do it? If he hurt her...

Isaac: I'm with Zeke. Spill.

Ethan: Majority rules. Tell us.

Asher: Keep your traps shut about it, especially you, Ethan.

Ethan: I swear if I talk, I'll give up my Lexie back massages privileges. Zeke can enforce.

Wait. Lexie was giving Ethan back massages now? I kept reading.

Asher: He fucking came down knowing he was going to break up with her. He pretended everything was fine then hit her with it after we dragged her out of the party and he brought her back here.

What? They had to drag Lexie out of a party? I kept reading.

Zeke: I don't remember where he lives. Give me his address, Asher.

Isaac: Pick me up on the way, Zeke!

Ethan: I'm going too.

Zeke: It was the 'seizures,' wasn't it?

Asher: Yeah. Ran like a bitch. He told her she had too many problems for him to deal with.

Her concerns from the family meeting made more sense now. That would have hit Lexie right in the heart. Dylan might as well have gutted her while he was at it. I grew tense as I fought the urge to hunt Dylan down myself. He made her feel like a burden when she was anything but. That piece of shit. I took slow calming breaths. I needed to be the calm one.

Zeke: Address NOW!

Asher: Zeke, don't tempt me. She cared about that fucker. I can hear her crying upstairs.

Zeke: I want blood.

Isaac: Seconded

Ethan: Third.

Zeke: Majority rules, give it up.

The last message was only a minute ago; I needed to be the calm one. The guys interfering without Lexie asking them to would be a disaster.

Miles: Majority does not rule this time. Lexie does. If she wanted to kick his ass, then she'd have done it or asked one of you to.

Asher: About time you picked up!

Zeke: What he said to her was fucked up!

Miles: Yeah, it was screwed up. But it's not about how angry we are right now. It's about what she needs. I'll be home in a few hours. I expect all of you to be at home and stay out of jail.

Ethan: You don't need to come back for this.

I exhaled. Might as well tell them now.

Miles: Autumn and I broke up. We won't be dating again.

Asher: Shit.

Zeke: Fuck.

Isaac: What the hell?

Ethan: What is with this week? Is it national breakup week or something? Next, we're going to hear that Riley dumped Zeke.

Zeke: Hey!

I grinned at that.

Miles: You all know Lexie. Is she going to sit around moping?

Zeke: No, she's going to want to hit something.

Miles: Take her for training tomorrow. I'll try and make it.

Asher: She gave me that necklace to give back to Dylan. Zeke?

Zeke: What?

Asher: You have dogs, right?

The conversation degenerated from there. I watched as the guys discussed how to send Lexie's necklace back to Dylan. It was going to be messy and disgusting. Then I thought of something.

Miles: Make sure he knows it's you guys doing that part, not her.

Asher: I was already planning a note. I can't hear her crying anymore.

I grinned. Dylan deserved it. If he couldn't appreciate her, then screw him. I leaned my head back and closed my eyes. A feeling of doom swept over me. Dylan broke up with her.

"I am so screwed."

EPILOGUE

$\mathcal{I}$ spent the next few days at Asher's house, working to get rid of the rest of those memories. Some nights I slept through the night, others I woke up screaming. When I woke up not remembering who I was, Asher was there, gently reminding me, and sometimes not so gently. It depended on what was happening. I saw a side of Asher that I had never seen before, and it made my heart race. It was probably nothing. Just... hormones or something.

During it all though, the guys were there. The twins for a cuddle if I needed one, or a laugh. Zeke for a kick in the ass. And Miles, sweet, handsome Miles, always gently reminding me to take care of myself.

Dylan called me two days later; I let it go to voice mail. He apologized for the things he said, that he was an idiot and he didn't mean it. I might have believed him, but the things he had said hurt like hell, and he knew they would. There was no excuse for hurting me that way. No, I was not calling him back.

The dead were still stuck, but I was working on it. They kept hanging around the house. I had a few nights of uninterrupted sleep before I caught Isaac salting a circle around the house with rock salt. Apparently, the guys and Rory had been taking turns doing it every day. I loved those big bastards. I took over, so they didn't have to do it.

We were going back to school soon, and I was looking forward to it. Winter formal was coming, and I was planning on going. Even if I didn't have a date. I wanted to have some normal. A little normal was just what I needed right now.

FOR THE LATEST NEWS ON THE VEIL DIARIES

Visit:

blbrunnemer.com

Or

https://www.facebook.com/BLBrunnemer-1575614369409677/

Or

https://twitter.com/blbrunnemer

I love to hear from my readers, so if you have a question or spot a grammar error,
Please let me know at:

Blb@blbrunnemer.com

www.ingramcontent.com/pod-product-compliance
Lightning Source LLC
Chambersburg PA
CBHW020624020726
47494CB00001B/32